# TREASON'S
# GIFT

The Moon in the Water
The Chains of Fate
Alathea
The Lodestar
Wintercombe
Herald of Joy
A Falling Star

# TREASON'S GIFT

## Pamela Belle

St. Martin's Press
New York

MAY 2 1 1993

Library of Congress Cataloging-in-Publication Data

Belle, Pamela.
    Treason's gift / Pamela Belle.
        p.    cm.
    ISBN 0-312-08913-9
    1. Great Britain—History—James II, 1685–1688—
Fiction.   I. Title.
PR6052.E4474T73   1993
823'.914—dc20                                    92-37736
                                                        CIP

First published in Great Britain by Random Century Group.

First U.S. Edition: March 1993
10  9  8  7  6  5  4  3  2  1

*For my parents,*
*Brian and Sylvia Belle,*
*with much love*

The quotations at the head of each chapter, and beginning each of the three sections of the book, are taken from Dryden's poem *The Hind and the Panther*, which is a religious allegory, written in 1687, in praise of Roman Catholicism.

# THE St. BARBE

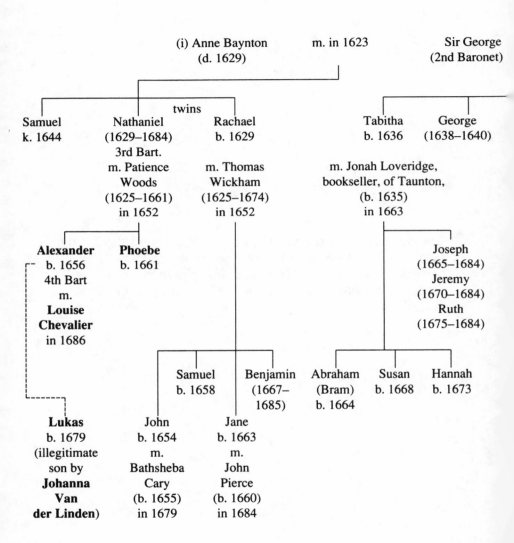

(i) Anne Baynton     m. in 1623     Sir George
(d. 1629)                         (2nd Baronet)

twins

Samuel    Nathaniel    Rachael        Tabitha    George
k. 1644    (1629–1684)    b. 1629        b. 1636    (1638–1640)
         3rd Bart.
         m. Patience    m. Thomas    m. Jonah Loveridge,
         Woods       Wickham    bookseller, of Taunton,
         (1625–1661)    (1625–1674)      (b. 1635)
         in 1652       in 1652       in 1663

**Alexander**    **Phoebe**                Joseph
b. 1656     b. 1661               (1665–1684)
4th Bart                      Jeremy
m.                         (1670–1684)
**Louise**                     Ruth
**Chevalier**                (1675–1684)
in 1686

               Samuel    Benjamin    Abraham    Susan    Hannah
               b. 1658    (1667–     (Bram)    b. 1668    b. 1673
                       1685)      b. 1664

**Lukas**       John       Jane
b. 1679      b. 1654      b. 1663
(illegitimate     m.         m.
son by      Bathsheba    John
**Johanna**     Cary       Pierce
**Van**        (b. 1655)    (b. 1660)
**der Linden**)    in 1679     in 1684

The characters in bold appear
in *Treason's Gift*

# FAMILY IN 1686

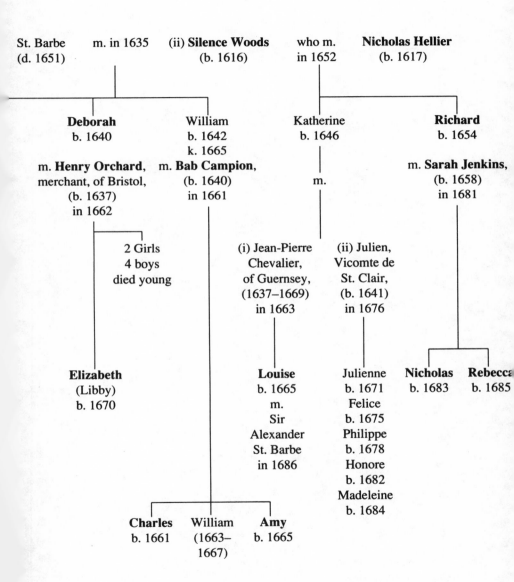

St. Barbe    m. in 1635    (ii) **Silence Woods**    who m.    **Nicholas Hellier**
(d. 1651)                (b. 1616)      in 1652      (b. 1617)

**Deborah**      William      Katherine      **Richard**
b. 1640        b. 1642       b. 1646        b. 1654
             k. 1665

m. **Henry Orchard,**   m. **Bab Campion,**            m. **Sarah Jenkins,**
merchant, of Bristol,    (b. 1640)                (b. 1658)
(b. 1637)          in 1661         m.         in 1681
in 1662

2 Girls      (i) Jean-Pierre    (ii) Julien,
4 boys        Chevalier,       Vicomte de
died young    of Guernsey,     St. Clair,
           (1637–1669)     (b. 1641)
            in 1663         in 1676

**Elizabeth**          **Louise**      Julienne    **Nicholas**    **Rebecca**
(Libby)            b. 1665      b. 1671     b. 1683      b. 1685
b. 1670            m.         Felice
            Sir        b. 1675
        Alexander    Philippe
        St. Barbe     b. 1678
         in 1686      Honore
                       b. 1682
                       Madeleine
                       b. 1684

**Charles**    William    **Amy**
b. 1661     (1663–     b. 1665
          1667)

# PART ONE

'This masquerade of mirth and love'

June–September 1686

# Chapter One

## 'No mother more indulgent'

'M'lady – 'tis a boy!'

She hardly heard their voices, so overwhelming was the sudden freedom from pain and effort. Someone wiped her face with a damp cloth as she lay back on the pillows, gasping, her eyes closed. Then, the import of the words trickled into her consciousness. 'A boy? Is – is he alive?'

For a moment no one responded, and she thought, with a sick stab of terror, that her worst fears had come to pass. But then, answering her, came the cry of her baby, so weak and thin that she could hardly hear it above the bustle around her, but nevertheless a signal of hope.

She struggled to sit up. The curtains had been drawn, shutting out the June sunlight, and the chamber was suffocatingly hot. The familiar people who had attended her in her labour were reduced in the gloom to dim shapes, blank and anonymous. Then, the plain, dough-pale face of her maid, Christian Birt, came towards her, smiling anxiously. 'Oh, no, m'lady – no, don't ee try a-sitting – do ee lie still now, 'tis all over.'

'I want to see him,' said Louise, Lady St Barbe, and the strength and urgency of her voice surprised both her and Christian. 'Please – let me see him, let me hold him – '

'Here he be, m'lady,' said the midwife. She was a middle-aged village widow who had borne a large family of her own, and the surprise summons to attend Lady St Barbe, who had been expected to command the services of an expensive man-midwife or physician from Bath, would enormously increase her confidence and prestige. 'Here be your little mite.' And with a curious expression, compounded of satisfaction and sympathy, on her plump, lined face, she put the bundle into Louise's outstretched arms.

She had known he would be small: he had been scarcely seven months in the womb, after all, and such infants were rarely born alive, let alone vigorous and healthy. But even so, she was completely unprepared for the lightness of him, the minute size of his head, that was surely no larger than an orange under the shock of straight black hair like an old chimney-brush, and the tiny hand that groped and curled around her little finger and clung on, as though that grip was all that anchored her son to the world. So small, so fragile, so weak, surely he was doomed.

She had planned to engage a wet nurse, as most wealthy women did, and to hand him over to the management of servants. But now, seeing him, feeling that astonishingly tenacious grasp of her finger, she knew that she could not do it. For he would need so much help to survive: and only she, his mother, could possibly possess enough will, and power, and love, to save him.

He opened his eyes and stared up at her, and she felt for the first time the strength of the bond between them, and the force of her adoration. The midwife was hovering, waiting to take him back: back, Louise thought suddenly, to danger, perhaps to death. With a sudden, fiercely protective gesture, she bent her head over her son's, and whispered softly to him, in the French that was her childhood tongue. '*N'aie pas peur, mon petit – Maman te gardera sain et sauf, je te promets.*'

'M'lady – shall I take en from ee now?' said the midwife, with a touch of impatience.

Louise, already utterly absorbed in her baby, brought her attention back with an effort. 'No – no, I've changed my mind. I shall feed him and care for him myself.'

'Thank God you're home, sir!' Abandoning his usual dignity, the butler came running into the stable yard as his master dismounted. Sir Alexander St Barbe looked down at him from his considerable height, and said sharply, 'What is it, Twinney? What's happened?'

'It's my lady, sir – her time's come early – the midwife's with her now, sir.' The butler gasped for a much-needed breath, and found it wasted: Sir Alexander dropped the bay stallion's reins into his hand, pushed unceremoniously past him, and ran into the house.

The head groom, Pardice, took the big horse's head, much to Twinney's relief, and gave him a considering look. 'How do it go, with m'lady?'

'I don't know,' Twinney confessed. 'But she's been in travail since this morning, and no sign yet, or none that I've heard. But the Widow Poole is known to be a skilled midwife, so let us pray that all will be well.'

''Tis too early,' said Pardice, his seamed and sunburnt face creased with worry. 'I *told* she, I told she over and over again, and so did Sir Alexander, she should never have kept a-riding, she were out this morning on that little yellow mare, and her pains started – but you know m'lady, she won't be told.'

'We must pray for her and the babe,' Twinney said stiffly, with a return to his professional dignity: it was hardly seemly to exchange gossip about their betters with the groom, particularly at such an anxious time. Inside the house, in the high, light chamber above the library, the heir to Wintercombe and all the St Barbe lands was about to be born: and he knew, as did the whole household, that it was of the utmost importance that both mother and child should survive the perils of a birth that had come too soon for the safety of either.

Alex St Barbe took the steep, winding stone stairs at a run. Not yet, not yet, not yet, his urgent footsteps beat the words into his mind. A seven-month baby would be small, feeble, marked for death: and for many reasons, not least for the child's own sake, he desperately wanted it to live.

Outside his lady's chamber, he paused to catch his breath, and saw, sitting hunched against the wooden wainscotting by the door, the small, forlorn figure of his bastard son Lukas. The boy jumped to his feet, his face ghostly white with fear. 'Papa – it's Louise – she's having the baby!'

'You shouldn't be here, Lukas,' he said, and the little boy's face crumpled suddenly into most uncharacteristic tears. 'I know – I know – but I'm so afraid she'll die!' he wailed, and cast himself into his father's arms.

Alex wanted, most urgently, to go to Louise, to discover what was happening, but Lukas was his child too, and in sore need of comfort. He knelt on the cool, polished wooden floor, his arms around the little boy, whispering reassurance. 'She won't die, Luikje – she won't die – not if I have anything to do with it.' He disentangled his son's arms, and gave him an encouraging smile. 'Don't worry – she's as strong as a horse.'

'I heard Christian say it was much too soon,' Lukas said, wiping away the tears with a valiant hand. 'And the midwife said it was dangerous.'

From behind the door, faint but unmistakable, came the muffled cry of a baby. Lukas gasped, his eyes wide, and a smile broke out suddenly on his face. 'Oh, Papa, listen!'

'I heard it,' Alex said, and smiled back. 'Maybe not so dangerous, after all. Stay here, Luikje, while I go in – and perhaps you can greet your new baby brother or sister, in a little while.'

The chamber that he knew so well was an unfamiliar landscape now, dark, shuttered, lit only by one or two inadequate candles. The baby wailed again, a feeble, fretful sound, and there was a murmur of voices. Alex made his way through the unlit antechamber, where the maid Christian usually slept, and stood unnoticed in the arched entrance. Four or five women, including his bailiff's wife, Sarah Crowe, were busy folding soiled linen, banking up the already sweltering fire, stirring a steaming pot in the embers. And in the bed where together they had known so much delight and pleasure, in the six months of their marriage, was his wife Louise.

She had never been beautiful, and now, her face moulded by suffering and exhaustion, she looked almost ugly, her aquiline nose very prominent and her olive skin a sallow, sickly colour even in the flattering golden glow of the bedside candle. But then the shapeless bundle in her arms stirred, and her eyes opened, and the expression on her

6

face, as she looked down at the baby, was as breathtakingly radiant as any Madonna's.

Involuntarily, he moved towards her, and the midwife, Widow Poole, glanced round. 'Sir! Be ee home already?'

'It seems I am,' he said drily, and threaded his way through their curtseys and bustle and concern to the bedside. 'Louise?'

At last she looked up, and he saw with sudden fear, and compassion, the tears on her thin cheeks. 'Oh, Alex – thank God – oh, I'm sorry – he's so small – '

'She bain't herself, sir, she've had a main hard travail, poor lady,' said the midwife, just behind him. 'Sir, I d' beg ee, don't ee sit down, please, your clothes, the baby – '

Ignoring her, and his dust- and travel-stained coat, Alex lowered himself on to the bed beside his wife. 'Let me look?' he said softly: and Louise, apparently unaware that she was weeping, turned the soft woollen folds back from the baby's face.

Red, crusty, unfinished, the eyes no more than slits, it hardly seemed human: and he could scarcely believe that such a minute creature could be alive. But he saw the movement of a tiny hand, and he heard a snuffling, difficult breath.

'You have a son, Sir Alexander,' said Sarah Crowe, answering his unspoken question. A slender, pretty young woman, she had given birth to her second child, a daughter, only six weeks or so before. She added, her voice soft with pity, 'I have known seven-month children live, and grow strong and lusty. My own sister's babe was such a one. Please, my lady – there is no need for despair.'

Louise gave her a grateful glance. Behind Alex, the Widow Poole, with a brisk and total lack of tact, said, 'Best send for Parson, sir, and christen the poor little mite as soon as ee can.'

As if even the act of baptism were a threat, Louise hugged the baby closer, her head bent over his, shutting out the hostile world. Alex touched her shoulder briefly, and got to his feet. Under his menacing gaze, the midwife's officious manner withered on the vine. She dropped her eyes to apparent contemplation of the floor, and a sullen flush suffused her face.

'There's no need for such haste,' Alex said, quite pleasantly. 'I shall inform Master Pigott, all in good time. Meanwhile, I think you and your assistants could best employ yourselves setting the chamber to rights, and doing all that is needful. Then perhaps my wife and son will be able to enjoy some peace and quiet after their ordeal.'

Notably subdued, the women hastened to do his bidding. Alex spared a glance for Louise, but all her attention was given to the baby: she had put him to her breast, and Sarah Crowe, kind and considerate, sat beside her offering encouraging advice. He turned away from them, and went to the door.

Lukas was still outside, of course, his face pale and expectant. Alex smiled at the boy, and put his finger to his lips. 'Come – come and greet your new brother. Then you can spread the news to everyone.'

Father and son walked into the chamber side by side, and Alex, his hand on the child's shoulder, felt, almost imperceptible through the cloth, little tremors of fear or excitement. The baby, its efforts to suckle apparently in vain, gave a feeble wail like a kitten, and Lukas gasped. 'Oh – isn't he *small!*'

'Small, but strong,' said Alex, denying, for both his sons' sakes, the voice of realism and truth unwelcome inside his head.

'And hairy.' Lukas glanced up at him, with a rather nervous smile. He was normally a very solemn, thoughtful little boy, with a gravity far beyond his seven years: to make such a remark, at such a time, revealed the tension and strain under which he had suffered since that morning. 'I thought new babies didn't have hair.'

'This one does.' Alex, seeing that Louise was still utterly immersed in motherhood, turned his elder son to face him. 'Lukas, I have an important task for you. Go tell everyone you can find, all over Wintercombe, that you have a new brother – and also tell Pardice that someone must ride into Bath straight away, to let your Aunt Phoebe know. Can you do that?'

'Of course I will, Papa,' Lukas said, and with a last glance at his stepmother and the baby, ran for the door, his excitement and relief at last overwhelming him.

If only everything were so easily arranged. Alex looked around the chamber. The midwife, unwontedly meek, was busy piling soiled linen in a basket, with the help of her assistants, and gave him a watchful glance: as if, he thought with rather grim amusement, he were a grenado ripe for explosion. They probably considered it unseemly for him to linger at such a time, but he did not give a toss for convention, or propriety, and never had.

His new son was crying feebly again. He went over to the bed, and Louise looked up. Her fine chestnut eyes were filled with fresh tears: once, she had never wept. 'He won't suck,' she said, with a sob. 'He just won't!'

'Be patient, my lady,' said Sarah Crowe softly. 'He's new, and bewildered most like – not all babies are born knowing what to do. We have the rest of the day to show him how.' She glanced up at Alex, and he saw the betraying pity on her face. Whatever her soothing words, she knew as well as the midwife of the fragility of hope.

In this chamber, at this time, he was an intruder. The thought came to him suddenly, forcefully, in waves of heat from the fire as the maid stoked it until the flames leapt roaring up the chimney to join the warmth of the summer afternoon. Later, when the baby was asleep and the midwife gone, he would return to talk to Louise. Apart from anything else, his son needed a name, whether his lifespan was to be measured in hours, or days, or years. And he, Alex, needed a drink.

Quietly, attracting no notice from his wife or his son, Alex left the chamber.

Sunset was approaching, and soon the curfew bell of Bath Abbey would be rung to herald the night. In her comfortable little house in Nowhere Lane, not far from the Cross Bath, Phoebe St Barbe was about to sit down for her supper when someone started hammering on the front door.

'I wonder who that is?' said her cousin Libby Orchard, a

9

startled look on her plump face. Visitors to this quiet and unconventional household were somewhat infrequent, and rare indeed at such a late hour.

'We'll discover soon enough,' Phoebe said. 'Mattie has gone to answer the door.' She glanced at Libby's well-rounded figure, and decided, not without mischief, that it would do the child no harm at all to fast a little longer. 'It sounded urgent – I'm sure supper will keep for a while yet.'

Libby's expression struggled between hunger and curiosity. Phoebe ignored her, and moved awkwardly to the door of the dining parlour, her stick providing the support that her twisted, almost useless leg could not. 'Mattie? Who is it?'

The maid came scampering in haste down the hallway, a piece of paper in her outstretched hand, and a look of dismay on her face. 'Oh, madam, 'tis young Earle from Wintercombe, and he d'have an urgent message for ee!'

Phoebe took the letter, aware of Libby avid beside her. 'Tell him to stable his horse in the White Hart, Mattie, and then come back here for supper – he won't have time to return before dark.'

'Yes, madam,' said her maid, and hurried off to do her bidding. Phoebe, with a sick presentiment of catastrophe, was left looking at the thick, leaping scrawl, stark across the paper and barely legible, of her brother Alex.

Libby said anxiously, 'Oh, Phoebe – is it bad news?'

There was no other reason why Alex would have written to her in such haste. She was conscious of a sudden, perverse longing to be alone. Libby was a dear girl, and extremely intelligent beneath the rolls of puppy fat, but if the letter did indeed bring ill tidings, Phoebe would have much preferred to avoid the consequent need for explanation, discussion, and repression of feeling.

'Aren't you going to open it?' Libby was asking, aflame with innocent curiosity. Phoebe was only nine years older, but at such times the gap between them felt centuries long. Slowly and deliberately, she broke the seal and unfolded the paper.

Alex had written with such speed that there were scarcely

10

three words to a line, and the quill had spluttered great blobs of ink along the margins.

Sister,
I must tell you that my dear wife was this afternoon, at about three o'clock, delivered of a son. He lives yet, but being come two months early, I cannot share her hopes for his future: although smallness at birth is not necessarily a disadvantage, as none know better than yourself.

Will you look out Doctor Peirce, and bid him come to Wintercombe straight away – and your own presence would also be greatly welcomed by Louise, and by your affectionate brother

Alexander St Barbe

'It's Louise,' Phoebe said, looking up from the paper. 'She's had her baby.'

'Already?' Libby's voice squeaked with astonishment. 'But it wasn't due until August!'

'Exactly. And Alex wants me to go to Wintercombe, tomorrow.' She glanced at her cousin. 'He doesn't mention you, but I'm sure you would be welcome too. Would you like to go with me? If nothing else, you can while away a few hours in the library. In fact,' she added, thinking aloud, 'we'd best assume that we'll be staying there for a few days at least. I imagine that Louise is well enough, but of course the baby must be very small and frail.' She smiled at Libby's anxious face. 'Although, as my brother reminds me in his letter, that alone need not spell disaster. I weighed only four or five pounds at birth, and was thought a poor life indeed for many years – and yet here I am still, hearty if not exactly hale. So, we must be hopeful, even if Alex cannot share our optimism. He was ever a realist.'

'Poor little baby,' Libby said sympathetically. 'Shall we make an early start in the morning, then?'

'As soon as we can,' Phoebe told her, with a rather bleak smile. 'So after supper, you had best pack what you will need, and go to bed in good time. Do I sound exactly like your mother?'

'Not in the least,' said Libby, whose parents were both large, jovial and overbearing. 'But please, please, Phoebe, can we eat now? I'm *starving!*'

The baby had eventually suckled a little, but not enough, and slept now in the carved wooden cradle which had once held his father, and his aunt, and his grandfather, and countless St Barbe children down the ages. The Widow Poole had taken her bag of silver and departed, promising to return in the morning, and only Louise's maid Christian was left, sorting through a pile of baby clothes that no one had thought to look at so soon. Most had proved to have the moth, or were otherwise unsuitable, and all were much, much too big. For now, the child was warmly swaddled, but he would soon need, if he survived, short coats, biggins, caps, bibs, clouts . . . Christian smiled tenderly at her mistress's first-born, and gently rocked the cradle with her foot.

The door opened. Louise had been dozing, exhausted both by the birth and by her increasingly desperate attempts to persuade the baby to feed, but at the sound she opened her eyes, and saw her husband approaching the bed. Only yesterday, her heart would have leapt at the sight, but now, drained and sick with anxiety for the child, she could barely muster a smile. 'Hullo, Alex.'

Christian had risen, and curtseyed: he nodded to her, glanced into the cradle, and then came to sit on the bed beside his wife. 'How do you feel now?'

'Tired,' Louise said. She had a curious sensation of distance from him, the man who had possessed such power over her senses, who had roused her passions to the point where she had cast aside all constraint, who had made her his mistress, got her with child and then, against all hope, had married her: at this moment he could have been any considerate stranger, politely enquiring after her welfare.

'You look tired,' he said, and smiled, and kissed her like a brother on the cheek. 'I won't stay long – sleep is the cure for it, after all. But there are things we must discuss.'

The baby snuffled and stirred, and Christian began to

rock the cradle again. Alex went on. 'The midwife told me that you wish to nurse him yourself. Is that wise?'

'What could be better for him than his own mother's milk?' said Louise, her quick anger suddenly rising, despite her weariness. 'Alex, he's so small – I can't hand him over to some wet nurse who won't really care for him, who might overlie him or neglect him – he needs so much love, and help, just to survive – and only I can give it.' She swallowed, trying to control her tears, and then added, more quietly, 'He did suckle a little, earlier. Sarah was very good, she showed me what to do, and in the end I think he took some milk . . . I know it is not the fashion for me to feed him, but all the authorities agree that a mother's care is best – and no matter what you or anyone else may say, I *will* nurse him myself!'

'Then I will give you all the support I can,' Alex told her. He took her hands in his, and smiled at her. 'Don't worry. I remember Phoebe when she was born, and she looked far more sickly – a little skinned rabbit, red and raw and wrinkled, with a cry like a starving kitten's – and she lived, and so will our son.'

'Our son,' Louise said, her voice distant, wondering. 'Which of those illicit hours in the Tower made him, do you suppose . . . Alex, what shall we call him? He arrived so early, we haven't even discussed it.'

'Not James,' said her husband drily. 'That would be altogether inappropriate, in view of the fact that His Majesty was so eager to have me executed. And to call him George, after my grandfather, would not endear me to Aunt Silence. What other names are in the family? Isaac, Samuel, William, Nicholas – or Jean-Pierre, after your father?'

'We could call him Nathaniel, after yours,' Louise said, watching him closely. She was well aware that for most of his life, Alex had been on the worst of terms with his father, and at Sir Nathaniel's untimely death, eighteen months previously, the estrangement had long been almost complete. But she had liked Alex's father, a spare, witty, abstemious man who had died much regretted and mourned by all his kin: save for the dissolute, rakehell only son whom he had unaccountably sired, and who had been such a grave disappointment to him.

But much had happened since Sir Nathaniel's death, and Alex had changed: the mere fact of his marriage showed that. The man of her first acquaintance, hostile and malicious, would doubtless have uttered some biting and contemptuous reply. But he was looking thoughtfully at the cradle, a slight frown between his black, winged brows, as if contemplating the aptness of it.

Nathaniel: so many syllables, such a large name for this tiny child. And yet, to call him after his grandfather seemed somehow to be symbolic of old debts paid and old wounds healed, and of a new beginning.

'Why not?' said Alex, turning the benefit of his sudden, dazzling smile upon her, the only woman amongst so many that he had loved enough to marry. 'Another Nathaniel St Barbe – and if the holy water does not drown him, the weight of his names assuredly will. An excellent suggestion, sweet Louise. Your grandmother will be so pleased – my father was always her greatest friend.'

'I know she will be,' Louise said softly, thinking of her grandmother Silence, who lived many miles to the south, in Chard. Louise's headstrong and passionate nature had been a sore trial to Silence, who was now seventy, and her granddaughter's liaison with Alex had caused her real grief. But the marriage seemed to have mended all the damage, despite Silence's initial misgivings, and the birth of a son and heir for Wintercombe would surely delight her.

If little Nathaniel did not die.

He would not die, not with all her fierce care and devotion lavished upon him. He *will* not die, Louise repeated to herself, like a litany. He is no smaller than Phoebe was, and less frail, and she lived. My baby will not die – I will not let him!

She lay wrapped in the warm feathers and quilts of the luxurious bed, and gathered all her strength, all her will and love and purpose, as if merely by doing so she could pour life and hope into the fragile occupant of the cradle.

And Alex, seeing that she had once more slipped away from him, rose softly to his feet and left the room.

Phoebe St Barbe, riding in a hired coach that had taken most of the day to travel the seven or eight miles from Bath, arrived on the following afternoon, with her cousin and companion Libby Orchard, and the maid Mattie. It had rained for much of the journey, increasing her discomfort, and by the time the jolting, badly sprung vehicle pulled up in the gravelled courtyard outside Wintercombe's north front, she was in one of her most mordantly waspish moods. Libby, who liked her cousin but stood in some awe of her, had sensibly kept quiet for the past two or three miles. Phoebe notoriously hated travelling anywhere, for her crippled leg made most movement more or less painful, and riding for any more than the shortest distances impossible. In Bath, of course, it was easy to hire a covered chair, and be carried smoothly and quickly through the narrow, crowded streets by two burly chairmen. But a coach, slow and expensive, was essential for journeys outside the city where riding was out of question, even though the steepness of the hills around Bath made such a method of transport very difficult and slow.

'Well, here we are at the ancestral home,' Phoebe said, as the ponderous vehicle creaked to a weary halt. 'You look very green, Libby – are you sure you're not ill?'

'I'm quite well, thank you, now that we've stopped,' the girl said. The coachman opened the door, bowing obsequiously in the hopes of a handsome tip, and she climbed down with relief and turned to assist Phoebe.

'I can manage quite adequately, thank you,' said her cousin. She ignored Libby's proffered arm and clambered awkwardly from the coach, leaning heavily on her stick. 'I wonder where my wretched brother is? Ah, there you are!'

Libby was even more in awe of Alex St Barbe than of his crippled but formidable sister. She had forgotten how tall he was, how vigorous and compelling his presence. More than two yards high, with very blue eyes and a face far too handsome for his own good, or anyone else's, he wore his own hair, densely black, rather than the fashionable excesses of a periwig. To Libby, quiet, sixteen and rather bookish, he was like a creature from another world. She sank into a reverent curtsey, hoping that he would not notice her and tease her: her tongue always became tangled at such moments, and suitable retorts only sprang to her mind hours later.

But today, obviously, he had other and more weighty matters on his mind. He kissed Phoebe with great warmth, and gave Libby a rather more perfunctory embrace, before taking his sister's arm to lead her inside.

'How are they?' Phoebe asked, concern sharpening her voice.

Libby saw Alex's quick frown, and a significant shake of his head. 'Louise – Louise is very well, considering. Doctor Peirce rode out this morning – thank you for telling him so promptly. He says she should make an excellent recovery – she's young and strong, and it was a comparatively easy birth, the baby being so small.'

'And the child?'

'Not so good, I'm afraid.' Alex paused as his sister negotiated the steps up to the porch, Libby following close behind. 'Louise is nursing him herself, which Peirce approves, but he is too feeble to suckle properly. She is doing her utmost for him, she has no other thought but his care, and she hopes most desperately to save him.'

They had reached the passage, dark and narrow, screened off from the Great Hall on their left. Phoebe stopped, and looked up at her brother. 'And you are not so hopeful?'

There was a brief, sad silence. Libby, quiet and unregarded behind them, saw a look of real, surprising grief on Alex's face. He said softly, 'No. Peirce told me privately that very few such babes survive, born so soon – although he did add that miracles do sometimes happen, even in these hectic, ungodly days, and that if Louise's care and love alone were enough, his future would be assured. But please, please, say nothing of this to her. It would break her heart . . . and besides, perhaps the miracle might happen, after all.'

16

'You should not doubt me,' Phoebe said, her dry voice almost concealing her own distress. 'Louise is my dear friend, remember. Have you christened the baby? Or have you some alternative and heathen ceremony in mind?'

Shocked, Libby stared at Alex. He gave his sister a tired smile that was a shadow of his usual mischievous grin. 'Parson Pigott came over this morning – I thought that it was best, given the rain, that the baby was kept warm and snug indoors. I had to pay the old dodderer double, but there was no alternative. We have named him Nathaniel.'

Phoebe looked at him for a long, significant moment, and then said, with an almost bitter smile on her face, 'I am glad of that. Even if the baby dies, I am glad.'

'I thought it would please you – you were so close to him. Now,' he added, turning to the housekeeper, who had appeared with a brisk jangling of keys, 'Abigail will show you to your chambers – you have your old rooms, Phoebe, on the other side of the Hall. And I will go tell Louise that you have arrived.'

Sarah Crowe was with her when he entered the chamber. The bailiff's young wife, with a small boy and a new baby of her own, had proved invaluable since the birth, and her patient wisdom had done much to encourage and hearten Louise in her efforts to feed Nathaniel. But the child was noticeably weaker than he had been the previous day, too feeble to do more than sleep, and cry in that faint, reedy wail, and struggle fitfully against Louise's breast. And something in him wished that his son would die, and soon, so that this terrible, heart-rending pretence could be abandoned, and Louise could begin to accept the bitter fact of his loss. Babies died all the time: every family, rich and poor, had experienced such tragedies. And, knowing that Nathaniel was almost certainly doomed, he had, from the moment he first beheld his son, tried not to allow himself the luxury of love.

Louise looked up as he approached. She had hardly slept the previous night, despite her exhaustion, and he saw dark shadows under her eyes and hollows in her thin face. But her expression was full of joy. 'Alex – look – he's suckling strongly now!'

It was true, the baby seemed to be taking milk, and Sarah was smiling too. Alex felt the first tiny stirrings of hope, and ruthlessly suppressed them. He said gently, 'I'm very glad of it. Louise, Phoebe has just arrived, with Libby. Would you like to see them, when Nathaniel has done?'

'Phoebe?' said Louise, absently. 'Oh, has she? Yes, I'd like to see her.' She did not sound particularly overjoyed, although over the past two years Alex's sister had become her greatest friend, despite their dissimilarity. 'I think he's had enough for the moment,' she added, looking down at the baby, who seemed to have fallen asleep.

Sarah Crowe rose from the chair by the bed. 'If you will excuse me, my lady, Sir Alexander, I must return home. My own babe will be wanting me.'

'Of course,' Louise said, and stretched out a thin, sallow hand. 'Thank you so much, Sarah, for everything. Can you come back later?'

'Certainly I will, my lady,' said the bailiff's wife, and with a curtsey to them both, withdrew.

Alone, save for Christian, who was sewing tiny shirts by the fireside, Alex smiled at his wife. 'I shall go tell Phoebe that you will be able to receive her shortly – if you are not too tired, that is?'

'Of course not,' Louise said, but she was not really listening: already, her gaze had returned to the tiny bundle cradled so lovingly against her breast, and her lips curved in an expression of infinite tenderness.

The thought crept like a traitor into his mind, as he left the chamber unnoticed. That wonderful smile had been for her son, now apparently the recipient of all her undivided love and attention: and she had all but ignored the man whom she had, not so long ago, professed to adore without restraint or reservation.

Phoebe, climbing the steep, spiralling stone stairs with the aid of her stick, and Libby's solid presence behind her to cushion any fall, was conscious of considerable apprehension. It seemed very likely that the baby would die, and she, who all her life had shied away from extremes of emotion,

18

loathed the thought of the sorrow that both its parents would surely suffer. Moreover, she was necessarily more clear-sighted and detached than her brother and his wife, and she could discern other difficulties ahead. Alex had not married Louise for the sake of the coming child, she knew, but most of Somerset assumed that he had. Would Louise, even armoured with all that vibrant self-assurance, be affected by the poisonous gossip that would surely come to her ears before long? And what of the disappointment that the loss of Alex's legitimate son and heir would cause him? He had hoped very much for a boy, she was certain, even if he had never said so. And just as little Nathaniel's death – *if* it happened, she reminded herself sternly – would greatly grieve his parents, so, conversely, there were other, more distant members of their wide family who would be delighted at the news.

'While there's life, there's hope,' Phoebe said to herself bracingly, with a wry smile at the triteness of the phrase, and entered Louise's chamber.

The girl's appearance, hollow-faced, gaunt and spectrally thin, shocked her deeply, though she had prepared herself for it. But at least there seemed to be no sign of the dreaded child-bed fever, and Louise's skin was cool and dry as she embraced her.

'A surprise visit,' said her sister-in-law, lying back against the pillows. There was a little animation in her face, a wan travesty of the old Louise who had dazzled and entranced the cynical, libertine Alex. 'Thank you for coming, Phoebe – and you too, Libby. The baby's asleep – you can look at him, if you like.'

Not by any means was Phoebe familiar with newborn babies, nor could she imagine herself ever wishing to be. But this tiny, tiny scrap, hardly larger than a kitten, was her nephew, the heir to Wintercombe, and his frail form bore the burden of a great many hopes. And, seeing him, she could understand only too well why Alex had not been optimistic.

Beside her, Libby drew in a wondering breath. 'Oh – he's so *small*!'

19

'Everyone says that,' Louise told her, rather defensively. 'But he's taking milk – and you were not so very much bigger, Phoebe, when you were born.'

'My dear brother called me "Feeble" for years,' she said tartly. Her eyes prickled suddenly, and she coughed to hide the sudden and completely unexpected rush of emotion, before turning back to face Louise. 'And at least you are able to care for him. Was it an easy birth?'

'So I've been told,' said her sister-in-law. 'Although it didn't seem so at the time. I feel well enough, but very tired – Nathaniel seems to cry most at night.' She gave a weary smile. 'I hope you approve of his name?'

Phoebe, who had been closer, and more dear, to her father than Alex ever was, took her hands and kissed her. 'Of course I do. Did you suggest it?'

'Yes – but Alex was quite happy, rather to my surprise.' There was a little colour, now, in Louise's cheeks, and she patted the chair beside the bed. 'Sit down, Phoebe, please – how is your leg? Have you found the Baths helpful?'

'There has been some little improvement, I think,' Phoebe said cautiously. Crippled from birth, she had long since come to accept her disability with resignation, humour and a complete lack of self-pity, recognising that although her physical horizons might be restricted, her intellect was unbounded. She spoke eight languages besides her own, corresponded with a variety of scholars on a vast range of subjects, and had welcomed the handsome legacy from her father that had enabled her to set up her own spinster establishment in Bath. Not only did it give her more opportunities for meetings with like-minded spirits, but the Baths themselves, hot and healing and especially good for ailments of joint and muscle, offered her the chance to ease the almost constant pain that had afflicted her all her life.

'Bath must be very busy at present,' Louise commented. 'Is there much company there?' Over the past months, pregnant, married, the mistress of a large and rambling manor house in the depths of the country, she had missed the bright merry life that she had enjoyed with her mother

20

and stepfather in France, and occasionally since coming to England. There had, recently, been precious little opportunity for dancing.

'Altogether too many people for my liking,' Phoebe said waspishly. 'I go generally to the Cross Bath, which is more convenient, and select, than the King's or the Queen's, but even so there's been scarcely room for a pin between the bodies, this last fortnight. Indeed, there was one gentleman so huge I hoped he would not slip and fall in, for then I'm sure all the water would have overflowed and we'd have been left high and dry – and as for his lady, she looked like a beached whale, and with her bathing gown on I'm glad there was no wind, or she'd have resembled a ship in full sail.'

Louise was smiling properly, even at such a thin joke, and there was a sparkle in her chestnut eyes. Heartened, Phoebe embarked upon a droll description, in her driest voice, of the horrors to be seen in Bath during the height of the summer season: the overdressed, the overweight, the men and women of fashion and those who would ape them, those who were genuinely ill and those who pretended to mysterious and interesting ailments: and those who preyed upon the company, the pickpockets, the whores and the gamesters and, more respectable, venal and dangerous than any of these, the doctors, apothecaries and barber-surgeons, and the keepers of inns and lodging-houses, who made such an excellent living out of the fashionably sick.

And Louise continued to smile, and even laughed once or twice, and produced some stories of her own, from her childhood in France, where the fops were more outrageous, and morals far more lax, than in strait-laced England. And as both Libby and Christian sat and listened, delighted, the atmosphere of fear and dread that had clouded the chamber since Nathaniel's birth was for a little while dispelled.

And then the baby woke, and began to cry, a sound so thin that at first Phoebe could not think what it was. Christian lifted him out of the cradle and brought him over to his mother, and Phoebe rose to her feet, beckoning to Libby. 'We have stayed long enough, for the moment. Let's go, and leave them in peace.'

21

'Are you going back to Bath?' Louise said, taking her son from the maid's arms.

Phoebe shook her head. 'Oh, no, no. We shall stay for as long as you wish it – until he is well, if you like. I'm sure Libby will find plenty to occupy her in the library.'

'As will you,' said Louise. 'Come back later, when I've had some rest. And if you can spend a little time with Lukas, I'm sure he would love it. He may have been feeling rather neglected since Nathaniel was born.'

'Indeed I will – and I'll be interested to see how his learning has progressed,' Phoebe told her. 'Come on, Libby, let's go inspect the library, and seek out all Alex's most interesting new books.'

We'll stay until Nathaniel is well, Phoebe had promised. But as she sat between Lukas and Libby in the library, listening to the eager voice of Alex's elder son declaiming fluently from *The Perfect Politician*, a life of Oliver Cromwell, she recognised with sadness that it was unlikely that her tiny nephew would ever be well. It was plain, even to her, that he was too weak to make any real attempt to suckle. Louise's care and devotion were laudable indeed, but she was, surely, deluding herself. And Phoebe, who had sat by her beloved father's deathbed, who had experienced grief and disappointment in plenty during her twenty-five years, dreaded the inevitable anguish that lay in wait for her brother and his wife, a day, perhaps two days hence.

That night, Nathaniel's slow, inexorable slide towards death gathered increasing momentum. He cried, but with fast-failing strength, and would not take the breast, despite all the efforts of Louise and Christian and Sarah Crowe, who had been summoned again. At last, towards dawn, he lapsed into an exhausted sleep in his mother's arms.

It was no longer possible for Louise to convince herself that he was strong and healthy, despite his size, or that he had suckled his fill: her breasts were aching, swollen and dripping with what he had not taken from her. Despite her promise, she had failed him: all her love, all her care, had not in the end been enough.

22

Her silent tears dropped on to the minute lace-edged cap that Christian had sewed for him, only yesterday. She had not slept now for a day and two nights, but rest was unthinkable. Nathaniel was drifting away from her towards death, and she would not let him travel this last journey alone, in the solitary splendour of his cradle.

Christian tried to persuade her to give him up, to sleep, but she resisted stubbornly, her arms sheltering her son, his insignificant hand, even now, circling her finger. Alex came at daybreak, his own face marked by a sorrow which she did not notice, and sat with her, but he was only a shadow, like all the others, a figure with no substance beside the beloved, fading reality of the baby in her arms. She saw Phoebe, once, but smiling now was beyond her reach, and the merriment they had shared so recently seemed to have happened to someone else.

Doctor Peirce rode out again from Bath, in happy expectation of a fat fee, and went away well rewarded, but shaking his head. The infant had a surprisingly tenacious hold on life, but there was nothing he could do, as he had known from the beginning. Lady St Barbe, fortunately, remained in good health, although he had taken it upon himself to draw Sir Alexander aside and utter a few tactful, well-chosen words upon the melancholia and other afflictions which often befell mothers in this unhappy but, alas, all too common situation.

'Melancholia? Louise?' said her husband, in tones of weary disbelief. 'It would be hard to imagine anyone less likely than my wife to suffer such a thing.'

'Nevertheless, sir, there is always some danger of it, however cheerful and resilient your good lady's nature may be,' said Peirce. 'However, let us hope that you are right. My heartfelt condolences, Sir Alexander, upon this lamentable occasion – although I am sure that you and your lady will be blessed with many healthy and robust fruits of your union in the future.'

Alex, from long practice, was adept at hiding his real feelings when he wished, and Peirce had no idea that his patient's husband was tempted to wipe the false sympathy from his face with a few brief and pungent words. He watched as the stout doctor rode away, and then climbed slowly up the stairs to see Louise.

She was sitting just as she had when Peirce had examined her and the baby: propped up on the pillows, the child in her arms. She did not look up as he approached.

He saw the change immediately. The baby was still, quite unmoving, and he could not discern even the almost imperceptible rise and fall of his chest. Gently, he bent and touched the limp, curled fingers. Once, they had grasped his, with an astonishing strength that had aroused his wonder. Now, they were quite unresponsive. To make sure, he laid his hand against the pulse-point on his son's neck. There was nothing.

'Louise?' he said, and the tone of his voice brought Christian's head up in alarm. 'Louise, my dearest love . . . I think he has gone.'

She made no movement to acknowledge his words, but sat as still and lifeless as their son, and only the flowing tears, pouring in a river of grief upon Nathaniel's head, bore witness that she knew, and understood, that she was a mother no longer.

# Chapter Two

## 'Endless anguish'

Nathaniel St Barbe, the second of his family to bear that name, though for a scant two days, was buried in the church of Philip's Norton, half a mile from Wintercombe, beside his grandfather and namesake, his grandmother, and other, more distant ancestors. As was customary, his tiny body had been wrapped in the white cloth he had worn for his christening, and the coffin, carried in his father's arms, was draped with a white pall. The household of Wintercombe formed a sad procession behind the corpse, while the church bells tolled and many villagers congregated in the churchyard to pay their respects and watch the show.

Louise was unable to attend his funeral: covention decreed that she should not appear abroad until her churching, a month after the birth, and in any case it was far too soon for her to rise from her bed. Doctor Peirce had left prescriptions for a variety of strengthening cordials and tonics, and instructions to eat plenty of good red meat. But for Louise, the most ambrosial of foods would have tasted as dust and ashes in her mouth.

Phoebe came up to keep her company, for it was a long and dreadful day. Alex's sister was so unlike her that their friendship had grown up unawares, until they had discovered its strength in the dark days of December, the previous year, when it had seemed very likely that Alex would be tried and executed for treason. Remotely, Louise was grateful for her presence, but nothing seemed to matter very much. No miracle, no effort of will, no amount of grief or mourning could return her dead son from the grave; and beside the vast aching agony of her loss and her guilt, everything else, her husband, her friends, her past and present life, seemed grey and insubstantial and of no account.

Phoebe, remembering her own sorrow at her father's death, knew she could do little to assuage Louise's grief, save to listen as her friend talked, her voice hoarse with despair, of the baby she had loved so briefly.

'It was my fault,' Louise said. She sat in the bed, her pretty, Turkish-patterned night-robe wrapped around her, her face hollowed and shadowed and lined so that she looked much, much older than her twenty-one years. 'I shouldn't have gone out riding – they told me, Alex told me, and Pardice, and Doctor Peirce – and I thought I knew better, and ignored them.' A tear slid down the side of her prominent nose, and dripped on to her hand. 'If I hadn't ridden on the day he was born – he would still be within me, and alive.'

'Surely that's not so,' Phoebe said. 'I know I'm ignorant in these matters, but you mustn't blame yourself – '

'But I do!' Louise cried. 'I do, and I'm sure Alex does.'

'Has he said so?' Phoebe asked, vowing to take her brother severely to task if he had indeed been so insensitive.

'No, he hasn't – we've hardly spoken since – since – '

'You *must* talk to him,' Phoebe told her, deeply disturbed. 'He is your husband, after all, you love each other – '

'Do we?' Louise's voice had diminished almost to a whisper. 'I don't know any more, Phoebe – I don't know. All I know is that Nathaniel is dead, and I promised him that I would save him and I didn't – I put a little piece of coral in his hand, something for him to hold – he clung on to my fingers so tightly, as if only I could help him – and I failed him, and now he's dead – and it's as if a great hole has been torn in my heart and it will never heal, and Doctor Peirce talks bracingly about growing strong and doing my duty and no reason why I shouldn't produce a string of healthy babies – as if that could make me feel better!'

'And you don't want any more babies?' Phoebe said, hoping that her disbelief was not too evident in her voice. Once, only a few days ago, her sister-in-law had been a lively, confident, assured young woman. Now, it seemed that the death of her baby had reduced her to this anguished husk, destroyed by grief and guilt and bitter fate.

She had thought that Louise was made of sterner stuff, and she had some sympathy for the good Doctor's point of view. Surely another baby, and soon, was the best way to assuage her sorrow and heal her loss?

But what do I know? Phoebe reminded herself. I am a dried-up spinster, leading apes in hell for sure, twenty-five years old and never even been kissed, let alone borne a child. All my knowledge is culled from books, most of them written by men, for whom the mysteries and complexities of womanhood are for the most part beneath their notice.

'No – no more babies – I only want Nathaniel,' Louise whispered, and buried her face in her hands.

For almost the first time in her life, Phoebe was at a loss. The expression of affection, whether in word or gesture, had never come easily to her: only recently had she felt able to acknowledge the strength of her feelings for her brother, who had made much of her childhood a torment. Awkwardly, wincing from a sudden twist of pain in her hip-joint, she leaned over and put her arm about Louise. 'You say that now – but soon you'll have another, and be able to forget.'

'I don't *want* to forget!' Louise cried. She pulled out of her sister-in-law's embrace, and stared at her with distraught, tear-filled eyes. 'I want to remember him always. And how can I have any more children when I can't bear the thought of Alex touching me?'

Her words appalled Phoebe. The affair, and then the marriage, between Alex and Louise had been characterised above all by an explosively mutual passion that had, at times, seemed to crackle like lightning between them. Well aware that for her to offer advice on such matters was akin to the late King Charles advocating celibacy, she said, 'You can't mean that.'

'I do,' said Louise, and an involuntary shudder ran through her thin body. 'I look at Alex, and I think of what we used to do – and I can't imagine feeling or doing such things ever again.'

'You *must* talk to him,' Phoebe said despairingly. 'He's not a monster – he'll understand.'

'But will he? Since the baby was born he's seemed like a stranger – so distant – I don't think he was even sorry when Nathaniel died – I know he blames me – ' She dissolved into a fresh torrent of weeping.

Phoebe was conscious of an unworthy and uncharitable impulse to scold her, to shake some sense back into her. She hastily repressed it, and said softly, 'That's a little inconsistent – how can he not care, and still blame you? You can't have it both ways. And I know, as surely as I know my own heart, that he grieves for the baby as much as you do.'

'How can he? He didn't give birth to him.'

'Of course not – but inside that careless, cynical shell is a man with the capacity to feel as strongly as you do, or stronger. Isn't that why you fell in love with him? For God's sake, Louise,' Phoebe said urgently, 'you did what no other woman has ever managed to do, you besotted him, he loves you, he married you, he forsook most of his pleasures for your sake – don't throw it all away now, just because of a child who never even really lived!'

It was a grievous mistake, she knew it before the words had died away into the hot, stuffy air. Louise looked as if she had been struck to the heart. She said, her voice shaking and the French accent suddenly very strong, 'Please go, Phoebe. I would like to be alone now.'

'I'm sorry, Louise – I shouldn't have said – '

'No, you shouldn't. Please go.'

Faced with implacable hostility, Phoebe had no option but to withdraw. She rose to her feet, fumbling for her stick. 'Louise – please at least try to *talk* to Alex – don't keep your grief to yourself.'

'You don't understand, so why should he? Now, please will you go?'

Recognising failure, Phoebe turned and made her halting way towards the door. Christian Birt was in the antechamber, sadly folding away into a basket the baby clothes that were no longer needed. Phoebe paused by her, and said softly, 'I think your mistress is in need of comfort.'

'I'll go to her,' the maid said at once, and Phoebe, with a last glance at the lonely, distraught figure in the bed, left the room.

She had no wish for company either, at this moment. Soon, the burnt wine, cakes, biscuits and sweetmeats would be set out for the funeral party in the Hall, and those mourners of sufficient standing to be invited back to Wintercombe would fill the place, eating and drinking. When she thought of the pitiful corpse of the child, the desperate grief of his mother, her stomach turned. She hobbled down the stairs and made her way out into the empty garden, to sit and to think.

She found peace on one of the stone benches placed around the pond garden, on the eastern side of the house. The sun shone fitfully between the high, bubbling white clouds that had been gathering all day, and the worn golden stone was temporarily comfortable. Images chased each other in her mind: the red encrusted skin of the dying baby, like some pathetic goblin: Louise, her sallow face made ugly by exhaustion and weeping, speaking of her indifference to the husband she had once passionately adored: and the expression in Alex's eyes, the pain he would not admit, when he had told her of the child's death.

Perhaps it was all nothing. Perhaps tomorrow Louise would summon up her gallant smile, put aside her grief, and welcome Alex with open arms. Somehow, that prospect seemed unlikely. The impulse to interfere, to offer well-meaning advice, was very strong, but Phoebe knew that she should resist it. There was only one person in the St Barbe family whose wisdom, diplomacy and strength might prevent Louise and Alex from straying into rough waters, if not on to rocks. But Silence, aunt to Alex and Phoebe and grandmother to Louise, was fifty miles away in Chard, and had recently been unwell.

No, Alex and Louise would have to deal with this trouble themselves. She had offered her small remedy to her sister-in-law, though it might perhaps have been done more tactfully, and it had been spurned. Possibly, on reflection, Louise would change her mind, and reveal her feelings to

Alex as she had done to his sister: Phoebe hoped very much that she would. But she could not force Louise to anatomise her emotions for Alex's benefit, any more than she could compel her brother to listen to her.

Still, she would make the effort, and talk to him tonight.

Supper that evening was an unhappy and awkward occasion. The funeral guests, a surprisingly large number given the lack of notice, and the fact that a mere chrisom child had been buried, had long since dispersed to their homes, well fortified with burnt wine and the magnificently frivolous refreshments that Alex's new French cook had provided. Louise, of course, would take her meal in her chamber, on a tray: and so only Alex, Phoebe, Libby and Lukas were distributed around the long oak table in the dining parlour that could seat a dozen and more without difficulty.

Alex occupied his usual place, at the head. It was evident to Phoebe, at least, that he must have been drinking steadily for some time. Before his marriage, he had been altogether too fond of the bottle, but he had never previously, even at his worst, been drunk in Lukas's presence. With a curious mix of foreboding and hope, she realised that this, in itself, revealed how deeply the death of Nathaniel had affected him.

She prayed that neither Lukas nor Libby would notice, although her young companion, quiet and observant, undoubtedly saw much more than one might think. But both children had attended the funeral, and were remarkably sad and subdued. Alex plainly did not intend to waste his breath in idle banter, but swallowed his wine as if it were water. Monsieur Leclerc had produced a fricassee of mutton and a particularly delicious fish broth, but his efforts were wasted. Phoebe found that she had lost her appetite entirely, and even Libby, usually so fond of her food, could only toy with what lay on her plate. She was heartily glad when Lukas's nurse appeared, to take him to bed, and Libby, with a wary glance at Alex which showed how much she had, in fact, understood, made her excuses and left soon after, muttering something about the library.

'Is that child ever seen without her nose in a book or in the trough?' Alex enquired caustically, as the door shut behind her.

Phoebe, devoutly hoping that Libby had not heard him, said sharply, 'That's unfair. She's a sweet girl, and very clever. I've been teaching her French, and Italian, and she's remarkably quick to learn.'

'Pity you can't teach her to shine in company, or to dress properly.'

'We can't all be witty and decorative,' Phoebe snapped. She, alone of her family, was not frightened by her brother in this mood, but she knew that she would have to tread very carefully. With considerable apprehension, she eyed the brandy bottle that Twinney, the butler, had placed in front of him before making a prudent withdrawal, and hoped that he would not drink too much more before she had said all that was in her mind.

He saw her looking, and said aggressively, 'If you plan to read me a lecture, my dear and sanctimonious sister, I should leave now before I say something unforgivable.'

'I have more sense,' Phoebe told him drily. 'What I wish to discuss with you concerns another matter entirely . . . Alex, I don't think I have said how very sorry I am that Nathaniel is dead.'

He finished the brandy in his glass, and shrugged with a carelessness that did not deceive her. 'It was inevitable, born so early. Easy come, easy go . . . babies die every day. How many has the Queen lost? Five or six, at least. Louise is only twenty-one, there's plenty of time.' A lascivious smile crawled over his face. 'I shall look forward to making them.'

Phoebe stared at him, appalled. She knew, none better, how he instinctively seemed to utter just those words that would be most offensive, and now, as ever, the best policy would be to ignore them. But she thought of Louise, upstairs alone with her grief, and her resolution grew stronger. She said carefully, 'Alex – have you seen your wife today?'

'She was asleep when I looked in earlier,' he said, pouring

31

himself another brandy with a hand that was not quite steady. 'Why? D'you think I'm neglecting her?'

'Yes,' Phoebe said bluntly. She saw his brows draw together, and added quickly, '*You* may think that Nathaniel doesn't matter – although I suspect that the reverse is true. *She* certainly doesn't – Alex, she is distraught, bereft, and she thinks that you don't understand how she feels.'

'Really. Surely that is between her and me?'

'Perhaps it is – but when two people I value seem to be at odds, then it is very difficult to stand aside and do nothing.'

'What a pity. Anyway, has it not occurred to you that I have had no opportunity to speak with Louise since the baby died? Rest assured, I will do so.'

'Tomorrow morning, I hope.'

'And what makes you think I'll be sober then?' Alex enquired, his eyes glinting.

'I don't – although I trust you have some small shred of decency left.' Phoebe told him. She found her stick and heaved herself upright, her blue eyes, so like his own, hard and uncompromising. 'And I think you have. You forget, brother, how thoroughly I know you, the good as well as the bad. I am well aware that this is all a pose – you affect not to care about Nathaniel, but the very fact that you are trying to drink yourself into oblivion tonight suggests otherwise. All I will say now is that if you care, it does not matter if you deny it to me, or to anyone else – but don't deny it to Louise. For God's sake, admit it to her, or you'll richly deserve any trouble you cause by your callousness – as she will not.' She paused, seeing the closed hostility on his face, and added forcefully, 'You profess to love her. Well, prove it.' And without waiting for his response, she turned and limped towards the door.

Alex forestalled her. He crashed to his feet with a force that knocked over his chair, and in a few hasty strides pushed in front of her, blocking her path. He was much taller, with all the physical strength and vigour that had passed her by: she had to tip her head back to look into his eyes, and what she saw there gave her some small encouragement.

'Of course I love her,' Alex said, his voice suddenly thick with emotion. 'You know that I do – you of all people – Phoebe, I am sorry.'

'Really?' she said, her cool voice the echo of his, earlier. For a moment, their eyes held together, identical sapphire blue, and then suddenly she smiled, and held out her hand. 'And so am I. We have spent too much of our lives at odds. Now that we are friends, I would not have that altered – especially on such a sad occasion as this.'

He smiled, rather crookedly, and she saw with a touch of exasperation that his neckcloth was distinctly dirty, and there was a tear in the sleeve of his grey suit. Alex, well aware that he possessed good looks and charm in abundance, had never taken much care over his appearance. For that matter, neither had she, but then silk purses were not to be made from sow's ears, no matter how splendid the clothing. If she had been blessed with her brother's powers of attraction, she would have dressed as finely as any lady of fashion.

'I will see her tomorrow morning,' he said softly, and took her hand and gave her a rather clumsy, brandy-flavoured kiss on one cheek. 'And I promise I will be as kind, and loving, and understanding, as any wife could wish.'

And Phoebe, making her slow way to her bedchamber, hoped most fervently that it would be enough.

For Louise, sleep brought no comfort. She dreamed of Nathaniel, of holding him once more alive, feeling the warmth and strength that he had never possessed and then, turning back the soft folded shawl from his face, saw not her child, but a grinning death's head, eyes empty, mouth gaping, eager to suck the life from her as well.

She woke weeping in horror, and Christian came running, candle in her hand. 'Oh, m'lady, m'lady, be summat amiss?'

Her maid had served her for nearly two years, but Louise shrank from telling her the ghastly details of her nightmare. She shuddered, feeling the depth of her loss anew, her empty womb, her aching, swollen, useless breasts, and shook her head. 'It's – it's all right, Christian – I had a bad dream, that's all. What time is it?'

The girl looked at the clock that stood on the mantelpiece, just out of Louise's sight. 'Almost midnight, m'lady. You've been sleeping sound, six hour or more.'

'Did I wake you? I'm sorry if I did.' Louise smiled at her, unaware that in the light of the single candle, her own face, haunted by grief and exhaustion, bore a chilling resemblance to the leering skull that had terrified her in her dream. 'I shall do very well now, Christian. Light that candle there, by the bed, and leave it burning – then you can go back to sleep.'

The girl obeyed. Louise watched as she padded back to the antechamber, and then lay back on the pillows. Sleep, now, was beyond her: she still felt drained, and utterly weary, but her mind, hollow with loss, would not let her rest. Over and over again, she relived the brief hours of Nathaniel's life, every movement, every cry, the hazy blue of his eyes, the astonishing grasp of his hand. He was gone: he lay now lonely and cold and dark under the stone floor of Philip's Norton church, with only the piece of coral for comfort, and she had failed him. Her fault that he was dead, her fault that he had been born too soon, with scarcely a chance of life: her fault, her fault, her fault.

Silently, she curled under the sheets and blankets, her hands wrapped across the place where he had lain inside her, safe and secure, until her selfish folly had ejected him into this harsh and unmerciful world, and killed him. And she wept in despair for her lost son.

She must eventually have slept after all, and this time the nightmare did not invade her dreams. She woke to daylight, and Christian's quiet Somerset voice saying, 'M'lady? M'lady, 'tis Sir Alexander here to see ee.'

And there he was, blotting out the morning sunshine, the man she had, in another, more carefree lifetime, loved and married: Nathaniel's father. She had wanted him so much: and now, rent and aching after childbirth and tragedy, she could not imagine ever again feeling the stirrings of desire, let alone passion.

34

He was very pale, and his eyes were shadowed: from this, and the lines about his mouth, she guessed that he had spent the previous night drinking. Since their marriage, he had been remarkably sober, as if the need for brandy had died away as his need for her burgeoned: but now, obviously, he had reverted to his previous habit.

Well, perhaps he did care: but still she had that sense of distance, of remoteness, as if he had become a stranger again, and she could no longer even guess at his thoughts. Talk to him, Phoebe had urged, almost in desperation. Talk to him, share your grief, don't hide it away inside yourself.

But she knew what he must be thinking, as Phoebe, disastrously, had revealed that she also thought. All this anguish and to-do for a baby who had lived for scarcely two days was unseemly, misplaced, extreme. And she shrank from revealing the full extent of her distress to a man who, as she had good cause to remember, could be appallingly and brutally cruel, using words as his weapons when another man, less sophisticated and intelligent, might employ fist and foot and bludgeon.

Besides, he must undoubtedly, and quite justifiably, blame her for killing his dearly wanted son.

'Hullo,' he said, and smiled. It was not the mischievous, dazzling, uninhibited grin which he could employ to such overwhelming effect, and which had first attracted her. This smile was weary, careworn, bleak. 'May I sit down?'

'Of course,' Louise said. She watched as he settled himself on the bed beside her, wondering why she still felt nothing, no touch of love nor of lust, at the sight of her husband. It was as if all her feelings had been poured into Nathanial's frail body, only to die with him.

'I'm sorry if I woke you,' he said, and took her hand in his. The touch was warm, yet almost impersonal. 'How are you this morning?'

'Quite well, thank you,' Louise said. She could not muster a smile, but at least there were no more tears: somehow, she could not bear the thought of weeping in his arms, for the sake of a child who had hardly even lived . . .

And for Nathaniel's death, she had already cried tears sufficient for a river.

'I wish he had not died,' Alex said softly. 'I do mean that, Louise. I am very sorry for his death.'

'Naturally you are. He was your son and heir, after all. And neither was it your fault – you told me often enough that I should not ride. I ignored you, and Nathaniel paid the price.'

'And so did you,' Alex said. There was an unaccustomed gentleness in his voice, and she shrank from the intimacy that it implied. 'And – Louise, I don't blame you. Doctor Peirce said that your riding made no difference.'

He had, in fact, stated the exact opposite, and Louise had overheard him saying as much to the midwife. She looked down at her hands. 'You know that's not true. If I had not ridden as frequently – even if I had given it up a week ago – Nathaniel would be safe within me still. Anyway, what does it really matter, in the end? He was only a baby, and babies die so easily.'

'Do you honestly think that?' Alex stared at her, his eyes very blue and intent. 'Phoebe said that you did not.'

'Did she? Well, of course I care: I carried him, and I bore him, after all,' Louise said. She swallowed, praying that tears would not betray her. 'But – but it would not be fitting, I think, to grieve so much for one so small.'

He was still looking at her, as if he did not believe her. Then he said quietly, 'Oh, Louise – you do not have to be so brave, you know.'

'Why not?' She managed a smile, bright and false and empty enough to disguise a breaking heart. 'Other women lose not just one baby, but two, or three, or more. If they can endure such loss, who am I to complain when only one has died?'

One of his fingers stroked the palm of her hand. 'Nathaniel was our first child,' he said, and his voice held a promise that once, not so long ago, would have set her blood singing. 'There will be others, soon enough. When you are ready, sweet Louise, and not before . . . Time will heal even this.'

She wanted to shout her denial, to say that no child could replace Nathaniel in her heart, that a hundred babies would not compensate her for his death. And her mind shrank from the prospect of making love again, of being pregnant, with all the attendant inconvenience and indignity, the sickness and the limits on her once carefree life, and the desperate care she would be forced to take, to ensure the safe birth of her babies, the terrible fear that they would succumb to the first passing chill or fever . . .

No, no, she could not face it, or Alex: not yet. One day, perhaps, but her grief and her loss were too recent: she could not look ahead when her mind, like her body, was still raw, agonised, bleeding. All she wanted to do was to curl up and weep, in darkness and alone, to indulge in the anguish that her pride could not now let her reveal to Alex. He had lost his son and heir, but the most important part of herself seemed to have been wrenched away from her, and nothing would ever be the same again.

'I'm tired,' she said, looking still at a place just beyond their joined hands, where there was a discoloured patch on the embroidered bedcover, and a few pulled threads. 'Please, can you leave me for a while? I would like to rest.'

'Of course,' he said at once. 'I shall come back later . . . and I'll try to choose a time when you are awake. I'm sure that Lukas would like to see you too, and Phoebe.'

'By all means,' Louise said bleakly, although she could not imagine, in her present mood of listless despair, what she would say to either of them. 'But now, I want to rest.'

It was not hostility: he had received that from her before, often enough, when they had first met. With a shock Alex realised, as he left the chamber, that her attitude to him had been one of indifference.

Nor, later in the day, did Lukas fare any better. Until Nathaniel's birth, and death, Alex's elder son had enjoyed a happy, affectionate, uncomplicated relationship with his stepmother that was more sisterly than maternal. But instead of the cheerful, smiling girl he loved, he found a wan, unwelcoming stranger who quite evidently wished him elsewhere.

Lukas was a very sensitive child, and he had already been much upset by the death of his baby half-brother. Phoebe found him, some time later, sobbing in a corner of the garden, and did her best to comfort him. 'Oh, Lukas, what is it?'

It took some time for her to understand what he was saying: his mother tongue was Dutch, and although his English was now fluent, and not so correct and formal as it had been on his arrival at Wintercombe, under the stress of the past few days he had reverted to his native language, which was not one that Phoebe had ever learned. But by dint of much gentle coaxing and encouragement, she eventually discovered what was wrong.

'I thought she would be sad,' Lukas said miserably. 'Papa said that she would be. But she wasn't – she just didn't want me there.'

Phoebe, with the memory of her own visit still painfully fresh in her mind, said sympathetically, 'I know. But, Lukas, try to understand – she *is* sad, very much so, but she doesn't wish to show it. She is being very brave.'

'But. . .' Lukas gulped, and went on. 'But she used to be my friend – and now she doesn't want to know me any more – she didn't say it, but I could *feel* it, and *see* it.'

'It's not that she wants to be cruel,' Phoebe said gently, after a painful pause. 'Nor does she dislike you now. But she is so unhappy because Nathaniel died, that there is no room in her mind for anything except her grief – no room for you, or me, or even your father. Can you understand that?'

Lukas wiped his eyes, and looked up at her with an earnest, tear-filled gaze as blue as Alex's. 'I – I think so. But – but I'm sad too.'

'I know you are, Lukas – I know you are.' Phoebe held him close, ignoring the pain in her hip that always afflicted her when she knelt. 'And so am I. But we can't, any of us, feel the same sorrow that Louise must be suffering. Remember how pleased and excited you were to think of having a baby brother, and how disappointed you are now, as well as sad. Well, poor Louise must feel ten, twenty, a hundred times worse – she was his mother, after all. So, you must try and imagine how unhappy she must be, and understand that she hasn't much time to spare for you and me at present.'

'I wish Nathaniel hadn't died,' Lukas said, after a pause. He had stopped crying, although his face was still very blotched and tense. 'But – I thought Louise would die too, and she hasn't. She *is* going to be well again, isn't she, Aunt Phoebe – isn't she?'

'Of course she is,' she said stoutly, hoping that her words would not tempt fate. Childbirth was a dangerous time, and so many mothers followed their infants to the grave. 'And one day, I'm sure there will be another baby brother for you to play with – one that will be as strong and healthy as you are.'

But Alex's own father had been a frail, undersized child, and Phoebe herself was hardly a shining example of sturdy vigour. She prayed silently that Louise would not be subjected, as so many women were, from the Queen downwards, to the agony of endless miscarriages, still-births, and babies who lived only a few hours, or days, or weeks.

'Aunt Phoebe? Can I ask you something, please?'

Her thoughts thankfully interrupted, she looked down at her nephew's solemnly enquiring face, and smiled. He was so like Alex, but without the malice and the restless, urgent nature that had driven her brother half across Europe in an attempt to escape the constricted views and prospects of his inheritance and his responsibilities. Lukas would be a scholar, perhaps even take Holy Orders: she could see him as a parson, earnestly arguing some abstruse point of theology with a pedantic parishioner. Since his father was a professed atheist, and interested in republicanism and other dangerous, treasonable ideas, the thought made her smile wider. 'What is it, Lukas?'

'When you go back to Bath . . . can I come and stay with you for a little while?'

He was devoted to Alex, and to Louise: that he should want to leave them, and Wintercombe, and his pony, even for a short time, showed how greatly the tragic events of the past few days had upset him. She hugged him close, for he was very dear to her. 'Of course you can, Lukas – of course you can, until Louise is better.'

And until Alex and his wife had bridged the chasm of despair that had opened up between them when Nathaniel died.

She found her brother in the stables, tending his favourite horse. The grey stallion, Pagan, had come with Alex from Holland, eighteen months ago, and had reigned over the Wintercombe brood mares ever since. His first crop of foals had been born this spring: according to Pardice, the head groom, they were highly promising, and an increasing number of local gentlemen were now asking for Pagan's services for their own mares.

Phoebe was not knowledgeable about horses, and she could not share her brother's enthusiasm for improving his stock, nor Louise's love of riding, that had led her to disaster. But even she was willing to admit that the grey was a magnificent beast. He was a big horse, powerfully muscled, with a keen, intelligent head and a proud white waterfall of a tail: and yet, unlike Blaze, the young bay stallion that Alex often rode, he was as gentle and amiable as the proverbial lamb.

From the look of her brother, his talk with Louise had not resolved their problems. Frowning, he was grooming Pagan's sleek dappled quarters, sweeping the soft brush over and over the gleaming hide until it was as highly polished as fine pewter. The big horse stood half asleep, one hind leg cocked, his whiskery nose in his manger, the picture of contentment.

As she had expected, Alex was not in a welcoming mood. 'What do you want?'

'To ask you a favour, on behalf of Lukas,' Phoebe said. She leaned on her stick and surveyed him. Even in a torn shirt and old breeches, his long black hair straggling untidily across his wide shoulders, he was a man of great power and presence. Easy to see why Louise, who despite her youth was no green girl, had fallen so heavily in love with him: easy, too, to understand why she had been the latest in a very long, and scandalous, line.

The latest but, Phoebe hoped, the last. She added, 'You have five grooms to perform that office.'

'So I have – but I prefer to do it myself, when time permits. So does Pagan.' He slapped the horse's rump. 'Move over, you sleepy old donkey.'

Without a flicker of resentment at the insult, Pagan shifted his weight from one hind leg to the other, and blew thoughtfully into his oats. Alex moved round his rump so that he was standing between his sister and the horse. He pushed the hair out of his eyes with the hand that was not holding the brush, and said, 'I can imagine what Lukas wants – to stay with you in Bath for a while.'

Startled, despite the fact that Alex often seemed to know his family's thoughts better than they did themselves, Phoebe said, 'Yes, he does. How did you guess?'

'Call it male intuition,' her brother said drily. 'It's a good idea – I'd have suggested it myself if he had not. He'll be happier with you than moping round my heels, and you can continue his education – it's been sadly neglected of late. I've had other things on my mind.'

'I would be glad to,' Phoebe told him. 'I'll make a scholar of him yet. And he would be better away from Wintercombe for a while. You may have noticed that the baby's death has upset him greatly.'

Alex looked at her, and raised his brows. 'When you resort to irony, dearest Phoebe, I quake in my boots. Of course I've noticed, for Christ's sake – he is my son, remember. But . . .' He paused, and she saw in his face the weariness and strain inflicted by the last few days. 'But, as I said, I have had other matters on my mind. Louise, first and foremost. I thought you said she was distraught?'

'She was, yesterday. Today, she seems to have come to some acceptance,' Phoebe said cautiously.

Alex gave a bark of mirthless laughter. 'Acceptance! Not the word I'd have used. When I spoke to her this morning, she was . . . lifeless, like an effigy, or a statue, mouthing

41

platitudes politely, like a stranger. And . . .' He turned abruptly, as if this were almost too much to bear, and swept the brush violently across the stallion's glossy quarters. His voice, when it came, was almost inaudible. 'When I touched her, it was all she could do not to flinch. And not so long ago, we were hardly able to keep our hands from each other.'

'I know – I remember,' Phoebe said drily. 'Alex – please, be patient.'

'I am not a patient man.'

'I know that too – but you must be, for her sake. She has suffered a very great loss, one that neither of us can really understand – give her time, treat her gently and lovingly, and she will come back to you.'

'I only hope that you are right,' Alex said. 'Because, little sister – and I tell you this in all honesty, and the knowledge that you are no gossip – because I do not think that I can bear very much more of her indifference – however understandable the cause of it.'

There was, Phoebe found, nothing she could possibly say to that. Words of sympathy stuck in her throat: she swallowed, and thought wryly of Alex, the careless, licentious libertine, notorious for the number and brevity of his liaisons, now struck to the heart by his wife's coldness towards him.

If the circumstances had not been so tragic, she might almost have mustered a smile.

She left the next day, in the hired coach, and Lukas went with her. The thought of a stay in Bath had wrought a considerable change in her nephew: his eyes sparkled with excitement as he took his place next to Libby, and he had bid his father a remarkably brief farewell.

Phoebe, with some compassion, had taken a little longer to say goodbye to Alex, and despite her intentions, had found herself giving some sisterly advice. 'Please, Alex, try to be patient – she must melt, eventually. At present, I think she is consumed by grief, and guilt – whatever appearance she may give. But in a week or two, when the first pain has faded, then I'm sure you'll find a change in her.' She looked up at his unresponsive face, and continued. 'I remember, when Father died – I saw nothing, did nothing, ate nothing, for days – I felt that there was no more purpose to life – and yet I did recover, and more quickly than I thought. Oh, I still mourned him, and do even now, but I realised that I had a life to lead, despite his death. And, sooner or later, Louise will come to the same acceptance.'

'Oh, Phoebe, you're as full of proverbs as an old goodwife,' Alex had said, unsmiling. 'And the mantle of Aunt Silence sits ill upon you – her wisdom comes from long and bitter experience.'

'Whereas mine is all garnered from books – I'm well aware of that,' Phoebe told him. 'Well, you can ignore me or not, as you choose. No one can mend matters but yourself, and Louise, and I will not interfere any more. But remember – I am ever at your service, should you need me.'

'I will remember,' he promised, and kissed her, and helped her with unobtrusive care and thoughtfulness into the coach. Her last sight of him, as the cumbersome vehicle rolled out of the gate in the early morning sunshine, was his tall figure, bareheaded and somehow very alone, standing on the gravel of the courtyard, watching them leave.

# Chapter Three

## 'Unfaithful ground'

Lukas had not stayed in Bath for so long before, and never at the height of the season, and he loved it. The promenading men and women of fashion, with their fine clothes and exquisite manners, fascinated him: so did the activity in and around the several Baths, each catering for a slightly different clientele. His aunt's favourite was the Cross Bath, not far from her modest but comfortable residence in Nowhere Lane. It was frequented by ladies and gentlemen of wealth and refinement, a far cry from the crowded hurly-burly of the King's Bath, and had a roofed gallery, from which those who did not wish to immerse themselves could watch the bathers, and listen to the music being played, with variable results, in the other gallery opposite. Since the water was less hot than in the other Baths, it was particularly popular on the warmest days of summer.

Lukas loved music, but it was not, alas, one of Phoebe's gifts. Libby, however, played the guitar, not very proficiently, but well enough to teach her young cousin the rudiments. In addition, his mornings were spent reading, studying, and practising his writing skills. He had arrived at Wintercombe from Holland just over a year previously, bilingual in Dutch and English, but otherwise entirely uneducated, unable at six years old even to write his name. But he had proved to have an excellent brain, which, though lacking his father's effortless, flamboyant intelligence, possessed a far greater capacity for hard work and concentration. He had desperately wanted to learn, and Phoebe had found teaching him to be unexpectedly and deeply rewarding.

Often, she looked at him with love, seeing the sleek black head so like his father's, and wondered how her brother could have sired this solemn, pleasant and kindly little boy. But he was undoubtedly Alex's get – his looks alone proclaimed it, along with the love that bound father and son so strongly together. From all accounts, the child's mother had been a woman of great beauty, foul temper and despicable morals, who had treated Lukas very badly. No, the many and delightful qualities which he possessed had been inherited from neither parent, but had developed, like a rose amongst briars, entirely from some seed of original virtue within himself.

In the afternoons, if the weather was fine, they promenaded, Lukas escorting his aunt and cousin with charming gravity. They strolled along the walks of Kingsmead, and ate cakes and syllabubs in the little houses where refreshments were served to the company of fashionable visitors to Bath. They browsed in bookshops and sat by the New Bowling Green, just outside the northern walls, watching the play of those more energetic than themselves. When Phoebe's leg was painful, which was quite often, she stayed at home, or went with her maid Mattie to bathe in the Cross Bath, and Lukas and Libby set out on their own, exploring the city.

It was a peaceful, comfortable existence. With relief, Phoebe saw the signs of her nephew's misery ebb away in the very different surroundings of Bath. But he did not talk about his baby brother, nor about his stepmother, and she did not like to broach the subject and thereby, possibly, undo all the good that the change of scene had done.

It was never very far from her own mind, and no amount of reading, of cheerful talk and busy idle days, could erase the memory of Louise, weeping for her dead child and later, more disturbingly, trying to deny and eradicate her grief: nor of Alex, doubly bereft of both wife and son. They were both intelligent people, who up until now had loved each other passionately, and Phoebe hoped very much that they would soon be reconciled. But she also remembered Alex's anguished words to her in the stable, and wondered how a marriage that had been so predominantly founded upon physical desire would fare once that desire, in Louise's case, seemed to have withered and died.

But what did she know? Crippled, intellectual, lamentably plain and thin and dowdily dressed, she had no wish for marriage, and certainly no one in their senses would want to wed her – even for the sake of the handsome legacy which her father had left her, not for a dowry, but to enable her to live her present congenial, selfish and independent life. There was one man, true, whom she had met last year in her quest to save her brother from the penalties of treason: a man as different from herself as it was possible to be, a courtier, some years her senior, widowed with a young son. His help and influence had probably saved Alex from the block, and she would always be grateful to him. But that such a man might want more than friendship, she could not believe, despite the fact that he had written to her regularly since her return to Somerset in January: long, interesting, news-filled letters, always signed, 'Your humble and most affectionate servant.'

No, Sir Hugh Trevelyan was her friend, and always would be: anything more, Phoebe felt, knowing herself and her limitations too well, was ludicrous and unthinkable. She sensed that Libby, with a young girl's wistful sense of romance, read far more into the relationship than it actually contained, and Alex had sometimes teased her about her courtly admirer. Phoebe, who was long inured to his jests, took no notice.

In Hugh's latest letter, he had expressed his hopes for the continued good health and happiness of Sir Alexander St Barbe and his lady, and for the successful birth of a son and heir. She would have to write and tell him that those hopes had ended with Nathaniel's death.

Phoebe sighed, and glanced again at the other letter that lay on the table, propped against the pile of books which she had employed to teach Lukas something of the complexitites of recent English history. It had arrived the previous afternoon, and she had at first feared, seeing her brother's distinctive sprawling hand, that it contained bad news. But there were only three brief sentences:

Dear Sister,

I trust that you are well, and my son Lukas also. I shall be coming to Bath shortly, and hope to take full advantage of your ever-generous hospitality. If Lukas wishes it, I shall carry him back to Wintercombe with me.

And he had signed his name below, with an entirely characteristic flourish that took up most of the rest of the paper. Phoebe looked at Lukas, who was curled up on the windowseat of her everyday parlour, head in the inevitable book. He had been excited at the news of his father's imminent visit, but his face, no doubt of it, had fallen when Phoebe had mentioned the possibility of his return to Wintercombe. 'Oh, Aunt Phoebe, must I?'

'Of course not, if you wish to stay longer – I'm sure your father will understand,' she had told him, smiling, and he beamed in response. 'Oh, good. I do so like it here!'

And she enjoyed his company as, mostly, she enjoyed Libby's. Alex would not mind: and Phoebe hoped that his suggestion meant that matters had mended between him and Louise.

The clock struck eight, with a soft, silvery chime. She leaned back in her chair and said, 'Time for bed, Lukas.'

'Oh, please, Aunt, can't I stay a little longer? Just till I've finished the page?'

'Bed,' she said, gently implacable. With a resigned sigh, and a yawn, her nephew shut the book and rose from the window seat. 'Very well. Good night, Aunt Phoebe – good night, Libby.'

When he had gone, she turned her mind again to answering Sir Hugh's letter. Almost immediately, however, her thoughts were interrupted by a sudden and urgent knocking on the front door. Libby's mouse-fair head went up like a deer's, and she stared at her cousin. 'Whoever can that be?'

'I don't know, but we'll soon find out,' Phoebe said. She got to her feet and limped over to the door that led out into the long, narrow hallway. The last time this had happened at such a late hour, it had brought them news of Nathaniel's premature birth, and she hoped that whoever stood outside now would not be the bearer of similarly bad tidings.

Mattie had forestalled her. As Phoebe entered the hall, she saw her maid slide back the bolts, lift the latch, and peer round the door with justifiable suspicion. Then she opened it wider, with a hasty curtsey. 'Why, Sir Alexander – we didn't expect ee here today!'

'No? Well, I trust your mistress is at home,' Alex said. He ducked his head under the lintel and smiled at his sister, standing outside the parlour door. 'Hullo, Phoebe. I see you are.'

She had already discerned his unsteady gait and slurred words. As the maid shut and bolted the door again behind him, Phoebe said swiftly, 'That will be all, thank you, Mattie.'

'On the cont'ry,' Alex said, turning to the maid. 'You can get me a bottle of wine, and a glass.'

Mattie glanced at her mistress, her eyebrows raised, and Phoebe sighed. 'Very well, Mattie. You may bring them to the front parlour – and make sure that neither Mistress Libby nor Master Lukas disturbs us.'

'Yes, madam,' said the maid, with a hasty bob, and scurried away towards the kitchen.

With a look of thunder, Phoebe pushed open the door to her best parlour, where she kept her books, and a bed for those nights when her leg was too painful to use the stairs. 'In there.'

'What's the matter, little sister? Not pleased to see me?' Alex removed his hat and aimed it at one of the wooden pegs projecting from the wall just inside the door. It missed, and he laughed, but made no effort to pick it up.

'Usually, I would be,' Phoebe hissed, and jerked her thumb at the open door. 'In there, before Lukas realises you're here.'

'Afraid I'll c'rupt him? Shame on you,' said her brother. 'Take my coat, will you?'

'No, I certainly will not,' Phoebe told him, her anger rising. 'What in God's name are you thinking of, to come here unannounced, and in that condition?'

'What con – condition?' Alex said, evidently inclined to be irritating. 'Do tell me, little sister.'

'You know perfectly well,' Phoebe snapped. Mattie arrived with the wine and two glasses on a tray, and she took it from her maid. 'You may go, Mattie. Tell Mistress Libby that Sir Alexander will be sleeping in the front parlour tonight – and she need not wait up for me, if she wishes to go to bed.'

'Yes, madam,' Mattie said, and with a wary glance at Alex, who was leaning against the panelling that lined the hallway, eyeing her enquiringly, she turned and made good her escape.

'In here,' Phoebe said again. She carried the tray into the front parlour, and set it down on the table. As she had expected, Alex followed her, his eyes on the wine. She turned to face him, noting his flushed face and unfocused gaze, and said furiously, 'I must be mad, letting you stay here. You're as drunk as a lord.'

'As a judge, surely,' Alex said, grinning. He walked over to the table and poured out two overflowing glasses of wine. 'Don't look so dis – dis'proving, sister – I've good reason.' He raised his glass, and she saw, suddenly, the wildness in his eyes. 'A toast to marriage, Phoebe – drink with me?'

She picked up the other glass gingerly, wondering how soon he would explode. 'Alex,' she said quietly, her own anger suddenly evaporated, 'Alex, what has happened?'

'Happened?' He swallowed most of his wine in one gulp. 'This isn't claret – you've been cheated.'

'Since I bought it from Libby's father, I rather doubt it.' Phoebe watched him empty his glass and pour out more, spilling a fair amount, and then repeated her question. 'What has happened? Why have you come here like this?'

'Happened? Nothing's happened – that's why,' Alex said. 'Nothing at all – ev'rything's just exactly the same.'

'But Louise – Louise is well?'

'Oh, well enough,' said her brother, with transparently false carelessness. 'Take my advice, Phoebe – never get married.'

'I hadn't intended to,' she said drily.

He went on, as if she had not spoken. 'I thought Louise would be different – I was wrong.'

'Different? Alex, what do you mean?'

'You haven't touched your wine,' he said, ignoring her. 'Don't be such a milksop – drink it!'

'I have no intention of drinking it,' Phoebe told him, and set her glass firmly back on the tray. 'Not until you've told me what's wrong. Oh, for God's sake, Alex, I know you drank a lot in the past, but when you married Louise, it seemed that all that had changed – and now something's wrong, it must be. I don't think I've ever seen you like this before, you can hardly stand – '

'Shows how much you've missed, doesn't it?' Alex said. 'God damn you, Phoebe, I've had enough of your in – int'rogation – let me go to Hell my own way, will you?'

'No,' she said, and stepped closer to him, ignoring the ache of weariness in her leg. 'No, I won't – you're my only brother, and I care about you, God knows why, and Louise is my dear friend – why is she "different"? What's happened? For Christ's sake, Alex, you can't burst in here roaring drunk and drop vague teasing hints and then refuse to tell me anything – what has happened?'

He stared down at her, swaying slightly, a frown on his face. 'I told you. Nothing. That's the reason, Phoebe – nothing – nothing at all.' He took another swig of wine and went on, almost to himself. 'I talked to her – I tried, believe me I tried – just like talking to a bloody wall. She won't let me in – oh, not lit – lit'rally.' His voice stumbled over the syllables and went on, thick with drunken desperation and bitterness. 'She's like a stranger, Phoebe – 's as if she never loved me, never loved me at all.'

'And you still love her?'

'Of course I bloody do, you fool!' He hurled the glass, still half full of wine, at the empty fireplace. It smashed against the stone, flinging a shower of glittering drops and fragments into the hearth. 'How could you understand? You're only a dried-up sexless old spinster, after all.'

It was true, but his words still had the power to hurt.

Phoebe stood her ground, pale with anger. She said furiously, 'I hope you don't mean what you say.'

'Oh, I do, I do,' said her brother unpleasantly. 'Ev'ry last bleeding word of it, sister Feeble.'

His use of the old cruel childhood nickname stung her into rage. Without stopping to think, she lifted her stick and swung it at his face. His hands went up to ward it off, but drink had slowed his reactions, and the wood smacked against his cheekbone with a force that sent him staggering back against the table. The wine bottle and remaining glass tipped over, sending red claret splashing like blood across her precious books, and her brother, his face hidden behind his hand, slid slowly to the floor.

All her fury gone, Phoebe stared down at him for a moment. Then she dropped to her knees beside him. 'Alex! Alex, I'm so sorry – are you all right?'

He did not reply: she touched him, stricken by remorse, and then realised that he was shaking with silent, helpless laughter. She pulled one of his hands away from his face, and saw with alarm the split, bleeding mark of her blow, slashing across his face just below the left eye. 'Dear God,' said Phoebe in horrified astonishment. 'Did I really do that?'

'I think you must've done,' Alex told her, gasping. 'How long have you been waiting for the chance to beat me to death?'

'About twenty-five years,' Phoebe said drily. She found a kerchief in the sleeve of her old, shabby black gown, and dabbed at the cut. Already the surrounding flesh was red, and swelling fast. Alex flinched away. 'Christ, that hurts. Let me before you do me any more damage.'

She watched as he staunched the blood with clumsy hands, and said again, 'I'm sorry.'

'Don't be – you were sorely provoked, and not for the first time.' He had stopped laughing, and his eyes, brilliantly blue beneath the dishevelled locks of black hair, were suddenly serious. 'Rest 'sured, I shan't call you Feeble again. I've been hurt worse than this before, by man or horse, but never by a woman. And I deserved it.'

'You certainly did,' his sister agreed. 'Has it sobered you?'

'A little – though I wish the room would keep still for a space.' He looked down at the bloodstained kerchief. 'Has the bleeding stopped yet?'

'Yes, but it's a nasty cut. You'll carry the scar of it for a while, if not for ever. How are you going to explain it away?'

'No idea – but I've no intention of telling the truth.' His eyes gleamed for a moment. 'That'd be altogether too hum – humil'ating.'

'Exactly – hardly in keeping with your pose as a hard-drinking, hard-living rake,' Phoebe told him. 'Alex, you may not remember this in the morning, but I'll say it, nevertheless. Please, please don't despair. It's only a fortnight since Nathaniel died. Louise hasn't had time to recover from the birth yet, let alone her grief. She can't just pretend that it never happened, that she wasn't pregnant, that she did not give birth. Please, be patient, give her time. She's very young, after all – and I don't think she has known such sorrow before.'

'Whereas we both have,' he said. 'Our mother died bearing you, and I have never forgotten the pain of it. And you – you lost Father.'

'I mourn him still,' said Phoebe. 'As he mourned the loss of you, to the end of his days – how he would have loved Lukas.'

'Don't reproach me with that,' Alex said, his voice suddenly hard. 'Phoebe, I am not proud of what I am, or have been or done. I just ask you to accept it.'

'You make it very difficult at times,' she pointed out. 'But can Louise accept it? Alex, let us be practical for a moment, and put muddy emotions aside. You need a son and heir. Lukas is a bastard, and Nathaniel is dead. Despite her loss, Louise is not, thank God, now likely to die of it, and besides, on your own admission, you love her. You *must* mend matters between you, or there will be no more children. And then, in spite of everything he did to you, Cousin Charles will have Wintercombe.'

There was a brief, fraught silence. 'D'you think I haven't

52

thought of that?' Alex said, with a sudden, angry gesture. 'But if that was all my worry, I'd be willing to wait for Louise for ever – or nearly for ever. Sweet Christ, Phoebe, is unreturned love so completely outside your experience?'

'Any love of that kind is outside my experience,' Phoebe said. 'But even I can see that all you can do is wait, and be patient, and if you love her, *tell* her, don't assume she knows it already.'

There was a long silence. Alex had turned his head away from her: all she could see was the ugly wound on his cheek, marring the clear line of bone below his eye. He said at last, so low that she could hardly hear him, 'I have told her. Again and again. It makes no difference.'

Phoebe laid a hand on his shoulder. 'Do you want me to come back to Wintercombe and talk to her? Perhaps she will listen to me.'

'Why? She didn't before.'

As Phoebe, annoyed, withdrew her hand, he turned towards her, and she saw the desperate appeal in his face: Alex, the cynical, the self-sufficient, the careless. 'I'm sorry, little sister – I'm in no state to talk. Can we discuss it in the morning? At this precise moment, I could fall asleep where I sit.'

'Well, I couldn't,' she observed, reaching for her stick. Using it and the table, she hauled herself upright. With rather more effort, Alex did likewise, and stood swaying gently, a steadying hand on her leather-upholstered chair. 'I should go to bed if I were you,' she added kindly, surveying her dishevelled and disreputable brother. 'It's not aired, though I don't suppose you care much about that. In case of necessity, there's a basin over there, on the little table by the door. I'll see you in the morning.'

'Don't bother to wake me,' Alex said, as she left. 'I doubt the last trump would do that.'

Phoebe snorted. 'Well, if you would prefer it, we can arrange to have an excellent imitation of it played outside your window at daybreak – '

'I'll commit murder if you do,' Alex said, with a laugh that sounded almost genuine. The echoes of it stayed in her mind until she had found her own way to her comfortable bed in the chamber above, and a rest that was probably, and most unfairly, a good deal more uneasy than his.

Lukas was overjoyed when he walked into the dining parlour the next morning and found Alex sitting there, rather pale and with an angry mark on his face, sipping coffee and talking to Aunt Phoebe. 'Papa!' he cried in delight, and bowed with a happy flourish. 'I didn't know you were here. What's happened to your face?'

'I met my just deserts,' Alex said, with a rather wry smile. 'But you can tell people that it was some desperate highwayman with a sword, if you like.'

'*Was* it?'

'No, alas – I could welcome a villain to cross swords with, and beat into submission,' Alex said reflectively.

'How's Louise?'

'Oh, well enough, though very bored, I fear. Doctor Peirce told her she must rest as much as possible, and you know Louise.'

'And Tubs?' Lukas asked, naming his fat skewbald pony. 'Does he miss me?'

'Not in the slightest – Pardice has turned him out into the orchard, and he's grown bloated on too much new grass. Why? Do you want to come back to Wintercombe with me, tomorrow?'

Lukas threw a quick glance at Phoebe that Alex did not miss. He smiled rather shyly at his father, and said apologetically, 'If you don't mind, Papa, I think I'd like to stay here for a while longer. Is that all right? I promised Aunt Phoebe that I'd teach her some Dutch.'

'Of course I don't mind,' Alex told him. 'But as I'm here, why don't you show me some of the sights of Bath? We have all day at our disposal, and I'm sure Phoebe, and Libby, would appreciate some time to themselves. And you can tell me why she wants to learn *Dutch*, of all the benighted languages.'

'It's Lukas's mother tongue,' Phoebe pointed out. 'And

54

since the husband of the heir to the throne is Dutch, it might one day prove very useful.'

'I don't care – any language that can render "Hamlet, I am thy father's ghost" as "*Omlet, Ik ben da Poppa spook*" is doomed to be the subject of ridicule. Well, brat, will you eat your breakfast, or shall I go out on my own?'

Not for the first time, Phoebe, watching him, marvelled at his powers of recovery. It was as if the offensive drunkard who had provoked her into striking him, only twelve hours previously, had never existed: and instead here was the brother she loved best, the attentive, teasing, humorous father who could raise delighted childish giggles even from such a serious little boy as Lukas. The unfairness and tragedy of Nathaniel's death struck her anew, and she sipped the scalding hot coffee and told herself that her suddenly watering eyes were caused only by its temperature.

Lukas normally ate with well-mannered deliberation, but he bolted his bread and cheese and announced, through the last mouthful, that he had finished.

'Then you may both go, and leave us in peace,' Phoebe said magnanimously, and watched as the child virtually towed Alex from the room. There was a brief bustle in the hallway, to do with hats and coats, and then the door slammed shut behind them.

Libby, who had sat silently eating at the end of the table, gave an audible sigh. Phoebe laughed. 'Yes, Alex can be very exhausting, even when he's on his best behaviour – and when Lukas catches his mood, he's just as bad. Well, I think I shall spend a quiet and pleasant morning with my nose in a book – will you join me?'

And Libby, with alacrity, assented.

Lukas was thoroughly enjoying himself. It seemed a very long time since he and his father had been alone together like this: in fact, he could not remember exactly when, though he thought it might have been a ride along the Wellow Lane in the spring. And all the pain and sorrow that had beset them since then fled away under the warm morning sunshine, and in the cheerful crowds of people thronging the streets.

His father apparently knew a great many of them: every few yards there was an exchange of pleasantries, and cries of, 'St Barbe, my dear fellow, how d'ye do?' Lukas was invariably introduced as 'my son', which raised several eyebrows. The boy, with a gleam of mischief, took his cue from Alex's teasing, light-hearted mood, and would fix the enquirer with a solemn, matter-of-fact gaze. '*Natural* son, sir.'

They arrived at the King's Bath in fine spirits. It was already too late in the morning for the fashionable, who liked to bathe early to avoid the crush, and the risk of staying too long in water contaminated by other, inferior bodies, but there were still many people immersed in the hot, bubbling, evil-smelling water. They paid a penny for a cupful pumped up directly from the springs beneath, said to be an excellent restorative and purgative. Lukas, who had not drunk it before, grimaced and pronounced in disgust that it tasted just as if eggs had been boiled in it.

'That's why it's so good for you,' Alex pointed out. 'The more disgusting the medicine, the more effective the cure.'

'Then that fiddler must be the best remedy of all,' his son said, grinning, as the offending musician, who had neglected to tune one of his strings finely enough, sent his instrument screeching into life. 'Can we watch the bathers, please?'

The Bath would be emptied at ten or eleven o'clock, but there were many men and women, mostly the elderly or the obviously sick, soaking in the sunshine and the warm greenish water. A small boy, stark naked and no older than Lukas, hovered expectantly. Alex fished a shilling from his pocket and flicked it into the Bath, and the child, in a flash, vaulted the stone balustrade and dived after it. Lukas, who could not swim and was secretly rather afraid of water, hung over the edge, wondering if he would find the coin. It did not seem possible, in those murky depths, but after an alarmingly long time the urchin's small head shot up, streaming water and screeching triumph, his hand held aloft with the coin clutched in his fingers.

'Ever thought of earning some pocket money?' Alex asked Lukas, with a teasing grin.

His son shook his head emphatically. 'No, I have *not*. I'm sure there must be easier ways.'

Alex laughed. 'You're right, there are.' Folding his arms, he leaned over the stone rail, gazing down at the boy, who was splashing energetically towards one of the 'slips' that led out of each corner of the Bath.

Lukas's eye was caught by a vast shape billowing out of the same slip: a woman enormously fat, her size increased still further by the stiff yellow canvas robe that all respectable female bathers wore. 'Look! Isn't that Aunt Bab?'

Alex followed his pointing finger, and his smile abruptly disappeared. 'Yes,' he said shortly. 'Time we were going, I think.' And he swung away from the balustrade and started walking back towards the steps that led up to the Abbey.

After a startled pause, Lukas raced in pursuit, nearly knocking over a rheumatic old lady with a stick. 'Papa! Wait for me!'

Alex turned at the top of the steps. 'I am waiting,' he said. 'Shall we walk in the Abbey? It's cooler there.'

Lukas would much rather have gone to the bowling green, or to one of the syllabub houses in Kingsmead, or browsed along the shops in Cheap Street and Stall Street, with their enticing sights and smells and glorious variety of tempting fripperies from far and near, but he had seen that look on his father's face before, although rarely turned in his direction. 'Very well, Papa,' he said, subdued and obedient, and the man and boy walked into the dim, cool, echoing void of the magnificent Abbey Church that dominated Bath.

There were a great many people parading there, laughing and chattering and greeting each other as if this were a place of public assembly rather than of worship. Lukas, who had learned from his years in the care, if it could be called that, of his Dutch mother, when it was advisable to keep silent, followed his father, bowing when he bowed, avoiding unwelcome notice. They strolled the length of the building without exchanging a word with each other, although several acquaintances complemented Alex on his son's handsome looks and exquisite manners, and emerged blinking into the light and heat of the day, just as the clock above them began to strike eleven.

Lukas glanced up at his father, and saw an encouraging change in the set of his face. Emboldened, he said tentatively, 'Please, Papa – no one's ever really told me – what *did* Aunt Bab and Cousin Charles and Cousin Amy do that was so terrible?'

Alex stared down at the boy, a frown on his face. 'Why do you want to know?'

Lukas swallowed. Secure in the knowledge of his father's love for him, he was not really afraid, but did not, even so, wish to incur his wrath. He took a breath, and said, 'I liked Cousin Amy. I wanted to see her again, but Aunt Phoebe says I can't, even though she lives in Bath too, now.'

Alex turned towards the gardens that lay to the east of the Abbey, just inside the city wall. After a while, he said, 'If anyone was innocent in the whole sorry tale, it was your Cousin Amy. And the reason you can't see her is because Aunt Bab won't allow it. She can't forgive me for what happened, you see – and I suppose in a way she's right to blame me.'

'But what *did* happen?' Lukas persisted.

They had come to the gravelled walk, shady and tree-lined, and there was no one within earshot. Alex stopped, his hands clasped behind his back, apparently studying the slender, grey-barked trunk of the nearest tree. He said at last, 'Cousin Charles wanted Wintercombe. He thought it should be his, because he had lived there for most of his life, and my father relied on him to run the estate. When I came back from Holland, after my father died, Charles's nose was thoroughly put out of joint – especially when I told him and Aunt Bab and Amy to leave. He was even more upset that I had fallen in love with Louise, because he loved her too.'

'I remember,' Lukas said, his face very serious. 'He hated you, and me too. I didn't know why then. Was it because you are my father?'

58

'Unfair as it may seem, Luikje, yes.' Alex began walking again, down the gravelled path between the neat trees, bustling with birds. 'And because he hated me so much, and wanted Wintercombe, and Louise, he tried to have me executed for treason.'

Lukas's face showed that a great many previously puzzling matters had now become clear. He said, 'That was when you were in prison, in the Tower of London. But they let you go, so Cousin Charles's plan didn't work.'

'No, it didn't – firstly because I wasn't guilty, and secondly because King James decided that I was worth more to him alive than dead. I paid a fine, or money for a pardon – what you call it rather depends on your point of view – and I was set free. But of course, once everyone else in the family realised what Charles had tried to do, they didn't want to have anything more to do with him.'

'And then he tried to kill you,' Lukas said, remembering. 'In London, when we were all staying at Sir Hugh Trevelyan's house.'

'Fortunately, he didn't succeed in that either. But as a punishment, and so that he would have no chance to try again, Aunt Silence told him that he must go into exile – leave England, and never come back. And that's where he's gone – to the New World, to start again.'

'It doesn't seem right,' said Lukas thoughtfully. 'He should have been put in prison for trying to kill you.'

'Well, Aunt Silence has a soft heart, and he is her grandson, after all,' Alex told him. 'She gave him the choice – to go to the New World, or to stay and be tried for attacking me. Not surprisingly, he chose exile. But Aunt Bab and Amy didn't want to go too – they decided to remain in Bath, in the house in the Abbey Green that I made over to them. And Aunt Bab won't have anything to do with us now.'

'That doesn't seem fair, when you could have had Cousin Charles put in prison, and didn't.'

'Oh, she adores Charles, she thinks I've been cruel and heartless – so we are no longer speaking,' Alex said. 'Is it all clear to you now? I left the Bath because I had no wish to be seen by Bab – she'd doubtless subject me to a torrent of public abuse.'

'Poor Amy,' Lukas said, after a pause. 'I wouldn't like to have Aunt Bab for my mother.'

'I don't blame you – neither would I. But Amy's a very pretty girl. She'll probably marry soon, and escape Bab's clutches. And, Luikje – '

'Yes, Papa?'

'I'm sorry if I seemed angry. I wasn't angry with you, not in the least.'

'I know.' His son grinned up at him, suddenly ebullient. 'Papa? Do you think anyone would mind if I *ran*? Just round the outside of the walks?'

'I doubt it – there aren't many people here, it's close to dinner time. Just mind those ladies over there.'

'Of course.' Lukas glanced at the two women, one very fashionably dressed, strolling towards them down a path to the left. 'Papa? One of them is looking at you as if she knows you.'

Alex followed his gaze. Seeing his interest, the fashionable lady smiled, and inclined her head coyly behind a very large feather fan in the latest style. 'Well, I'll be damned!' he said softly.

'Who is it, Papa? Do you know her?'

'An old acquaintance – a *very* old acquaintance. You do your running, Luikje, and I will exchange a few courtesies with Lady Burton.'

Obediently, Lukas set off at a decorous trot. As he passed the women, he saw that the lady with the fan was very beautiful, with a profusion of dark curls and an exquisitely pale, heart-shaped face. She smiled radiantly at him as he passed, and he thought, as he ran to the end of the path, that she seemed to be very friendly and pleasant.

'Sir! As I live, Sir Alexander St Barbe!' Charlotte, Lady Burton, sank into an elegant curtsey, entirely devoid of subservience. Her eyes glanced up at him, and she smiled. 'I might ask you what you do here, sir – and is that charming boy by any chance your son?'

The years had not changed her: still the same easy,

teasing, flirtatious manner, the same flower-perfect face and soft laughter, and the hint of greater and more intimate favours in every roguish glance, the light touch of a delicate gloved hand, the flutter of her outrageous fan. Four years ago, when he had been living in London, toying with treason, he had encountered her at Whitehall, and had embarked on a scandalous, passionate affair with her. Then, they had been well-matched, both being young, good-looking, amoral and pleasure-seeking. The liaison had set even Whitehall buzzing, until two almost simultaneous disasters: the discovery of a supposed Whig plot to kill King Charles and his brother, the Duke of York: and the return, from diplomatic service in Germany, of Charlotte's middle-aged, influential and insanely jealous husband. Alex had judged it prudent to remove himself to Holland, a country he already knew well. There, he had joined one of the English regiments in Dutch service, and stayed for two years before his father's death pulled him reluctantly back to Wintercombe, to take up his inheritance.

And to encounter the envy and enmity of his cousin Charles: and the enchanting, effervescent vitality of his cousin Louise, whom he had made his wife.

He took Charlotte's hand. 'My natural son, as you might guess. His mother is Dutch, but he lives with me now. Shall we walk, and talk?'

'I would be delighted, sir,' said Charlotte, with a flutter of very long, dark lashes. She was still breathtakingly beautiful: and he knew, from the sidelong, speaking glance she sent him, that he could have her again, whenever he wished.

'So, what are you doing here in Bath?' he enquired. 'Have you come for the company, or to take the waters?'

'Oh, I am here for the company – I have bathed, once or twice, but I favour rather different diversions,' said his former mistress, with a smile that indicated exactly the path of her thoughts. 'No, it is my poor husband, alas, who has been advised to come here by his physicians. He suffered an apoplectic fit last winter, and it has left all his right side

61

palsied – arm, hand, leg, everything, nor can he now speak.' She made a little grimace of distaste. 'He can only make the most disgusting noises, and his valet must carry him and tend him like a baby, for he can do very little for himself. So – he bathes every day, morning and evening, and I am left to take the air, and find my own amusements, while he takes the waters.'

Alex glanced at the other woman, who was following them at a little distance. From her submissive demeanour and plain dress, he assumed her to be a servant, or a companion. Charlotte laughed. 'You need not worry – Dickson is perfectly discreet. She knows what will happen to her if she is not, and even in Bath she would be hard pressed to find another situation, without a character. And so, Sir Alexander, I have told you my recent sad history – what is your news? I heard that you are married – to a French cousin, was it?'

'That is correct,' Alex said. He thought of Louise, her smile, her laughter, her essential honesty, the wild, reckless life in her that he had thought unquenchable, until Nathaniel died. And the thought came to him, that it would not be a true betrayal, for she seemed to care nothing for him any more . . .

'So, we shall have to be circumspect,' Charlotte said. Her smile was as dazzling as Louise's had once been, but more calculated; on the other hand, she was so very beautiful. And minute by minute, his senses were remembering more and more of the luscious body so cleverly concealed, yet revealed, beneath the caerulean silk of her fashionable mantua, and the almost transparent white tippet that protected her plump bare shoulders from the sun. If the sin of lust could be made flesh, it would surely assume the tempting glance, the teasing voice and voluptuous curves of Charlotte Burton: and he knew already, without guilt or remorse, that it was a temptation which he did not want to resist.

Lukas was coming back, at the same neat trot. Charlotte said, 'A handsome child. He looks very like you. And he lives with you? What does your wife say to that?'

'She dotes on him,' Alex told her, although the last time

Louise had seen Lukas, she had taken no more notice of him than of a piece of furniture.

'And you and your wife have no children yet?' Charlotte asked, in a casual tone that did not deceive him.

'No,' Alex said. 'None, as yet.' He had no intention of telling her about Nathaniel: that tragedy was still too raw and painful to be served up as a titbit of news, to invoke protestations of insincere sympathy and regret. He had no illusions about Charlotte. Unlike Lukas's mother, she was not malicious, but she was as naturally and unthinkingly selfish as a flower, existing only in terms of her vanity, her beauty and allure and the gratification of appetites which, even at the dissolute Court of the previous King, had caused comment. He had not been the first of her lovers, nor the last, and beside Louise, she was pure dross.

But the Louise whom he had married perhaps no longer existed: and with every step, desire for Charlotte burgeoned in his mind.

'Hullo,' Lukas said, coming to a halt in front of them. He removed his hat and made a charming French bow, his black hair shiny in the sun.

'Lady Burton, may I present my son, Lukas van der Linden?'

'A great pleasure, sir,' said Charlotte, smiling at the boy. 'You run very nicely, Master Lukas – I would love to see you make another circuit of the walks. That is, if you are not too tired by your exertions.'

'Of course not, madam,' Lukas said, with an answering grin, and set off once more with a flourish.

Charlotte's large blue eyes followed him. 'A delightful boy,' she said. 'So – you are in Bath for a few days, sir?'

'I had intended to return home tomorrow.'

'Ah, yes – your estate is hereabouts, is it not? Well, perhaps your wife is pining for you.'

'I doubt it,' Alex said, and the bitterness in his voice took him by surprise.

Charlotte glanced at him assessingly. 'I see. Then she will not be averse to your staying in Bath for a while longer, perhaps?'

Alex, with sudden helpless anger, thought that Louise had probably not even noticed his absence: or, if she had, felt only relief that he had gone. He said, with a creditable return to his earlier, careless manner, 'Of course not. And besides, I had already resolved to spend a little more time here, enjoying the company.' He smiled at her. 'Especially when the company is as delightful as at present, Lady Burton.'

Charlotte fluttered her fan coyly. 'La, sir, you do me too much honour.'

'I do not flatter you, madam. And I am sure that my sister will not mind if I further impose on her hospitality. She lives near the Cross Bath, and since she is in poor health, she often takes the waters twice a day – as does your husband, so you said?'

'Most regularly, sir – up at sunrise, back for a purge and a sweat in his chamber by ten o'clock, and out again at five for the evening bathe . . . you could set your watch by him,' said Charlotte, with a quick, significant glance. 'He does not visit the Cross Bath, however – he prefers the heat of the King's Bath, whatever the weather, and we are handily lodged in the Abbey Green, with Mistress East – do you know it? Our chambers are very well appointed and spacious, with a kitchen, and our own entrance to the side, all very private and convenient.' She fluttered her fan again, and glanced at Alex to ensure that he had understood. 'Well, sir, here is your son once more, so I must bid you goodbye, and return to see how poor Sir Anthony does. We have been here ten days, and there is little improvement thus far, although if we stay for the remainder of the summer, perhaps he will recover some of his faculties.'

'I trust he will, madam.' Alex bowed, very formally. 'Goodbye, Lady Burton – I don't doubt that we shall meet again, very soon. Tomorrow morning, perhaps?'

She curtseyed, with a far from formal smile on her lovely face. 'That will be most pleasant, Sir Alexander. I shall greatly look forward to it. Until then, sir, goodbye.' And with a last coy flick of her fan, a swish of heaven-blue silk and a lingering sweet aroma of rosewater, she was gone, gliding elegantly away along the path towards the Abbey Green, her maid following.

'Who was that lady? Do you know her well?' asked Lukas, returning breathless to his father's side a moment later.

'Yes, I used to know her when I was in London, some years ago.'

'I like her smile,' Lukas said with approval. 'And she's very beautiful, isn't she? Is she lodging here in Bath?'

'She is, yes.'

'Then perhaps we'll see her again soon,' Lukas said, sounding pleased.

'Yes,' he said, with the vision of Charlotte Burton glittering, wickedly seductive, in his mind. 'Yes, I am sure we shall.'

# Chapter Four

### 'Covering adultery'

'M'lady?'

Louise opened her eyes, blinking, clogged and stupid with sleep. Christian stood by the bed, an expression of some concern on her face. 'You asked I to wake ee,' she went on. ''Tis almost dinner time, and a fair fine day.'

'Is it?' Louise said, without much interest. But she could see sunshine on the warm oaken wainscotting clothing the walls of her chamber, and sparkling on the little Dutch picture that Alex had brought back from Holland.

Once, she had loved that painting, a scene so real that it seemed to be a glimpse through a window, frozen in time and oils: two children laughing over some game with a ball in a courtyard, watched by a bored cat and an excited dog. Before Nathaniel, it had celebrated all her joy and her hopes of happiness. Now, it seemed only a bitter, cruel mockery of those false, deluding dreams.

'M'lady?' Christian said, her voice unusually tentative.

Louise looked at her again. She had never been on particularly close terms with her maid, an efficient, plain, rather reserved girl whose demeanour did not encourage the exchange of feminine confidences. Once Louise, self-sufficient and headstrong, with her own dangerous secrets to conceal, had been quite happy with this state of affairs. Lately, however, she had sometimes regretted a little that she and Christian were not on more friendly terms: for there was no one, no one at all in the whole world, who seemed to understand the depths and compass of her misery.

'Yes?' she said listlessly. 'What is it?'

'Beg pardon for presuming, m'lady – but have ee thought to send a letter to Mistress Hellier?

Startled out of her apathy, Louise stared up at her. 'To my *grandmother*, do you mean? Why ever should I?'

Christian, committed, said doggedly, 'Because she be a tarblish wise and kindly lady, and all d'know it. She could help ee, if nobody else can.'

'I don't need help,' Louise said, denying the small, lonely voice, deep within, that cried frantically that it was just what she did need. 'I'm perfectly well, thank you, Christian – nothing's wrong that plenty of rest and sleep won't put right.'

'If you say so, m'lady,' the maid muttered, chastened. 'Do ee wish to be dressed now?'

'In a little while, thank you,' Louise told her, in a voice which effectively squashed any further unwelcome suggestions.

But it would not suppress her thoughts. Phoebe had warned her: and although all her sister-in-law's knowledge came from books, her judgement of people, their feelings and needs and thoughts, was surprisingly acute. And she had driven Phoebe away, as she had also driven Lukas and Alex away, with the exclusive, obsessional power of her grief. She had thought that time alone, to think and remember and, eventually, to accept, would heal her loss. But with no one to talk to – for Sarah Crowe was busy with her own baby, who had fallen ill – her sorrow had filled all her waking hours, monstrous, terrifying, exhausting, so that there was no room for anything or anyone else. She had tried to escape into sleep, but her dreams woke her weeping: and even the golden reality of daylight, and Wintercombe, seemed remote and pale beside the great stone of misery weighing down heart, mind, life itself.

As Christian had said, Silence, her grandmother and the matriarch of the St Barbe family for over forty years, was famous for her wisdom and strength and kindness. She had seen much in her seventy years, and she had borne seven children, of whom two had died in early childhood, long ago. She surely would understand Louise's overwhelming grief, and be able to help her back to some semblance of normality.

But her grandmother lived in Chard, fifty miles away, with her second husband. And she had recently been ill: the troubles of last year – one grandson transported for treason after the Duke of Monmouth's failed rebellion, another who had tried to kill Alex in a jealous rage – had weighed much on her spirit. She could not be expected to travel such a distance, even along summer roads, and Louise knew that if she asked for Silence's advice by letter, her grandmother would feel compelled to give it in person.

There was another alternative, of course. In a few days' time, Louise would be churched, a ceremony she dreaded, to give thanks for her recovery from the birth, even if her baby had not been so fortunate. Then, custom dictated that she could appear in public once more, and travel. She would take the Wintercombe coach, and go down to Chard, where she had stayed so happily last year, and where there were no memories of Nathaniel to arouse her grief. She could see her other cousins in Taunton, and play chess and backgammon with her grandfather, and ride with her uncle Richard along the leafy lanes of south Somerset, and rebuild her heart and her soul.

The more she thought about it, the more attractive the idea seemed. But she could not tell Alex: he would not understand, he would think that sorrow had turned her wits, and he would want, at the very least, to accompany her. And still her flesh shrank at the thought of the other things he would surely want, to ensure that he would soon have another heir, to displace his hated cousin Charles once and for all . . .

But if anyone could heal her anguish, and her marriage, it was her grandmother. Suddenly, at the thought of revealing her distress to that wise, compassionate woman, the great burden seemed already to lift a little from her shoulders. Her mind began, with something almost like eagerness, to plan the journey.

There was one possibility, however, that would wreck her schemes. Alex had taken himself to Bath a few days ago, ostensibly to visit Phoebe and collect Lukas, but in reality, she was aware, to escape a situation that he found intolerable. He had sat with her, talked to her, he had told her of his love, had spoken of the children they would make in the future, and sketched in quiet, unwontedly gentle words a Wintercombe filled with infant laughter and tumult. It was not his fault that all mention of such things aroused in her only revulsion from the act of conception, and fear of the pain and agony and danger of childbirth, and the possibility of more dead babies. She had tried to feign indifference, but she knew that he was aware that even a casual touch made her shudder.

So, he had gone to Bath, and she had been glad of the consequent relief from guilt. In his absence, she could sink further into her torpor of misery, and forget that one day she would have to drag herself back to reality. But she knew in her heart that she was behaving unreasonably, that he had offered her help, love, sanity, and she had turned her face away. She would not blame him if he stayed in Bath indefinitely: but at the least, she hoped that he would not return to Wintercombe until she had made her escape to Chard, for he would undoubtedly disapprove of her plans, travelling so far so soon after the birth, and do his best to prevent her.

She looked up, with a new sense of purpose, and saw her maid still watching her, the look of concern lingering on her face. Louise tried a smile, and found that it did not hurt. 'Christian, you have set me thinking, and you are right. Bring me a pen and paper, and I will write to my grandmother now.'

Mistress East's lodging-house, in the Abbey Green, was most conveniently placed for those more wealthy sufferers who wished to have easy access to the King's and Queen's Baths, without being so close as to be discommoded by the noise and bustle which invariably surrounded them in the height of the season. It was a handsome edifice, built against the old city wall in the local yellow stone, with an enclosed formal garden surrounding it. A side entrance gave on to a narrow alleyway leading to the broad expanse of meadow and garden between the city wall and the River Avon, and it was a simple matter to enter the Burtons' lodgings discreetly, without calling at the main house.

Alex knew that Charlotte cared not a fig for scandal, and still less now that her husband had been reduced to an impotent and palsied shell. She would delight in flaunting her latest conquest, would wish to parade round the Abbey or in Kingsmead on his arm, and he had no intention of allowing her to make their affair public: not when his wife would come to hear of it. Although, he thought with some bitterness, as Charlotte's maid opened the door to his knock, perhaps the discovery of his adultery might shock Louise out of her indifference.

There was no doubt: it was Louise he loved, Louise he wanted, Louise for whom he had a passion and desire beside which his lust for Charlotte seemed as tawdry and sordid as if he were to offer her money for her body. But he had done his best to penetrate that dreary indifference, and she had taken no notice. Now, angry, baffled and hurt, he was about to embark on an affair which, he knew very well, was at least partly an act of revenge.

No, he was not proud of what he was: but, as he had told Phoebe, patience was not one of his virtues, despite his long-dead mother's name. Nor was chastity, nor temperance.

He had left Lukas in Phoebe's charge, explaining that he had business to attend to, and had walked away from the house, and the sharp eyes of his sister, without a twinge of shame or regret. And now, seeing Charlotte *en déshabillé* in all her luscious, tempting glory, her gaze blatantly enticing, her knew that the next hour or so would be extremely pleasurable for them both.

And so it proved. Charlotte was an exceedingly skilful bedfellow, with that lustry greed which he had found so exciting four years ago, and a range of tricks that a Covent Garden whore would be hard pressed to match. In her arms, he could forget Louise, who had also possessed skill and wiles, though not to the same degree of harlotry, and whose desire had been swiftly transmuted into a passionate love that had, in turn, ignited his own.

70

He could forget her for a while, but afterwards, he looked at Charlotte as she lay sleeping in sated and naked abandon: the plump, pale body, so different from his wife's lean, wiry figure, strong and active from so much time in the saddle: the artful disarray of her curls: the lovely face that had enticed so many men: the perfumed cosmetics which Louise, relying on the attraction and charm of her personality, had used only sparingly, and with a subtlety that Charlotte entirely lacked: and felt a sudden surge of disgust and anger. No coin had changed hands, but he suspected that he would have felt less self-loathing if it had.

And yet, he reminded himself, why should he be ashamed? In fashionable circles, licence and promiscuity were the mode, for both men and women, and he who remained obstinately faithful to his wife was a rarity, the subject of amazed, mocking gossip, assumed to be too timid or inadequate a lover to indulge his appetites as others normally did.

He had spoken his marriage vows sincerely, believing that with Louise, young, passionate, infinitely desirable, in his bed, he would find it easy to forsake all others. But that had been half a year ago and more, and the Louise who had stood by his side at their wedding, brilliant and beautiful in her happiness, was not the woman he had left at Wintercombe.

He had grieved for his son too: she did not have a monopoly of mourning. The sight of that tiny baby, the thatch of black hair, the minute, tenacious fingers, had moved in him a love that was frightening in its power. Knowing that the child was certainly doomed, he had repressed the feeling almost immediately, but not soon enough to prevent a real sense of loss, of sorrow and regret, at Nathaniel's inevitable death. He loved Lukas, but Lukas's mother had been a vile-tempered trollop, who had mistakenly thought that by bearing his son, she would be able to coerce him into marriage. How much more might he feel for the children of Louise, whom he loved to distraction still, despite her present indifference?

She will not always turn away, a voice whispered

71

comfortingly in his mind. Time will heal her: time is all that is needed. But he wondered, with bitterness, how many days, weeks, months, years, would intervene before his Louise was restored to him.

Softly, careful not to wake the slumbering Charlotte, he slipped from the bed and quickly pulled on his clothes. He cared little for his appearance, save on important or ceremonial occasions, and his habitual style of dress was casual, even slovenly, rendering the services of a valet unnecessary. He had no patience with the endless niceties of fashion which obsessed those fops with nothing better to occupy their time, and he had noticed, long ago, that his careless garb seemed to make no difference to his ability to attract women.

He stood for a moment, looking down at his mistress, who had begun, very gently, to snore. Love, and pleasure: Louise, and Charlotte. There was no denying, he had behaved very badly, but that was nothing new. And while Lady Burton remained in Bath, teasing and tempting and above all available, he knew that he would continue to take what was offered.

With a twisted smile, he turned and left the chamber.

Silence Hellier, who had once been Lady St Barbe and mistress of Wintercombe, as her granddaughter Louise was now, finished reading her letter and said, 'Poor child!'

Her husband, Nick, glanced up from his account book. Nearly seventy, he was white-haired but still kept the sparse, wiry vigour of his youth. 'You mean Louise? How is she?'

Silence stared down at the frantic, hasty scribble that was so disturbingly unlike her favourite granddaughter's usually swift and elegant hand. After a while, she said, 'Much troubled, I fear. The loss of the baby seems to have affected her spirits very badly.'

After more than thirty years of marriage, Nick Hellier was attuned to the slightest nuance of the wife's voice. He put down his pen and came to her side. 'Still? It is surely a month at least since the poor infant died.'

72

'There speaks a man,' said Silence, with affectionate mockery, but he saw the tears in her eyes, behind the spectacles she wore for reading and sewing, and put a gentle hand on her shoulder. She went on, drily. 'However you may try, you cannot really understand what any woman suffers who loses her baby – even one stillborn, or miscarried before her time. Nine months of hope, of joyful expectation, a day or more of pain and effort, and then – nothing, no child to cradle in your arms, to feed and love and cherish and protect, nothing but an unmarked grave in the churchyard, and a procession of well-meaning people telling you to have another as soon as possible, babies die all the time, why grieve for them?'

'My God,' said Nick, shaken by the strength of feeling in her voice, 'was I really so insensitive when poor little Anne died?'

'Of course not,' Silence said, smiling up at him. 'You knew that I loved her, and you gave me so much comfort. She only lived for a week, but I shall always wonder what she would have been like if she had survived. Most men are not like you, though, and they dismiss a woman's deepest feelings too easily. I fear that Alex has proved to be of that company.'

'Well, yes,' said Nick, who did not know his wife's nephew and granddaughter's husband very well, and on the whole was glad of it: the man had an appalling reputation, and his company, while at his best lively, inventive and amusing, could also be exhausting, difficult and downright offensive. His own youth had been spent soldiering, in the Royalist army as well as in Europe, and he was no saint, but he enjoyed his present comfortable, untroubled existence to the full, and the turbulence that Alex always seemed to create was thoroughly unwelcome.

Besides, Silence had not been well of late, troubled with shortness of breath and an inability to sleep soundly, and he knew, from long experience, that she would always feel impelled to help any of her wide family, should they need her. Unfortunately, with so many children, stepchildren and grandchildren, there was usually someone, somewhere in Somerset, who wanted advice, assistance or comfort.

'She would like to come and stay here for a while,' Silence said. 'She writes – rather incoherently, I'm afraid – of wanting peace, and time, and healing. Would you mind very much if she paid us a visit?'

'Here?' said Nick, surprised. 'But surely, so soon after the birth – '

'She is young, and healthy, and seems to have recovered her strength – in body, if not in mind. I don't see why she should not, and a coach journey will do her less harm than riding.'

'That's true, at least. And if she comes to Chard,' Nick pointed out, gently teasing, 'you will be saved the trouble of traipsing fifty miles to Wintercombe to be with her.'

'So I will,' Silence said, and smiled up at him with a love unquenched by the long, long years they had shared together. 'And it will be so good to see her again, however sad the circumstances. We have not stirred from here since we returned from their wedding in January.'

'Nor will we,' Nick said firmly. 'The mountain is fixed now – let all your Mahomets of grandchildren come to us, instead.'

Louise, Lady St Barbe, an unlikely Mahomet, arrived at her grandparents' house in Chard as she had planned, at the end of July. The weather was bright and showery, not too hot, and the journey had been surprisingly easy.

Alex had not returned to Wintercombe, but he had written to her, three times, from Bath. She had never received any letters from him before, and the arrival of the first, the day after her decision to visit Chard, had surprised and alarmed her. But his huge, flamboyant scrawl contained no demands, no mention of the future: he wrote only of what he had seen in Bath, what he and Lukas had done, and a stream of witty gossip that caught her unawares and made her smile, before she remembered that she was supposed to be grieving. He ended, in a characteristic flourish, by stating his everlasting, undying and infinite devotion, and signed his name with an impressive proliferation of curlicues and ornamental swirls. Nowhere had he

74

had stated when he might return to her, for which she felt at once grateful and guilty.

The second was in similar vein: the third suggested a possible trip to London, in the autumn. It was not a prospect that filled Louise with joyful anticipation, although once she had craved the brilliant gaiety of fashionable company. Now, like a wounded animal, she wanted only to hide until her hurts were healed.

And so, she had made her plans, and left Wintercombe the day after the sad, pointless ceremony of her churching, with only her maid, the coachman and the young groom, Henry Renolds, for company, and turned her face to the south, away from Alex and all that he owned and represented.

Chard in summer was lovely, the garden, her grandmother's pride and joy and creation, all brilliant with scent and colour, and the quiet green countryside promising rest and peace. The Wintercombe coach drew up outside, and suddenly she could wait no longer. She pushed the door wide, stumbled past the startled servant who was opening the tall gates, and flung herself into the arms of her grandmother, who had been waiting anxiously for her since the groom had ridden on ahead to bring word of their imminent arrival.

Silence was skilled at disguising her feelings, but the change in Louise shocked and appalled her. She stared at the plain, gaunt, tearful wreck of her once vivacious and attractive granddaughter, and said in horror, 'Oh, my poor child – you must go to bed, straight away.'

The effort of organising her journey, the exhaustion that was the inevitable result of three days in a jolting, uncomfortable coach, and above all the strain and anguish of the past weeks, had drained away every last vestige of Louise's will and spirit. She was safe, she had found her haven, and for the moment nothing else mattered. Stumbling like a sleepwalker, she allowed herself to be led into the cool, whitewashed hall and up a steep flight of creaking stairs to the chamber which she had been given on her previous stays here, overlooking the garden. Her grandmother's maid, Fan Howard, helped Christian to undress her, while Silence mixed up a potion to ensure sound rest and ease the pains of a troubled, grief-stricken mind. Although it was bitter and gritty, she drank it to the dregs, and was asleep before the curtains had been drawn round the bed, shutting out the fading evening sunlight.

She slept until the next morning, and awoke aching, still tired, and yet strangely refreshed. Outside, it seemed to be raining: she could hear drops spattering against the window panes and, far off, a reflective mutter of thunder. For a while she lay still, savouring the sense of refuge, the feeling that she was no longer alone. She had escaped from a terrible nightmare, and now she could begin to regain her strength.

It took time, of course. She found herself hungry, and ate all that was set in front of her: Silence knew what would restore an invalid's appetite, and every dish was tempting and delicious. She slept a great deal, but suffered no more of the hideous dreams that had tormented and disturbed her rest at Wintercombe. She sewed, a skill she had acquired with the greatest reluctance and had always, previously, practised resentfully if at all, and found the intricate, careful creation of an embroidered purse strangely soothing. Her grandfather spent some time reminding her of the pleasure involved in playing the spinet, which she had hardly touched since leaving France, nearly two years previously. With Nick and her uncle Richard, Silence's youngest surviving child, she embarked on battles over backgammon and chess boards, and refreshed her memory of piquet and other, less respectable games of hazard, played for shillings and groats. She devoured the lighter books in her grandparents' small collection, much of it poetry, and found herself disproportionately delighted when Richard, visiting their Loveridge cousins in Taunton, brought back from her Uncle Jonah's bookshop a fat, four-volume romance in French that she had never read. She discussed matters of fashion with Richard's wife Sarah, an energetic, happy young woman with few interests beyond the domestic: but, to their uncomprehending disappointment, showed no interest in Sarah's two children, Nicholas, who was a lively three, and Rebecca, nearly a year old and just beginning to haul herself upright.

With increasing satisfaction, Silence watched her granddaughter gain weight, lose the hollows under her cheekbones and the shadows around her eyes, and acquire a little colour in her sallow face. After a fortnight at Chard, Louise had begun to recover her looks, and no longer appeared ten years older than her actual age. But she still lacked the sparkle and mischievous humour that had once made her such a delightful companion: and she had yet to unburden her cares to her grandmother.

Silence had a gardener's patience, and knew that when the time was ripe, and the opportunity presented itself, Louise would talk to her. And the chance came on a pleasant morning in the second week of August.

It was just after the household had broken their fast, and the sun was still low in the sky. The night had been clear, with a heavy dew, and as soon as she had eaten, Silence had gone outside, armed with knife and basket, to cut carnations before the heat of the day. There were a man and a boy to perform routine duties in the garden, but she had always regarded it as her domain, and advancing years and failing health had not affected her reluctance to delegate any task of importance.

The walks were empty, the servants busy weeding in the kitchen garden beyond, but her eyes, still sharp for seeing at a distance, spotted a patch of solid black within the honeysuckle arbour in the western corner of the garden, sited to take advantage of the morning sun. After a moment's reflection, Silence set her basket carefully on the gravel beside the knot of carnations, still bursting with colour despite the lateness of the season, and strolled casually down the path towards her granddaughter.

Louise was sitting quietly, her eyes closed, her body relaxed against the rough wooden seat inside the arbour. At the sound of Silence's footsteps, she looked up, and then smiled briefly. 'Hullo, Gran'mère. I thought you were going to gather carnations. I'm afraid I took the liberty of stealing one.'

77

Silence noticed the splash of crimson in Louise's corsage, cheerful against the sombre black gown she had worn ever since her arrival at Chard. Hoping that it was a good sign, she smiled in return. 'Well, I shall turn a blind eye, just this once. Do you mind my company? I shall go back to my carnations if you prefer.'

'No – no, please come and sit down – there's plenty of room,' Louise said, moving into the corner of the seat and patting the space she had left.

Silence eased herself carefully down on to the rustic boards, and tucked a stray tendril of honeysuckle back into the tangled trellis beside her. 'It was made for two, after all,' she observed. 'Nick and I have spent many an idle and happy hour here.'

'A lovers' seat,' said Louise, and looked down at her hands, at the thick band of deep yellow gold around one long, slender finger, that Alex had placed there eight months ago. She added, 'I wonder if he knows yet that I have left Wintercombe.'

'You've been here for more than a fortnight,' said Silence in surprise. 'Of course he must know – even if you didn't tell him. You didn't, did you?'

'No,' Louise said, very quietly. 'I – it's difficult to explain – I wanted to escape – he was in Bath, visiting Phoebe and Lukas, and I thought that if he knew, he might try to stop me, or come with me. So as soon as I was churched, I left, before he returned. I didn't even write to him – I don't really know why.' There was a painful pause. 'I wish I had, now.'

'Will he find out where you've gone?'

'I made no secret of it – someone at Wintercombe will tell him,' Louise said. She lifted her head and stared urgently at Silence, 'Oh, Gran'mère – I don't know what to think any more! I loved him – I loved him utterly and passionately, I really did – and yet when Nathaniel died, it was as if all my feelings had died as well, and only grief was left – I had no *room* for him, Gran'mère, I shut him out, and now that I feel better, I wish so much that I had not!'

'Is that why he went to Bath?'

78

'Yes, I'm sure that it is. At the time, I was glad of it,' Louise said. She sighed, and Silence saw that her eyes were heavy with tears. 'I hurt him very badly, Gran'mère – I know that I did. He loves me, and he couldn't bear it any longer – so he left.' Her voice wobbled, and she fought for control, while Silence waited with compassion, too wise to make hasty interruption.

At last, with a visible effort, Louise managed a smile, albeit a rather weak and watery one. 'When you came up the path just now – I was thinking of him – and when I heard your footsteps, I hoped for one mad moment that it might *be* him – as if I were a little girl again, and thought I could have what I wanted just by wishing for it, if I tried hard enough. And yet, if he did walk down the path now, I don't know what I could possibly say to him, to undo all the hurt and damage and harm. In the circumstances, "Sorry" is such a puny, inadequate little word.'

'You can write to him,' Silence suggested. 'Apologies are so much easier to put on to paper than to speak face to face. And besides, I am not entirely sure that all the fault is yours.'

Louise stared at her in surprise. 'But I drove him away – why should it be his fault?' She produced a shadow of her old, mischievous smile. 'But you've never really liked or trusted Alex, have you, Gran'mère? Admit it, you never wanted me to marry him.'

'I do freely admit it – at first I did not. To be frank,' Silence said drily, 'the idea filled me with horror. But that was before I discovered that you were not quite the innocent I had assumed – and that he, too, was not entirely the debauched rake he appears to be, despite his excellent and convincing imitation of it. I recognise that he has a heart, even if it isn't exactly unsullied gold, and I know that he does love you. But he is a man, and even the most sensitive and perceptive of men may have difficulty in understanding a woman's particular feelings. Your letter to me was not entirely clear, but you could not hide the fact that you thought he did not understand or appreciate the extent of your grief for Nathaniel – and that I was the only person who could help you.'

Louise was twisting her wedding ring round and round her finger. In a voice so quiet that Silence could hardly hear it, she said, 'You were – and you have. I thought at first that I'd never get over it – I could think about nothing save Nathaniel, I couldn't eat, or sleep properly, or do anything – I was lost. Alex tried to help me, but I wouldn't listen. And he kept talking about having more children – and I couldn't face that, I couldn't bear the thought of more waste, more grief, more pain. And it still frightens me.'

After a while, Silence said gently, 'I do know what you are suffering. I have borne seven children, and two of them died young. George was two, old enough to walk and talk, so that it was not a baby that I lost, but a *child*, a *person* in his own right, whom I remember as clearly as if he had just left me. And Anne, who came unexpectedly, after Richard, when I thought my child-bearing years were over – she lived hardly longer than Nathaniel did, but I think of her with regret even now, I will never forget her, and at her death I was distraught. And I know that I have been so fortunate. Few women can live out their allotted span with five children grown to maturity – although William of course was killed more than twenty years ago – and a quiverful of grandchildren. There were fourteen alive at the last count, and soon to be more, for Sarah has told me that she is to have another, early next year.'

Smiling at the thought, she went on. 'Grief and pain cannot be avoided, Louise, they are inevitable in this sinful world, and must be borne as best we can. You have lost Nathaniel, and you will think of him always, with longing, and regret, and sorrow, as I still remember poor Anne, and George, and as my daughters will think of the children they have buried. Tabby reared six, and lost three when they were almost grown, and then Bram, as good as dead, transported to Barbados. And Deb had six stillborn or who died very young, and only Libby left to her. Any child you bear will carry all the burden of your hope and your terror, and you never cease to fear for them, all your life long and theirs. If you cannot face that responsibility, then you should not have children, and you should not have married Alex.'

Louise, she saw with relief, had reacted to her sharpness with anger. She said hotly, 'Of course I can face it! I did think that I couldn't – that I couldn't bear any more sorrow. But here, over the past two weeks, I've been able to think clearly – and I know what I want now.'

'And that is?'

'I want to go home,' Louise said, her voice firm, her face resolute and all of a sudden aflame with hope and purpose. 'I want to begin again, and – not *forget* Nathaniel, I can never do that – but to *accept* that he is gone, and to look to the future. Do you think that it's possible? Will Alex take me back, after I've hurt him so much?'

'Sometimes,' Silence told her, smiling, 'even when we are old enough to know better, a little magic can still work its wonders. Some things can be conjured up, just by the strength of our desire – and perhaps love is one of them. Write to Alex, tell him what you have just told me, and I do not think you will find that your efforts have been in vain.'

As Alex had known, the presence in Bath of Charlotte Burton, available, ardent and attractive, was a temptation which he at first did not try to resist. But after he had taken advantage of her offer some half-dozen times, a creeping sense of where his careless adultery might actually lead was beginning to infiltrate his mind.

It was to a large extent prompted by Charlotte herself. Discretion, modesty and restraint had never numbered amongst her characteristics, and to be fair, they were not his virtues either, nor his wife's. But a modicum of conceal-ment was vital, for Bath was a small city of some three or four thousand inhabitants, many of whom knew him by sight. And there were several who were much better acquainted with him than that, amongst them, of course, his sister Phoebe, with her sharp, suspicious mind, and his aunt Bab, who was not only his enemy, but a foolish and idle woman addicted to malicious gossip. And as if that were not enough, she lived in a small house on the Abbey Green, just over the way from Charlotte's lodgings.

He had not actually encountered her, but he had met her

pretty, vacuous daughter Amy, on his way to see his lover. Amy, who had once harboured a girlish, innocent and disastrous *tendresse* for him, which he had done nothing to discourage, had gasped, and blushed, and veered aside as if she feared he would throw her down and rape her there and then, in broad daylight with crowds flowing past. Alex, succumbing to the demon of dangerous mischief who was his more or less permanent companion, stepped into her path and bowed. 'Good day to you, fair Cousin!'

Amy had never been able to tell flattery from jest from malice. Completely at a loss, she trembled and fluttered into a curtsey like a dying bird, while her maid, a stick-like girl whom he did not know, glared at him disapprovingly.

'And where are you going this fine morning, Cousin Amy? Pray permit me to accompany you.'

The last thing he wanted, with thoughts of the coming hour with Charlotte occupying his mind, was to endure even the briefest moments of Amy's witless chatter: simpering blonde innocence had never attracted him. But, as he had expected, there was no risk that she would take up his offer: she was too thoroughly beneath her mother's thumb for that. She stared at him reproachfully with large hazel eyes that all too frequently filled with tears. 'Surely you cannot imagine, sir, that I would lower myself so far as to accept even that small courtesy from such as you? After what you have done to my poor brother, and my mother too, I fear even such chance acquaintance as this is to be avoided at all costs.'

Alex, aware of the curious faces and keen ears of many passers-by, smiled mischievously at her. 'After what *I* have done to your mother and brother? Surely you cannot have forgotten that your dear mama spread it about that I was not my father's son, and that your upright and honourable brother did his best to murder me?'

It was not entirely fair: after all, in the last year's sorry tangle of lust and hatred and greed, Amy had been the one person entirely blameless. Her reaction was completely predictable: with a muffled sob, she pushed past him and hurried away, her maid in brisk attendance.

Whistling a bawdy tune, Alex had gone on his careless way, and in the heat of his reunion with Charlotte, all thought of the encounter had been burned from his memory.

But Charlotte herself, a few days later, had brought it forcefully back to his mind. There was to be a gathering, the following afternoon, on the bowling green at Kingsmead, and she wanted Alex to escort her there. He had never enjoyed bowls, preferring more vigorous pursuits, and said so, but she was not satisfied, and pressed her case. She could not go alone, it would not be seemly: and what possible harm could result from their appearance together in public on such a respectable and decorous occasion?

'I made a condition with you, when we first agreed to this,' Alex said, lying back against the pillows, his posture deceptively lazy and relaxed while Charlotte, sitting bolt upright beside him, all her charms amply displayed without even a sheet to cover her, radiated indignant insistence. 'I required the utmost discretion. Once I start squiring you round the town, gossip will have ample to feed on, and rumour will put two and two together and make the right answer, however circumspect we might be – and you, dear Charlotte, have never been circumspect in your life.'

'It will all be perfectly proper,' she said, pouting prettily, and tossing her glossy curls. 'I swear I will do nothing to make anyone guess the truth.'

'You won't have to,' Alex pointed out. 'Your reputation is more than sufficient. Any man in your company who is past childhood and not actually blind, decrepit and senile is immediately assumed to be your lover. And since I have ill-disposed relatives who live only a few yards away from this house, not to mention my sister, and my son, all exposed to Bath's seething cauldron of gossip, I have no intention of doing as you ask.'

Charlotte, as was her habit when thwarted, enchantingly lost her temper. She sparkled, she blazed, she shouted, she stamped her foot, all to no avail. Alex dressed without comment as she pleaded, cajoled and finally, with a tragically martyred expression, burst into tears.

83

It was a display that had melted many stony masculine hearts, notably her husband's, before the apoplexy struck him down. But Alex had seen her performances before, and was unimpressed. 'Have you ever thought of going on the stage, my dear? They'd pay a fortune at Drury Lane for talents such as yours.'

Charlotte, arrested in mid-flow, glared at him. 'How dare you!'

'Oh, I dare very easily. And I'll tell you something else, my sweet seductress, that's even less to your liking. I will not succumb to your demands inside this chamber, or outside it. I insisted on discretion, and if you will not oblige me in that, then I will no longer oblige *you*.'

'What do you mean?' she said sharply. 'Explain yourself.'

'Gladly. I have enjoyed our diversion, but that's all it is – a diversion. I can very quickly become bored, dear Charlotte, and you are beginning to bore me. The swiftest way to bid me farewell for ever is to indulge in another tantrum. I really wouldn't, if I were you.'

'Well, if you would only do as I wish,' said his mistress, her voice catching appealingly in her throat, and her eyes downcast, 'then there would be no need for . . . for persuasion.'

'And if I have nothing more to do with you,' Alex said brutally, shrugging on his coat, 'there's no need for it either.'

Before he could evade her, she was beside him, using the lure of her body to ensure success where all her other arguments had failed. Once, not so long ago, her brazen wiles would have excited his passion: now, as he had warned her, he was beginning to find her lack of honesty and subtlety tedious. He removed her groping fingers, and held her hands, clutching at the air, in a grip that was not intended to be gentle. 'Enough, Charlotte.'

'Let go!' she cried, and suddenly, with satisfaction, he saw genuine anger in her face. 'Let *go*, you bastard!'

'Not until you've listened to what I have to say. I did not intend to finish our liaison yet, but I will do so now if you persist with this stupid suggestion.'

'It's *not* stupid!' Charlotte protested. 'I want to show you off – we make such a handsome pair – '

'A pair with you is exactly what I have no wish to be. We made a bargain, remember? We are together only within this chamber, and at certain hours. At all other times, in all other places, we are polite strangers. Is that understood, madam? Or the affair ends, here and now.'

Tears of pain, or mortification, stood in her eyes. At last, she said sulkily, 'Yes, Alex. I understand.'

'Good.' He released her, and gave her a light, dispassionate kiss on one soft, flushed cheek. 'I'm glad – I would not have us part enemies, so soon. Until tomorrow morning, dear Charlotte?'

'Until tomorrow,' she repeated, her tone still subdued and resentful. He smiled, and left her.

He would have to end it, and soon. Already he had stayed in Bath for more than a fortnight, far longer than he had intended, and it was plain that he was rapidly wearing his family's tolerance to the bone. Lukas, of course, still enjoyed his company, but even he was beginning to question his father's unexplained absences, and it was surely only a matter of time before Phoebe, already suspicious, made an accurate guess at the truth. And in passing almost under the windows of his aunt Bab's house every time he went to his assignation with Charlotte, he took an appalling risk. Bab detested him, and if she knew of his adulterous liaison with such a notorious and promiscuous woman, she would take great delight in telling Louise, in fullest detail, exactly what he had done.

Yes, it was past time to end the affair, one of the least savoury, least praiseworthy episodes of a less than creditable life. He could justify his behaviour to himself, when not thinking too deeply, with any number of reasons and excuses. But at the end of each day, staring into the dregs of whatever bottle he had emptied that evening, the bitter truth leered up at him, inescapable, unpleasant, menacing. He loved Louise, with a power and a passion that had astonished and delighted them both, and at the time when she most needed him, he had deserted and betrayed her.

Tomorrow, he would end it.

He walked swiftly away from Mistress East's lodging house, with the prowling stride that was so distinctive, and did not see the avid, malicious eyes that watched him leave, as they had watched for days, from the house across the Green where his cousin Amy St Barbe lived with her mother Bab.

# Chapter Five

## 'Appeals to sense'

Louise found that her grandmother, as ever, had been quite right: it was much, much easier to apologise on paper than to do so face to face. She had always been wilful and rebellious, unwilling to accept advice or to admit her fault, and the thought of humbling herself, even to Alex, was most unwelcome. But a piece of paper could not spurn her, or laugh, or be angry, or offensive, and she would not have to watch his expression as he read it.

But she had had so much time to think, here at Chard, time to find again, within herself, the depths of love and hope that she had once believed to have vanished for ever, with Nathaniel. Her baby was dead, and she mourned him, and would always do so. But at first her obsessive grief had turned inward, selfishly excluding everything else, and above all, her husband. Now, however, with her grandmother's help, she had somehow managed to crawl out of that terrible slough of despond, and into the daylight. She was ready to return to Wintercombe, to enter the world again, and to contemplate Nathaniel's death with her sense of proportion regained. Yes, it was a tragedy, but one all too commonplace. If it did not happen to her again, she would be fortunate indeed. And she felt that with Alex's help, that she had rejected two months ago, she was strong enough to face her future.

And next time, Louise thought, dipping her quill into the inkpot with firmness of purpose, next time I will abandon all thoughts of riding at once – I'll be carried to church in a litter, I'll even keep to my bed, to ensure that I don't lose any more babies.

She had thought a great deal about what she would say, and at last the words flowed from her pen. When Silence knocked and entered, to wish her goodnight, she was writing busily. Her grandmother took in the scene, Louise's fierce figure hunched over the paper, and said quietly, with a smile, 'Is it going well?'

The girl glanced round, a rather rueful expression on her face. In the candlelight, Silence was pleased to see, she looked almost pretty, and certainly far more animated than before. 'I think so – I hope so. But it's almost impossible to find just the right words – not to sound too abasing, or too insinuating – or, on the other hand, too like myself!'

Silence laughed. 'I would remind you that Alex has a very well-developed sense of humour – one of his more endearing qualities. If you humble yourself too thoroughly, he will surely tease you for ever more. And if he does truly love you, he will welcome you back whatever you say. I should not worry too much.'

'He may love me,' Louise said drily. 'But he can't possibly overlook the fact that I ran away from him without leaving any word as to where I was going. Most men would be enraged by that.'

'But Alex is not most men,' her grandmother pointed out. 'You may well be pleasantly surprised. And no, I do not wish to peruse your efforts. I will leave you to finish it in peace, and a boy can take it to Wintercombe in the morning. Goodnight, Louise, and sweet dreams.'

'Goodnight, Gran'mere,' she said, and watched the door close, chewing the end of her quill, before returning to her task.

The repeating clock by her bed had chimed midnight before she was at last satisfied. It was not a long letter, but she felt that it honestly conveyed her confused feelings and, above all, her desire to return to Wintercombe and start afresh. She had expressed her apologies, sincerely but not too abjectly, and her hopes for the future. And she had signed it, 'Your loving wife, Louise.'

Yawning, mind and body drained by the effort of composition, she folded it and sealed it with a blob of melted wax, into which she impressed the signet ring which had belonged to her father, Jean-Pierre Chevalier, a

Guernsey sea-captain who had been drowned early in her childhood. The bold curves of his crest, a knight in full armour, glittered in the soft red wax. She dipped the quill again, and wrote the superscription. 'Sir Alexander St Barbe, at the Manor of Wintercombe near Philip's Norton in the County of Somersetshire. To be left at the George for collection.' And below, as an afterthought: 'If Sir Alexander be not yet returned to Wintercombe, please ensure that this is delivered to Mistress Phoebe St Barbe's house in Nowhere Lane in Bath, as soon as may be.'

She had told a sleepy Christian that she could retire, an hour or more previously. With a last, fond look at the letter lying on the table, she pulled off her loose embroidered night-robe, blew out the candle and snuggled down into the warm comfort of her feather bed. Tomorrow, that letter would set out on its journey northwards: in two days, or three, with luck, Alex would receive it. And then, at last, their marriage could begin again, unfettered by past tragedy.

'I'll make sure your precious wife knows *every* detail of what has passed between us!'

Charlotte had not taken the news that their affair was ended particularly well. She made a wonderful picture, standing there clothed in her anger, and very little else save for a brief and almost transparent chemise. Alex observed the tossing curls, the passionate eyes, the furious yet provocative posture with some amusement. 'Will you, now? What a prospect.'

'Yes, I will!' Charlotte cried. 'Every single thing!'

'I'm glad your memory is so precise. You'll have to rely on it exclusively, after all, in the days ahead. I am leaving Bath this afternoon, and I do not intend to return for some while.'

'I'll spread the truth all round the company here if you do,' Charlotte said. She saw the look on his face, and abruptly her manner changed from threats to wheedling. 'Why must you leave? Have I offended you? Our pleasure is surely not finished yet.'

'For me it is,' Alex told her. 'Charlotte, you are a woman of the world, you know as well as I do that affairs such as ours are transient at best. And Bath is thick with gentlemen who'd do for you exactly as I have done, and far more eagerly. Or have you had most of them already?'

She gave him a sulky look. 'I don't want them. I want you.'

'Forgive me, dear Charlotte, for laughing, but your presentations of undying passion grow ridiculous, and they deceive neither of us. Let us at least part with good grace, and no pretence, as we agreed at the outset. And I swear to you now, if so much as a whisper of this intrigue reaches my ears, or my wife's, I shall know exactly who has spread such a rumour, and believe me, madam, I shall be merciless. Do you understand me?'

She looked up at him, pouting. After a long, hostile pause, she nodded. 'Yes.'

'Good. I happened to see your husband in the King's Bath yesterday – I must say, he was looking very well. Either the waters have wrought a dramatic improvement in his condition, or you have greatly exaggerated his infirmities. Certainly, he is not the palsied wreck of your affecting description – and, I should imagine, he is still perfectly capable of inflicting considerable punishment upon his wayward wife, should he learn of her recent indiscretions.'

For almost the first time in the course of their affair, genuine emotion showed on Charlotte's face. 'What do you mean?' She came up close to him, forgetting to employ her swaying, seductive walk. 'You wouldn't tell him, Alex – you wouldn't!'

'Oh, yes, I would, believe me.'

'But you know what he's like – how jealous he is – he nearly killed poor Jack Murray, and he would have killed you if you hadn't gone to Holland.'

'I doubt he would,' Alex said with a grin. 'Whatever the other gaps in my education, I can assure you that my swordsmanship was not neglected. I had many reasons for going to Holland, and Sir Anthony's urgent desire to slaughter me was just one of them. Anyway, while he's not an incapable invalid, neither is he the man he once was. He might not be able to challenge me to a duel, but he can undoubtedly make your life extremely unpleasant. You are a promiscuous little trollop, my dear Charlotte, but you are still Lady Burton, you have wealth, position, comfort. Think on what might happen to you should your husband decide to reward you for cuckolding him again.'

Charlotte had gone very pale. She said, her voice stripped of all artifice, 'That would be a disaster for me – I couldn't bear it – he'd take me back to that Godforsaken, draughty old pile of stone in Yorkshire and leave me there! Alex, I swear to you, I *swear*, that I will say nothing of this, ever, to anyone. I *swear* it!'

'Though not upon your honour, I hope,' he said, and smiled, and kissed her lightly. 'Goodbye, Charlotte. I hope I have given you pleasure, as you have assuredly given it to me. I am only sorry that I was forced to threaten you – I had much rather part friends, as I had hoped.'

'We are, still,' she said, and gave him one of her coy, enchanting smiles, that sat as if painted upon her pallid face. 'Goodbye, Alex.'

She watched him go, still with that false smile covering her fear and anger: and when the door had finally closed behind him, flung herself on the bed, pummelling the pillows in a rage of frustration and disappointment. There were other men in plenty, as she had said, but beside Alex, vivid, amusing, overwhelmingly attractive, they all seemed to be pale shadows of his brilliance.

'Damn him, damn him, *damn* him!' Charlotte cried into her pillow, but she knew that she was quite powerless to influence her erstwhile lover. He had always gone his own way, without deference to the wishes and interests of others, and there was nothing, nothing at all that she could do to change his mind.

Besides, she was much more frightened of her husband, who was jealous, vindictive, and quite capable of packing her off home to Yorkshire for ever, exiled from the glittering life of Court and fashionable society, so that she might as well be dead.

The prospect was so appalling that, as Alex had well known, her complete silence was ensured. Never, while Sir Anthony lived (and how often, over the past few years, had she prayed for his end), would she reveal anything of this liaison to anyone.

She might be helpless where Alex was concerned, but there were other men in Bath. They might provide some entertainment over the next few weeks, even if not at the same supreme level of gratification. Charlotte was nothing if not practical, and had never made a habit of yearning after the unattainable. Alex had left her, and there was nothing she could do about it. Therefore, she would suppress her anger and disappointment at his rejection of her, and take her delightful skills and enticements elsewhere, perhaps to a man less attractive but more easily influenced.

She lay back on the battered pillows, and began, with a thoughtful expression, to review the varied men of her acquaintance at present residing in Bath.

In the comfortable little house in Abbey Green, within sight of Mistress East's lodging-house, Bab St Barbe turned away from the window and waddled heavily over to the table. She had kept watch for nearly three weeks now, ever since she had seen her nephew's unmistakable figure, tall, wearing his own hair and a characteristically understated grey suit, walking unobtrusively into the Green and knocking on the side door of the lodgings over the way. Curious, she had stationed herself the next morning at an upstairs window, with a splendid view of all the comings and goings at the houses around hers, and was rewarded by a second glimpse. Knowing Alex's habits, an assignation seemed to be the most likely reason for these furtive visits, and Bab, who had built up a considerable network of acquaintances, informers and gossips, soon discovered that a certain Lady Burton, young, attractive and possessed of a sick and elderly husband and a notorious reputation, resided in Mistress East's longings. With considerate satisfaction, she had continued her vigil, noting the days and times of his visits, always when the cuckolded husband was safely

92

absent at the Baths. Alex did not come every day, but she saw him sufficiently frequently to be certain that this was no passing moment of pleasure, but a full-blown and passionate affair.

There was one person, not at present in Bath, who would be most interested in the adulterous activities of Sir Alexander St Barbe. With an eager smile on her plump face, Bab drew pen, paper and ink towards her, and began to write.

My dearest son,

I have today seen further evidence with my own eyes of the sinful and wicked congress of your cousin Sir Alexander with a certain Lady Burton, a most notorious woman with whom, I am told, he has had carnal relations before. Naturally, I have said nothing of this to our dear and innocent Amy, nor yet to Lady St Barbe, who is in any case said to be still lying sick at Wintercombe after the death of her son. However, in the fullness of time, and of course with your knowledge and approval, I feel it is only right she should be told of the depths of her husband's wickedness, and moreover in her time of greatest sorrow and need. I know of your continued regard and affection for her, and I feel that it would be only natural if she were to turn to you, as an old friend, should her husband's perfidy become known. I shall write more on this another time. Meanwhile, I remain ever your loving and devoted mother,

Barbara St Barbe

With a smile she sealed the letter, using the crest of the despised family into which she had married, and who, for more than twenty-five years, had done their best to make her feel an outsider, William's regrettable mistake, given a home out of charity. All that time, her own feelings of resentment and dislike had festered, suppressed while her dead husband's half-brother, Sir Nathaniel, was alive, but come to full flower under the brutal and insensitive treatment of his son Alex.

But though Bab's dear and only son Charles had been forced into exile, he had not gone as far as was thought. Silence, Bab's misguided Puritan mother-in-law, had told him to take ship for the New World, to begin afresh far from Wintercombe and all he had ever loved. Silence, however, was not all-powerful in the St Barbe family, whatever she might like to think. Charles had taken her money and said goodbye to his grieving mother and sister, and found a ship sailing from Bristol to Virginia. But only Bab and Amy knew that the vessel, *Susan and Mary*, was also due to call at Cork, in Ireland, before sailing across the Atlantic. And there, Charles had disembarked, and made his way to Dublin, the centre of the English administration in Ireland. An enthusiastic Catholic, he had obtained an excellent post in the government, and looked likely, from his account, to do very well for himself. Already he had bought land, made some fortunate investments, and was well on the way to becoming a rich man.

Bab knew, however, that despite the cheerfully optimistic tone of his weekly letters, Charles was desperately homesick. He longed for Wintercombe, for his beloved mother and dear sister, and above all for Louise, the cousin whom he adored, and who had betrayed his love and trust, fornicating with his enemy Alex, and then marrying him. The news that their only legitimate child was dead, that the marriage appeared to be in trouble after a scant eight months, and that Charles was still the next heir to Wintercombe, would delight her son. Perhaps soon, if all went as Bab hoped, he would be able to return from damp, provincial Ireland, and take up his rightful place once more, at the home of his ancestors.

With vindictive satisfaction, she addressed the letter, smiling. Soon, soon she would see him, and they could take their vengeance, at long last, on the man who had brought her and her family to the brink of ruin.

Phoebe heard the news that her brother was to return to Wintercombe that afternoon with a certain sense of relief. She was very fond of him, rather against her better judgement, but it was something of a strain to have him stay in her once peaceful household for upwards of three weeks, disrupting her orderly life, driving poor shy Libby deep into her shell, upsetting Lukas with his unexplained and suspiciously regular absences, and several times returning very late at night, considerably the worse for drink. She knew that he was desperately worried about Louise, and hurt by her indifference to an extent that those who were deceived by his habitual manner of cynical arrogance would find impossible to believe. But, being Alex, he had a strange way of displaying his deep distress. From long and bitter experience, she knew better than to nag or to pry, but when he told her that he was returning to his wife, she decided to be honest. After all, in an hour or two he would be gone, and they would be prey to his savage and unpredictable moods no longer.

'Good,' she said pointedly. 'You should have gone back two weeks ago.'

Alex raised his black brows and grinned. 'You never said anything.'

'Since when have you ever taken any notice of what I tell you? Except, of course, to do the opposite. Well, since you're going anyway, I'll say what's been in my mind for weeks. Louise needs you – she may not know it, but she *does*, Alex, she *does*. And in time, she will realise it. Perhaps she already has, and you will find her on the doorstep with her arms open wide to welcome you.'

'Perhaps,' Alex said. 'Perhaps not.' And his eyes, a vivid and gentian blue, were bleak and unhopeful.

He left after dinner, on his fiery bay stallion Blaze, who had spent the past three weeks out at grass on a farm beyond Kingsmead, and who badly needed the exercise. It was seven miles to Philip's Norton, a comfortable two hours' ride, but Blaze's exuberance reduced the time considerably, despite the steepness of the way up into the hills on the south side of Bath.

He had left Lukas behind, for whatever lay ahead for himself and Louise, whether reconciliation or a final, bitter estrangement, was between them alone. Lukas, who loved them both, might be deeply hurt and disturbed if matters turned out badly. If they did not, then he would send for his son as soon as possible.

He arrived at Wintercombe well before supper time, and dismounted with a flourish in the courtyard. Blaze, muddy, lathered and for once too exhausted to make any attempt to bite or kick, was taken away by one of the young grooms, and with a curious mixture of hope and dread, Alex entered his house in search of his wife.

Everything was quiet, somehow lifeless. He had not been concerned for his possessions in his absence: both inside, under the direction of the butler Twinney, and Abigail the housekeeper, and outside in the fields, where his bailiff Crowe presided, everything was quite capable of running like clockwork, whether he was in residence or not. He dropped his riding coat and hat on to a chair in the Hall, and paused, listening to the stillness around him, before calling out, 'Hey! Anyone at home?'

Suddenly, there were hasty footsteps from several directions, a flurry of voices, and then the housekeeper, smoothing her apron, hurried into the Hall with a great jangling of keys, her face flushed and flustered. She curtseyed apologetically. 'Why, sir, we didn't expect ee – beg pardon, sir, welcome back.'

'Thank you, Abigail. Is my lady in her chamber?'

A look of consternation appeared on the housekeeper's face. 'But, sir – I thought you knew – '

'Knew? Knew what?'

'She've gone, sir – gone two week and more – she upped and left and went to Chard to visit Mistress Hellier. Your lady bain't here, sir, tis the truth. She've gone.'

The letter was despatched, carried for the sake of speed by one of her grandfather's grooms, and now all Louise could do was to wait. She had never been a patient person, and the long hours weighed leadenly on her. The weather had turned rainy, so that her restlessness could find no outlet in riding, nor even in a brisk walk in the garden. She tried to sew, to read, to play the spinet, but her limited powers of concentration had slipped away from her, and the pastimes which, only a day ago, had seemed diverting enough were now unbearably tedious. She paced from window to window, gazing out at the drenched garden, and snapped at young Nicholas when he dared to ask her to play some childish game with him. Silence watched this tense, irritable girl with relief, and did not interfere despite Sarah's bewildered, reproachful looks, because at last, after nearly three weeks at Chard, this was the old Louise returned with a vengeance, possessed of all her faults but also, overwhelmingly, her urgent vitality.

It might take two days for the groom to reach Winter-combe, and two days more for Alex to return – always assuming that he was there, that he would receive her letter, and above all that he would not spurn her offer of reconciliation. So many imponderables, so many doubts, that she knew she could not hope to see him before the end of the week, or, realistically, long after that – if at all. And yet she could not settle to anything, could not rest, could not sleep, but prowled around her grandparents' house like a caged animal, desperate for release.

Two days after her letter had been sent, she was awake at dawn, and up for breakfast before anyone else, save a few sleepy and startled servants. It was raining again, a light and rather timid drizzle from patchy clouds. To the west, beyond the walled garden and behind the tall trees in the hedgerow bordering the lane leading to the house, there were even one or two streaks of blue sky.

'Enough to make a pair of Dutchman's breeches?' said Silence, coming into the dining room to see her grand-daughter peering hopefully out of the window. 'Then it might be fine in an hour or two. Or at least, that's what the old gardener at Wintercombe used to say, and he was usually right in matters of weather. I wrote all his saws down in my gardening book.'

'If it does turn sunny later, I would like to go riding,' Louise said, in a voice that admitted no dissent. She turned abruptly away from the window, and flung herself down in her chair with a rueful smile. 'I can't have slept for more than a few hours last night, but I feel so full of energy, I think I'll burst if I have to spend another day cooped up indoors. And don't look so worried, Gran'mère, I'll take one of the grooms with me.'

'Always assuming that he can keep up with you,' Silence commented. She sat, observing the scatter of torn pieces of bread on Louise's plate, the half-eaten cheese, the cold neglected collops of bacon. 'But at least eat something more, or you'll faint from hunger before dinner time.'

'My stepfather doesn't break his fast in the mornings,' Louise said, through the cheese. 'He says it's a meal for peasants off to the plough, not for noblemen. He takes a little chocolate, and perhaps a roll, but no more.' She grinned. 'Maman always eats heartily, though.'

Silence thought of Kate, her beloved youngest daughter, brown and vital and laughing, whom she had not seen for many years. Binnick, the family had called her as a child, using the Somerset word for a minnow, and Louise had inherited that quicksilver quality, the mischief and the chestnut eyes and reckless spirit, together with something more serious, more sensitive, that might have come from her Guernesiaise father.

Silence prayed, with fervour, that Alex would respond to his wife's letter and come to Chard as soon as possible. But despite Louise's loyalty, she knew that he was unreliable, thoughtless, and quite capable of astonishing and casual cruelty. Even if he truly loved Louise, there was no certainty that he would instantly leave Wintercombe and rush to a reconciliation. He was probably even now dallying in Bath, or sleeping off a night's carouse, and the pleas of his neglected wife would fall on oblivious ears.

'It's *still* raining,' Louise said. She rose and peered out of the window again, an expression of intense frustration on her face. 'Oh, why won't it *stop!*' she banged her hand on the stone sill, and winced. 'Ouch. I shouldn't have done that quite so hard. I think I'll go practise on the spinet.'

Poor spinet, Silence thought ruefully, as her grand-daughter strode briskly from the room. A few moments later, the sounds of the instrument being purposefully thumped, with more fervour than skill, echoed through the house, and made her smile with some sympathy. There was no doubt that a long and vigorous ride would do much to release Louise's overwhelming burden of energy.

After dinner, the sun came out properly at last, and with immense relief Silence watched Louise urge her horse out of the stable yard, followed by a rather resigned-looking stable boy, kicking his own mount in pursuit. In this mood, the girl was too wild and restless to make congenial company for anyone, save possibly a heathen dervish. Hoping, probably in vain, that Alex would soon descend on them all and whisk his wife back to Wintercombe and a renewal of connubial bliss, Silence turned away from the window and went in search of her daughter-in-law Sarah, who had requested her presence in the still room.

Revelling in her freedom, Louise had to force herself to keep her mount to a decorous trot. The lanes around her grandparents' house, which lay to the east of Chard, a little way from the Crewkerne road, were muddy and treacherous after the heavy rain earlier in the week, and she had no wish to ruin her smart riding-habit, made in a rich golden yellow that enhanced her olive-skinned, rather exotic appearance. This was the first time she had worn it since the middle of her pregnancy, and it had been remarkably gratifying to have Christian do up the score of tiny jet buttons and view again, sleek in the mirror, the supple, slenderly graceful figure of which she had always been proud. Louise had surveyed her reflection for a long, thoughtful moment, seeing nothing to give anyone the frights, and then descended eagerly to the stables, and the willing but steady young black gelding which had been allotted to her for the length of her stay.

She had waited so long for this hour or two of liberty, to feel the warm summer sunshine on her face, the breeze stirring in her curled dark hair, to smell the rich aromas of the fields, the wet earth and vegetation, even the dungheaps and the occasional, inevitable stench from some decaying dead animal in the hedgerow. This was a country of small, steep valleys and snug closes of pasture or arable, tiny squares and strips of yellowing grain, or the red Somerset cattle, a pleasant contrast to the lush green of the fields in which they grazed, and Louise gazed about her with delight, seeing even the most humble beast or building or hedgerow flower as symbol and proof of her return to life.

Her horse was eager for a canter, and her arms ached from holding him in. Ahead, the road ran up towards the distant bulk of Windwhistle Hill, with a broad fringe of grass. She glanced at the bored young stable lad behind her, and said briskly, 'You can stay here, Jan. I shall ride up to that clump of trees, and then back.' She added, seeing his doubtful expression, 'I shall be in plain sight all the time, so you will be able to rescue me if I come to grief.'

'Aye, m'lady,' the boy said, in the thick local dialect that was even more difficult for her to understand than the speech of most of the Wintercombe servants. He pulled his mount to the side of the road, and let its reins run loose so that it could crop its fill of grass. As Louise readied herself for the gallop, he fished inside his coat and brought out pipe, tinderbox and tobacco. Hoping fervently that he did not indulge his habit when in her grandfather's stable, she urged the black into a trot, then into a canter.

This road was in fact part of the main highway which ran from Exeter all the way to London, and on a fine, warm afternoon such as this, it was comparatively busy. Ahead of her were a small group of men, probably farmers, riding east in the direction of Crewkerne: a couple of wagons, drawn by oxen, labouring up the hill: a man, two boys and several dogs attempting to control a flock of perhaps two hundred sheep: and a solitary horseman just breasting the crest of the ridge. There was no chance of an extended gallop, and every prospect that all these worthy folk would be scandalised at the sight of an apparently unaccompanied lady, well-mounted and impeccably dressed, thundering past them. But she had always delighted in shocking people, and this broad, open, sweeping highway was a temptation too great to withstand. Besides, it was down that hill that Alex would come, in a few days' time, in answer to her letter.

If he came. If he had even received it yet. If he wanted a reconciliation, and the chance to start afresh. She pushed all the writhing doubts firmly to the back of her mind, and gave the black gelding a flick of her whip and sounds of encouragement.

He was fresh, and eager, and needed no second bidding. She had a glimpse of startled bucolic faces as they passed the group of farmers at a full gallop, and approached the flock. One of the shepherds looked around, and shouted something. Louise pulled on the reins, found no response, pulled harder. The black, thoroughly enjoying himself, took no notice. Divots of soft turf spun from his driving hooves, and flecks of foam splattered on to Louise's flying skirts. There was no path through the sheep, who with typical ovine stolidity filled the road from hedge to hedge, but there was a rather tumbledown gate to one side, just before the wall of fat woolly rumps. Louise had no idea if the black could jump, but the old wildness was singing in her blood, the same glorious recklessness that had in the past inspired her to take huge risks and, usually, succeed. She steered her mount towards the gate, and he pricked his ears, shortened his stride, and sprang over the ramshackle timber like a deer.

Fortunately, it was pasture on the other side, occupied by some surprised-looking heifers. With the indignant yells of the shepherds, and a cacophony of barking dogs diminishing behind her, she let the horse carry her up the hill, parallel with the road, until the next hedge, high and thick and quite impassable, brought even the black's exuberance to a halt.

Louise, exhilarated, but also rather relieved that no harm had come from her audacity, took several deep breaths to calm her racing heart, and patted her mount's soaking neck. And then, from the road beyond the hedge on her right, came a voice she knew like her own.

'I'm surprised I still have a wife to greet, sweet Louise, if that's how you've been gallivanting about the countryside of late.'

Beyond belief, beyond hope, it was Alex.

No prospect of calming her heart now. Suddenly, she found herself shaking so much that it was impossible to move. With a supreme effort, she kept her seat and a hold on the reins, but any more was temporarily outside her power.

'Louise? Louise, are you all right?'

Remotely, she realised that his tone was sharp with concern. Furious with herself for revealing her weakness, she forced her head round to face the road, and saw him on the other side of the hedge. He was riding his bay stallion Blaze, and every line of him was eloquent and familiar and yet somehow strange, different, as if she were seeing him in a painting, delineated with the remote and crystalline clarity of a Dutch artist.

'I'm all right,' she said. The words emerged with surprising normality: to her own ears, she sounded merely breathless.

'You don't seem to be,' Alex said. 'Is there another way into that field, apart from the one you so precipitately leapt over?'

'I don't know – I didn't look.'

Louise could discern little from his face, which was turned away from the sun, and moreover shaded by the brim of his hat. His voice, however, contained several strands of expression: exasperation, irony, concern, amusement, and something else. 'Well, if you're not too shocked to ride back to the gate, or whatever it was your nag jumped, I'll meet you there. If, of course, I can negotiate the sheep. Oh, and Louise?'

'Yes?'

'Practise a *little* common sense, and open it this time?' He grinned at her suddenly, and turned away before she had the opportunity to think of a suitably rude and cutting reply.

At least she had stopped herself shaking now, and her mood had changed to one of indignation. He knew perfectly well that she was an extremely competent horsewoman. And if he thinks me incapable of persuading my horse over a rickety three-foot gate, Louise thought, with rising annoyance, then I shall make him eat his words.

102

She turned the black and trotted him back down the field, keeping out into the middle of the rough pasture. Alex, as he had predicted, was being delayed by the sheep blocking the road: she could hear his complaint, delivered with all the high-handed arrogance of which he was capable, and the placating replies of the shepherds. Grinning wickedly, Louise put her mount at the gate, with a great deal more confidence and forethought than she had employed earlier, and he popped over it as neatly as if he had been jumping such obstacles all his life.

By the time Alex had threaded his way through the sheep, his errant wife was sitting smugly on her horse by the side of the road, waiting for him. She had managed to muster at least the outward appearance of calm: she had arranged the heavy golden folds of her skirts to hide the worst of the mud and foam with which the black's high spirits had showered her, and her hat was tilted at a jaunty angle. She watched her husband approach with a sense of disbelief. Silence had told her how some things might be conjured up purely by the power of longing for them: and in proof of it, Alex, who could not possibly have received her letter yet, was here now, on the high slope of Windwhistle Hill, staring at her with his desire naked on his face, and a smile of appreciation stretching his long mouth. 'I'm glad to see that you took notice of what I said.'

'Why should I?' Louise sensed that her voice lacked his humorous tone, and hastily adjusted it, without much success. 'I may have vowed to obey you, once, but I never intended to keep my promise.'

'You wouldn't be Louise if you did.' He paused, and then said, suddenly urgent, 'Why, Louise? Why did you leave?'

His bay stallion was very near now, and she found that she did not dare to look at his face at such close quarters. She made a pretence of brushing flecks of foam from her skirts, and said at last, 'I couldn't bear it any longer. I know I should have told you what I wanted to do, but I thought that you would try to stop me – and once I knew that I must come here, to Gran'mère, it seemed to be my only chance to – ' She stopped, swallowing the word 'escape', and found, to her humiliation, tears rising to the surface. 'Alex, I'm sorry – I know it was wrong and thoughtless and stupid, but I truly think that I would have run mad if I had stayed at Wintercombe any longer.'

'Look at me,' he commanded. Afraid to reveal her distress, she shook her head. 'Louise, look at me. *Look* at me, damn you – I thought so, there's a huge gobbet of mud on your cheek, and I'm sure you'd like this to wipe it off.'

Astonished into rather feeble laughter, she lifted her head and found his hand extended, kerchief at the ready. With unwonted obedience, she accepted his offer and scrubbed the dirt and tears from her face, trying not to catch his eye.

'There,' he said, pushing the returned kerchief back into the pocket of his riding coat. 'You can face the world once more, your beauty undimmed. And don't dare apologise to me again – I am at fault, not you. I should never have left you alone like that – I should have stayed, and done a great deal more to help you recover.'

Expressions of regret were so completely alien to all she knew of Alex that she could only stare at him in amazement. Unabashed, he smiled at her, the boyish, mischievous, overwhelmingly attractive grin that had first enchanted her as a child, and had later snared her adult heart. 'You look as if you don't believe me. Shall I spell it out again, slightly different? I treated you very badly, and I am deeply sorry for it. In your place, I would probably have gone a deal further than Chard, and made sure that I left no trace at all. I don't forgive you, because there is nothing to forgive – I can only beg humbly and sincerely for your mercy.' His eyes, very blue and compelling, gazed hungrily into hers. 'Although I must confess, sweet Louise, that I do not make a habit of thus abasing myself.'

Amid the churning tangle of emotions that were threatening to overpower her, she found herself smiling. 'No, you certainly don't. Oh, Alex, I don't want apologies or regrets or even forgiveness – I want to begin again – I shall never forget Nathaniel, but I have come to accept his death, I want to move on, and think about the future rather than the past. I wrote to you, but only two days ago – you can't have received it yet – am I making sense?'

'Not much,' Alex said. His hand, still encased in an ancient leather riding gauntlet, shiny with much use, came out to touch hers, with gentleness. 'But I have read your letter. I recognised your grandfather's groom – we met on the road just beyond Shepton yesterday, and he gave it to me. He's a couple of miles behind me.'

'So why did you set out for Chard if my letter hadn't reached you?'

Alex stared at her for a moment. Then he said with mock exasperation, 'Because I was coming to fetch you home, of course. What did you think I would do? Sit at Wintercombe all alone, twiddling my thumbs and waiting for you to return? Not exactly my style, you must admit. Oh, Louise, this may be the time, but it is certainly not the place to say all this, but I'll tell you anyway, before your young guardian arrives – he's obviously decided that I'm some ruffian who's molesting you.'

She glanced over her shoulder to see the stable boy, his face set in a threatening scowl, riding up the hill at a laboured trot. Alex went on, his voice low and impassioned. 'I love you, and I want you, most desperately and beyond all measure. You may not believe me, but it's the bare and honest truth. We can talk later, but I need to know – I must know.' His gaze, urgent and demanding, held her attention. 'Louise – do you still love me?'

Once, not so long ago, she had doubted it. Now, faced with the vivid reality of him, his size, his overwhelming personality, the supremely attractive power of his presence, there was only one answer that she could possibly give.

'Yes,' she said, and smiled. 'Yes, I do love you.'

His answering smile was dazzling, and he urged his horse closer. 'Then will you kiss me, my own dearest lady?'

Their lips met, briefly, and then were abruptly wrenched apart as the bay stallion, notoriously bad-tempered, chose that moment to object to his enforced proximity to Louise's horse. There was an explosion of squeals, and the black, nipped viciously on the rump, tried to retaliate with his hooves. It took a while to calm them, by which time the groom had arrived, and the moment was lost.

But not for ever: his eyes, his smile, told her that as soon as opportunity offered, he would take her in his arms, touch and kiss her, make love to her . . .

And, stranded between hope and fear, she found herself dreading the moment when they would next be alone.

# Chapter Six

## 'The paths of paradise'

All the way back to her grandparents' house, perhaps three miles from where she had encountered Alex, Louise kept up a determined flow of small talk and banter, covering her inward turmoil. Part of her welcomed the man riding beside her, keeping his horse just out of biting and kicking distance from her abused and resentful mount, welcomed him with a wild and desperate longing to share, at last, her grief and loneliness, and to rejoice in the love and friendship he offered to her. But there was also, running dark and deep beside these more positive feelings, a fear that threatened to overwhelm them.

Once, her passion and desire had been the equal of his, and together they had achieved a level of delight and pleasure in their lovemaking that neither of them had known before. But Nathaniel's birth, and death, had driven all such thoughts from her mind. She loved Alex, but even now, in his presence and under his spell, she did not know if it would ever be possible to attain again the glory they had shared.

Her terror of it, of cruel disappointment, of failure, stayed with her like a grim shadow. He wanted her, and every movement, every glance, betrayed his desire for her. But when they had kissed, though briefly indeed, she had felt nothing, no frisson of lust, no stirring of the blood. She feared that the passion she had once felt for him was dead, and impossible to rekindle: and she knew that it would be the worst betrayal of all, to counterfeit ecstacy in his arms.

Besides, she did not think that she would be able to pretend.

As they rode into the stable yard, her apprehension increased. She had thought herself cured, in these few weeks, of the malaise which had afflicted her after Nathaniel's death, and she had assumed that it would be easy to welcome Alex into her arms and her bed, almost as if nothing had ever come between them. And now she realised that it was rather more complicated than she had thought: nor was she fully recovered.

The horses were led away, and Alex took her arm. The stables here lay a little distance from the house, and there was a gate in the wall to their right, leading to the garden. 'Will you walk with me for a while, my lady?'

'Of course,' Louise said, and allowed herself to be drawn into the colourful, sweet-scented enclave that her grandmother had so lovingly created around her home.

There seemed to be no one about, and the mullioned windows of the house gazed blankly down on them. Suddenly desperate to keep their conversation on a safely trivial plane, she said, 'Where is Gerrit?'

Gerrit Thyssen was her husband's Dutch manservant, and usually accompanied his master everywhere, so his absence was surprising. Alex said, 'He's gone to Holland. I sent him over there before I went to Bath. There's some business that needs attending to, and I have no other Dutch speakers in my employ – although Lukas is supposed to be giving Phoebe lessons.'

'Will that be her seventh language, or her eighth?'

'Ninth, I think, not counting her native tongue. Oh, and the Waspish.'

Despite her nervousness, Louise laughed. They had strolled some way around the perimeter path, avoiding the intricate walks between the knots at the centre of the garden, and now the arbour, made for lovers, was almost upon them. Smoothly, Alex guided her towards it, and when they were within the sheltering tangle of honeysuckle, took her in his arms.

She could not resist, but neither could she respond. She submitted passively, trying to summon some feeling, as his mouth came down on hers, and his hands caressed her with increasing urgency. But it was useless: with despair, she knew that any whore could have put up a better show.

But she was not any whore: she was his wife, and she loved him, and she would not pretend or deceive, however much her honesty might hurt. And he knew: he lifted his head, and said softly, 'Louise – what's wrong?'

Miserably, she stared up at him. She was tall, but even her height, unusual in a woman, could not match his six feet and two inches. She saw the spare, virile beauty of his face, the remarkable eyes, the lines around them and his long, mobile mouth that betrayed his past excesses, his humour and his wilfulness: a man she loved despite his manifold faults and vices, a man who had once possessed such astonishing power to arouse her. And she wondered why, now, her senses seemed to be dead, when her most desperate wish was to respond to him with equivalent passion.

She said helplessly, 'Nothing. Everything. I don't know, Alex – I don't *know*!'

'But you love me.' It was a statement, not a question. Mutely, she nodded.

'In my admittedly wide experience, ladies do not usually respond to the caresses of their lovers with all the ardour of a sack of meal,' Alex said, and his sudden, tender smile robbed the words of their brutality. 'What frightens you? Because you *are* frightened – and don't try to deny it, I can sense it, and see it in your face.'

She had thought, once, in the innocence of being in love, that theirs was an equal partnership, despite the fact that he was nearly ten years older than she was. But faced with his insistence, and his acute and disconcerting perception, she realised suddenly that she had always, perhaps, been a little afraid of him: of the strength of his character, of his capacity to hurt and to harm, and, most of all, of the power which he held over her emotions.

Confused and unhappy, she turned her head away, expecting some expression of anger or impatience. But he made no movement or sound, and in the end, she gathered all her courage and looked at him. His face was still and thoughtful, but his eyes, meeting hers, were frighteningly intense. He said, 'Louise – you must *talk* to me. How can I know what is wrong, and what you want of me, if you will not tell me?'

'I don't think I can,' she whispered, feeling her eyes fill with tears.

'Why not? What frightens you?' He stared down at her for a moment, and then said, 'Louise – do *I* frighten you?'

She had vowed to be honest with him, but admitting this newfound and unwelcome truth was far from easy. At last, unable to speak, she nodded.

'*I* frighten you?' Alex had his hands on her shoulders still: their grip tightened, and she winced involuntarily. At once he let her go, and turned away with a savage gesture. '*Why?* The Louise I knew – the Louise I married – *nothing* frightened her. What's happened? What's changed? What, God help me, have I done?'

'Nothing,' she said, feeling the tears falling again. It had all gone wrong, he was angry with her, their longed-for reconciliation had failed, and she would have given the world and all it held to be back on the slopes of Windwhistle Hill, so that she could have the chance to make matters different.

Alex swung round to face her, and with a great effort she stopped herself from flinching away from him. For what seemed like an hour, they stared at each other, and she saw the appeal, the desperation in his eyes, and wanted with all her heart to give him what he most desired: the old, reckless, carefree Louise, with her fire and gallantry and unashamed, uninhibited lust.

But that Louise had died with Nathaniel: and no amount of pretence, no number of wild leaps over rickety gates, could bring her back. She could not deceive him, and she would do her best to tell him the truth, however alarming his reaction to it might be.

She said slowly, trying to explain, 'I *do* love you. I want more than anything to – to show it, as you would wish. But . . .'

'You are afraid? Is that it? Of the act itself, or of the possible consquences?' His voice was more gentle, and she gathered her courage.

110

'Of both. I don't think I could bear to – to lose another child. And . . . it's as if all my senses have been numbed, since Nathaniel died.' She faced him, head high, intent on her faltering, difficult task. 'I *want* to feel as I used to, before – I want to, so much. But it's all dead, lifeless, gone.' She gave a small, bitter smile. 'Like a sack of meal.'

He said nothing, and she waited bleakly for the inevitable explosion. Instead, to her surprise, he smiled. 'Is that all?'

'*All?*' Astonished and goaded into annoyance, she glared at him. 'What do you mean, *all?*'

'Well, the world has hardly ended, has it?' he pointed out. 'Louise, has no one told you that this often happens to women who have suffered a difficult birth, or lost a child?'

Blankly, she shook her head.

'Haven't you had a talk with your grandmother?'

'Oh, yes, but – ' She stopped, and gave a rather rueful laugh. 'The secrets of our bed were not under discussion.'

'I should hope not. Aunt Silence is no Puritan, whatever appearances might indicate, but she does not share our lack of inhibition. However, the good Doctor Peirce mentioned something of the sort to me, by way of a warning, and I understand that such feelings are surprisingly common. You may think now that your old ardour will never come back – but it will, I promise you it will.'

Such was the certainty in his voice that she could almost believe him. 'Perhaps,' she said reluctantly. 'But when?'

'Tonight?' His eyes glinted wickedly. 'In your bed-chamber, at eight o'clock, shall we say? After supper, at any rate.'

'I can't!' Louise said, trying to fight her sudden, rising panic. 'Alex, please – it's too soon – I can't!'

'I know,' he said, and planted a brief, loving kiss on her brow. 'But trust me – please, sweet Louise, trust me, try not to be frightened of what you can or can't feel – trust me, and all will be well. Can you do that?'

Remotely, there was a sparkle of hope. And because she loved him, and wanted to make everything right between them, as it had been only two months ago, she took a deep breath, and nodded. 'Yes, I will try. But, please,

111

Alex, don't expect too much of me – I don't want to pretend – '

'Do you think I wouldn't know if you did?' he said, and grinned, and held out his arm. 'I think we had better make our presence felt in the house, or they will be imagining that you've been abducted. And don't forget what I said – *trust* me, don't resist, and it will all come right in the end, I promise you.'

And as he escorted her back towards the house, Louise found herself, in spite of all her confused doubts and fears and misery, beginning to assume some of his own belief and optimism.

In happier times, she would have been amused by the rather wary welcome which her grandparents, with Richard and Sarah, gave to Alex. Living fifty miles from Wintercombe, they did not know him very well (although his fearsome reputation was another matter), and much of his adult life, after all, had been spent in London or in Europe.

The children, however, suffered from no such inhibitions, and the hour or so before supper was spent in noisy, gleeful horseplay in the garden, with Nicholas and little Rebecca laughing, squealing, chasing and being chased, while the other adults looked on in some bewilderment, astonished that Alex, the dissolute and vicious, should prove so completely and endearingly at ease with small children. And Louise, watching her husband swing an ecstatic Nicholas around him until dizziness overtook them both and they collapsed in an effervescent heap, felt at once an aching sense of loss and regret, that he should have been denied such future delight with his dead son, and a new determination to give him the children that he so greatly desired.

And if, to conceive, she had to submit to his passion without response, well, she would endure it, and hope that one day her old desire for him would be reborn.

Supper was a surprisingly cheerful meal, with young Nicholas, on a stool at the end of the table, still apt to giggle at unexpected moments. As in his letters to her from Phoebe's house, Alex entertained them with a variety of anecdotes and descriptions of the denizens of Bath, both permanent and temporary, and made them all laugh. And Louise, seated opposite him, tried to eat, though without much success, and watched him enchant the company, and knew that whatever the message of her senses, her love for him was undiminished.

She drank several glasses of wine, and found herself able, eventually, to join in the conversation, and even to make one or two dry jokes. Suddenly, the prospect that lay before her did not seem so dreadful. Her fear, after all, lay within herself: it was her own failure that she most dreaded, and somehow she was sure that he understood, and could accept it. And this Alex, delightful, charming, witty, was the one she loved best, very different from the angry, impatient stranger of whom she had been so frightened. She knew, after all, that he loved her. Trust me, he had said: and for once she intended to obey him.

The chamber next to hers had been made ready for him, and her grandfather had generously offered the services of his manservant, which Alex, never particularly careful of his appearance, had firmly refused. Normally, the time after supper was spent reading, sewing, playing cards or strolling in the garden: but her husband, rising from the table, announced his intention of retiring immediately.

It took Louise by surprise: she stared at him, and he smiled, and stretched out his hand to her. 'Louise and I will see you in the morning.'

She permitted herself to be led from the dining parlour, and up the handsome wooden staircase to the bedchambers above. Her maid was busy laying out nightclothes and turning down the bed, and looked up, startled, as the door opened. 'Oh, m'lady, I didn't expect – '

'Thank you, Christian – that will be all for tonight,' Alex told her. The maid curtseyed, gave her mistress a quick, friendly glance, and left the room. There was no key in the lock, but he took a piece of paper from the table, folded it into a small, fat wedge, and pushed it behind the latch. 'Now we can't be disturbed.'

Louise, standing in the middle of the floor, wondered at

113

her own outward calm. Inside, however, she was quaking as if, she thought with sudden annoyance, she were a sheltered virgin on her wedding night, not an experienced married woman.

Alex turned away from the door and surveyed her. She had changed out of her riding habit into a mantua of peacock-blue silk, cool and slippery and low-cut, her favourite amongst a very extensive collection of clothes. He said, smiling, 'You look superb. That colour becomes you very well.'

'Thank you,' Louise said. Her mouth was dry, and she wanted more wine: her courage was beginning to ebb.

'Don't worry,' he said, and walked towards her, still smiling. 'I told you – trust me. I will do nothing to hurt you, or alarm you, or distress you – and if you do not wish me to do anything, anything at all – you have only to say, and I will stop. Do you understand?'

She nodded, her eyes wide and stark with apprehension. He stood very near and tall, and even though his words were reassuring, at such close quarters she could not help feeling overwhelmed.

'How long is it, sweet Louise, since you were last seduced?' Alex enquired. 'Or is it a new experience?'

He grinned at her, and she found an answering smile. 'I can't imagine that you have ever had to persuade anyone before.'

'Indeed not – I can hardly walk down the street without lust-crazed women hurling themselves at me,' Alex said. 'And patience, I must admit, is an alien virtue.'

He reached out, and touched her cheek. His fingers were warm, but she shivered suddenly. Very gently, his eyes holding hers, he drew his hand down the side of her face, and through the thick, artfully arranged curls that framed it, caressing her as if she were indeed some shy virgin. It was strangely comforting to stand there so close to him, yet not held, only stroked, and with such tenderness. Gradually, as his hand explored the contours of her face, she began to relax, and some of the tension left her body. He pulled the pins deftly from her hair, and she felt a sudden sensation of

114

release, and freedom, as the heavy ringlets cascaded down around her shoulders. Then he drew her into his embrace, but not to kiss her, his lips brushed her ear, and he whispered, 'All right?'

She nodded, still feeling comforted, protected, sheltered within his arms. As lightly as a drifting feather, he kissed her hair, her brow, her eyelid, her cheek, her ear, the nape of her neck, and suddenly she shivered again, but not from fear. He drew away at once, his face questioning, and she smiled. 'Please – don't stop.'

'Sure?' he said, and when she nodded, bent his head to kiss her.

At first, as in the arbour that afternoon, she felt nothing. And then, almost unnoticed, sensation stirred, and woke. Her hands came up, slowly, to touch his shoulders, and her body moulded closer to his, almost of its own accord. When it ended, he smiled at her, his eyes dark with desire, and his hands strayed down her shoulders, lingered over her breasts, and then descended to the slim knotted sash that fastened her mantua. She held his gaze as he untied it, letting it fall to the floor, and then slid the sleek blue material down her arms. As it followed the sash, with a soft whisper of silk, he reached behind her to undo the laces of her stays.

Louise's heart began to quicken. She stood as still as a statue as Alex removed the constricting garment, leaving her clad only in her chemise and the cream and blue flowered petticoat which went so well with the peacock mantua. Then, he took her hand and led her, unresisting, to the bed.

Never before had she been wooed with such gentleness and patience: never had she been touched, caressed, fondled as if she were a piece of fragile Cathay porcelain which would be broken with excessive carelessness or haste. She allowed herself to be divested of her remaining clothes, and laid back upon the pillows, while he swiftly pulled off his shirt and breeches. Then he came to lie beside her, and she tensed, expecting that this amazing, wonderful tenderness would give way now before the urgency of his

115

desire. But he propped himself on one elbow, and began again to stroke her naked body, first her face and hair, then her neck, and her shoulders. And as his touch, soft, almost tickling, reached her breasts, she became aware that she was holding her breath, waiting for the exquisite sensation of pleasure that, suddenly, she remembered so well.

And with the thought, it was there, walking like a ghost beneath his fingers, and she sighed in wondering delight. Woken, her own desire began to take wing.

Still, his eyes were intent upon her: he had not spoken, there was no need of words, for touch and expression were all that was necessary between them. His hands explored her breasts, leaving a trail of white-hot fire on her skin, and then slid lower. And with every inch her longing grew, and she moved involuntarily, craving further sensation. But he smiled again, teasingly, and his fingers continued their slow, subtle journey, while she moaned, and gasped, and her hunger rose to impossible heights, and the anticipation of rapture became almost too much to bear.

And then, when she felt that she could wait no longer, when her need for him was overwhelming, he slid inside her, and began the slow, rhythmic movement that her body remembered so well, and to which it responded with increasing ardour. If there was pain, she did not realise it: and fear had long since been vanquished by his touch, his love and his patience. Overcome by passion, she forgot everything save for the inexorable surge of pleasure that burst into sudden and glorious flower, and her cry of joy and triumph came at the same moment as his.

She wept, then, for love and relief, and happiness that her heart's desire had been granted: and fell asleep in his arms, free of care at last, with the echo of his words soft and rapturous in her ear. 'Oh, Louise, my most sweet and glorious Louise, I love you so much.'

It was dark when she woke, her mind coming slowly back to life. There was a full moon, soaring high in a clear starry sky, and it poured light almost as brilliant as sunshine on to the bed. Alex had moved away from her a little, and lay sprawled on his back, his black hair coiled on the pillow, the

116

sheet twisted around his lean, powerful body. Even in sleep, there was a subtle smile on his lips: he looked relaxed, and fulfilled, and uncharacteristically at peace. For a long time, she sat watching him, remembering with delight, and rekindling desire, how with such infinite skill and tenderness he had reached beneath the surface of her fears and anxieties, to raise again her powerful sensuality. And she knew that, whatever the world might say or think, Alexander St Barbe was a man entirely worthy of her love.

At last, she put out a hand, and touched his arm. 'Alex?'

He opened his eyes, robbed of their startling colour by the cold silver light, and turned his head drowsily to look at her. 'Hullo, sweet Louise. What is it?'

She let her fingers stray with wanton impudence across his skin, and saw understanding leap joyfully into his face. She was well aware of the moonlight, outlining and enhancing her slender naked body and laying secretive shadows under her small, prominent breasts, and smiled wickedly down at him. With a sudden soft laugh, he pulled her into his embrace, and they made love with a swift, feverish urgency that was in utter contrast to the slow-burgeoning desire she had experienced earlier. And as she drifted once more into sleep, her head pillowed on his shoulder and his arms encircling her, she knew that at last they were whole again, and healed, and united in love.

For a week they stayed at Chard, hardly aware of the slightly bemused looks of the rest of the household, moving in their own exclusive sphere of happiness. If anyone thought it strange, or remarkable, that they spent so much time in the bedchamber, or walking, arms entwined, in the garden, or kissing with luxurious abandon in the shelter of the honeysuckle arbour, no comment was made in their presence. But once or twice, through her daze of delight, Louise saw her grandmother's glance resting on her, and knew that they possessed her wholehearted approval.

It was a time of joy, a time of enchantment, eclipsing the despairing, unhappy months since Nathaniel's death to such effect that her previous misery seemed now to be no

117

more substantial than some transitory nightmare, to be banished by the sunshine and glory of the day.

A week, and then the idyll was ended, and they must at last return to Wintercombe. But she was no longer afraid of reality, or of the future, for Alex's love and tenderness had transformed her life.

Dublin was a city second only to London in the isles of Britain, with much new building, and a flourishing trade. But to the man walking alone to his lodgings in the soft, drizzling evening light that seemed so peculiarly Irish, the well-built stone and timber houses that he passed might have been the meanest hovels, and the people who still crowded the streets were, in his opinion, for the most part illiterate savages, who could not even speak comprehensible English.

He was a young man, not tall, and sturdily built. His suit, in a fine blue cloth with silver buttons and braid, proclaimed him a gentleman, as did the ordered curls of his blond periwig, and the polished buckles on his shoes. He was fair-skinned, blue-eyed, conventionally good-looking, but given an air of grimness by the repressed, bitter set to his mouth. Beggars, of whom there were many in Dublin, had learned to avoid him, and the contemptuous sweep of his silver-topped cane.

As a gentleman, it might have been expected that he would hire a chair, or a hackney, to carry him through the filthy streets. But since his lodgings were very close to the Castle, where the Lord Lieutenant conducted the business of government, and where he worked as a clerk, there was little point in wasting good coin to transport him a few yards. Charles St Barbe dressed well, because he liked to, and because a man's standing was denoted more by his clothes then by anything else: not for him the ink-stained broadcloth of most clerks. His chief interest lay in the gathering of money, and already, after only nine months in Ireland, he had a finger in several lucrative pies, somewhat to the detriment of the native population, and a growing sum deposited with a goldsmith in Castle Street.

The house where he lodged was, like most buildings in the old part of Dublin, constructed of timber, with a steep tiled roof that, not so long ago, had been covered in thatch. Its owner, Mistress Maguire, was a middle-aged Catholic widow, childless and still comely, who had taken a fancy, half romantic, half maternal, to the silent young Englishman who occupied her ground-floor rooms. Over the past months she had tried, without success, to gain his confidence, to discover what tragedy (for surely nothing else could have caused him to be so serious, so grim, so reticent) lay in his past. Her fair, handsome lodger was, in consequence, the subject of much interested gossip and speculation amongst the Widow Maguire's circle of cronies, and the agreed verdict was that he had been disappointed in love.

They were partly right, but it was not only his cousin Louise's rejection of him that had driven Charles St Barbe into exile. His desire for Wintercombe, his home since early childhood, the place he loved best in the world, was the other mainspring of his life. He had wanted both, and had been encouraged to think that they were his for the taking. His uncle, Sir Nathaniel St Barbe, had employed him as his steward and secretary, relying upon him to run his affairs, and Charles had not unnaturally assumed that Wintercombe and all its lands would come to him.

But his uncle's death, and Alex's return from abroad, had shattered Charles's dreams. Disillusioned, sickened and disgusted, not only by Louise's betrayal but by Alex's treasonous activities, Charles had informed on him to the authorities after the collapse of Monmouth's pathetic rebellion. He had done his duty as a loyal and honest subject, but his family, all save his mother and Amy, had turned on him as though he, and not Alex, were the traitor.

But now he had seized his chance. He had money, presence, and valuable administrative skills and experience: moreover, he was a Catholic, and under the Catholic King James, those of the Old Religion were encouraged. It had been surprisingly easy to obtain a comparatively lowly but responsible position in the government. It had been even easier, with the money he had inherited from his uncle, as well as the two hundred pounds Silence had given him to make his new life in Virginia, to make careful and profitable investments. Many ships plied between Dublin and the west coast of England, a few days' voyage away: and Wintercombe was only fifteen miles or so from Bristol. If circumstances changed, he could be home within a week.

His mother, in her regular letters, kept him apprised of all the gossip about the family he had left behind. He learned of Phoebe's removal to Bath, to set up her own household in a most unconventional manner that, in someone less ill-favoured and spinsterish, would have been quite shocking, and her engagement of their cousin Libby Orchard as her companion.

Charles had no interest in them, nor in the activities of his other cousins in Bristol, Taunton and Glastonbury. News of Louise was what he most craved, as Bab was well aware. Although she privately detested the girl, considering her a wanton hussy, she had always given her beloved only son the greatest indulgence, and Louise was his obsession. Over the months, Charles had read of her progressing pregnancy, her reckless refusal to give up riding when big with child, and, with a grim mixture of satisfaction and pity, of the early birth and almost immediate death of her baby. If he had lived, Alex's son would have supplanted Charles: but the entail that Sir Nathaniel had placed upon Wintercome meant that, until Alex fathered another legitimate son, like it or not, Charles was his heir.

It was this hope that had sustained Charles in the hated, alien surroundings of Dublin. Alex was still young, only just thirty, but men who followed his way of life, drinking and wenching to excess, frequently came to bad and premature ends. And if there was the slightest chance that Alex might die, or go on his travels again, then Charles would take ship for England, to claim what he had always considered to be his right.

Mistress Maguire was waiting for him when he entered her dark, oak-panelled hall, her handsome oval face alive

120

with curiosity. 'There's a letter here for you, Master St Barbe – from your mother?'

So much had she deduced over the past months, though he had never actually told her who wrote the fat weekly epistles, in a remarkably ill-spelt scrawl. 'Thank you, madam,' Charles said, taking it without a smile.

The door of his chamber banged behind him with curt, uninformative finality, and the widow sighed. One day, surely, she would discover why a young man who, apparently, enjoyed every advantage in life – money, looks, health, intelligence – should be so cast down by adverse fate.

Charles had no servant: it was another unnecessary expense, and besides, his flesh crawled at the thought of some uncouth Irishman, by definition a savage even if he was a fellow-Catholic, performing personal ministrations. He cared for his own clothes, dressed himself and his periwig, had himself shaved by a neighbouring barber, and hired street boys by the hour to run errands or take messages. The widow's own servants cooked and cleaned for him, and their silent, deferential and yet somehow hostile presence was irksome enough. He was, after all, an Englishman, albeit a Catholic one, and since the massacres of Cromwell, thirty years ago, the English had been bitterly resented by most Irish men and women.

Alone in his large, comfortable chamber, he sat down at the table, lit a five-branched candlestick, and opened his mother's latest letter.

Her news was not entirely unexpected, given the knowledge of his cousin's reprehensible habits, but even so, Charles was shocked. To embark on such an affair after only a few months of marriage, and with his wife ill in childbed, was utterly despicable, and entirely typical of Alex's character. He grew hot with pity for Louise, lying sick, bereaved, neglected and betrayed, and still, presumably, under the pathetic illusion that her wicked husband was loving and faithful. He had begged her to leave Alex, and had warned her that this would happen, and still she had married him. And now, sooner even than he had thought, he had been proved right.

121

His immediate impulse was to go to her side, to comfort her with his own steadfast love and devotion, and heal her hurt. But a moment's reflection convinced him of the folly of such a move. She would not believe him, and Alex, who was still a man of wealth and influence despite his treacherous past, might well have him thrown summarily into prison. After all, only last Christmas Charles had tried to kill him, and almost succeeded. Several other people knew of that attack, and might, deluded as they were, bear witness against him. Charles knew that he was in the right – if anyone deserved death, it was Alex – but the might of the law would be invoked against him.

No, he would have to wait until Alex was out of the way, absent from Wintercombe temporarily or, God willing, permanently, before he could return to comfort Louise. But there was still good reason to be hopeful. The baby was dead. Alex had committed adultery, of which his wife was apparently still in ignorance. If Louise could be told of that betrayal, it might at last turn her against Alex – and if they became estranged, then of course the prospect of further children was unlikely. Alex would be tied to a wife who hated him, and with luck would soon drink himself to death, or succumb to the pox, or a riding accident, or an outraged husband: and then, Charles would inherit Wintercombe, and Louise.

He opened his writing case, sharpened a quill, and dipped it into the inkwell. His careful, secretary's hand curled elegantly across the thick paper.

My dearest Mama,
    Thank you indeed for your most welcome letter of the seventh of August, which I have only now received, ten days later. The news which you send is most sad, and shocking. It grieves me deeply to think of poor Louise so betrayed, and in ignorance of her husband's wickedness. I do feel it best that you acquaint her with the unfortunate truth as soon as opportunity presents itself, so that she may tax him with his adultery. It may indeed be that he will be

122

encouraged to mend his ways, although this, I fear, is most improbable – the dead will rise sooner. But take care how you tell her, for he is an evil man, and has no love for us, and will not scruple to do you harm if he can.

Pray give my most affectionate regards to Amy, and tell her that perhaps, with God's will, we may soon be reunited. Until that hopeful day, I remain,

Your entirely devoted son,
Charles St Barbe

He sealed and addressed it, and left it on the table: it could be slipped into the government postbag tomorrow, and would reach her very soon. Then, as there was still a little while until supper, he removed his shoes, his coat and his periwig, and lay down on the bed, to occupy the time in delightful contemplation of all the ways in which Sir Alexander St Barbe might best be forced from this world to the next.

# Chapter Seven

## 'Some secret revelation'

'The Queen Dowager will visit Bath this week,' Alex said to his wife over the dinner table, a fortnight or so after their return to Wintercombe. 'And I think Lukas would like to be rescued. He's been staying with Phoebe for more than two months now, and he must surely have managed to teach her all he knows of Dutch.' He smiled at her, across an expanse of white linen, gleaming pewter, polished silver, and the remains of a particularly succulent saddle of lamb. 'What say you to a jaunt to Bath? I'm sure you're ready to face the world again.'

The Queen Dowager, widow of the late King Charles, was a middle-aged, retiring and notably frumpish woman who had never, even in her youth, been in the forefront of fashion, but her arrival in Bath would inevitably bring a trail of courtiers and ladies and gentlemen of quality in her ample wake, with the consequent social round of dancing, theatrical performances, card playing and less respectable pursuits. Louise said doubtfully, 'Surely you have never been of her circle?'

'Hardly – the confidants of an ageing Papist Portuguese widow are certainly not to my taste. But Sir Hugh Trevelyan is to be of the company, and I am sure,' Alex said, with a mischievous grin, 'that my dear sister will be in need of a chaperone.'

Louise shook her head in mock reproof. 'Phoebe has no need of my protection, nor yours. Sir Hugh is a good friend – a very good friend, since he procured your release from the Tower. But I can't believe that he means any more to Phoebe than that.'

'Everyone, my sister included, seems to think that because she has a crippled leg, a bookish mind and a sharp tongue, she is incapable of giving or receiving affection,' Alex pointed out. 'But Sir Hugh has spoken of her to me in the most glowing terms, on several occasions. So far, Phoebe has remained stubbornly blind to his regard for her, but perhaps some more time in his company will change her opinion.'

'I doubt it,' Louise said, finishing her raspberry tart. 'Phoebe could have the handsomest men in England clamouring for her hand, and she'd take no notice. Alex, she isn't – she isn't *designed* for marriage! If she were a man, she'd be some crusty old scholar, teaching at Oxford perhaps, and getting more and more testy and eccentric with every passing year.'

'And I thought you were her friend!'

'I am, I love her like a sister, but she – she isn't a *feminine* woman, Alex, she's too – '

'Clever?'

Louise stuck out her tongue at him, cheerfully childish. 'You know very well what I mean. I just can't imagine a sophisticated courtier like Sir Hugh being romantically interested in Phoebe, however much he may want a mother for young James.'

'Perhaps he's looking for a cheap tutor,' Alex suggested, with a sly grin. 'Why go to the bother and expense of hiring one when your wife speaks eight or nine languages, and has a comprehensive understanding of mathematics, astronomy, geography, history and the natural sciences?'

'Alex!'

'Well, she's given Lukas an excellent grounding in all subjects, and considering he was completely uneducated when he came to England, he's become quite a scholar himself – not to say a pedant.' His voice softened reflectively. 'I miss him – and that pony of his has grown so fat on too much grass and no exercise, he looks fit to burst. Well? Shall we descend on poor Phoebe for a few days, and further the course of true love?'

'You know full well that if you mention anything of the sort to her, she'll never speak to Sir Hugh again.'

'Oh, I doubt that, somehow,' Alex said, and raised his

125

glass. 'To my dear sister Phoebe – may her days of spinsterhood soon be over!'

Since their return from Chard, Alex had been remarkably good company: loving, attentive and witty. They were lovers again, in the truest sense of the word, touching often, looking when touch was not possible, and laughter was frequent. Almost every day they rode out together, Louise accompanying Alex when he visited outlying farms, or went to inspect horses, and the days, although busy of course with the running of the house and estate, always afforded ample opportunity for enjoyment of each other's company.

And the nights . . . Her loins grew warm just thinking of what they did, the passion, the closeness, the delight and laughter and extremes of pleasure, gladly given and joyfully received. There was no sign yet of another child – perhaps it was still too soon after Nathaniel's birth – but surely it could not be long. And her body ached for another baby, as it ached, more specifically and intensely, for Alex, every night.

Yes, love had completed the healing that her grandmother's compassionate wisdom had begun. She would never erase the memory of Nathaniel, but she could think of him now without weeping, and the renewal of her marriage had given her hope and confidence for the future.

'Is it too soon to dance, do you think?' she said. Although she had never been a slave to polite convention, she was now Lady St Barbe, and appearances were important: even her mischievous, heedless mother Kate had realised that, eventually.

'We've never danced together, have we?' Alex said thoughtfully. 'In that case, sweet Louise, it certainly isn't too soon. Shall we go tomorrow? I'll send Henry Renolds over with a message, so that poor Phoebe isn't completely taken by surprise.' His eyes gleamed. 'And while we're there, you can take the waters. They may not have worked a cure for the poor Queen Dowager, but they're said to be an excellent aid to conception.'

'I hope you don't see me in one of those frights they call bath-gowns,' Louise said, grinning. The stiff yellow canvas garments, designed to conceal every vestige of a woman's shape from curious eyes, would undoubtedly incite no one's lustful thoughts.

'For shame – I'd assumed you were planning to enter the King's bath in a state of naked grace. Oh well,' Alex said, with an exaggerated sigh, 'I shall have to content myself with my own private viewing. Are you busy this afternoon? No? Well, I'll see you in my chamber in five minutes – and no dawdling, mind!'

It was not, Louise felt certain, the way that most married couples behaved, retiring to bed in broad daylight, and doubtless providing the entire household with ample fuel for gossip. But when Alex beckoned, his blue eyes narrowed with unashamed lechery, he summoned up the same desires in herself, and she would have made love on the Hall table if he had suggested it. Knowing Alex, wickedly inventive, she suspected that it was only a matter of time before he did.

They rode to Bath the next day. It was the first time that they had seen Phoebe since their return from Chard, and although she knew about their reconciliation, because both Alex and Louise had written separately to tell her of it, her expression was still somewhat wary as she welcomed them within her house in Nowhere Lane.

In the noise of the joyful reunion between Alex and Lukas, however, her doubts vanished, and she greeted her brother and his wife with unalloyed delight. At last, she thought, looking at Alex's unshadowed, glorious smile, at Louise's sparkling eyes and glowing face, at last everything has turned out right for them: they have put Nathaniel's death behind them, and made their lives anew.

And a small, unwelcome worm of envy moved within her, before she could repress it. After all, she herself had chosen her path: she had eschewed the softer, female destiny of marriage and motherhood, vowing to dedicate her life to the pursuit of knowledge. She had a mind superior to most men's, and a face that would never launch any ships: and moreover, she despised those many women who made a virtue of ignorance, stupidity, and blind

127

submission to their husbands. She wanted no man's rule in her life: she had seen little enough of the world, but she knew that the loving and passionate friendship that bound Alex and Louise together was rare indeed, and her own chances of enjoying such a marriage scarcer than alchemist's gold.

So why had the news, in his letter last week, that Sir Hugh Trevelyan was soon to visit Bath, lightened her days and kindled in her scrawny breast an unreasonable and ridiculous sense of anticipation? The only man she loved, now that her father was dead, was her brother, and that was a difficult and battered emotion that only served to prove, after twenty-five years of dislike, tormenting and abuse on both sides, that blood was thicker than water.

Sir Hugh was a friend, no more, despite Alex's raised eyebrows and sly wink, and she had no intention of degenerating into one of those dried-up, love-starved spinsters who notoriously conceived inappropriate and undignified passions for unsuitable men. She was entirely above that sort of thing.

So when Sir Hugh Trevelyan came to pay his respects, three days later, she greeted him with smiling friendship, and managed entirely to conceal the sudden lurch of her pulse when her maid Mattie announced him. Alex and Louise had gone out, and she suspected that their absence had not come about by chance: she would not have put it past her brother to have suggested to Sir Hugh, whom he had met that morning in the Abbey, that this afternoon, at a little after three, would be an excellent time to call.

She had last seen him in London after Christmas, at Alex's wedding, and the intervening months had not changed him at all. He was a tall man, broadly built, with the ostentatious and extravagant dress of the courtier, all gold buttons and elaborate, costly trimmings and frothing lace at neck and wrist. Indeed, the buckles on his shoes, and the carved silver head of his ebony cane, would not have disgraced a king. It was all a pose, however: he was a Gentleman of the King's Bedchamber, and had a position and status to maintain, but a shrewd, cynical and witty man of the world lurked beneath the preposterous curls of his periwig, and he had done Alex, and thereby Phoebe and Louise, a signal service in procuring her brother's release from the Tower.

'My dear Mistress St Barbe – your most humble, affectionate and devoted servant, ma'am,' he said, on the threshold of her parlour, and bowed with a flourish. Phoebe did not dare look at Libby, who had never met Sir Hugh or anyone remotely like him before, and whose eyes were doubtless popping out of her head. She favoured him with an ironically brief curtsey, and invited him to sit and take refreshments.

'Indeed I will – and I will do more, if I may,' said Sir Hugh, smiling. 'I chanced upon your brother and his charming wife and son this morning in the Abbey, as they may have told you, and Sir Alexander took the liberty of inviting me to sup here this evening.'

'Oh, he did, did he?' said Phoebe. 'Unfortunately, he neglected to tell me of it, which is entirely typical of Alex – but it makes no difference, Sir Hugh, because you'll be gladly welcome.'

'I had not thought otherwise,' said her guest. 'And this, I presume, is your cousin Mistress Orchard?'

Annoyed with herself for forgetting the conventions, Phoebe presented a flushed and tongue-tied Libby, who was always shy and mouse-quiet in strange company. For a while, they talked of trivial matters: the weather, which this summer had been the usual varied English mixture of sun and rain: the condition of the roads between London and Bath: the health and happiness of Sir Hugh's motherless son James, at present staying with cousins in Suffolk: and the scholastic achievements of Phoebe's nephew and protégé Lukas, whose chance meeting with young James Trevelyan in Hyde Park, nearly a year ago, had begun the friendship between the two families.

Phoebe very much wanted to ask Sir Hugh about affairs of state, and in particular about the Bishop of London, who had recently been suspended by the King's new Ecclesiastical Commission for refusing to punish one of his clergymen, who had dared to preach against Roman Catholics. Sir

Hugh was very close to the King, but she knew that he did not feel much loyalty to his sovereign, and certainly did not share his religious views. But doubtless Alex, with his dangerous republican and atheistical opinions, would instigate a most lively conversation at supper.

Which, of course, he did. It had always amused Phoebe that her brother, who had publicly declared that he owned no God and therefore did not care a toss for how, or whom, other people worshipped, should identify so strongly with the cause of the Dissenters, who, after all, were the moral descendants of those Puritans whose beliefs could not have been more different from Alex's own.

But there was, she supposed, some logic to it, for Dissenters, being made up of a great variety of more or less peculiar sects – Baptists, Anabaptists, Quakers and so on – desired only to worship as they pleased in peace, and had no wish, unlike those of the Anglican, or indeed the Catholic persuasion, to impose their beliefs on anyone else. Certainly the Papists in France, headed by King Louis, were fervently persecuting the Protestant Huguenots, so that vast numbers of them had been forced to flee into exile: this was one reason why Louise's mother Kate, though she herself had turned Catholic, had sent her Protestant daughter to England, two years ago. It was widely supposed that King James aspired to emulate his cousin Louis, and convert his subjects to Catholicism by force. To do him justice, so far James had shown no sign of wishing to do so, although he had greatly favoured certain Papists at Court, sometimes beyond the bounds of common sense, given the level of popular prejudice.

'The Ambassador to the Vatican, for instance,' said Sir Hugh, growing expansive as Phoebe's excellent claret went round. 'Now I admit that, by its very nature, such a position should go to a Catholic, but there were many gentlemen at Court, myself included, who would have been happy to fill it – and many Papists, too, of good sense and high standing. Yes, they do exist – how a man worships, after all, should be between him and God, and should not affect his duties, or his public conduct.'

'Ideally, yes,' Alex pointed out. 'In practice, alas, almost never.'

'How would you know?' Phoebe enquired, smiling at him. 'You've never worshipped anyone, or anything, in your life.'

'And whom did His Majesty send?' Sir Hugh continued, with a sigh. 'The Earl of Castlemaine, a Papist of course, but one so noble and intelligent that the chief achievement of his life to date has been to allow our late King Charles to set horns on his head. The man's a standing joke – God knows what the Pope thought.'

' "Here comes another Englishman, ripe for having the wool pulled over his eyes by King Louis",' Alex said caustically. 'I'll grant King James is a devout and pious man, but compared to his late brother he's a small child let loose in a den of lions. And if there's one person more dangerous than a religious bigot, it's a stubborn and stupid religious bigot.'

Libby, Phoebe saw with a quick glance, was sitting quiet and unnoticed in her place, drinking it all in. She was only just sixteen, but she was observant, intelligent and thoughtful, and was doubtless even now forming her own opinions. A pity that her excellent brain would probably be wasted in marriage to some smug young merchant. Libby, being her parents' only child, would inherit a considerable fortune at her father's death.

'In a way, of course, the King's case is sad,' Sir Hugh was saying. 'A more devoted Catholic never breathed, and whatever people may say, I'm sure that he realises that he will never convert this country by force. All he can hope for is to make life easier and more pleasant for Papists, and even then he knows full well that it will all end when he dies, and Protestant Mary comes to the throne. He's almost fifty-three and not in the best health. In five years, or ten, everything will have changed, and we will wonder why we were so alarmed.'

'He may be fifty-three, and an old man,' Louise pointed out. 'But the Queen isn't – she's not much older than Phoebe. Why shouldn't she have another child?'

131

'She's had five already, and they all died,' Phoebe said, and regretted it as soon as the words had left her mouth.

But Louise only smiled rather sadly. 'Then perhaps hope will once more triumph over experience.'

There was a slightly awkward pause, and Sir Hugh, unusually, looked rather discomfited. He said slowly, 'That, I suppose, is possible – Her Majesty miscarried only a few months ago. But it does not seem likely that she will produce a living child, let alone one that is strong and healthy and, of course, male. The poor woman seems to have been perpetually pregnant since her marriage, and perpetually disappointed. Nor is her health good.'

'Which leaves the way clear for your friend Dutch William,' said Phoebe, looking slyly at her brother. 'And then, perhaps, instead of being just another country gentleman of the Whig persuasion, you'll occupy the very same position as Sir Hugh does now – but under a different king, of course.'

'I doubt it,' Alex told her, leaning back in his chair with a fresh glass of claret. 'I have no ambitions beyond the desire to cultivate my acres in peace, and breed the fastest horses in England. Oh, and to make love to my sweet Louise.'

He smiled at his wife, and raised his glass to her: and Phoebe, with that unwelcome pang of envy, saw the love and desire plain on his face, and knew that no one would ever look at her with such longing.

The Queen Dowager had entered Bath in state, with bells ringing to welcome her, and the way strewn with herbs and flowers. She stayed, as did most royal visitors to Bath, in the Abbey House, with its private entrance to the Baths, and a flock of richly dressed and elegant ladies and gentlemen descended on the inns and lodging-houses of the city, beginning to empty because of the lateness of the season.

Louise, in her two years in England, had lived a very quiet existence compared with the gaiety and dazzle of her stepfather's château in France, where the days had been crowded with fresh faces, dancing, musical performances of every kind, plays, cards, hunts, amusements. She had grown used to the slower pace of English country life, and besides, the company of Alex and Phoebe was an entertainment in itself.

But to dance with her husband, whom she found to excel at this as at most things, was a new and delicious experience. She saw the fashionable women eyeing him longingly, and smiled with delight, for she knew that he was hers, heart and body and soul, for always and for ever. She ordered several new gowns, took particular care over her attire, and revelled in the admiration and envy that surrounded her and Alex whenever they appeared in public. It was almost as if the ghastly months after Nathaniel's death had never happened: but there was a new maturity beneath her mischievous sparkle, a quality of sadness which the old Louise, young and heedless, had never experienced. It lent her an aura of mystery which only increased her allure.

Charlotte Burton was still in Bath. The health of her elderly husband had improved somewhat over the summer months, and he was determined to continue his twice daily baths until the season ended. Charlotte, bored to distraction, had found no one with whom she could even contemplate a liaison. Somehow, after Alex, they all seemed so dull, so insipid and uninteresting. Still, it would not be long before they could return to London, and meanwhile, as an insurance, she was particularly attentive to her husband, spending much time reading to him, or keeping him company after his sessions in the Bath, when his physician had prescribed two hours of sweating in a hot room. Sir Anthony, grateful for her devotion, declared himself happy for his wife to see her own friends at times when he was asleep, or resting.

She was walking in the Abbey, one dull morning in the third week in September, the breeze outside chilly enough to be an unwelcome reminder of the oncoming winter. Her maid, as usual, followed behind, and she was escorted by a friend of Sir Anthony, Sir John Pritchard, a stout and elderly gentleman who suffered from the gout, but who had been a great rake in his youth, and who had a vast fund of

133

*risqúe*, not to mention bawdy, anecdotes and jokes. In consequence, Charlotte rather enjoyed his company, and the two had long ago acquired the habit of conversing in a flirtatious banter that was amusing but would never lead anywhere, despite Sir John's appreciative glances at her ample bosom.

They were approaching the west door when a party of people came into the Abbey, and with a lurch of her heart, Charlotte saw that one of them was Alex. Another, a young woman who walked with a stick, was like enough to him, though without his good looks, to be his sister, of whom he had sometimes spoken. There was the boy Lukas, and a fat, plain, mouse-haired girl who had the air of a companion or servant: and a richly dressed man whom, she was certain, she had seen at Whitehall.

And the woman on Alex's arm, in a mantua of rich crimson and cream brocade, dark and striking and exotic even in the gloomy light of the church, must surely be his wife.

Charlotte felt a sharp stab of jealousy. She could not mistake the expression on her erstwhile lover's face as he smiled at Louise, and it was a look he had never bestowed on herself. And really, she thought, with a vain toss of her head, the girl's not even beautiful! With that brown skin and Roman nose, she could be a Spaniard, or a gipsy. Whatever does he see in her?

The answer might lie in her smile: it dazzled even Charlotte's jaundiced eyes. And then the child had noticed her, and was tugging at his father's sleeve in a very forward way, and he turned his head, and saw her.

Charlotte, well prepared, made her curtsey with studied malice. Alex, also skilled at the dissembling arts, displayed only polite surprise. 'Why, Lady Burton – I have not seen you for so long.'

The introductions were performed with the usual courtesy, and Charlotte remembered that Sir Hugh Trevelyan was a Gentleman of the King's Bedchamber, and a man of some influence in Whitehall. He undoubtedly knew her name, and, to judge from his shrewd glance, her reputation as well. The sister, Phoebe, who leaned on his arm, was a sour-looking young woman, dowdily dressed, with uncomfortably sharp blue eyes, very like her brother's. Charlotte, after one glance, dared not meet her speculative gaze again. She was tolerably certain that Mistress St Barbe had guessed altogether too close for comfort.

Alex's wife, however, was evidently too deep in love to notice anything untoward. Whatever had caused the rift in their marriage, and driven Alex to seek consolation in Charlotte's arms, had now, evidently, been amply repaired. There would be no hope of a resumption of the liaison: and much as Charlotte would have liked, from sheer frustrated lust, to take Lady St Barbe aside and reveal the full story of her husband's recent adultery, she had no intention of doing so. If she did, Alex would undoubtedly carry out his threat to tell Sir Anthony, and then Charlotte would be packed off to exile in the bleak Yorkshire house, where the wind whistled through the window-frames even in the height of summer, and the last word in fashionable attire was a ruff and a sugar-loaf hat . . .

She shuddered briefly, and forced herself to smile, and make polite conversation to Alex's wife, who had admired her striped silk mantua. There was no denying, Lady St Barbe had a charm and vivacity that more than compensated for her olive complexion and prominent nose, and she possessed, in addition, a pair of very fine chestnut-brown eyes that had no need of enhancement. She discussed the latest modes with knowledgeable enthusiasm, in an accent faintly but unmistakably foreign, and it soon became apparent that, although English, she had spent most of her life in France, and had a French stepfather. Charlotte realised suddenly that at another time, in other circumstances, she might well have wished to become better acquainted with this girl: it was difficult not to like her open, friendly manner.

The thought made her uneasy, as did the assessing glances which Alex's sister occasionally sent in her direction: and with the excuse that her husband would soon be expecting her return, she bid them all goodbye, and with some relief left the Abbey on Sir John's steady arm.

'An old acquaintance, Alex?' Louise asked, as they continued to stroll slowly up the aisle of the Abbey, allowing Phoebe, led by Sir Hugh, to keep pace. 'She's exceedingly pretty.'

'A *very* old acquaintance,' Alex said, with a grin. He had no intention of ever letting Louise find out about his more recent affair with Charlotte: a liaison that he now deeply regretted. However justifiable it had seemed at the time, whatever excuses he had made to himself, the fact remained that his adultery was despicable, even in his own eyes, and Louise would be greatly hurt if she ever discovered it. Which, if Charlotte kept her vow of silence, she never would.

'You were lovers, once,' Louise said softly, glancing up at him, her eyes gleaming. 'A woman can always tell these things. Was she the one with the jealous husband, whom you went to Holland to avoid?'

'The very same. And pretty she may be, but beside you, sweet Louise, she is completely eclipsed.'

She laughed at his extravagant tone, but the look in his eyes told her, beyond all doubt, that he spoke the truth. Her heart glowing, she leaned her head briefly against his shoulder, and her finger caressed his sleeve.

A little way behind them, Lukas said to Phoebe, 'I like Lady Burton. She has a lovely fan, made from a peacock's feathers, with eyes in them.'

'Has she?' Phoebe raised her brows in surprise. 'I did not notice her carrying it just now.'

'Oh, no – she had it when Papa and I met her in the Abbey Gardens,' Lukas explained, with fatal innocence. 'She asked me to run – she said I ran very nicely.'

'Did she? When was this?'

'Oh, weeks ago – when Papa was showing me round Bath. When I grow up,' Lukas said with enthusiasm, 'I would like to marry someone like Lady Burton.'

'You'd be well advised not to, young man,' said Sir Hugh drily. 'Pretty she may be, pleasant she certainly is, but

136

faithful? Never in a thousand years. She has had more lovers than the old King and the new one put together, by all accounts, and her unfortunate husband is too sickly to do anything about it. If I were you, Lukas, I'd forget all about Charlotte Burton, and find some nice girl who'll adore you, and won't run off with the first handsome man to crook his finger.'

'Oh,' said Lukas, crestfallen, his illusions sorely dented, and walked silent in front of them, scuffing his feet until Phoebe told him to stop.

She was certain, now, that Alex had indeed had an affair with Lady Burton that summer: sometimes, she thought angrily, I could strangle him. But Louise obviously does not know, and not for anything would I shatter that newfound, glorious happiness.

But if he ever does it again, Phoebe decided as they reached the chancel, and began to walk back along the nave, then I shall not scruple to confront him with it. He loves Louise, she loves him: what utter, utter folly to risk throwing everything away for the sake of a trollop like Charlotte Burton.

Amy St Barbe was not often permitted to venture out unaccompanied by her mother, but this errand was too important to be left to a servant. With a feeling of considerable trepidation, she made her way through the crowded streets of Bath to the small house in Nowhere Lane in which her cousin Phoebe lived.

Although the two girls had shared a childhood at Wintercombe, they had never been close: indeed, it would have been difficult to find anything they had in common, apart from kinship. Phoebe, plain and intellectual, was the very opposite of blonde, pretty, innocent Amy, four years younger and with no thought in her head beyond the latest fashions, and the amiable, Catholic young man who had recently begun, with her mother's blessing, to pay court to her.

A year ago and more, she had fancied herself in love with her rakehell cousin Alex, and it had been so humiliating to discover that he had no interest in her at all, save as a way of angering her brother Charles. The experience had made Amy sadder, and a little wiser. Her new suitor, Edward Carne, was fair-haired, mild-mannered, and obviously very taken with her. No one could possibly be more different from Alex, and she was heartily glad of it. After what he had done to her, and to poor dear Charles, she loathed him beyond words.

But she had always regarded Louise as her friend, and she had much appreciated the lessons in French which her cousin had given her. She had a few young, female acquaintances amongst Bath's small Roman Catholic community, but after the dashing, vivid, cosmopolitan Louise, they seemed boring, flabby and provincial. But she was Alex's wife now, and Amy, knocking on Phoebe's door with an apprehensive hand, wondered if Louise would refuse to receive her.

The maid, Mattie, who had once served Amy as well as Phoebe, looked astonished to see her, but allowed her into the front parlour. 'Lady St Barbe bain't at home, Mistress Amy, but I'll tell Mistress Phoebe.'

Alex's sister was even more gaunt and forbidding than Amy remembered, if that were possible. However, she smiled courteously at her cousin. 'This is something of a surprise, Amy. To what do we owe this visit?'

Avoiding her eyes, which reminded her unpleasantly of Alex, Amy said hesitantly – 'I – I have a message from Mama, for Louise. She wishes to let bygones be bygones, she said, and sends an invitation to Louise to take tea with her, tomorrow afternoon.'

'Really?' Phoebe's spiky brows rose in patent disbelief. 'That doesn't sound like Aunt Bab at all. I'm sorry, Amy, but I will not play the hypocrite. What does she want of Louise?'

'Want?' Amy gazed at her in genuine bewilderment. 'Mama doesn't want anything, save to be friends again. We are all kin, she said, and she wishes to be on better terms with Louise. That's all, I'm sure.'

'I doubt it,' Phoebe said acidly. 'But I will pass your

138

message on to her, Amy. In the mean time, I have an engagement to meet a friend in a very few minutes, so I cannot linger, nor do my duty as hostess, I regret to say. Will you kindly excuse me?'

Amy, feeling more than a little hurt by this briskly polite rejection of her overtures of friendship, found herself firmly ushered into the street, her maid by her side. Phoebe's parting words undermined all her remaining confidence. 'Do not be too put out if Louise does not accept your mother's invitation, nor even reply to it.'

Phoebe herself, allowing Mattie to dress her in her outdoor tippet and hood, found to her surprise that she was wound up with anger, as tensely as a clock spring. After all that Bab had done, her warping of Charles's mind, the slow drip of her poison into his heart, the malicious whispers of gossip about Alex's parentage, did she seriously consider that her dubious olive branch would be accepted? Despite Charles's obsession with her, Louise had come to fear him, and his attempt to murder Alex in cold blood had utterly destroyed any remaining sentimental affection which she might have harboured for him. Phoebe was certain that she held Bab in similar contempt, and she had never been truly friends with Amy, whatever the girl might like to think.

Phoebe's quick, logical mind reached the inescapable conclusion. Either Bab was indeed making genuine overtures of reconciliation, in which case she must be uncommonly saintly or uncommonly stupid, or she had another, more devious motive for wishing to see Louise. And Phoebe, as cynical and realistic as her brother, strongly suspected that her aunt was plotting mischief again.

It did not require a supreme effort of intellect to guess what that mischief might be. Phoebe was tolerably certain that she had guessed correctly about Alex's recent liaison with that pert little trollop they had met yesterday in the Abbey. And if Bab, too, had discovered it, or suspected . . . it would be entirely in character for her to take her revenge on Alex by telling Louise of his infidelity.

Phoebe frowned, thinking ahead, plotting action and reaction, assessing personality and motive exactly as if, she realised wryly, she were engaged in a game of chess. She had two choices: to tell Louise of the invitation, or to keep quiet. If she did tell her, Louise would probably refuse to go, in which case Bab, thwarted, might well try to contact her again: or, more unlikely, she might accept, and her present state of wedded bliss would then be shattered when Bab poured out, with predictable glee, the full tale of Alex's perfidy.

There was also, of course, the remote chance that Bab knew nothing of any affair, and was merely making a genuine, if rather clumsy attempt to bring together the two feuding branches of the St Barbe family.

If that's the case, then I'm a Dutchman, Phoebe thought grimly. She's up to no good, I'm sure of it.

With a small, resolute smile, she decided to say nothing to anyone of Amy's unexpected visit, and to instruct Mattie to do the same. Not for anything would she give that repellent woman the opportunity to further her own malicious ends.

Bab waited in high expectation, even after her daughter's discouraging account of her reception by Phoebe. As the time appointed approached, with no word from Louise, and departed without a sign of her, she realised that the wretched girl must have ignored her invitation: or, just as likely, given Phoebe's apparent hostility, the message had not been passed on to her. Some other way must be found of approaching Louise directly, and soon: there was no telling how long she and Alex would remain in Bath, and Bab knew that, once Louise was back at Wintercombe, the chances of convincing her of Alex's treachery would be greatly diminished.

She made enquiries amongst her cronies, ever eager for a gossip, and learned that Sir Alexander and Lady St Barbe were a shiningly devoted couple, obviously much in love, and never seen apart in public. Bab ground her teeth, longing for the opportunity to wipe the fond smiles from their faces. She had always disliked Louise, who despite her lack of classic beauty had completely eclipsed dear, pretty

Amy: and Alex, who had cheated Charles out of his birthright, was the devil incarnate, and more than deserved any punishment she could devise for him.

She spent some time wondering how best to set her vengeance in motion: and at last her urgent prayers were granted. Inspired, she took up pen and paper.

The note was delivered to Nowhere Lane the following morning by the small boy who generally slaved over Bab's pots and pans. As instructed, he slipped it into the hands of his counterpart in Phoebe's kitchen, who was somewhat better treated and better paid, with the request that it be passed to Lady St Barbe as soon as possible, but only when she was quite alone. The boy, curious, and pleased with the groat he had been given for his trouble, soon found his opportunity, and slipped the sealed note into Louise's hand. 'And don't ee tell norry one, m'lady – tis a despeard dark secret!'

Alone in her chamber, Louise stared with interest at the grubby, crumpled piece of paper. A dark secret: she smiled at the memory of the child's shining eyes and hoarse, eager whisper, and pushed her thumb under the seal.

No superscription, no signature, and a scrawling hand which she did not recognise. 'Be in the Abbey Garden alone, this afternoon at two of the clock, if you would learn something greatly to your advantage.'

It was intriguing: it gave promise of amusement: and Louise, in her present joyous mood, found it irresistible. With a grin, she tossed the note into the cold hearth, and looked forward with pleasurable anticipation to discovering what lay beyond this mystery.

Easy enough to slip away from the rest of the party, as they promenaded by the King's Bath, with the excuse that she had a headache, and would return to Nowhere Lane to lie down. As the Abbey clock above her struck the hour, she walked into the garden, and stood, shading her eyes against the brilliance of the September sun, already regretting the impulse that had brought her here. Was she the victim of some pointless prank, or was the anonymous writer of the note amongst the people strolling along the gravel paths, in the welcome shade of the trees?

No one beckoned her, no one came rushing up, and she began to suspect that someone, somewhere, was laughing at her expense. She was about to turn away when a voice hailed her from one of the wooden seats placed along the south-facing wall of the garden.

'Lady St Barbe!'

Louise stared at Bab in astonished recognition. It was nearly a year since she had last seen her aunt, and this grotesquely fat, overdressed woman, spreading over the bench like an obese toad, was even more repulsive than she remembered. Suspicious, but unwilling to be downright rude to her, she walked over, giving only a cool inclination of her head in greeting. 'Good afternoon, Aunt. What brings you here?'

'I wished to speak to you in private,' Bab said, and indicated the space beside her with a welcoming smile that Louise instinctively mistrusted. 'Please, sit beside me. I have been waiting for the opportunity to talk to you, and this seemed to be the only way. Did you receive the message that Amy took to you?'

'*Amy?* I haven't laid eyes on her for about a year,' Louise said. She remained standing, looking down with narrowed eyes at the fat woman. 'But I did have a message this morning. Did *you* send it?'

'I did – and I pray you will forgive the secrecy,' Bab said, with an exaggerated sigh. 'But my fears are confirmed by your words. I sent Amy to your cousin's house, yesterday, with an invitation for you to come and take a dish of tea with me. As you were not at home, she spoke with Phoebe. It seems that your sister-in-law did not see fit to pass the invitation on to you.'

'I expect she had good reason,' Louise said curtly. She had been alive with curiosity, but now, discovering that the writer of that mysterious note was only her aunt, whom she disliked and distrusted, she felt a disappointing sense of anticlimax. 'Neither I nor Phoebe bear any malice against Amy personally, but you must realise that after what Charles did, there can no longer be any friendship between us.'

'My dear son was treated very cruelly,' Bab said, her voice suddenly full of distress. There was no doubt of her maternal devotion, however extreme or misguided, and Louise felt a surprisingly strong surge of sympathy. To save her son from the grave, she would have done anything, walked to the edge of the earth, sold her soul, prostituted her body: and Bab's unconditional adoration did not, now, seem so wicked or unnatural. With her new maturity, she realised that in all this unpleasant history of love and betrayal, greed and hatred, there was no one truly evil, no person completely past redemption, and nobody blameless and beyond reproach.

'I think Gran'mère was being cruel in order to be kind,' she said quietly. 'In the New World, he is far away from me, and Alex, and Wintercombe. He can forget all about us, and begin his life again.'

On Bab's fat, unlined face a curious, smug expression briefly appeared. 'It was most cruel,' she repeated. 'His only crime, to love too much . . .'

She glanced at Louise, a look which plainly revealed her bewilderment that her beloved son should have chosen such an unworthy object for his adoration. 'And to wish for justice for his family,' she added, a catch in her voice. 'And his reward, to be forced into permanent exile, never to see us again – so cruel, so cruel.'

'You forget – he betrayed Alex, he tried to murder him, and he tried to coerce me into marrying him,' Louise said bluntly. 'If you have nothing to say apart from lies and half-truths, raking over old ashes – then I do not wish to continue this conversation any further.'

She turned, but Bab's hand shot out with surprising speed to detain her. 'Wait!' her aunt said forcefully. 'Wait, and listen to the news I have for you, madam, and then perhaps you will think of my poor son less harshly.'

'I don't wish to hear any more of your malicious lies – and Charles deserved everything that happened to him, and more.'

'*Listen*, I said, you hussy,' Bab hissed, and her fat white fingers gripped the fine flowered silk of Louise's sleeve.

143

'Your fine husband, who seems to love you so much, so I'm told – well, he loves you so little that he's been fornicating with another woman behind your back – and a married woman, what's more.'

'Alex?' A sudden sick feeling of fear clawed at Louise's stomach. 'Don't be stupid, you spiteful old gossip. He wouldn't be unfaithful to me, I know he wouldn't.'

'You can't ignore the truth,' Bab said, smiling, her eyes glittering with malevolent satisfaction. 'Do you know of a notorious Lady Burton? I see you do. Well, she lodges just over the way from my house in the Abbey Green, and with my own eyes I saw him visit her – and only when her husband was safely out of the way in the Baths. And you can't pretend he was just passing the time of day – not when he spent upwards of an hour with her, several times a week, mornings and afternoons too. *And* came out again looking like a cat that's been at the cream bowl.'

She was still grasping Louise's mantua. With a sudden exclamation of horror, the girl tore herself free and took a step backwards, out of reach of the pudgy, pale fingers like a clutch of bloated termites. 'I don't believe you,' she said desperately. 'Alex knows Lady Burton, yes, and he did have an affair with her, but it was years ago – and we met her in the Abbey yesterday, and he told me of it himself!'

'But not about this latest liaison, I'll be bound,' Bab said gloatingly, seeing that despite Louise's denials, her words had struck home. 'Perhaps you ought to come back with me, madam, and keep watch yourself – he'll come creeping up to her door this afternoon, if he thinks he's free of you, and you can see for yourself how worthless his love is.'

It was too much. Louise slapped her aunt's face with a strength increased by rage, and distress, and disgust: and then, before Bab's astonished wail of pain had ended, whirled and ran away from the garden, as if she could escape the hurt, the disillusionment, the revulsion that the news of Alex's infidelity had caused her.

Overwhelmed by nausea, she vomited into the gutter, and found she was weeping. Someone touched her arm, and asked, with slyly knowing concern, if she needed his assistance. She straightened, and shook him off with a fierce epithet, and walked away shuddering, with the tears pouring down her face. People stared as she brushed heedlessly past them, but she did not see them: the only image filling her vision was Alex, his dark hair tangled over his shoulders, his sleekly muscled feline body making love to that plump lascivious whore who had smiled at her yesterday, and politely pretended friendship . . .

She found herself by the river: somehow, without realising it, she must have crossed Mitre Green, and passed under the East Gate. Now she stood here on the bank of the Avon, just upstream from the weir and Monk's Mill, staring at the sluggish brown waters, the jetties and boats, the green cow-spangled expanse of Bathwick Meadow on the other side, as if she had never seen them before.

One of the fishermen, hat in hand, approached her. 'Can I help ee, madam?'

'No, thank you,' Louise told him, with impatience. As he continued to stare at her, she added savagely, 'Don't worry, I won't throw myself in. Now go away.'

'Yes, of course, madam,' the man said, and retreated, bowing, his face at once curious and obsequious.

She turned, and hastily wiped the tears from her cheeks. There was a foul taste in her mouth, that no amount of pure water or fine wine would be able to wash away. He had betrayed her, while she was lying sick and miserable at Wintercombe – he had taken up with a woman who, despite her fine clothes and lovely face, was no more a lady than any street drab, and then, compounding his felony, he had lied to her, he had come from Charlotte Burton's bed to her own, he had reawakened her senses, he had given her happiness beyond all measure, and all the while the memory of his adulterous affair must have been fresh in his mind . . .

He had mentioned, before their marriage, the possibility that he might not be faithful to her. And she, secure in her powers of attraction, certain of his love and desire for her, had laughed lightly, refusing to believe that he would ever stray from her bed. Now, she cursed herself for her foolish naïvety, and blamed the blindness of love that had led her to believe that a man notorious for his womanising would instantly change his ways, once married.

But nothing, no self-reproach, could erase the bitter sense of betrayal. Trust me, he had said: and she, poor deluded idiot, had followed him obediently, joyfully, back into the world, back to the sensual delights to which he had introduced her last year. He had given her happiness, but its bright gold was false, counterfeit, bought with treachery and deception.

There was, the still, small voice of reason reminded her, always the chance that Bab was lying. But she did not think so: something in the woman's vehement, gloating certainty told her that her aunt had spoken the truth.

And if I was a fool to trust him, Louise thought angrily, he was double the fool, to think that he could conduct an affair almost under Bab's nose, without her discovering it.

But, of course, he might not have cared that he would be found out: and since it was inevitable that she would then gleefully inform Louise at the earliest opportunity, the conclusion seemed obvious. Either he did not mind news of this adultery reaching his wife: or he had assumed that, if she did learn about it, she would not be hurt.

He'll find out soon enough what I think, Louise said to herself, her rage increasing. But not here: not in Phoebe's house with her eyes too sharp upon us, where every word of a quarrel would be overheard. I'll go back to Wintercombe, today, now: he can follow me there, and then he'll learn in private exactly how I feel about this treachery.

And with the thought of immediate action salving, a little, the pain inside her, she turned away from the river, and walked purposefully back through the busy streets of Bath, to her sister-in-law's house.

# Chapter Eight

## 'The horror of the night'

The letter was brief, curt and uncompromising, and the words had been written with a passion that had dug holes in the paper, and spluttered a storm of ink across it.

'She's gone back to Wintercombe,' Alex said, lifting his gaze from the note in his hands.

At the door of his chamber, Phoebe stared at him in astonishment. 'Louise has gone back to *Wintercombe*? In God's name, why?'

'I don't know – she doesn't say.' Alex screwed up the paper and flung it into the hearth. It landed next to a similarly crumpled ball: he looked at them both for a moment and then, walking over to the fireplace, picked up the one which he had not read.

As he unfolded it, his sister limped over to stand beside him. She said sharply, 'That's Bab's hand – I'd swear to it.'

'*Bab*? But this reads like an assignation,' Alex said. He added grimly. 'Something of a surprise, I should imagine, to go to a meeting expecting some importunate lover, and find that overdressed lump of lard awaiting you.'

'Bab sent Amy here, two days ago, with an invitation for Louise,' Phoebe said slowly. 'I didn't pass the message on, because I thought it could not be a genuine overture of reconciliation – I strongly suspected that Bab might be trying to make mischief again.' She looked up, fixing her brother with her uncomfortably penetrating stare. 'It seems that I was right. And the question is, what has she said to Louise to provoke such a furious reaction?'

Alex said nothing. Phoebe went on cautiously, sensing his rising anger. 'I think I can guess, though. Does it perhaps concern that young woman whom we encountered in the Abbey yesterday?' And then, as he still did not speak,

147

she added in exasperation, 'Alex, I'm not stupid. I strongly suspect that you had an affair with her, when you were here in July, and if that's true, and Bab has discovered it and told Louise, then I suggest you forget everything else and go after her and make amends – if you can.'

Abruptly, he ripped his aunt's letter across, again and again, and scattered the pieces over the floor. He said, in a deceptively calm voice that Phoebe recognised with deep foreboding. 'You are right, of course. I did renew my old – friendship – with Charlotte. But for a short while only, and when my conscience began to trouble me, I ended it. And I made the little trollop swear never to tell anyone.'

Phoebe, seeing the look on his face, felt briefly sorry for Lady Burton. She said, 'Surely she could not have informed Bab directly? They are hardly likely to be on terms of intimate friendship, or even acquaintance.'

'No,' Alex said shortly. 'But perhaps Charlotte need not have told her, after all – she lodges in Abbey Green.'

'She *lodges* in *Abbey Green*? So you conducted an affair with her almost under Bab's windows, and she the biggest purveyor of scandalous gossip in the West Country, not to mention your worst enemy, and you expected her not to *notice*? Dear God,' Phoebe said incredulously. 'And I once thought you possessed some intelligence. Did you *want* to be found out?'

'Of course I didn't. And don't think,' Alex said savagely, rounding on his sister with a face so pale and contorted with fury that she flinched, 'don't think that I don't regret I ever set eyes on Charlotte Burton again – because I do, most bitterly, I regret seeing her, I regret bedding her, and above all I regret that Nathaniel died, for then none of this would ever have happened.'

By now, Phoebe was likewise so enraged that all thought of guarding her tongue had vanished. 'My God, brother, you are utterly despicable! What man who has any shred of decency or humanity about him leaves his sick and grieving wife alone for six weeks and beds some pretty lightskirt who's as notorious for her lack of morals as you are? And then tries to use the baby's death as an excuse for his adultery? I wouldn't in the least blame Louise if she barred the door to you and refused to see you – I'm not at all sure I can bear the thought of your company myself.'

For a moment, such was the wildness in his eyes, she thought he would strike her. Then he said, through his teeth, 'Don't worry – you won't have to. I'm going.'

The door had been left half ajar, she realised too late. Alex flung it wide, to reveal the frightened faces of Lukas and Libby on the landing beyond. With an oath, he pushed them aside, and ran down the stairs at a speed which surely risked a broken neck. The street door slammed so hard that the windows rattled, and he was gone.

Phoebe found that she was shaking. With an effort, she reduced herself to a poor semblance of calm. Then Lukas, his face crumpled with distress, flung himself sobbing into her arms, soaking her dress with his tears. Mechanically, she stroked his hair and muttered soft and useless words of comfort, while wondering, with sick dread, what would happen when the two volatile spirits of Alex and Louise next collided.

Louise had taken a small bag of clothing, her maid Christian, and a groom from the White Hart as escort: her flight from Bath might be precipitate and impulsive, but she was not completely foolhardy. There were still some four or five hours of daylight left, ample time for the journey to Wintercombe, even if she never urged her horse above a trot. But it was not until they had climbed up the Hollow Way, and had reached the high, bare, sheep-scattered downs that lay between Bath and Philip's Norton, that she could safely give her mare Saffron her head, and expend some of her furious energy in a wild gallop along the grassy verge of the highway, while the servants plodded far behind.

At last, even Saffron's speed began to fail, and Louise pulled her up where the road began to descend into the Midford valley. She patted the mare's sweat-soaked neck, and turned to look for Christian and the groom. The two tiny figures would take a long time to catch her up, and she was glad of it. For the moment, solitude was essential.

149

He had betrayed her. All the excuses, all the reasons she could muster could not erase that bare, hideous truth. He loved her, or said he did, and yet he had leapt into that harlot's bed at the first opportunity.

She must be realistic: she must. She was his wife, so they were bound together, indissolubly and for all time. And she still loved him: suspected, indeed, that she would still love him whatever he did, however many women he bedded, because in the end he would always come back to her. And for those glorious nights of tenderness and pleasure, however spurious the emotion, she, poor idiot, would forgive him anything. She was in love, and could not help it, however much she might rail against her fate.

And besides, she thought grimly, how many men these days *were* faithful to their wives? Her stepfather had fathered two bastard daughters upon her own mother, before his first wife died and they had been able to marry. Up and down the land, men blithely fornicated with women of all kinds, from whores to ladies, and their wives were regarded with astonishment and derision if they dared to complain. She was bound to Alex: she shared his name, his position, his house, all the comforts and status of marriage to a wealthy man. To demand his exclusive love, as well, seemed to be asking for gilt on the gingerbread.

But she had put her faith in him: he had spoken of his love for her, and she had believed him. Poor, gullible deluded fool that you were, she thought bitterly, knowing that if she had not trusted him so completely, her present sense of hurt and betrayal would not be so agonisingly deep.

The sound of hoofbeats intruded into her mind. She looked round, wondering why Christian or the groom should be moving at such a speed, and saw with a shock of dismay that it was Alex.

He was riding Blaze, the big, fast, unruly bay stallion. The horse had obviously been galloped at a furious pace, for he was black and white with sweat and foam, and when her husband reined him in, a few yards from Saffron, he stood with heaving flanks and hanging head. Above the animal's drooping neck, Alex's face was a white, set mask. 'Louise. We must talk.'

150

She glanced behind him, and saw that the two servants had halted their horses, well out of earshot. He said, 'I've told them to keep their distance. And at least out here it's far more private than Wintercombe.'

There was a shepherd, perhaps fifty yards away, leaning on his crook and surveying them with bucolic interest. Louise looked at the sun, now sinking towards the west, and twitched Saffron's reins. The mare began to walk on, down the hill. Above the suffocating thud of her heart, she heard Alex swear under his breath, and then Blaze's head appeared beside her. He said sharply, 'Louise! For God's sake, won't you listen?'

'I am listening. I have no wish to be benighted on these hills, that's all,' she told him. 'Well? What have you to say for yourself?'

There was a short pause, and then he said, 'I take it that your sudden and unannounced departure from Bath was caused by something that Bab told you this afternoon?'

'It was.' She spoke with flat hostility, staring straight ahead. Not for anything, just now, would she let him see the extent of her hurt, as well as her anger. 'So – are you going to tell me the truth? Or do you still think me so foolish and gullible and besotted that I'd believe your denials?'

'No, I don't – and I never did. The truth is this.'

He had drawn level with her now, and she could see him out of the corner of her eye. She stared resolutely between Saffron's yellow ears, determined not to be swayed by the urgency and desperation plain in his voice, as he continued. 'The truth is that, yes, I did have an affair with Charlotte Burton. But I ended it, more than a month ago, and I have no intention of ever bedding her again – a decision which she understands, and accepts. You have no reason to be jealous of her – it is over, finished, in the past.'

'And what is your excuse? Did she seduce you? Or are you weary so soon of your marriage vows, or of me?' Despite all her efforts, Louise could not keep the note of hurt and bitterness from her voice.

'I never promised fidelity,' Alex said. 'You know that.'

'Oh, I *know* it – but I had not *expected* it!' She managed to

151

calm herself a little, and went on, more quietly. 'I trusted you – I thought you truly loved me. And only a few months after our wedding, you think so little of me that you would bed a woman like *that*?'

'I have no excuses,' Alex said forcefully. 'I betrayed you, I lied to you, and I am desperately sorry for it. I regret very much that I did it.'

'You do now that you've been found out.' Louise clenched her hands on the mare's reins, and prayed that she would not burst into tears. 'And you couldn't even pay me the compliment of being discreet! You must have *known* that Bab was bound to see you – and tell me! Didn't you *care* that I knew? Did you *want* me to be the subject of that dreadful woman's gloating gossip? To have all Bath looking at me pityingly from behind their hands – "Poor Lady St Barbe –so upset by her husband's adultery – but what else could she expect, marrying a man like that?" Well,' Louise cried, her voice cracking, 'I *did* expect you to be faithful! I loved you, I thought you loved me, and whatever the way of the world, I cannot believe that love and betrayal go hand in hand, save perhaps in your distorted view. They certainly don't in mine.'

'I didn't want Bab to find out – most emphatically, I did not.'

'Well, she did, and she told me, with great glee – and I felt such a fool, as stupid and naïve as any milk-and-water virgin. You made me so happy, so very happy,' Louise said, as the pain and tragedy of it overwhelmed her, and her voice sank to a whisper of despair. 'You made me happier than I had ever thought to be, and it was all an illusion, false, a mockery – you don't care for me in the least!'

'I do – believe me, I do.' Alex caught at Saffron's rein, snatching the mare to a halt. 'Louise – I love you. Even when I was with Charlotte, and I thought you were lost to me, it was you I loved.'

'You chose a strange way of showing it, then, to bed that whore!'

'I make no excuses for that. Tempation was placed in my path, and I failed to resist it. You don't have to tell me that it

152

is a despicable weakness, but both of us are aware of it. I can't promise that it will never happen again – I know myself too well for that. What matters is that the Charlotte Burtons make no difference, no difference *at all*, to what I feel for you.'

'But they make a difference to *me*! I feel cheapened, devalued – as if I were worth less to you than I thought.' At last, despite all her efforts, the tears were beginning to flow. She wiped her face with the back of her hand, and cried passionately, 'You can offer me all the justifications under the sun, or none, I don't care, I don't want to hear them – the fact remains that you betrayed me, you betrayed me when I trusted you, and it *hurts*, Alex, it hurts as much as if you'd stabbed me, and I don't think I can ever trust you again, and if this is only the first time and you plan to bed a harem full of women, well, I don't think I can face the thought of it!'

She brought her whip down on Saffron's round, sleek rump. Startled, the mare leapt forward, and galloped down towards the village and stream at the foot of the hill. The bay, exhausted by the effort expended in catching up Louise, could do no more, and Alex knew it.

He sat and watched her flying figure, the skirts of her riding habit wildly flapping, her hat clinging precariously to her head. Almost, he hoped that she would fall, so that he could pick her up, and hold her, and comfort her, and somehow undo the terrible hurt that he had caused her.

But she did not fall. She glanced back, before the bend in the road took her out of his sight, and when she saw he was not following, slowed Saffron to a more decorous trot. When she had disappeared, he turned Blaze, and rode back to where Christian waited with the groom. They could go after her, and make sure that she came to no harm: it was only three or four miles further to Wintercombe, and she would reach it before sunset.

He, though, had other plans. The servants passed him, their faces studiedly blank. When they, too, had vanished around the corner, he urged Blaze down the hill. Midford had an alehouse, and he knew from past experience that its keeper had a secret and illicit store of brandy tucked away in his cellar. At this moment, he could not face the prospect of the next inevitable, wounding, bitter quarrel with Louise, without a glass or more to deaden the pain.

By the time Louise reached Wintercombe, it was almost dark. Saffron had cast a shoe, and she had been forced to dismount and walk her the last two miles. Then the groom had stayed with the mare at the smith's forge in Philip's Norton, while Louise went on, with Christian, riding his old hired nag. The two women had arrived at Wintercombe unheralded, to a dark and silent house, and it had taken Twinney some time to realise that his mistress had returned, and required lights, fires, supper, and an aired bed.

Well-trained and discreet, the butler had learned to hide his surprise, this past year or two: since old Sir Nat's death, in fact. He had firm opinions about the various members of the family he served, but kept them strictly to himself.

Something had happened, again, between Lady St Barbe and Sir Alexander. She was alone, save for her maid, and he was not surprised when she requested a quiet, simple supper in her chamber. He bade her goodnight with warmth, and not a little sympathy. As an afterthought, he added one last question. 'Will Sir Alexander be returning tonight, my lady?'

Louise turned wearily. Twinney had already marked the signs of tears: he saw now that she was utterly exhausted, her face drained of colour and shadows smudged deep under her eyes. She said bleakly, 'I don't know, Twinney – I really don't know.'

And if he does, the butler thought sadly, returning to the cosy haven of the servants' hall, with its fire and gossip and air of peace and relaxation, he'll be in an evil mood for certain – and I for one have no intention of getting in his way.

Up in her chamber, Louise ate her supper – bread, cheese, a cold chicken, apples and pears – with little appetite and less enjoyment. The ride from Midford, after her encounter with Alex, had afforded her further opportunity for thought, and she had tried to consider her situation objectively.

He had committed adultery. Many might say, so, what of it? Nine men out of a dozen had probably done as much in their first year of marriage, and their wives, if they knew, accepted it as an unfortunate but unavoidable fact of life. It was their duty, after all, to love their husbands for better, for worse, and if the man strayed, well, the marriage bond, children, a home, meant that he would always return to her between his liaisons. Most marriages amongst the better sort were not, after all, undertaken for love: perhaps, for such women, their husbands' lack of fidelity was not a matter of great concern. And when the old king, and the new, had both flaunted their mistresses and fathered troops of publicly acknowledged bastards, it seemed rather petty to make so much to-do over a brief and unimportant affair that was now finally over.

But she had not married for dynastic reasons. She had married because she loved Alex, body and soul and heart, with a passion that had overwhelmed her senses and destroyed all caution, a passion that, she thought, had been returned in equal measure. She had assumed that she was different from all those dull, domestic, stay-at-home wives, content to have their husbands take their pleasures elsewhere, so long as dignity and propriety were not offended.

And a large part of her anger had sprung from the fact that she had been reminded, brutally and humiliatingly, that she was not different at all. Her marriage, that had promised such joy and excitement and adventure, was in fact just the same as those of the housewives whom she had covertly despised.

It's not fair! she had cried to herself, tramping along the high windy ridge between Charterhouse Hinton and Philip's Norton, her maid and the groom toiling behind her. Not fair, that what was sauce for the gander most definitely could not be sauce for the goose. Alex could bed ten different women in a week and escape censure, as long as he did it with a modicum of discretion. If she so much as fluttered her fan in the direction of another man, she would be branded a loose woman by the pillars of respectable Somerset society. Thirty years ago, they had gossiped about Alex's mother, so that Bab had even convinced herself that he was not Sir Nathaniel's son. And poor Patience St Barbe had only been guilty of an excess of beauty, and an irrepressible lightness of heart.

She could not pay Alex back in his own coin, not because of scandal, but because, underneath all the hurt and anger and bitter sense of betrayal, she knew that she still loved him. And because she could not, would not change him into someone less difficult, less dangerous, less exhilarating, she must, at last, accept what he had done, and come to terms with it, and make her peace with him.

Christian helped her undress for bed: usually, when Louise was alone, the maid slept on a truckle bed in the antechamber, but she had told Christian to use one of the other bedchambers instead, in case Alex appeared after all.

Once the girl had left, she blew out the candle, closed the bed-curtains, and lay back upon the pillows. It was not late: the church clock, half a mile away, had recently struck eight, but she was exhausted, her legs ached from the unaccustomed walking in riding boots, and wildly vacillating emotion had sapped all her remaining energy. As she drifted into welcome sleep, she wondered where Alex was. He might have gone back to Bath: more likely, he was in some taproom somewhere, drowning his sorrows. If so, she hoped that he would not appear at Wintercombe until the following morning.

But, eventually, he would come back to her. In that quarrel on the hill above Midford, she had had the last word. She knew Alex well enough to be certain that, if for no other reason, he would want to redress the balance.

She slept, deeply and dreamlessly, until something woke her. She lay in the thick blackness behind the bed-curtains, thinking stupidly that morning must have come, and wondering why it was still dark.

There was a noise, too distant to be in the room with her, too near to be ignored. She stiffened, then relaxed, her mind fully awake by now. It could only be Alex, returned in

156

the middle of the night. She scrambled out of bed, found the tinder box, and managed to light the candle. Her eyes slowly made sense of her chamber, the familiar shapes of the furniture, wall-hangings, curtains, hearth. There was no one else there.

Another sound came from the room beyond, which was nominally Alex's, and where he had slept during her illness. She walked across to the door and opened it, holding the candle high.

It was indeed her husband. He was standing by the half-tester bed, clad only in shirt and breeches: the rest of his clothes lay strewn across the floor. His eyes narrowed when he saw her. 'Good evening, madam.'

'It was you, then, and not some thief,' Louise said. She might have decided, in her heart, to forgive him, but not before she had given further rein to her anger. She added, with a chill in her voice, 'Where have you been?'

'It's no concern of yours,' Alex said. 'But I'll tell you anyway. There's a certain alehouse in Midford, excellent cellar, friendly landlord, very friendly serving girl.' He smiled, and it was not pleasant. 'Aren't you just dying to know what we did?'

Louise had realised, belatedly, that he was very drunk. Suddenly rather frightened, but determined not to reveal it, she lifted her chin and said flatly, 'No, not in the least – and nor do I really care.'

'Oh, but you do,' Alex said, in the slurred, drawling voice that had betrayed him. 'You'd care if I so much as smiled at another woman, wouldn't you?'

'No,' Louise said. She stayed where she was, intent now on maintaining an air of calm and proportion. 'I care that you betrayed me – I care that it was that repellent woman who had the pleasure of telling me. But I don't want to put chains on you, Alex – I never did.'

'Didn't you? But you trapped me into marrying you – the prospect of a son, who so tragically died – half of Somerset probably thinks you tricked me – '

'You *know* that's not true!' Appalled at the injustice, Louise took a step forward, her candleflame guttering. She

157

had seen Alex in this drunkenly offensive mood before, she knew what he could do, but never, never before had it been turned on herself. Horrified, her voice shaking, she said urgently, 'It's nonsense – you know it is. I didn't tell you I was pregnant until after you asked me to marry you. And, God help me, I agreed.'

'Regretting it now, sweet Louise?'

She stared at him, seeing with stark clarity his dishevelled appearance, the untidy hair, the creased, unfastened shirt revealing the long, hard, powerful body beneath, the impression of wildness, of danger, of something dark and ungovernable within him that was about to be unleashed.

He began to walk towards her. 'I know I am,' he went on. 'I regret I ever set eyes on you – because if I can't live with you, I don't think I can live without you either.'

He was very close now, and she could smell the brandy on his breath, see the fine lines around his eyes, and the fury within them. Really frightened, she backed away, wondering if she could lock the door between the chambers, if there was a key, a bolt, anything, she could not remember . . .

With a heroic effort, she snatched at her failing courage, and said with firm and deceptive calm, 'Alex, you're drunk. Go to bed, sleep it off, and we'll talk in the morning.'

'No – we'll talk now. Now, d'you hear me? And don't keep backing away from me.'

'Your breath stinks like a stillery,' said Louise unwisely. 'And I have no intention of staying to bandy abuse with you – it'll only lead to trouble, and more things to regret.'

'You'll stay,' Alex said, and his hand shot out to grasp her wrist. 'You're my wife, aren't you? Then you'll stay.'

The candleflame leapt wildly as she struggled against his grip. But even in his cups he was much the stronger, and she was jerked against him with a force that made her cry out in pain. But he only had hold of one hand, and in the other was her small pewter candlestick. In wild panic, she swung it at his head. He flung up his other hand, and the metal and hot wax hit his arm and bounced off on to the floor, with a sharp clatter. The flame vanished, and they were in darkness.

She had fought with him in the past, but in play, in bed, laughing together. This ghastly travesty was in earnest, and now she only wanted to escape. What he wanted, as she struggled and twisted, kicked and bit, became horribly clear when she was slammed backwards against the ridged panelling of the wall, with a force that knocked the breath from her lungs. Then, he grasped both her wrists in one hand, and with the other took hold of the neck of her chemise, and ripped it downwards.

Sick with fear and horror, she cried frantically, 'No, Alex – please, no!'

But the dark shadow looming over her said venomously, 'Shut up, you little bitch, while I teach you a lesson you won't forget in a hurry.' The fine holland linen, too fragile to withstand such brutality, rent under his assault, and she felt his mouth and hands rough and greedy on her skin. In a frenzy of terror, she fought wildly, until an impatient blow smashed across her face. Her head crashed back again into the wall, and for a moment she thought that he would kill her. Then, he pushed her to the floor.

It did not take long: dazed, half-conscious, she was incapable of further resistance. As he rolled off her, she heard someone whimpering, and realised with distant surprise that it was herself.

The darkness was complete: she could see absolutely nothing. Something wet and sticky, probably blood, felt cold on her face, and every bone, every muscle, every surface seemed to throb with pain. Sick, defiled, she lay paralysed, fearing that he would attack her again. She wanted to crawl somewhere, anywhere, a dark hole where there might be comfort and safety and oblivion, but she could not move: she lay on her back on the hard boards of her husband's chamber, and wondered remotely if she were dying.

Noises in the dark penetrated her pain and inertia: stumbling footsteps, and the sound of retching. A window opened, and a chilly draught raised goose-bumps on her naked flesh. Somehow, she forced her unwilling body to obey her, and slowly, gasping with pain and effort, she

159

managed to sit upright against the wall. She must get away, flee, put a locked door between herself and the violent and brutal man whom, only yesterday, she had loved and desired, and who now had been transformed into this evil monster.

'Louise?'

His voice, hoarse and barely above a whisper, was hardly recognisable. She strained her eyes, and made out a dark, amorphous shape against the dim square of the window. Renewed terror froze her limbs, and she could only crouch against the wall and wait for him to find her.

'Louise?'

He was much closer, and her fear began, perversely, to be replaced by anger. She imagined him groping for her in the dark, and said desperately, 'Don't – don't come near me!'

'It's all right – I won't hurt you.'

She laughed bitterly. 'Do you think you haven't hurt me already? I said, don't come near me – don't touch me!'

On her last words, she felt his fingers on her thigh, and struck out blindly, wildly, hitting him away. 'I said, don't *touch* me!'

'I won't,' he said, still in that very altered voice.

She went on, the words tumbling out, incoherent with rage and fear and disgust. 'Go on, go away, I hate you, do you hear? Go away, never touch me, I never want to see you again!'

'Louise – '

'Get out – Charles was right all along – you're just as he said you were, a monster, evil, I wish you'd died in that battle, I wish I'd never met you, never married you, never loved you, I must have been mad, I wish you were dead!' Her voice cracked with anguish, and she fought to retain the last shreds of her self-control. 'Don't you understand me? It's over, finished, done – you've destroyed everything – now get out and don't come back!'

For a dreadful instant, she thought that he might attack her again. Then there was the abrupt sound of movement, and retreating footsteps, and the door shut. And at last she was finally, irrevocably alone.

Christian found her a few moments later, lying sobbing as if her heart was broken. Without comment, but with revealing gentleness, her maid helped her to her bed, and put ointment on the bruises that covered her body, and bathed the cuts and swellings that disfigured her face. When the weeping had at last drained away, she gave her a warming, soothing posset, and dressed her in a clean chemise to replace the ripped and bloodstained garment that Alex had despoiled. Louise submitted to her ministrations bleakly, numbly, seeing nothing, while her inward gaze looked at her life, her hopes, her happiness, her future, destroyed by one man's lust and anger, one woman's temptation, another woman's desire for vengeance.

As Christian slipped the chemise over her head, she heard the sound of hooves, distant and diminishing, and knew that Alex had taken her at her word, and left her life for ever. As she curled up in the lonely softness of the bed she had so often shared with him, she thought helplessly of all they had done together, the love and joy and infinite pleasure that she had thought invulnerable: and wept anew, until she slept, for everything that had gone, and would never be again.

Five days later, Sir Alexander St Barbe, sitting half-drunk in a notorious London tavern, was approached by an old friend, Tom Talmarsh, whom he had known years ago, when the Green Ribbon Club had fomented republicanism and plotted against the lives of King Charles and his brother, then the Duke of York, now the second King James. An important message must be carried secretly to one of the English exiles in Amsterdam, and since Alex was well known to have friends and business interests in Holland, he could visit the Low Countries without rousing suspicion. Would he oblige?

'Of course,' the other man drawled, pouring himself more brandy. 'England stinks like a cesspit at present. I'll be glad to breath pure Dutch air for a while.'

The message was given, hands shaken on it, and a bottle of fine claret opened in Talmarsh's honour. The evening passed in reminiscence, of a time when he did not know Louise, and blurred into a fog of wine and brandy fumes that could not, even in this quantity, bring welcome oblivion. Alex walked unsteadily back to his lodgings, filled with confused feelings of rage and desperation and, above all, sick self-loathing and disgust, while the voice of his wife, beloved despite all he had done to her, echoed in his mind forever, sounding the death knell of their marriage. 'Get out – don't come back – I never want to see you again!'

Well, she would have her desire. He had not really wished to leave Holland, two years ago: only the prospect of snatching Wintercombe from under Cousin Charles's nose had, in the end, persuaded him to take up his inheritance. Louise had provided good reason to stay, and to become a respectable country gentleman. Without her, he had no interest in his wealth, his possessions, his estate. At least in Amsterdam he might eventually come to forget her, if he had to drink the city dry in the process.

He embarked on the *Anna Maria*, of Rotterdam, two days later, and did not dare to look back at the flat, grey, receding land that held his home, and his wife, and his two sons, one living, one dead.

And on the same day, a hundred miles and more to the west, a week after her husband had brutally raped her, Louise was forced to recognise the unpalatable and un-welcome truth. She was not, after all, free of Alexander St Barbe: for she was once more carrying his child.

# PART TWO

'Winged with vain desires'

December 1686–February 1688

# Chapter Nine

## 'Barefaced envy'

After a year in Ireland, Charles St Barbe stepped on to the Key at Bristol, his light-blue eyes shining with delight, and took a deep breath. No matter that the smells that invaded his lungs were for the most part unpleasant – river mud, rotting fish, decaying seaweed, human excrement, the reek of the tannery – all seemed as sweet as roses to the returning exile. This was English air and, however foul, it meant that he was home.

It was early evening, but the Key was, as usual, thronged with workmen, sailors, whores, onlookers, passengers. Too late to set out for Bath now: Charles beckoned to the sailors carrying his boxes and baggage, and led them through the crowds to his Uncle Orchard's house in Small Street.

Like all the buildings in this part of the city, it was tall, half-timbered, with four storeys, each jutting out above the last, so that there was only a slender glimpse of sky in this narrow street, and it was already gloomy half an hour before sunset.

Charles hammered upon the stout studded door. His aunt and uncle were not expecting him, but he was sure of his welcome. They had not been involved in the family feud, and Uncle Orchard greatly valued his matrimonial kinship with the wealthy St Barbes.

And indeed, he was greeted with great warmth. His father's sister, his aunt Deb, was a big, stout woman, with red cheeks, a beaming smile, and a manner that brooked no nonsense. Small wonder that her only surviving child was a quiet girl with her nose forever in a book, and very little to say for herself.

He gave Deb a considerably edited account of his sojourn in Ireland, omitting entirely his reason for going there, and

165

then, with a convincingly casual air, asked for news of the rest of the family.

His aunt was as fervent a gossip as his mother, but, as even Charles had to acknowledge, she entirely lacked Bab's malice. He listened, trying not to appear too bored, to her long account of how Libby was enjoying her stay in Bath with dear Phoebe, and her own recent journey to Chard to see her mother and stepfather, and how well Silence was keeping considering her advanced years, and that sweet girl Sarah's latest pregnancy. Then there was a long digression on the Taunton cousins, the Loveridges, and news of their son Bram, transported to Barbados for his part in Monmouth's rebellion. Charles, who had considered Bram's punishment to be unduly lenient in the circumstances, had to conceal his irritation as his aunt described how well the boy was doing on the island, how he had bought land and made money and hoped to return to England when the political climate allowed. Equipped with a substantial bribe to purchase his freedom from bondage, he had managed to escape the dismal fate of his less fortunate fellows, much to Charles's secret disgust.

Just when he thought he would have to ask her directly, Deb switched from a confidential discussion of the Wickhams at Glastonbury, concerning the recent serious illness of her sister Rachael, who had never recovered from her adored half-wit son Ben's death on the battlefield of Sedgemoor, and launched into a sympathetic description of Louise's plight, left alone for so long at Wintercombe while her husband jaunted round Europe.

'And they've not been wed a year yet,' said his aunt, with some indignation. 'If I were Louise, I'd be tempted to stray myself, give Alex a taste of his own medicine – and so soon after the poor little baby died, too! So sad, don't you think, that dear, dear Nat's son should have turned out so bad? Do you realise, Charles, he had a mistress in Bath this summer? Yes, indeed, I could hardly believe it myself, but apparently it's quite true. Your mother told me all about it when she came over to visit us last month. I feel so sorry for Louise. Still, I'm sure she'll be delighted to find that you're home at last.'

'I hope so,' Charles said, with some confidence. True, the last time he had seen her, the love of his life, she had been kneeling in the filth of a London alleyway, supporting Alex in her arms, her face full of horror and hatred, turned against himself. She had been blind, then, to her lover's faults: indeed, shortly afterwards, she had married him. Presumably now her eyes had been opened, and she doubtless thought of Alex with the contempt he so richly deserved. And Charles, who had been right about him all along, would surely be welcomed back with friendship, if not more.

After a night in Henry Orchard's warm and comfortable house, well fed and rested, he made arrangements for most of his considerable baggage to be transported to Bath, said a fond farewell to his aunt and uncle, and set out on a hired horse to ride the last few miles.

He knew that he must go first to his mother's house in Bath. He owed her so much: her letters had kept him sane in dreary Dublin, and her information about Alex's adultery had directly caused the rift between Louise and her husband. But the thought of Wintercombe, its stone walls turned to the colour of honey under this weak and fitful December sun, was a lure so strong that he almost succumbed. Just over the hills to his right, an hour or so's ride, lay his heart's desire. After so long, so much grief and frustration and mishap, it was hard indeed to turn his horse away from all he had ever wanted, and to keep to the wet, muddy highway between the hills that led to Bath.

He had sent one of Uncle Henry's apprentices ahead to warn of his arrival, and when he dismounted outside the Abbey Green house, his mother and sister were there at the door to greet him. As usual, Bab's welcome was suffocatingly effusive, and, to his considerable embarrassment, conducted on the doorstep in full view of curious, amused neighbours and passers-by. At last, he managed to draw her inside, and shut the door.

His mother, alternately laughing and crying, had expanded considerably in the past year. In contrast, Amy had lost much of her girlish plumpness, and looked neat, trim and slender in a pretty flowered gown. She was obviously delighted to see him, even if her welcome lacked Bab's overwhelming raptures, and he soon discovered that one reason for her joy was that she wanted to be married, and had been told by her mother that the betrothal must wait for Charles's return, and approval.

It was not until just before dinner that he was able to find a quiet moment to speak to his mother privately, in the parlour. Amy was an innocent, and although he was fond of his pretty little sister, there were matters which he did not wish to discuss in her presence. He shut the door and addressed Bab in a soft whisper. 'I've spoken to Aunt Deb, and she told me that Alex has gone overseas. Is that certain?'

'Of course it is,' she said, with a huge smile of self-satisfaction. 'He's been gone for nearly three months now, as I told you in my letter, and it seems very unlikely that he'll return. If you want to visit Wintercombe, dearest, you'll be quite safe.' She gazed eagerly, greedily up at him. 'Twinney is courting my maid Beck Richeson – she passes all the news on to me. There's been no word from that man since he left in September, until a letter last week to the lawyer, Cousins. Louise is at Wintercombe all alone, though Phoebe has paid her several visits. Drifts about like a wraith, so Twinney says, and all her looks have gone – not that she was beautiful in the first place, mind you.' She glanced slyly up at her son, noting his suddenly stern face. 'Why not go to Wintercombe tomorrow? She'll be glad to see you, beyond a doubt. Who else can she turn to? You're the man of the family now. You can steward the estate, as you did after Nat died. Twinney says that Louise has no head or heart for business, and the place is in sore need of a guiding hand. And if the poor girl lacks a housekeeper, or female companionship, well, I for one would be delighted to return. And so, I am sure, would Amy.'

In this she was wrong, for her daughter, anxious to escape into matrimony at the earliest opportunity, realised that a return to Wintercombe would mean that she saw dear Edward very much less frequently than at present. Besides, the beloved home of her childhood seemed now a dull rustic backwater compared with Bath, even a Bath almost bereft of fashionable visitors in the depths of winter.

She was too good-natured to stamp her foot or indulge in a display of temper, but she wept, quietly and persistently, until Charles, torn between mother and sister, said with some irritation that if she loved the fellow so much, why not marry him? He was a Catholic, he came of a wealthy and respected Bath family, and while not the glittering prize he had always wanted for his sweet Amy, if her happiness was in danger then he was prepared to agree to the match.

That dried Amy's tears with miraculous speed, and the next few days were spent in detailed negotiations with the bridegroom's father. Berkeley Carne kept a prominent and luxurious lodging-house by the King's Bath, besides fingers in numerous other lucrative pies, and Edward, although his younger son, was not expected to have to make his own way in the world. Amy, with the four hundred pounds left to her for her dowry by her uncle Nat, and her exalted family name and connections, was, fortunately for her, considered to be an excellent wife for Edward, and the matter was settled two days before Christmas, with the wedding arranged for the second week in January, at the Abbey, and a private Mass afterwards.

Amy, of course, was overwhelmed, and went about in a daze of happiness, talking incessantly about the pretty house in Box that her future father-in-law had leased for the happy couple, the details of its furnishings, the improvements she would make to it, the clothes she would wear at her wedding and the guests she would invite, until Charles began to wish that she had never set eyes on Edward Carne. He pined for Wintercombe, for Louise, for his rightful place in the world: he felt he would suffocate here in this very female household, thick with interminable conversations about matters that seemed so desperately trivial. What did the colour of Amy's wedding gown matter, or the number of invitations, or whether the celebrations would be held at this poky, undistinguished house or at the Carnes' infinitely grander establishment, conveniently empty of lodgers at this time of year? Everything he desired lay almost within his grasp, a few miles away, and yet he was pinioned here, effectively as distant from his Grail as he had ever been in Dublin, and far more frustrated.

In desperation, he suggested to Amy that she send an invitation to Louise, and she agreed with alacrity. She was less eager to include Phoebe amongst the guests, but since Libby and her parents would be coming, Alex's shrewish sister could not very well be omitted.

To his relief, though, Phoebe despatched a curtly polite note regretting that her untimely indisposition would prevent her presence on the happy day, and conspicuously omitting to wish the couple good fortune for the future. More surprising, and a cause of great disappointment to Charles, was the letter that arrived from Wintercombe. Louise, Lady St Barbe, would not be able to attend, but sent her affectionate regards to Amy, and her hopes for a happy, long and fruitful married life.

So Charles would have to wait still longer to see her. He spent the days before the wedding in a fever of irritable impatience that his sister did not notice, and his mother ignored. He longed to be free of this small and dirty city, with its tiny shops, its narrow crowded streets, the faint but unmistakably sulphurous reek of the Baths, and the rather raffish, faded air that the place always wore out of season, when the brilliant people of wealth and fashion were no longer available to distract a fastidious eye from squalor, neglect and poverty.

At long last the day arrived, and even Charles had to admit that his sister, arrayed in a cornflower-blue gown, and a sable tippet on which he had been forced to squander a ludicrous amount of money to avoid floods of tears, had never looked lovelier, or more happy. Edward Carne seemed a pleasant young man, with an air of steady maturity about him: he was five years older than his bride, and plainly adored her. With a sour feeling of jealousy lurking beneath his breastbone and spoiling the taste of the lavish wedding breakfast, which had also cost him dear, Charles stared glumly at the joyful pair, and wondered why such good fortune, after all his struggle and striving, still eluded him, while it had apparently dropped like a ripe plum into Amy's passive and undeserving lap.

But he was fond of his sister, and tried, though without much success, not to dampen her delight. The effort of being pleasant brought on a savage headache, and he watched Edward and Amy being ceremonially bedded at Berkeley Carne's house through a fog of megrim. Afterwards, with the raucous laughter and bawdy jests still battering his ears, he shouldered his way out into the dubiously fresh air of Bath, and walked back in the rain to his mother's house in the Abbey Green.

Tomorrow. Tomorrow, if it rained, even if it snowed and there were drifts three feet deep on Combe Down, he would hire a horse and ride to Wintercombe, and at last, at long last, after the most miserable year of his life, he would see Louise again.

'M'lady?' Christian Birt stood deferentially in the doorway of the winter parlour. 'M'lady, a visitor for ee.'

Something in the tone of her voice, at once disapproving and excited, roused Louise's interest. She looked up from her book, and saw her maid's face. 'Who is it, Christian?' Despite everything that had happened, her heart had quickened. Was it Alex?

But her husband would not have waited to be announced, as if he were a stranger. Alex would have walked in, with that prowling, restless, hasty stride, his clothes disordered and slovenly, his hair tangled, and given her no option to refuse his presence. Involuntarily, she shivered. He had treated her abominably, as if she were some street drab not worth paying for her favours, he had betrayed her, he had hit and hurt and abused her, and even after everything he had done, her treacherous body remembered other things, and her heart leapt against her wishes . . .

She reminded herself, grimly, of that terrible last night, and said again to Christian, 'Who is it?'

The maid took a deep breath. 'Master Charles, m'lady.'

The book, a history of the French wars of religion,

written in that language, slid off Louise's lap. She bent hastily to pick up, and said in amazement, 'But he's supposed to be in Virginia!'

Christian had been with Louise on the night that Charles had attempted to kill Alex. She knew everything that had happened, and that Mistress Hellier, for his own good as much as in retribution, had forced Charles into exile as the price of his freedom from a well-deserved punishment at the hands of the law. She said, her voice heavy with disapproval, 'So thought I too, m'lady – but there he be, in the Hall, large as life and twice as stomachy, and though I told en as how ee wouldn't likely see en, he woulden take no for an answer.'

'He hasn't changed, then,' Louise said wearily. She got to her feet with care, and smiled rather bleakly at Christian. 'Well, he can see me, though I doubt he'll like what he sees. And after all, I can hardly turn him away in this weather, can I?'

Outside, the rain beat with renewed enthusiasm on the windows, and the leaping fire smoked and hissed. Christian, who over the past few months had become much more of a friend to her mistress, smiled back. '*You* might not, m'lady, but I bain't so kind. Be ee certain you want to see him?'

'No, Christian, I'm not – but I suppose I must,' Louise said. She stared into the hot core of the fire, holding out her hands to it. 'Can you ask Abigail to arrange for refreshments, and another place for supper? And . . . I would rather not be alone with him.'

'I understand, m'lady,' Christian said, and a look full of significance passed between the two women. Then the maid bobbed a curtsey, and went out.

Louise stood still by the fire. It poured out its heat, but even this fierce radiance was powerless against the chill that invaded her now. For months, she had hardly thought of Charles: the once pleasant, rather reserved young man who had seemed to be her friend and who, under the force and pressure of Alex's malevolence, had been transformed into a murderous desperado. Silence had sent him to the New

172

World, to start again, to take the opportunity to repent, and forget.

But it seemed that he had done neither, for he was here: he must have heard from Bab of Alex's departure, and seized his chance.

She realised, suddenly, that he could not possibly know about the collapse of her marriage: it had happened four months ago, and surely even the swiftest ship would take longer than that to sail to Virginia and back again. He must have returned for some other reason, and of course, learning from his mother that both Wintercombe and Louise were now unprotected and apparently his for the taking, had wasted no time in coming here to stake his claims.

Well, he will not have either of us, she vowed grimly. She turned, and with a deliberate resolution that the old, careless, wild Louise had lacked entirely, sat down again in her chair, hands decorously folded in her lap, and waited.

The door duly opened, and Christian entered, her face set in the blank mask of dutiful servitude that she wore in public. 'Master Charles St Barbe, m'lady.'

She had last seen him in that alley, maddened and obsessed by his hatred for Alex and his passionate longing for her, and for Wintercombe, his face contorted and twisted into something far more menacing and evil than ever Alex had seemed to be – until the night when he had raped her. And she wondered suddenly whose dark blood ran slyly in them both, whose the strain of violence that Alex had not bothered to hide, and that Charles had concealed too well . . .

The young man standing before her, stocky, apparently self-confident, his expensive and tasteful clothes splattered and darkened with mud and rain, seemed to bear no resemblance to that other Charles, crazed, desperate, ruthless. His eyes, Bab's pale and rather prominent blue, were glowing with joy, and he bowed with a flourish that was almost worthy of Alex. 'Oh, Lou – it's so wonderful to be home at last!'

She stared at him in angry astonishment. 'For you, it

173

might be. I'm amazed you have the effrontery to show your face here, Charles. Why have you come back?'

'I wanted to see you, of course,' said her cousin. He glanced at Christian, who had unobtrusively taken up one of the chairs by the window, and added in a hissing whisper, 'I must talk to you – in private. Can't you get rid of her?'

Louise gazed up at him with a calm that successfully disguised her anger and her fear. She did not think that Charles would actually try to harm her – after all, he professed to adore her – but he was capable of enormous obstinacy, and his blind obsession with her had alarmed her considerably in the past. There was something horrible about the way that her supposedly stolid, reserved cousin had pestered her, begged her, and assumed that she would come to her senses and love him. She repressed a shudder, and said firmly, 'No, Charles. Christian will stay here. She knows what has happened in the past, after all, and she is no gossip. Whatever you have to say will not go beyond the three of us.'

Charles's eyes flickered to Christian, who had taken up some sewing and turned her head to the light. He said, with the note of pleading she had so much disliked, 'Please, Lou – I *must* talk to you. Alone.'

'No. Either you say it here and now, or you don't say it at all.'

For a moment, his gaze held hers, and then, seeing her implacable expression, he looked away, his hands twisting and maltreating the brim of his hat. His voice, when it came, was like a sulky little boy's. 'Oh, very well – if you insist.'

There was a knock, and one of the housemaids brought in a tray, laden with small spiced pies, steaming and fragrant, and a mug of hot mulled ale. She set it on the table, curtseyed, and withdrew.

'Supper will be served at the usual time,' Louise said. 'I thought you would be in need of some sustenance meanwhile. You may stay here tonight, Charles, as the weather is so foul – I have a duty of hospitality, after all. But tomorrow, you must return to Bath.'

174

'No,' Charles said. He dropped his dripping hat and riding coat on to a chair, and stood stubbornly facing her, ignoring the food. 'No, I will not leave tomorrow. Wintercombe is my rightful home, and now that Alex has gone, it is in sore need of a master.'

Louise stared at him, and a sick dread began to invade her heart. Short of summoning the grooms, and having him physically ejected, she knew that there was little she could do immediately to prevent him staying. She might beg, plead, cajole, argue, but he would be immovable, certain that he was in the right. She could instruct Crowe, the bailiff, to refuse to carry out his orders: she could send to Bath for the family lawyer, Philip Cousins: she could apply to a magistrate. But all these remedies were uncertain of success. Crowe was competent, but had said, several times, that he wished Sir Alexander were home to give him some direction, and he would probably welcome Charles's return. Cousins would certainly take her part, but the wheels of law ground exceedingly slowly. It might be months, perhaps years, before Charles could be removed from Wintercombe. And in the mean time he would sit at her table, eating her food, collecting her rents, assuming the responsibility of the estate as subtly and efficiently as he had done after their uncle's death, so that the tenants and servants and workers, ignorant of the truth, would wonder why she wanted so desperately to be rid of such a capable manager, who was her cousin and had only her interests at heart.

And who was also the next heir to Wintercombe.

But only for a while: for five more months, in fact. And then the child, Alex's child, who had begun to stir in her belly, perhaps conceived on a night of love, perhaps in that last terrible act of rape, would be born. If a boy, it would inherit Wintercombe, and supplant Charles. If a girl, then under the terms of the entail that her uncle Nat had placed on the estate, Charles would still be the heir.

Looking at her cousin's greedy, self-satisfied face, Louise hoped very much that the baby would be born healthy, and male. She said, with rising anger, 'Wintercombe is *not* your

175

rightful home. It is mine, and I do not choose to share it with you. Crowe is an excellent bailiff, and has managed very well in Alex's absence. We have no need of your . . . assistance.'

'Oh, yes, you have,' Charles said. He took a step forward, and Christian, who had been listening to the argument, looked up sharply from her sewing. 'Are you still deluding yourself? After all he did to you? Oh, don't deny it, Lou, I know what happened. I was right about him, all along – he treated you like dirt, he lied to you and betrayed you and beat you, just as I knew he would – you can't *still* cling to his memory, Lou, you can't – no loyalty could possibly survive all that.'

She did not ask how he knew about Alex's brutality: she was well aware that despite Christian's discretion, her distress and her bruises could not have been hidden from her household. Twinney, a kindly man, would have told his sweetheart Beck Richeson, and she, undoubtedly, would have passed on the sordid tale to her mistress Bab. But at least the rape, most dreadful and humiliating of all, remained a close-kept secret between Louise and her maid.

She said, with a determination she did not feel, 'That is none of your business. Alex is still my husband, and Wintercombe is his, not yours. I am merely keeping it for him until he returns.'

Charles laughed incredulously. 'Until he returns! Do you really think me so stupid, Lou? The whole of Somerset knows he'll never come back. He'll come to a bad end somewhere, in some squalid tavern on the point of someone's sword, or drink himself into the grave, and then Wintercombe will be mine in truth.'

'Will it?' Louise said. Pointedly ponderous, she rose to her feet. She was only four months gone with child, but already her waist had thickened noticeably, and when she stood like this, deliberately pushing her belly forward, her condition was very obvious.

It was certainly obvious to Charles. His mouth opened in astonished dismay, and he stared at her as if he had never seen a pregnant woman before. She surveyed his discomfiture with a sense of incongruously gleeful satisfaction, and said with a smile, 'As you can see, there may yet be another heir to Wintercombe, and there is nothing short of murder, Charles, that you can do about it.'

'It – is it – it is Alex's?'

'Of course it is,' Louise said angrily. 'What kind of whore do you think I am? This is his child, and I pray it will prove to be stronger and more fortunate than poor little Nathaniel was. Well? Does this put a different complexion on all your schemes? Or are you planning to go beyond trying to murder an unarmed man, and put an end to my baby's life?'

Charles had gone greyish-white. He said, in a hoarse, shocked whisper, 'Of course not – it's disgusting, unthinkable – I wouldn't dream of it!'

'Wouldn't you? Well, I don't want to take your word for it.'

'You *know* I wouldn't! Alex – Alex was different – he's evil, he deserved it – but an innocent baby – of course I wouldn't harm a hair of its head, Lou!' He swallowed, and added, in a slightly calmer voice, 'It might be a girl.'

'It might – or it might be a boy. The chances are more or less evenly matched, I believe. We'll just have to wait until June to find out.' Louise looked at him coldly, aware of an unworthy but gratifying sense of power. Like this, almost grovelling for her favour, he did not inspire fear, only a pitying contempt. But she must never, ever forget the forces that drove him, the perverted ideals and desires which had impelled him to betray and attempt to murder his cousin, and to blackmail her into marriage. Now, he seemed almost harmless, and she knew that his horrified revulsion was quite genuine. But she could imagine how his twisted logic might, if the child proved a boy, provide him with excuses, persuade him that it would be better, kinder, fairer if the obstacle to his dreams could be quietly and mercifully put aside . . .

Oh, yes, Charles was dangerous, maybe more so than Alex, because he seemed so plausible, so reasonable, and his worst thoughts and plans were hidden, perhaps even to himself, beneath a cloak of mild normality that only slipped at moments of great stress. Even now, he was once more in control of himself, turning that bland, persuasive mask towards her. 'Louise – you would not turn me away? Your own cousin?' He smiled appealingly. 'Oh, Lou, you know it is the sensible solution, to let me stay here. You cannot expect to take Alex's place, and certainly in your condition it would not be proper or seemly to do so. You should rest, and not worry yourself about the business of managing Wintercombe's affairs.'

'Crowe has been quite successful in doing just that, for the past four months,' Louise pointed out. 'And I have been particularly careful of myself, this time. Anyway, what business is it of yours? The child may supplant you, after all – and neither are you its father.'

'No – but I wish I was,' Charles said, and the sudden, passionate hunger in his voice raised the hairs on her neck.

The stared at each other for a long moment, while Christian, all pretence of sewing abandoned, looked on with alarm. Then Louise said sharply, 'Don't, Charles – don't be ridiculous. I am another man's wife, and I will hold to that, in spite of everything. And even if I were his widow, do you think I would ever choose you? You may have been right about Alex, although it was churlish to remind me of it, but that does not make me any more likely to look on you with favour. Less, in fact.'

Charles's pleasant face was creased in bewilderment, like a small boy's, and she struggled to remind herself, again, of how deceptive his appearance could be. He said, 'I don't understand you, Lou – I don't understand! You were my friend – I thought we had a fondness for each other! Why can't you let me comfort you, at least?'

'I don't think anyone could comfort me,' she said, bleakly bitter. No one, save Alex: the Alex she had thought she knew so well, who had surely loved her so passionately. And in a few minutes of horrifying violence, he had torn apart all her certainties, all her beliefs, and left her stranded in a void where nothing was true, or trustworthy. Not even her own feelings could provide an anchor, for despite her anger and disgust and grief, she still missed him desperately. She had pulled herself back to some semblance of normality by concentrating her mind on the daily life of the house, and on her baby. She dared not think beyond the birth: if the child died, and she was once more bereft, she did not know how she would survive it.

No, she was no longer the old, wild, reckless Louise, joyfully dancing through her giddy, carefree days, taking risks in everything, whether in love or on horseback. In the last year, and especially in the last few months, she had grown up: grief, betrayal, loss had sharpened and hardened and strengthened her. She doubted whether her mother, who had not seen her for more than two years, would recognise her once wayward, glittering, superficial daughter. Surely she was quite capable of dealing with her importunate cousin.

She added firmly, 'I do not want you here, Charles. Can you understand that, at least? You do not live here any longer, and although you may stay the night, you must leave in the morning. Your home is in Bath, with your mother.'

'And if I stay?' he said obstinately.

In this mood, he reminded her of one of her small brothers, refusing to go to bed. She realised, from the vantage-point of her own new-found maturity, that there was much that was childish in Charles. Despite his solidly adult appearance and manner, he still yearned for what he should not have, and was prepared to break all the rules to achieve his desires.

'You can't stay,' she said, with mounting exasperation. 'Apart from anything else, it would not be seemly. I thought you cared about such things – can't you see that if you impose on me, while Alex is not here, it will give rise to gossip?'

Charles looked astonished: evidently, the thought had not occurred to him. He said hastily, 'Of course, it would be perfectly proper. I would make sure of that. You need have no fears on that score, Lou – none at all.'

'Oh, I have no fear of *you*,' she said, with a dismissive confidence that was not entirely genuine. 'But you know, none better, how malicious tongues can seize on a perfectly innocent situation and distort and exaggerate it out of all proportion.'

Her pointed tone had no effect: Charles looked entirely unrepentant. 'My mother was reporting the plain and unvarnished truth,' he said. 'And she has done you a considerable service, after all. Without her information, you would still be blind to that reptile's wickedness.'

'Yes,' she said vehemently. 'And Alex would still be here, and I would be in ignorance, and happy. Charles, can you not understand that I do not *want* you here? You are *not* my friend, I find you alarming and ridiculous and as thick-skinned and obstinate as a rhinoceros. And as for your mother, she's utterly beneath contempt. All she wanted was the chance to revenge herself, and make me hate Alex. And before God, I wish she'd taken her horrible insinuations and hypocrisy and malice and gone to the New World with you, instead of causing all this pain and misery.'

'I didn't go to the New World,' Charles said smugly. Her attack on his mother seemed to have passed him by completely. 'I disembarked in Ireland. I've been in Dublin for the past year.'

'You promised Gran'mère that you would go to Virginia – and she even gave you two hundred pounds to help you start a new life! What will she say?'

'She's in no position to say anything,' Charles said. 'She's seventy, after all – she won't leave Chard again. What can she do?' The smile of satisfaction became broader. 'Why don't you accept it, Lou? I have come home, and here I will stay, and look after you.'

For a moment of blind rage, she thought she might throw something at him: preferably something heavy, that could hurt or maim. She heard herself shouting, 'You haven't listened to a *single word* I've said! This is *my* house, Charles, mine and Alex's, and I do not *want* you here! Do you understand, or are you even more stupid than you seem? I hate you, I loathe you and all you've done, I find you completely repugnant, and I'd rather sleep in a ditch than share Wintercombe with you!'

The smile had gone from his mouth, she saw with glee: then his expression hardened, and he said in quite a different voice, 'Well, you may live to eat your words, for I am not leaving. You'll have to accommodate me, Louise, because there's no alternative. You can hardly have me ordered out at gunpoint, after all. Now, I think I will go and change for supper, and we will have our meal in a civilised manner, and say no more about it, for there is nothing you can do to prevent me living here, and my mother too if she chooses. You'll only make yourself look ridiculous if you rail against the inevitable, so why not make the best of it, and be friends again?'

Incredulous, she stared at him, and saw only his bland, smiling, reasonable mask, as impervious as rock. But she knew that he could be goaded, that his insufferable air of self-righteousness could be shattered, because Alex had done it.

He had tried to kill Alex, and had almost succeeded. She shivered suddenly, her hands crossed over her belly, where the baby who might stand between Charles and Wintercombe lay safe. She said coldly, 'You may take supper in the dining parlour, if you like. I am retiring to my chamber. Goodnight, Charles.' Still so furious that her hands itched and tingled with the desire to strike him, she swept past, and out of his presence.

In the confines of her chamber, she could not sit quietly: she prowled restlessly round the walls, pausing to stare out at the lovely terraced gardens, bleak and wet and dead in the cold January rain, and wondered what to do. She was alone here: Twinney and Crowe might take her part, but she could not rely on it. They had both been here for some time, and to them Alex was the interloper, the stranger, and not Charles. Moreover, they had both shown, by their kindness to her, that they thoroughly disapproved of her husband's behaviour. Why should they distrust Charles, who had looked after the estate so well, before and after Uncle Nat's death, and whose attack on Alex in London was a secret known only to the few people who had witnessed it and its aftermath?

There was only one thing she could do, if Charles insisted on remaining at Wintercombe. She would not stay here to endure his obsessions, his hatred of Alex, his arrogant assumption that she was a poor fool blinded by infatuation and misguided loyalty, and that sooner or later she would inevitably come to love him.

And above all, lurking ever present at the back of her mind, there was the terrible fear that one day his perverted, devious mind would provide him with adequate justification for harming her baby . . .

She stopped her endless pacing, and faced Christian, who had sat and watched her mistress for the past half-hour with considerable concern, while she wrestled with her thoughts. 'I'll not endure more than one night under the same roof with him! We'll go to Bath tomorrow, Christian, to stay with Mistress Phoebe again, and try to find an answer.'

The maid came up to her, a frown on her broad country face. 'Do ee think it wise, m'lady? The baby . . .'

'I know, I know,' Louise said despairingly. 'But what can I do? He's left me no choice – oh, he thinks he has, but I can't stay here with him, I can't! And the most dreadful thing is that I don't trust him. I can't help feeling that the baby and I will be safer going to Bath in that jolting coach than staying here with him.'

And Christian's nod of agreement was at once reassuring and deeply disturbing, for it told her that she was not being fanciful about the danger that Charles might pose to Alex's child.

# Chapter Ten

## 'Unrighteous title'

The Englishman had already visited several taverns and drinking houses in this disreputable quarter of Amsterdam, each one more dubious than the last: filled with fat Dutchmen, bellies straining their coats and shirts, swilling beer by the gallon, fondling similarly enormous young women, all with that solidly bovine expression that he found so dull after the liveliness of most English girls. There was a great deal to admire in the Low Countries, not least the astonishing cleanliness of most houses and streets, the joyous, healthy children, and the enormous variety of pictures, often beautifully and skilfully painted, to be found on the walls of parlours, chambers and hallways. But the women . . .

Tom Talmarsh was a connoisseur, with a discriminating taste. He liked his ladies to be witty, well-dressed, and preferably blonde, slender and petite. There were many yellow-haired Dutch girls, but, alas, he had yet to meet one who was both slender and witty. He had come to the conclusion, some time ago, that this deficiency had much to do with the huge quantities of beer that everyone, including the women, seemed to wash down morning, noon and night.

And not only beer. The smell of it was mixed in this tavern with the sharper, aromatic tangs of a variety of exotic spirits, and all overlaid with a suffocating fug of pipe smoke, through which the tapsters and serving girls pushed with their pewter jugs of wine and black-jacks of beer. The noise was like a wall: everyone seemed to be either shouting a toast at the tops of their voices, or singing bawdy and drunken songs with similar enthusiasm. Talmarsh took a deep breath, set his shoulders, and plunged into the packed room. Surely one Englishman, drinking alone, would be conspicuous enough to have been noticed, even in this mêlée?

It took him ten minutes and much exercise of his rather primitive Dutch to ascertain that the man he sought was not in this room, at least. Then, belatedly, he realised that, mangled somewhere in the pandemonium around him, there was music: and yet he had seen no musicians.

He grabbed a passing tapster and yelled at him. On the third attempt, his voice hoarse, he managed to make himself understood. The man jabbed a finger at a door in the darkest corner, and held out his hand. Talmarsh thrust a coin into it, and with a leering smile the man led him past a table crowded with roisterers, opened the door, propelled him through it, and shut it behind him.

The din was instantly muted, and the music leapt suddenly into prominence. In one corner sat a rather makeshift band of fiddle-players, scraping away on their instruments, while a young man with a harsh but tuneful voice sang a humorous song of astonishing obscenity to a simpering, painted girl who gave a singularity unconvincing display of coy innocence. When he had finished, to bawdy cheers, she sang a reply rather less melodic, and even more blatantly suggestive.

Talmarsh's keen soldier's eyes peered into the murk. There were tables and benches around the sides of the room, crowded with whores plying their trade and customers drinking and selecting the wares on offer, and the space in the middle was thronged with dancers, many more or less inebriated. He smiled, rather grimly, elbowed his way through the staggering dancers, evading a number of importunate hands, and arrived at a table in the corner furthest from the musicians.

The man sitting there was whispering something to the girl pressed against him, and Talmarsh, not without some trepidation, rapped smartly on the table to attract his attention.

His quarry turned his head, and surveyed him. For a moment, Talmarsh wished that he had not gone to such trouble to seek out his old friend, for there was a darkness, a look of savagery and danger, in the other man's eyes. Too late, he remembered the nights in London, the wild young blades of the Green Ribbon Club, the duels and the drunken violence in which, too often, this man had taken a leading part.

Well, he himself had been guilty too, often enough. And they were men of supposedly more sober years now: he himself was thirty-five, and the other, though hardly sober at present, some four or five years younger.

'May I sit?' Talmarsh enquired, and Alex St Barbe nodded. A serving girl, buxom even by Dutch standards, brought a glass and a fresh bottle of wine. He took a cautious sip, and found it to be a surprisingly good Rhenish. These 'musicos', as they were called, were little better than brothels, notorious places where the wine was invariably expensive and usually well watered, and customers were frequently robbed.

'I have an arrangement with the owner of the house,' Alex said, smiling as he saw Talmarsh's appreciative expression. 'Best wine – and girls.' He said something in Dutch to the one beside him, who giggled. Talmarsh had already noted that she was by far the prettiest in the room, and moreover, with a tinge of envy, that she was blonde, petite, and slender. Alex had always been the kind of man who attracted the most desirable women, apparently without conscious effort.

'I've been looking for you for some while,' Talmarsh said. He had observed that the man opposite, although flushed with drink, had not entirely drowned his wits in his wine cup. Even when inebriated, Alex's intelligence was a force to be reckoned with.

'Well, now you've found me.' Alex leaned back in his chair, the long clay pipe dangling loosely from his fingers. 'What do you want?'

Talmarsh hesitated, and concealed it with another gulp of Rhenish. Years ago, he had been good friends with Alex St Barbe. His captaincy in the Coldstream Guards had not prevented him from enjoying the pleasures of London, and

185

he had flirted with treason, honing his Whig principles, on the fringes of the Green Ribbon Club and the disreputable company who met at the King's Head in the Strand, and the Rose Tavern in Covent Garden. Alex had been one of the leaders, but his abrupt departure to exile in Holland, nearly four years ago, had, according to gossip, more to do with his seduction of someone else's wife than with his part in Whig conspiracy. Since then Talmarsh, his own career somewhat chequered, had heard occasional reports. A string of mistresses in Amsterdam, a bastard son: then the death of his father, return to England, and embroilment in Monmouth's rebellion. There had even been a spell in the Tower, but, characteristically adroit, Alex had evaded the treason charge that he probably thoroughly deserved, and returned a free man to enjoy his Somerset estates. When Talmarsh had met him at the Rose, last September, and given him that secret message to take to Holland, he had assumed that Alex would return immediately to England. So what was he still doing here in Amsterdam, notoriously the refuge of disaffected Englishmen with prices on their heads?

'A quiet drink, and a talk,' Talmarsh said. He looked at the girl, and Alex grinned. 'Don't worry – she doesn't speak a word of English, and she's as stupid as they come – but charming, eh, Annetje?'

Another simpering giggle, and Talmarsh began to feel less envious. He glanced around the room, careful not to catch the eye of any of the unattached whores, and saw no one who could possibly have been an English spy. Indeed, the most suspicious-looking character present was sitting opposite him. In his dishevelled grey coat, and with his noticeable height and good looks, Alex St Barbe would always turn heads. Talmarsh, middle-sized, lean and observant, possessed the opposite ability, to blend with his surroundings.

In a soft, unremarkable voice, he described the present situation in both England and Holland, and Alex listened with apparent interest, although Talmarsh noted irritably that his eyes often wandered, and the level in the jug of

Rhenish was sinking fast. Annetje, bored, grew bold with her hands, and Alex, with a sudden sharp word, pulled her off and sent her packing.

She flounced away after a few choice phrases, in search of a more attentive customer, and Alex leaned forward, his face bright with unholy amusement. 'So – you resigned your commission in the Guards, because you thought the King would use the army as it has been used in France, to set up an arbitrary and absolute power. Now you're in the pay of the States General, and you've forsaken the English army. D'you want me to take up my former commission in Bellasise's Regiment?'

'Not at present,' Talmarsh said. He surveyed the other man, and wondered, suddenly, just how far he could be trusted. Had the price of that freedom from the Tower included a promise to inform on the Whigs and rebels who had been his associates?

He added curiously, 'You have a house and lands in England – why leave all that and come back here?'

'My reasons for returning to Amsterdam were strictly personal.' Alex drained his glass and shared the last of the Rhenish between them. 'You're not married, are you?'

'No,' said Talmarsh, startled. 'Are you?'

'Oh, yes, for my sins – and let me give you a piece of very sound advice,' Alex said, with a sudden savage bitterness in his voice that took his friend aback. 'Never, ever get wed, for there'll only be grief and misery and captivity for both of you. And never, never, never fall in love with your wife – for that way lies the worst pain of all.'

Talmarsh stared at him, and Alex stared back, his gaze acutely uncomfortable. 'A toast,' he said thickly. 'A toast to my sweet wife Louise – and may she speedily find a better and more gentle lover than ever her husband has proved to her.'

'You can't mean that!'

'Oh, yes, I do – better if she forgets me, better we never meet again, better she thinks I'm dead, than I hurt her as I have done already,' Alex said. He swallowed his wine and smiled, an expression which raised the hairs on Talmarsh's

187

neck. 'Trouble is, I can't forget her – I could drink Holland dry, have every whore in Amsterdam, and still I'd see her looking at me whenever I close my eyes.' He stopped, and stared down at the empty wine jug, and then, with sudden rage, picked it up and hurled it at the sawing fiddlers.

The ensuing brawl was one which, afterwards, Talmarsh remembered with a mixture of astonishment and appalled delight. Beset by a mob of screeching whores and their customers, Alex St Barbe flung chairs and tables with gleeful and malicious abandon, and fought with a complete lack of courtesy that surprised even Talmarsh, when he had the leisure to notice it. Then, using the flats of their swords, they extracted themselves from the mêlée before the city bailiffs arrived to break it up, and ran down a back alley, over several dank and dirty canals and across a couple of dim and disreputable streets, before slowing to a walk, and then a halt.

Behind them, the sounds of uproar were muted by distance. Talmarsh, catching his breath, said with unwilling admiration, 'Where in God's name did you learn to fight like that?'

'At school in Bath, I regret to say.' Alex leaned against a convenient wall, his face a study in amusement and wild mischief. All the savagery and bitterness that he had revealed in the musico had vanished, apparently exorcised by the violence. 'I'm sorry, Tom – you expected a quiet evening over a couple of jugs of Rhenish, and instead you escape a pack of howling harlots by the skin of your teeth.'

'Don't apologise,' Talmarsh said drily. 'I don't recall any evening spent in your company that could possibly be described as quiet. Where are your lodgings?'

'Just behind the Zuiderkerk, not far from here,' Alex told him. 'I've a most excellent French brandy – care to sample it?'

And although Tom Talmarsh had fully intended to keep a clear head that night, he found himself agreeing with enthusiasm.

'I trust you slept well?'

188

His host's voice penetrated Talmarsh's comfortable doze. He opened his eyes, squinting against the pale brilliance of an April morning, and beheld Alex, in shirt and breeches, looking calm and unruffled and quite unaffected by the night's carouse, save in a certain heaviness around his eyes. Aware that he himself had a considerable headache, Talmarsh grunted and sat up with caution. Brandy always affected him adversely, and it was a drink he usually tried to avoid. A few glasses of claret never left him with this megrim, nor with such a sour taste in his mouth and a queasiness in his belly.

'This will improve your view of the world,' Alex said, and indicated a pot of steaming, aromatic coffee on the table by the bed. 'A sovereign remedy for all drink-induced ills. My manservant will assist you, if you wish.'

Some while later, washed, dressed and refreshed, Tom Talmarsh joined his host at a table in the dining parlour. Unlike most of the English exiles, Alex was evidently not short of money: the rooms were comfortable and well-furnished, with the usual quantity of good pottery and pewter, walnut furniture in the fashionable French style, and a number of very fine pictures. His mother had furnished her house at Ham with lavish opulence, and Talmarsh had disliked her clutter of ornamentation, and the ostentatious display of wealth. The Dutch, despite the shortcomings of their womenfolk, undoubtedly knew how to decorate their houses with style, taste and restraint.

'There is a maidservant who comes in to cook and clean,' Alex told him, seeing his interested inspection of the spotless room. 'As plain as a mule, before you ask.' He crumbled the bread that a local baker had brought hot and fresh to the door at sunrise, and then looked up, his eyes on Talmarsh. 'I apologise for my behaviour last night. Drink has the usual effect of loosening both my tongue and my restraint.' He smiled thinly. 'I would not wish anything I said concerning my private affairs to become public knowledge.'

'Don't worry,' Talmarsh said. He drained his coffee, which was made in the English manner, strong and black

189

and a welcome change from the anodyne brew, diluted with milk and spices, which was fashionable in Holland. 'As you may remember, indiscretion is not one of my vices. At any rate, I know now that I can trust you – you are obviously not here to spy on the English exiles.'

'For the King?' Alex gave him a startled glance, and then laughed rather bitterly. 'Has even my reputation sunk so low that you suspected me of that? If I weren't in a reasonably good mood this morning, I'd call you out for it.'

Uneasily aware that he had overstepped the invisible bounds of honourable conduct. Talmarsh said swiftly, 'Don't be ridiculous, man – I know you're not one of James's agents. They're an evil pack of weasels, ferreting out men who've fled from arrest and persecution, and sending the details back to London so that the King can petition the Prince of Orange to return them to England. They're not beyond a little discreet abduction, either – if you have any reasons other than, er, marital ones to be in Amsterdam, I should take great care.'

'Have no fear – I'm here of my own free will, and can return any time I wish – if I want to,' Alex said. 'Forget what I said last night, Tom – embarrassingly personal, if I remember. No wonder you never told me the real reason why you were looking for me.'

Talmarsh stared at him, an unwilling smile on his face. 'You noticed that.'

'Of course I did. I was drunk, but not completely befuddled. So, it must be something that you don't wish to be broadcast around Amsterdam's most notorious musico.' He leaned back, smiling. 'Go on. Trust me.'

'It's little enough. There's a group of us in London, army officers, men like yourself, people with Whiggish or republican sympathies, subtle and clever enough to remain safely in England.'

'Thank you for your flattery,' Alex said drily.

'They mislike the way the King's rule seems to be tending. They meet at the Rose, in Covent Garden.'

'Where we met last autumn, if I remember.'

'Some call themselves, though not in public, the Treason

Club. At the moment, we do little save drink and talk. But there may come a time, not long hence, when that is not sufficient.'

'Why? The King is elderly, and not likely to last much longer – he's known to be in poor health. And then the Princess of Orange will inherit the throne, and all James's efforts to establish Popery will come to nothing.'

'You may play devil's advocate, Alex, but it's by no means a certainty, and you know it. The King might live ten more years. He might even get his wife with child again – she's still young, after all. And besides, if matters in England continue as they have done, the army riddled with Catholics, the laws flouted, Protestantism plainly in danger, then it may be that the people themselves will decide that enough is enough.'

'Civil war?' Alex looked at him sharply. 'I think not. There are too many who remember the last one with horror.'

'The English have fought one war against Popery and arbitrary power,' Talmarsh pointed out. 'And killing kings can become a habit. The late lamented Charles the Second survived to die in his bed because he was quite without scruple, ready to appease and compromise and lie and deceive to keep his throne. James is stiff-necked, stupid and devoted to a religion and a way of government that most Englishmen fear and loathe. If the moment comes when we can take no more, then there is one person to whom all Protestants can look for help – the Prince of Orange.'

'Who has his plate heaped high here, fending off the unwelcome attentions of King Louis.'

'Perhaps. But you know him, you were a regular visitor to his court. Would he come to our assistance, if asked?'

Alex considered the matter. 'I have not seen him since my arrival here – but I have no reason to think that his mind has changed on the subject. He has dedicated his life to ensuring the survival of Holland against the designs of the French. All his strategies, all his policies and alliances, are directed to that end. If he wants England, it is because he must believe that its possession will help him in his struggle

191

against Louis.' He grinned suddenly. 'The good Bishop Burnet has apparently persuaded the Princess that her duty now is to her husband, and not to her father. If William moves against James, she will raise no objection, whatever her private distress. And it is she who is the next heir to the throne, not William.'

Talmarsh sipped his coffee thoughtfully. 'All this is pure speculation, of course, but a blind man could see the direction matters are taking in London. How long have you been here?'

'Since September last year. Seven months.'

'Well, even in that short time, things have changed. Rochester and his brother have been dismissed from the government and the Privy Council, as you may have heard, and Sunderland reigns supreme. And he, of course, will do everything his royal master says. There is even talk that he is contemplating converting to Rome.'

'I know.' Alex threw him a sly glance above the steaming cup. 'His wife, remember, is in regular correspondence with our old and mutual friend, Harry Sidney. And one by one, all the King's servants, in his household and in his council, are being gently persuaded to turn Papist – or lose their positions.'

'How do you know that?'

'I have a very reliable informant – one of James's Gentlemen of the Bedchamber, in his service many years, whose loyalty has been strained beyond the breaking-point. He has no intention of becoming a Catholic, but he is certain that, sooner or later, he faces a choice between his religion or his position. And strange to say, cynical man of the world that he is, I think in the end his religion will win.'

'And so the King is surrounding himself with others of his own persuasion and similarly blinkered vision,' Talmarsh said slowly. 'A recipe for disaster if ever I heard it – and the situation in the army is much the same, which is one of the reasons I resigned my commission.' He leaned forward, his eyes intent. 'Well, are you with us? Or are you going to sit in Amsterdam until you rot in a stew of Holland spirits and tobacco, and take no part in affairs of state? You had the ear of the Princess of Orange, not so long ago. You have a contact in Whitehall, and you were a member of the Green Ribbon Club, with all that implies.'

'So?'

'So, you are ideally placed to act as one of our go-betweens. Harry Sidney would be another, but he's in Germany at present, and besides, he's too well-known. Sound the Prince and Princess, gently, as to their intentions. Wring what information you can from your friend in Whitehall. You must know many of the exiles here. Who can be trusted? And of course, if you are indeed free to come and go as you please, what is to prevent you returning to England, to sound out support in Somerset and the West?'

'With every town still carrying the blackened and festering remains of the men Jeffreys caused to be hanged in the last rebellion, I doubt I'd find anyone prepared to oppose the King.'

'But this will not be a rebellion,' Talmarsh said. 'This will be an invasion.'

'To the men of the West, little difference – treason by another name, that's all, and punishable as such. You forget several things, Tom. Firstly, I do not wish to go anywhere near my former home. Secondly, the Prince will not risk anything, least of all the country he loves, on some wild lunatic scheme as that fool Monmouth did. He will not help you unless he is certain of success. And finally, I am a republican. What makes you think that I will happily eject one king, only to put another in his place?'

Tom Talmarsh stared at him. A slow smile curved his mouth. 'Knowing you, pure devilment.'

Alex laughed, and tossed his empty cup into the air, catching the fragile oriental porcelain a second before it smashed on to the table. 'Who knows? Perhaps, Tom, you may be right. Even in Amsterdam, life can be tedious at times – and seven months is too long to brood on the past.'

'Then are you with us?'

'You damned fool, Tom – of course I'm with you,' Alex said, and spun the delicate cup with accuracy into the hearth. 'And thus may all our enemies end, smashed on the

rocks of righteousness, and similarly high-flown sentiments.'

And Talmarsh, seeing the sudden fierceness on his face,
had the impression that Alex was thinking of foes quite
different from his own.

Phoebe St Barbe had not been very surprised to find her
sister-in-law Louise once more on her doorstep. Only two
days previously she had found out, quite by chance, that
Charles had unexpectedly returned just before Christmas,
and was living unobtrusively at his mother's house. She had
at once sent a message to warn Louise, but it seemed that
Charles had forestalled it.

She listened with angry astonishment to Louise's
description of their cousin's intransigence. And then her
anger had ebbed away as her brother's wife turned to her
and confessed, in a voice barely above a whisper, 'And the
worst of it – when Christian told me that I had a visitor – just
for a moment, I thought it was Alex – and I was *glad*,
Phoebe, God help me, I was *glad*!'

Phoebe repressed the brisk comment that had immediately sprung to her mind. Telling Louise that she was a
fool would do no good at all. She controlled her tongue and
said gently, 'Does that disturb you?'

'Of course it does! After what he did to me, I thought – I
*knew* that I hated him. Everything we had shared, all the
love, the companionship, the laughter – all tainted for ever
by one night, because I discovered what his real nature is,
and all my hope and happiness turned out to be false, just a
mockery, based on illusion.' She gave a small, bitter laugh.
'And of course, Charles couldn't resist reminding me that
he'd been right about Alex all along. It was at that moment
that I was most tempted to smash a candlestick over his
thick pate. But, Phoebe, I feel so –so humiliated. Duped,
deluded, abused like some poor spineless female in those
interminable romances that Amy used to read – like Amy,
in fact. I thought I had more spirit – I thought I was worth
more. And yet I have the horrible feeling that if Alex walked
into this room now, I would leap up and rush to embrace

him. Instead of which, I should be pointing a pistol to his head – and pulling the trigger.'

'If you don't do it, I will,' Phoebe remarked caustically. 'But have you considered this? You were much in love with him, after all – and there is a poem which tells us that "love is not love, that alters as it alteration finds". And he, too, was much in love with you. Perhaps it was because he loved you that he acted as he did?'

Louise made a noise of deepest derision. 'He chose a very strange way to show it.'

'Perhaps. But love, so the poets say, brings not only the capacity to make each other happy. You don't have to experience it to realise that lovers have the power to hurt, to cause terrible pain and grief to those whom they adore – *because* their love is so overwhelming.' She smiled, suddenly wry. 'Who am I, a dried-up old maid, to sit here and pontificate on love to you, of all people? But I think I know more than a little of human nature, and Alex, after all, is only human – no saint, but no devil either, whatever Charles may feel. And for the sake of the baby, if for no other reason, I think you should try to contact your husband. You did marry him for worse, as well as for better.'

'If I'd known the worst in advance, an ox-team wouldn't have dragged me to the church. I don't want to see Alex again, I told him so, and thank God he took me at my word. I've heard nothing from him since he left Wintercombe that night, and I've no idea where he could be, save that Philip Cousins told me that he's gone overseas.'

'Hugh knows,' Phoebe said.

Louise shot her a suddenly shrewd glance. She did not comment on her sister-in-law's familiar use of the courtier's unadorned Christian name, but said calmly, 'Does he? Have they been in correspondence, then?'

'Apparently so, though in somewhat clandestine fashion, I understand. There are those in Whitehall who would not appreciate that their letters indicated merely an old friendship. I note that you do not ask where Alex is.'

'I told you – France, Spain, Germany, Cathay – I don't care.'

' "Methinks the lady doth protest too much",' Phoebe quoted, with some satisfaction. 'I'll tell you anyway – he's in Amsterdam, doubtless renewing his acquaintance with the fleshpots there. Does he know about the baby?'

Slowly, Louise shook her head.

'Perhaps he should. After all, it might be his heir. And perhaps, also, he should be told about Charles. I have the unpleasant suspicion that Alex is the only person who could kick him out of Wintercombe.' She fixed her sister-in-law with an intense blue stare. 'Louise – I know he has treated you abominably. I know you told him that you never wanted to see him again. But you are still married to him: you are carrying his child: and in his absence, you are responsible for Wintercombe. You cannot just walk away from the St Barbes and wash your hands of us, like Pontius Pilate. You are one of us now, like it or not, and you must face reality. We can't allow Charles to get away with it.'

The fear and anger which had fuelled Louise's flight from Wintercombe had by now largely evaporated. Sitting here in Phoebe's snug, comfortable back parlour, with its cushions and roaring fire and air of utter safety, the threat of Charles and his usurpation of her home and her rights seemed very remote, and somehow nothing to do with her any more. She heard herself saying, 'Why not? He'll run the estate better than I could – and certainly as well as Alex.'

'Louise!' Phoebe was obviously horrified. 'You can't do that! You said yourself that he drove you out.'

'Yes, but he didn't intend to. He wanted me to stay. Oh, don't misunderstand me – I detest him, I hate his manner, that awful combination of adoration and condescension, as if I were as pretty and witless and malleable as Amy – and I loathe what he did to Alex and to me. Even if he was right about Alex, it doesn't excuse attempted murder. But Wintercombe is *not* my responsibility, Phoebe – it's a burden, and I would have found it too heavy to carry on my own before much longer. Alex obviously doesn't want it, and neither do I – Charles does, and now he's in possession, what does actual ownership matter? He's a good and efficient manager, he won't waste the estate's resources.

And I can't face the thought of airing all our foul linen in a court of law, in an attempt to force him out.' Aware of Phoebe's frown, she essayed a smile. 'My mother was born at Wintercombe, and fled from it at seventeen. I can't think of it as my home, Phoebe – home, for me, is the St Clair château in France. Perhaps when the baby's born, I'll go back there.'

Phoebe was staring at her. Finally, she said, 'If you do, I think you'll find you were mistaken. Surely your place now is here, in Somerset? Anyway, I was under the impression that life for a Protestant is at present very difficult in France.'

'Then perhaps I'll do as my mother did, and turn Catholic.' Louise looked down at her hands. 'If you find it difficult to believe anything any more, changing your religion is easy – just the exchange of one set of mummery for another.'

'You sound remarkably like Alex,' Phoebe pointed out, with a return to her usual astringent tones. 'Let me be plain and honest with you, like it or not. You are married to my brother, with all the duties and rights and privileges that being Lady St Barbe entails. I accept that he has been unforgivably cruel, but I strongly suspect that he is suffering for it. After all, he has destroyed his own happiness and future, as well as yours, in a few moments of drunken violence, and he is far too intelligent to be unaware of it. And here is Charles, whose mother engineered the estrangement between you, stepping in pat to take advantage of it. He has no *right* to Wintercombe, he is a usurper, and if he installs his dreadful mother there and lives off the fat of the land, he's no better than a thief. Out of principle, if nothing else, we should try to prevent him, or the law of this land counts for nothing.'

Louise knew, in her heart, that Phoebe was right, but the thought of the battle ahead appalled her. She said reluctantly, 'I suppose so.'

'Good. And out of principle, also, you should write to Alex. I'm not asking for forgiveness, or a reconciliation, or anything similar – I recognise that at present you feel it's

197

impossible. But at least *tell* him about the baby – *tell* him about Charles. You don't have to do anything else. Hugh will make sure the letter reaches him. If he then wants to return, well, that is for the two of you to negotiate. But, whatever his sins, it is not fair to leave him in ignorance. I'll give you ample time to write, but I warn you – if in the end you cannot bring yourself to do it, then I will.' She studied Louise closely, noting the signs, controlled but obvious, of considerable distress, and then said gently, 'What are you so afraid of? Alex himself? Or the emotions he inspires?'

And Louise, after one startled glance at her overly perceptive sister-in-law, burst into anguished tears.

After that first discussion, Phoebe let the matter rest, knowing that it would not be far from Louise's mind and hoping that, sooner or later, she would come to a decision. But she went, without the other girl's knowledge, to see the family lawyer, Philip Cousins.

He was well acquainted with both Charles and Alex, and listened without much surprise to her concise and pungent account of recent events. However, he could offer Phoebe little hope. 'It does indeed appear that, if your cousin is living at Wintercombe, and spending the money from the estate, then he is doing so without the authority of the owner, and is in illegal possession. However, with Sir Alexander absent overseas, and Lady St Barbe unwilling and indeed unable to eject him by force, we have no alternative but to pursue the matter through the courts. And I warn you, it could well take years, and eat up all your income. Besides, you are not even certain of success. Sir Alexander might be held to have forfeited his right by his departure, and since Charles is a Papist, well, regrettable though it may seem, under the present King it is quite possible that pressure will be exerted on his behalf. His Majesty is eager to extend Catholic influence in the country, and has already appointed Papist magistrates, despite the requirements of the law.'

'So we may beggar ourselves to no purpose?' Phoebe said grimly. 'I see. Well, my brother had best be persuaded to come home, as soon as possible. He may not be on speaking terms with his wife, but if Louise is carrying his son, the child's inheritance is in danger. Thank you, Philip, for your help and advice.'

'Such as it is,' the lawyer said apologetically. 'The saying "possession is nine-tenths of the law" is, alas, peculiarly appropriate in this case. If I were you, Mistress St Barbe, I would seriously consider hiring some discreet and efficient assassin.'

And Phoebe, who knew him well, was startled to see that he was not entirely joking.

While Louise sat quietly in the house in Nowhere Lane, reading or sewing or talking to Libby or Lukas, Phoebe exerted herself on her brother's behalf. Local Justices were consulted, but gave the same answer as had Philip Cousins. Without the complaint of Lady St Barbe, or her husband, nothing could be done. And Louise, who had sunk into an uncharacteristically dreamy lethargy which Phoebe supposed charitably to be connected with her pregnancy, seemed to think that Charles was welcome to Wintercombe, so long as he did not come in search of her.

But as the weeks slipped by, and the time of her child's birth crept inexorably closer, Louise's conscience began to wake. She had tried to defend and repair her broken heart by pretending that she did not care, by shutting out all thought of Alex and Wintercombe, as well as Charles. Here in Phoebe's house she was safe from the stormy, terrifying emotions that had led her to such extremes of happiness and despair. Here, she could draw up her strength again, and prepare herself for the arrival of the baby. And Phoebe, after that initial, uncomfortable harangue, had wisely left her alone, to make her decisions in peace.

The days lengthened, and spring warmed the air: the point at which Nathaniel had been born was reached and safely passed, and the child within her kicked lustily. She suspected that so vigorous a child might well be a boy, and if so, Phoebe was right: for his sake, if for no other reason, Wintercombe must be wrested from Charles, and returned to its rightful heir, even if Alex never set foot in England again.

And he did have a right to know: although by his behaviour he had forfeited her love, still the baby was his, and perhaps conceived in delight, before that brutal rape had destroyed everything that had preceded it.

Still, it was extraordinarily difficult to bring herself to send him even the barest information. The unpleasant truth was that she did not want to write, did not wish to communicate with the man who had hurt her so deeply, and thereby reopen wounds that were only just beginning to heal. Here in Phoebe's house, living from day to day, trying to pretend that this was not just a temporary refuge, she had at last managed with difficulty to forget, most of the time, what Alex had done to her in September: indeed, sometimes that brief episode seemed to have taken on much of the horrific but unrealistic quality of a nightmare, and she found herself wondering if it had actually happened.

No, if her husband was indeed in Amsterdam, he was better there, unseen, as distant from her life as if he were dead. A letter might break the spell, and bring him back to England: and whatever her treacherous heart might feel, she truly never wanted to see him again.

The presence of Lukas in the household made matters worse. She loved the child, but his close resemblance to his father was very unsettling, as was his frequent expression of bewildered distress. The rift between Alex and Louise had upset him very much, and it was obvious that no amount of patient and expurgated explanation by Phoebe could assuage his deep sense of betrayal. Louise felt very sorry for him, and was careful not to discuss Alex in his presence. Nor did her stepson, whose manners were usually impeccable, ply her with awkward questions: but several times she saw him looking at her with sad reproach, further nagging at her already burdened conscience.

She suspected, too, that Phoebe was active behind her back. Guiltily aware that she, not her crippled sister-in-law, should have been dutifully making efforts to remove Charles from Wintercombe, she tried to ignore Phoebe's unexplained absences, her purchase of several weighty treatises on legal matters, and the visits of Philip Cousins which always began with long discussions in the front parlour, with the door firmly shut. Surely Phoebe's patience could not last for ever: sooner or later, her façade of sweet reason and understanding was bound to crack, and then, Louise knew, she would be soundly and deservedly scolded for her descent into apathy and torpor.

But still she could not bring herself to write, and thereby to admit to herself, to Phoebe, and most of all to Alex, that communication with her husband might yet be possible.

And then at last, her procrastination was overtaken, on the first day of June, when the first pains assailed her, and announced that very soon her baby would be born.

# Chapter Eleven

## 'Protracted punishment'

If Alex St Barbe had wished to forget England entirely, Amsterdam, full of his fellow-countrymen seeking a refuge from intolerance, or the unwelcome attentions of the law, was not the best place to go. But it was a city he knew well, and it had proved surprisingly easy to slip back again into his old dissolute life amongst the exiles, drinking and whoring and talking treason in the smoky taverns and musicos of the Jewish quarter and around the harbour. He spoke fluent Dutch, he had a Dutch servant, and he was possessed of considerable funds forwarded from his banker in London. It was inevitable that indigent exiles should begin to congregate at his comfortable lodgings, to partake of good wine and excellent brandy, perhaps even a bed for the night if they had imbibed too well. Alex had made it plain that his hospitality would not extend further than that: he had no intention of becoming a charitable institution for the benefit of poverty-stricken English and Scottish republicans and Whigs.

Tom Talmarsh had returned to England, and the dangerously named Treason Club at the Rose Tavern. Theirs was, and always had been, a slightly wary friendship, founded on considerable respect for each other's capabilities, tempered by an appreciation of the ruthlessness that existed in them both, more overtly in Alex. He knew that Talmarsh still did not entirely trust him: and, also, that it had been a little unwise, in that mood of drunken bitterness, to reveal the extent of his vulnerability concerning his wife. Not that the details of his treatment of her would have shocked Talmarsh, who was a man of the world, and had served in Tangier, an experience guaranteed to open anyone's eyes to the infinite and horrible variety of evils which men could inflict, particularly upon women. But his admission of anguished regret must have shattered the aura of careless self-sufficiency that had taken him the better part of twenty years to construct. He suspected that Tom's mistrust was based on the conviction that Alex had gone soft, and had lost the hard edge of devious ruthlessness that had made him such a successful conspirator in the glorious days of the Exclusion Crisis and the Green Ribbon Club.

He knew all this, and yet still, at inconvenient moments, the spectre of Louise, laughing and teasing and inviting, would slip into his mind, catching him unawares with the sharp agony of loss. Even now, more than half a year after he had raped her, his self-disgust was capable of sinking him into a mood so black and savage and despairing that no quantity of brandy could drown it. He had forfeited all right to her love, all prospect of future happiness, and he had no one but himself to blame. It was a bitter pill indeed, to face the fact that he had done such harm, for reasons that now seemed ludicrously slight: wounded pride, a desire to assert himself, to obtain power over her, unleashed into violence by drink. And he had driven her away for ever, and exiled himself here, in this crowded and cosmopolitan city, with no prospect of reconciliation. What he had done might not be regarded as at all reprehensible by such as Talmarsh, or the disreputable men with whom he spent his time: but between himself and Louise there had been love, and desire, and the beginnings of something more, a closeness and friendship that might well have cemented them together more strongly, as the years passed and the initial intensity of their passion inevitably faded. And by beating her, and raping her, he had smashed all affection, all companionship, as irrevocably as if he had taken a hammer to one of the ubiquitous blue and white china pots that decorated his lodgings.

He would not return to England, still less to Wintercombe: his pride would not allow him to humiliate himself, to beg for her forgiveness for something that was utterly unforgivable. Better she forget him, and take a lover who would treat her kindly and cherish her joyous vitality, that he had done his best to extinguish. And if he died without a direct heir, and Charles inherited Wintercombe, he thought he would not care very much. The place was only a pile of stone and mortar and glass, after all: his aunt Silence might love it with a passion that should be more properly reserved for people, but it was just a house like many others, and had no magical power over him.

No letters came from his wife, which did not surprise him: and none, either, from Phoebe, which did. He found that he missed his sister's astringent, often brutal honesty more than he cared to admit. Sir Hugh Trevelyan wrote, rather guardedly, of affairs at Court, mostly trivial gossip: but occasionally a more informative letter would arrive, sent by channels other than the official post, which would doubtless be watched, and letters opened. By the same secret route, he had several missives from Talmarsh: and in June, mindful of his promise to his old friend, rode down to the new palace at Het Loo, to see the Prince and Princess of Orange.

In his previous years of exile in Holland, he had served in one of the English regiments in the Dutch army, rising to the rank of major, and had resigned his commission only with considerable reluctance, to take up his inheritance on the death of his father. He had come to know William of Orange quite well – as far as anyone could become acquainted with such a reserved and private man – and to respect and appreciate his formidable efficiency and administrative gifts, as well as his single-minded defence of his country, threatened by the encroaching power and aggression of the King of France. The Prince's opinion of Alex was rather more in doubt. He notoriously gave his absolute trust only to those closest to him, like Bentinck, or Count Zuylestein, who had shared his lonely childhood, and to his beloved wife Mary, Protestant daughter of King James. Alex suspected that Prince William considered him to be a good officer – promotions within the six English and Scottish Regiments were attained entirely on merit – but disliked and distrusted his openly republican sympathies.

The Princess, however, was much more approachable, and he had always been able to make her laugh. William was not at home when Alex arrived: he was indulging in his favourite pastime, hunting deer and boar in the forests of Gelderland that surrounded his new palace. The building itself was not complete, but the gardens, in which the Princess took a keen and active interest, had already been laid out with geometrical precision where once, only two years ago, had been rough grass and heathland around an old hunting lodge. The elaborate waterworks and fountains which the Prince and Princess planned had not yet been built, but the knots and parterres between the gravelled walks were filled with summer flowers in a glorious array of colour.

On this pleasant afternoon, the Princess and her maids were walking along the formal paths, engaged in a lively and probably gossipy conversation, punctuated by bursts of laughter. Alex waited at a few flowerbeds' distance while the official spoke to her, and then was beckoned over by Mary herself, with her usual refreshing lack of ceremony.

'Sir Alexander!' she said with evident pleasure, as he bowed low, aware of the interested looks and whispers of the maids of honour. 'What a delight to see you again, after so long. How have you been keeping? Will you walk with me for a space?' And, with a quick glance at the gaggle of ladies, she added, 'You may stay here, for the moment. Sir Alexander is an old friend from England, and we have much to discuss.'

William's wife was a tall young woman, one of the few people, of either sex, who could approach Alex's height. The Prince of Orange himself was half a head shorter than Mary, which made them an ill-assorted couple, although they were devoted to each other. He had not expected it, but her tall figure and dark curling hair, her liveliness and friendly manner all reminded him a little of Louise, although the Princess was considerably plumper, and more beautiful. At her gracious invitation, he took her arm and led her along a path between parterres packed with

205

different coloured flowers, bright yellow in one, gaudy red and white in another, all shimmering with eager bees and butterflies.

'I did not know you had returned to Holland,' Mary said with a smile. 'Surely you have an estate in Somerset now?'

'I do, madam – but I found that I preferred life in Amsterdam,' Alex told her. She was justifiably curious, and he was beginning to regret his decision to speak with her, rather than wait for her husband's return from hunting. William's taciturn reserve might, on reflection, have been much easier to deal with than his wife's genuine interest in someone whom she regarded as an old friend.

'Then I am at one with you in that,' Mary said. 'I could not endure to live in England now. In my memory, it seems so – so dirty, somehow, so wild and full of licentiousness – very unlike our clean and sober Dutchmen.' She glanced at him, with another smile. 'Though not always so sober, I cannot deny – but then you would know more about that than I, Sir Alexander.'

'Perhaps,' Alex said. His reputation had never been a secret, and he suspected that the virtuous Mary felt a certain pleasurable sense of daring, walking like this with a notorious rake. 'But rest assured, madam, in your gracious presence I am never less than the soul of propriety.'

'That's just as well – my ladies gossip like a pack of fishwives,' said the Princess, and giggled. 'And the gossip says, Sir Alexander, that you have a wife. Surely that cannot be true?'

'I assure you, madam, it is.'

'Who is she? How long have you been wed? Is she here with you in Holland?' Mary, who had the reputation of a chatterbox, rattled her questions off without pause for breath.

Alex deliberately paused, and made his reply as measured and unemotional as he could. 'She is my cousin, my mother's sister's grandchild, and her name is Louise Chevalier: she was raised in France, where her mother still lives, but was sent to her kin in England as life grew too difficult and dangerous for Protestants, under King Louis.'

'That vile, persecuting Papist,' Mary said fervently. 'So, did you meet her in Somerset?'

'I did – and married her in January, last year.'

'And you have brought her to Holland?'

'No, madam – she stays at home.'

Mary paused, and looked at him. She had received a somewhat perfunctory education, but she was intelligent and perceptive, and genuinely warm-hearted. She said with a frown, 'Surely, Sir Alexander, being so recently married, you do not wish to be parted from her for long?'

'It is indeed a matter of some regret to me,' he said.

'And have you any children yet?' Mary's tone was slightly wistful: a miscarriage, some years ago, had ended her only pregnancy, and it was now accepted that she would never be a mother.

'A boy, who died,' Alex said: and although he had thought that the grief of that momentary life had long since faded, he had a sudden and poignant vision of Nathaniel, so tiny, so frail, the unfinished red skin and the shock of black hair, and Louise's face, fierce, desperate, willing him to live.

If Nathaniel had survived, he would not be standing here now, he would be at Wintercombe, and Louise would still love him.

'I am so sorry,' said the Princess, gently and with real compassion. 'But I do hope that you will have others, who will be more fortunate.'

For a moment, he was tempted to tell her that such a prospect was unlikely, to say the least, while he and Louise were estranged. But he could not reveal his marital difficulties to her sympathetic gaze. He said, 'I hope so too, madam.'

Mary gave him a shrewd glance, but said no more on the subject. Instead, she turned the conversation to the gardens, describing the fountains and statues that would grace these walks very soon, and then to the palace itself, already rising behind them, its understated elegance, very modern and very Dutch, masked as yet by a tangle of scaffolding. They had reached the end of the walk, and

207

turned to retrace their steps, before he was able to broach the matter for which he had ridden all the way from Amsterdam.

The Princess paused, her brown eyes puzzled. 'Why do you ask me, Sir Alexander? Surely you should speak with my husband, when he returns this evening? I have little knowledge of such business, and small desire to learn.'

'Perhaps I should, madam,' Alex said. 'But I feel that His Highness would look upon my suggestion more favourably, were it to be put to him through your agency.'

Mary was still looking very doubtful. 'I do not see why he should, sir. I know he has held you in high regard in the past, or he would not have raised you to the rank of major.'

'But he has no love for those who hold republican beliefs, has he? The English exiles in Amsterdam are a disreputable crew, poor, drunken, quarrelsome, and no lovers of kings, or indeed of any form of authority, or they would not be there in the first place. He wishes to keep his distance from us, and I do not blame him.'

'And do you count yourself of their company? I had assumed that you were here from choice, rather than necessity.'

'I was under some suspicion at one time, yes, but no charge was ever brought against me, and as far as I know I am free to return to England whenever I wish – for the present, at least. The King your father no longer has any interest in me, and besides, my imprisonment was due entirely to the jealous malice of my cousin, who hoped to appropriate my estates. No, my reasons for being in Holland are quite legitimate – and private.'

The intelligent, thoughtful brown eyes studied him. 'I see,' said King James's elder daughter, who had inherited neither his obtuseness nor his obstinacy. 'But if you wish now to act as an intermediary between my husband and certain . . . factions in England and Holland, then it is quite probable that suspicion will fall on you again. You may not be able to return home openly, even if you might wish to do so. Are you sure that is what you want, Sir Alexander?'

'Quite sure, madam,' Alex said grimly.

He talked with the Princess for a while longer, and then, at her suggestion, managed to obtain a private hour with Dijkvelt, the Prince's emissary, who had recently returned from a visit to England. It was a discussion of considerable profit to them both, and was interrupted by the arrival of William, fresh and triumphant from the hunt, and in an excellent mood.

When Alex left Het Loo the following day, he carried with him not only the good wishes of the Princess Mary, but her husband's approval and instructions for the intelligence network which Tom Talmarsh had proposed. William had many lines of communication, more or less secret, between himself and his friends in England, but he was well aware of the vital importance of reliable information, and this link between the army Whigs in London and the republican exiles in Amsterdam filled a small but vital gap in his web. And although Alex had now committed himself to conspiracy, with all the dangers and inconveniences that attended it, he rode away through the forests of Gelderland with a surprisingly light heart. At last, after the dark, haunted months of bitterness and remorse, he had a purpose to his life: and if it led to permanent exile from England, even if it led to his death, at that moment he did not greatly care.

He did not return directly to Amsterdam, but turned his horse south-west, towards the Hague, where there were certain officials whom William wished him to consult. And when his business with them was done, he succumbed at last to curiosity, and also to the promptings of his abused conscience, and went in search of the luxurious house near to Het Oude Hof, that had once had been as familiar to him as his own home.

He gave his name to a very ugly maidservant, and was left in a hall whose furnishing, in the fashionable French style, reminded him sharply of the lavish and overbearing taste of his aunt Bab, all softness and gilt and drapery, very different from the sparse, whitewashed beauty of the traditional Dutch interior. The maid returned, and with knowing smiles ushered him into the presence of the lady of the house.

He had first met Johanna van der Linden ten years ago, when she had been young, delectably pretty, and already practised in the arts of lust and deception, with a string of rich and elderly lovers in her past. Their affair had been passionate and stormy, and for a time he had been genuinely in love with her, while she, hoping to bind the handsome young Englishman closer to her, had allowed herself to become pregnant. But her initial allure had quickly faded when he discovered that she had continued to take other lovers, despite her protestations of eternal fidelity. Something of an irony, Alex thought grimly, in view of his subsequent behaviour.

The baby, Lukas, had meant nothing to Johanna in himself, but was merely an encumbrance, once her reason for conceiving him had vanished in one final, blistering quarrel with Alex. But although their affair was over, he had ensured that his son was well provided for. During Lukas's childhood, he had often visited him, and the boy, neglected and unwanted by his mother, had transferred his love and allegiance to Alex, who had played with him, taken him for walks in the woods and by the dykes and sand-dunes along the sea shore, and taught him to speak English as well as Dutch. And when Alex had returned to England to assume his inheritance, he had sent his servant Gerrit to take Lukas away from the mother who had treated him so unkindly, and bring him to Wintercombe.

He had not seen Johanna for nearly three years, and her appearance was a surprise. Always ripely plump, she had put on a great deal of weight, and he saw with malicious satisfaction that she was nearly as fat as his aunt Bab. Her once pretty face now bore a faint and ludicrous resemblance to a pig's, but without the sow's expression of smug contentment. There were frowning lines between her thinly plucked brows, her golden hair had a brassy tinge, and her mouth was set in a peevish mould.

'I'm surprised you have the gall to appear here again, after what you did to me,' she said resentfully.

Alex gave her a formal bow that had much of mockery in it. 'I came merely to find how you did, and to give you news of Lukas. If you did not wish to see me, you could have turned me away.'

Johanna fluttered her dyed eyelashes with grotesque coquetry. 'I never bar my door to attractive men – you know that.'

'I have good cause to,' Alex pointed out caustically. 'I don't intend to waste any more of your time, Johanna. I will say merely that Lukas is well and thriving, shows signs of a gift for scholarship, and never mentions you save with dislike and contempt. Is that what you wish to hear?'

'You took my baby away from me,' Johanna cried, and tears sparkled prettily in her blue eyes.

She had always been able to give an appealing display of grief, and Alex made a derisive noise. 'Spare me, madam. You hit him, you locked him in cupboards, you told him you wished he had never been born. No woman alive could have been a worse mother, and it is to his credit, not yours, that he is such a pleasant and well-mannered child. With Lukas gone, you have your freedom, and I should enjoy it to the full before age and greed catch up with you. Goodbye, Johanna – I do not expect that we will meet again.'

He left, with her cries of 'Alex – wait!' echoing down the stairs. He had no compunction about being cruel to Johanna: she was hard, rapacious and callous, and the affair had been founded entirely on mutual lust. It seemed that she still found him attractive, despite her dislike: he himself would rather have bedded the lowliest sailor's drab.

He lodged in a simple inn that night, and thought much of the son he had left behind in Bath. It occurred to him, for the first time, that the hurt he had done to Lukas, abandoning him without a word, must be almost the equal of the pain he had inflicted on Louise. Worse, perhaps: for how could such a sordid and unpleasant tale ever be explained to a child of eight, who doted on both his father and his stepmother?

He must write to Lukas, with some account of his

absence. He was beginning to understand that when he had attacked Louise, more than his life and hers had been shattered.

In a distant, thoughtful mood, he rode back to Amsterdam. The sun seemed unusually and oppressively hot, and he felt very tired. He had left Gerrit at his lodgings, preferring his own company on the ride to Het Loo: but as the long, dusty miles rolled slowly on, he began to wonder if that had been wise. Apart from injury, and the effects of too much wine or brandy, he had hardly suffered a day's illness since childhood: and now it was creeping up on him menacingly, like a footpad.

He had hoped to reach Amsterdam by nightfall, and the thought of lying sick and helpless in some squalid roadside tavern did not appeal. He ignored the raging headache, the shivering that assailed his body despite the heat of the sun, the increasing feeling of disorientation, and temporarily cured his thirst with a jug of beer purchased from an alehouse.

His hired horse, no Blaze or Pagan, plodded on, paying little heed to his urgings, and oblivious to his plight. But at last, as the sun dropped down towards the west, he discerned the distant spires and smoky smudge of Amsterdam, humped on the horizon of this flat, marshy country, dominated by the overwhelming vastnesses of sky and sea.

He found himself suddenly longing for Somerset, with the sweep and bulk of the seven hills around Bath, the secret valleys and infinitely changing views. But his right to that land was gone for ever: he had chosen his path, in a moment of drunken rage, and now, however bitter the result, he must accept it. And if he died here, of this fever, then Louise would be free of him, and probably glad of it . . .

With an effort, he dragged his mind from maudlin self-pity, and realised that the long journey was nearly at an end. The gates of the city were open still before him, the curfew had not sounded yet, and in a little while he would be home.

'Not home,' he said, and did not realise that he had

212

spoken aloud, and in English, until he saw the surprised stare of a passing peasant.

It took all his considerable reserves of will power and determination to fight against encroaching collapse, to keep upright, to pretend that nothing was wrong, to remember the way through the narrow streets to his lodgings, and to steer his weary mount in the right direction. Afterwards, he had no recollection of doing so: one moment he was riding into the city, the next he was sitting staring at the familiar brown paint of his front door, wondering bemusedly how he was going to dismount, if he did not fall off his horse first.

Then Gerrit was there, solid and utterly reliable, his round, typically Dutch face anxious. *'Mynheer, was is er aan de hand? Bent U ziek?'*

'Something's wrong,' Alex said. The street was behaving oddly, it would not keep still, and there was a peculiar singing noise in his ears. 'Help me down, would you?'

Fortunately, Gerrit's knowledge of English, although imperfect, was equal to this instruction: for the moment, Dutch was quite beyond Alex's capabilities. Somehow he slid off the horse's back without too much loss of dignity, and managed, with his servant's assistance, to stumble up the few steps to the hall.

He had been cold earlier, under the heat of the sun: now, sitting on a chair inside the evening coolness of the house, he felt as if he were cooking in a furnace. Gerrit hovered, a piece of paper in his hand, and said something in Dutch.

Alex stared at him in bewilderment. For the past ten years he had spoken the language almost as fluently as his own, but suddenly it made no sense to him at all. 'Try English,' he said.

His servant handed the piece of paper to him. 'Mynheer – from England – for you.'

He found a letter lying in his hands, addressed to him in the elaborate curlicues of Sir Hugh Trevelyan at his most urbane. At the top, however, his name was written in the spiky, unfeminine and forceful hand of his sister Phoebe.

Gerrit was saying something unintelligible to Clara, the

213

maid who came in every day to cook and clean. Ignoring him, Alex opened the letter and frowned at the words. Despite his efforts, they seemed to lurch drunkenly in and out of focus. He pushed the hair out of his eyes, and tried again, with more success.

'Dear Brother,' Phoebe had begun, in her characteristically blunt style. 'I consider it my duty to inform you, since your wife cannot do so at present, that yesterday evening, at nine o'clock, she was brought to bed of a healthy child, a daughter.'

Her words jostled incomprehensibly inside his head and then, suddenly and overwhelmingly, made sense. He shut his eyes, disbelieving, and then opened them and stared again at the letter, wondering if there was some mistake.

No: despite the feverish disorder threatening to overturn his wits entirely, the words were not the product of his imagination. Louise had borne him a baby, a girl: alone, and without telling him, she had successfully negotiated the hazards of pregnancy and produced the child for which they had both longed. It did not matter that it was not a boy, although no baby could ever completely replace Nathaniel, nor undo the damage his death had caused. It was enough to know that there was a healthy child, and that Louise was no longer alone.

He sat still for a moment, astonished by the intensity of the emotions overwhelming him. Joy, and grief, and the unspeakable bitterness of regret and remorse: and above all, a longing to see her, and the baby, and put right what had no hope of ever being mended, to call back time, to return to a happiness that he would never, ever recover.

He had not wept since he was a small child: but now, beset by illness and this wonderful, unexpected news, he came very close.

Gerrit touched his shoulder. 'All right, sir?'

He found his voice, somehow, and was surprised to find that it sounded almost normal. 'Yes, Gerrit – it's my wife – she's given birth to a daughter.'

His servant's ruddy face split into a glorious smile. 'A daughter? A baby? *Het is heerlijk, heerlijk!*' He turned to

214

Clara, and began a long and excited explanation, while Alex, with an effort, concentrated on the rest of Phoebe's letter.

You may or may not care to know that the birth was easy and quick, that Louise is so far very well, and that the child is large and lusty, with much black hair and a marked resemblance to her father, poor infant. I have not been told the full tale, I know, of the quarrel between you and your wife, nor do I wish to be, for you have evidently committed some unforgivably dreadful act of mistreatment, and she shows no desire to contact you, even to inform you of the child's safe arrival. Neither have I any desire to interfere in your private affairs.

However, there is one other matter of importance, which I feel most urgently that you should know. Charles has returned to Wintercombe. He arrived a while after Christmas, and is now ensconced there with, it seems, the blessing of all save myself and Philip Cousins. Louise would not stay there with him, and has washed her hands of the matter. She is at present lodged with me in Nowhere Lane, but talks of returning to her mother in France when the baby is older. I have tried to dissuade her, but at present she is firm in this purpose.

Charles is obdurate, and will not be moved. He is living in your house, off your rents, and ordering your servants. He will doubtless be overjoyed to learn that the baby is not the boy who would have supplanted him, and that he is still therefore your heir.

Only you, it seems, can eject him from Wintercombe, for all recourse to the law has so far failed. I would appreciate some word from you on this matter, if only to say that you have turned your back on Wintercombe and all your inheritance, so that no more time, money and effort be spent in this vain task by your unaffectionate sister,

Phoebe St Barbe

Compared with the news of the baby, the information about Charles's return seemed somehow irrelevant. His eye fell on a postscript below Phoebe's uncompromising signature. 'Louise has named her Katherine, in honour of her mother. I believe she intends her to be known as Kitty.'

Kitty St Barbe: his daughter, a sister for Lukas, a first great-grandchild for Silence. As clearly as that earlier memory of the dying Nathaniel, he had a different vision, of another baby, rosy with health, crying lustily, her small fat hands beating the air: and above her Louise's exultant, joyous face, shining with the love he himself had forfeited nearly nine months ago.

It was the last entirely lucid thought in his mind for some time. Gerrit and Clara, greatly concerned, intruded again with medicines, remedies and suggestions. More for the sake of peace than anything else, he allowed himself to be undressed and put to bed. He had, afterwards, a dim recollection of a man in physician's black standing over him. Someone had uttered the dread word 'smallpox', and Alex tried to say that it could not be that, he had already had the disease years ago in early childhood. But somehow his words seemed to make no sense, and as in a nightmare, no one was listening.

After a long, confused interlude that might have lasted for hours, or days, there was another doctor, examining him with brisk competence. He still could not understand Dutch, but the man seemed to be certain of his diagnosis, whatever it was, and Gerrit was nodding with evident relief. Then Clara made him swallow a drink of peculiar and astringent bitterness that made him struggle and choke and cough before he lapsed once more into delirium.

The remedy must have worked, though, for gradually the strangeness and the heat ebbed from him, and he slept, and woke to find Gerrit bending over him, looking pleased, and telling him that the worst was over.

He was speaking Dutch, and Alex realised that he could understand it. In the same language, he asked, 'How long have I been here?'

'Four days, Mynheer, and we thought you were dying.

216

That first doctor told us it was smallpox, the fool, and nearly killed you.'

'I had it when I was two years old,' Alex said. He moved his hand, with some effort, to indicate the place at the side of his forehead, partly concealed by the fall of his hair, where the faint, unmistakable scars remained. 'The signs are there, if he'd bothered to look. What was it, if not smallpox?'

'The marsh fever,' Gerrit told him. 'It's very common here, he was surprised you hadn't had it before, Mynheer.'

'Perhaps I've been lucky,' Alex said. He lay in the softness of the bed, enjoying the feeling of cool lassitude which enveloped him like a blanket. 'So what was that drink Clara gave me? The devil's own brew, by the taste.'

'You remember that?' Gerrit said. 'You were raving, Mynheer, for days – I did not think that you even knew where you were. Doctor van Vas prescribed a dose of Jesuit's Powders, he said they would work a miracle, and he was right.' He smiled, with heartfelt relief. 'Thank God Clara had heard of him, and called him in. Most doctors are quacks, but that one is a master. He saved your life, no doubt of it.'

'Then I must thank her, and present my apologies for being such a difficult patient. Is Doctor van Vas returning to see if his remedy was successful?'

'He said he would call in this evening, Mynheer. Now, would you like anything to eat?'

Alex, with some surprise, realised that he was ravenously hungry. Very soon, Clara brought a tray of nourishing delicacies to tempt his appetite, and he was in the process of cleaning his plate when Doctor van Vas was ushered in.

The physician was young and possessed of a brisk, breezy manner that inspired more confidence than most doctors. He pronounced Alex cured, for the present, but warned that the marsh fever had a habit of returning over and over again, until the body had expelled the noxious humours which caused it. 'Usually, Mynheer, each bout of ague will be a little less severe than the one which comes before it, until it dwindles away altogether. However, in some

217

circumstances the fever may become more serious, indeed may endanger your life. Excessive drinking, for instance, often has a most deleterious effect. If you are a gentleman of immoderate habits, I strongly recommend that you alter them immediately. The occasional carouse may not do you much harm – it is the prolonged, heavy and regular indulgence which may kill you before your time. At the moment, you are strong and healthy, and well able to fight off the fever, with the aid of the Powders which I gave you. But if your body is weakened by persistent debauch, before long the Powders will be useless, and the fever will triumph.'

It was a warning which Alex knew he could not afford to ignore. Already he had begun to drag himself out of the abyss of drunken despair in which he had wallowed since his return to Holland. He had thought that death would be welcome, in whatever guise: now, threatened with it in earnest, he knew that life, however bereft of love and purpose, was infinitely preferable to the grim alternative. The fever was a salutary reminder of his mortality, and provided a most excellent motive for amending his dissolute habits. He had no intention of abjuring the pleasures of wine, or brandy, entirely, but if spending each night in an increasingly inebriated blur would do him, as well as the cause he had just joined, serious harm, then he would take the doctor's advice.

He spent several days in pleasantly idle recuperation, regaining his strength, reading and sleeping a great deal. And when he was well enough, Gerrit helped him to dress, and he sat at the table in his chamber, with his little inlaid writing desk before him, and took out Phoebe's letter.

Until he held the evidence in his hand once more, and knew that his memory had not played him false, he had hardly dared to believe that it was true. Louise had given birth to their daughter, on the second day of June, nearly four weeks ago now: and according to his sister, both mother and child were in excellent health.

Today, almost recovered from the debilitating effects of the fever, he could confront the implications of the baby's

218

birth in a more calm and rational frame of mind. It was pointless to yearn for the past. He must accept, once and for all, that although he and Louise were joined together in matrimony until death sundered them, they could never again live together as man and wife. Despite what he had done to her, he loved and respected her too much to contemplate forcing his presence, or his attentions on her for a second time against her will. He hoped that the child would survive, and that her arrival had given Louise some small consolation for the end of her marriage. And since the baby was a girl, she would not tie his wife to Somerset, and Wintercombe: if Louise wished to return to France with her daughter, she could leave the turbulent St Barbes with a clear conscience.

But although Wintercombe would never pass to Kitty, she would still inherit a considerable fortune at Alex's death, made up of those parts of his estate, mainly in and around Frome, Bristol, Wells and Mendip, that were not subject to entail. The rest, Wintercombe and those lands lying immediately about it, would go to his nearest male heir. And Charles, anticipating events somewhat, was already in possession.

In view of the deep and bitter mutual loathing which he shared with his cousin, Alex was surprised that the news had not affected him more. It was as if, by leaving Wintercombe that night, he had forfeited all rights to the home that was his inheritance. Even if Louise returned to France, he did not think that he would ever go back. He could not deviate from his path now: his future lay in Holland, or beyond it, and he would no longer waste his time in futile regrets, for that way, as the poet had said, lay madness.

No, Charles could have Wintercombe and all within it, even the beautiful horses on which he had once lavished such love and care, and which he had intended to form the foundations of a breed unequalled in Somerset, or indeed in England. He would even abandon his magnificent grey stallion Pagan to the tender mercies of his cousin, who had no interest whatsoever in anything equine.

Alex smiled wryly to himself. At this moment, the loss of his favourite horse caused him more regret than Charles's illegal occupation of Wintercombe.

The ancient and lovely house where he had been born, small and yet rambling and inconvenient, seemed very remote now, and irrelevant to his life here in Holland. Charles was welcome to it: for if Alex could not share Wintercombe with Louise, and their children, he did not want it at all.

# Chapter Twelve

## 'Possession of his just estate'

'Isn't she delightful?'

Phoebe had as much interest in babies as she had in most female and domestic matters: in other words, very little. She looked at her niece's replete face, with a dribble of regurgitated milk emerging from the corner of her mouth, and said with heartily false enthusiasm, 'Of course she is.'

Louise glanced up at her, and grinned. 'Liar,' she said affectionately. 'All babies look alike to you – wailing at one end and messy at the other. Your interest in Kitty will only begin when she's capable of holding a pen and learning Latin.'

Phoebe laughed. 'You exaggerate – a little. I confess I have few maternal instincts, but I do find her quite diverting at times – and as fascinating as a seedling, when you have no idea what it will grow into.'

'She'll inherit the worst traits of both parents, I suspect,' Louise said, looking down at the baby who was now the light of her life. Sometimes, her love for Kitty seemed to overwhelm her, so powerful it was almost suffocating: and with love had come the darker side of the coin, the fear that all mothers knew, even if they did not openly acknowledge it. So many babies died, so many children. She herself had lost Nathaniel, and had nearly run mad with grief, although she had known in her heart from the beginning that he was doomed.

But Kitty was so very different: a sturdy, healthy, solid child with deep creases around her chubby wrists and ankles, an insatiable appetite, and a smile that already seemed designed to captivate everyone who saw her. She had survived, with robust success, the first hazardous

221

weeks of life, and Louise had begun, daringly, to admit to herself that Kitty might be destined to live a while longer.

The baby was asleep now, and she tucked the shawl closer around her and handed her back to the nurse, Betty, a kind and cheerful Bath girl with plenty of experience of looking after babies (she had eight younger brothers and sisters, all living). As Kitty was carried tenderly away to her nursery upstairs, Louise rearranged her chemise and the loose informal robe which she wore in the house when company was not expected.

She had been very eager to nurse the baby herself, and Doctor Peirce thoroughly approved her unfashionable decision: there was no food better for babies, he had said with avuncular satisfaction, than a mother's own milk. At first, Louise had enjoyed the closeness thus encouraged between her and her daughter, but now, more than two months after the birth, she was beginning to find the necessary restrictions on her life a little irksome. It was summer, if such a wet and stormy season, all extremes of rain and wind, heat and thunder, could be dignified by such a description, and Bath was full of company. She was young, after all, and the contented lethargy that had accompanied her pregnancy, and lingered through the weeks immediately after Kitty's birth, was beginning to drain away. She had still not recovered her former reckless vitality, though: oh, she would dance again, and laugh, and ride, but never with the wild joy which she had experienced before the loss of Nathaniel, and of Alex.

'You seem pensive.'

Phoebe's voice broke in on her thoughts, and Louise looked up with a hasty smile. 'Perhaps. I was thinking that the time has come to find a wet nurse for Kitty, or to begin weaning her. I would like to be able to go *out* occasionally, without worrying about whether she needs me. The season is halfway through, and I am beginning to feel like a Mohammedan's wife, immured for ever behind high walls.'

'Good,' Phoebe said at once. 'I never thought that complete domesticity was quite your style. Kitty is thriving, and will continue to do so under the care of some kind

222

and reputable wet nurse, I feel sure. And did you know that the Queen plans to take the waters here, very soon? Perhaps the King, too.'

'No, I didn't.' Louise found interest, even excitement, waking in her mind. A royal visit meant courtiers, dancing, entertainments: the gentry for miles around would descend on the city to kiss the monarch's hand and pay their respects, and shopkeepers always made a particular effort to stock up with tempting luxuries. The latest fashions would be on parade, and an air of festival would pervade the streets.

And a certain Gentleman of the King's Bedchamber would doubtless appear at the house in Nowhere Lane, to open another chapter in his curious relationship with Phoebe.

She looked up at her sister-in-law, and saw, as if for the first time, that she had put on a little weight recently. The dowdy black gown did not hang so loosely, and there was even a trace of colour and some plumpness in her cheeks. With sly mischief, Louise said casually, 'Have you had a letter from Sir Hugh?'

'Yes, I have – one arrived this morning, as a matter of fact.' Phoebe sat down in the windowseat, overlooking the tiny bare patch of ground that was all her house could boast in the way of a garden. 'And – I have a confession to make.'

Her voice was not in the least light-hearted. Louise stared at her, feeling her heart begin to beat a little faster. 'Yes?' she said.

'Just after Kitty was born, I wrote to Alex. It was evident that you had no wish to contact him, and I thought that it was only fair that he should know that he has a daughter.' She stopped, frowning, and added with exasperation, 'Don't look at me like that, Louise! Whatever he did, and I know that it was appalling, he is not a monster, and he loves Lukas. Did you really want to keep him in ignorance of Kitty's existence?'

'No,' Louise said at last, very quietly. 'No – I didn't.' She sighed and looked up, her chestnut eyes full of sadness. 'I'm sorry, Phoebe. I know I should have written to him months ago – but I couldn't bring myself to do it. Can you understand? I don't want to see him again – and I was afraid that if I wrote to him, especially if I told him that I was pregnant, he would come back to me. And . . .'

'Don't you want that?' Phoebe prompted gently.

'No! I couldn't bear it – I'm happier now!' Louise said fiercely. 'I have Kitty, I have my freedom – I don't want to let him back into my life, and allow him to hurt and betray me all over again.'

'Then you must still love him,' Phoebe said, studying her with a shrewd and perceptive eye.

Louise flushed. 'No – no, I can't! Phoebe, I didn't want to tell you this, but it seems I must. He didn't just hit me that night – he raped me, too, he used me like a common whore, and I can never forgive him for it – *that* was the betrayal, not that Burton woman. I might have forgotten her, given time, but to force himself on me . . .' She shivered suddenly. 'It tainted everything that had gone before, somehow – all the love, the affection, the tenderness – all false. How *can* I love him, after that?'

'I don't know,' Phoebe said, shocked despite herself. She had never harboured any illusions about her brother's vices, but she had not thought him capable of raping the woman he apparently adored. Belatedly, she realised that she had done Louise an injustice. There was indeed little chance of a reconciliation after such a brutal violation of love and trust.

'I'm sorry,' she added, rather inadequately. 'I didn't realise – I should not have written behind your back.'

'It doesn't matter,' Louise said, with an air of unhappiness that suggested that in fact it did matter, very much. 'You are right, as usual. He should know about Kitty. And I do have some feelings for him still, loath though I am to admit it – I must, or I would not fear that he could hurt me. I have tried and tried to extinguish it – I have hated myself for it. But I cannot deny that if he came back, my first reaction would be joy.'

'And your second?'

Louise smiled wryly, and spread her hands in a very

224

Gallic shrug. 'I fear that I would call him every name under the sun, in at least three languages. And then . . . I suspect that I would fall into his arms.' She gave a bitter laugh, tears sparkling suddenly in her eyes. 'Phoebe, what is wrong with me? Why can't I hate him? Why do I still dream of him almost every night, and wake weeping for him? Why do I watch Kitty, and see how like him she is, and rejoice in it? Why, oh why do I find it impossible to forgive him, and yet I can't forget him?'

'Because he's Alex,' Phoebe said rather grimly. 'I have had similar problems, though not to such an extent, all my life. He attracts people like moths to a flame, and when their wings are singed and their hearts broken, they still return for more. But in time, perhaps your hurt will heal – and certainly Kitty will help.'

'I hope so,' Louise said bleakly. She fiddled with the ribbons decorating the front of her robe. 'But I feel for the first time that I am in control of my life now. I may be alone, but I have Kitty, I can manage my own affairs perfectly well. I am content, Phoebe – it is all due to the baby, I know, but I have survived, and I can start my life again, sadder perhaps, but wiser too. If Alex returned . . . he would disturb everything, set everyone at odds again – I would be buffetted about like a ship in a storm, and Kitty would be the first to suffer.'

'It might not happen like that,' Phoebe pointed out. 'Louise – I said that I had written to Alex. I haven't had the chance to add that with Hugh's letter this morning came his reply.'

'Alex? Alex has written to you?' Louise had flushed again, revealingly. 'What – what does he say?'

'Very little – he's not exactly verbose,' Phoebe told her. She pulled a rather crumpled piece of paper from the pocket of her gown, unfolded it, and read in the dry, unemotional tone that usually disguised somewhat stronger feelings:

Dear sister,
    I thank you for your letter. Please convey my hearty congratulations to Louise upon the birth of our

225

daughter, and tell her also that she need have no fear of ever seeing me again. As to our cousin, he may enjoy Wintercombe as he pleases, since he remains my heir. If I cannot live there with Louise, I have no desire to live there at all. I have written also to Philip Cousins, to tell him of my wishes. You may therefore cease your efforts on behalf of your ungrateful brother,

Alexander St Barbe

There was silence after she had finished. Outside, a pigeon cooed gently, and Phoebe could hear, more distant, Betty singing a lullaby upstairs. She looked at Louise, and saw, without surprise, that she was struggling to suppress tears. She said gently, 'He still cares for you very much, I know. Why not write to him?'

'I told you why not!' Louise cried. 'I don't want him to make me unhappy again!' And with a sudden whirl of furious energy, she leapt to her feet and ran from the parlour.

Phoebe sighed, folded up the letter, and replaced it in her pocket. She had no doubt that, eventually, Louise would allow her heart to overrule her head, and contact Alex. But she thought with anger of what her brother had done to his wife, and of his hardly less despicable affair with Charlotte Burton. Louise might admit at last that she wanted him back: Phoebe was certain that Alex wanted to regain his wife's love. But did he deserve it?

The answer must surely be in the negative.

And yet, and yet . . . he was her brother, and despite everything, she had still some concern, even some affection for him. Perhaps he had learned something from the consequences of his appalling behaviour, although in view of the fact that he was now thirty-one, and apparently set in his dissolute ways, she rather doubted it.

So why, then, did she hope so much that he would one day be reconciled with his wife, when for Louise's sake she was tolerably certain that it could only be a tragic mistake?

But his uncharacteristically spineless capitulation,

handing Wintercombe over to his bitterest enemy, had made her incandescent with rage. Charles deserved to have charge of such an important, cherished and valuable possession even less than did Alex, if that were possible.

Louise had taken refuge with Kitty in her nursery, so Phoebe put on her outdoor tippet and with her maid Mattie in attendance, marched round to Philip Cousin's house in Westgate Street.

He had received his own letter from Alex, somewhat more detailed than hers: and there was, he told her unhappily, nothing he could do. Her brother's instructions were lucid, and quite explicit. It did not seem as if he had taken leave of his senses.

'He must have been drunk, then,' was Phoebe's caustic comment. 'Philip, for God's sake, this is *Wintercombe* he's handing to Charles on a platter, not some worn-out piece of family silver! You know what Charles did, what he's like – why should he enjoy his ill-gotten gains at Alex's expense?'

'Because Sir Alexander seems to want it,' said Cousins, with gloomy resignation. 'Believe me, I can't understand it either, but his wishes are quite clear, and I cannot in all conscience ignore them, much as I would like to.' He looked up at Phoebe, his face grim. 'And I, as a slightly more detached observer, might add that this situation may well not continue for ever. What if your brother changes his mind? Or if he and his wife are reconciled, and a son is born? Unless we are all very careful, I can easily foresee endless years of lawsuits and bitterness, and the riches of Wintercombe sucked away in the process. Many a family that once was wealthy has been beggared by such disputes. And in my experience, there is no feud so bitter, or prolonged, or unnecessary, as that between kin.'

'As I have good cause to know,' Phoebe pointed out. 'Philip, there must be *something* we can do. Surely Charles can't be allowed to get away with such barefaced theft?'

'We cannot go against your brother's wishes,' Cousins repeated unhappily. 'Even if he later changes his mind, and decides to return.'

Phoebe's face had become suddenly thoughtful. She

pondered for a moment, and then smiled. 'I have an idea. It might not work, and there is also the chance that Charles will notice it. But we can't sit tamely by and do nothing, and at least our consciences will have been salved, a little. If Alex stays in Holland permanently, so be it – that is his choice. But if he does ever change his mind, and wish to return, perhaps if you can do this it will be easier to put things right.'

'Tell me,' the lawyer said: and a slow, delighted smile dawned on his face as Phoebe described to him, in devious detail, exactly how Wintercombe might be saved for Alex, after all.

Charles St Barbe stood in the gravelled courtyard that lay outside the north front of his home, and breathed a deep sigh of satisfaction.

He had won. After all the grief and pain of the past two years and more, he had finally turned the tables on his cousin. Alex was in exile, permanently, and Charles was in full and legal possession of Wintercombe.

The news had been brought that morning by the family lawyer, Philip Cousins. Charles had never liked the man, who knew altogether too much about events in the past, and whose face always seemed so hostile and disapproving when speaking to him, and he had found it impossible to contain his delight at Cousins's discomfiture. After months spent fruitlessly trying to eject Charles from his rightful home by due process of the law, he had had the ground sliced from under his feet with a vengeance by Alex himself. Through stiff lips that indicated that he was bitterly aware of the humiliation, he had curtly informed Charles that he had received a letter from Sir Alexander St Barbe, stating that he did not intend ever to return to England, far less his ancestral home. Therefore, Charles should be confirmed in possession of it, and the revenues from the entailed portion of the estate paid to him for his use in their entirety, as if he were the owner. The moneys from Alex's other possessions, Cousins had added, were to be divided, some to maintain him in exile, the rest to support his estranged wife and his daughter Katherine.

'I don't believe it!' Charles gazed in stupefied joy at the lawyer, who by now was looking thoroughly miserable. 'Have you got his letter? Show it to me!'

With bad grace, Cousins handed it over. There was no doubt whatsoever about the thick, sprawling hand, unquestionably that of Alex. Nor were the contents in the least ambiguous. Even so, Charles read the letter three times, just to make absolutely sure, before handing it back. Smiling broadly, he said, 'No, there seems to be no doubt about it – his instructions are quite explicit. Have you brought the deed with you?'

'I have it here, with a copy for Sir Alexander.' Cousins's assistant, a thin young clerk, pulled the parchments from his bag. The precious document was, to Charles's secret relief, written in English, in an ornate hand, with many 'wheretofores' and 'notwithstandings'. He skimmed briefly through it, seeing in the convoluted legal phrases the final proof, the confirmation that he had defeated Alex, that right had triumphed over might, and that Wintercombe was his.

The butler, Twinney, was called in as a witness, along with the young clerk, and Charles put his neat, painstaking signature at the foot of both copies, just above that of Cousins, who had signed as Alex's legal representative. Wax was heated, the seals impressed, and the parchment lay in Charles's tender hands, the key to his happiness, the most valuable thing he had ever held.

He was pointedly and condescendingly gracious to Cousins, his defeated enemy, offering him wine, refreshments, even dinner. The lawyer politely declined, with an expression that indicated his urgent desire not to remain at Wintercombe one moment longer than was absolutely necessary. Charles escorted the two men to the door, his delight spilling over, a broad smile cracking his face. He was about to bid Cousins goodbye when he remembered something. 'And how has my cousin Phoebe received the news that Wintercombe is now legally mine?'

'With commendable equanimity, sir,' Cousins said coldly, and rode away from Wintercombe in some haste, as if to stay longer would somehow expose him to an unpleasant infection.

He was exceedingly grateful to Phoebe. He loathed the thought of Charles at Wintercombe quite as much as she did, and her solution to the problem was simple and, knowing her cousin, quite likely to succeed. It had been surprisingly easy to insert, amongst the dense and complicated language that the conventions of the law demanded, a brief clause to the effect that the transfer was to be reversed immediately if, at any time in the future, Alex wished to reclaim his inheritance, and that Charles was permitted to enjoy Wintercombe and its fruits only by the continued good will of his cousin.

And, as Phoebe had predicted, and hoped, Charles had been much too amazed and delighted to give the precious document more than a cursory glance. Alex's intentions, so plainly stated in his letter, had been proof enough: Charles would certainly never imagine that Cousins, whom he seemed to regard as someone slightly more elevated than a hired lackey, would presume to insert his own safeguards into the deed. He might reread it at his leisure, but the lawyer doubted it: and meanwhile he had the copy, signed, witnessed and dated at the same time as the original, as incontrovertible proof. If Alex ever returned to reclaim Wintercombe, Charles would have to give it up.

In view of the man's infuriating and self-righteous smugness, Philip very much hoped that Alex would come back.

There was one member of the St Barbe family, of course, who would be much concerned to hear the news from Wintercombe. Both Phoebe and Louise, however, had decided to give Silence a heavily edited account of recent events. Chard was a long way from Bath, and they knew very well that if Charles's usurpation, with or without Alex's consent, became known to her, she would instantly set out, despite her age and increasing infirmity, to mend matters between the younger members of her warring family. Louise shrank from the prospect of explaining to Silence exactly what Alex had done to her: and without that knowledge, her grandmother would never understand the depth of the estrangement between them, or the impossibility of any reconciliation. She would certainly try to eject Charles, to persuade Louise to travel to Holland and submit to her husband, she would try to make everything at Wintercombe as cosy and safe and peaceful as it once had seemed.

And Louise knew that the pattern had changed for ever. She did not want to witness the unhappy and humiliating spectacle of her beloved grandmother attempting the impossible, and probably wearing herself into the grave in the process. She had written to Silence to tell her of Kitty's birth, and that she was at present staying with Phoebe in Bath: and from the warmly congratulatory message she had received in return, she hoped that for the moment Silence was content with such limited information.

Eventually, of course, she would find out that Alex had deserted her granddaughter: but by then, Louise hoped that the wounds would be less raw and painful. And, of course, there was always the possibility that she would take Kitty to see her own mother, in France.

But despite her defiant words to Phoebe, she could not rid herself of the growing sense that her stepfather's lovely, gracious château was no longer her home. Home was Wintercombe, even with Charles in possession: home was the narrow, jostling streets of Bath, and the round, high green hills of Somerset, that cupped the city all about like a sheltering hand. She thought in English now, not in French: only her olive skin and a certain flamboyance of dress still marked her out as foreign, for her Gallic accent had all but vanished, to be replaced, as Lukas delighted in telling her, by a distinct Somerset burr. She still occasionally found herself longing wistfully for French conversation, French manners, French elegance: but it was three years since she had said goodbye to her mother and gone in search of an English husband. If she returned to France, Kate would not fuss, or interfere, or even ask awkward questions, but so much had happened in those three years, and Louise knew that she had grown up, and apart, and away from her own family.

231

No, she realised now that she wanted to stay in Bath, with Phoebe, if her sister-in-law did not mind: it was not always easy to guess at her feelings, but Louise was sure that, so far, she had not outstayed her welcome. Indeed, since Libby had recently returned to her parents in Bristol, and Lukas, much to his delight, had begun to attend the Free School, she thought that Phoebe welcomed her company.

As for the future, she could not think of it yet: it was enough to live from day to day, watching her daughter grow. But Alex had ensured that she would be well provided for, so she had plenty of money at her disposal, and could afford to rent a house for herself, if necessary. She had found a most satisfactory wet nurse for Kitty, a kind and ample woman who lived just round the corner. And she found herself contemplating the visit of the King and Queen and their Court, only a few days distant now, with a sense of pleasurable anticipation.

Charles, confirmed in possession of Wintercombe, was also looking forward to the King's imminent arrival in the West Country. His Majesty's interest in military matters was well known: indeed, there were many grumbling voices who complained that King James had made an excellent soldier and should have stayed one, rather than trying to rule the country with the limited talents, both his own and other people's, at his disposal. Charles, who admired the King for his devotion to order and authority, and to the Roman Catholic religion which they shared, took no notice of such mildly seditious talk. James would probably be eager to view the site of the skirmish that had been fought at Philip's Norton during Monmouth's rebellion, two years previously. While in the village, he would undoubtedly need to dine, or at the least take refreshments. What more suitable host than the new, and Catholic, owner of Wintercombe, unquestionably the finest house for miles around?

Unfortunately, the only courtier he knew was Sir Hugh Trevelyan, who had been such a good friend to Alex when he was under threat of trial for treason. Charles could

232

expect no favours from him. But Amy's father-in-law, Berkeley Carne, proved most helpful, and suggested that he write to Father Petre, a Jesuit who was universally loathed by English Protestants, both for his fanatical devotion to his religion, and for the fact that he was the King's confessor and apparently wielded enormous influence behind the scenes. Alternatively, a friendly ear at Whitehall might be found in the person of Henry Jermyn, now Lord Dover, who was a Catholic convert and had been close to the King for many years.

Charles, who had been born into his faith, and suffered for it, had little time for courtiers who converted, no doubt, for reasons that had more to do with personal advancement than personal conviction. However, he swallowed his contempt and wrote properly humble and effusive letters to both men, stressing his loyalty to the King and to the Catholic Church, and praying for the opportunity to kiss His Majesty's hand on the field of an important conflict during the late rebellion.

Then, with golden vistas opening before him, Charles rode into Bath to spend money. After a lifetime of scrimping, it was wonderful to order three or four new suits in fine silks and satins, a dozen neckcloths and shirts of the most expensive Holland linen and Bruges lace, shoes, canes, hats and, most important of all, two periwigs in the most extravagant style, with long ringlets down the back, and of a fairness to match his own hair. Charles had worn a wig for years, but his present one was no longer in the latest style, and looked a little tired and old beside the imposing confections which adored the heads of the fashionable gentlemen thronging Bath at the height of the season. Supremely conscious of the link between status and apparel, he had always scorned the slovenly style of dress which Alex affected, and still more the eccentricity of wearing his own hair, like a tradesman or a Dissenter.

Emerging from Bath's most expensive tailor, lighter in pocket by several hundred guineas, Charles felt a vast sense of self-satisfaction. When the King came to Philip's Norton, as he surely must, he would be welcomed by a

233

gentleman of his own faith, strenuous in his loyalty to the crown, and dressed as fine as any courtier. James notoriously favoured Catholics, and he wanted to promote men of that religion to positions of responsibility all around the country. No longer did prospective Justices have to swear allegiance to the Church of England, and a magistracy was the least of Charles's ambitions. He was young, able, and an efficient administrator. His work in Ireland had been excellent, and he knew that it had been noticed. He rode home dreaming of positions at Court, a title, all the wealth and influence which could now be his for the asking, and never once thought of Louise.

He was greeted by Bab with the enthusiasm that always inspired, in the reserved Charles, a certain uneasy discomfort. She adored him, her faith in him had made the year of his exile almost bearable, and she had instilled in him an unshakeable belief in his own worth and the righteousness of his cause, but he still found her overwhelming. Nor did he like being kissed and fondled as if he were still a little boy, while Twinney and the other servants hovered, smirking behind their hands.

He had eventually given in to her entreaties, and had installed his mother at Wintercombe some months previously, with guilty reluctance. It had been so much more convenient, and liberating, to have her eight miles away in Bath, to be visited once a week. Sharing Wintercombe's rambling space with her was suffocating and restricting in the extreme, and he was often forced to hide his growing irritation. He owed her everything, after all, and it smacked of base and unfilial ingratitude to keep her away from the home she had never wanted to leave.

Signs of her touch and taste were everywhere: like her son, Bab enjoyed spending money on display, and relished luxuries like gold-embroidered cushions, fine silver, costly oriental porcelains, fashionable French pictures of improbable landscapes. A good proportion of Wintercombe's yearly income had already been lavished on its refurbishment, and now Bab was talking about rebuilding the medieval house in the latest classical style. Charles, who loved Wintercombe as it was, and who had already been alarmed by the swags of rose-coloured drapery that seemed to festoon every window, had been obdurate in his refusal. Besides, their income would not support it. If he had been able to command the revenues from the rest of the estate, it might have been possible, but Alex had kept those for himself, and for Louise and the daughter he had never seen.

That did not stop Bab dreaming, aloud, of the splendidly ostentatious mansion she would like: nor of the grandchildren she hoped would inherit it. And Charles, having attained part of his heart's desire, found himself increasingly frustrated by the fact that Alex, though in exile, was inconveniently still alive. Until he died, Louise would not be free to marry again: and Charles wanted no other wife.

In idle moments, he had wondered about hiring an assassin, but the difficulties and dangers of such a step were enough to discourage him. Still, there was no harm to his soul in praying fervently, every night at his devotions, that his wicked and dissolute cousin would soon drink himself into a well-deserved early grave. God was on Charles's side, and, sooner rather than later, God would surely oblige.

'A letter came for you this afternoon, dearest,' his mother said now, with eager curiosity. 'Brought by a servant in livery, all the way from London! Could it be news of the King's visit, perhaps?'

Charles hastily hushed her. He had wanted to keep his hopes secret, in case something went wrong, for he had no wish to be the subject of amused and pitying gossip in his household, or in the village. But too late: he heard the curious, eager whispers as he led his mother to the privacy of the winter parlour, overlooking the garden, so that he could peruse the letter away from prying eyes.

Father Petre had written with gratifying warmth, welcoming Charles's protestations of loyalty and devotion, hailing him as a standard-bearer in the holy army of Catholics who, few as yet, would undoubtedly soon grow to irresistible proportions and return this schismatic and unfortunately heretic country to the Faith. As for the invitation to Philip's Norton, His Majesty had already expressed a wish to view the battlefield, and would undoubtedly, all being well, include a visit in his crowded itinerary.

It was not a promise, but there was no doubt in Charles's mind. Many years before, the wife of the first King James, Anne of Denmark, on an excursion from Bath, had dined at the Manor Farm, and the chamber where she had rested was still pointed out, with superior pride, as the Queen's. Now Charles, head of the St Barbe family for a scant six or seven months, had achieved a royal visit to Wintercombe, to be remembered for generations to come.

In a mood of quiet but fervent elation, he began to plan, with Bab's enthusiastic help, the lavish welcome which they would extend to King James and his entourage.

On Thursday, the eighteenth of August, 1687, King James the Second entered Bath in state, to be greeted by his Italian wife, Mary of Modena, who had arrived in the city the previous day. The church bells had been ringing since daybreak, in joyous anticipation: His Majesty might be regarded with dislike and mistrust in some quarters, but a royal visit was undeniably an excellent excuse for a celebration, and the Mayor and Corporation would spare no expense. The way was scattered with sweet-smelling herbs, flags and banners decorated almost every house, and the streets were lined with cheering citizens, enjoying the respite from their normally humdrum lives, and shouting 'God save the King!' until they were hoarse. They were rewarded by an almost endless stream of gilded, painted and resplendent coaches, carrying the courtiers. The King's, naturally the most magnificent of all, was escorted by the soldiers of His Majesty's Lifeguard, tricked out in red coats with gold and silver lacing, and their prancing glossy horses, matched for size and colour, had bright ribbons woven into their manes. Above them, the crimson damask colour of the troop was heavy and glittering with bullion.

The King was welcomed at the Guildhall by the Mayor

and Corporation, and there were several flattering and laudatory speeches, presentations by local dignitaries, and a Latin oration composed and delivered by a pupil of the Free School, chosen both for his extreme youth, and for his precocious command of the language. And Louise and Phoebe, watching Lukas's moment of glory from the upper windows of the Guildhall, both felt enormous pride in his achievement, although tempered with a certain sadness that Alex could not see his son carry off the occasion with a clear and unfaltering voice, and enormous aplomb.

The King, a tall man with a rather long and lugubrious face, spoke very pleasantly to Lukas when he had finished, and gave him a purse of silver, explaining that it would pay his school fees for a few years at least, although His Majesty had added, with unwanted humour, that in view of Lukas's already remarkable erudition, the money might well prove unnecessary. Then the Queen gave him a kiss, which was not at all to the boy's liking. As he explained afterwards to his stepmother and his aunt, he was now eight, and too old for that sort of foolishness. 'And besides, she smelt so strongly.'

'She smelt?' Louise wrinkled her brow with amused perplexity. 'You mean, she hadn't washed?'

'Oh, no, she was clean enough, I suppose,' said Lukas. 'But so much rosewater and orris root – ugh!'

He looked affronted as both Louise and Phoebe burst out laughing. 'She was very pretty, though,' he added grudgingly. 'But she's so old!'

'She's not yet twenty-nine,' Phoebe pointed out. 'Hardly three years older than I am. Certainly not too old to bear another child, whatever anyone says.'

'So that's why she's come to Bath? She hopes to conceive an heir?'

'Of course she does, whatever the doctors say.' Phoebe looked at her nephew, who was still clutching the bulging purse which the King had presented to him. 'Why don't you put that down, and go see your friends? I doubt anyone will steal it here.'

'Very well, Aunt,' Lukas said, reluctantly. They

eventually persuaded him to exchange his best suit for one less vulnerable to energetic usage, and he hurried out to meet his schoolfriends, no doubt to tell them all about his encounter with royalty.

'To think it's little more than two years since he arrived at Wintercombe unable to read or write,' Phoebe said, as the street door banged unceremoniously behind her nephew. 'He's only been at the school for a few months, and yet Master Baker says that he already has the learning of a boy three or four years older. And, just as important in my view, he's well liked by the other pupils.'

'It's all due to the excellent grounding he has received from you,' Louise told her, smiling.

Phoebe shook her head. 'I claim no special gift. Teaching Lukas is like filling a dry sponge with water – he's so eager and apt to learn. Let's hope that he has inherited Alex's better qualities, as well as his intelligence, and not his vices.'

Louise was not given the chance to disagree, for the outer door had crashed open again, to admit her stepson, flushed and joyful. 'Look who I met by the Cross Bath!'

And with him, in the full dazzling splendour of his Court attire, topped with a wig that must have required several heads of hair for its construction, was Sir Hugh Trevelyan.

When the welcome had died down, he congratulated Lukas on his oration. 'You have the better of me, young man – my education was sadly deficient, and I regret to say that I could understand barely one word in three of your Latin.' To the boy's disappointment, he had not brought his son James with him, but had left him in Suffolk with his cousins. He accepted Phoebe's invitation to sup with them that evening, and was ushered into the best parlour, looking out on to Nowhere Lane, with its books neatly arranged on new shelves, and a set of upholstered and comfortable chairs in fashionable walnut. Lukas was persuaded to return to his friends, with the promise that he would be allowed to have supper with the adults that evening, and Louise and Phoebe settled themselves with a pot of chocolate and excellent cakes, to hear the latest news and gossip.

238

Louise still found it difficult to believe that the courtier harboured a more than friendly interest in her sister-in-law. Surely he would prefer some fine lady with a fat dowry and influential kin? But of course Phoebe was wealthy, although to look at her, shabbily dressed and living in comparative simplicity, one would never think so. And if the King should die, with a consequent change in the government, then Alex, with his Whig sympathies and undoubted ability, might well rise to a position of power.

If he could ever acquire a legitimate outlet for all that formidable intelligence and energy, it might be the making of him.

As if her thoughts had directed his, Sir Hugh mentioned his name. 'No, I have had no letter from Alex for some time. However, I have spoken recently with a man who met him in Holland, a few months ago. Have either of you heard of Tom Talmarsh?'

They shook their heads, and he went on. 'He's the second son of the Duchess of Lauderdale – she who was born Elizabeth Murray, and owns Ham House, a lovely place on the Thames near Richmond. Her first husband, before Lauderdale, was Sir Lionel Talmarsh, who had a fine estate in Suffolk, not far from my brother's house near St Edmundsbury. This Tom Talmarsh is nothing at all like his mother, who's a high-handed, greedy, meddling woman, addicted to politics and intrigue. He was in the army for a while – rose to be lieutenant-colonel in the Royal Fusiliers, then resigned last year in protest at Papists being encouraged in the army. He's hoping for a commission in one of the English regiments in the Dutch service – and came across Alex when he was in Amsterdam in April.'

'Where?' said Phoebe, in her usual direct fashion. 'Some sordid tavern?'

'Something of the kind, I believe,' said Hugh drily. 'And although Talmarsh implied to me that the meeting was accidental, I don't think that it was. He's well known to be a stalwart Whig, as Alex is, and meets with a group of like-minded men, mostly soldiers, in a tavern called the Rose, in Covent Garden.'

'I've heard Alex mention it,' Phoebe said. 'Hugh, what exactly are you saying? Is my brother up to his ears in conspiracy again?'

'Over his head, I would say,' he told her. He finished his chocolate, and set the fragile china cup, prettily decorated in blue and white, down on the table beside him. 'I don't know exactly what he has been doing, but he may be acting as a link between the Whigs still in London, and the Prince of Orange. And I did not have this from Talmarsh – he is exceedingly cautious and discreet, and I know that he does not trust me. After all, I owe my rise at Court to Henry Jermyn, who is now Lord Dover, and a notable Papist, very high in the King's favour. No, my information on your brother's activities came from Sunderland, the King's Secretary of State.'

There was a small ominous silence, as they digested the implications. Phoebe spoke first. 'So he's been up to all kinds of no good in Amsterdam, and Sunderland knows of it? Then there's small chance of him ever being able to return to England, even if he might want to.'

'Exactly,' Hugh said. 'I have written to Alex to tell him this, and to warn him. It is by no means unknown for the King's agents to try to abduct or even kill troublesome exiles – indeed, there was an attempt last year to snatch a man called Peyton from Rotterdam, and bring him back to face English justice. It was only foiled because he had had the foresight to become a citizen of the country, so the abduction was illegal, and they had to let him go. Alex, as far as I know, has no such protection, and I advised him to obtain it.'

'And where do you stand, Sir Hugh?' Louise asked curiously. 'We know you are a good friend, and you did Alex a signal favour in the past, but can we trust you? Or are you another of His Majesty's stalking horses?'

Phoebe was looking at her with some indignation, but Hugh grinned. 'Oh, I can understand your doubts, my Lady St Barbe. After all, I am apparently a loyal and valued member of the King's household, and it's hardly surprising that both you and Tom Talmarsh, not to mention several others, regard me with some suspicion. Shall I make a clean breast of it, and state my position quite honestly?'

'I'm sure that I, at least, would greatly appreciate it,' Phoebe said, with her usual dry irony. And Louise, looking from the magnificent courtier to the plainly dressed young woman who sat opposite him, realised suddenly that the two were, after all, exceedingly well matched.

'And I can, of course, rely entirely upon your total discretion?' he went on.

As Phoebe nodded, Louise rose and went swiftly to the door. There was no furtive spy lurking with ear pressed to the keyhole. Sir Hugh laughed as she sat down again. 'No eavesdroppers, I'm glad to say.'

'Good – for although I suspect my days at Whitehall may be numbered, I would not like to be dismissed earlier than absolutely necessary.' He paused to accept the second cup of chocolate that Phoebe had poured for him, and then continued. 'As I said earlier, I owe my position to Henry Jermyn, Lord Dover as he now is. He obtained a post for me as Gentleman of the Bedchamber to His Majesty when he was Duke of York some thirteen or fourteen years ago. I have only a small inheritance, although my late wife was something of an heiress, and this seemed to be an excellent opportunity to rise in the world. As indeed it has turned out – King James was most generous at his accession to the throne, and I have the lands and the knighthood to prove it. But despite this, I feel no especial loyalty to His Majesty. I may not be a religious man, but I am no Papist either, and I have some respect for the laws of the country. I do not like the way things seem to be going. And there has been a great deal of pressure on me, especially in recent months, to turn Catholic. I have refused, and intend to go on refusing: and sooner or later, the King will dismiss me, and replace me with one of his own faith.' He smiled cynically. 'Perhaps, who knows, even a certain Charles St Barbe. Did you know that he has invited the King to Wintercombe?'

'No, I didn't,' Phoebe said, after a startled pause. 'But, on reflection, it would certainly be in keeping with Charles's ambitions. He must think that being a Catholic

241

gives him a considerable advantage.' She smiled with rather bitter irony. 'Can you imagine Charles the Justice, Charles the Member of Parliament, even Charles the Courtier?'

'All too clearly,' said Louise. 'It seems so unfair – and yet Alex has handed Wintercombe over to him, it's all legal, and there is nothing we can do. He has almost everything he has ever desired – the wages of sin, it seems, are Wintercombe, and the King's favour.'

'Which, if he plays his cards aright, he will have in full measure,' said Hugh. 'His Majesty was apparently much impressed by his protestations of devotion, and has every intention of taking the opportunity to see the site of the skirmish at Philip's Norton, and inspect his most loyal subject in Somerset at the same time. He asked me if I knew the man.'

'And what did you say?' Phoebe asked, looking at him narrowly.

'I spoke the truth: that I had encountered him once, very briefly, under somewhat unfortunate circumstances, and that while I knew him to be a most devout Catholic, and a firm believer in the rule of law and the authority of government, I could not vouch for his more personal qualities. I'm afraid the King assumed that I was prejudiced against your cousin because of his religion, and refused to listen to further explanation.' Hugh coughed. 'I regret to say that His Majesty is not amenable to persuasion, once his mind is set on its course. And he suffers from the same fault as many of his subjects: save that when they look on a man and see only that he is a Papist, the King divides his court and his country into friends and heretics.'

'And Charles, of course, being Catholic, is his friend,' Louise said. 'And entertaining the King at Wintercombe will be the crown of his achievement. I am very glad that I won't be there to see it, or I would be sorely tempted to wipe the smug smile off his face with a cudgel.'

'I shall tell you how it goes, for I shall certainly be one of the party,' Hugh said. 'He plans to ride over to Philip's Norton tomorrow, or the day after, and he has already sent some of his household to Wintercombe, to arrange the visit.'

'Well, the villagers will enjoy it,' Phoebe pointed out. 'Most of them may be hostile to Papists, but they love a good show – like the people of Bath today.'

'And the King is eager to display himself in as good a light as possible, hence this Progress around the West. Although since his idea of courting popularity is to have Father Huddlestone preach a Papist sermon in every church they pass, I somehow doubt anyone will think the better of him for it. Well, I shall have to leave you now, and return tonight for supper. I am lodged with the King and Queen and the rest of their train in the Abbey House, and I think a barrel of herrings would be less tightly packed.'

At the door, as he took his leave, he gave them both an affectionate embrace. 'And remember this – I am still your good friend, and Alex's, and I will use what little influence I can, while I still have the chance. But I fear your cousin Charles is just the kind of man the King wishes to encourage – and dubious episodes in his past, even his occupation of Wintercombe, will count for little beside his loyalty and devotion to the King, and to the Catholic faith. Charles is a rising star, and I fear he knows it only too well.'

# Chapter Thirteen

## 'A fair behaviour, and a fluent tongue'

His Majesty King James the Second rode into Philip's Norton on Saturday, the twentieth of August, just before dinner time. He received with gracious waves of his hand the cheers of the villagers, their ranks swelled by a goodly proportion of the people of Wellow, Beckington, Farleigh, Hinton and even Frome, although that town in particular was a notorious nest of sedition and Dissent.

At the entrance to the village, more than two years previously, the soldiers of Monmouth's raggle-taggle army had erected a barricade and kept the might of the royal forces at bay for several hours. Here, the King was met by a party of local dignitaries: the vicar, Parson Pigott, a bent, white-haired old man who was so deaf he could only hear what was shouted directly into his ear: Master Flower, of the Manor Farm, a stout and respectable gentleman squeezed into a suit that had, all too obviously, been made for him when somewhat younger and thinner: and Charles St Barbe, the self-proclaimed lord of the manor of Wintercombe, to the north of the village.

Sir Hugh Trevelyan, in company with most of the other courtiers, was not used to long hours in the saddle, and had been silently cursing his royal master's enthusiasm for riding for some time. Still, it was undoubtedly quicker than a procession of coaches would have been, up and down the high hills between Bath and Philip's Norton, and His Majesty, in uxorious mood, was eager to return to his wife that evening. Hugh looked around curiously, seeing the substantial stone houses and well-fed, well-dressed people of a prosperous village. Despite what Phoebe had said about their devotion to the Protestant religion, their welcome seemed hearty enough. The sun shone, swallows and swifts

244

soared and swooped along the street and in the unfathomable blue of the sky, and down in the valley the ringers were earning their beer with a glorious cascade of bells.

Hugh had only once seen Charles St Barbe, on a dark December evening, just after his attempt to murder Alex. This confident gentleman, as sleek and well-groomed as a pampered cat, was so different from that wild-eyed, dishevelled and desperate man that he had to look twice before he was certain that they were, indeed, one and the same. His new authority and wealth, however ill-gotten, undoubtedly suited Alex's cousin: he was chatting with the King, indicating with generous sweeps of his arm the relative positions of the two armies who had fought here, while Master Flower, a little to one side, looked sulkily on.

As Hugh had suspected, Charles St Barbe was exactly the kind of man whom James held in high regard. He spoke to his sovereign with just the right mixture of flattery and deference, he was young, his apparel was impressively splendid, he was handsome, able, and an ardent Papist. By the time the royal party had toured the rest of the village, James had unbent as far as it was in his nature to do so, and was smiling and talking very warmly to Master St Barbe. Only one thing had, for a moment, dissolved his good humour, and that was the sight of the shrivelled, blackened remains of some of the twelve men hanged in the village for their part in Monmouth's rebellion. They had been there so long, almost a year, that most of the inhabitants no longer noticed them, and in any case, none of the grisly quarters and heads belonged to local people. Those few from Philip's Norton who had joined the rebels had escaped justice because the village constables, sympathetic to their situation, had mendaciously replied to the enquiries of the Sheriff, saying that no one they knew had been so wicked and foolish as to rebel against their lawful sovereign.

The King, however, was obviously more squeamish. With a frown, he surveyed the gruesome remnants, and then gave orders that they should be taken down at the first opportunity, and given decent burial. 'And I shall issue similar instructions to all the Justices in the West Country.

These good people have learned their lesson, I am certain. I feel sure that they are now my true and loyal subjects.'

There was a cheer from the onlookers at this, which the King acknowledged with another gracious gesture. And indeed, here in this quiet village, so typical of the thousands up and down the country, that doomed rebellion seemed in retrospect to be nothing more than a momentary aberration, a solitary flaw in the smooth, even, unchanging texture of the countryside. Yet Hugh Trevelyan, watching the confident smiles of the King and his host, knew that it was not: knew that, under the surface atmosphere of welcome and loyalty, there lurked a deep and abiding mistrust of James, his courtiers, and above all his Papist advisers. All seemed so peaceful: but how much would the people of England accept from this authoritarian and bigoted Catholic, before he goaded them once more into revolt?

At Wintercombe, the venerable stones were hung with banners and garlands, and the servants crowded the courtyard, cheering with sycophantic enthusiasm to welcome His Majesty and his entourage. Hugh was surprised by the comparatively small size of the place: it seemed humble and unassuming beside the spacious beauty of the house in Suffolk where he had been born, and where his half-brother Francis Heron now lived. Somehow, he had imagined that the Wintercombe over which the St Barbes had fought so bitterly, and which was the source of the family's wealth, would be much larger and more grand than this ancient, lovely and unpretentious house.

They were greeted by Charles St Barbe's mother, a monstrously fat woman wearing a quantity of jewels, paint and patches that would not have disgraced a Whitehall whore half her age. By her side, somewhat overawed, was her daughter, a very pretty girl, blushingly shy, and her new husband, one of the Carnes of Bath. Hugh knew that Edward Carne's elder brother, Francis, had been chosen by the King to be Master of the Free School in Bath. Apparently the Corporation, not to mention the pupils and their parents, were furious, for the existing Master,

246

William Baker, was a clergyman of impeccable learning and morals, and of course a Protestant. By the King's express command, this popular and respected man was to be ejected against the wishes of the people of Bath, to be replaced by a young man – Francis Carne was only just in his thirties – of little learning, less reputation, and, the crowning insult, a notorious Papist.

King James, to judge by his air of satisfaction, fondly imagined that his Progress into the West Country had endeared him to his subjects in these parts. If he continued to behave with such scant regard for their wishes, or for their natural prejudices, Hugh suspected that their good will and loyalty would soon be seriously strained. His Majesty's brother, the late King Charles, had had faults in plenty, but bigotry, stupidity and gross misjudgement had not numbered amongst them.

They dined in the Hall, a splendid feast: the fatted calf, not to mention pig, lamb, chicken and carp, had been killed for the delectation of His Majesty. The food was brought in by troops of maids and servants, all dressed in sky-blue livery with crisp white linen, evidently purchased specially for the occasion. To Hugh's experienced eye, this day must have cost Charles St Barbe a small fortune, not to mention the money spent on his own and his family's clothes: money that, in the view of Alex's sister, did not belong to him. Charles had laid out with a lavish hand, in full hopes of his due reward: and Hugh, who knew his royal master only too well, was certain that his investment would be amply returned.

Hugh was a cynical man: nearly fifteen years immersed in the glittering, sordid corruption of Whitehall could have had no other effect on him. But for a while now, he had been aware of a growing inward weariness, a rising distaste for the world in which he moved with apparent ease. He had no principles, and yet this overdressed, decadent, self-seeking company was beginning to bore, even to disgust him. A court at which men like Charles St Barbe could obtain approval and advancement was no longer to his liking.

I must be getting old, he thought ruefully. But he knew that, if he were not dismissed from the King's service, he would continue at Court. He might, in idle moments, hanker after the fresh green fields of Suffolk, innocent of corruption or intrigue: but he belonged at Whitehall as the carp on his plate had belonged in water, and would expire without it.

Besides, he owed it to Phoebe to do what he could for her brother. While he still had useful contacts and influence, he would employ them, discreetly and to the best of his ability, to thwart Charles's overweening ambition.

The King left Wintercombe replete, and well satisfied with the day's events. The tour round the village had been most illuminating and interesting, and the cheers of the inhabitants, simple peasants though they were, had greatly warmed and heartened him. And young St Barbe had fulfilled all his expectations: personable, devout, loyal, a man to be fostered and encouraged. If only, James thought with a sigh, there were more Catholics of his stamp spread across the country, his mission would be made so much easier.

Still, it would be a simple matter to reward St Barbe as he deserved. He was a little young and untried, as yet, for a court position, but experience of local responsibility, as a Justice of the Peace, would prepare him for the future. Of course, all men who aspired to such posts were obliged, by law, to swear their allegiance to the Church of England, and naturally no devout Catholic could comply. But he, the King, had the power to dispense with such requirements, and indeed had already done so several times, as part of his avowed policy to introduce Catholics to positions of authority. It would take as little to make Charles St Barbe a magistrate as it had done to appoint Francis Carne Master of the Bath Free School. And very soon, as more and more Catholics rose to prominence, and were seen by his suspicious and prejudiced subjects to be as capable and trustworthy as any Protestant, the hostility against them would dwindle away from lack of substance, and his dream of returning England to the true religion would be appreciably closer to reality.

It was not, alas, a dream shared by the majority of his people. And the good citizens of Bath, who were hardly famed for sedition or radical Dissent, were still more offended when their Abbey Church, on the day after the King's visit to Philip's Norton, was used to stage a display of Popish superstition. With great ceremony, James touched a procession of poor people to cure the King's Evil, a practice now regarded with some doubt by many physicians: and to make matters worse, during divine service Father Huddlestone, the Roman priest who had attended the previous King on his deathbed, preached a Papist sermon with missionary zeal. Those Catholics in the congregation, amongst them the King and Queen and a considerable proportion of their court, listened avidly, as did the Carne family, Charles St Barbe and his mother, and the other members of the tiny Romish community in Bath. The rest looked on with interest, or shocked amazement, or disgust, according to the degree of their prejudice.

Afterwards, many lingered outside the Abbey, or walked in the gardens, discussing what they had just witnessed. Lukas, who had a child's simplicity of belief, was outraged that a Papist ceremony should have been allowed to take place in a Protestant church, and his outspoken indignation turned several heads as they emerged into the bright sunlight outside the Abbey's ornate west front. Hastily, Phoebe hushed him. 'Not here, Lukas, not now. We can talk about it later, if you like, but for now I think it would be more tactful to hold your peace.'

Louise, dressed in her best summer mantua, in a strikingly striped yellow and white silk, had already noticed several pairs of masculine eyes lingering appreciately in her direction. Since giving birth to Kitty, her figure, once lean and almost boyish, had filled out considerably, and the demure lace of her tippet no longer fell almost flat from her shoulders. Enjoying her new freedom from maternal duties, she gave her stepson one of her dazzling, mischievous smiles. 'Shall we walk in the Abbey Garden,

Lukas? And perhaps we might even have time to go down by the river before dinner.'

'You will have to excuse me,' Phoebe said, as Sir Hugh Trevelyan, his face somewhat flushed, appeared at her side. 'I do not feel equal to a stroll this morning, even if the sun is shining, and I am sure that I shall be adequately escorted home. Dinner will be at eleven, and I shall see you then. Goodbye!'

Lukas and Louise watched as she was led away, supported by her stick and by Sir Hugh's stalwart arm, and grinned at each other. The couple were so wildly mismatched: Phoebe thin, limping, black-haired and plain, Sir Hugh tall, solidly built, and resplendent in a green suit heavily encrusted with gold lacing and buttons, topped by a vastly extravagant periwig. And yet, curiously, they did not look in the least comical together.

'My lady,' said Lukas, with the grave and charming formality which he could adopt at will, 'pray permit me to escort you to the gardens.'

'*Enchantée*, Monsieur van der Linden,' Louise said, laughing, and gave him her arm.

There was a man in the crowd who had been looking at her intently: she possessed an infallible instinct in such matters, and could sense the warmth of his regard. Careful not to give him open encouragement, she had risked no more than a brief glance at him, noting only that he was young, dark, and very fashionable dressed, with a short wig in the French style. Handsome, certainly, and once she would have been attracted to him.

More and more, she was realising that despite what he had done to her, and utterly against her wishes, she was still, somehow, in thrall to Alex.

She hated herself for such stupidity, she hated him even more for possessing such power over her even at this distance of months, and miles. But she suspected now, with anger and frustration and bitter regret, that no man would ever again engage her emotions, her heart and her soul, as Alex once had.

She put her thoughts firmly aside, determined to enjoy

the morning sunshine: it had been such a dreadful summer, often wet, windy and cold, that this bright warmth was a most welcome change. Lukas was, as usual, an entertaining companion, and it was not his fault that he bore such a heartbreaking resemblance to his father. She wondered if Alex as a child had been like this, and then smiled wryly, chiding herself for her foolishness. What hope of a fresh start, of any amusement in this glittering company, if she was still yearning, like a lovesick schoolgirl, for a man whom her mind, if not her heart, regarded with loathing?

'Oh,' Lukas said, in the middle of his chatter, and stopped dead.

A man stood in front of them, just at the entrance to the Abbey Garden, and for a moment, in the brilliance of the sunlight, and dazzled by the silver braid on his blue coat, she did not recognise him.

Then, she saw that it was Charles under the ludicrously elaborate wig. Involuntarily, her hand tightened on the child's, and Lukas glanced up at her, his sapphire-blue eyes anxious.

'Hullo, Lou,' said her cousin and the longing note of adoration in his voice made her heart sink. 'I hope you don't mind me meeting you here – I've been so looking forward to seeing you again.'

'Unfortunately, I can't say the same,' Louise told him, trying to make her tone as chilly and discouraging as possible. 'Now, if you would kindly excuse us, Lukas and I wish to continue our stroll in peace.'

Charles ignored her. His eyes, a rather protuberant grey-blue, rested imploringly on her face. 'We're cousins, Lou, if nothing else – there is no need for such coldness.'

'Is there not?' Louise drew herself up to her considerable height, and stared at him challengingly down her long nose. 'I do not wish to remind you why I should feel such hostility towards you, Charles, with half of Bath passing by us, but you surely cannot pretend that it is possible for us to be acquainted, let alone friends. Now please stand aside.'

'No, I will not!' His voice had risen a fraction, and Lukas's fingers tensed on hers. 'No, Lou – not until you've listened to me. Come back to Wintercombe – it's your home, you belong there. I'll make you more than welcome, I promise you, you won't have to live in that poky little house – '

'And what about Kitty? Will you welcome her, too?'

'Kitty?' Charles stared at her in bewilderment. 'Oh, yes, the baby. Well, you won't have her with you, will you? She's at nurse.'

His dismissive tone stung Louise's quick temper into life. 'Of course Kitty would be with me. Her nurse only lives round the corner from Phoebe's house, and I see her for several hours a day. Did you think I would forget her as readily as you seem to have done? She is my daughter, as well as Alex's, and wherever I go, so does she.'

Charles had flushed. 'But – I thought – '

'You thought that because Alex and I are estranged – which was *your* doing, and your horrible mother's – I would happily cast Kitty aside. Well, you're wrong, Charles – *you* may think her of no account, but I can assure you that I do not. And even if I did, I have no intention of ever again setting foot over the threshold of Wintercombe while you remain in residence.'

'Louise, please, don't be angry.' Charles was almost abject now, his eyes beseeching her. 'Wintercombe is mine, legally. Alex has given it to me. Face reality, Lou – he'll never come back, he'll live out his days in a drunken stupor in Holland, and we're all well rid of him. Forget him, Lou –forget him, and come back to Wintercombe.'

Impassioned, his voice had become rather loud, and several people had paused to stare with frank and dis-courteous curiosity. Lukas's normally pale face was rosy with embarrassment. Louise said furiously, 'You are flogging a very dead horse, Charles. Now, let us pass.'

He did not move, but stood there, stout and stubborn, blocking their path. To her dismay, she recognised several faces in the growing crowd around them: once more, the St Barbes would provide ample fuel for the gossip rife in Bath. With a sick feeling of rage and despair, she said, '*Please*, Charles. People are looking.'

'Is this – gentleman – bothering you, Madame?'

The voice was deep, smooth, and unmistakably accented. Louise turned to find the dark man who had been watching her earlier, his face a picture of well-bred concern.

'A little,' she said, surprised and suddenly worried. Such men of honour and fashion usually thought nothing of fighting duels on the flimsiest pretext, and however much she loathed Charles, she did not wish him to be fatally transfixed by some short-fused Frenchman. 'But pray do not trouble yourself, sir – he is my cousin, and means me no harm.'

'Really? Appearances would seem to suggest otherwise,' said her deliverer, with raised brows. 'But in any case, Madame, the question is academic – your cousin has gone.'

A stir in the throng of people indicated where Charles, thinking better of his stand, was elbowing his way into the Abbey Garden. Louise gave the Frenchman one of her most dazzling smiles, and saw his face light up in response. 'My sincerest thanks, sir. You intervened at a most opportune moment, and we are very grateful to you.'

'It was nothing, Madame – any true gentleman would have done the same.' He smiled, and bowed with elaborate courtesy. 'Edmond Everard, Madame, at your service. And you are Lady St Barbe, I understand.'

'I am – but how did you know?'

'Madame, a lady so enchantingly beautiful cannot remain anonymous, even in this city full of beauties. Permit me, please, to escort you in this lovely garden.'

She had Lukas with her for a chaperon, and besides, she was a married woman. Doubtless people would notice, but some of the Bath gossips would discuss her to her detriment even if she never stirred out of doors. And it was a long time since such appreciative masculine admiration had been directed at her, without complicating emotions attached.

She smiled at him. 'Of course, Monsieur Everard – I would be delighted.'

Lukas was looking rather doubtful as she gave the Frenchman her arm. Since Alex's abrupt departure, he had been almost comically protective towards her, as if trying to assume the role which his father had so brutally abdicated. She sent him a reassuring grin. 'How fortunate I am – now I have *two* handsome gentlemen to lead me!'

They made a leisurely circuit of the Abbey Gardens, attracting not a little attention from those strollers who had earlier formed an audience to her quarrel with Charles. Louise had never taken much notice of people who had nothing better to do than to gossip about her: indeed, like Alex, she often had the regrettable impulse to provide such scandalmongers with suitably shocking smoke for their fires. She smiled charmingly at an elderly, prune-faced widow, a near neighbour in Nowhere Lane, who was well known for her assiduous spreading of malicious rumour, and nodded to another, younger woman who was everyone's friend to their face, and a vicious foe to their back. Lukas stepped beside her with the grave reserve he always adopted in the company of strangers, and she was able to converse, in a most amusing way, with Monsieur Edmond Everard.

He told her that his family lived near Blois, and this provided an immediate link between them, for she had spent some time at a Protestant school in that city, a sore trial to her teachers. For three years now, she had thought herself English, she had English friends and had married an English baronet, and until this chance meeting she had felt only mild nostalgia for the country in which she had grown up. But it was not until she caught sight of Lukas's baffled, politely indignant expression that she realised that, without being aware of it, she had begun to talk in French. And of course Monsieur Everard, with great wit and fluency, had responded in kind.

Lukas was bilingual in Dutch and English, and his Latin was now extremely competent, but he knew as yet only the barest essentials of French. With a pang of guilt, Louise switched hastily back to her mother's tongue. 'Forgive me, Lukas – it is so long since I have been able to converse with someone from my own country.'

'But you are English now,' said her stepson, still with that faint look of hurt bewilderment.

'No French man – or woman – can ever lose their first attachment to the land of their birth,' said Everard, with a friendly smile at the boy. 'Just as you are English, and wherever you travel in the world, English you will remain.'

'But I'm not English,' Lukas explained, with that touch of pedantry that both Louise and Phoebe found so endearing. 'My mother is Dutch, sir – although my father is English.'

Louise realised, belatedly, that she had not introduced him. 'Lukas is my stepson, Monsieur Everard – my husband's son's.'

'His *natural* son,' Lukas said seriously, his wide, sapphire-blue eyes frowning at the Frenchman.

Louise realised suddenly that he did not like Monsieur Everard. It would be easy to dismiss it as the immature judgement of a child, but she loved the boy, and respected his feelings. She disengaged her arm from the Frenchman's, and said with a smile, 'I regret, Monsieur, that we must leave you now – we shall be dreadfully late for dinner as it is. But we are most grateful for your assistance this morning. Matters might have turned out very awkwardly, had you not come to our aid.'

'It was nothing,' Everard said, with that rather too handsome smile. 'And since my intervention has led to this very pleasant conversation, and to a better acquaintance with a most beautiful and charming lady, then I could dare to say, Madame, that I am glad that your cousin behaved so boorishly. *Au revoir*, Lukas – *au revoir*, my Lady St Barbe. I feel sure that we shall soon meet again, and I look forward to it eagerly.'

'And I also, Monsieur,' Louise said. There was an exchange of courtesies, he kissed her hand, and smiled at her, and walked away through the promenading Sunday morning crowds.

They were not, in fact, late for dinner, but walked back to Nowhere Lane quite quickly. For a long while, Lukas was silent, lost deep in thought: then, as they crossed Stall Street, he said suddenly, 'Louise – did you like that man?'

255

'Monsieur Everard? Yes, he seems most pleasant – and he certainly arrived at a very opportune moment.'

'I suppose so,' said Lukas, frowning.

'But you didn't like him? There's no law which forces you to like people, you know – I won't be upset if you don't.'

'Well . . . I didn't very much,' said her stepson at last. 'He seemed too – too smooth and slippery, somehow. All politeness and courtesy and nothing else, as if there wasn't anything *behind* him.' He gazed up at her with disarming honesty. 'I can't explain it any better, Louise – I just didn't *like* him.'

'Well, I can't personally see any reason, as yet, to *dis*like him,' she pointed out. 'So we shall just have to agree to differ. And I must say, it was wonderful to talk French to a Frenchman again. No doubt of it, few English people can speak the language without tearing the pronunciation to shreds.'

Lukas gave her a sudden grin that reminded her, with pain, of Alex. 'Including Aunt Phoebe?'

'Oh, Phoebe is the exception that proves the rule. She'd make sense of the Tower of Babel.'

He laughed at that, his usual good humour apparently restored. 'I'd like to learn more languages – I can't imagine anything worse than travelling in a foreign country and not being able to understand what people were saying. Will you teach me French, Louise?'

'Of course I will – but with school every day from six to five, and study at home besides, how will you find the time?'

'Oh, I'll find it,' said Lukas confidently. 'And after French, I'd like to learn Italian perhaps, and Spanish, and then German – I want to learn everything in the whole world!'

She could not laugh at him: his enthusiasm shone like a beacon from his face. She said, smiling, 'It'll take a lifetime, you know – several lifetimes.'

'I don't mind – trying hard is the important thing, Papa always says.' The life abruptly drained out of his face, and

256

he stared up at her with anguished eyes. 'Louise – is he ever going to come home?'

'I don't know,' she told him, with sad honesty. 'Oh, Lukas, I don't know.'

'Do you know where he is? I asked Aunt Phoebe and she said she didn't, but I don't think,' said Lukas miserably, 'that she was telling me the truth.'

'He may be in Amsterdam,' Louise said reluctantly, unwilling to compromise her sister-in-law. 'But we're not absolutely sure.'

'Could I write to him?'

She realised now that, in her own rage and despair after Alex's departure, both she and Phoebe had failed to appreciate the depth of Lukas's own sense of betrayal and loss. He had adored his father, and Alex had appeared to love him deeply. How must it feel to a child of eight, who had led a largely rootless, insecure and loveless existence, to have the one stable prop of his life abruptly withdrawn? He was mature, intelligent and sensible, and had coped admirably with his father's disappearance. Guiltily, Louise recognised that all his feelings must have been repressed, too successfully and for too long, behind the polite childish mask that had always served him well.

'I don't see why not,' she said, with an encouraging smile.

Sir Hugh was staying for dinner, and she somehow did not care to mention the unfortunate encounter with Charles, nor the timely intervention of Edmond Everard. Lukas, who had reverted to childhood after their curiously adult conversation on the way home, did not mention it either, but devoted himself hungrily to his food.

She thought about the handsome Frenchman. His dark good looks did not appeal to her, but his witty and amusing talk was much more to her taste. And she found herself wondering how soon, in the restricted public places of Bath, she would meet him again.

The King left the city the day after those unfortunate Papist ceremonies in the Abbey church, escorted by the gentlemen

257

of his court, Sir Hugh Trevelyan amongst them. He intended that this Progress would take him through the western and north-western parts of the kingdom, before returning to Bath in two weeks' time.

In his absence, the Queen settled down to enjoy her sojourn in the city, intent on presenting herself in as charming and unthreatening a light as possible. Every morning, attended by her ladies and several daughters of notable Bath citizens, she bathed in the waters of the Cross Bath, at the end of Nowhere Lane, while people crowded the gallery above to watch. After this public ceremony, she usually dined at her lodgings in the Abbey House, now rather less packed, and received all those local dignitaries, and their families, who were eager to wait on her and kiss her hand. Often she would be driven through the villages and hamlets in the hills and valleys around Bath, showing herself to her husband's subjects and, she hoped, impressing upon them an indelible picture of her smiling, gracious and undeniable beauty.

Even those who mistrusted her husband and all his works – and in this Puritan area of Somerset, there were many – professed themselves charmed by the Queen. Phoebe, however, was not so easily swayed. She had always despised those who uncritically worshipped royal pomp and display, and refused to join the crowds who gawped at the Queen, in her all-concealing canvas gown, immersing herself decorously in the warm, sulphurous waters that she hoped would help her to conceive the Papist heir for which she and the King, and few others, longed so much. Nor did Phoebe wish to attend Her Majesty as she strolled through the Abbey Gardens, or played dignified and tedious games of bowls with her ladies: indeed, she grumbled, with a morose misanthropy worthy of some crusty old hermit, that the Queen's presence had quite upset all her modest pleasures, since it was impossible to go anywhere in Bath without tripping over Maria Beatrice, her court, or a troop of sycophantic admirers.

With Phoebe in self-imposed seclusion, surrounded by books, and Lukas once more spending his days at school,

Louise was left much to her own devices. By now, after more than six months' residence in Bath, there were several acquaintances on whom she could call, women who could be greeted with amicable conversation when encountered in the gardens or in Kingsmead, or browsing along the crowded rows of shops in Cheap Street or Stall Street, but no one who could replace Phoebe as friend and confidante. She did see her cousin Amy several times, usually squired by her stalwart Papist husband. But she made obvious attempts to avoid Louise whenever possible, and when they did meet, face-to-face in the doorway of a mercer's shop, Amy blushed, muttered some polite greeting, and made a hasty withdrawal.

So there was, on the face of it, little opportunity for Louise to do more than hover on the edge of the social whirl in Bath, like a pauper child peering through the window of a baker's shop. But not for long: it was only a day or so after their first meeting that she again encountered Edmond Everard.

With her maid Christian as escort, she had been watching a match in progress between various members of the Queen's household, on the bowling green under the east windows of the Abbey. She noticed him amongst the crowd opposite where she stood, and in a few minutes he was by her side, bowing, and they were exchanging pleasantries like old friends, before lapsing once more into French.

Christian, of course, could not understand a word of it, but, unlike Lukas, she did not consider it a discourtesy. She walked a little way behind them, her sensible Somerset face a placid, emotionless mask, while her mistress jabbered away in an incomprehensible foreign tongue, and her gestures and mannerisms grew more gallically and expansively distant from English reserve as she talked.

And Louise, aware that already this meeting with Everard was bringing her into unknown and uncharted waters, was glad that her maid was loyal and discreet. Christian would not ask awkward questions, and would not gossip. Somehow, the thought of conducting even a harmless and amusing flirtation under the beadily disapproving stares of her husband's sister and her husband's son made her feel acutely uncomfortable.

But despite the small, wicked voice at the back of her mind, informing her that what was sauce for the gander should also, in fairness, be sauce for the goose, she had no intention whatsoever of embarking on an affair with the handsome Monsieur Everard. Smooth and slippery, Lukas had called him, and she sensed that he might be right. Nor did his darkly regular looks appeal to her, despite the dazzling whiteness of his teeth, and his exquisitely fashionable apparel. Alex, tall, slovenly yet impressive, possessed an arrogant, careless and wholly masculine beauty that seemed to have spoilt her for anyone else. But the Frenchman was excellent company, and as he escorted her again round the Abbey Garden, she slipped back into the past, to become once more the vivacious, witty and entrancing Louise who had flirted outrageously with half the aristocracy, young and old, in the Loire valley, and professed not a care in the world.

The old widow was there again, and gave the pair a very penetrating glare as she passed. Doubtless she had already consigned Lady St Barbe to that portion of Hell set aside for adulteresses. Louise favoured her with another wickedly wide smile, and a gracious inclination, worthy of the Queen herself, of her immaculately coiffured head.

'An acquaintance of yours, Madame?' Everard asked, with a raised eyebrow that perfectly indicated what he thought of the widow's primly pursed mouth, but was too well-bred to say.

Louise was tempted to giggle, but repressed it sternly. She said, with a light irony to match Everard's, 'No, Monsieur – I make her empty days more interesting, that is all.'

He smiled openly at that, his appreciation frank on his face. And Louise, who had once thrived on masculine admiration as a flower welcomes sunlight, tossed her head coquettishly with an archness that would have made Alex laugh out loud, and added, 'And you, Monsieur Everard? Do you also lead an – *interesting* life?'

She learned a little more about him, although he was not especially forthcoming, and she knew better than to give her curiosity full rein. He told her something of his family near Blois, confirming what she had suspected, that he was of the bourgeoisie, his father being in the legal profession. Edmond himself, a younger son, had had to make his own way in the world. He seemed equally at home on the fringes of the French Court and the English, although he was very vague about his precise function in such exalted circles. He had also, it seemed, travelled widely in Europe, and was familiar with Spain, Italy and, more surprisingly, Holland.

And it was in the course of this part of their conversation that he said suddenly, 'My pardon, Madame, if this question should seem impertinent – but your name is not a common one in England, and I must confess to some curiosity. While in Amsterdam, some months ago, I encountered an Englishman called, if I have it aright, Sir Alexander St Barbe. Has he some kinship with you?'

With considerable effort, Louise managed to conceal her reaction. She turned her chestnut eyes to his, and said coolly, 'He has, Monsieur. He is my husband.'

'Your husband!' The smooth, urbane Frenchman seemed almost disconcerned. 'But forgive me, Madame – I had assumed – I did not know that Sir Alexander had a wife. He did not seem – '

'To be the type of man who would be married?' said Louise, and despite all her care, a note of bitterness entered her voice. 'Well, Monsieur Everard, he is married to me. When precisely did you see him?'

He had recovered his poise. 'In April, I think it was, Madame. He had, if you will forgive me for saying so, acquired a considerable reputation in Amsterdam.'

'That does not surprise me,' Louise said drily. She had no desire to satisfy Everard's obvious interest in the unpleasant details of her brief marriage, but she found herself urgently, desperately hungry for news of Alex. And apart from those few curt communications with Phoebe, and the third-hand report originating from Thomas Talmarsh, this was all she had heard for nearly a year.

261

She managed to keep her face still and her voice light, and added, 'Where did you meet him?'

Everard coughed. 'I regret to say, Madame, that it was in a house of ill repute. He apparently haunts such places – they are called musicos in Holland, most sordid establishments, where those who are so inclined may drink, and wench, to their heart's content, while some vile group of peasants screech away on their fiddles.'

Louise did not ask what the Frenchman had been doing there. She said, apparently drily amused, 'It sounds just the sort of place that Alex would like – wine, women and song, all under the same roof.'

'It amazes me that you can seem so light-hearted,' Everard said, regarding her with raised brows. 'English women are not usually so tolerant.'

'But you forget, Monsieur, that I am not truly English – I am a Guernesiaise by birth, and French by breeding, and a very different attitude prevails in France,' Louise pointed out. 'Did you speak with my husband?'

An ominously dark cloud had swept in front of the sun, and already the strollers in the Abbey Garden were looking anxiously up at the sky, wondering if they would have to take shelter in the Abbey. Everard glanced at the thinning crowds, and gave her an apologetic shrug. 'I regret to say that I could not, Madame. He was, I fear, very drunk, and moreover his attentions were, how shall I put it, otherwise engaged.'

'You mean he was surrounded by whores,' Louise said mischievously, wondering if he would be shocked. 'Don't worry, Monsieur Everard – I am under no illusions whatsoever concerning my husband's activities. We each have our own life to lead, and our chosen path to follow.'

'Then – forgive me, Madame, if I should seem impertinent – but do I collect that you are estranged from your husband?'

'Not precisely,' Louise told him: she had already decided to avoid the unpleasant truth. 'But for the moment he lives in Amsterdam, and I live in Bath at his sister's house, with our daughter.'

'Your daughter? You have a child? *C'est ne pas possible!*'
Everard gazed at her with frank admiration, and lingered,
too long for her comfort, on the newly generous swell of her
breasts. 'I did not imagine that a lady so young and so
beautiful could already be a mother.'

'Your flattery is outrageous, Monsieur. But since I am all
of twenty-one years old, the fact that I have a baby daughter
should not be so astonishing.'

'A baby? Then your husband has not yet seen her?'

'Alas, no.' She had meant it to sound as carefree as the
rest of their conversation, but a betraying sadness escaped
all her efforts at suppression. Kitty, who was thriving in the
care of her wet nurse, who had black hair and chestnut eyes
and a happy nature, who smiled so entrancingly at her
mother, had never seen her father, and quite probably
never would.

And that seemed to her, suddenly, to be the greatest
tragedy of all.

'Forgive me, my dear Lady St Barbe – I did not mean to
upset you.'

Furious with herself for her weakness, Louise blinked
back the tears and gave him her gallant, dazzling smile. 'I
cannot pretend that I do not sometimes regret it, Monsieur.
But my daughter is beautiful and healthy, and I have much
for which I can be thankful.'

'Does your husband know that the baby exists?'

'Of course he does,' Louise snapped, and then smiled
wryly. 'It is my turn to apologise, Monsieur. I have talked a
great deal too much about my own tedious affairs, and now
it looks as if it will soon be raining. Shall we agree to adjourn
to the Abbey, and there turn our conversation to lighter
matters?'

Everard was too much the chivalrous gentleman to ignore
her request, and adroitly embarked upon an amusing and
scandalous story concerning the King's late mistress,
Catherine Sedley. It made her laugh, and she managed, quite
successfully, to repress the sudden sadness that had overwhelmed her under the sycamore trees of the Abbey Garden.

But later, the feeling returned. It seemed likely, from

Everard's unflattering description, that Alex had embraced all his old dissolute habits with a vengeance, his wife and child forgotten or disregarded. But she knew the twists and turns of his complicated character, and the thought remained to haunt her. What if Phoebe was right, and he did in fact regret most bitterly what he had done to her? Was he drinking himself into an early grave, when one letter, one word from her might bring him back?

She had thought that she did not want him to return. She had told him that she never wanted to see him again, and she had meant it with utter sincerity, at the time.

But they had been apart for nearly a year, and as her initial rage and disgust had faded, so her doubts had crept in unawares. She missed him, the Alex she had thought she knew, and loved, the tender, witty, considerate lover who had wooed her with lust and laughter, the passionate friend, a man who had made his own rules and followed them until, in one ghastly drunken rage, he had shattered them so brutally that she could never trust him again . . .

She did not know what to think. She did not know what to do. She knew only that she wanted time to run back, to the days before Nathaniel's birth, so that she could do things differently.

And that was a gift never granted in this world, or beyond it. A line from a play entered her head, and stuck there, echoing her regret and her grief. 'Oh, call back yesterday, bid time return.'

It was probably by Shakespeare: Phoebe might know, and Alex, who had a surprisingly wide acquaintance with such things, certainly would. That was an irony which made her smile, briefly and bitterly.

But what could she do? She would not write self-abasing letters, begging him for a reconciliation, when the fault was his. She could not, despite the urgings of her reckless and impulsive spirit, abandon her baby, so dearly loved, and sail alone to Amsterdam to comb the taverns and stews and drinking-dens for a man who would, quite possibly, reject her with all the sneering cruelty of which he was capable. She was not yet so desperate.

264

But she could encourage Lukas to write to him: that could do no harm. And she could clothe her broken heart with levity and cheerfulness, and continue her entertaining conversations with Monsieur Edmond Everard.

# Chapter Fourteen

## 'Love produces care'

In a city as small and close-packed as Bath, where gossip thrived and festered like mould on stale bread, it did not take long for the news of Lady St Barbe's association with a handsome Frenchman to reach the ears of her sister-in-law. Phoebe paid little attention to the sort of scandal that was life's blood to many of her neighbours, but the words of the Widow Wiltshire, spoken over dishes of her abominably weak tea, could not be ignored.

Phoebe normally gave the woman only the briefest of greetings, purely for the sake of courtesy. She knew that her neighbour strongly disapproved of the St Barbes in general, and Phoebe and her brother in particular: Alex for his demonic reputation, Phoebe for her shocking disregard of convention in setting up her own establishment, instead of being content to remain at her brother's beck and call for the rest of her days, as a genteel pensionary at Wintercombe. She and Louise had always laughed at Mistress Wiltshire's barely concealed malice, and had invented imaginary conversations between the widow and her cronies. 'And to think of it, the hussy has even *learned a heathen language!*'

But her neighbour had obviously been waiting for the chance to impart this particularly juicy titbit, and she had almost dragged a reluctant and protesting Phoebe into her house, a few doors away. At last, with wry resignation, and the intention of recounting the conversation later to make Louise, and perhaps Hugh, laugh over it, she had allowed herself to be drawn inside, and plied with pallid, lukewarm dishes of tea.

And Mistress Wiltshire, amid much hand-fluttering and insincere apology, informed her that her sister-in-law was conducting an affair with some fine French courtier, right under her very nose.

From her earliest years, victim of her tormenting brother, Phoebe had been adept at hiding her true feelings when she wished. Not by one gesture did she betray that this was news to her: she surveyed the Widow Wilshire's avid, triumphant face and said pleasantly, 'I know all about this affair, as you call it, so your information is no surprise in the least. It is merely a matter of acquaintance – the man is an old friend of Lady St Barbe's family in France.'

'It seemed to me to be rather more than mere acquaintance, my dear,' said the gossip, with a barely concealed sneer.

Phoebe put down her dish of tea, unfinished, and rose to her feet. The chilly arrogance of her expression reminded the older woman that she was the daughter of a baronet, whereas the Widow's husband had been a mere mercer and shopkeeper. 'Did it indeed, madam?' she said coldly. 'Pray tell me, since you are so interested in my sister-in-law's private affairs – how could you tell? Are you such an expert in adultery? From your own personal experience, perhaps?'

And with the Widow's furiously indignant protests fading behind her, Phoebe had limped from the house as fast as she could, before her anger got the better of her dignity and she did the repellent woman actual harm.

But, like it or not, there might well be a grain of truth in Mistress Wiltshire's story: even in Bath, there was rarely smoke without fire, and often a veritable conflagration. Uneasily aware that of late Louise had been much on her own, and had had ample opportunity to create scandal, Phoebe waited until after supper that evening, when Lukas was studying in his chamber, to broach the subject.

'I hear you have a new escort,' she said, in her usual direct fashion.

To her surprise and dismay, Louise blushed. 'How did you know?' she said, looking rather guilty, as if well aware that she had been in the wrong. 'No – don't tell me – that dreadful old woman who lives over the way.'

'Mistress Wiltshire, yes, she told me with great glee this

afternoon,' Phoebe said. She surveyed Louise, who had assumed a definite air of bravado. 'Well? I'm on fire to know more myself. Who *is* this handsome Frenchman who's been squiring you round the Abbey Gardens? By the way, I told the woeful Widow that he was an old friend of your family. I don't think she believed it for a moment.'

'I don't suppose she would,' Louise said. 'His name is Edmond Everard, he comes from Blois, where I went to school, so you were almost right – and he is exceedingly amusing company, and that is all.'

'Nothing more?'

'Oh, Phoebe, of course there isn't – a little harmless flirtation, that's all. I've only met him a few times, and he makes me laugh – he's travelled widely, he's a man of taste and fashion, and it is beyond anything pleasant to talk French to a Frenchman again – but that is *all*.' She glared at her cousin. 'You can't tell me you actually *believe* what that woman says.'

'I certainly don't – but all the same, is it altogether wise to be seen in the company of such a man?'

It was certainly not wise to say so. Louise's quick temper, already on the defensive, flared into life. 'That's rich, coming from you – I'm sure she spreads just as many rumours about you and Sir Hugh! Anyway, when have either of us ever cared about what such people think? She should be beneath our contempt and our notice, she's just like Bab. You aren't my keeper, Phoebe, any more than your brother is – I shall do as I please, and see whom I wish, and there is nothing you can do to prevent it!'

She sat glaring at her sister-in-law, her face flushed, her eyes glittering with anger. And Phoebe, who also possessed a temper, but kept it under rather firmer control, said mildly, 'I quite agree with you. I'm sorry, but my curiosity got the better of me. If this Monsieur Everard has such witty conversation, why not really give the gossips something to talk about, and invite him here for supper?'

So Edmond Everard, rather to his surprise, arrived at the house in Nowhere Lane the following evening, clad with a magnificence that drew all eyes in the street, and made

Mistress Wiltshire, peering from behind her shutters, bristle with righteous indignation. The hussy – not two years married, and with a new baby – to encourage the attentions of such a man with such shameless, brazen . . .

Here, words failed Mistress Wiltshire entirely, and she retreated from the window, urging her maid to bring her a reviving tot of Holland spirits.

Lukas, of his own wish, had taken his supper up to his chamber on a tray, and was deep in the mysteries of Caesarean grammar. Phoebe had discovered that he had already met the Frenchman, and had his considered judgement lurking in the back of her mind. 'I don't like him very much. He's like one of the boys at school, who makes himself very pleasant and friendly to you when he wants something, but you know he couldn't really care less about you.'

For a child of eight, it was an opinion remarkably astute, and she could see exactly what he meant.

Phoebe greeted Everard in her excellent French, and from then on, by tacit agreement, the conversation was conducted in that language. She knew that she would be of no interest to Monsieur Everard, and so it proved. Wit in a woman was permisssible, so long as she was attractive as well, but to be so formidably plain, and intellectual to boot, was altogether beyond the pale. From politeness, she was included from time to time, but almost all the talk flew between Everard and Louise, in a swift, expressive and idiomatic flood that even Phoebe once or twice found hard to follow. She watched, and listened, and drew her own conclusions.

There was no doubt in her mind that Louise had spoken the truth: there was, as yet, no more than friendship between them. But it was quite obvious to Phoebe that Everard was attracted to her sister-in-law: the warmth of his appreciation, his courtly and outrageous flattery, his lingering glances, all conveyed the same message. Louise, laughing, lively, even beautiful, was apparently quite unaware of his regard, save for one or two watchful looks when she thought that Everard would not notice. Her own manner was friendly, open, slightly flirtatious. Phoebe, amused despite herself, realised that she knew exactly what she was doing, and could judge to a nicety just how far she could go before the game became dangerously close to reality.

She knew better, now, than to warn Louise against him: she had told her to beware of Alex, once, and look where that had led. So long as Louise kept Everard at arm's length, she would be safe. But the Frenchman had the look of a man who would be only too willing to seduce an attractive and apparently deserted wife, and for all Louise's sophistication and worldly wisdom, she might be unable to resist him.

And be unable, also, to resist the temptation to pay Alex back in kind.

Phoebe hoped grimly that she would have more sense than to waste herself on this vain popinjay who could be anyone, perhaps an adventurer who milked his conquests of their wealth before departing in search of another willing and gullible victim. She wondered how long it would be before the King returned to Bath, with Hugh Trevelyan in his train. She felt in sore need, at present, of his practical, friendly support.

Upstairs, in his chamber, Lukas heard the talk and laughter below, and frowned over the paper on the table in front of him. It was nothing to do with Caesar: he had decided, after Louise's encouragement, to write to his father.

He chewed the end of the quill, and wondered if he had spelt it all correctly, whether he had done the right thing, whether these few painstaking lines would bring his father home. He read them again.

Dear Papa,

I hope you will be joyed to learn that I have prospered in school. I had the great honour to be chosen from amongst all the boys, to write and read an Oration in Latin to the King His Majesty, when he came to Bath last week.

270

Was that too boastful? But he was only stating the truth, and his Aunt Phoebe had taken him to task often enough about hiding lights under bushels. He went on:

My Aunt Phoebe is well, though she complains mightily about the ladies and gentlemen of the Court, who crowd the Baths so that we poor natives cannot come near them. Sir Hugh Trevelyan has been here, but went away again with the King on his Progress, and we hope that he will shortly return. My sister Kitty grows apace – she was a little red wrinkled thing when she was first born, and cried all day, but now she is out to nurse, and smiles at us when we visit her, and I have even heard her laugh. My lady stepmother calls her Kitten, though none I ever saw looked so strangely, with neither fur nor whiskers, yet I dare say she mews like one.

Lukas smiled, rather pleased with this whimsical flight of fancy. Perhaps Papa would laugh, when he read it. He dripped his quill in the ink and continued, in his clear, round, schoolboy hand.

My lady stepmother is newly acquainted with a Frenchman, Monsieur Edmond Everard, who saved us from an unfortunate dispute with Cousin Charles in the Abbey Garden. He is come to supper, and all sounds very merry. I do not like him over much, he is too eager to be our friend, but my lady stepmother says she likes his company, and certainly he makes her laugh, which she has done too little since you left.

Now his heart was running away with the pen, the words pouring faster than he could write, so that the nib stuttered and blotted the page.

In truth I think she misses you sorely, though she will not admit it, and so do I, and Aunt Phoebe too, and we all wish that you would leave Holland and come home and put Cousin Charles to flight so that we may all live at Wintercombe again and be happy, like we were before you went.

271

In a rage of reproachful misery, he signed it, 'Your sorrowful and abandoned son, Lukas van der Linden', and then put his head in his hands, the quill dropping unnoticed to the floor, and wept in despair.

Phoebe heard him. She had left Louise and Everard, with Christian an impassive chaperone, to talk over cups of chocolate in the parlour, and come upstairs to ensure that her nephew was in bed. The sounds of grief emanating from his chamber were so unusual that for a moment she thought she had misheard. Then, realising with anxiety that there was no mistake, she knocked and went in.

He was sitting slumped at the table, sobbing his heart out, and obviously unaware of her presence. She saw the letter, and read it over his shoulder, with growing pain and sympathy, as well as guilt. She and Louise had both neglected him: they had assumed that Alex's abrupt departure had barely affected him at all, since he had seemed so cheerful. To judge from that sad, pathetic letter, the reverse was the case.

'Oh, Lukas,' she said softly, and touched his shoulder. 'He'll come back – he *will*.'

He turned up to her a face made swollen and ugly with anguish. 'How do you know, Aunt Phoebe? How do you *know* that? He doesn't *want* to come back – he never wanted to leave Holland before, when my grandfather died, and now he's where he always liked to be best, and he'll *never* come home!'

There was nothing she could say but platitudes that he would not believe.

He went on, gulping angrily. 'And that Frenchman, I don't like him, I don't trust him, but Louise does – how could she? I thought she loved Papa, I thought he loved her, I thought he loved me, we were so happy together – what happened, Aunt Phoebe, why did it all go wrong?'

And she could only hold him, and try to explain, in terms he could understand, and in ways that would not hurt him, that love was not always lasting, that people could not be perfect, and that his father was the least perfect and reliable of all.

*

The letter that Lukas wrote, still blotched with his angry, hopeless tears, was sealed and left in Phoebe's letter box for the return of Hugh Trevelyan, who could send it on its way without risking the official post. If Alex was indeed now suspected of conspiracy, any message to him ran the risk of being opened: and although Lukas's letter contained nothing that would interest the prying eyes of the King's agents, Phoebe could not bear to think that his childish pleas might be the subject of coarse comment and ridicule.

The King and his entourage returned to Bath, with great pomp and ceremony, on the sixth of September: and shortly afterwards, Lukas's letter was sent on its way by devious and unofficial channels involving, amongst others, a private messenger, a London coffee house, and an English sloop plying out of Maldon, in Essex, to Rotterdam.

And thence, more conventionally, to the house near the Zuiderkerk in Amsterdam, where lodged Sir Alexander St Barbe.

The company at dinner, on the day that his son's letter finally reached its destination, more than a month after it had been written, would look strangely assorted to an outsider's eye. They were of completely different generations: Alex himself, only just past thirty, and Tom Talmarsh, a few years older: Harry Sidney, now forty-six: and, apparently rather out of place, a man who, in his time, had possessed the power to shake governments and alter the course of history.

John Wildman was sixty-four, white-haired but still undeniably vigorous. He had been a major in Cromwell's army, a leader of the Levellers, and, more recently, an associate of Harry Sidney's elder brother Algernon, executed by the late King Charles for his republican beliefs. For forty years, Wildman had been a thorn in the side of authority, he had plotted with Monmouth and Shaftesbury, his pamphlets had thundered against royalty and popery, and he lived now in prudent exile in Amsterdam, still writing, still plotting, and above all still alive.

The four men were hardly bosom companions. Sidney,

although a convinced Whig, was, unlike his executed brother, no republican, and he plainly mistrusted Wildman. Talmarsh knew Sidney, who had been general of the British regiments in Holland until quite recently: and Sidney, wit, diplomat, apparently devoted to a life of dissolute idleness, in fact possessed the complete confidence and trust of the Prince of Orange, a man as different from him as it was possible to be.

Alex, lounging at the head of the table, a glass of brandy for once untouched at his fingertips, was the link between them. He had known both Talmarsh and Wildman in the heady days when the members of the Green Ribbon Club, led by the Earl of Shaftesbury, had virtually ruled England: and Sidney had been his commanding officer during his years in one of the English regiments in Dutch service. He was well aware that this meeting was unlikely to be entirely friendly, and that Wildman, notoriously cautious and taciturn, would probably contribute little to the discussion.

As in fact had proved to be the case: nor did Harry Sidney, complimenting his host on an excellent dinner and very fine brandy, prove to be much more forthcoming. He shared the Prince's distrust of the more extreme republicans, and his utter and instinctive discretion, and his gift for intrigue, were the equal of Wildman's.

Talmarsh, recently in England, had talked the most. He had given them the latest news from Windsor, where the King was now in residence after his sojourn in Bath: the Queen, apparently, was still there, diligently taking the waters and praying for a Papist heir to the throne. James was determined now to remove all the legal barriers that prevented Catholics from taking an active part in public life, and to this end had sent enquiries to all gentleman of consequence in the Kingdom.

'Three questions,' Talmarsh said. 'First, if elected to Parliament, would they agree to the removal of the penal laws against Catholics, and the repeal of the Test Act, so that Papists may enter Parliament and hold office, without the King's special dispensation. Secondly, would they assist the election of men who support the removal of these

274

laws. And, thirdly, would they be prepared to live in peace with their neighbours, of whatever religion, as the King's Declaration of Indulgence urges them to do.'

'He won't find many to disagree with that last question,' Alex pointed out. 'The first two are, of course, rather more controversial. His Majesty obviously wishes to have a compliant and fawningly loyal Parliament at his beck and call. Whether the good electors of England will bow to his wishes is another matter.'

'Well, the questions have only just gone out,' Talmarsh said. 'I doubt even the King will know what the answers will be, until after Christmas. And if they are not to his liking, well, he is King, and can ride roughshod over the laws as he pleases. He has done it already, forcing a Papist on the Fellows of Magdalen in Oxford, and allowing men to assume office without having to take the Test. The whisper is that he will issue new charters to those boroughs that oppose him, and so ensure that men who support him are elected.'

'And if he has a parliament full of toadies,' Sidney observed, sipping his brandy, 'then he will not rest at the abolition of the Test Act and the penal laws. I'm giving away no secrets when I say that the Prince is very concerned for the rights of his wife as the heir to the throne. If there should be any change to the succession . . .'

'The Queen is unlikely to produce an heir now, surely?' Talmarsh said. 'All England knows why she's gone to Bath, and why the King visited that Papist well in Wales – they're hoping for a miracle, and the age of miracles is long past.'

'The Queen is only twenty-nine, and not barren – although all her children have died, at least she is capable of bearing them,' Sidney pointed out. 'That, of course, is one reason for the Prince's concern. He is also worried about the Princess Anne – there has been much pressure on her to turn Papist. To her eternal credit, she has resisted her father's blandishments very stoutly, but it shows where his mind is walking. Who is to say that a submissive Parliament might not be persuaded to nominate a Papist heir, in place of the Princess of Orange? The Queen of Spain, for one – she is the King's niece.'

275

'The country would never stand for it,' Talmarsh said sharply. 'A Papist, a foreigner – '

'But how do we know?' Sidney leaned back in his chair. 'Are the gentlemen of England, doubtless now snugly abed, prepared to oppose the imposition of a Popish, France-loving dynasty? Or are they too fond of their quiet lives, too fearful of starting another civil war? No one has asked them. King James will ask them, this autumn, whether they are prepared to lick his boots and let Catholics into the government and into office. The Prince would very much like to know their answers – and also their answers to rather different questions.'

'Dijkvelt went to England in the spring – I thought that was the purpose of his mission,' said Talmarsh.

'He conferred with many peers, yes, and with men in high places,' Sidney told him. 'But they are few, and they can do little on their own, without the support of the gentry. Count Zuylestein has recently returned with more information, but the Prince is most anxious to learn what ordinary squires think and feel – men with great influence in their own counties, even if they are strangers in Whitehall. You, Tom, have your contacts in London and in the army and the navy, and very valuable they are, but the Prince wishes to extend his network of intelligence.'

He was looking at Alex as he spoke, and his host smiled suddenly, with mischief. 'And he is prepared to trust me? I thought he considered me to be a dangerous republican, like the Major here.'

Wildman snorted derisively. 'I'll not deny I mislike kings, but given the choice I'd rather have Dutch William on the throne of England than that Papist bigot.'

'You are all trusted,' Sidney said, his incongruously sharp eyes lingering on each of the other three men in turn. 'You, Tom, can come and go between England and Holland with impunity: your role is invaluable, and may prove vital should circumstances alter for the worse.' He glanced at Wildman. 'There are others, too, exiles for one reason or another, whom the Prince wishes to employ in this matter. You, sir, are a marked man, of course – but the Prince knows that you have many friends and contacts both here and in London. You must be able to suggest safe and trustworthy men to do his bidding.'

'Perhaps,' said Wildman curtly. The cautious habits of a lifetime of conspiracy, that had frequently saved his neck, were obviously hard to lay aside. 'I shall give it my consideration.'

'And you?' Sidney turned to Alex. 'You are in Amsterdam of your own free will, and you too can come and go as you please.'

'That may not be the case,' Alex said. 'I have a good friend at Whitehall, as you well know – and he has warned me that Sunderland is aware of my activities here, innocent or not. At the very least, he is suspicious – and if I enter England openly, I have been told that I risk arrest.' He smiled thinly. 'There are old scores to pay off, even though I was pardoned for whatever I was supposed to have done during the late unfortunate rebellion. So if I do return to England, I will have to do so under another name, and in a part of the country where I am not known – therefore, neither in the West Country nor in London.'

'We can discuss the finer points of the matter at a later date,' said Sidney. 'For now, I can tell the Prince that I have the agreement and co-operation of you all – and when the time comes, you will doubtless be informed of your duties through the usual channels, and with the usual discretion. I need not tell any of you gentlemen, of course, to preserve the utmost secrecy. The Prince has always insisted on it, and the success of his intelligence network has proved its worth.' He smiled. 'Happily for us, King James seems to be rather more unfortunate in his choice of agents – or more careless.'

Not long afterwards, Alex's disparate guests departed, and the maid Clara came to clear away the remains of the meal. Behind her, Gerrit hovered, a packet in his hand. 'This came for you while you were dining, sir. It is from England.'

The writing on the outside was Hugh Trevelyan's, and the seals were intact, although Alex had little faith in such supposedly incontrovertible proof that the letter had not been tampered with. But the route that the courtier used for his clandestine correspondence was quick, secret, and apparently so far undiscovered. Since he still held all his posts and offices at Whitehall, the fact that Sir Hugh Trevelyan, Gentleman of the King's Bedchamber, was in regular communication with Whig exiles and radicals was probably not yet known to James, or to Sunderland.

Alex thanked his servant, and took the packet into the small room, overlooking the narrow sunless yard behind his lodgings, that he used as a study.

There was a close-packed page from Sir Hugh, giving all the latest news and gossip from Court, scandal rubbing shoulders with more important information, and all described in his dry, witty style. Some of it, of course, was already known to the Prince and his advisers, but there was much that was useful, and Alex always passed his friend's letters on to the Hague, to join the voluminous correspondence from the many people in England, often surprisingly highly placed, who kept the Prince of Orange fully apprised of affairs in England.

As usual, a second sheet contained news of a more personal kind. Hugh had stayed in Bath with the King, and had seen much of Phoebe and, of course, Louise. The quality of life in the little city, the rounds of pleasure and entertainment, the gossip and rumour, and all the atmosphere, close and heady, of a place devoted entirely to the amusement of its guests, rose evocatively off the page. He needed only to close his eyes to conjure up the bustling streets, the sulphurous smell of the Baths, the noise of shopkeepers and traders, the whores and pickpockets jostling respectable citizens, men of fashion, ladies of the Court – often whores, too, under the skin – and the sick and diseased of every station in life, from beggars and paupers to gentry and aristocrats, hoping for a cure.

Nostalgia was the most pointless and futile of emotions, and he had no truck with it. But Hugh's description of the royal visit to Wintercombe, and the lavish welcome given to the King by its present incumbent, prompted a different feeling.

Of his own free will, Alex had assigned the better part of his inheritance to Charles. He had renounced England, and settled once more in Amsterdam, where he had always felt comfortable and at ease, where toleration was a virtue rather than a vice, where he could conduct his life exactly as he pleased, and dabble in treason without, yet, the fear of retribution to hinder him.

So why, now, this inconvenient wave of, for want of a better word, homesickness? He had chosen his fate, however bitter, and accepted it: why now kick against the pricks, and long for what he could never enjoy again?

Perhaps his offer to go to England in the Prince's service, given without much thought beyond the wish for some purpose and structure to his life, was a symptom of this deeper desire, for home, for Wintercombe, for the astringent friendship of his sister and the uncomplicated adoration of his son: and above all, a passion unslaked for a year, for the love of Louise.

No use regretting: no use, either, in drowning his bitterness in brandy. In the aftermath of that first bout of marsh fever, a mood of despairing darkness had seized him. Ignoring the advice of Doctor van Vas, he had resorted to the bottle again, and he remembered little of those three or four weeks, save that he had been almost continuously drunk. Then the illness had returned, with greater virulence, and only the doctor's skill had saved him. This time, his warning had been harsh, and specific. If Alex continued to drink to excess, the fever would come back again and again, with increasing severity. Sooner or later, he would die of it.

This time, he had taken notice. Apart from anything else, he did not wish to give his cousin the satisfaction of knowing that he had died the drunkard's death which Charles had always predicted. And for the past few weeks, since his recovery, he had, by his previous standards, led an exemplary life, to Gerrit's evident relief. The musicos no longer tempted him, and he retired to bed sober, nine times out of ten. So far, the fever had failed to return.

Certainly, he would need all his wits about him if he were

to go to England to spy for the Prince of Orange. As Sidney had said, William demanded the highest standards of secrecy and caution from the men chosen for such missions, and in consequence he was the best-informed man in Europe, more so even than King Louis. Alex, thinking about it with a wry smile, knew that the meeting just ended would never have taken place if he had been still sunk in debauchery, and was glad of it. Anything, even a task as dangerous as this might well prove to be, was preferable to drinking his life away in the squalid taverns and musicos of Amsterdam.

A third piece of paper, folded and sealed, had fallen to the floor. He picked it up, and saw Phoebe's swift hand, devoid of flourish or elegance, across the outside of it. 'Knowing your situation from Hugh, I wonder if I should send you this – but I promised that I would, and it may serve as a reminder to you of those whom you have so carelessly discarded.'

No signature, no sign of affection, but he had long ago come to expect no more from his sister, whose nature, like his own, was scarcely demonstrative. With a sudden, wild hope, he broke the seal, and found that the writing inside was not that of Louise, but the careful, childish hand of his son Lukas.

It did not take long to read it. He stood quite still for some while afterwards, the paper in his hands, and the pain of loss, of guilt, of the knowledge that he had failed his son and callously abandoned him, settled on him like a leaden weight. The child needed him, his unhappiness poured off the page, and Alex had been too absorbed in drunken despair to write to Lukas, as he had intended to. Then he had fallen ill again, and somehow he had forgotten about his son, and what the boy might be suffering.

He would write to Lukas, now, this afternoon, to apologise, and to reassure him. And even if he could not return to England openly, it would surely be possible to send Gerrit to Bath, to bring his son back. It would interrupt his studies, of course, but from the sound of it, Lukas could easily catch up later. He glanced down at the

280

letter again. '. . . the great honour to be chosen from amongst all the boys, to write and read an Oration in Latin to the King His Majesty . . .'

Love for his son was not a recent emotion: Lukas had long ago joined that very restricted company for whom Alex felt deep and lasting affection. But this sensation of pride in the boy's achievements was definitely new to him. He himself had never shone at his studies: he had a mind which acquired information effortlessly, but only when it interested him. There had been precious little in the curriculum at the Free School to engage his attention, and he had long since forgotten most of his Latin and Greek, preferring, like Phoebe, to learn more modern languages, and to dabble in the new sciences. As a boy, he had scorned and derided those who studied industriously, and obeyed the schoolmaster in everything. It was something of an irony to discover that he could be proud of his son's scholarly success.

His eye fell on the paragraph further down the page. 'My lady stepmother is newly acquainted with a Frenchman, Monsieur Edmond Everard . . .'

He had hardly noticed it earlier, but now the words seemed charged with especial significance. Edmond Everard. Where had he heard that name before?

A moment's thought convinced him that it had been here in Holland, quite recently, and in an ominous context. He scanned the page again, more closely. '. . . Too eager to be our friend . . .' It certainly sounded as if this mysterious Frenchman had deliberately sought Louise out.

And why not? She was attractive, lively, entrancing. But Lukas's suspicion came plainly off the page, and the boy, though young, was an instinctive judge of character.

Then he remembered. The previous English ambassador to Holland, Bevil Skelton, had arranged the abduction, nearly a year ago now, of Sir Robert Peyton, one of the more prominent and influential Whig exiles. He had paid some junior officers of the English regiments to do the deed, but the attempt had failed because Peyton had loudly and publicly asserted his rights as a naturalised citizen of Holland.

And Skelton's agent, who had lured Peyton to Rotterdam for the ambush, had been one Edmond Everard, a Frenchman.

A spy, in the pay of England certainly, and probably also a creature of King Louis. It seemed rather unlikely that such a man would ingratiate himself with the wife and family of another Whig exile for pure amusement. It was too great a coincidence. If this Monsieur Edmond Everard were indeed the same man – and it should be possible to find out easily enough – then Phoebe and Louise should be warned.

The news was disturbing, but it seemed that he had no reason for jealousy. And although he had once wished, in his most despairing moments, that Louise might find a more constant and gentle lover, that uncharacteristically altruistic desire had long since disappeared. He did not want anyone else to have her, to kiss and fondle her, to arouse the passion that he had set alight in them both. He could not bear the thought that another man might make love to her: and if Everard had an ulterior motive for winning her friendship, then he surely had less cause to be jealous.

He must be extremely careful now. He did not think that he was being watched or followed, but King James's agents could not all be stupid or indiscreet, despite Sidney's cheerful words. And at the first opportunity, he must tell Harry about Everard.

Sidney, consulted later that day, was likewise inclined to err on the side of caution. 'It sounds likely that this Everard is the same man as Skelton's agent. I know very little about him, save that he's French, around your age, and extremely handsome in a suave, oily sort of way. A great man for the ladies, so I've heard.' He glanced shrewdly at Alex. 'Not the sort you'd like to find paying court to your wife, I'd wager. And, as you say, the fact that he has apparently sought her out deliberately is unlikely to be coincidence. What are your chances of persuading your lady to send him packing?'

'Very slender, alas,' Alex said grimly. He had never discussed his marital problems with Harry, although as a man of the world, his friend must have guessed the situation fairly accurately. Sidney's lifeblood was intrigue, and he would certainly have made it his business to discover exactly why Alex had returned to Holland, just as he made the personal affairs of all the Prince's other potential spies a matter of concern. Presumably, his direct approach to Alex meant that his enquiries had been satisfactory. But would the news that his latest agent's wife was the subject of interest from one of King James's known spies change his mind?

It seemed to have made no difference. Sidney received without comment the information that Alex was not on speaking terms with his wife, and said, 'In that case, there is little you can do to keep Everard at bay. I would strongly advise you not to contact your wife – you may place her, and yourself, in danger by doing so. Is there someone trustworthy who is close to her, with whom you *can* communicate?'

'My sister Phoebe. She's no fool, and she could give an oyster lessons in discretion, where necessary. Moreover, she's in regular correspondence with my Whitehall contact.' He smiled. 'If you are ever in need of a female spy, you could find none better.'

'I'll remember it,' Sidney said drily. 'But if you can send your sister a message, to warn her about Everard – as obliquely as possible – then if she's as sensible as she seems, she can take the necessary steps to protect your wife from this man. But for the safety of both ladies, not to mention yourself, it's advisable that they know as little as possible.'

It meant, of course, that if he went to England, there could be no clandestine meetings, for the safety of Louise and Phoebe would be endangered. And in any case, that momentary hope had sprung from his heart, not his head. He had always known the brutal truth, that there could be no return, no going back, no miraculous reconciliation, however desperately Lukas might desire it.

# Chapter Fifteen

## 'Innate antipathy to kings'

Maria Beatrice, Queen of England, left Bath in the first week of October, to rejoin the King at Windsor. Many people in and around the city, had been charmed by her stately Italian beauty, and her gracious manner. More, alas, were still deeply suspicious of her husband.

Despite the well-organised flood of loyal addresses to the King, from the Dissenters and Quakers of Bath, Taunton, Somerset, Wiltshire and other places throughout the kingdom, thanking him for his recent Declaration of Indulgence towards their religions, there was a low, sullen murmur of displeasure from those who did not trust James, and those, the vast majority, who did not trust Dissenters, Quakers and Papists either, and resented the King's attempt to woo them. Everyone knew that His Majesty wanted a parliament that would obey his wish to repeal the Test Act and the penal laws, so that Papists, and Dissenters could take a full part in the government of the country, in the parish as well as in Whitehall. And if the solid Anglican, Tory squires and burgesses would not oblige him, then King James was, it seemed, prepared to alter the charters and corporations of every town and city in the land, so that grateful and obedient men would be elected to do as he wished.

And then, compounding the deep sense of unease, as the year began to draw to its end in cold rain and shortening days, rumour began to circulate in Whitehall. The whisper spilt outwards into the country, and was received with shock, astonishment, and disbelief.

The Queen's visit to Bath, and her husband's pilgrimage to the well of St Winifred, had borne fruit. Their prayers had been answered, and the miracle had happened. After four miscarriages and four dead children, and three years since her last pregnancy, Maria Beatrice was once more with child.

Soon rumour was confirmed, although not yet officially. The Queen became unwell, and the doctors, desperate to avert another miscarriage, bled her. The danger retreated, and just before Christmas, the King wrote joyfully to his daughter Mary in Holland to tell her the good news.

All over England and in Holland, and further afield, the participants paused in their subtle, shifting game of politics and alliances, to assess this new and unexpected development. If – if – the child was male, and carried to full term, and lived, then the position of the Princess of Orange as her father's heir was overturned. And the men who had too readily assumed that James would have no Papist successor to continue his policies realised that the Queen's pregnancy changed the situation entirely. The King was not young, was not expected to live very much longer, and they had confidently looked forward to the reign of the Protestant Princess in a few years' time.

Now, it seemed that England might be doomed to a Papist dynasty.

That supremely subtle, clever and determined man, William of Orange, was also by nature surpassingly cautious. For some time now, the English nobles who had visited his court had urged him, more or less openly, to invade their country and save the Protestant religion. Mindful of Monmouth's dismal fate, which he had done nothing to prevent, he had refused. It was entirely probable that the Queen would again lose her child, but by no means certain. And more than one adviser made the comment that the Jesuits, who supposedly wielded the real power in Whitehall, would not permit Maria Beatrice to give birth to anything other than a healthy son, even if he was not her own.

William would not commit himself, not yet. But there was no harm, and probably a great deal of advantage, to be gained by sending a group of trusted agents to England, to discover the mood of the country following this latest news.

285

At the beginning of November, Harry Sidney, still welcome at both courts, returned to Whitehall, bearing a letter for the King, his official business. Unofficially, he had instructions to reopen contact with as many of the discontented peers as possible.

And other men, less prominent but almost equally valuable, slipped across the North Sea as autumn turned to winter, braving the gales and foul weather. A Scot called James Johnston took up residence in London, with an intricate web of informants at his disposal, and a carefully planned route for his letters back to Bentinck, William's chief of staff, to ensure that they were never inspected by the authorities. Even if they had been opened, the contents seemed innocent enough, full of apparently trivial business matters. But certain words used in certain points in the letter would tell those who knew the secret that there was another message, written in invisible ink, to be revealed by soaking the paper in a special solution.

Johnston, and the other agents, were under orders to report on all aspects of English news that might possibly be of use to the Prince: the progress of the Queen's pregnancy; the appointment of the loathed Jesuit, Father Petre, to the Privy Council; the answers to the King's three questions that were beginning to trickle back to Whitehall; possible dates for an election; the likely composition of a parliament. They were also required to assess the impact of the many pamphlets circulating that autumn, in defiance of official censorship. 'A Letter to a Dissenter' advised them that the King's offer of toleration was merely the bait in a trap: 'You are to be hugged now, only that you may be better squeezed at another time.' The arguments of the anonymous author (it was, in fact, the Earl of Halifax) were lucid and clever, but were they convincing? All over the country Dissenters, basking in the unaccustomed glow of royal favour, were busy manoeuvring themselves into positions of influence, hoping for real power for the first time in nearly thirty years.

Sidney at Whitehall, and in aristocratic households, Johnston in London, Talmarsh and his friends at the Rose

Tavern, all worked to further the interests of the Prince of Orange, now seen by many as the only hope of saving England from a Papist future. And on a darkening December evening, a small Dutch vessel anchored just off Harwich, and beneath the cloak of nightfall a boat was lowered, to slip away secretly to the marshy shores of the River Orwell. It carried a cargo of pamphlets entitled 'Their Highnesses the Prince and Princess of Orange's Opinion about a General Liberty of Conscience', which stated William's position on the subject with a firmness and clarity that made him appear reasonable and trustworthy to both Anglican and Dissenter, while his father-in-law seemed by comparison to be an inflexible bigot. Fifty thousand copies had been printed in Amsterdam, and in Suffolk, as everywhere else in England, demand for them was insatiable.

And, sharing the small rocking boat with several boxes of this inflammatory publication, was Sir Alexander St Barbe.

In dark or daylight, the rainy marshes of the Suffolk coast, smelling sharply of salt and seaweed and echoing, even at this hour, with the calls of curlew and plover and duck, looked very similar to those of Holland. In his own country, Alex had never been further east than London, but he had recently spent some time at the Hague, being briefed by Bentinck. This was a well-established secret route, both for illegal pamphlets and for illegal immigrants. An isolated farm lay on the further edge of the marshes, well secluded from prying eyes. There, he would obtain rest, a meal, a horse and a guide. And at sunrise tomorrow, he would leave on the first stage of his journey through Suffolk.

No one knew him here, but an alias was only wise: the name of Alexander St Barbe had been notorious in London, and there might be unfriendly ears anywhere. So he had become a merchant, normally trading between Bristol and Holland, who had come to the east coast to seek out new markets. And he did not think that anyone would recognise his real self in the ordinary persona of Samuel Orchard.

The marshes might look the same, but this was England:

in this country, his wife, his son, the daughter he had never seen, lived a few days' ride away to the west. And it was undeniably pleasant to hear English spoken all around him once more, even in this harsh, uncouth dialect with, surprisingly, a certain resemblance to Dutch.

It had been a long voyage, against the prevailing westerly wind. Gratefully, Alex accepted a simple but plentiful supper, a comfortable bed, and slept the sleep of the just, or the exhausted, without recourse to more than a mug or two of beer. And in the morning, refreshed and undeterred by the cold and the rain, he rode to Ipswich with his guide, the farmer's son. A week or so in the town, the guest of a draper whose sympathies and links with the House of Orange and the Whig cause were not generally known to his friends, and then he would move on, to the house near St Edmundsbury belonging to Francis Heron, who was Hugh Trevelyan's half-brother.

Bath, with winter approaching, was a pale shadow of its lively summer self. The courtiers and men and women of fashion had long since returned to Whitehall, or to their own estates. Now that the Queen's pregnancy had become generally known, however, it was noticeable that even on cold days the waters of the Cross Bath, where Maria Beatrice had been so spectacularly cured of her infertility, were unusually crowded with barren women, hoping for a similar miracle. The people of Bath, who depended on the reputation of the waters for their continued prosperity, were torn between smug satisfaction at this public demonstration of the Baths' powers, and dismay at the prospect of a Papist heir to the throne.

Despite her continuing confusion about her feelings for her husband, Louise had enjoyed the past few months. All through September and October, she had been entertained by the company, flattery and good conversation of Edmond Everard. She had managed, quite successfully, to ignore the doubts and suspicions of both Phoebe and Lukas, and also, with more effort, the small insistent voice at the back of her own mind.

288

It nagged her, though, whenever she was not with him, asking why he had sought her out, why he continued to escort her and call upon her, without making any move to transform a friendship into an affair. Not that she would welcome a liaison: she had no desire to complicate her life still further. Yet, paradoxically, she could not help feeling a little piqued that his eloquent admiration had not proceeded beyond mere words. Was she losing her powers of attraction?

And he seemed surprisingly eager to encourage a reconciliation between her and Alex, several times urging her to write to her husband and invite him home. In the end, she had to tell him, quite sharply, that it was her private business, and he did not mention it again. But it was hardly the behaviour of an importunate lover.

It was only a game, after all, and she knew the rules: she had played it often enough in France, laughing, flirting, dazzling any number of men, without any real risk of entanglement. The danger arose when passion entered the balance, and distorted sense and judgement. It had happened to her twice in her life, and both times had ended in disaster. However, she had long since successfully evicted her married French lover from her heart. Alex was much more difficult to forget.

At the end of October, Everard left Bath, saying that he had business in London which would keep no longer. He wrapped the news up in flowery phrases about her *beaux yeux* that brought a smile to her face, hiding the undeniable feeling of disappointment. When he had gone, she mooned restlessly about the house for some days, causing Phoebe no little annoyance, and then decided on impulse to pay a long overdue visit to Chard, to see her grandparents.

She took the baby, Kitty (who fortunately seemed to have inherited the robust constitution of both her parents), the wet nurse, and her maid Christian. Despite the lateness of the season, it was a pleasant and uneventful journey, and Kitty, her eyes wide with infant astonishment, even loved the jolting coach.

Louise had intended to stay only for a week or so, but the

delighted welcome of Nick and Silence, not to mention her uncle Richard and his growing family, changed her mind before she had even been escorted inside the house. When Silence asked her how long she would be staying, she answered immediately. 'At least until after Christmas.'

Nor did she regret her impulsiveness, although once the initial euphoria of welcome had died down, she realised that all would not be as cosy and pleasant as she had imagined. It was fifteen months since she had last seen her grandparents, and both of them seemed much older, somehow, than she remembered.

But their minds were still as sharp as ever, despite encroaching age, and it did not take Silence long to ascertain that the evasive answers which her favourite granddaughter had given for over a year to her questions about Alex's whereabouts concealed the collapse of their marriage. And, being Silence, it did not take long, either, for her to broach the subject with Louise.

It was a cold, wet November, so the garden was not available for exercise, or for private conversation. Louise instead spent much time in the nursery, with her small cousins Nicholas and Rebecca, as well as their baby brother John, who was nine months old. Needless to say, Kitty was fussed over by the two older children, and revelled in all the extra attention. And her mother, who enjoyed childish company, and missed her own young half-brothers and sisters in France, entered into the spirit of their romps and games with a happy loss of dignity that surprised the nursemaids.

Silence, watching her from a comfortable position on the windowseat – this damp weather did her joints no good – wondered if Louise's fine French friends would recognise this laughing hoyden, dressed in an old gown, with an apron already grubby and ripped in one corner, and her hair coming unpinned. Alex also possessed that endearing ability to enter a child's world, and the adoration of his son Lukas had been his reward.

Her eyes strayed to Kitty, sitting on the floor surrounded by cushions, thoughtfully chewing on her coral as she watched the entertainment with huge, astonished brown eyes. Her first great-grandchild was a delightful baby, with her father's black hair and a placid sweetness of nature that was inherited from neither parent. Silence wondered, unhappily, whether this child, first living member of a new generation of St Barbes, would also be the last.

Louise, protesting exhaustion, left the fray, and Nicholas and Rebecca were called to order by their nurse. She sat down beside her grandmother, holding aching sides. 'Oh, how I enjoyed that! It won't be long before Kitty is old enough for wild games, too.'

'She's a lovely baby,' Silence said. 'You must be very fond of her, and proud.' She paused, and added gently, 'What a shame that she lacks her father.'

Louise flushed deeply, something she very rarely did. 'Yes, it is,' she said, keeping her voice neutral.

The nursemaids were busy with the children, so this was as good a chance as any. Silence went on softly. 'I'm afraid that age has not made it any easier to pull the wool over my eyes. Alex has been in Holland for over a year now, and he has never seen his daughter. You cannot tell me that is the behaviour of a loving and devoted husband. What has gone wrong?'

If anything, Louise had gone a deeper shade of red. She turned to stare out of the rain-streaked window. Silence waited patiently, knowing that tears, or an angry outburst, were less likely in the presence of the nursemaids and the children.

'I'm afraid I can't tell you precisely,' said her granddaughter, at last.

'I'm not prying,' Silence said. 'But out of love for you, and Kitty, and even for Alex, I would like to be told the truth. Have you parted on bad terms?'

Louise nodded.

'And is it likely to be permanent?'

Her granddaughter brushed a casual hand across her eyes. 'Yes.'

Silence surveyed her, frowning. At length, when Louise had won her struggle for composure, she said, 'May one ask why?'

'It's private,' Louise said, still staring out of the window. 'All I can say is that we quarrelled, and he's gone, and is unlikely to return. Ever.'

'But he adored you,' Silence said, in bewilderment. 'Being Alex, of course, he didn't always show it, but he genuinely loved you very deeply, I would stake my life on it.'

'That's what I thought,' Louise told her bitterly. 'You'd never have guessed it, though, from what he did to me – so I told him to go.'

'And now, I think, you are regretting it?'

There was a very long pause. Eventually Louise sighed and shrugged, with a wry smile. 'Yes, despite everything – and conducting an affair in Bath with some well-born trollop was only the half of it – despite everything, I miss him desperately, and I do want him back. And, *mon Dieu*, how I despise myself for being his adoring slave, even now!'

'But you are not his slave,' Silence pointed out. '*You* refused to put up with his behaviour, *you* told him to leave. That is hardly the action of a submissive slave.'

'I know. But I still love him – my heart is still enthralled, whatever arguments my mind may summon against it. I look at Kitty and wish that he could see her, and love her, as he loves Lukas. And Lukas, too, misses him so much. He wrote to Alex, two or three months ago.' She smiled bleakly. 'I am still trying to muster the courage to do so myself.'

'Why not? It can do no harm, surely. And if you told him to leave in the first place, the chances are that he is sitting in Amsterdam, missing you as much as you are missing him. Life is too short for such a waste.'

'That's what Phoebe said – that he might be unhappy. But we've had various reports, from certain mutual acquaintances, and it appears that he is amusing himself perfectly well without me. And there is an additional complication – he might not be able to come home, even if he wanted to.'

'Why not?'

'According to Sir Hugh Trevelyan, he has been engaged

in intrigue against the government – and this fact is known in Whitehall. It's quite possible that if he returned openly, he would be arrested for treason.'

'I see. And you cannot go to Holland?'

'Not unless I am certain of my welcome,' Louise said frankly. 'However much I may wish to see him again, I have no intention of setting sail on a fool's errand, only to find him drunk and whoring in some tavern, having forgotten all about me. The only proof I have that he regrets what he did is a line in his letter to Phoebe. He said that if he could not live at Wintercombe with me, he did not want to live there at all.'

'Ah, yes, Wintercombe. I was coming to that,' said Silence. 'You may all fondly imagine that down here in Chard, apparently confined to the house, I no longer have any interest in what happens amongst my family. The silence on the subject of Wintercombe has been positively deafening – especially as I have had several letters from your aunt Deb, the first nearly a year ago now, mentioning Charles's return from foreign parts, and his subsequent activities.'

Louise had become very still. She cast a guilty glance at her grandmother. 'We decided it was best not to tell you.'

'Why not? I may be old, and a great-grandmother now, thanks to Kitty, but I am not in my dotage. I have had innumerable unpleasant shocks in my life, and I do like to think that I am robust and resilient enough to withstand them. So – Charles took my money and went to Ireland, not to Virginia? Hardly a surprise, given his devious nature – and his obsession with Wintercombe, and with you. I suppose his mother informed him that Alex had gone, and it was safe to return? I thought so. Did she also have anything to do with the quarrel between you and Alex?'

'She told me about his affair,' Louise said, clenching her fists in sudden anger. 'And the more I think of it, the more I feel a fool – for taking it so seriously.'

'Why should you? Nick has, to my certain knowledge, never been unfaithful to me, nor I to him – but I can well imagine my reaction if he conducted an adulterous liaison under my nose. No, I don't blame you for being angry, for feeling bitter and betrayed. But your thoughts have changed, have they not? And where there might be a chance of reconciliation, I think, for Kitty's sake, and for Lukas's, you should take it.'

'It's not so easy as that.'

'When was life ever easy? *Write* to him, Louise, at least let him know that you have changed your mind. Then a reply is up to him. Whether you hear anything or not, you will know what he thinks.'

Louise sat quiet for a moment, lost in thought. Then, she sighed, and turned to Silence, a rueful smile on her face. 'Perhaps you are right – and I will never have any peace here until I agree, will I? Very well, Gran'mère. I will write to him today.'

It was a lengthy and tenuous line of communication between Louise and her husband: first to Phoebe in Bath, thence to Sir Hugh, at present in Whitehall, hanging on to his court position for as long as he could while beset by proselytising friars and Jesuits: and so, secretly, over the stormy winter seas to Holland.

Her letter, painfully constructed after many false starts and pauses for thought, took four weeks to arrive at Alex's lodgings in Amsterdam, and by then it was too late: he had already been in England three days.

Gerrit, left behind despite his protests, put it carefully in his master's study to await his return, along with all the other messages, from correspondents in several countries. Then he went to the kitchen, to resume his slow, patient courtship of Clara. But his thoughts remained with Alex, and the dangers that he faced. Would he return safe to Holland, to find his wife's letter? Or was he even now in custody, facing the hideous death prescribed for traitors?

In Whitehall, just before Christmas, the campaign to persuade Sir Hugh Trevelyan to convert to the Roman religion reached its peak.

Ever since his return from Bath, he had been the subject of 'closeting', as it was called in Whitehall. Of course, he was by no means the only person to be thus harried: far better people than he, from the King's daughter downwards, had received the unsubtle attentions of a variety of proselytisers. Hugh found himself cornered in succession by Father Petre; his old friend and mentor Harry Jermyn, now Lord Dover; Sir Nicholas Butler, another recent convert; a procession of elderly Catholic lords, mostly in their dotage and with powers of persuasion to match; and finally, the King himself.

Hugh had known for a long time that, eventually, his lucrative Court position was doomed if he did not become a Catholic. In preparation, he had lived as frugally as he could whilst still maintaining the necessary display of splendour. His various offices, yielding a considerable income, had paid for the purchase of parcels of land dotted around the outskirts of London, including one which he had recently sold on for building, at an excellent profit. He had also bought a small estate in Suffolk, not far from St Edmundsbury, to which he would be able to retire, when dismissal came, with his son James.

Financially, then, his future was secure, but the thought of spending the rest of his days in rural seclusion, even with his beloved son, did not appeal. He had lived the life of a courtier, glittering, superficial, even influential, for fifteen years, and at the age of forty-three he suspected that he was too old to settle to the tedium of the country. His half-brother Francis, after the turbulent years of the Civil War, had adjusted to it well, but he had an intelligent and loving wife to keep him company. Hugh's dear Susannah had died years ago, and he was beginning to wonder if the time was not approaching to seek another.

There was one woman, of course, who would be his friend, companion, adversary: but lover, or wife? He knew that Phoebe St Barbe, with her keen, unfeminine mind, her sharp, acid wit and fierce independence, would laugh a proposal of marriage to scorn. And, try as he might, he could not think of another, amongst all his wide acquaintance who would suit him so well.

Still, the question was purely hypothetical. He would not

295

wish to subject Phoebe, whose health was precarious, to the stresses of life at Whitehall, and the artificial glitter of marriage to a courtier. And if he were to be dismissed, his prospects of future advancement were negligible under the present King.

The latter possibility was now seeming more and more likely. He had summoned up all his skills in diplomacy and tact to deal with those insistent, and at times downright infuriating Catholics, never answering them directly, never saying what he thought, always giving the impression that he was a possible, indeed a probable, candidate for conversion. At times, it had been difficult to conceal his resentment. His religion, such as it was, should be his own business, and this constant prying and harrying and nagging had set up the opposite reaction to what had been intended. His family were famous in Suffolk for their obstinacy. The greater the Papist's efforts, the less likely he was to do as they wished.

King James was, like most genuine converts, an enthusiast. To him, Catholicism was the only true religion, and those who did not follow it were unquestionably damned for all eternity. He had no understanding of the extraordinary level of hostility and prejudice against Catholics that prevailed amongst the great mass of his people, to whom Papists had been bogeymen since the Armada and the Gunpowder Plot, if not the fires of Smithfield. It was a measure of the King's own blindness that he was convinced that if only Catholics were placed in positions of influence and power, and the tenets of the Catholic religion widely disseminated in pamphlet and pulpit, then his island full of heretics would see that there was nothing to fear.

They, of course, with equally blinkered partiality, saw His Majesty's efforts only as the prelude to a campaign of forcible conversion, as was happening even now in France.

But there was no one left in the Privy Council bold enough to tell James about this catastrophic mutual mis-understanding: and Hugh, who had no great respect for his sovereign's intelligence, suspected that the King would not pay them any attention if they did.

With an inward feeling of resignation, he looked at his master's rather cadaverous face, illuminated by his eagerness to expound the truth and beauty of the Catholic religion, not to mention its more material advantages, and listened with his usual urbane courtesy as James waxed increasingly lyrical on the subject of salvation.

'I will, naturally, think very deeply about what you have told me, Your Majesty,' he said, when the King had at last paused in his exposition. 'But you can understand, I feel sure, that I need time for serious consideration. It is no light matter for a man to change his religion, when his chances of eternal life may be at stake.'

'You've been giving it serious consideration for months,' James pointed out peevishly. 'Surely the truth should be apparent to you by now?'

'Alas, no, Your Majesty,' Hugh said, allowing irony to creep into his voice: the King famously lacked any sense of humour. 'I am no St Paul, and neither is this the road to Damascus. Conversion is a difficult matter for me, and I need time to search my soul.'

James stared at him, frowning. At length, his petulance still evident, he said, 'I still feel that you have had long enough. So many of my friends have seen the light, and if you will not, or cannot, then I can only assume that you are my friend no longer.'

'Be assured, Your Majesty, of my undying loyalty,' Hugh said swiftly.

James looked at him, and shook his head sadly. 'I am persuaded of your sincerity in this, Sir Hugh. But you have served me well and faithfully all these years, and I have amply rewarded you for your devotion. Why are you still so stubborn?'

Time. He needed time, to come to a final decision, and to consult with his son. The boy was only ten, but he already had a good understanding of the world, and it was his inheritance, his future, which might be at stake. Christmas was only a few days away, and at Goldhayes they always kept the old festive customs, with much greenery and feasting and merriment. At Goldhayes, he would talk it over with young James, and with his half-brother Francis, and his niece Alathea, who had once been a fashionable artist before her marriage, and who understood the ways of Whitehall.

'If I may beg a favour, Your Majesty?'

The King was obviously reluctant to countenance further delay, but eventually he assented. Hugh had leave to go to Suffolk for Christmas, in return for his promise that when he came back to Whitehall, in two or three weeks' time, he would give his final answer.

But as he rode out of London in his coach, freshly painted and refurbished because it was cheaper than buying a new one, he suspected already what that answer would be. His position and influence at Court was useful not only to himself. And in matters of religion, as in almost everything else, he had long, long since cast all thought of principle out of the window.

Why else, after all, would he have continued in service for fifteen years to a man he both disliked and despised?

In Bath, Phoebe prepared to spend Christmas quietly, in the company of her nephew, who had two weeks' holiday in honour of the season. The weather was mild for December, but damp, and the pain in her joints was unusually severe. She went twice daily to the Cross Bath, and found that the waters brought her some little relief.

At least Lukas was not left alone, for he had acquired many friends at school and almost every morning one or other of a group of about half-a-dozen would be at the door, asking him to come and play. Phoebe suspected that often they got up to mischief, along the river bank amongst the fishing boats, or in the fields around the city, but she knew better than to ask. Her nephew was growing away from apron strings, revelling in the companionship of other boys, and she rejoiced in it. She had once thought that he might have difficulty in making friends, being so used to the company of adults. And to be hard-working and studious was never a popular trait. But Lukas, it seemed, had inherited his father's gift for inspirational leadership, though without the darker aspects, and she noted that the other boys seemed to defer to him quite naturally.

Against all the odds, it appeared that Lukas would turn out very well indeed. But he obviously still missed Alex: often, Phoebe would see him sitting over his books, staring into space, an expression of such complete desolation on his face that she longed to take him in her arms and comfort him. Usually, however, she refrained. School, and the natural process of maturity, had ensured that except in moments of acute distress, her nephew no longer welcomed such 'babying'.

But at least Alex had written to him. The letter, with another for Phoebe, had arrived at the beginning of December. Lukas showed her his, laughing and crying at the same time, and she thought that if her brother could have seen his face at that moment, he would abandon Holland for ever, and return to his son. It was a long letter, for Alex, nearly a whole page, full of interesting titbits of information, and congratulations on Lukas's success at school. And it ended with the cautious hope that the boy might, perhaps, join him in Amsterdam next year.

For weeks, Lukas went about with happiness incandescent behind his eyes, the precious paper tucked in his breeches pocket, to be taken out and read and reread until the creases wore through, and he knew it by heart. Phoebe pointed out that it would fall to pieces unless he kept it in a safer place, so Lukas bought a little wooden box out of his allowance, to keep the letter in, with a key which he wore on a string round his neck. He so evidently expected it to be the first of many that Phoebe's heart ached for him.

She did not show him her own letter, saying only that it was private. Lukas respected that, and did not attempt to pry further. She was very glad of it, for Alex's message, in language characteristically blunt, was brief, and frighteningly clear.

Edmond Everard, the Frenchman who had befriended Louise that autumn, and who had, to Phoebe's relief, left the city some weeks ago, was almost certainly a spy. He was undoubtedly in the pay of King James, he had been concerned in the attempted abduction of an English exile in Holland, and there were reasons to suspect that he was also working for the French King.

'In short,' Alex had written in his swift hand, 'he is a dangerous man, and his friendship with Louise is unlikely to be the result of coincidence. He may try to use her to persuade me home, or to harm me in some other way. I think it best not to tell her of this, unless you have no choice, for the less she knows, the better. But keep her away from him if you can.'

And under his sprawling signature, he had added, 'Burn this.'

She had obliged at once, but his words returned again and again, etched on her mind with disturbing significance. It both angered and frightened her, to think that Louise, and probably the rest of the household as well, was the subject of hostile government surveillance. But she felt also that her judgement, and her nephew's, had been vindicated. There had always been something too smooth, too glib, about Monsieur Everard, although Louise, revelling in his entertaining company, had been blind to it.

Despite what her brother had advised, Phoebe doubted very much that she could warn his wife against Everard without giving her the true reason for it. Louise was wayward and wilful, and open disapproval of the Frenchman, even a vague insinuation of danger, would only reinforce her desire for friendship with him. But at least the situation would probably not arise, for Everard had been gone for over a month now, and Bath in the winter, out of season, was a quiet, shabby, rustic place, host only to the unfashionable, and the genuinely sick. Such a man of mode, on the fringes of the Court, was unlikely to return here now unless his business was especially urgent. And as Christmas approached with no sign of Everard, Phoebe began to relax. Perhaps his absence was an indication that, however unlikely it might seem, the Frenchman's attentions had no ulterior and sinister motive.

Anyway, Louise was safe at Chard, and enjoying herself. Her letters, written regularly once a week, were full of family news and gossip, and Kitty's latest achievements. She apologised to Phoebe for staying away so long, and her sister-in-law wrote back to tell her briskly that she could stay at Chard for as long as she wished. Silence and Nick would undoubtedly want to see as much as possible of their granddaughter, and their first great-grandchild, and Phoebe was more than content to spend Christmas quietly with Lukas, pottering amongst her books and taking the waters.

When Hugh's letter came, in the middle of January, she was alone in the house, save for the servants: Lukas was at school, and Louise still at Chard. It arrived not by the post, but was brought by his own servant, so she knew that it must contain news that required considerable secrecy. She sent the exhausted man to the kitchen, in Mattie's capable charge, for a good hot meal. Then she sat down in her parlour, by the warm, comfortable fire, sea-coal glowing red and cheerful at its heart, and slid a knife under the seal. What information did Hugh have for her, that he could not trust to the post? Did it concern Alex?

She scanned down the lines written in her friend's elaborate hand. It seemed at first to be merely Whitehall gossip, chiefly the official confirmation of the Queen's pregnancy, until the third paragraph.

There is a man now often seen at Court, who speaks most warmly of your brother's lady wife, in terms which have aroused some curiosity and comment. Having a friend's concern for her reputation, I took it upon myself to broach the matter with him, and I am glad to say that he has now seen the error of his ways. As I am not a quarrelsome man, his faint-heartedness was most welcome to me, though you may be sure that he still thinks me most eager to protect the lady's good name, at point of sword if necessary. But take good care should he return to Bath and attempt once more to ingratiate himself with her, for I fear, from things that I have heard whispered, that more than her reputation might be endangered thereby. However, he has apparently now gone overseas, to France so they say, and so I hope you are well rid of him, though you may be certain that there will be others ready to take his place.

This cryptic passage must surely refer to Edmond Everard, and only confirmed the warning that Alex had already given. The thought of Hugh challenging anyone, even the smooth Frenchman, to a duel, almost made her smile, but his information was deeply disturbing. At least Everard had been a known danger, to be avoided, encouraged or deceived as necessary. But now almost anyone might be spying on them, keeping them under suveillance, waiting for the mistake, the error of judgement, the careless word or deed that might spell disaster, danger, death to Alex in Holland.

Feeling faintly sick, she forced herself to read the remainder of the letter. Hugh had spent Christmas at the home of his brother in Suffolk, there was news of his son James, a dry comment on the parlously wet state of the roads, and then a reference that puzzled her.

While I was at Goldhayes, I was able to renew my acquaintance with our old friend Master Orchard, lately come into these parts on business, after some fifteen months travelling overseas. He asked to be remembered to you, and spoke of you very fondly, but regrets that his business will not allow him to return to his home in Bristol at present.

Phoebe stared at the letter in bewilderment. Orchard. That was her Uncle Henry's name, and he was a merchant in Bristol. But to her certain knowledge, he had not been overseas for years, and was probably even now in his warehouse, inspecting his most recent consignment of wine. Nor was she particularly intimate with the wider Orchard family, amongst whom there was no one who could remotely be described as an 'old friend'.

And then light poured in on her. '. . . fifteen months travelling overseas.' Alex had been in Holland for precisely

302

that length of time. It was *Alex* whom he had met in Suffolk, under this alias: and that explained the warning about Everard, and the elaborate precautions Hugh had taken to ensure that the letter did not fall into unfriendly hands. And even if it had, his reference to her brother was couched in terms that only those closest to him would understand.

So, Alex had at last returned to England, doubtless for some nefarious purpose not unconnected with the Prince of Orange, and was even now skulking in Suffolk under an assumed name, while his wife, his son, his estate, even his sister, were all in desperate need of him . . .

But of course he could not come home. Even if he were not spying for William, he was still a marked man, in danger of arrest for treason if his presence in England was discovered. But if he cannot appear in Bath, Phoebe thought, astonished by her sense of anger and urgency, then I shall go to him. It's high time he learned exactly what I think of him, and I shall tell him the full extent of the distress and harm he has caused to Louise, and Lukas. And there's the matter of Wintercombe, too. How could he allow Charles to usurp his rights? Even if he is unable to return to us, he cannot so easily escape his responsibilities, and the consequences of what he has done.

She read the letter again, carefully, to ensure that she had not leapt to unwarranted conclusions. Then she screwed it up into a tight ball and pushed it with the poker into the depths of the fire. Once the thin pale spear of flame had died away to ashes, she took a deep breath, marshalled her considerable mental powers, and began to make plans.

When Lukas returned home from school at dusk, flushed with the raw cold outside, he found his aunt packing her bags. He stood at the door of her chamber, bewildered and distressed, and stared at her. 'What's happening? What are you doing?'

Phoebe had rehearsed this moment in her mind a hundred times, but she hated the thought of lying to him, and for a moment her resolution faltered. Then she pushed the last of her old shabby black gowns into the bag, buckled the straps with an air of determination, and turned to face him.

Her unease at the situation ironically brought a sadness to her face which was entirely appropriate for the falsehoods she was about to utter. 'Lukas, I'm afraid I have to go to London – tomorrow morning, early. It's Sir Hugh – I had word today that he's very ill.'

'Oh, Aunt Phoebe, I'm so sorry.' Lukas dropped his satchel and came to put his arms around her.

His sincere attempt at comfort was nearly Phoebe's undoing: she sniffed, scrabbled in her pocket for a handkerchief, and blew her nose with noisy thoroughness. 'Don't worry too much, it doesn't seem to be mortal,' she told him. 'But the message from his brother said that he was asking for me, so I have to go.'

On the other side of the bed Mattie, who knew the truth, kept her head down and folded clothes industriously. Phoebe smiled wanly at her nephew. 'Don't worry about yourself. I've been to see Matthew Ryder's mother, and she is very happy for you to lodge with her while I'm away. I shouldn't be gone for longer than a week or two.'

'I'd much rather Louise came back so that I could stay here,' Lukas said unhappily. 'Matthew's my best friend, but his father is very strict and stern. You aren't allowed to talk at table.'

'Very few children are – this household is an exception,' Phoebe pointed out. 'But Louise is quite happy and settled at Chard, and she won't want to bring Kitty back here in this weather. Please, Lukas, stay at Matthew's house – I'll arrange to have your things sent over there tomorrow, and you can go home with him after school. This house will be shut up, and I'll give the key to Mistress Richards next door.'

He still looked unhappy, but resigned to his fate. With heartfelt relief, and guilt, she knew that he had accepted her lies, and answered his questions about Hugh's supposed illness vaguely, saying only that the message had not been specific, but that it seemed to be some kind of severe fever.

Although she still loathed the necessity of such deception, it was essential if anyone should be watching their movements. A hasty trip to London to visit a sick friend would seem quite innocent, and would arouse, at worst, only slight suspicion. If she took Lukas with her, or, even more dangerously, told Louise, then Edmond Everard's replacement, if he existed, would surely realise why and where she was going, and she would lead him straight to Alex. To cover her tracks, she had already ensured that all her friends and neighbours in Nowhere Lane knew of the purpose and destination of her journey, in case someone asked awkward questions.

Certain that she had thought of everything, she retired early to bed after a light supper, leaving her nephew poring over the long passage of Tacitus which he must learn for tomorrow.

Lukas usually enjoyed Tacitus, particularly the section on the barbarous British, but tonight the dense Latin held no attraction for him at all. Something in his aunt's manner today had disturbed him, although he assumed that she was upset about Sir Hugh's illness. Like every other member of her family, except Phoebe herself, Lukas had confidently expected the courtier to offer for her hand, one day. What if he were dangerously ill? Even worse, what if he died?

Completely unable to concentrate, he gave up and closed the book. It was not late, and he felt too restless and uneasy for sleep. Perhaps Mattie would still be in the warmth of the kitchen, sewing or reading, and he could persuade her to let him have a cup of chocolate. Comforted and hopeful, he took his candlestick and made his way to the rear of the house.

The kitchen was small, and had no oven, so bread, pies and other baked meats had to be provided by the baker or the cookshop. Mattie sat in front of the fire, humming to herself and stitching at one of Lukas's shirts: and, as he had hoped, a gently steaming kettle hung over the flames.

She would not be persuaded at first: chocolate was so dear, in such short supply, the cabinet where it was kept was locked, and she had no idea where the key was . . .

'It's on that hook over there,' Lukas said with a grin.

305

'Please, Mattie, it's such a cold night, and I'd like something warming to cheer me up – and I expect you would, too.'

The maid relented, as she had intended to do all along. She was very fond of Lukas, who had all his father's looks, charm and energy, without, it seemed, any of his more unpleasant qualities. She had liked the thought of lying to him as little as had Mistress Phoebe: the boy doted on his father, pined for him, and not to take Lukas to Suffolk, not even to tell him that his beloved papa was in England, struck her as heartless and cruel. Her mistress had explained the necessity of it, but Mattie was privately sceptical. She had great respect for Mistress Phoebe's intelligence, although to be so clever was surely unnatural in a woman, but this talk of spies and treason and danger seemed far-fetched in the extreme. That smooth Frenchie had left Bath weeks ago, and Mattie was certain that his only reason for calling had been to make eyes at Lady St Barbe.

Despite her misgivings, though, she had said nothing, although the little boy's innocently concerned face had almost brought tears to her eyes. Now, as he sat opposite her, sipping the thick, fragrant chocolate and talking anxiously about Sir Hugh Trevelyan, whom he clearly liked, Mattie's resolve weakened further. She hoped that the conversation would not turn to Lukas's father: but since Alex was never far from his mind, it was almost inevitable.

'I'd like to go back to Holland,' the boy said wistfully, into a companionable pause. 'I've almost forgotten how to speak Dutch, and I'm not even sure I could understand it any more – my head's all filled up with Latin now. But did you know, Mattie, that Papa had asked me to join him in Amsterdam, next summer perhaps?'

'Your aunt said something of it to I, Master Lukas.'

'I *do* miss him so much,' he went on, with heavy sadness. Normally, he kept his feelings as much as possible to himself, but it was so easy to confide in Mattie, round, comfortable, and full of friendly sympathy. 'I wish he hadn't gone away – I wish he would come back to us. I *worry* about him so much.'

The thought of Lukas, eight years old and precociously solemn, being concerned about Alex, past thirty and more than capable of looking after himself, might at another time have brought a smile to Mattie's lips. She looked at him, seeing the blue eyes so suspiciously bright, the yearning misery in his face, and came to a decision.

'I shouldn't be telling ee this, Master Lukas,' she said softly, putting her needle down. 'But I will, so long as ee don't breathe a word of it to no one – particularly not to your aunt. She don't want ee to know, but I'll tell ee now, and put the smile back on your face.'

'Tell me what?' He was suddenly all eagerness and hope, like a puppy. 'Please, Mattie – tell me *what*? Is it to do with Papa?'

Committed, the maid still hesitated. 'Do ee swear not to speak a word of it?' she said, very seriously.

'Of course I do – but please, Mattie, please, *tell me*!'

She took a deep breath, aware that this indiscretion would displease Mistress Phoebe mightily, if she ever learned of it. But she could not bear to see the poor child so unhappy: and so she said quietly, 'Yes, Master Lukas, 'tis your father. He be in England, and your aunt be a-travelling tomorrow to see en.'

'Then – then Sir Hugh isn't ill?'

'Not that I know of, he bain't, Master Lukas.'

'But she lied to me! Aunt Phoebe lied to me! Why didn't she tell me Papa was in England?'

Mattie had anticipated this question. To speak of spies and danger sounded ludicrously overdramatic, and Master Lukas was a very down-to-earth child. But she knew she must give him some good reason, so she said with calculated vagueness, 'Mistress Phoebe did think that Sir Alexander would be put in danger if she didn't go in secret, and alone.'

'Alone?' Lukas's face was a study in outraged bewilderment. 'But she's taking you, Mattie! And even if she couldn't take me, why didn't she *tell* me?' Tears stood in his sapphire-blue eyes. 'I can keep a secret, she could have *trusted* me – I wouldn't have told *anyone*!'

'Maybe she thought you'd want to go with she,' Mattie

307

said. 'But even aside from keeping it a secret, 'tis a long, long way to Suffolk, and I d'reckon she were thinking of your schooling.'

'Suffolk?' Lukas said in surprise. 'Isn't Papa in London, then?'

'No, he bain't – he be at Sir Hugh's brother's house near St Edmundsbury, so your aunt said.' And what he be doing there, thought Mattie, who strongly disapproved of Alex, the Devil only knows.

'I *would* like to see him,' Lukas said wistfully. 'But I suppose I can understand why Aunt Phoebe didn't want to take me too.'

'Don't ee dare tell she that I've told ee,' Mattie reminded him urgently. 'I weren't supposed to say aught – she'll be all a-hoh if she find out.'

'She wouldn't dismiss you,' Lukas said reassuringly. 'I *know* she wouldn't – you're part of the family. But don't worry – I won't tell her, I promise. You're quite safe.'

'Thank ee, Master Lukas,' Mattie said. She smiled at him, and the boy smiled back, in perfect and friendly understanding.

# Chapter Sixteen

## 'Launch into the deep'

At dawn the next day, Phoebe St Barbe, with her maid Mattie, left Bath in a hired coach: and Lukas, determined to conceal the fact that he knew the truth, waved them goodbye and then trudged off to school, well muffled up against the wind and rain of January.

On the way to the Northgate, he stopped briefly at the White Hart in Stall Street, and left a sealed letter for posting on to his stepmother in Chard. It had taken him some time to compose a message that would, he hoped, be clear to her but not to anyone who might open it with hostile intent. Everyone knew that mail travelling by the ordinary post was at risk of clandestine inspection by the authorities: presumably, that was why Sir Hugh's message had been brought by his own servant.

Lukas could not command such a luxury, but he hoped that no one would bother with a message so obviously the work of a child. And he prayed, desperately, that Louise would understand what he had written, and act upon it. He could not go to Suffolk alone to see his father: he needed his stepmother's help and support. And he was able to contemplate the rather bleak prospect of a stay at his friend's house with equanimity, even eagerness. For in a week's time, if all went well, Louise would return to Bath, and they could set off together to find his father.

Life at Matthew's house was not so bad as he had feared, for the stern and terrifying Master Ryder was in Bristol on business, and Mistress Ryder and the other children were friendly and sympathetic. But the cold, dark days crawled past, and there was no word from anyone, although he called every morning at the White Hart. By the end of the first week, he was beginning to wonder if his letter had gone

309

astray: or, far worse, if it had been opened, and his father captured as a result.

Lukas was not usually given to such alarming flights of fancy, but his state of excitement and expectation made him very susceptible to the unwelcome excesses of his imagination. January became February, milder, but very wet, and he hoped that the lack of any reply from Louise was caused by the undoubtedly awful state of the roads. Chard was fifty miles away – how long would it take for his stepmother to travel to Bath? Two days? Three? Even a week?

And then one evening, just before hope had finally expired, he came back with Matthew to the house in Westgate Street, and found Louise waiting for him.

She looked rather tired, but there was a light in her face that he had not seen for over a year, since his father left them. He ran into her arms, and she hugged him in a tight, fierce embrace, her eyes wet. 'Oh, Lukas, it's so good to see you again! Do you want to come home with me?'

He nodded, not trusting himself to speak: Matthew was watching, and Matthew would never let him forget it if he burst into tears. He packed his one small bag, said a grateful goodbye to Mistress Ryder, and left their house with winged and buoyant delight.

'I'm sorry I took so long,' Louise said, as they made their way down the dark street, the Ryders' kitchen boy walking in front of them to light their way safely home. 'But your letter didn't reach Chard until last Friday, a week after you'd written it – the roads were flooded, apparently. Then I had to organise the journey, and my grandfather's coach turned out to need repairs to one of the wheels and the axle, which took another day or so – and although the floods had gone down by then, we thought ourselves lucky if we made ten miles in a day.' She smiled at Lukas with breathless brilliance. 'Still, I'm here now, and I only hope that it isn't too late. But if nothing else, at least I've rescued you from the clutches of Master Ryder. Is he as fierce as he looks?'

Lukas, hoping that the kitchen boy was not listening, grinned. 'Fiercer. But he's been in Bristol until yesterday, so I didn't mind too much.'

'Well, I'm glad of that.' She laughed, and hugged him again as they came up to the door of Phoebe's house in Nowhere Lane. 'And I'm glad, too, so very, very glad and grateful, Luikje, that you wrote to me.'

Only his father had ever before used the Dutch diminutive of his name, but he found that he did not mind it in the least from Louise.

The house was a little musty from being shut up for two weeks, but Christian had lit fires and opened windows, and the beds were freshly made, with a warming pan placed in each one to air it. Kitty was there with her nurse, who was spooning a rich egg posset into her wide mouth. When she saw her brother, she hid her face in the nurse's shoulder, and then peeped out to look at him with round chestnut-brown eyes that were exactly the same colour as her mother's. Lukas grinned, and made hideous faces, and she chuckled and all but choked on her spoon.

'Supper first,' Louise said. 'Then, we'll make plans.'

The meal had obviously been brought from a chophouse, for the meat was rather tough and the pies cold in the middle, but Lukas devoured it with as much enthusiasm as if it had been a banquet. Kitty, who seemed to have taken the long and difficult journey in her stride, was put to bed, and Lukas, Christian and Louise sat in the back parlour, where there was a truly ferocious fire blazing, and the shutters closed against the rain outside.

'Tell me exactly what happened,' Louise said to her stepson, as soon as they had settled themselves.

Lukas glanced at Christian, and the maid smiled at him. 'Don't ee fret, Master Lukas – I can be so quiet as the grave when 'tis needed, and I will.'

So he launched into his account of Sir Hugh's message, and its aftermath. 'I know it was supposed to be kept a secret,' he finished. 'Mattie told me that Papa might be in danger if the King came to hear that he was in England. But I couldn't try to find him on my own, so I wrote to you. Will you come with me?'

'Of course I will,' Louise said. 'We'll go together, as soon as it can be arranged. Christian will come too, naturally, and Kitty, with her nurse. I'll have to tell people the same story that Phoebe told – that we've gone to give comfort to Sir Hugh in London. Once we're there, we can go on to Suffolk to find your father.'

'What about Sir Hugh? Will we tell him anything? You see,' Lukas explained earnestly, 'Mattie said that Papa was at Sir Hugh's brother's house near St Edmundsbury in Suffolk, but I don't know the name of it. How will we find it if we don't ask Sir Hugh?'

'His half-brother is an important man – people are bound to know him,' Louise said. 'I think it's best if we don't call on Sir Hugh. He might advise us against it, or even try to stop us. No, the fewer people who know the truth, the better. I'll speak to Master Carne in the morning, and tell him that you'll be absent from school for a few weeks, and I'll make all the other arrangements too. With luck, we should be able to leave Bath the day after tomorrow. And before long, if all goes well, we'll reach Suffolk, and find your father.'

'I hope he's still there,' Lukas said, but his shining eyes and eager face spoke eloquently of his belief that the success of their quest was certain.

St Edmundsbury was a handsome town, full of substantial houses well built in both brick and half-timber. It also possessed a fine market square, dominated by an inn called the Angel on one side and the flint walls and gateway of the defunct Abbey on the other. After nearly a fortnight of travelling, however, none of the occupants of the hired coach were in any condition to admire the scenery. As it rolled to a halt in the courtyard of the Angel, dripping copious quantities of mud and water, they roused themselves from a stupor of jolted exhaustion, stumbled down the steps, and staggered into the warm and welcoming embrace of one of the most famous establishments in Suffolk.

Louise had had perforce to use her own name when hiring a coach in Bath, but it had been easy, in the crowded anonymity of London, to take another under the alias of

312

Mistress Woods, her grandmother's maiden name. And it was as Mistress Woods, with her stepson Luke, daughter Katherine and two servants, that she reserved a capacious suite of chambers on the first floor of the inn, overlooking the marketplace, and ordered a hearty supper to be sent up to them.

The landlord himself escorted the trio of serving women with their loaded, steaming and delicious-smelling trays. Louise, her heart thumping so hard she wondered that it had not forced its way out of her chest, made polite conversation with him as the table was laid. It proved easier than she had feared to ask him, with every appearance of casual interest, whether he knew of the brother of her old and dear friend, Sir Hugh Trevelyan, who lived somewhere in these parts.

'Trevelyan? Ah, I know him, Mistress. His brother is Master Heron, at Goldhayes,' said the landlord, to her utter relief. 'You know him, then?'

Louise saw the curiosity in his face, and spoke carefully. 'I know *of* him only. Sir Hugh is a longstanding friend to me and my family, but I have never met his brother. However, as we are travelling in these parts, it would be a matter of courtesy to make ourselves known to Master Heron. Is he a hospitable man?'

'He's famous for it hereabouts,' said the landlord, who was an elderly, birdlike little man with the eager look of the habitual gossip. 'Well liked, and respected, for all he's led a wild life in his youth. I could tell you some stories, Mistress Woods . . .'

For longer than they wanted, she and Lukas listened while their food grew cold, as the landlord described the Herons of Goldhayes. Francis Heron, the present head of the family, was a man in his sixties, though in excellent health, and he lived there now with his wife and his widowed sister. His son and heir, recently married, resided with his wife and baby son somewhere near Oxford: another son was a captain in the navy, and there were also two daughters. One was married to a well-respected Bury doctor who lived just round the corner from the Angel, with six children, all girls, save the first and the last: and the other, Mistress Sophie, widowed while still very young, was one of the Princess Anne's ladies.

The gleam in the landlord's eye indicated that Francis Heron's younger daughter was a prime subject for scandalous gossip, but Louise was not to be drawn further. She thanked him in mid-flow, slipped a generous sum into his palm to compensate him for his disappointment, and firmly asked him to leave.

At last, they had a measure of privacy, and could plan their campaign. The garrulous landlord had not mentioned any mysterious or suspicious strangers, and Sir Hugh's half-brother seemed to be a pillar of the local community, well loved and greatly respected. Surely such a man would not be harbouring traitors, or encouraging the interests of the Prince of Orange?

But they had travelled from one side of England to the other, and now that they were so close, Louise had no intention of running home cowardly, her plans abandoned and her hopes unfulfilled. She looked at Lukas, who was almost too tired to eat, and gave him her bravest and most gallant smile. 'Well? Shall we try our luck at Goldhayes tomorrow? It's only a few miles away now.'

'Shouldn't we send word to Sir Hugh's brother first?' Lukas objected. 'Isn't it very impolite to turn up un-announced?'

'Not necessarily, no. If he's as hospitable as the landlord said he was, he'll make us very welcome. After all, it's not as if we're lying to him – Sir Hugh *is* a very dear friend. And besides,' Louise added, 'I want to surprise your father. *If* he's there.'

'If?' Lukas swallowed a yawn behind his hand, and gazed at her with some anxiety. 'But what if he isn't? What if we've come all this way for nothing?'

'I hope, I hope very much that he will still be at Goldhayes. But Sir Hugh wrote to Phoebe weeks ago, remember. Your father may have moved on to some other house – or he may even have gone back to Holland. I don't know, Luikje, and I have no intention of undoing all our

314

careful conspiracy by asking the landlord! But even if he isn't at Goldhayes, Sir Hugh's brother will surely know where he's gone. And perhaps Phoebe will be there, too. Tomorrow, we'll find out for certain, one way or the other.' She smiled at him as he yawned again. 'But for now, I think we all need a good night's rest. You look as if you're about to fall asleep at the table.'

That brought a rather sheepish smile to her stepson's pale face, and he obediently stumbled off to bed in the chamber already occupied by Kitty and her nurse. Two maids came in to settle the fires for the night, and clear away the remains of their meal, and Louise, yawning herself although it was hours before her usual bedtime, retired thankfully to the warmth of the Angel's most comfortable feather bed.

But the thought remained with her, sharp and painful, even as she drifted into an exhausted sleep. She had told Lukas that she wanted to surprise Alex. She had not told him the true reason for planning their unheralded appearance at Goldhayes: that Alex might not welcome them – or, far worse, that he might seize the opportunity to leave before they arrived.

'I can see it, I can see it!' Lukas's head was thrust so far from the window of the coach that he was in serious danger of falling out. Louise, her nerves already on edge, seized his coat and pulled him back in, more brusquely than she had intended. 'Lukas! Don't – please don't behave like some noisy street boy.'

Anger made her voice loud, and he thumped down on the seat, looking at her with injured astonishment. 'I'm sorry, Louise,' he said, swallowing hard. 'I forgot.'

His crestfallen expression made her ashamed of her loss of temper, and she gave him an apologetic smile. 'I'm sorry I shouted at you, Luikje. But I do think we ought to be on our best behaviour, all of us. Tell me about Goldhayes – what does it look like?'

'It's big – very big and grand, much larger than Wintercombe – and it has two wings coming forward at either side, with a funny little tower at each end, and it's

315

built of red brick, rose red, not bright red,' Lukas told her. 'Do you think Sir Hugh's brother will receive us? Or is he too important?'

'Just you remember, Luikje, that I am *Lady* St Barbe, and you are the son of a baronet, even if your parents were not married,' Louise said firmly. 'In any case, a true gentleman will always receive visitors, even uninvited ones, with courtesy and kindness – and from what the landlord of the Angel was saying last night, Sir Hugh's brother is a man who would give us a warm welcome even if we were in rags.'

'And we're not,' said her stepson, looking down with satisfaction at his best suit, in dark red with gold braiding and buttons, and the shoes with shining buckles to match.

Louise also wore her finery, a striped mantua of heavy green silk, with a fur-lined hood, muff and tippet to keep her warm. She grinned at him reassuringly. 'No, we're not, are we? And my mother always says that you can go anywhere, do anything, without let or hindrance, so long as you have the right clothes and the right manner to carry it off. Even calling at the house of a man we've never met, who hasn't any idea who we are, in search of someone who shouldn't be there, and might not be there anyway . . .'

'I hope he is,' Lukas said fervently. 'Oh, Louise, I do hope so much that he is.'

'And so do I,' she said, as the coach rumbled, with a suddenly hollow sound, over a bridge that presumably spanned a moat. And now they were drawing up in a gravelled forecourt, very like that in front of Wintercombe, save that the walls that surrounded her as she descended from the coach were not made of golden stone, but of a warm, rather faded brick.

As Lukas had said, Goldhayes was large and grand, but also very beautiful. There were just enough examples of asymmetry – oddly placed chimneys, a tall oriel window off-centre beside the stone porch, several strands of un-official ivy climbing the walls – to give the house an air of welcoming informality. Louise took this all in with a brief glance, not wishing to be seen gaping awestruck like a bumpkin. After all, she was familiar with Versailles, unquestionably the most splendid palace in all Europe. She smiled at Lukas, and took his arm, and together, with Christian a few steps behind, they walked to the porch.

She had wondered about leaving Kitty behind at the Angel: it was remarkable enough to arrive uninvited at Goldhayes without an eight-month-old baby in attendance, and although her daughter was usually very good, she was teething at present, and apt to be fretful. In the end, at Lukas's suggestion, she had compromised, and told the child's nurse to wait with her in the coach: the sun was shining, and it was a mild and pleasant day for February. As peevish wails arose behind them, Louise was glad that she would not have to face Alex with a squalling infant in her arms, rendering all attempts at civil conversation, let alone reconciliation, absolutely impossible.

A butler, large, young and formidable, admitted them and asked their business. Louise, with sublime and deceptive confidence, gave him her assumed name, and asked if it might be possible to speak with Master Francis Heron.

'The master is not at home,' said the butler, in a voice so deep and portentous that it seemed to come from the ground beneath his feet. 'However, Mistress Heron is above stairs, in the gallery, and although she has guests, she may be prepared to speak to you. What business may I state, madam?'

'We are friends of Sir Hugh Trevelyan, paying a visit of courtesy only,' Louise said, and waited, with a thundering heart, as the man ascended the staircase leading from the hall, with as much dignity as if Heaven were his destination.

Lukas had come to stand very close to her, his face as pale as ashes and his eyes bright with mingled apprehension and excitement. At least he is sure of his welcome, Louise thought. Alex has never failed to be kind to him, has never treated him brutally.

Whereas she . . . She had a sudden horrible vision of that last night, his drunken violence, the rape which had, to her bewilderment and shame, failed to destroy her love for him, and her knees began to shake. Why had she done this? Why

317

had she wilfully reopened this just-healed scar, to hurt and bleed and suffer again? She could have stayed in Bath, watched Kitty grow up, flirted enjoyably with any man she chose, taken lovers, lived a life of pleasurable luxury free from danger, and few people, in these licentious days, would have thought any the worse of her. And instead, she had crossed England, enduring the discomforts and dangers of a prolonged winter journey, to a house where no one knew her, just for the chance, remote and uncertain, of seeing him again.

And he might not want her, he might well be angry, she had probably put him in jeopardy by embarking on this foolish wild-goose chase . . .

Or he might have been longing for her. And even as that possibility warmed her chilled heart, Lukas's hand pressed her arm, and she saw the butler returning with that studied deliberation. Yes, Mistress Heron would be delighted to receive her: she was in the long gallery with some of her grandchildren, but she had ordered refreshments to be brought, and the footman would escort Mistress Woods and Master van der Linden upstairs.

Wintercombe was ancient, far older than Goldhayes, and could boast nothing like the great gallery which stretched the width of this house. It was lined with pictures of, presumably, past Herons, in the ruffs of Elizabeth's day, the silks and lace and lovelocks of forty years ago, and the studied informality favoured by more modern artists. And at the far end, where a fire burned cheerfully, a small, grey-haired woman in a russet silk gown sat surrounded by children.

She rose to greet them with a very pleasant smile. Her eyes, on either side of a nose as aquiline as Louise's, were dark and humorous, and her voice had a dry, amused quality. 'Ah, Mistress Woods! Any friend of Hugh's is a friend of ours, and you are most welcome. These are my granddaughters – I'll say their names, and then send them packing so that we can talk in peace. Frances, Lucy, Grace and Harriet, come to stay to give my poor daughter a rest – she's just been brought to bed of a son, and about time too, after all these girls. This is her elder boy, Sandro.'

A handsome blond child of about thirteen bowed lavishly, his dark eyes sparkling.

'And Hugh's son James – but I see you know each other.'

The fair-haired boy who had befriended Lukas, two years ago in London, and so initiated the link between the Herons and the St Barbes, was staring at Louise and Lukas in puzzlement. 'I remember you! You were Mistress Chevalier then, weren't you? And Lukas – Lukas, your father is here! Is that why you've come?'

Mistress Heron's face was a study in bewilderment. 'Your father? Who is he? There is no one here called van der Linden.'

James looked round at the gaggle of girls, variously red-haired and blonde, who were staring at him and at Lukas and Louise with unabashed curiosity. 'If you'd all go away,' he said, with heavy patience, 'then I'll explain. These are *adult* matters.'

His cousins glared at him, and the smallest, who was about three and had hair the colour of oranges and an abundance of freckles, screwed her face into a hideous leer and stuck out her tongue.

'Hattie!' said her grandmother reprovingly. 'That's most impolite, and before our guests, too. Sandro, Frances, do take them all away, please.'

The elder boy and his sister, who had very pale hair and an air of responsible gravity shepherded the younger ones away down the gallery. Once they had gone beyond earshot, Louise turned to Mistress Heron with an apologetic smile. 'I'm afraid that we're not exactly as we seem – as James has already indicated. My name is Louise St Barbe, and this is my husband's natural son, Lukas.'

'So your husband is Sir Alexander St Barbe, who has also come to Goldhayes under a name not his own,' said Mistress Heron. Her eyes, brown and shrewd, rested thoughtfully on Louise. 'Well, as he is still Master Orchard to all but myself and my husband – and James, of course – then you had best continue to be plain Mistress Woods. Does he know that you were coming to see him?'

'No, I'm afraid he does not,' Louise said honestly. She

had liked her hostess on sight, the warmth and down-to-earth intelligence evident in her face, but she did not wish to reveal all her marital difficulties, even to this friendly woman. 'He has been in Holland for over a year, and I have had very little news of him. He has not even seen his baby daughter yet.'

'You have a baby? You hardly look old enough,' Mistress Heron said with a smile. 'What age is she? What is her name?'

'She is called Kitty, and she is nearly nine months old.'

The conversation turned innocuously to infant matters, for Mistress Heron professed great interest in Kitty and her accomplishments – could she crawl? Stand? How many teeth did she have? A pair of maids in identical blue gowns brought trays of refreshments, tea, cakes, and a mug of small beer for Lukas. He was then drawn away by James, eager to renew their friendship and to introduce him properly to Sandro, and soon all seven children, the three boys and the four girls, were playing some restrainedly noisy game of tag at the other end of the gallery.

Louise let slip that Kitty was at this moment outside in the coach, and her hostess immediately suggested that she be brought inside to be shown off. 'Although my daughter's girls, I'm afraid, are heartily sick of babies at present, and will find the arrival of another sadly tedious. But if your baby is teething, perhaps we'll talk awhile first – we have serious matters to discuss.'

She sipped her tea, and surveyed Louise, who was nibbling a biscuit and trying to appear relaxed and at ease, without a hint of the questions and fears jostling and tumbling in her mind. 'I take it,' she went on, 'that you are well aware of the danger in which your husband stands, if his real identity and the reason for his stay here become public knowledge?'

'Yes, of course I am,' Louise said softly. 'That's why I have called myself Mistress Woods.'

'I thought so. And if he were to be discovered, or betrayed through carelessness or malice, then you must understand also that my husband, and a great many other people in these parts, would also be put in danger – not to mention the network of intelligence that the Prince of Orange has spent so many years painstakingly building up.' She looked at Louise assessingly. 'I must doubtless risk offending you by saying this, but I have to make it perfectly clear to you, for everyone's sake, including your own. From things that your husband has said – and more from what he has *not* said – I have received the impression that you and he parted on bad terms. Don't worry, I have no intention of prying into your private affairs, and if you have come here to attempt a reconciliation, then I wish you the very best of luck. But I must be sure in my own mind that you will not betray us, for whatever cause.'

'Of course I wouldn't!' Louise said angrily. Lukas, at the far end of the gallery, heard her and looked round: she waved at him reassuringly, and he returned to the game. Acutely aware of the older woman's scrutiny, she added, more quietly, 'You are right – I do hope for a reconciliation. And if that proves to be impossible, then at least my conscience will be clear – and he will have seen Kitty.'

'I hope very much, for your sake and his, and the baby's, that you will be successful,' said Mistress Heron, smiling. 'I do apologise for the necessity of my inquisition, Lady St Barbe, and I hope you understand the reasons for it. Now, before we send for Kitty, we must descend to practicalities for a moment. I'm afraid your husband is not here at present – he has gone over to Newmarket with Francis, on the pretext of inspecting a horse, but with other purposes entirely. They should be back in time for supper, however. And you are, of course, more than welcome to stay here for as long as you wish, and your baby and your charming stepson as well. How like his father he is!'

'He possesses all Alex's better qualities,' Louise said drily.

Mistress Heron raised an eyebrow at her tone, but made no other comment. Instead, she suggested that their baggage be fetched from the Angel, and that the story that Louise was a friend of Sir Hugh Trevelyan be continued for public consumption. 'Of course, you will have to pretend that you and your husband are merely acquainted. If all goes well and you are reconciled, you may find it difficult to disguise your feelings, in public at any rate.' She gave Louise a friendly, conspiratorial smile. 'But I remember only too clearly what a trial it is, to keep love a secret, and the more so when you have every right to display your affection. And so I propose that you and your baby and stepson occupy the little suite of rooms just round the corner from where we are sitting – they are comfortable, and there is a chamber each for the children. And since all our guest-chambers are in the same part of the house, you will find your husband just a door or so distant. Will that suit?'

Louise was overwhelmingly grateful for Mistress Heron's kindness and understanding, and said so. A new feeling of hope was waking in her heart. Against all her fears, her journey had not been in vain. Mistress Heron was her ally, and Alex was here: she would see him tonight. Whatever happened then, at least the difficulties and dangers of the past weeks had been to some purpose.

Kitty was brought in at last, and prevailed upon to dry her tears and chew on a hard rusk to ease her sore gums, whereupon she managed to favour the company with a rather watery smile. The eldest of the girls, Frances, bore her off to the windows to look out at the deer grazing in the park, and Louise remembered that Phoebe, too, had intended to come to Goldhayes in pursuit of Alex. She turned to her hostess, and said softly. 'Has my sister-in-law also been here?'

'Your husband's sister? No, she has not, but don't worry about her – she wrote to him here, from Hugh's house in Westminster, a week ago and more. I gather that she had a difficult journey from Somerset, and was hoping to come on here, but needed to rest and recuperate before attempting a further spell in a coach. And I think, although I am not sure, that your husband wrote back to her, asking her to stay in London.'

'Perhaps he would rather I had stayed in London too,' Louise said bleakly. 'Because I *have* put him in danger by coming here, even if I am merely Mistress Woods.'

'Nonsense,' said the older woman briskly. 'Your visit has nothing to do with him. You are here as my guest, and as an old friend of the family, just as your husband's sister would have been. Indeed, since Hugh always speaks of Phoebe with the greatest affection and regard, we were all most disappointed not to have the chance to meet her.'

Louise was, secretly, rather relieved that she would not have to face Phoebe as well as Alex. After all, her sister-in-law had gone to great lengths to ensure that Louise did not learn of Alex's presence in Suffolk, and she and Lukas, not to mention Mattie, would certainly incur the full force of her wrath if she found out.

But then, why should she be angry? Louise thought, with some indignation. She has been pressing me for a reconciliation for months. Alex is my husband, I have every right to see him, and I have been very careful to avoid rousing suspicion.

But she knew, as the day crept on inexorably towards the hour when she would see him again, that her impulsive journey risked his rage with far more justification than any displeasure Phoebe might feel. For it was Alex who would be in danger if his identity became known, whether through his wife's carelessness or by other means, and he had already suffered the hostile attentions of the authorities. They had been lenient two years ago, in return for a large fine: but the King surely would not allow him to escape justice a second time, no matter how much money was offered for a pardon.

Pale with apprehension, she took Lukas and Christian aside, and told them that they were to stay at Goldhayes tonight, and perhaps longer, and of the importance of continuing secrecy. The longer they lingered here, the greater the chance of discovery, and Louise had already decided that, whatever happened, they could spend only a few days in Suffolk at most.

Of course, it was quite likely that she would pack her bags tomorrow, tail between her legs, and all her hopes burned to ashes in the heat of his anger, his rejection, and his scorn.

Their baggage arrived from Bury late in the afternoon, and she dressed for supper with great care: a mantua in flowered red and silver tabby satin, with a plain silver underskirt, and her best sable tippet warming her shoulders and disguising, to some small degree, the low cut of the mantua. Lukas, to his dismay, would be supping separately, with the other children, and she had to explain that this was the safest course. It would be hard enough for Louise, well prepared and adult, to pretend that Alex was almost a stranger to her: how much more difficult would it be for a boy of eight?

Despite his desperate wish to see his father, he agreed rather miserably, and went off with the kind and reliable James making valiant efforts to seem cheerful.

Louise, almost as pale as her stepson under her smooth, olive-gold skin, glanced for the last time in the mirror, and then went in search of her hostess.

There were several people whom she did not know gathered in the long gallery, but Alex, to her mingled disappointment and relief, was not amongst them. Mistress Heron introduced her to her husband's sister, Mistress Ashley, a white-haired woman in widow's black, and to a cousin, Master Graham, a tall, grizzled bear of a man with a strong accent that Louise could not place. His wife, also tall and still possessed of a grave and serious beauty, was Irish, and apparently Mistress Heron's oldest and dearest friend. Louise, making polite conversation and giving a necessarily expurgated account of her friendship with Sir Hugh, found the gathering of these people, veterans of the civil war, curiously touching and endearing. Would she and Alex one day live in comfortable old age at Wintercombe, talking of their grandchildren and reminiscing about the old days to youngsters who had no understanding of what they had experienced?

Somehow, bearing in mind her husband's dangerous way of life, not to mention his complete disregard for his health, she rather doubted it.

And then, as if her thoughts had conjured him up in a puff of hellfire, there were footsteps on the stairs, and two men, both tall, one young and the other old, appeared in the gallery. She stood stock still, stiff with fright, clutching her carved ivory fan like a shield, and watched Alex walk towards her.

He moved still with the prowling, careless grace that haunted her dreams, and his eyes were as blue as ever. But his hair was different, changing his appearance so completely that she thought for an instant that she had gone mad, that this was a stranger with Alex's face. Never, for as long as she had known him, had he worn anything but his own hair, defying fashion and following the example, so Phoebe had once told her, of the Prince of Orange. But now, the elaborate ringlets of a modest but modish periwig curled on his shoulders, in a colour somewhat lighter than his own densely black hair.

Stunned, she could only stare at him as he approached. Then Mistress Heron was at her one side, making formal introductions. 'My dear, may I present Mistress Woods, who is a friend of Hugh? My husband, Francis Heron – and this is Master Orchard, with whom I believe you are a little acquainted.'

'We have met,' Alex drawled, with exaggerated politeness, and bowed over her hand. As he straightened, she felt the full force of his gaze, sapphire blue and glittering with malice. 'How – delightful to see you again, Mistress Woods.'

No flicker of surprise showed in his eyes: somehow, he must have been warned of her presence at Goldhayes. She saw that his face had altered, subtly, showing more clearly the marks of dissipation, and also something else which, in this brief moment, she could not identify.

Her wits seemed to have left her: she knew she must behave normally, and not stand here gaping at this man who was supposed only to be a vague acquaintance. But under the overpowering spell, once more, of his presence, she felt as if her limbs had turned to lead.

Mistress Heron came to her rescue. Smiling, she took Alex's arm. 'Did you find what you were seeking, in Newmarket?'

After a pause, he turned to his hostess, and Louise realised that she had occupied all his attention, as he had held hers. It must surely have been blatantly obvious that this was not just a chance meeting between old friends, but something much, much more: and yet no one seemed to have noticed anything amiss.

A maid had brought a tray of wine glasses, and she took one gratefully, glad of the chance to collect her thoughts, and make some sense of her feelings.

It seemed that he still had the same effect on her, undiminished by separation, or, more disturbingly, by his past brutality. She sweated, her knees shook, her heart thudded: she was in thrall to him, and did not know whether to laugh or to weep because of it. She did not dare to cast more than a swift glance or two in his direction, and then in any case was claimed by Francis Heron.

For a man in his sixties, master of a great estate, he was refreshingly informal and friendly, like his wife. He engaged her in small talk, and then led her over to some of the pictures distributed along the walls of the gallery, to acquaint her with past members of his family. As a breed, the Herons tended to long noses and forceful characters, and many of them bore a marked resemblance to the man standing beside her. With amusement, she noted also that he looked very similar to his half-brother, Hugh Trevelyan, if rather more lean.

'Hal Heron the pirate – or privateer, rather,' said her host, indicating a most formidable gentleman, dark-haired and scowling, in the ruff and doublet of Queen Elizabeth's time. 'My nephew Oliver would have liked to emulate his exploits, I fear, but has settled instead for the life of a country squire in Essex. My son Edmund is the sailor, he's a captain in the navy. This is my father, and I regret to say that it's an excellent likeness of him.'

The harsh, forbidding features were not those of a man easy to love. Louise glanced at Francis Heron, and he smiled. In his youth, he had evidently been very good-looking, and even now, in a fair periwig, his charm and friendliness of manner were most attractive.

'But you are not at all like your father, sir,' she said drily, and he laughed. 'Not in the least, thank God – although my eldest brother Simon was, and in consequence his last years were friendless and miserable because he had driven us all away, for one reason or another. But here we all are, in the portrait Van Dyck painted of us fifty years ago and more – a handsome group, don't you think?'

Four boys and a girl stared solemnly out of the canvas, for ever immortal in the innocent radiance of childhood. She recognised her host immediately, the fair-haired boy with an enigmatic, secret expression in his grey-green eyes, somehow set apart from his darker brothers and sister. It was more difficult to detect a resemblance between the painted little girl beside him, fresh and glowing, and the white-haired, sad-eyed widow talking to Mistress Graham behind her.

'My sister Lucy was a great beauty in her youth,' said Francis Heron softly. 'But she only ever had eyes for one man – and he, alas, died three years ago. That is my eldest brother Simon, the solid-looking lad is Edward, who was killed at Edgehill, the first battle of the civil wars, and the little one is my younger brother Jamie, who died in the siege of Colchester, almost the last – save for Worcester Fight, of course, but by then Simon was in exile in Holland, and I had beaten my sword into a wedding band, and decided upon a quiet and blameless life.'

'My grandfather fought at Worcester,' said Louise, thinking of Nick Hellier, who could not be much older than the man standing beside her. 'It must have been so strange, and terrible. I saw a little of one skirmish during Monmouth's rebellion, two years ago, and that was dreadful enough. I cannot imagine our peaceful England transformed into a battleground.'

'Nor could anyone in 1641, before King Charles finally fell out with his parliament,' Francis Heron pointed out, his voice grim. 'And that is why I am so concerned now to find a peaceful solution to the troubles that have overtaken us. If left to himself, King James will plunge us all into bloodshed once more, through sheer stupidity and obstinacy. Like a

327

great many men, your husband included, I have come to the view that our only hope lies in the Prince of Orange and his wife.'

There was no one within earshot, but his voice had dropped to a whisper. Louise said, equally softly, 'I have never concerned myself greatly with politics, sir, but I was bred a Protestant in France, where my mother still lives, and I have seen the miseries that a bigoted Papist can cause to ordinary people. So if the Prince can save England both from war and from Popery, then I am wholeheartedly in his support.'

'Good,' Francis Heron said, with a smile. 'My wife has managed, very briefly, to convey to me something of your situation. I can only wish you luck. And perhaps it may hearten you to learn that whenever your husband has mentioned you – which is seldom, for he is not a man who is inclined to reveal much about personal matters – he has spoken of you with affection, and regretted that circumstances have enforced a separation.'

'It was not enforced,' Louise said sadly. 'Save by me. And now, if it is not too late, I hope to heal the breach between us.'

'I do not think, from the way he looked at you when you met, that it is too late,' her host said. 'He knew you were here – my wife contrived a moment downstairs just now to tell him, so that surprise would not give him away. I suspect the precaution was probably unnecessary – Sir Alexander, from my admittedly brief acquaintance with him, appears to be a master of dissimulation. The Prince invariably chooses his emissaries well, and wisely. And now, "Mistress Woods", it is time for supper, I think – and afterwards, I feel sure that a lady of your resourcefulness and enterprise will be able to contrive a meeting in private with your husband.'

The dining parlour at Wintercombe was small, cosy and intimate. Meals at Goldhayes were served in a huge, echoing room with an enormous table stretching from one end to the other, and more family portraits gazing down from the walls. Louise sat between Francis Heron and

Master Graham, with Alex opposite, next to Mistress Heron. The food was excellent, varied and well cooked, and served as a succession of courses in the French manner. Unfortunately, she found her appetite, usually healthy and omnivorous, had all but deserted her, and the succulent roast carp and delicious-looking fricassees and ragouts could not tempt her. She could not help noticing that Alex did not seem to be eating very much either, but that his wine glass was frequently refilled. She dared not address him directly, or make him the object of her attention, but she sensed that he was likewise avoiding her eye.

She made conversation with Master Graham, whose accent, it appeared, was Scots, while a suffocating fear began to grow inside her. What would they say to each other, in private at last? Would they fight, argue, part bitter enemies? Or would it end in each other's arms?

She had no idea: she could barely make sense of her own feelings, let alone his. And she had a quick temper, as did he: they might both say things in the heat of a quarrel that they did not mean, and would afterwards bitterly regret.

And the wine he was consuming, unobtrusively and steadily, filled her with foreboding, for she knew only too well how drink could inflame his anger.

At long last, the interminable meal ended, and the ladies retired once more to the long gallery, leaving the men to enjoy a bottle of brandy. Louise, knowing Alex's fondness for it, did not dare to look at him. She glided with deceptively casual grace in Mistress Heron's wake, and wished herself safely back in Bath, in Phoebe's acerbic company, and free of the unpleasantness, the complications and the disruption that always seemed to accompany Alex, wherever he went.

They played cards, which was a welcome distraction. Louise enjoyed piquet and whist, although she had rarely had the opportunity recently, as Phoebe did not play. She found all her old skills returning, and won several games. Then the children joined them, briefly, to say goodnight, the four shining little girls, the two older boys and Lukas, thin and dark, and as much out of place amongst the orange

329

and yellow heads around him as Francis Heron had been in that lovely portrait. They bowed or curtseyed, kissed their grandmother, and walked decorously off to bed.

Lukas approached Louise: as he embraced her, she whispered, 'Go to bed – I'll see what can be done.'

He gave her a quick, secret, longing smile, and made his way back to their chambers, where Kitty was probably already asleep.

The four women played a few hands more of whist, and then Mistress Graham, who lived at the Home Farm on the other side of the park, made her excuses and went downstairs to collect her husband. There was still no sign of Alex, and Louise, feeling sick with apprehension, rose to take her leave of Mistress Ashley and her hostess, pleading tiredness.

'We keep country hours here,' Thomazine Heron told her. 'By nine o'clock in winter time, everyone is in bed and snoring. I hope you have everything you need – I have sent a maid to make sure the fire is banked up and that the beds are warmly aired. And don't worry about rising late tomorrow – you may break your fast an hour before dinner, if you choose. At Goldhayes, our guests can do as they please – within reason, of course!'

Lukas was waiting for her in her chamber, in his nightshift, his face downcast. 'I've seen Papa,' he said, his voice rather muted.

She stared at him apprehensively. 'Have you? What did he say?'

'He – he didn't seem very pleased that we'd come here,' Lukas said unhappily. 'He wasn't friendly at all – and he'd been drinking, I could smell it on his breath.' His chin wobbled. 'Oh, Louise, he's angry with us, I know he is. He doesn't want us any more!'

Her worst fears confirmed, she held him while he sobbed miserably into her chest. At last, he drew away from her and wiped his eyes, struggling for calm. 'I'm sorry, Louise – it's just that I've been looking forward so much to seeing him again – and I wanted you to come back together – and I don't think it will happen, I really don't.' He gulped despairingly. 'He said he wanted to see you – in his chamber – as soon as possible. He – he won't hurt you again, will he?'

She had not realised how much Lukas had guessed about the cause of their estrangement. She gave him what she hoped was a reassuring smile, although inside she was quaking with apprehension. 'Of course not, Luikje,' she said. 'Not if I can help it. Don't worry – I'll do my best to explain why we've come, and perhaps he'll soften. He still loves you, I know he does.'

She gathered her failing courage around her like a cloak, and bid Lukas goodnight. 'You go to bed now, and try, please try not to worry. Tell Christian not to wait up for me.'

'I will,' he said, with a watery smile that wrung her heart, and made her suddenly very angry with Alex. Even if she deserved to be the object of his hostility, Lukas did not.

She watched as he trailed dejectedly back to his chamber, and then went out into the passage. She did not know which of the doors led to Alex, but only one of them showed a light underneath.

Of her own free will, out of love, or compulsion, she had started this business. And now, she should end it, one way or another.

Condemned men must feel like this, on their way to hang at Tyburn. She took a deep, despairing breath, and knocked on his door.

A pause, and then his voice. 'Come in.'

She lifted the latch, and walked in, and faced her husband, alone and in privacy, for the first time since he had raped her.

'What the hell d'you think you're doing here?' said Alex St Barbe.

# Chapter Seventeen

## 'A dangerous guest by night'

He sat in his shirtsleeves at a table by the window, a pile of papers in front of him, quill in hand. He had taken off his periwig, and it lay discarded and rather sinister, like a piece of someone else's head, over the back of the chair opposite, along with his coat and waistcoat. The shortness of his hair, cropped for comfort under the wig, disturbed her: she still could not adjust her mind to this drastic alteration in his appearance.

But his voice, and the malice within it, had not changed at all. With a feeling that she had nothing to lose, she rose to the challenge and lifted her chin, the light of battle in her eyes. 'I came to see you. Lukas told me you wanted to speak to me – so, here I am.'

'Don't wilfully misunderstand me – you know very well what I mean. What are you doing at Goldhayes?'

Apparently unafraid, she met the full blue malevolence of his stare, and wished she had not. 'I came to find you.'

'I was under the impression that you never wanted to see me again.'

'I thought so too – at the time.' Louise took a deep breath, hoping, praying, that behind his aggressive wall of hostility lay something very different. 'Make no mistake, what you did was utterly despicable, horrible – you betrayed all the love and trust I had for you, and I still don't know if I will ever be able to forget it – or to forgive you for it.'

To her surprise, it was his gaze that left hers. He got abruptly to his feet, and turned towards the fireplace. His voice was rough and brutally uncompromising. 'If that is the case, I repeat – why in God's name did you come here? Do you *know* that you may have put our whole enterprise in jeopardy by doing so?'

'I have been extremely careful,' Louise said. She stared at his back, the fine linen of his shirt, characteristically creased, barely disguising the taut muscles of his shoulders and arms as he gripped the mantelpiece. And intuition flared suddenly, setting light to a wild and unlikely feeling of hope.

'So you think – "Mistress Woods".' He bent to pick up a poker and stabbed savagely at the fire. It leapt up greedily at his bidding: as if, she thought inconsequentially, he were some secret sorcerer, with the ungovernable elements at his command. Then he swung round to face her, his eyes furious. 'And this Frenchman – this Monsieur Edmond Everard who was so entertaining, so flatteringly attentive – did it never cross your mind that he might have some motive other than climbing into your bed?'

She stared at him angrily. 'How dare you! He was never in my bed, nor was he ever likely to be! Who told you about him? Phoebe?'

'No, it was Lukas. But at least my dear sister had the sense to warn me that she was on her way here – and to stay in London when I told her to. How did you discover I was at Goldhayes? Not from her, I'll wager.'

'Lukas found out, somehow, and wrote to me – I was at Chard, with Gran'mère and Gran'père.'

'You should have stayed there. Well? What about your French lover?'

Louise said indignantly, 'He was *not* my lover! He was good company, yes, but it was no more than a pleasant flirtation. Anyway, what business is it of yours? You're not exactly innocent of adultery yourself, are you? What possible right have you to be jealous?'

Alex laughed. 'None at all, it seems. I might on some occasions be magnanimous enough to believe that he was not your lover, but I am not feeling particularly benevolent tonight.'

'That's plain to see. Shall I repeat it again? Everard was never in my bed – and nor was he ever likely to be, whatever he might have thought.'

'That's just as well – because your precious Frenchman,

333

my dear, is in the pay of the King of England, and the King of France.'

There was a long, appalled silence. Louise felt all her righteous indignation trickle away into fear. She said at last, 'Do you mean – Edmond is a *spy?*'

'To put it bluntly, yes. I suspect he sought you out deliberately, to try to glean information about me – so your fluttering eyelashes were not the lure, whatever you might like to think. Was he in Bath when you left?'

'No – he went back to London in November, he said he had business to attend to.' A thought struck her, and she added, 'So that was why! It puzzled me – he kept trying to persuade me to write to you, and ask you to come home.'

'So that I could be arrested and tried for treason, no doubt,' Alex said drily. 'Just as well you didn't – not, of course, that I'd have taken any notice. Hugh had already warned me that my activities were known in Whitehall. So, perhaps there is a small chance that you have not led the King's men straight to me.'

He brushed his hand across his face, as if pushing nonexistent hair out of his eyes. He looked suddenly desperately weary, and sick at heart, and she realised, with alarm, that he had recently been rather ill. He went on, 'Is there anything in that immaculate head of yours, beside men and fashions and horses? Do you know how much depends on my presence here being kept secret? The fate of two nations certainly, perhaps three, or even four. And you put it all at risk for the sake of a foolish whim.'

'You're being unfair,' Louise said. She wanted to be angry again, but found she could not. His need of her was so plain, and yet he did not seem able to admit it, even to himself. She added urgently, 'It was no whim, Alex. I knew that I might be putting you in danger. I was as careful as I could be, and I am sure that no one here, apart from Mistress Heron and her husband, knows who I am – or that I am your wife.'

'For better, for worse,' Alex said, and the bitterness in his voice wrung her heart. She cried in sudden anguish, 'Yes, I am your *wife!* Had you forgotten? *That* cannot be altered, whatever has happened between us – we are bound together for all time. But I came to find you for Kitty's sake – do you want her to grow up fatherless? In some little house in Bath, all noise and crowds and smells and disease, when her birthright is a childhood at Wintercombe? And there is Lukas to consider too – how could you hurt him so much? Despite everything, he still loves you – his face just now was pathetic, as if you had kicked him in the teeth – he is your *son*, Alex, do you want him to turn against you too?'

'It's time he learned the truth about me,' Alex said. 'The father he has always idolised is a drunken, whoring bastard, and not worth anyone's love, least of all his. Let him forget me, Louise – in the long run, it would be kinder.'

'You can't mean that! It would destroy him – and besides,' Louise said, her fists clenched, her heart thundering, 'it isn't true, whatever impression you like to give. Don't betray him because you can't bear to face up to your responsibilities.'

'At the moment, this mission for the Prince is my only responsibility. And besides, you told me to go, remember? And I went.' He turned away, his hands moving blindly amongst the papers on the table. 'You said just now that you would never forgive me, or forget what I did to you. Well, neither can I forgive myself. It was my boast, once, that I had never taken any woman who was not willing. That is no longer true. And to the end of my days, however long or short they may be, I will regret it more bitterly than anything else I have ever done in my life.'

She could not speak. She heard the truth and emotion raw at last in his voice, and knew that, like her, he had paid for that night of drunken brutality, and that he was still paying. And she realised too that now, for her at least, forgiveness was possible after all, for in some strange and disturbing way, the balance between them had changed.

He had turned away: he would not look at her: and she knew why. At last, the time was ripe for the first move, and she must make it.

But not quite yet. 'I will go tomorrow,' she said at last,

hardly above a whisper. 'And never trouble you again. If you wish it.'

It was raining outside: she heard, in the pause, the tiny rustling against the windowpanes, behind the shutters, like grains of sand in an hourglass.

His back was still towards her, his knuckles clenched white on the table. 'It might be best,' he said, his voice dropped as low as hers.

She walked over to him, so close that she could see the ragged movements of his shirt, as he fought to control his breathing. She said, 'Let me speak plain. I have changed my mind. I discovered, to my dismay, that what you did has made no difference to what I feel for you. I tried to hate you, I tried to forget you, but I could not. And so – I have come here to make peace.'

He still said nothing, but she heard a sudden harsh intake of breath. And moved by love, deeper and more indestructible by far than she had ever imagined, she put her hand on his shoulder.

Alex turned then, in one swift clumsy movement, the papers scattered in disorder on to the floor, and pulled her into his arms. Joyously, she returned his embrace, pressing her body against him. He was whispering her name, over and over again, like an incantation, his hands stroking her hair, her back, as if he could not believe the reality in his arms. Overwhelmed by an astonishing rush of emotion, she wept into his shoulder.

'You're making me wet,' he said suddenly, and laughed, and drew away from her a little, though he kept hold of her hands. She looked at the wide damp patch on his shirt, and he added, 'So unhappy, sweet Louise?'

His smile was joyous, dazzling: it had snared her heart, long ago, and held it in spite of disaster and separation. She wiped her eyes, and said, halfway between laughter and tears, 'The opposite of unhappy. Despite everything, I love you – I have never stopped loving you.'

'Fool that you are,' Alex said, but there was no bitterness now in his voice. 'God, I don't deserve this – I don't deserve you – I could never dare to hope that this hour would ever come. I dreamed, once, that you loved me again, and woke with ashes in my mouth, knowing it must be an illusion. Will I wake from this, do you think?'

'I doubt it, somehow,' Louise said, and pinched his hand gently. 'Did you feel that? This is real, and neither of us are asleep – although I must say you look as if you need it.'

'Do I?' He grinned at her like a schoolboy. 'At the moment, I feel as if I could climb mountains, ford rivers, walk on water – but that is probably the effects of the wine.'

'And not my sweet self? For shame, husband.' She slipped one of her hands from his, and traced the faint, indelible marks on his face, the lines between nose and mouth, the shadows under his eyes. 'Have you been ill? Or is that, too, the effects of the wine?'

'It may well be – but, yes, I was ill last year – I had a couple of bouts of the marsh fever in Amsterdam.' He glanced at her, his smile suddenly fading. 'After the second, the doctor told me to moderate my drinking habits, or the next would undoubtedly carry me off. And until tonight, I have managed to obey him.'

Louise said, trying to hide her astonishment, 'Why did you make an exception of tonight?'

'You know very well why. I needed Dutch courage to face you and your quite justifiable wrath – and if I was in consequence somewhat offensive, I can only crave your pardon, sweet Louise.' He drew her hand to his mouth and kissed her fingers gently, one by one. 'Am I forgiven?'

'For that, at least,' she said tartly. 'But I am glad that you have given up drinking so much – tonight excepted, of course. In excess, it does a man no good.'

He smiled wryly. 'I have always been well aware of it. But it's strange – I thought that my future held nothing of further interest, lacking you, but when that quack told me plain what would happen to me if I continued to get drunk four nights out of five, I discovered that life was very much more attractive than the alternative.'

'Edmond said that he saw you once, in Amsterdam,' Louise told him, frowning. 'His description was not . . . flattering.'

'I'm not surprised. Until July, most of my time passed in a blur of brandy and geneva. I don't remember seeing him, but that doesn't mean I did not, if you understand me. The King of France could have tapped me on the shoulder and I wouldn't have noticed, save to share the bottle with him. But I do know a little about him. He was agent to Bevil Skelton, who was the King's ambassador to Holland until quite recently. Skelton is an extremely dubious character, like his minion – the Prince couldn't bear him. And William is surprisingly tolerant.' He smiled. 'He tolerates me, after all, and despite everything, he has trusted me with this mission.'

The shadow of it lay between them suddenly, and Louise shivered. She said slowly, 'So you cannot come back to us? Phoebe said that you could not.'

'I doubt it, at present. Charles would not give up Wintercombe without a bitter struggle, and he'd doubtless seize the opportunity to denounce me as a traitor. And since some of my activities are well-known to the King and his henchmen, I do not think my liberty, or indeed my life, would last very long.' He stared down at her, his face suddenly filled with longing. 'Oh, Louise, I want – more than anything in the world, I would like to pack my bags, and forsake the Prince of Orange, and treason, and danger, and ride home with you and Kitty and Lukas to Winter-combe. I have missed you so much – wanted you so much – and even now, I can hardly believe that you still love me.'

'Oh, I do,' she said, and smiled wryly. 'If my love could survive that night, then it can survive anything. But please, Alex, please don't take that as a licence to do as you want.'

They stared at each other for a long, searching moment: then he said softly, urgently, 'I swear, by all the gods I do not believe in, that I will never use you so evilly again. I was drunk that night, and angry with myself, and with you for being in the right – can you understand that? And I have had a long, long time, since then, to do penance for my crime. You have given me another chance, Christ knows why, and I'll be damned if I waste it.'

She knew that he spoke the truth: but knew, also, that

338

trust, once so violently shattered, could only be rebuilt, slowly and laboriously, from the ordinary bricks and mortar of shared lives, with all its small joys and sorrows. And yet they must soon part again, with no certainty of further reunion.

'I will not hold you to any promise,' she said, a challenge in her voice. 'I would not presume to it. But if you treat me like a whore again, I will fight like one – and *I* will call the tune.'

For a moment, she thought that she had demanded too much. After all, words now were easy, promises could be freely uttered. She had forgiven him, she loved him, she wanted him, but his need for her was desperate. And a man in such straits might say anything, in the stress of the moment, to gain his heart's desire.

'Very well, my lady piper,' he said, and smiled suddenly. 'Although, as I'm sure you've guessed, I would swear to draw the stars down and net them in your hair, if only I could hold you in my arms again.'

She smiled back at him. 'Am I to take it, then, that you love me? For you have not yet told me so.'

'You bloody fool,' Alex said, with affectionate exasperation. 'Of course I love you – more than anything else in the world, or beyond it, I love you. What more do you want?'

There was no mistaking the look in his eyes, and she knew that her own desire must be as plain: her body ached for him, as it had ever since she had seen him riding up to Wintercombe on his grey stallion Pagan, almost exactly three years ago.

His eyes held hers, silently asking her leave: and with a huge glorious joy leaping up in her, she flung herself into his embrace and his kiss.

She had wondered, when her imagination had reached this point in their reconciliation, what would happen – would her response to him still be as powerful, as deep and overwhelmingly passionate as it once had been?

The answer was never in doubt, for her need was as urgent as his, and her desire the match of his own. Somehow, his mouth linked to hers, he turned the key in the door and then began to undress her, his hands exploring slowly yet hungrily, seeking their mutual pleasure. The fur tippet fell discarded to the floor, followed by, a little later, the flowered tabby mantua with its beribboned stomacher and silver underskirt. They never reached the bed: there was a warm, pattered Turkey carpet on the floor beside it, and they made love there, with wanton disregard for comfort, for dignity, for anything save the imperative satisfaction of their desires.

Afterwards, they lay tangled together, pressed skin to skin, content with this consummate closeness. Speech would be superfluous: better to stay silent, luxuriating in the sensual languor that followed lovemaking, than to risk breaking the spell, returning them to harsh reality with an ill-chosen word.

He fell asleep, his head heavy between her breasts, and she had not the heart to disturb him, despite her increasing discomfort. So many thoughts crowded in her head, feelings and memories, all confused, of other times and other places: his beautiful chamber at Wintercombe, when they had first become lovers: the green bed-curtains in his quarters in the Tower, only in name a prison, where Nathaniel had been conceived: and the whitewashed, oak-panelled room at her grandparents' house in Chard, when they had begun to repair the damage that Nathaniel had wrought.

So many times they had lain together like this, and yet now it was different. Now, she had been in control of her senses, to give or withhold her body as she chose. And though she wanted him as much as she ever had, despite the rape, she had at last become mistress of her own desires. And he knew it: despite his hunger for her, his overpowering need and desire, he had waited on her word.

Once, she had feared him, feared the hold he had over her, feared the strength of her love for him. And now she lay beneath his warm, sleeping weight, heard the soft, regular sounds of his breathing, felt the prickle of his hair against her skin, and knew that they had become equals, for all her illusions had been scorched to ashes, and she still loved him for what he was.

He stirred at last, and she smiled, and stroked his hair with the hand that was not trapped beneath his body. He muttered her name, and she smiled more widely. 'At least you have not confused me with some fat Dutch whore.'

'That's the trouble with Dutch whores,' Alex said, sleepily, into her breasts. 'They drink so much beer . . . Have you been imbibing too, sweet Louise?'

'No, of course not! Why?'

'There's more of you than there used to be, I'll swear.' He rolled over and sat up, studying her as she lay on the rug, glad of the liberty to breathe freely and deeply again. 'Yes, I was right. Distinctly inflated – especially here – and here.'

She giggled, and twisted playfully away from his touch. 'Your hands are cold. You have Kitty to thank for it – I hope you don't think I have grown too fat?'

'Not fat, certainly,' Alex said, eyeing her judicially. 'But a little more – how shall I put it? – buxom, I think. Don't mistake me, I like it.'

'I can see that,' Louise pointed out tartly.

He laughed. 'How very observant of you. Shall we try the bed, this time? It's been provided for us, after all, and it seems churlish not to use it.'

And later, when the quilts and blankets had fallen to the floor, and the sheets, rumpled and soaked with sweat, had been kicked aside, and they lay quite still, not daring to move for fear of falling untimely over the edge into a final extremity of pleasure, he whispered into her ear, his voice fierce and impassioned, 'It has *never* been like this, ever, with anyone else – dear God, how I love you!'

And she smiled wickedly, and moved, just a little, but it was enough: and as he gasped and control toppled away from both of them, she was aware of a secret, unworthy feeling of triumph amidst the convulsions of delight.

They spent the night in sleeping and in making love, with a voracious and inventive passion that astonished them both, although, as Louise pointed out, they were merely making up for lost time. And when, finally spent, too exhausted and sated and drowsy to do more than lie in each other's arms amid the wreckage of the bed, they watched dawn creeping into the chamber, they both knew that they must return to the world, and think of matters other than the joyous gratification of long-withheld desires.

'I ought to go,' she said dreamily. The increasing light was beginning to reveal, almost imperceptibly, the contours of their surroundings: the candles, unnoticed, had long since expired.

'Must you?' He was lying on his belly, one arm draped across her, his head turned close to her face. 'It's early yet.'

'I can hear people moving. And it would look strange indeed if I was seen slinking from your chamber, when we're supposed to be mere acquaintances.'

'You could imply that I was struck by a *coup de foudre*?' Alex suggested, a smile in his voice. She saw that, despite the lack of sleep, his fine-tuned face was subtly relaxed, and infused with a new contentment, lazily abandoned to the aftereffects of overindulgence in sensual pleasures.

Louise shook her head. 'No risks. You know that must be the rule. Too much is at stake – you said so yourself.'

'Well, go I suppose you must,' Alex grumbled. 'Though how I shall be able to encounter you at the dinner table and keep my hands away from your luscious body, I can't imagine.'

'Neither can I – which is why I must leave Goldhayes today,' Louise said.

There was a brief pause, and then Alex propped himself on one elbow and looked down at her, love and longing and the foreshadow of parting grief plain on his face. 'Oh, Louise, how shall we bear it? But you are right, you must go today, or we shall give ourselves away, we cannot help it.'

She found, despite her new strength, that tears were filling her eyes. She tried to blink them back, but he had noticed, and touched her cheek where one had already left a shining track towards her tangled hair. 'Don't cry,' he whispered. 'Please don't, sweet Louise, or I shall be tempted to do likewise. You must return to Bath, and I to Holland – my duties here are all but accomplished, anyway. And perhaps one day soon we shall all be together again, at Wintercombe.'

342

She looked up at him, and slowly moved her head in sad denial. 'You know as well as I do – better – that cannot come true.'

'Why not?' Alex leaned forward and kissed her with sudden and exultant passion. 'I will tell you this, on the understanding that it goes no further – not to Hugh, nor to Lukas, nor even to my dear sister Phoebe. Between us, and us alone.'

She nodded, holding her breath.

'The Queen, as you know, is pregnant. She is past the time most dangerous for a miscarriage, and it is now more likely than not that she will give birth to a child. A child who will found the new Papist dynasty to rule over England.'

'It might be a girl – or it might well die. All her others have, poor woman.'

'So it might. But understand this, sweet Louise – many people believe that the Jesuits will not allow the Queen to give birth to anything other than a healthy baby boy.'

His words slid slowly into her sleepy mind, and woke her. She said, suddenly alert, 'You mean – if it does turn out to be a girl, or dies, they will nevertheless produce a healthy boy?'

'That is undoubtedly what will be thought, even if the child is genuine. In any case, the Prince of Orange has all but decided to act, when the time is right. With England turned Papist, he and a few German states stand alone against France, and King Louis's bigotry and aggression. He cannot afford to lose his wife's expectation of the English throne. That is why I, and many other agents, are here secretly – to discover how much support the Prince could command, were he to come to England to secure the Princess's rights.'

'You mean, invasion?'

'William doesn't put it quite so bluntly as that,' Alex said drily. 'He has poor Monmouth's sad fate ever present in his mind, and he has no intention of launching himself and his army into a void. He will come when the time is right in Europe, when King Louis's attentions are engaged elsewhere – and he will come at the express invitation of the

343

chief men of influence and affairs in this country, outside – or inside – the Court. And if that means war, well, war it must be now, to avoid greater evils and more bloodshed later.'

Louise thought of what Francis Heron had told her, and shivered suddenly. 'And I suppose that you will be in the thick of it?'

'Of course I will – when the Prince comes to England, whether this year or next, then I shall be at his back. My quarrel is not only with King James and Popery, remember. The only way of kicking Charles out of Wintercombe is to kick his master out, too. If I go back with you now, I shall be laid by the heels as a rebel and a spy. But if the Prince invades, and wins, then Charles, not I, will be the loser and the traitor.'

'Surely there must be some other way to get Wintercombe back.'

Alex shook his head. 'No, dear lady – no other way – unless you were to give me an heir, and claim it on his behalf.' He grinned suddenly. 'And after the wonders and excesses of last night, that must surely be a definite possibility.'

She smiled back. 'I hope so – oh, I do hope so. But even if there is no child, we have Kitty.'

'Tell me about her,' Alex said softly. 'Phoebe said in one of her letters that she looks like me, poor infant.'

His words were light, but the expression on his face was not. Holding his gaze, her own emotions close to the surface, she said, 'She has your face and my eyes, and the best of her belongs to neither of us – she is sweet, and happy, and altogether a delight. I will introduce her to you, although she will probably be rather shy at first – she always is, with strangers.'

'But I am not a stranger,' Alex said, his voice suddenly bleak and raw with longing and regret. 'I am her father – and I swear to you, and to Kitty and Lukas, that somehow, whatever happens, I will try to repair the hurt and damage that I have done to you all. And as soon as I am dressed, I will attempt to mend matters with Lukas. He has never deserved such treatment – I abandoned him without a word, I failed to write to him until it was almost too late, and last night, as you quite justifiably pointed out, I behaved with despicable unkindness.' He paused, and she saw remorse and self-loathing stark on his face. 'I would not blame him if he never wanted to speak to me again.'

'But he will – I know that he will.' Louise, her eyes wet, reached up her arms to him, and drew him down into her embrace. 'He loves you, as I do – and loving you, can also forgive you, whatever you have done. Oh, Alex, you should be so proud of him – he has excelled at school, he shines at his studies, he works hard, and he's very much liked and admired by the other boys.'

'I am proud of him,' Alex said. 'Quite unjustifiably so, for his achievements owe nothing to me, and everything to himself – and to your care and Phoebe's tuition.' He turned his face into her shoulder, his breath warm against her bare skin. 'Is it possible? *Is* it possible to turn back time, to make it as it was before? I know I don't deserve your love, or Lukas's – can we make our lives whole again, and be happy?'

'I don't know,' Louise whispered. His arms were clasped tightly about her, and she felt him struggling to control the uneven, desperate rhythm of his breathing. Her own eyes were overflowing with tears, for all they had so wantonly thrown away, and thought lost for ever. 'Oh, my dearest love, I don't know – but Gran'mère once told me that some things could be conjured up against all hope, as if by magic, if you desired them strongly enough. And love and happiness, she said, might number amongst them. Do you think that could be true?'

'Of course it is,' Alex said. He lifted his head, and smiled, and the overwhelming power of his feelings, glowing in his face, took her breath away. 'I longed more than anything else in the world to regain your love, although I thought it was impossible – and here I am in your arms, and you love me still in spite of everything, and so life and hope are restored to me. And though I must very soon say goodbye to you and the children, I can face the future now without dread, even without you, because I know that you are no longer lost to me.'

It was then that reluctantly, but by mutual consent, they rose from the bed where they had each given and received such pleasure, and dressed for the day that lay ahead, with all it contained of parting and sweet sorrow. Then, Alex sought out Lukas, and spoke to him in private. Louise never discovered what was said, but it seemed to have repaired the hurt and harm that had been done the previous night, for Lukas, gaining and losing his father in the space of an hour, was nevertheless self-evidently consumed with happiness.

After that, she took Alex to see Kitty, who stared at him with owl-round chestnut eyes, and grumbled because her gums were sore. He laughed, and removed her from her mother's arms, and within a few moments had reduced her to helpless mirth by pulling hideous faces at her, combined with a little judicious tickling. 'Unquestionably your daughter,' he said, at last handing her back to Louise. 'Already an incorrigible flirt, even though she's barely into short coats.'

But despite his light and casual air, she saw that he was deeply affected by this first encounter with the daughter who might be – Louise had never been sure – the result of the rape that had almost destroyed their marriage. And at their parting, in the privacy of his chamber, her greatest regret of all was that he had missed so much, and would miss much more, of Kitty's childhood.

She had arrived at Goldhayes apprehensive, fearful of the storm that might break over her head, afraid that she had put Alex into danger. And she left with Lukas the next day, heads high and hearts full of joy as well as sadness. For in finding Alex, their worlds had been restored to them. There was firm hope now, where none had existed before, and despite the grief of parting, they felt a great and abiding sense of happiness.

As Alex had suggested, they went first to see Sir Hugh Trevelyan in London, and found Phoebe there, acerbic and sharp as ever, and with no trace of fatigue or illness in her face. She took one look at her sister-in-law and her nephew, and said drily, 'I can see your journey wasn't wasted.'

Louise blushed rosily. It had taken them four days to reach Westminster, and she had assumed that the glorious afterglow which had shone back at her from the mirror in her chamber at Goldhayes had long since faded. She glanced at Lukas, and he said, grinning, 'We found Papa, and he wasn't really angry with us.'

'Wasn't he? I am surprised,' Phoebe said. 'You're fools, the pair of you, and I don't dare ask how you knew where Alex was, nor why he was forbearing enough not to send you packing the moment he set eyes on you.'

'He did want to,' Louise told her. 'But I, er, persuaded him otherwise.'

'We wanted to stay at Goldhayes for longer, Aunt Phoebe,' Lukas added. 'But we had to leave the next day – it was too dangerous, we wouldn't have been able to pretend that we didn't know Papa very well.'

'So, you only had a day?' Phoebe commented, her thin eyebrows climbing. 'Your powers of persuasion must be considerable, for you to part friends after so short a time.'

'A day was enough,' Louise said.

'And a night?' said her sister-in-law wickedly. 'Yes, I can see by your face that all is well again between you and my reprobate brother – and how very pleased I am for you both.'

Surprisingly, she held out her arms. Lukas sprang into her embrace, and after a pause, Louise joined him. Phoebe so rarely demonstrated her affection: like Alex, she preferred to hide her emotions behind a casual, sharp-tongued mockery. And like him too, her love was given to few, but absolutely.

Much later, when Lukas was in bed, the two women retired to a small parlour where they could have a quiet and private talk: Sir Hugh was at Whitehall that night, but would be back in the morning. And without the constraint of her stepson's presence, Louise was able to discuss her meeting with Alex as fully as was necessary, although some

347

events, of course, would always remain utterly private between her and her husband.

But not private enough, given Phoebe's usual bluntness and perspicacity. 'So you were reconciled in bed, were you?' she enquired, pouring each of them a dish of hot, bittersweet chocolate. 'Well, I can't say I'm surprised. You and Alex were always drawn to each other like iron to magnet – despite all the sparks.'

'And there were plenty of those,' Louise said. A reminiscent smile curved her mouth, and the joy in it gave her a transitory beauty. 'He was concerned for the risks to himself and to us, yes – but in the end he admitted to being pleased to see us.'

'You do surprise me there,' said her sister-in-law, settling herself more comfortably on the cushions. 'And was he full of remorse?'

'Yes,' Louise said.

Her emphatic intensity gave Phoebe some pause. She looked at her brother's wife for a long moment, and then said, without a trace of her earlier sarcastic tone, 'Genuinely so? Then he has changed.'

'He has,' Louise said slowly, thinking of the man, tired, vulnerable, desperate with longing and desperate to hide it, whom she had faced initially in his chamber at Goldhayes. 'He has been ill – he has all but stopped drinking because of it.'

'My God,' Phoebe said, startled. 'Are you sure it's the same man? My debauched brother?'

'Oh, it was certainly Alex,' Louise told her, grinning. 'Despite the periwig.'

It was the first time that she had ever seen her sister-in-law completely disconcerted. She stared at Louise for a while, and then began, rather helplessly, to laugh. 'No – I don't believe it! *Alex?* In a *wig?* I can't possibly imagine it – he's never worn one in his life.'

'But he does now, I swear it. And it's a very effective disguise – I hardly recognised him at first.'

'Of course – and everyone knows that he wears his own hair, like the Prince of Orange does. He's not such a fool, is

348

he?' Phoebe said, her composure regained. 'It's just as well, given that if he's caught, he'll probably hang.' She looked sharply at Louise. 'I trust you were aware of that fact, before you set out so blithely for Goldhayes?'

'Not really, no,' Louise said, honestly. Over Phoebe's derisive snort, she added, 'But I do now. He told me something of what he is doing. He also said that his task was nearly complete, and he would be returning to Holland very soon. My arrival had nothing to do with it.'

'Well, let us hope that he has already left,' Phoebe said grimly. 'Hugh told me this morning that there is report of spies and suspicious persons seen in Essex and in Suffolk, and the King is despatching several men to investigate, and apprehend them. Of course, Hugh has sent a warning to his brother at Goldhayes, but it may not arrive in time – or it may be intercepted. In which case, we shall shortly be haled off to the Tower – or, if we are really unlucky, to Newgate.'

The dish of chocolate, a drink she loved, had grown cold in Louise's hand. She said, her voice uncharacteristically uncertain, 'How – how did this news come to the King?'

'Hugh doesn't know – but it reached James about three days ago, from Ipswich, I believe,' Phoebe said. She leaned over and took the dangerously listing cup from the other girl's lax hand. 'Don't worry – from the sound of it, I don't think that either you or Alex were the cause. But it may make it very much more difficult for him to leave the country safely.'

Louise turned haunted eyes on her and said unhappily, 'Are you *sure*? *Sure* it was not me? I'd never forgive myself, ever, if anything . . . happened and I was to blame for it.'

'No one can be absolutely certain,' Phoebe told her, with brisk common sense. 'But Hugh thinks not. Nor is it anything to do with your Frenchman – did Alex tell you about him? I see he did. No, Everard has gone back to France, so Hugh says, and good riddance.'

'Alex was under the impression that he was my lover. Did you tell him that?'

Phoebe loked at her, and then shook her head. 'No. But I

349

did say that Everard had the potential to be so – and I also told him that if he was, then Alex had no one to blame but himself. I take it he is now assured of your fidelity?'

'I think he is,' Louise said. She felt sick with fear for him, imagining him arrested, imprisoned – and executed. And she was also furious with herself. How lightly and thoughtlessly she had gone in search of him, thinking only of her own wishes, and never of the risk to him and his mission. How could she have been so stupid?

But a memory of that sleepless, wonderful night sidled into her thoughts, and Alex's face afterwards, a man finally at peace with himself and with her, all the demons laid to rest. And her heart knew, even if her head did not, that she had been right to find him, right to trust to her longing and her instinct. For by doing so, whatever the danger, she had restored purpose to both their lives. They had now a common aim: to return to Wintercombe, to oust Charles, and to live once more together in their rightful home, with Kitty and Lukas, and with the children that would surely follow them in the future.

'So,' said Phoebe, her voice still drily casual, 'what shall we do now? Assuming, of course, that Alex is safe, and that we ourselves have avoided suspicion.'

'Return to Bath, I suppose,' Louise said, regretfully. Despite all her other concerns, she had remembered that London was only a mile or so down-river: London, with all its diversions, its heaving, bustling mass of people, and above all its shops, filled to the rafters with every imaginable article of fashion, designed to tempt the frivolous, and those with long enough pockets to indulge the extravagant and luxurious taste at present à la mode. Beside such wealth, Bath was a rural and unsophisticated backwater with ridiculous pretensions to grandeur.

Phoebe laughed suddenly. 'But no need to leave in haste, I think. Hugh has promised to take us to the theatre, and dancing at Whitehall – and for that you'll surely need a new gown, or two, or three. Lukas is scholar enough not to suffer from missing another week or two of lessons, and we have told our friends in Bath that we have gone to London,

350

after all – they'll think it strange indeed if we come home without any new finery.'

And so, at her sister-in-law's unlikely behest, Louise attempted to submerge her worries about Alex in an orgy of spending. She bought a multitude of new mantuas in the latest style and in the most fashionable materials, and suits for Lukas, who was fast growing out of his old ones. And for Kitty, who had just learned to crawl and whose nurse could not keep pace with the resulting damage to her clothing, she also purchased an ingenious device, a high square frame with a wheel at each corner, intended to encourage the baby to walk.

March continued, cold and dry, and as no word of arrest reached them from Suffolk, Louise and Phoebe began to relax. Alex was surely by now safely back in Amsterdam. And some three weeks after the momentous meeting at Goldhayes, confirmation reached them, in the form of a letter from Thomas Talmarsh, who had gone to Holland, against the King's wishes, to take up his commission in one of the English regiments in the Dutch service. He had seen Alex, who was safe, and well, and sent his most loving and affectionate regards to his dearest wife, and his sister, and his son and daughter.

It was little, but it was enough. One day, Louise promised herself, hugging her joy in the lonely, comfortable expanse of her bed in Sir Hugh's house: one day, we will be together again, all of us – and at Wintercombe.

One day, if the Prince of Orange comes.

# PART THREE

'To ripen green revenge'

June 1688–April 1689

# Chapter Eighteen

## 'Imperious need'

The Carnes were a wealthy family, and spent with a lavish hand: the christening party for their newest member, Edward's first-born son James, was awash with food and drink, and the celebrations had continued all day.

There were bells ringing outside, but not for this child's birth. Only three days after young James Carne's protracted and difficult arrival in the world, the Queen had borne a healthy, lusty boy. The prayers of the King, and of all English Papists, had been answered: a Catholic dynasty was now assured.

The Mayor and Corporation of Bath, well aware which side their bread was buttered, ordered the Abbey bells to be rung and bonfires to be lit, and if they felt any dismay or foreboding at the prospect of a succession of Papist rulers presiding over a Protestant country, they took good care not to reveal it. But in the Carne household, the rejoicing was redoubled, and delighted guests drank the health of the new Prince of Wales, and confusion to his enemies, in finest claret and Rhenish wine.

In the middle of the festivities, the baby's uncle found time to slip away to the chamber upstairs where his sister rested in lonely splendour. It was only six days since the birth, and she could not yet appear in public. Charles felt envy, rather than pity, for Amy and Edward had their son and heir, while he, as yet, had none, and no prospect of it while the husband of the woman he loved would not oblige him by dying.

He cast a swift, yearning glance into the cradle, where young James, hairless and outstandingly ugly, slept in milk-sated abandon, and then approached his sister.

Amy submitted listlessly to his fraternal kiss. A difficult

355

pregnancy and birth had had a catastrophic effect on her looks. She was now decidedly fat, with a tired, peevish expression that reminded Charles unhappily of their mother, at present downstairs boring some blameless Carne relation with the interminable details of her various ailments, both real and imagined.

He had been genuinely fond of his sister, but since her marriage they had seen each other infrequently, and now there was little common ground between them. He spent almost all his time at Wintercombe, immersed in the business of the estate, and in trying to discourage his mother's ever more extravagant plans for the house. Amy, meanwhile, had been occupied by family duties. And now, this weary, plain, discontented girl did not seem to be his lively, pretty, innocent little sister any more.

He asked all the usual fatuous questions about the baby, and was surprised by her apparent lack of interest in her offspring. If I had a son, Charles thought, gazing with renewed and jealous longing at the cradle, I would love and cherish him, not talk about him as if he were something of no account.

After a while, he ran out of questions, and there was an awkward silence, filled by sudden wails. A buxom wet nurse appeared to lift the baby and carry him away, and shortly the noise ceased, to be replaced by the faint and, to Charles, disgusting sounds of sucking. To cover his embarrassment, he said, 'Do you ever see Louise? You used to be friends, once.'

'We were,' Amy said, and her eyes, accusing, seemed to blame him for it. 'I've seen her often, though, in the street. You can't avoid it, after all, Bath is such a small place.' She gave him a weary look, in which he hoped he had imagined the malice. 'Why don't you call on her? You say you're in love with her, yet you've been behaving as if she no longer exists. As you've made the effort to visit me, you might as well save yourself another journey, and see her too.'

He had not realised how much she resented his long absences, and hastily apologised, but she was in no mood to

356

be cajoled, and turned her face away peevishly. 'I'm tired, and I want to sleep. Can you go now, please, Charles?'

He had done so much for her sake: he had found her a wealthy husband, he had dowered her with generosity, and this was his reward. Hurt and angry, he turned and strode from the chamber without another word. The merry-making downstairs was still noisily in progress. He ignored it, and the cheerful calls of Amy's brother-in-law Francis, and walked out into the street.

On this early evening in June, it was warm, and still crowded. The house where Louise and Phoebe lived was not far: down Stall Street, a turn to the right, and more or less straight on to Nowhere Lane. He was at the door, his hand raised to the knocker, before his anger began to diminish, and he hesitated, wondering if this was wise.

He had not seen her for so long: since that unfortunate encounter in the Abbey churchyard, in fact, and it had been . . . He paused, counting, and realised that it was nine months since the King's visit to Bath. Nine months, in which all his high hopes and ambitions, he saw now, had gradually trickled away. He still had Wintercombe, true, and he had been made a magistrate, but there was no court position yet, and no hope, although he had tried to use what little influence he possessed, of standing for election in the coming parliament. And all his wealth was likewise streaming, in a rather faster torrent, through Bab's greedy fingers.

His mind had been so thoroughly occupied with more mundane matters that he had hardly thought of Louise for weeks at a time. Now, at her door, his love rose up with renewed vigour, and her image filled his mind: his lovely, laughing, lively cousin, with her gallant, flyaway smile, and the touch of the exotic that had always fascinated him, her French accent, her olive-gold skin, her gestures, the mistakes she still sometimes made with her English, the bright gowns clothing her slender body like flowers, the innocence and friendship that they had once shared, before Alex had corrupted her . . .

Why, oh why, had he not come here before? Why had he left it so long without seeing her again? A confused wave of unbearable yearning and anger and regret swept over him, and he hammered on the door.

Louise's maid Christian answered it. When she saw him, she shook her head. 'No, Master Charles, they bain't at home.'

But he had heard her voice, down the hall, asking who it was, and then she appeared from a doorway, her hair casually knotted, a loose gown flung round her. And beside her, tottering with the uncertain steps of the very young, was a baby in short coats, with a profusion of dark hair and a smile unmistakably her father's.

If it had been a boy, he could have picked it up and dashed its brains out against the wall.

The violence of the thought appalled him, and he stared at the infant with horror and loathing. Not in the least disconcerted, she pointed at him, her delight evident, and gabbled something.

Louise bent, with a graceful, fiercely protective gesture, and picked up her child. She said, 'Don't let him in, Christian, shut the door on him.'

'I can't, m'lady – his foot be in the way!'

Charles pushed the maid aside and walked in. Louise stood in the hall, her face hostile. She said furiously, 'How many times do you have to be told, Charles? Get out!'

He smiled at her, knowing that sooner or later she would come round – a little more time, a little more persuasion, was all that was necessary. To his shame and sorrow, he had neglected her, his mind taken up entirely with the business of Wintercombe, and his other concerns. Now, as his gaze devoured her with renewed adoration, he knew that he must devote more time to winning her back.

'Oh, Lou,' he said, 'why can't we be friends?'

'Ma,' said the baby, regarding him with bright-eyed interest. 'Ma-ma-gaga-yada-dada!'

'Can you not absorb this one fact into your obstinate and stupid skull, Charles? I may have been your friend once, before I knew what you really were – '

'Before Alex debauched you, you mean!'

'But I loathe you now. Do you understand, or are you still

gripped by your pathetic delusions? I *hate* you, Charles, I detest and despise and revile you – and I can assure you that I shall never change. Never, never, *never!*'

'Bababab – yaya Mama!' said the baby, with satisfaction.

In a sudden rage, Charles was tempted to tear her from her mother's arms and fling her to the floor, but that would hardly endear him to Louise, so he desisted, and said with patient reasonabless, 'You don't mean that, Lou. *You* are the victim of delusion, not me. Alex has betrayed you, he's never loved you, his desertion is proof enough of that – '

'What do you know about it?' she said sharply. 'You know *nothing*, Charles, *nothing* of what lies between me and Alex, the good as well as the bad. It is my business and mine alone – and your spiteful interference has done damage enough.'

'Lou, please – '

'And don't call me that – it implies there's still some bond of affection between us.'

'But, Lou, I love you, I always have – why can't you understand that? All I have ever done I have done for your sake.'

'So all this coil of serpents is my fault, is it?'

The acid in her voice would have withered any man less in thrall to the blind urgings of his heart. Charles ignored it, his hands spread in desperate appeal. 'Lou, *listen* to me, for God's sake! I *love* you! And I will always be your friend – even though you spurn me now, there'll be a time when you will *want* to turn to me – believe me, there will!'

'Not if the skies fall and the world shatters and you and I are the last people left on earth, would I turn to you,' she said venomously.

The intensity of the emotions swirling around her was beginning to have some effect on the baby's initial friendliness: she was now gazing at Charles with an expression of the gravest doubt. Then, with a whimper, she pressed her face into her mother's shoulder. Over her tangled black hair, Louise stared at her cousin with implacable enmity.

'You're upsetting Kitty,' she said. 'Now kindly leave, before I send Christian for help.'

'I wouldn't hurt you, Lou – you *know* I wouldn't!'

'I grant that you might not lay violent hands on me – but you have done your utmost to harm everything I love,' Louise said bitterly. 'You and your mother have wrecked my marriage, deprived me of my home and my husband of his right, and I wouldn't trust you not to hurt Kitty from sheer spite – and if I ever bore a son to Alex, you'd soon convince yourself that you were doing him a favour by murdering him.'

'No!' Charles cried in horrified denial. 'No, Lou, *no* – I would *never* harm a baby – how can you say that, how *can* you? I'm not the monster, I'm not depraved and evil – *Alex* has hurt you, *Alex* has deprived you of your home – I didn't take Wintercombe from you, he *gave* it to me!'

'And one day, he will take it back,' Louise told him. In her arms Kitty, her happy, placid, smiling Kitty, had begun to howl. 'Enjoy it while you can, Charles, for sooner or later, Alex will return to kick you out!'

'How can he? He's an acknowledged traitor – oh, yes, I've heard what he's been doing in Holland. I'd be within my rights to shoot him at the door.'

'But he might not be a traitor for ever,' Louise said, and then stopped, reining in her temper, despite the rage that was shaking her uncontrollably. She tightened her arms about the baby, trying in vain to soothe her crying. She wanted to call for Kitty's nurse, but she was upstairs, busy with the inevitable sewing and washing and mending, and besides, the fewer who witnessed this unpleasant and undignified scene, the better.

Charles was looking at her intently: then he said, 'Do you mean the Prince of Orange? His nose has been thoroughly put out of joint by the birth of the Prince. He'll never have the throne now, and the King has more than enough strength to repulse him if he's foolish enough to try and take it by force. He'll suffer Monmouth's fate if he does, and end on the scaffold. No, Alex will never see Wintercombe again, he'll skulk in Holland till the end of his days – and may they be brief, and miserable!'

'How dare you, Charles – go on, get out, leave, *go* – I have nothing left to say to you!' Suddenly sick of futile argument, she turned and ran back into the parlour, slamming the door behind her. There was no key, but she put Kitty down, despite her screams, grabbed a piece of paper from the table, and with shaking hands folded it again and again until it was thick enough to jam the latch.

Outside in the hall, she could hear Christian's voice, heavy with disapproval and dislike. 'I think you had best go now, sir – *now*.' And then, at last, the sound of the street door crashing shut.

Kitty was sitting on the floor in a paroxysm of distress, hiccuping, her face red and shiny with tears. Louise swept her into her arms, and pulled the paper out from the latch. She almost wanted to laugh at the horrible absurdity of it – that she should be forced to bar the door against Charles, whom she had once thought to be kind, considerate, steady and reliable, and her true friend.

The events of the last three years had taught her different. She had realised that her cousin, gripped by obsession and self-delusion and the blind conviction that he was in the right, and that nothing should stand in his way, was as dangerous as any lunatic. Alex, despite all he had done, still possessed some moral sense, some conception of right and wrong, even if his ideas were somewhat unconventional. He had acknowledged his fault, and atoned, and had learned his lesson. She remembered that he had not dared to hope that their marriage could survive his brutality: he was aware of the consequences of what he had done, and had accepted them as his just deserts. His love was given to her completely, irrevocably and for all time. And his feelings for her were the mainspring of his life, a force for change and the growth of maturity and responsibility, the focus at last of all that formidable intelligence and energy.

Charles, in contrast, had obtained Wintercombe by trickery and betrayal, he had even attempted murder, and given the opportunity would doubtless try to kill Alex again. And still he could not see any wrong in his actions, could not understand why she recoiled from him as from a poisonous viper. Indeed, he seemed to take great satisfaction and pride in what he had done, with the blinkered and bigoted outlook of the absolutely self-righteous.

'He must be mad,' she said aloud, into Kitty's dark, wispy curls.

And Christian, the sober and sensible, entering the room at that moment, nodded in serious agreement. 'Yes, m'lady – I d'think he be truly rampin' mad.'

Louise saw again, with a shiver, Charles's urgent face, his insistence that he was right, his utter disregard for her own opinion, indeed for anything she had said, and felt a stab of real fear.

Phoebe, with Mattie in attendance, returned from a pleasant and relaxing wallow in the Cross Bath, nicely glowing, the ever-present ache in her hip almost vanquished. Her mood of well-being was instantly destroyed by Christian, who met her at the door, an expression of considerable anxiety on her face. 'Oh, Mistress Phoebe, thank God – could ee go straightway to m'lady? That Master Charles have called, and he've put she insuch a puzzivant.'

'Charles? *Here?* Why, in God's name?' Phoebe demanded sharply.

Christian shrugged her bewilderment. 'I don't know, madam. He did seem almost mazed to I, and the poor baby was a-crying fit to burst, and he woulden go. M'lady will tell ee what happened better nor I.'

Phoebe hurried into the back parlour, expecting to find her sister-in-law at the least upset, even weeping. Louise was sitting by the window, reading, and although she was very pale under the lightly golden skin, she seemed otherwise quite composed. She put the book down, and said, 'Has Christian told you?'

'Yes, she has – Charles can count himself lucky that I wasn't here.' Phoebe studied the younger girl for a moment, and then said, 'Are you all right?'

'Yes, I am – I was so angry with him, I didn't have the time to feel really frightened until after he'd gone. He threatened to kill Alex if he ever showed his face at Wintercombe, he told me over and over again that he loves me, he still thinks that everything he's ever done has been right and that once I grow out of my supposed infatuation with Alex, I'll fall into his arms, and he doesn't *listen*, Phoebe, he doesn't listen to a single word I say . . . I think perhaps that he's a little mad,' Louise said, and shivered. 'I know he'll come back, again and again, he said he would – and I'm frightened, I'm really frightened – not for me, but for Kitty – he looked at her as if he wanted to kill her too, and she knew it, poor little thing, it took me and Bess half an hour to calm her down after he'd gone – and if he finds out . . .'

Her voice tailed away, and she looked at Alex's sister with fear. Phoebe said gently, although she had already guessed, 'Finds out what?'

And Louise said, just above a whisper, 'I'm pregnant. And now I don't know what to do.'

Phoebe, looking at her, knew that to offer any display of emotion would only release the tears. She said briskly, 'I thought as much. You haven't been eating well, although I have noticed that your enthusiasm for milk possets and cheesecakes has bordered on the depraved. That one night at Goldhayes, I take it?'

Louise nodded, with a trace of her old, joyfully reminiscent smile. 'That night,' she said. 'And if Charles finds out, he'll realise that Alex was in England – and that we're not estranged after all.'

'What does that matter? Alex is safe in Amsterdam now, we know that. And Charles must surely have realised that despite all his efforts – and Alex's – you have been reconciled.'

'You don't understand,' Louise said. 'I'm not afraid for Alex, or for me. I'm afraid for the baby.'

There was a brief, horrified silence. Then Phoebe said, 'Not Charles – surely, not even *Charles* would stoop so low – '

'But if the baby is a boy – Alex's heir – then in law he could supplant Charles. And even if Charles didn't feel endangered by him . . . Oh, Phoebe, I saw the way he looked at Kitty – she's only a baby, scarcely a year old, and he loathes her because of who her father is. How much more would he hate a boy? Especially if he stood to take Wintercombe from him – especially if he were the proof that Alex and I were reconciled? And Charles is still obsessively jealous.'

'I still can't believe that he would deliberately harm your child – born or unborn,' Phoebe said slowly. 'If, God forbid, anything were to happen – if you miscarried, or the baby died, then he would be glad – Charles is certainly mean-spirited enough for that. But to hurt a baby, an innocent – even his warped sense of self-righteousness has not embraced such a hideous crime as that.'

'Perhaps not,' Louise said wearily, after a pause. 'Perhaps you are right. But I saw him today, I saw what he is like, and you did not. He is so obsessed with me, with Wintercombe, he will do anything. Phoebe, this child is so precious to me, I cannot afford, I don't *want* to take the risk!'

'Very well,' said her sister-in-law, masking her very real concern with an air of practical common sense. 'Even if the danger Charles presents is a figment of your imagination – and I do accept that it might be real, horrible though the thought is – even if he has no intention of harming your baby, your *fear* that he might is genuine enough. So, I think we must remove from Bath before he discovers the truth. The signs are evident already, to anyone who suspects: in a month's time, it will be so obvious that no number of loose gowns will disguise your condition for long. When will it be born?'

'Some time in November,' Louise said. She looked up at Phoebe. 'I should be so happy – indeed, I *was* happy, until Charles came. I want this baby so much, and so does Alex – I haven't written to tell him of it yet, I needed to be sure that it was going well. And now Charles has ruined everything.'

'Not at all. We can go to London, stay with Hugh again –

I don't think even Charles will follow you so far, with Wintercombe to look after. He's been guarding the place as jealously as a dog with a bone, for fear that we, or Alex, will steal it back. You'll surely be safe in London, and you seem healthy enough – I shouldn't think that the journey will present a problem. And if you're still worried about the baby, we can easily rent a house in one of the villages – Chelsea, or Knightsbridge, well away from Westminster and the City, and far more pleasant and salubrious.'

She smiled at her sister-in-law, and Louise smiled reluctantly back. 'You seem to have it all planned, all organised already. What can I do but agree?'

Charles spent a restless and sleep-free night at the Carne house, and rose the next morning with a haggard face and a raging headache, although, ever abstemious, he had drunk no more than a glass or two of watered wine the day before.

There was no one he could talk to, no one at all, about the thoughts and feelings that filled his head to bursting point. He wanted to scream at the hideous face of temptation, beckoning him into mortal sin. If the miracle ever happened and he were to be once more presented with the opportunity to kill Alex, that would be no crime: he would be doing his duty, and a favour to everyone. But to wish to harm his daughter . . .

And there was worse. Last night, tossing in his bed, he had thought of Louise, in her old gown and casually knotted hair, of the aura of allure and enticement that surrounded her despite her informal attire, and, God help him, his imagination had leapt lustily in, undressing her, fondling her, forcing himself upon her, ignoring the protests that would surely turn to cries of joy . . .

He wanted her so much. It was no longer possible to pretend to himself that his adoration was chaste, that he wished to preserve that air of innocent friendliness which he had always loved in her, until Alex seduced her. That attraction, it was obvious, had been purely physical, an expression of lust and desire. Surely he, Charles, could also rouse her passion? She claimed to hate him, true, but he did not believe it. After all, love and loathing were two sides of the same coin.

It was a while before a small, lonely inner voice of reason reminded him that the name for what he contemplated was rape, an ugly word for an ugly deed. Contrite, he prayed for forgiveness, and for freedom from his impure thoughts, and passed the day wrestling with his conscience, with apparent success.

But the next night was filled with more dreams, hideous yet enticingly erotic, of Louise struggling in his arms, the moans of despair which became moans of pleasure, her resistance at last destroyed by the irresistible force of his passion. He rose early, heavy-eyed and grim, and went to seek out Father Anselm.

His confessor, by the nature of his priestly duties, had heard many unpleasant things in his life, but even he seemed shocked by Charles's savage, despairing account of the lustful dreams, sleeping and waking, which haunted him. 'My son, this is wrong – most wrong, and wicked, and sinful – to desire this lady – and she your cousin, and a married woman – who by your own admission has done nothing to encourage you! You must truly repent, and do penance, and pray most humbly and earnestly for God's forgiveness, for your immortal soul is in peril if you give way to such devilish temptation.'

Knowing it to be true, he spent much of the day in prayer, as Father Anselm had demanded, but to no avail. As the soft June dusk began to fall outside, he rose to his feet, stiff and sore and weary, and tossed the final rags of his conscience to the demons.

The house in Nowhere Lane was dark, shuttered and obviously uninhabited, but he hammered on the door for some time, with increasing rage and desperation. At last the elderly woman who lived opposite put her head out and told him snappishly to stop that noise, it was no good, they'd gone.

'Gone?' Charles glared at her as if she were personally responsible. 'When? Where?'

'This morning, to London, so Mistress St Barbe said,'

the woman told him, with malicious satisfaction. 'So you can give over making that racket, it's fit to wake the dead in their graves.'

In his fury, he felt his hand lifting to strike her. But she saw the murderous look on his face, spat with gleeful accuracy right at his feet, and slammed her door before he could give way to his overwhelming rage and frustration.

Louise was gone: she had taken fright, and fled from him. For a wild moment, he thought of following her, but then he realised that it could be a trap. If he rode to London, he might spend weeks searching for her in vain, and return to find her firmly ensconced with Alex at Wintercombe, his mother ejected and homeless.

It was a chance he could not afford to take, even for the only woman he had ever wanted, the only woman, it seemed, that he could not have. Wintercombe, after all, was his supreme prize, the symbol of his triumph over the forces of evil embodied in his cousin Alex, and he would cling to it despite the lustful temptations offered to him by Louise.

The summer of 1688 was equable and placid, neither unduly wet nor uncomfortably warm. But although the weather was calm, London was not: and when Louise, Phoebe and Lukas arrived, on the nineteenth of June, they found all the city in a ferment.

Preoccupied with her worries about Charles, and Alex, and the possible dangers to the child within her, Louise had paid scant attention, these last few weeks, to events in the wider world. But even she, looking out at the streets of Westminster, could sense the air of tension in the crowds in King Street. There were knots of people deep in discussion on every corner, pamphlets and broadsheets being openly waved, hawked or recited, and everywhere, permeating even the raucous babble of London, the sound of the jaunty, catchy tune that she had already heard Lukas whistling in Bath.

'What's happening?' she asked, as the coach drew up outside the entrance to Bell Court, where Sir Hugh lived.

Phoebe cast her eyes up to heaven in mock exasperation.

'You mean you don't *know*? Well, I'm sure that Hugh can tell you much better than I can.' And more than that, despite Louise's impatient questions, she would not say.

Sir Hugh Trevelyan greeted them with his usual affection and friendliness. He told Lukas that his son James was at present staying with him, and doubtless a tutor could be engaged to keep their noses to the grindstone. At this, the boy's face registered a comical mixture of delight and dismay, until Hugh took pity on him, and assured him that he was merely joking. Then, they all ate a hearty supper, during which Louise tried to contain her curiosity, and both Phoebe and Hugh frustratingly kept the conversation on a trivial plane. It was not until the two boys had gone to bed that the three adults adjourned to a small, private parlour where they could talk undisturbed.

'It's the Bishops,' Hugh said in answer to Louise's urgent question. 'They've been arrested, and they're to be tried at the end of this month. All London is in an uproar.' He looked at her, and added, 'I can see you are still mystified. Shall I explain further? If Phoebe will permit me, of course.'

'I shall add my groat's worth of comment, where appropriate,' said Alex's sister tartly. She wore, amazingly, a new mantua, in a strong shade of blue figured silk that echoed her eyes and suited her very well. Earlier, Louise had tactlessly failed to hide her astonishment at seeing her fashionably dressed for the first time in her life.

The look of amused affection that now passed between Phoebe and Hugh was full of significance. 'In that case,' said the courtier, 'I had better make haste, for fear of interruption.'

He was less extravagantly clad than usual, in a suit of silvery grey that was almost plain, and to Louise his resemblance to his half-brother, Francis Heron, was very marked: the same fair wig, the same long face, and above all the same deceptively sleepy-looking grey-green eyes. She tried to imagine Phoebe married to him, and failed entirely.

'I hope you're listening, Louise,' said her sister-in-law pointedly. 'After all, this account is for your benefit entirely

368

– unlike you, some of us have been keeping our ears to the wind, these last few weeks.'

'I've had other matters on my mind,' Louise told her. 'And besides, politics has never interested me – as well you know.'

'But you should be interested – for Alex's future, and yours, depends utterly on what may happen in the next month or two. Now pay attention, for I don't suppose Hugh will want to say it twice.'

Her amused, bantering tone failed to arouse Louise's indignation. She took a sip of the rich Portuguese wine that they had been given, and turned her face to their host. 'I am all ears, sir – pray begin. Which Bishops are these, and why have they been arrested?'

'There are seven of them, led by the Archbishop of Canterbury, and including your own Thomas Ken, the Bishop of Bath and Wells. And their crime is that they refused to order their clergy to read the King's latest Declaration of Indulgence to Papists and Dissenters, which he commanded should be read from every pulpit in the land in May and June.'

'But we never heard it.'

'Exactly. The Bishops gave the lead by petitioning the King not to issue the Declaration. They fear that he means to strike at the Church of England, and infiltrate it with Papists. If the Declaration were to be meekly read in every church, it would indicate that the King was supreme, and the clergy merely his mouthpiece. But it's become far more than that now. The Bishops feel that for too long, King James has been allowed to undermine the authority of the Church, and the time has come to make a stand.'

'And the King has arrested them?'

'Yes, on the eighth of June. Very cleverly, they refused to give sureties, and so he was forced to send them to the Tower, or drop the charge against them. As James is determined to assert his authority, no matter what the cost, he has effectively made martyrs of them. In fact, while they were in the Tower, they had a constant stream of important visitors proclaiming their sympathy and support. They are now at liberty, but their trial is set for the end of this month, and much depends on the verdict.'

'What is the charge to be?' Louise asked.

'Seditious libel. The argument runs that, by petitioning the King, the Bishops have implied that he is incompetent, and cannot govern properly. The Bishops will doubtless claim that they were only acting within their rights as loyal subjects. In fact, the legal niceties mean little. What matters is whether they are convicted, or acquitted. On the word of the jury, the future of England will hang.'

'If they are found guilty, the King of course has won,' Phoebe said. 'He will assume a mandate to continue his policies. He is determined to be rid of the Test Act, once and for all, and the fact that the Prince of Orange has declared himself in favour of it has merely hardened his resolve. Towns up and down the country have been given new charters so that when the elections are called, they will send men to Parliament who will do the King's bidding in everything. After the Test Act is repealed, many are convinced that this country will have Popery foisted on it – and if persuasion does not work, then the King, or those who come after him, will eventually resort to force.'

'As is happening in France,' Louise said slowly. 'But for myself, I have no gripe against Papists – my mother is one now, after all.'

'Yes, but she converted to conform with King Louis's decrees,' Hugh pointed out. 'I gather from Phoebe that she would rather have remained a Protestant, but since she has no particularly strong feelings on the matter, found it more convenient to turn Catholic. How many do you think would follow that road, here in England? Few people are made of the stuff of martyrs. I myself have kept my position at Court by pretending to Papism, because Alex persuaded me that the interests of the Prince of Orange would be best served by so doing. But as soon as some sanity, by whatever means, is restored to this government, or when there is a greater change, I will revert with relief to the faith of my ancestors.' He grinned suddenly. 'For a rational, cynical man like myself, it is a considerable trial to be forced to suffer such superstitious mummery – and a still greater annoyance to be forced to pretend to believe in it.'

'My cousin Bram – the one who was transported to Barbados for his part in Monmouth's rebellion – he said to me once that what he abhorred, in any religion, Papist or Presbyterian or Anglican, was people forcing their convictions on others who were unwilling,' Louise said. 'And I agree with him. I wish everyone could be left in peace, to worship as they think fit, or not at all, without interference from Kings, or bishops, or from their neighbours.'

'My sentiments exactly – your cousin sounds a lad of sense,' Hugh commented. 'Have you heard from him at all?'

'Very little, but he seems to have made the most of adversity, and at least he was able to buy his freedom, although of course he cannot at present leave the island.' Louise smiled, thinking of her young, exuberant cousin, whose idealism had led him to follow Monmouth until the bitter end, and beyond, when greater men had deserted his cause, or betrayed their comrades for a pardon. 'But of course, if times change, he may be able to return.'

'We are being very coy,' Phoebe pointed out acidly. ' "When times change", "A greater change" – what we all really mean is, "When the Prince of Orange comes".'

And that meant war. Louise thought of the lush green hills and valleys of Somerset, despoiled by fighting and destruction and fire, as they had been more than forty years ago. Men like Francis Heron had suffered that nightmare once already in their lives – why should they wish to plunge England yet again into the peculiar barbarity of a civil war, brother against brother, father fighting son?

Because the alternative was worse: the gradual demolition, by trickery and bribery and force, of everything that so many people held dear: the rule of law; the sanctity of property; and above all, the safety of the Protestant religion. The King had already amply demonstrated his contempt for all three. How much further would he go, to fulfil his dream of a papist country?

And now he had a son, to carry on his work and his

371

dynasty. She thought of her own unborn child, a son too, perhaps, to be his father's heir, and understood only too well how the arrival of the little Prince had changed everything.

'And will he come?' she asked Sir Hugh.

That consummate courtier smiled. 'I do not know for certain, Louise. But the birth of the Prince of Wales has made it much more likely, and the fate of the Bishops will also play its part in his decision. Of course, he is watching events here very carefully, and he still has agents and informants everywhere. I feel sure that he will only intervene if he is certain of ample support from men of property. Monmouth's fate does not appeal to him.'

'Alex said much the same,' Louise told him.

'I am sure he did – he is the Prince's man, after all, and he should know. There are many things stirring now, coming out from under stones, since the King's son was born. Men are saying openly that his arrival was too opportune, that he is not the Queen's child at all, but the son of some tradesman smuggled into St James's Palace in a warming pan, and therefore no more a prince than you or I. Even the Princess of Denmark is saying so, according to my niece Sophie, who is one of her ladies. But in her case, the reason could well be jealousy. The poor Princess miscarried again a few months ago, and it is hardly surprising that she is bitter about her stepmother's inconvenient fertility. And she has already written to her sister of Orange, to tell her that the pregnancy was false, and that the Prince of Wales is not the Queen's son.'

'And is he?' Phoebe asked.

Hugh smiled wryly. 'Well, I was present at the birth, along with scores of other courtiers, male and female, although the view of those of us at the back of the chamber was necessarily somewhat restricted. But I heard the Queen groaning and crying in labour, and those sounds cannot be pretended – nor the wails of a newborn baby. Those who believe otherwise are, alas, deluding themselves – their wish has been father to their thought. The King, of course, is convinced that his son's birth is a sign of God's approval of his work – and he is filled with redoubled enthusiasm for his policies.'

'It will end in war, and worse, if he is not stopped,' Phoebe said softly. 'And he must be stopped – you know that, Hugh, as well as I do. The question is – what will *you* do?'

He looked at her, and smiled. 'I think you know that full well, my dear Phoebe. But, distasteful and dishonest as it may seem, for the moment I am going to play the hypocrite and pretend to be as Romish as the rest of them, with Henry Jermyn and all the others. For as your brother pointed out, if I am still a trusted servant of King James, I am of more use to the Prince of Orange than I would be if I followed my heart and resigned. More than that, I do not wish to say at present – but the wheels have begun to move at last.'

Phoebe stared at him, frowning. 'What of the army? The King relies on it, and on the navy too – they are largely his creation, after all. Where will they stand, if the Prince invades?'

'No one knows – yet,' Hugh told her. 'But there, too, the wheels are turning. The King has done his utmost to strengthen the army, and ensure its loyalty – if you remember, he appointed many Irish and Papist officers, and Alex's friend Talmarsh, along with many others, resigned his commission in disgust. Then he demanded, a few months ago, that the six English and Scottish regiments in the Dutch service be sent back to England. Of course, the Prince of Orange had no intention of letting them all go – they are a highly trained, highly disciplined body of men, far more so than that brawling rabble camped on Hounslow Heath, whatever the King may like to think. William, however, is no fool, and he allowed those officers who wished it to return – thus ridding himself of all those whose loyalty to him was in doubt. Some, too, may have gone as his spies. And the vacant commissions have been filled by men of great ability, whom he can trust absolutely – Tom Talmarsh, for one, and another friend of his, John Cutts, who fought under Monmouth. They have links with a group of young army officers who meet at the Rose Tavern, in Covent Garden – ah, I see you know it.'

'I've heard Alex mention it, once or twice,' Phoebe said drily. 'Don't they call themselves the Treason Club?'

'Yes, I believe so, although I don't think they want that name generally known,' Hugh said. 'I do not know how much influence they wield in the army at large, but I do know that Lord Churchill has a great deal. And his wife is Lady of the Bedchamber to the Princess Anne, and enjoys her confidence and her devoted friendship.'

To Louise, this glimpse of the connections, the tentacles of intrigue and conspiracy wound under the apparently smooth surface of everything the King trusted, was at once frightening, and exhilarating. James had seemed impregnable, secure, backed by his army and the authority of his position as King, however illegal his acts. And yet all the time men like Hugh, like Alex and Talmarsh, were burrowing under his castle of sand at the behest of the Prince of Orange, to bring it all crashing down when the time was ripe.

'So, you are implying that the army may not prove loyal,' Phoebe was saying. 'But are there not rumours of a purge?'

Hugh looked at her with admiration. 'Your ears are sharp indeed . . . Yes, there are, though only a very few straws in the wind at present. It's logical enough – the King has new-modelled his Court, his Universities, his judges, his towns. Even his Parliament, when it is elected, will consist of men hand-picked for their loyalty and their complete obedience to his every whim. He will surely now turn his attention to the army, and the navy as well. Soon all the officers will be Irish Papists, ready to enforce his decree. And if the Prince of Orange is to have any chance of success, let alone of avoiding bloodshed, then he must act before the army is purged of disloyal officers. I told Alex that, and he has doubtless passed the information on. As for the navy . . . well, I do not know, although my nephew Edmund sends me regular reports. Very few captains or sailors are Catholic, but on the other hand, they have no love for the Dutch after the wars of King Charles's reign. But somehow, whatever happens, I do not think that the Prince will long delay his intervention. When he judges that the time is right, he will move swiftly, and overwhelmingly.'

'And then,' Phoebe said to Louise, smiling, 'you will see Alex again.'

Strange, to think that her future, her husband's future, depended on so many unknown people: on army officers, weighing their military honour and their loyalty to the King against their devotion to the Protestant religion; on gentlemen and courtiers who, like Hugh, would watch and wait and send vital information, to cast their die when the time came; and above all on one man, small and hook-nosed, unhealthy and plainly dressed, at whose nod England might be plunged once more into civil strife, as bitter as that which had afflicted their grandparents, many years ago.

Alex might be killed before she ever saw him again: but if invasion offered their only chance of a lasting reunion, and of winning Wintercombe back from Charles, then it was a risk he must take. She could only pray that her bold, reckless husband would not put himself into unnecessary danger. And there was one piece of news that might very well persuade him to be more careful of his safety.

Tonight, she would write to him, and tell him of the coming child.

# Chapter Nineteen

## 'Instructed to rebel'

On the twenty-ninth of June, the Seven Bishops, led by the Archbishop of Canterbury, faced their accusers at the Court of the King's Bench. The place was packed, people standing in the corners, filling the galleries, craning for a better view. Counsel for His Majesty claimed very hotly that any petition to the King which called his prerogative and dispensing power into question must be a malicious libel intended to stir up sedition: counsel for the Bishops held that they had merely exercised their rights as citizens, and that the power of the King to dispense laws on his own, without recourse to Parliament, struck at the heart of the Protestant, even the Christian religion in England, and at all the laws of the land besides.

The four judges, summing up, split equally: two, the Chief Justice and Judge Allibone, a Catholic, found for the King, and the others for the Bishops, one of them saying that if the King indeed held such a dispensing power, it certainly did away with the need for parliaments, but he himself had never read of such a thing in all his life.

The jury, composed of worthy Middlesex knights and squires, listened closely to the argument, and were then shut away to consider their verdict. They deliberated all night, and it took until six in the morning to convince one recalcitrant that the rest of the jury were right. They refused to give their verdict in private, but insisted on returning to the open court, which even at that early hour was full to bursting point with a mass of hushed, expectant people.

The verdict was asked, and given. 'Not Guilty!' the foreman shouted, well aware of the implications of his words. All around him, the crowd exploded into shouts and cheers. The Solicitor General was booed and hissed, and such was the uproar that no further business could be done for more than half an hour. The Bishops, vindicated, made their way in triumph from the court, with people down on their knees before them to ask their blessing. All over London bells rang, guns were fired off, and bonfires lit although expressly forbidden: most audacious and insolent of all, a crowd burned an image of the Pope under the windows of St James's Palace. Everywhere, even amongst the army camped on Hounslow Heath, people rejoiced as the news spread. The Church of England had been delivered from its enemies, and from the King.

And the day after the Seven Bishops' triumphant acquittal, seven different men sat round a table to compose a letter to the Prince of Orange. It spoke eloquently of the danger in which they were placed, growing daily worse, so that they desired to find a remedy before it was too late to help themselves. People everywhere were deeply and generally dissatisfied with the Government's conduct in every sphere, so that nineteen men out of twenty wished for a change, and were prepared to rise in support of it if only they could secure some protection and assistance. Most nobility and gentry were of the same opinion, and would come at once to William's aid, were he to land in England. The King's army was riddled with disaffection, many officers continuing to serve only for the sake of their pay, and the common soldiers averse to Popery. It was certain that, in the event of an invasion, there would be many deserters in the army, and amongst the seamen as well. And as for the baby Prince of Wales, not one in a thousand believed him to be truly the Queen's.

In short, the time was ripe for the Prince's intervention, although certain difficulties and dangers were obvious: it was inevitable that the scale of the preparations needed in Holland would cause some alarm at Whitehall, and known malcontents and supporters of the Prince might well be arrested.

'So,' they wrote, 'if Your Highness shall think fit to adventure upon the attempt, there must be no more time lost in letting us know your resolution concerning it, and in what time we may depend that all the preparations can be so managed as not to give them warning here.'

And beneath, the seven men had placed their ciphers in the code that all William's spies followed, indisputable evidence of treason. The Earls of Devonshire, Danby and Shrewsbury; Lord Lumley; Henry Compton, the firebrand Bishop of London; Edward Russell, who had carried the message from Holland that William would invade if invited by men of power and influence; and Henry Sidney, whose secret network of spies and agents had fed a constant stream of intelligence back to the Hague, keeping the Prince better informed of events and opinions in England than was its own King.

The letter, which meant certain disaster, probably death, for its signatories if discovered, was given to Arthur Herbert, an admiral whom James had forced to resign, and who had been William's man for some time. He had been forbidden to leave the country, but found it easy to slip away to Holland unsuspected, in the guise of a common sailor, and to lay that momentous piece of paper in the hands of the man to whom all England now looked for deliverance.

As the summer crept inexorably towards autumn, rumours abounded in Whitehall. The appointment of Admiral Herbert to a command in the Dutch fleet aroused much speculation: so did the intense activity in Holland, where sailors were being recruited and ships fitted out. The Dutch ambassador told the King that the fleet would be employed against the Danes, corsairs, the French, in fact anywhere but England. For a while, at least, his assurances placated James, who could not believe that his own daughter and her husband would prove so undutiful.

He was the only one so optimistic. Everyone else, in London, in the country, even at Court, thought otherwise, and the prospect of a Dutch invasion was discussed openly, and with confident enthusiasm, by gentry and ordinary people alike.

A certainty, it was said: the only doubt was when.

Louise, growing fat and lazy, as she herself confessed, spent the summer months listening, as she had never listened before, to the news, comments, gossip and rumours that assailed her ears.

During these months, Hugh Trevelyan entertained many guests for dinner, or a quiet supper. Amongst them was Count Zuylestein, the Prince of Orange's envoy, who arrived incongnito on foot under a greatcoat and a broad-brimmed hat, to be closeted with his host for over an hour before appearing for the meal. And, one warm evening, a remarkably handsome, blond, witty man, a little older than Hugh, was introduced to Louise as Henry Sidney.

He bowed over her hand with a very charming smile, and said, 'I believe, ma'am, that I am acquainted with your husband.'

She had heard Hugh mention him often, in admiring and respectful terms, as the chief architect of the Prince's intelligence service in England. If William were to invade, he would owe success to this man. She looked at the elegant curls of his wig, the sensual mouth and the silk coat heavy with gold lacing, and wondered that such a man of the world, apparently only interested in pleasure, could excel at intrigue and conspiracy.

But of course, Alex gave the same impression: and Alex, as she had cause to know, was likewise much more than he appeared on the surface.

'I have not seen your husband for some time,' Sidney said, drawing her aside. 'In Amsterdam last year, in fact, and since then our paths have not crossed, for we have both been intent upon our own affairs.'

'And other people's?' Louise said, with a lift of her brow that drew Sidney's appreciative chuckle. 'Yes, indeed, ma'am, although neither of us, I feel, is sufficiently indiscreet to speak of it openly, even here in safe company. But your husband is a man of some parts, if I may be so bold as to comment. It's a crying shame that his talents are running to waste in Amsterdam. In different, happier times, he might well be called upon to take his rightful place as a player upon the public stage. And between you and me,

379

ma'am, such an elevation will be the making of him. I feel
he will go far – far indeed. And there are others, rather more
exalted than I, who think the same.'

'You are very kind, sir,' Louise said, and smiled warmly
at Sidney, with the dazzling brilliance that caused even that
seasoned and notorious womaniser to catch his breath a
little. 'I pray that he may one day be given the chance.'

It was an exhilarating thought. She imagined Alex in
Parliament, or at Whitehall, applying his mind and his
gifts, for perhaps the first time in his life, to matters that
were legal, and influential, and above all worthy of him. For
too long he had dabbled in treason, conspiracy, danger:
now, if the Prince's grand design were to succeed, Alex
might well be rewarded with some high office or position.

But nothing in this world was certain, and she would not
tempt Fate, ever cruel and capricious, with too much hope.
She added, 'Pray tell me, sir – do you return to Holland
soon?'

He nodded. 'In a few weeks, yes, I hope to do so. Do you
wish me to seek out of your husband? I shall be delighted to
oblige you, ma'am.'

'That is exactly what I was going to ask you,' Louise said.
'I am most grateful to you, sir – if I give you a letter, will you
convey it to him?'

And so, while the Court removed to the comparative peace
and fresh air of Windsor, and Louise and Phoebe, with
Lukas and Kitty and James, had Sir Hugh's Westminster
house to themselves, Henry Sidney slipped discreetly back
to Holland, carrying messages and correspndence, amongst
them, the letter that Louise, in the privacy of her chamber,
had spent many careful evenings writing, and rewriting, so
that no word would be wasted, and nothing omitted.

Alex was at the Hague when Sidney arrived, part of the
circle of agents and advisors who surrounded William, and
so he was able to deliver Louise's letter in person, with a
smile and the comment that he did not think that Alex
would find it contained ill news.

It ran to three pages, in her swift and individual hand,

full of loops and short cuts and idiosyncratic spelling and syntax. And she had made it a declaration and an affirmation of her love, and her joy at the coming child.

He read it over and over again, treasuring the thought of the night that had joined them once more, indissolubly, all that passion and delight to be given flesh, before the year was out, in the birth of another baby. It would have been madness to write back to her openly, using the official channels, but Admiral Herbert had reorganised and enlarged the secret courier network by which spies and letters and illegal pamphlets could be smuggled into England using Dutch fishing boats. And so, late in September, his reply reached her after a very roundabout journey, rather battered and smelling powerfully of herring.

My own sweet Louise,
I am joyed beyond all measure and all counting at your news, and hope that everything goes well with you, and with your Great Belly (as those of no sensibility, such as my sister, will call it). Keep Lukas at his studies, and kiss Kitty for me, and tickle her now and then as a remembrance of our meeting. Does she walk yet, and talk? Every hour that passes, every day, I miss you more, and long for you with all my heart. And be sure of this, dear love, that matters here proceed apace, and if nothing miscarries, you shall very soon be troubled once more with your passionate, devoted and most affectionate lover,
Alexander St Barbe

Louise, putting the letter down, felt the foolish tears prickle at her eyes, and fumbled hastily for a kerchief. She had found each of her pregnancies to be quite different: with Nathaniel she had bloomed, Kitty had made her sick and lethargic, and this baby had not only kicked her lustily night and day for months, but had rendered her extraordinarily vulnerable to emotion. She, who once had rarely cried, wept now at everything: a child's funeral; the pigeons flying across the sunset in Hyde Park; a dead cat by the roadside; the strains of sweet music from an open window; a ridiculous and overacted tragedy at the theatre in Drury Lane; and at Kitty's earliest unaided steps and first, almost unintelligible, words. And this yearning, affectionate letter, so full of unspoken hope and unashamed love and tenderness for her and for his children, touched her soul's heart. Alex, the careless, the callous, the cynical, could at last admit openly his need for them all: and she closed her eyes and prayed that he would survive the darkness and the danger drawing in upon them, as inevitably and relentlessly as the days diminished into winter.

For a long time, it had seemed as though the King, obsessed with his plans to ensure the election of a complaisant parliament who would obey his every command, was the only man in Europe who did not think that the Prince of Orange planned to invade England. It was late in August before James, faced with certain evidence from Holland and the urgent insistence of his ambassador, and King Louis's special envoy, began at last to comprehend that the danger might be real. Certainly, the fact that the Prince and Princess had now, much to his distress, cast open doubt upon the birth of the Prince of Wales, was reason enough to suspect them of ill will.

Reluctantly, James realised that war was possible, but was still unable to see how his son-in-law's plans could succeed. The memory of Monmouth's unhappy fate would surely serve to discourage open rebellion, and without support in England, even the strongest invasion had no hope of victory against his army. Satisfied that he and the realm were safe, the King and his ministers continued with their preparations for the meeting of Parliament, for which the writs were to be issued on the nineteenth of September.

In Holland, activity was intense, and increasing, until in the flat marshy creeks and rivers around Rotterdam, fifteen thousand men, with their arms, horses, baggage and provisions, were ready to embark. At long last, the King of England and his ministers were forced to recognise the scale of the danger being so efficiently prepared against them on the other side of the North Sea. Still, however, they could not believe that the Prince would actually achieve his aim. There had been no successful invasion of England for over six hundred years, and winter was rapidly approaching. The October gales would make the crossing virtually impossible for the barges and transports now being hired in vast numbers in every Dutch port. Surely only a madman, or a fool, would hazard such an enterprise so late in the year: and William, as even James must admit, was neither stupid nor insane.

But as September drew to its end, the stream of information from Holland could no longer be denied. Finally forced out of his complacency, James issued a proclamation, denouncing the imminent invasion of 'strangers and foreigners', 'purposing an absolute conquest of these kingdoms'. Military preparations were set in motion; the writs for a November Parliament were recalled; the hated Ecclesiastical Commission was dismantled; and those towns and cities which had been forced to accept new charters and franchises found their old ones restored to them.

These obvious symptoms of panic did not impress the vast majority of James's subjects. Hugh Trevelyan commented drily that if the King was incited to such a drastic reversal of his policies by the the threat of an invasion, what might he be persuaded to do by the time William's forces actually landed?

'Turn Protestant, perhaps,' Louise suggested tartly. Sitting by the fire in Hugh's private parlour, draped in the loose informal robes she wore now when in private, it was hard to discern that she was even pregnant, still less that the baby was due in six weeks' time. Phoebe, studying her, thought that she looked very well, her face glowing with health, her eyes bright with hope. The official announcement of imminent invasion had changed everything, had made the prospect at last a certainty, and had therefore brought a reunion with Alex much closer.

'I doubt even James would prove so craven,' Hugh said. 'The trouble is that he has listened to reason too late. Even if he is sincere in what he says – and I for one doubt it – even if he means to mend his ways in the future, everyone believes he's making the empty promises of a naughty boy when he finds himself threatened with punishment. And now that William's arrival seems a certainty, instead of some longed-for but elusive Holy Grail, the rats will be leaving the royal ship with a vengeance.'

'And you?' Phoebe enquired, with bland and spurious innocence. 'When will you depart?'

'That, dear lady, is my business and mine alone, despite the affection and regard in which I hold you. But I do think that it is time for you to leave London.'

'Leave? Why?' Louise sat upright abruptly. 'We are close to things here, we have all the gossip, the news – if we go back to Bath, we'll hear nothing!'

'But you'll be safe.' Hugh, deadly serious for once, leaned forward to address the two women. 'The likeliest chance is that the Prince will land somewhere on the east coast, or sail up the Thames. Whatever happens, he will aim first at London, and the King will do his best to stop him. There may well be a great deal of fighting, in or around the city. And even if there is not, I should imagine that once news of the Prince's landing reaches London, the mob will rise in his support. The houses of prominent courtiers will certainly be amongst their chief targets, along with Papist booksellers and chapels – and you won't turn their wrath aside by protesting that your husband is fighting with the Prince. At best, you'd be abused, manhandled, put out on the street. At worst . . .'

He did not finish, and did not need to. Louise's imagination had supplied her with ample details, to judge by her sudden pallor. She said slowly, shaken, 'And you are well known to be a convert to Popery. You're right, Hugh – it isn't safe. But – couldn't we find somewhere else to stay? Why do we have to go back to Bath? Charles may pester me again – '

'I've no desire, believe me, to force you on to the Bath coach at the point of a pistol,' Hugh told her. 'But think of the children – Kitty, Lukas, the new baby. I'm sending James back to Suffolk. Even though he may be closer to the place of invasion there, he will still be much safer than he would be in London. Also . . . if things go badly wrong, and my secret adherence to the Prince is discovered, then I will certainly be imprisoned, and all of my friends will fall under suspicion. If you return to the West, you will probably be out of their reach, for the present at any rate. I think that if you are not safe in Bath, then you are not safe anywhere in the Kingdom.'

'He's right, you know,' Phoebe added. 'You must see that, surely, Louise – and if Alex has a duty to you, to keep himself as safe as he can, then so have you likewise to him – and to the baby. As for Charles, I'm sure we can keep him at bay until Alex returns.'

'But to risk a coach journey . . .' Louise, well aware that she was fighting a losing battle, stared unhappily at her sister-in-law. 'Remember what happened to Nathaniel.'

'If I remember correctly, it was your *riding* that precipitated his untimely birth. And in any case,' Phoebe pointed out, with ruthless logic, 'surely the appropriate method of travel for one in your condition is a horse-litter? I'm sure London can furnish one of those for hire – or perhaps Hugh can arrange for you to borrow the Queen's.'

'A *horse-litter*?' Louise stared at her indignantly, and then gave a wry grin of capitulation. 'Well, I suppose if I must suffer such an ignominy, it is all for a good cause. For the safety of this baby, I will do anything, even that. But under protest, you understand – if I did not have my responsibility for the children to consider, I would not stir from London, whatever the danger.'

'Why? Because you think that you'll see Alex sooner if you stay here?' Phoebe asked. 'Well, I suspect that the chances of William marching unopposed into Whitehall are remote indeed. And unless that happens, you'll be reunited as quickly in Bath as here. After all, his first task, if all goes well, will be to take possession of Wintercombe.'

Louise had forgotten that. She said reflectively, 'So of course he will come to Bath as soon as he can, even if he doesn't know I'm there. Perhaps by then the baby will be born.' She winced suddenly, and added, 'That is, if it

385

doesn't kick its way out now, rather than await the usual course of events!'

Not long afterwards, she went to bed, leaving Hugh and Phoebe sitting comfortably in their cushioned chairs, either side of the fire. There was a pot of coffee on a trivet in the hearth: he bent, and refilled their dishes. Phoebe, sipping hers, studied his long, expressionless face, and then said quietly, 'When should we go?'

'As soon as possible, I think. Of course, no one knows when the Prince *will* land, but it must be soon, before the weather worsens beyond all hope of success. And there is always the possibility that he will not be able to sail at all, if the gales begin too early. In which case, he has lost all his advantage, for James will have the whole winter to prepare for his coming.'

'And the situation in Germany might have changed – the French King may be able to come to James's assistance.'

'Exactly. At the moment he's involved in war with the Emperor, which means that the Prince of Orange can do what he likes. But his first duty is to Holland – if Louis threatens his country, then William will have to abandon his plans of invasion.'

'*Why* is he invading? Oh, I know all the superficial reasons – but what does he *want*? Does he want the throne? Or a regency? Or just a free Parliament? Does anyone know?'

'No one save William himself, I suspect. And since I've only met the man once, when he came to marry the Princess, nearly ten years ago, I can't claim to judge his qualities or his character. But it's certain he is self-possessed, and cautious, and secretive, to a very great degree – and owns a strength of mind and of will which, I suspect, my royal master lacks entirely.'

'Alex admires the Prince – and there are very few thus favoured.'

'You surprise me,' Hugh said drily. He drank his coffee, his eyes on the hot heart of the sea-coal fire, his face suddenly and unwontedly sombre.

Phoebe wondered what he was thinking. They had been

386

friends for three years now, and had always agreed well, but mostly on a superficial level. He, always the courtier, always careful to give little away, had directly revealed almost nothing of his inner thoughts and emotions. She knew, from careful and perceptive observation of his expression, his voice, his hands, that he loved his son, and his niece – the female artist, whom she would one day dearly like to meet – and his half-brother Francis Heron and his wife. He had spoken of his own dead wife, James's mother, almost casually, but she had sensed the real pain still alive beneath his brief words. Open avowal of such feelings seemed impossible for him: and in that, he was much like her brother.

And like herself. She, too, found it difficult to show affection, save to the very few, like Alex and Louise, and Lukas, to whom she felt most close. And even as she recognised, wryly, the similarity between them, and the consequent obstacle to any further development in their relationship, he turned to her and said quietly, 'Phoebe – I have something to ask you.'

His voice was quite devoid of light-heartedness, or irony, or cynicism. Her heart jolted, and she admonished it sternly. He wanted her to arrange for the litter for Louise, or to carry a clandestine message to some West Country conspirator, or to find him an obscure volume or pamphlet in the bookshops she haunted around St Paul's and in the back streets of Covent Garden. But instead he looked at her directly, and said, 'Will you marry me?'

Stunned, Phoebe wondered if she had misheard him, or if he had run suddenly mad. She stared at him speechless, in absolute disbelief, and managed at last to say something. '*What?*'

It came out as a despairing and unintelligible squawk, and she gathered all her considerable mental powers from the four winds where he had scattered them, and tried again. '*What* did you say?'

'I asked you to marry me,' Hugh said, calmly matter-of-fact. 'As you very well know.'

Phoebe put her hands together and pressed, hard, until

the bones protested. She was certainly awake. She said, with more than her usual bluntness, 'Hugh – in God's name, *why?*'

'Why not? We are both adult, independent people. We rub along together tolerably well. And it would be pleasant to have some happy event to look forward to, once all this is over.'

'You mean, when the King has sent William back to the Hague with his tail between his legs, and you and Alex are dead, or refugees with prices on your heads,' Phoebe said caustically, her normal composure almost recovered.

'Why are you so sure it'll fail, of a sudden? My conversations with Alex, and other men who know the Prince well, lead me to the conclusion that he would not consider an invasion unless it had an excellent chance of success – and, being the paragon of efficiency that he is, William will spend, indeed is spending money like water to ensure his victory.' Hugh surveyed her rather quizzically. 'But we are straying off the point, my dear Phoebe. I asked you a question. All you have done is to fire questions back. Will you give me a straight answer, or more evasions?'

'I wasn't evading the point – just stupefied with disbelief,' she said. 'Hugh, you must surely be mad. I'm no fit wife for any man.'

'That's what you have made yourself believe, I suspect. From this man's point of view, you look admirably fit. You've as good a grasp of politics as I have, probably better, you're exceptionally well informed, you have a mind of your own, you can converse intelligently with the great, if not necessarily the good, you are witty, tolerant and wise, and above all, you have for a brother a man who, if William succeeds, will be able to convince him that I thoroughly deserve a place at his Court.' He grinned at her. 'Well? Any more excuses, or have you scraped that particular barrel clean?'

'Certainly I haven't,' Phoebe said resolutely. To her horror, she was in real danger of bursting into tears, something at all costs to be avoided: she had last wept at her father's death four years ago, and then only in the privacy of her bedchamber. She went on, with some force, 'I have no knowledge of housekeeping – Mattie does it all for me.'

'No matter – we can hire a housekeeper. Or my niece's sister-in-law will be more than happy to olige.'

'I'm crippled,' Phoebe said doggedly. 'Doctor Peirce told me that I would be unlikely to bear children.'

'I don't believe a word any doctor says – save for my niece's husband, he's an old and dear friend of mine, and a man of sense. Anyway, I have James, and he is more than adequate. Any more objections?'

'Yes. I'm old, and ugly. You'd be better off with some pert beauty who'll ornament your table and your bed,' Phoebe said, with the brutality of desperation. 'Someone who won't look like a scarecrow, and who can give you a string of sons! Isn't that what men want?'

She had not meant to sound so bitter. He looked taken aback, and she regretted her words, too late. He said slowly, 'Some men. Not all, I promise you. And not this man.'

'It doesn't matter,' Phoebe told him, as strongly as she could. 'It's very kind of you to offer, Hugh, but no. I won't consider it. I have no desire to marry, and never have had, nor ever will have. And feeling sorry for me is the worst of all reasons for marriage.' She got clumsily to her feet, feeling for her stick, and praying that he would not notice her shaking limbs. 'And now I think it's time for me to go to bed. Goodnight, Hugh.'

As fast as she could, she hobbled from the room: and only when she had at last achieved the splendid loneliness within her bedcurtains, with Mattie retired to a truckle in the closet, could she indulge in the shameful relief of silent, bitter tears.

It took some time to organise the hiring of a litter for Louise, as well as a coach for the rest of the party, and so it was not until a week later that the small group of St Barbes left Westminster on the painfully slow journey back to Bath.

It had been a most difficult time for Phoebe. Mortified by

Hugh's proposal, which he had surely made only out of pity, she found that she could hardly bring herself to speak to him, let alone attain her former ease in his company. He in his turn was too practised a dissembler to reveal any hurt or affront at her new coldness and distance, but she had, once or twice, caught him looking at her with what seemed to be genuine pain in his expression.

Almost, then, she relented, for there was no denying that she did hold him in high regard: he had been a true and dear friend to her and to her family, and she hated the thought that her rejection might have given him genuine grief.

But surely, surely, he could see, when he cast his clear, cynical eyes on the circumstances, that it was absolutely impossible. Affection, yes, regard and respect, yes, liking, certainly: she felt all these things for Hugh Trevelyan. But love, of the kind that Louise had experienced with Alex, soul-scorching, all-consuming, as wild and glorious and uncontrollable as a thunderstorm, that was not, and never would be, for her. Shrewish and intellectual, never mind her physical disabilities, she was not made for romance, for passion, for the intensity of feeling that had united her parents, and her aunt Silence with Nick Hellier, and all those others who were fortunate enough to marry for love.

It was when her thoughts had reached this stage that she faced the unwelcome truth: what Hugh had offered her was not, despite what he had implied, a business arrangement between friends. She had not imagined the look in his eyes: he loved her, God alone knew why. She had thought herself safe from the most desperate lecher, and Hugh, with all his failings, was certainly not one of those.

She looked in her mirror then, seeing the same Phoebe as she had always seen: the fine skin, pallid with ill-health and indelibly marked by almost constant pain; the thick black hair that had never hinted at a curl; the thin, sharp face; the large and brilliant blue eyes that were undoubtedly her only good feature, and which she shared with her brother. Despite them, she was plain beyond all remedy, and she had never felt the slightest desire to mend matters. Paint, patches, curling papers and tongs, fine clothes and the artful employment of padding and tight lacing were ridiculous: they would not disguise her damaged hip, nor her essentially uncomfortable personality. Passion and desire were ludicrous and grotesque in such a body: she tried to imagine herself kissed, fondled, caressed, and flinched away from the idea, humiliated and appalled. Why, oh why, had he spoken? Why had he declared himself? Why could he not have kept things as they were, safe and comfortable, a friendship where the issues discussed were those of the intellect or affairs of state, and inconvenient and embarrassing emotions were left severely alone.

Angry with him, more angry with herself for being so affected by his proposal, she spent much of that last week in an even worse temper than usual. Louise and Lukas at first ascribed her mood to pain, for the weather was raw and cold, and her joints always ached abominably in such conditions. But at length, on the night before they left, her brother's wife was constrained to ask Phoebe what was wrong. Why was she barely speaking to Hugh? What had he done to offend her, despite all his kindness?

'I suggest you mind your own business, and keep that very long nose out of my affairs,' Phoebe said, with a venom the equal of Alex's at its absolute worst.

She saw Louise's hurt, indignant expression, and knew that she had gone too far, but was too weary and miserable to remedy the matter. All she wanted was a sound night's sleep, and freedom from pain, both in her body and in her confused, unhappy mind. In the last few days, since the full implications of Hugh's proposal had finally become clear to her, her normally clear and pragmatic brain had become sadly disordered, and she hated it.

For her part, Louise had observed the lamentable change in her sister-in-law, and now drew her own conclusions from it. Indeed, her tacit and understanding sympathy might well have betrayed that she had guessed altogether too accurately for comfort, had Phoebe not been so preoccupied with her own thoughts.

So when Louise had been helped into the litter, warmly

wrapped and the leather curtains laced tight against the wind and rain, and Kitty, Lukas and the maids packed into the hired coach, Phoebe was more than glad to be leaving Westminster. It would take perhaps a fortnight to reach Bath, because of the extreme slowness of the horse-litter, but already her mind had raced home to her own cosy little house, her books, her correspondence with like-minded scholars, and blessed freedom at last from the disturbing and unwanted emotions which Hugh Trevelyan had roused in her reluctant breast.

On the same day that Hugh committed a most disastrous error of judgement by proposing marriage to Phoebe St Barbe, Prince William of Orange issued his Declaration of Intent. Much thought and labour had been expended on this vital document, which must not antagonise or alarm any of the disparate factions opposing King James. The conspirators in England had supplied the first draft, and this had been embellished and altered at the Hague until it could appeal to Tories and Anglicans, Whigs and Dissenters, and unite all those who wished for a free Parliament which would restore to this troubled and fearful country stability, harmony and a proper regard for law and property rights.

William, whose main concern, though he kept it from all but his most intimate advisers, was to secure the throne of England for himself and his wife, did not wish to be at the beck and call of any Parliament, however free, but his acute political mind knew that no other rallying cry would ensure the success of his design. Careful not to upset those who would see in his actions a threat to the life and person of the King, his Declaration emphasised the role that James's 'evil counsellors' had played in oversetting the religion, laws and liberties of the realm, and in turning James's heart against his daughter and son-in-law. It was therefore for his own safety, as well as for the preservation of the Protestant religion, that William proposed to invade.

The Declaration was careful, yet unambiguous, and scathing in its dismissal of the 'pretended Prince of Wales'.

392

To complete it, William, rather against his better judgement, had employed the advice not only of his close advisers, both English and Dutch, but of men whom he would never normally have trusted with so important a task, the Whig and republican exiles. Although he disliked republicans and regarded Whigs with some suspicion, they represented a powerful and influential faction, and in these circumstances he was prepared to listen to their suggestions. Unfortunately, most were only interested in rousing old hostilities and paying off old scores, and the form which they wanted the Declaration to take would undoubtedly alienate many good Protestant and Tory squires.

He was not entirely surprised to find that the lone voice of sense amongst the exiles belonged to Sir Alexander St Barbe. Long ago, when the man had served in one of the English regiments in his army, William had marked his undoubted ability, and promoted him to the rank of major. His avowedly republican and atheist principles did not endear him to the Prince, but neither did his opinions necessarily present a barrier to advancement. William was an excellent judge of men, and so far his confidence in St Barbe had not been misplaced. He had served in the army with efficiency and distinction: he had carried out his duties in England as a secret agent with absolute discretion, and his information about the East Anglian gentry had been both comprehensive and invaluable. There were, true, numerous unsavoury tales about his private life, but the Prince never paid heed to such tittle-tattle. Henry Sidney had a similar, though rather less lurid, reputation, and it had proved an excellent cover for his activities.

And so it was with Alex St Barbe. Those who knew him only by repute dismissed him as a womanising drunkard with no thought in his head beyond the next whore or the next bottle. But the Princess, who was gentle, lively and religious, liked St Barbe, and had never been given cause to reproach him: nor had William seen him the worse for drink, or found that his excesses, even if they were as spectacular as reported, interfered with his duties. And since there were always spies to keep watch on other spies,

393

the Prince was also aware that since his secret sojourn in England, and for a while before it, Alex St Barbe had moderated his private behaviour to a considerable degree. He had been ill, which might have some bearing on it: and the Princess, who had recently talked with him, had told her husband that Sir Alexander was much affected by his enforced separation from his wife and children, whom he dearly loved.

William, who harboured similar feelings for his own wife, was less inclined to disbelieve this than might have been thought. And certainly Sir Alexander had altered, was no longer the wild, reckless, gifted rake who had first come to Holland ten years ago. The man who sat at the table beside the radical John Wildman, pointing out the flaws in the veteran's argument with pleasant but inexorable logic, was one in whom William felt he could place considerable trust and responsibility.

So, when the disgruntled Whigs, Wildman, Mordaunt and the rest, were filing out, he indicated that Sir Alexander stay behind. And a few minutes later, in the absolute privacy of the Prince's closet, William stared dispassionately at the man in front of him, not so much younger but emphatically taller and more attractive than himself, and said quietly in Dutch, 'I have another duty to lay on you, and one which will be both difficult and very dangerous. If you are caught, you will undoubtedly hang.'

'Then I shall have to be exceedingly discreet,' Alex said. 'I take it you want me to help in the distribution of your Declaration?'

William gave one of his rare smiles. 'You are quite correct, Sir Alexander. It is a task which I can give only to the most brave, the most secret, and the most able of my friends: you now know, therefore, of the absolute trust and confidence which I place in you. And there are, besides, certain rumours concerning my intentions which I wish to be disseminated in England. It would be politic, for instance, to ensure that my royal father-in-law thinks that my troops will land at any point of the compass save where I actually *intend* that they shall land. Do you understand me?'

394

'I understand you very well, sir,' Alex said, and smiled. 'When do you wish me to go?'

'Not immediately – the Declaration must be printed first, and final preparations made. But with God's help, and an east wind, the ships and transports will be ready in perhaps two weeks, so it will be just before then. You should put your affairs in order and be ready in, say, five or six days. I trust that is possible?'

'Entirely possible, Your Highness,' Alex said. Despite his assumption of sober gravity, he felt the old wild exhilaration spring to life inside him. It was six months and more since he had returned to Holland, and there had been precious little to do after those first few weeks at the Hague, imparting everything he had learned in Suffolk to the Prince's advisers. He had missed Louise intensely, although their separation had become more bearable now that he knew beyond a doubt that she loved him. And there was Lukas, and Kitty, whom he had seen only once as a baby. She would be growing, with the astonishing rapidity of small children, into a little girl: when next he saw her, would she be walking, talking, even learning her letters?

The news that Louise expected another child had raised his spirits and his frustrations alike still higher. Surely this time it must be the healthy boy who would put the keystone into the arch of his future, just as the disputed Prince of Wales had answered the hopes of King James. He was too much a realist, however, to place all his hopes on the child's birth, for so many babies died, and their mothers too. Louise would be in danger: and when he thought of her supple, agile body, newly and lusciously mature, her laughter and the brilliance of her eyes and her smile, teasing and mischievous, and her glorious and uninhabited enjoyment of their lovemaking, he knew that if she died in bearing this child, as his own mother had died bearing Phoebe, then his world would indeed be ended. For nowhere else, in all England, or France, or on any shores of the earth, would he find another to match her: and other women, not even the most voluptuous, skilled and comely whores in all Holland, could no longer tempt him.

But now, the waiting was over. He was to travel secretly to England, to prepare the way for the Prince's invasion. It would not, yet, bring him to Louise: but at least he would be busy, working for the day when King James might be brought to see reason, and when his devoted servant Charles St Barbe could at last be forced to relinquish Wintercombe to its rightful owner.

# Chapter Twenty

## 'Beset with dangers round'

The pinnace *Griete* was built for fast sailing and ease of handling amidst the shallow waters and treacherous sandbanks of the Dutch and English estuaries around the North Sea. As she had so often done before, especially that year, she made the brief crossing from the fishing village of Maensluys, on the Maas, to the coast of Essex, entirely unsuspected by any customs officer in the land of her destination. She had carried pamphlets and spies, and had taken Admiral Herbert secretly to the Hague with the invitation to William: now, she was loaded with several thousand copies of the Prince's Declaration, and the person of Sir Alexander St Barbe, whose task it was to distribute them, and certain contradictory rumours, throughout the eastern parts of England.

His previous exploits might have left some trace, so he was not now in the guise of Master Orchard, merchant of Bristol. With a fine sense of irony, he had put on the sober black and plain linen of a Protestant parson, and called himself Thomas Marlow. His hair, now growing again after he had abandoned the periwig, had been lightly powdered to give the impression of a man going grey, and at least ten or fifteen years older than his actual age. He had also acquired a stoop, both to increase his clerical appearance and to diminish his unusual height, and from somewhere in the depths of his erratic education had dredged a stock of suitable Biblical quotations.

Tom Talmarsh, called to view his transformation, found his mannerisms frighteningly convincing, and said so with amused admiration.

'My tutor at Oxford,' Alex told him, clasping his fingers together in mock humility. 'He was forever washing his

397

hands, so, and we used to call him Pontius. Well, Tom? Would you recognise me?'

'I doubt your own wife would,' said his friend. 'There's only your eyes, but you can't do much to change them.'

'No?' Alex took a pair of spectacles from his coat pocket, and balanced them on his nose. The glass had been subtly smoked, Talmarsh saw, to reduce the impact of that vivid and distinctive blue. He whistled appreciatively. 'Perfect. Now I wouldn't know you if we met head-to-head in the street.'

'Good,' Alex said. He shed the spectacles and the priestly manner like a cloak, and sprawled into a chair. 'Brandy, Tom?'

'If it's as excellent as your stock in Amsterdam, yes. So – when are you going?'

'Tonight.' Alex passed a glass to Talmarsh. 'I suggest that we drink to a long life and victory for the Prince of Orange, and confusion to his enemies!'

With fervour, Tom echoed him and they drank, while outside the October winds whipped down the narrow street in the Hague where Alex lodged, carrying with it a burden of leaves, rubbish, and the salty smell of the sea.

Alex said softly, 'It's blowing from the east at present – but if it should change, the fleet will be trapped in harbour. How much longer before all the preparations are complete?'

'A week, perhaps less,' Tom told him. He was colonel of one of the English regiments in the Dutch army, and this brief hour after dinner was the first he had been able to snatch for days. 'My God, Alex, you should count yourself lucky to be out of it. Men, horses, provisions, hay, arms – all to be collected, ordered, embarked, and nothing forgotten – and you know how the Prince is obsessed with efficiency. There's even a bridge, in sections, and a smithy. He's thought of everything – and you'll be glad to hear that brandy and tobacco have not been forgotten.'

'How else is he to keep his officers happy? If the winds prove contrary, we may spend more time at sea than we'd bargained for. Do you suffer from seasickness?'

'No, thank God, but if the weather is at all rough, I

should think nine parts of my regiment will be hanging over the side.' Talmarsh eyed his companion, who was engaged in refilling their glasses. He was tempted to ask more questions, but decided against it: the less he knew of Alex's clandestine activities, the better. He added, grinning, 'There's also a printing press gone aboard. The Prince is very conscious of the value of reliable information in winning men over to his cause.'

'As I'm well aware,' Alex pointed out. 'But have you actually paused to *think* about what he is doing, Tom? To embark on an expedition such as this, with the weather fast deteriorating, leaving Holland virtually defenceless, should King Louis turn his attentions northwards? How many men in England, however they may grumble, will actually rise in William's support, when it comes to the point? A lot of lip-service has been paid to the cause of Protestantism and a free Parliament, but do all those comfortable lords and squires care enough about such things to fight for them? It's a very wild and risky gamble for the Prince to take. If he wins, he wins England. If he loses – he loses everything. And so much depends on fortune – and on the weather.'

'He is certain that God is with him,' Talmarsh said, thinking of the Prince's absolute belief in his divinely ordained destiny that had, with one or two brief relapses, carried his momentous enterprise thus far. 'But you, of course, don't believe that.'

'Well, I don't believe that King James has God at his right hand either,' Alex commented drily. 'But at least William, unlike poor faint-hearted Monmouth, has the courage of his convictions. And money to spend, and the wisdom and foresight to know how to spend it.'

'It's cost over a hundred and fifty thousand guilders just to hire the transports. The Prince is a very rich man, but this undertaking has called upon all his reserves. If it fails, he'll be a pauper.'

'Or dead,' Alex pointed out. 'And so may I be . . . Tom, will you do something for me?' As his friend nodded assent, he continued. 'The plan is that I stay in England for just a week or so, no longer, and come back to rejoin the army before it sails. If anything should happen to me, will you arrange for this to be given to my wife? I have put her direction on the packet. I know that she is at present staying in Westminster, but she may well return to Bath if the situation in London threatens to become dangerous. In any event, that address will find her sooner or later.'

Talmarsh took the thick wad of paper. He said slowly, 'Your chances of survival are probably better than mine – but, yes, I will do my best, if it should become necessary. I hope and pray that it does not.'

'So do I,' Alex said, with his sudden, boyish grin. 'Believe me, Tom, so do I. And let us also hope that no one will discern that Parson Marlow's mild and meek manner hides that desperate traitor and spy Alexander St Barbe.'

Talmarsh had left shortly afterwards, bearing the letter for Louise, and Alex had made his final preparations. His servant, Gerrit, was to take his baggage on board one of the three ships allotted to the Whig and republican exiles, who had been encouraged to join the expedition to swell the numbers of English and Scottish troops. If all went well, the *Griete* would carry him, and any intelligence he had managed to gather, back to Maensluys in time to take his place amongst them. And after so long, so much planning and delay and frustrating inaction, he was more eager than anyone, save possibly the Prince himself, to see the dream of invasion at last become a reality.

King James, finally convinced that his son-in-law, with the full support and connivance of his own daughter, was planning a hostile and imminent invasion, had panicked. As October advanced, his concessions flew thick and fast: he even made overtures of reconciliation to the bishops who had opposed him so implacably. Unfortunately, he had left it too late. Measures so frantically and hastily taken could very easily be countermanded once the danger had passed, and older people clearly remembered his ill-fated father, the first King Charles, who had just as urgently and

400

insincerely promised anything to his opponents, in order to gain time and advantage.

Despite the desperate attempts of the Government to suppress it, copies of the Prince's Declaration were everywhere, circulating in London's taverns and coffee houses, passed from hand to hand in the street, and, most impudently of all, distributed through the official channels of the Penny Post. The Prince was coming to save them from the Papists, and to restore peace and the Protestant religion. His army, which rumour claimed to number fifty thousand men, lay waiting in the harbours of Holland for the easterly wind which would bring them in triumph to English shores. No one knew where they would land, but suggestions abounded: Yorkshire seemed most likely, or Suffolk, being nearest to the Dutch coast.

The King, not knowing what to believe, or what to do, and still unable to comprehend the full scale and immediacy of the danger, strengthened his garrisons in ports that might be vulnerable – Hull, Portsmouth, Bristol, Yarmouth and the Medway – and thereby weakened his field army, which was being mustered in readiness around London.

In the middle of all the activity at Whitehall, Sir Hugh Trevelyan pursued his usual duties with his usual urbane competence. If he had been at all upset by Phoebe's summary rejection of his proposal, he gave no sign of it. Indeed, he spent much time, when not at court, entertaining a surprising variety of people at his Westminster house.

Among them was a middle-aged man who had visited him before, and in a similarly furtive manner. Count Zuylestein was supposed to be back in Holland, but had secretly returned, on a pinnace called the *Griete*, at the beginning of October. Very few people knew that he was in England, let alone of his visit to one of the King's trusted courtiers, and such was the care and discretion employed by all those working for the Prince's cause that no word of his presence in England reached the ears of the King or his ministers.

Sir Hugh was rather more open about the belated dinner

party he held to celebrate his niece Sophie's birthday. She was a member of the Princess Anne's household, and was known to the Heron family as the Merry Widow. Seven years ago, she had married, quite openly for the sake of convenience, a rich and elderly gentleman who had died only two months after their wedding, with no heir save his young and delectably pretty wife, to whom he had left his money, lands and respectability.

Sophie, with her dark curls and dimples and long, lazy, lascivious eyes, had since cut a swathe through the susceptible gentlemen of Whitehall. Her name had been scandalously linked with every rake at court, from King Charles downwards, and rumour had asserted that she was Sunderland's mistress, then the Lord Chancellor's, then Lord Dorset's. Hugh strongly suspected that in fact she had only rarely succumbed to temptation, and then from policy rather than for love. To any leading questions, she would laugh and smile and toss her head, and give absolutely nothing away: Hugh had long since stopped asking her, and contented himself with sending brief and expurgated reports home to her father at Goldhayes.

At his suggestion of a birthday dinner, Sophie had protested indignantly that she did not in the least wish to mark the passing of another year by any sort of celebration. Her uncle pointed out, with ruthless charm, that she was only thirty-two, but that rumour might easily be persuaded to add another few years to that total.

'You wouldn't, you wretch,' Sophie cried, with apparently genuine alarm. 'It's trial enough attaining such an advanced age – *promise* you wouldn't, Hugh, and I'll agree to anything.'

So, with a grin, he had vowed faithfully to keep her age a deadly secret, and told her whom he wished to invite. Sophie, who was no fool, sent him a very sharp glance, but kept her counsel.

It was a surprisingly military company for such an occasion. The only other lady present was Sarah Churchill, Sophie's friend and also a lady-in-waiting to the Princess Anne of Denmark. She was twenty-seven, the same age as

Phoebe, but had been married to John, Lord Churchill, for more than ten years, and was the mother of several young children. With her flaxen hair, blue eyes and lovely face, she presented a delightful foil to the dark and vivacious Sophie, but there was nothing insipid about Lady Churchill, who was well known to possess considerable and unfeminine intelligence, and enormous strength of character.

Accompanying her, of course, was her husband, Lord Churchill. He enjoyed the King's confidence, but had also sent secret assurances of his loyalty and support to William of Orange. The other guests included Thomas Langston, lieutenant-colonel of Princess Anne's Horse, and a leading light in the Treason Club; Jack Howe, whose brother Emmanuel was a captain in the Prince's army; Henry Wharton, of the Earl of Lichfield's Foot, and his brother Thomas, who had helped to compose the annoyingly catchy tune at present being whistled all over London; Charles Godfrey, who had married Churchill's notorious sister Arabella, and who always acted as Tom Wharton's second in any duel; and Richard Savage, Viscount Colchester, acknowledged leader of the Treason Club and a lieutenant-colonel of the Life Guards.

It was a long and productive discussion. To Hugh's relief, Sophie did not attempt to flirt with anyone, not even Langston, who was clearly taken with her. She accepted compliments with her usual grace, and spent much time in pleasant and trivial discourse with Sarah and with her uncle. Lady Churchill, Hugh suspected, would probably have preferred to take a greater part in the military talk flying around the table, but for once contented herself with an occasional remark that revealed her alertness, and the depth of her understanding.

The officers were confident that between them, and with the help of others whom Langston had organised into a semi-secret association, they could arrange for a considerable portion of the King's army to go over to William of Orange, when the time came. Hugh knew, none better, how such desertions would strike at the confidence of

James, who was devoted to his troops. And according to Langston, his navy, whom the King relied upon to prevent the Dutch fleet landing, was likely to prove just as disloyal.

Hugh had been in James's service for upwards of sixteen years, and John Churchill for even longer. And yet neither of them felt the faintest pangs of an inconvenient conscience as they plotted his downfall. The King, obstinate, bigoted, unblessed with humour, intelligence, charm or perspicacity, had alienated almost all those who were closest to him by his blundering miscalculations. Even his daughters, particularly Anne, who had been threatened with forcible conversion to the Catholic faith, had turned against him. It was her safety that they were now considering, for when the Prince invaded there was some danger that she would be seized by the King's supporters, and used as a hostage to bargain with William.

Sarah Churchill professed herself more than happy to arrange for the Princess's escape from Whitehall, if the need arose. Hugh looked at her firm, lovely, wilful face, that had always reminded him a little of his dead wife Susannah, and knew that she could be relied upon to manage such a responsible duty with her usual clever competence.

As the daylight waned, so his guests made their various farewells and left, with some discretion: James's intelligence service was notoriously lax, or the conspiracy against him would never have been able to proceed this far, but there was still the remote possibility that a watch had been kept on their comings and goings. Tom Wharton lingered unobtrusively until the last, and then spoke quietly, for Hugh's ear alone. 'I was asked to tell you this. It means little to me, but it may to you. The Rose, and ask not for Master Orchard but Master Marlow. And you should act upon it as soon as may be.'

It did indeed mean something. When Wharton had gone, Hugh called for his valet: and when he stepped out of his house to a hired hackney in King Street, a little while later, few would have readily recognised this shabbily dressed, anonymous man in a brown coat and cheap periwig as Sir Hugh Trevelyan, the luxurious courtier.

He got out of the hackney at Charing Cross, and walked swiftly through the crowds along the Strand, keeping a careful watch. Only when he was certain that he had not been followed did he change direction and plunge into the warren of streets and alleys around Covent Garden. Even here, his sense of caution did not desert him, and when he came to Russell Street, near the Playhouse in Drury Lane, he took care to approach his destination by the back way.

At the Rose Tavern he found the landlord, a man who was naturally, given the nature of his establishment, a model of absolute discretion. 'I seek not Master Orchard, but Master Marlow. Is he here?'

'And you are, sir?'

'My name is Trevelyan.'

Coin changed hands, and he was bidden to wait for a while, before a tapster came to conduct him upstairs. They passed rooms from which came the subdued, earnest rumble of voices, and others which, to judge by the sighs and giggles emanating from them, were reserved for activities altogether different. A door at the end of the gallery showed a light underneath: the tapster knocked twice softly, and opened it. 'Your guest, sir.'

Sitting within, doing justice to a considerable meal, was Alex St Barbe.

He rose as Hugh entered, and held out his hand. 'So Tom Wharton gave you my message. I take it you were not followed?'

'Not to my certain knowledge – I took some pains to avoid it.' Hugh surveyed the younger man with a smile. 'What in God's name have you done to your hair? Surely the cares of Holland have not turned you prematurely grey?'

'Powder,' Alex said concisely. 'Master Thomas Marlow is forty-five, and in Holy Orders.'

Hugh gave him a startled look, and then chuckled in delight. 'A brilliant choice of disguise, I must say. No one with any knowledge of your past activities would suspect.'

'I don't think anyone has. I've been in the country for a week, and I'm set to leave the day after tomorrow – and so far, all has gone according to plan. I would not have taken

405

the risk of asking for this meeting, but there is information I need quickly, which I can get from no other source.' He indicated the food and wine. 'Will you join me? I asked for a second plate and glass, and there is more than enough for two.'

Hugh had eaten a considerable dinner, but found himself ready for a little more. He sat down, and helped himself to roast fowl and a dish of kidneys. Alex poured him wine, which he found to be an excellent sack: and in the soft voices of conspiracy, they talked.

'The army,' Alex said. 'Tom Wharton told me of your gathering this afternoon. Have they given any indication of what will happen, come the invasion? The Prince has received a number of assurances, but he needs to be certain of desertions on a large scale. He has only some thirteen or fourteen thousand men, despite the inflationary rumours I have been spreading – and the King's army is three times that number.'

Hugh gave him a concise account of what had been promised at Sophie's dinner earlier, adding details of the navy's position, gleaned from his nephew Edmund Heron, who was captain of a fourth-rate frigate.

Alex listened intently, committing it all to memory. 'Excellent. The numbers are not especially great, but such things often start small, and then it's like rolling snowballs down a hill. What of the effect the desertions are likely to have on the King?'

'There are some men, Churchill for instance, whose defection will cut him to the heart. It's hard to predict – adversity and betrayal may stiffen his resolve, in which case the struggle will be a long and bloody one. Or it may deflate him like a pricked bladder. If that happens, then I suspect the Prince will find England handed to him on a plate.'

'Which is what he wants, and is working for – a quick and bloodless victory. He cannot afford to engage his men and resources in a prolonged campaign. Does the King still trust you?'

'I believe so – especially since I took your advice, and began attending Mass,' Hugh said, and his mouth curled in a rather self-mocking smile. 'I have now transferred my allegiance, such as it is, to Dutch William – but it leaves a sour taste in the mouth, even so, to play the hypocrite and pretend loyalty to King James. I seem to have acquired some sense of scruple in my old age.'

'Really?' Alex said, and grinned evilly. 'I must beware, when I approach my forties – always supposing I reach them, of course – of the dangers of too much attention to conscience. It's never troubled me yet.'

'You surprise me,' Hugh said drily. He paused, and then added quietly, 'If there is nothing else you wish to know, I would appreciate your advice, on a private matter of some delicacy.'

'*My* advice?' Alex stared at him in amused disbelief. 'My God, Hugh, you must be desperate. Even the briefest acquaintance with my past should serve as a warning that any sense of delicacy is unknown to me. What concerns you? Some importunate lightskirt flinging herself at your head?'

Something in the set of his friend's face gave him a clue: Alex put his glass down and whistled softly. 'It's Phoebe, isn't it? Hugh, you haven't declared yourself?'

'Unfortunately, I have,' said the courtier, with a wry and twisted smile.

'And what did she do? Hit you? Or run away?'

'Neither. She told me very distantly that she was not interested in marriage – '

'Are you telling me that you proposed *marriage*? To my sister? And you still have a head on your shoulders? She must have been very forbearing.'

'She was,' Hugh said, the smile still more twisted. 'For the remainder of her stay, she could barely bring herself to speak to me. She and Louise have gone back to Bath, by the way – they left on Monday. Louise did not wish to go – I think she felt that it would be easier to contact you in London. But with the child due next mouth, Phoebe and I thought it best to send her back – she'll be safer in Bath than here, whatever happens. She was well, and happy, but not very eager to ride in a litter.'

'In a horse-litter? Your powers of persuasion must be exceptional – Louise regards them as one degree better than a hearse, and the last resort of the senile and the mortally ill.'

'She realised that for the baby's sake it would be best,' Hugh told him. 'Neither of us knew, of course, that I would see you so soon – if I'd realised, I would have been able to give you some message from her.'

'It's just as well – I doubt you'd have persuaded her to leave by any means if she'd been aware that I was in the vicinity,' Alex said. 'But before you go, I will give you a letter for her, if you can wait while I write it.'

'I'd be delighted to oblige.' Hugh surveyed his friend, who was engaged in finishing the last crumbs of a particularly excellent plum pie, and then added, 'On one condition – that you tell me what I can do to persuade your sister to talk to me, even if the question of marriage is abandoned. If I'd known she'd be so offended – '

'Oh, I doubt very much that she's offended,' Alex said. 'She's probably scared out of her wits.'

'*Phoebe?* She's not frightened of anything.'

'Oh, yes, she is,' Alex told him. He leant back in his chair, his hands linked behind his head. 'My little sister is terrified of any emotion. She likes to think that she has such illogicalities well in hand and firmly under her control. Doubtless your offer of marriage came as a very unwelcome reminder that she is not entirely the soulless intellectual she would have everyone, including herself, believe. Friendship she will give freely, so long as there are no ties or conditions or demands attached. Love, however, is a very different matter.'

'I made no mention of it.'

'A good move in this case, though with many women it would have meant disaster. But she is extremely observant – perhaps she has seen through your usually excellent disguise?'

Hugh, facing those very penetrating eyes, felt suddenly and distinctly uncomfortable. He said firmly, 'I put it to her as a matter of friendship only. People must be speculating

408

about us, and I did not wish her to be the subject of malicious gossip.'

'So you offered her marriage to protect her good name? I can't think of any reason she would scorn more. Admit it, Hugh – you love her, and she has realised it – and *that*, not marriage, has frightened her.'

For a long moment, the courtier's grey-green eyes held Alex's gaze. Then he laughed, and gave a wry shrug of his shoulders. 'You may be right. I'll be honest with you – after my dear Susannah died, I thought I was safe from ever loving again. And Phoebe is so very, very different – there is nothing of softness or sentiment in her at all. But I have come to value her, to respect and admire her – and despite all her protestations, I would like nothing better than to make her my wife.'

'With all the possessiveness that implies,' Alex said slowly. 'It's her independence she clings to – she never wanted to be tied to a man, to have to do his bidding. She would need someone who would let her have her freedom, to speak and write and read as she pleased, to study and correspond with those old grey scholars who write to her from all over the country, and beyond – someone who would not chain her to domestic duties, and who would treat her as an absolute equal, not as a subservient and inferior female. Someone who would not fuss over her disabilities, or make undue allowance for them. And above all, someone who would not demand too much from her, too soon, for what you ask of her, she may never be able to give you. Are you that man? Answer me honestly, for she deserves it, and I will not permit her to be made unhappy.'

Hugh stared at him. At last, he said, 'I don't know. I do know that all I wish for is her happiness, and if she would be better off as she is, with only our old friendship between us and no more, then I will accept that, and be content. I told her that I did not need any more children – '

'And yet she loves Lukas,' Alex said softly, his hand playing with the stem of his wine glass. 'She has convinced herself that she does not want, indeed cannot have, any children – but in her soul's heart, I suspect that she

409

desperately desires a child.' He gave Hugh a sudden and encouraging grin. 'My sister Phoebe, despite outward appearances, is a mass of confusion and contradiction within. I have no idea how you can set about mending matters between you, especially at a hundred miles distance, but you have my blessing on anything you care to try. If you should ever offer her marriage again, however, beware – present it as coldly and unemotionally as possible, a convenient union of like-minded friends, and you might, just might, succeed. Remember what she fears above all, and avoid any mention of love, or ties, or duty.'

'I will try,' Hugh said ruefully. 'I have only myself to blame – I handled the matter very ineptly, and for one who earns his living being diplomatic and subtle, that's a disgrace.'

'I can hardly crow at your expense, though – I nearly lost Louise for ever,' Alex pointed out. 'And it was entirely my fault – my own crass, drunken stupidity. The only good to come of our estrangement was that, eventually, I began to see the error of my ways.'

'I noticed that you were not so free with the wine.'

'I can't afford to spend my time in a drunken stupor – too much depends, now, on my conduct here.' Alex grinned suddenly. 'If the Prince is successful, then doubtless I'll be tempted to celebrate his victory in style. For the mean time, I intend to stay as sober as a judge – if not Judge Jeffreys. Will you drink one last health with me?'

He raised the glass, and his voice dropped abruptly to a whisper. 'The Prince of Orange, and may he triumph in all his endeavours!'

And Hugh, the trusted servant of the King, drank to the success of his sovereign's son-in-law, and enemy.

In Holland, the invasion fleet waited impatiently for the capricious winds to shift back to the east, and carry them across the sea to England. The Prince, who trusted implicitly in the will and favour of God, bid a dignified but emotional farewell to the Assembly of the States General, and, in private, to his beloved wife Mary.

410

In England, King James, also believing that God was on his side, watched the weathercocks of Whitehall each day, and saw with satisfaction that the wind was still blowing hard from the west.

But the gale that kept the Dutch in harbour also swept boats easily out of the east-coast ports of England, and over the wild grey North Sea: and on a cold Sunday morning, the fourteenth of October, the *Griete* slipped unobtrusively out of the mouth of the River Blackwater, avoiding the ships of the navy stationed about the Nore, and scudded before the wind, close-reefed, on the eastward voyage that she had made so often before. It was the King's birthday: and the rushing high clouds, whipped across the sky, could not disguise the strange shape of the sun as it rose, marred by a partial eclipse.

Unlike many of his more superstitious countrymen, Alex St Barbe did not believe in omens, good or bad: but many people that morning marked the blemish on the sun, and remembered the significance of the date, and whispered that such a thing was surely a sign of divine displeasure.

And two days after the *Griete* made landfall at Brill, the Catholic west wind suffered a conversion, and began to blow, erratically, from the east. It took three days to make all ready, for the men had been sitting idle in their transports for so long that further provisions were required: but at last, on Saturday, the twentieth of October, the invasion fleet spilled out of the Maas estuary.

Thousands of people stood along the low dykes and banks that protected Holland from the savagery of the sea, and watched them sail for England. Fifty warships led the way, guarding the convoy of transports and smaller vessels. There were almost three hundred ships in all, and the grey horizon was crowded with sail. And on the frigate *Brill*, Prince William of Orange turned his thin, ugly face eagerly towards England, and his destiny, and whatever God's will should ordain for his enterprise.

The whole fleet covered some twenty miles, and took all day to leave the Maas. The wind, freshening, had changed again, and blew now from the south-west, hardly

411

convenient for the Prince's carefully laid plans. If it continued thus, they would make landfall on the coast of Yorkshire. But he had been compelled by the lateness of the season to snatch even at this slender chance, rather than to wait in endless futility in harbour, hoping for an east wind that might never come. His philosophy, at its heart, was essentially simple. If God wished him to prevail, then he would, and the invasion would succeed regardless of the vagaries of the wind.

And the wind, ever fickle, altered yet again. The day after the fleet's departure, it veered back to the west. The ships battled on northwards, in rising seas, and as night approached they were assailed by a violent and terrifying storm that continued until the morning.

The vast fleet was scattered. Battened down under hatches and panicking in the wildly lurching seas, many of the horses were injured, or suffocated from lack of air. There was no alternative: to survive, each ship must run before the tempest, and try to take refuge at the nearest friendly port.

News of the disaster that had befallen the expedition soon reached England, and the King's hopes rose high. Surely this God-sent storm had finally ended his impudent son-in-law's pretensions, at least until the spring. Lord Dartmouth, in command of the navy, had taken up a new station at the Gunfleet, just off Harwich, and was full of confidence: he assured James that the Dutch, their ships battered or wrecked, could not possibly sail again so late in the year, and risked complete destruction if they did.

Emboldened by accounts of the loss and devastation which had afflicted William's fleet, James called for witnesses to his son's birth to testify before the Privy Council that the child was genuine. And he dismissed his chief minister, Sunderland, who had lost his nerve when invasion became a certainty, and had urged the King to make further and even more humiliating concessions to his opponents. It was evident that, with the Prince's threat removed, James would soon reverse his policies again, and continue on his steady, inexorable progress towards absolute and Papist rule.

On the same day that the Dutch fleet had made its abortive foray from Brill, Louise and Phoebe arrived at last in Bath.

Adverse weather had meant very slow progress, but at least the gentle jolting of the horse-litter had not affected the unborn baby, who was still bruisingly active. Louise found, rather to her surprise, that it was pleasant to be back in Phoebe's comfortable and cosy little house. Here she could take her ease and wait, with a contented patience once entirely foreign to her restless, impulsive nature, for the birth of her third child.

Lukas went back to school, with four months' absence to make up. Kitty, now nearly a year and a half, was walking with competence, and had learned how to climb stairs, if not to come down so readily. She had lost much of her baby chubbiness, and her resemblance to her father was becoming much more pronounced, especially in the wide, brilliant mischief of her smile. Her chestnut eyes, however, were exactly like her mother's, but her sunny, easy-going personality was entirely her own. The house frequently echoed to her shrieks of delighted laughter at some favourite game or rough-and-tumble, and Louise wished, more than ever, that Alex could be with them, to share in the delight of his daughter's childhood, and to lend his wife his support and comfort as her time drew near.

But Alex was in Holland, or perhaps even now at sea, part of William's invasion fleet, if the wind had changed. She knew, though, that he had recently been in England, for she had received a brief, loving letter from him, soon after their return to Bath.

'Some may call me a traitor,' he had written, 'but you may be sure of this, my own sweet Louise, that I will never more prove a traitor to your love. And although my past transgressions may have driven us apart, yet I feel now that, like the child you carry, this enterprise is treason's gift, to bring us all together again, at Wintercombe. And the thought of that day is the motive and mainspring of my heart. I am yours for ever, sweet Louise, to be both master

413

and slave of your desires – and remember this, whatever should befall us, that I love you beyond all measure.'

Treason's gift: the odd phrase stuck in her mind, long after she had laid the paper gently, and with hope, in the inlaid box which contained all her most precious keepsakes: his other letters, a lock of Nathaniel's hair, black and fine, and another of Kitty's, as deep and dense a colour, but with a soft and springy curl to it, like a spaniel's. And as she replaced the lid, she thought of the baby within her, the gift of Alex's treason, and so vigorous and unruly that it must surely prove to be their longed-for son. When would she cut a lock of his hair, to place it with the others? And would Alex, traitor and enemy of the King, ever see his fourth child?

With the rest of England, she noted the change in the wind, and wondered what it would bring. October was nearly over: surely it was too dangerous now to set sail for England? She prayed that the expedition would not come to disaster, for if ships foundered in stormy seas, then all aboard them would be lost, and no amount of care would save Alex from drowning in the ice-cold waters that lay between Holland and his own country.

Charles had spent all summer at Wintercombe, his mind festering under the burden of his obsessions. Louise had escaped him, for the moment, but he could not forget her. Even in his dreams she haunted him, sometimes as the lively, friendly girl with whom he had fallen so hopelessly in love, but more often as the debauched slut that Alex had made of her, leering obscene yet tempting suggestions that caused him to spend an increasing amount of time on his knees, desperately trying to expiate his sins.

His once-vaulting ambitions had withered in the blast of his desire to possess her. To his mother's dismay, he excused himself from his duties as a magistrate, ignored the suggestion of Master Carne that he put himself forward for election to the coming Parliament, and retreated more and more to the close, stifling atmosphere within his chamber. There, candles burned day and night before an image of the

Virgin Mary, who had failed to deliver him from his overwhelming lust and desire.

At the end of October, he received an unexpected note from his sister Amy. It was afternoon when it arrived, and a prudent man would have waited until the following morning before setting out on any journey, but Charles had long since abandoned prudence. He called for his manservant, Robert Warren, and ordered horses to be saddled. Then, leaving his aggrieved mother, and his bailiff, with whom he had been discussing the sale of some land, he rode hotfoot out of Wintercombe, towards Bath.

Louise. His gelding's hooves beat out the syllables of her name. Louise, Louise, Louise. She had returned to Bath, and he must see her, he must. His mount, pushed too hard, cast a shoe at Midford, and he left the animal in Warren's charge and pressed on alone on his servant's horse. Dusk was approaching as he rode down the steep Hollow Way and across the bridge into the city, and the lanterns and lights gleamed fitfully across the wind-ruffled water. Soon, they would shut the gates for the night, and the curfew bell would toll. He urged his weary horse up Stall Street, and left it in the capable care of the head ostler of the White Hart.

He was in feverish haste, but the inn yard was buzzing with news, and when he caught the gist of it he lingered, listening with increasing glee. Then, he hired a stable boy to light his way, and walked the short distance to his cousin Phoebe's house in Nowhere Lane.

Unlike the last time he had come here, the house was not empty and dark: a friendly lamp burned by the door, and there was light behind the shutters. He rapped the knocker loudly, and when Louise's maid answered it, pushed past her and into the hallway.

She was squawking like an indignant fowl. He ignored her protests and said, 'I've come to see Lady St Barbe. I know she's here – take me to her at once.'

'She won't receive ee!' The maid caught angrily at his arm. 'You can't come a-bursting in here, sir, you bain't wanted – do ee go now, afore I call the Watch.'

415

'I have important news for her,' Charles said. 'Where is she? In the back parlour? Don't worry, I'll find her.'

'Charles! What in God's name are you doing here?'

It was not Louise but Phoebe who had swept into the hall, her eyes blazing blue and a small red spot of anger aflame on each sharp cheekbone. 'If you've come to see Louise, she's not available. Now get out.'

'I couldn't stop en, madam,' said the maid urgently. 'I tried, but he were too strong for I – shall I call the Watch?'

'Yes, Christian,' Phoebe said. 'Run as fast as you can.'

Charles made a lunge for the girl, but she dodged his clutching hands and fled, the wind-blown door crashing shut behind her. Breathing hard, he stared at Alex's sister, trying to master his own overpowering anger. With considerable effort, he injected a note of calm reason into his voice. 'I'm sorry, Phoebe, but I have some news which Louise should hear. And you, too. Will you let me speak to her, before the Watch arrives? And then, I promise, I shall leave.'

'I have no faith in your promises, Charles,' Phoebe said, with scornful contempt. 'And I repeat – Louise is not available. She is a little unwell, and has retired to bed early.'

'You're lying,' Charles said, through his teeth. 'I refuse to leave until I've seen her – so where is she?'

'Here I am,' said Louise's voice, and she stepped into the hall, to stand next to Phoebe.

No garment, now, could hide the advanced state of her pregnancy. Aghast, Charles stared at her swollen body. His mouth worked convulsively, and he spat abuse at her, his voice thick with horror and disgust. 'Whore! Slut! Now I understand why you ran away to London – you were too ashamed to show your face here! Whose child is it? That smooth Frenchman's bastard, eh? Oh, yes, my mother told me about him.'

Louise was white, but very calm: only Phoebe, standing next to her, noticed that she was trembling with rage. She said, loudly and clearly, 'That is a gross slur on my honour, sir. The baby is my husband's and none other.'

'*Alex's* child?' Charles stared at her in appalled disbelief.

416

'No – no, you lying trollop, it can't be Alex's – he's in Holland!'

'So he may be now – but he has also been in England, for a short time. And despite all your efforts to estrange us for ever, we were reconciled – with the result that you can see.' Louise walked forward until she was only just out of his reach: Phoebe said something, and she laughed. 'Don't worry – I shall take good care that he doesn't touch me.'

'Alex was in *England*? When?' Charles took a step forward, and Louise lifted her hand. To his horror, he saw that she held a small lady's pocket pistol, pointed unwaveringly at his stomach.

'It's primed, loaded and cocked,' she said, and her voice was in deadly earnest. 'And for my child's sake, I will not hesitate to use it. You heard what Phoebe said. Now get out.'

'But, Lou, you can't – we were *friends* – ' Charles heard the desperate, pleading note in his voice, and was filled with bitter hatred, for himself and for the man who had turned her against him, and ended his hopes. 'You wouldn't dare – you *couldn't*!'

'No? Try me,' she said, and he saw the glint in her eyes, the resolute set of her mouth, and knew that he lacked the courage to call her bluff. He took a step backwards, and then another. 'Please, Lou – wait – I have news for you, news that changes everything! Wait, please, until you've heard it – and then I'll go, I swear it, and leave you in peace.'

The angle of the pistol did not alter. He saw the small black hole at the end of the barrel, imagined the smoke and flame and deadly bullet that one twitch of her finger would propel into his body, and broke into a sweat.

'What news?' she enquired coldly.

Phoebe echoed her. 'Say it quickly, and then go. What news?'

And even amidst his own fear, the earlier satisfaction returned gleefully to his voice. 'The Prince's fleet set sail from Holland ten days ago. A storm blew up and scattered them. The word is that many ships and transports were sunk, and thousands dead or missing. So you can abandon

417

any hopes of invasion until the spring – and with any luck, your dear husband was one of those who drowned!'

She had gone deathly white, but still her aim did not waver. She said, her voice low and desperate, 'I don't believe it – you're lying to me. Alex isn't dead – I would *know* if he was dead, I would *know* it!'

'Perhaps you would,' Charles said, a sneer in his voice. 'But even if he is not, it will be a very long time before he sets foot in England again, if at all. And be assured that I am praying that he did die in that storm, for no man ever deserved it more!'

He turned and flung the door wide on the windy night. And as he slammed it shut, he heard sounds of bitter grief and anguish break out behind him, and was glad.

# Chapter Twenty-One

## 'A prosperous gale'

Rumour had confidently spoken of destruction or damage to the entire Dutch fleet, of the deaths of many men, and the end to all William's hopes of invasion. As the news filtered through the towns and villages of England, the Protestants who had looked to him for deliverance were cast into despair. In contrast, Papists everywhere, but especially at Whitehall, rejoiced in the Prince's downfall.

But rumour had lied. The storm had indeed scattered William's ships, but none had sunk: some three or four hundred horses were dead, and much time had been wasted, but it was no disaster. The battered vessels limped back into port, and over the next few days gathered once more in the Maas estuary, waiting for another change of wind. Many of the Prince's friends, as well as the ordinary soldiers and sailors, were disconsolate and demoralised by this setback. William himself, however, was still convinced that God walked beside him. He did not lose his nerve, but remained steady and confident, and gradually his example heartened his force.

Soon, the unwelcome news reached Whitehall. William's fleet, far from being destroyed by the storm, had been miraculously spared, and was now ready to sail again. Once more, the wind hesitated, then changed to a brisk, easterly breeze. And on Thursday, the first day of November, the ships left the Maas for the second time, their bows aiming for the shores of England.

For a while, the Dutch armada sailed north-west, stopping to pick up a passsenger from a small pinnace which had sailed from England the previous day, hoping to intercept the fleet. Count Zuylestein, the Prince's friend and trusted agent, climbed aboard the *Brill* and hastily

419

briefed his leader on the present situation in England. Then, obedient to the Protestant wind, now blowing with increasing force from the east, the three hundred ships, with their men, their horses and arms and provisions, the tobacco and beer, equipment and clothing necessary for a winter campaign, turned westwards.

The sun was shining and the wind had moderated a little when they entered the Straits of Dover, and people flocked to the cliffs to marvel at the spectacle, for such a quantity of ships had not been seen in these waters for a hundred years. And yet there was no sense of doom, of the fear and hatred which had filled the hearts of almost everyone in England when the first Armada sailed: for this time, the ships came to deliver them from Popery, not to inflict it upon them.

From ten in the morning until dusk, the fleet passed between Dover and Calais, their banners bright and brave in the sunlight, and the distant cheers of the English spun across the gently rocking water, to mingle with the drums and trumpets sounding from the ships. Cannon fired in salute, and the guns and smoke made some wonder if battle had been joined.

But the navy was still gathered off Harwich, impotent, trapped by the same Protestant winds blowing their enemy unmolested down the English Channel. The Dutch fleet sailed along the south coast for two days, and dropped anchor serenely in Torbay.

It was Monday, the fifth of November, the day after William's birthday, and an auspicious date in all Protestant English calendars. The Prince surveyed the efficient unloading of the horses, and felt supremely confident. After that one false start, God had so far amply blessed his enterprise: the weather was calm and fine, even warm for the time of year, the English fleet had been evaded without difficulty, and he knew, from the information given by Zuylestein, St Barbe and his other agents, that the King had sent most of his forces to the other side of the country, in expectation of an east-coast invasion. There would be no opposition to his landing: he could set up his headquarters nearby, perhaps at Exeter, and wait for the promised support to come flooding in.

On the sixth, an exhausted messenger arrived in Whitehall with the news. Despite everything, despite the superiority of the English navy, William had made a safe and successful landfall.

James was not so devastated by this information as many had predicted. His fleet would soon arrive off Brixham, and bombard his son-in-law's army as it struggled ashore. And even if that miscarried, William was surely doomed. With the dreadful example of Monmouth fresh in their memory, the men of the West Country would never rise in his support. Moreover, even such a vast array of ships could not possibly have carried enough soldiers to threaten the Royal army, which numbered some forty thousand, for the most part well trained and equipped. Neither was their loyalty in question: he had made the army his special care, it was his creation, and it was devoted to his service.

James issued a proclamation reminding his subjects that it was treason to give supplies or assistance of any kind to the Dutch enemy, and began, with no undue haste, to muster his troops on Hounslow Heath, before beginning the slow march westwards. He could ensure that he was fully prepared for battle, and defeat William of Orange at a time and a place to suit his convenience.

The Prince, meanwhile, was disembarking his men. The country people, doubtless indeed remembering Monmouth, at first did not offer him much help, but did not hinder him either. They were much impressed by the fact that many of the Prince's army were English, or Scots, rather than the Dutch enemy they had been led to expect, and even more by the fact that provisions were paid for promptly. The King's soldiers were notorious for their lax discipline: they brawled, raped, duelled, murdered and robbed almost with impunity, and garrison towns usually had cause to regret it. These men, however, were obviously well under their commander's control.

Four days after the landing, they marched into Exeter, and found that most of its wealthier inhabitants, including the Bishop, had fled. Those who stayed behind beheld a splendid sight, for the Prince, well aware of the advantages of a good display of military might and crowd-pleasing spectacle, had taken care to organise an impressive entry.

The whole procession took three hours to enter the city, and it was long past nightfall before the officers of the Prince's staff had found quarters for all the men. William himself, with his closest friends and advisers, lay at the deanery, just by the Cathedral, where a thanksgiving service had earlier been held. The rest of the army, some fourteen or fifteen thousand, were packed into whatever room the good citizens of Exeter, and the villages round about, could afford them, with every inn yard filled to capacity with baggage and horses. All those who had dealings with the invading army noted their decorous behaviour with approval, and rejoiced in the fact that provisions and billets were bought with good silver, rather than rudely taken.

The Dutch, for their part, were shocked that such an important place should be so filthy, with unlit, muddy backstreets and mean, dilapidated houses, quite unlike the gleaming paintwork and neatly swept throughfares of even the humblest town in Holland. They had already been amused, however, by the pipes that everyone, even young children, seemed to smoke here, and heartened, despite the wet weather, by the obvious warmth of the people's welcome.

But, as Monmouth had discovered to his cost, the enthusiasm of artisans, peasants and tradesmen would not be enough. Where were the lords and gentry, the deserters from the King's army and the men of power and influence, whose promises of support had tempted the Prince of Orange to this dangerous and foolhardy enterprise?

The Prince had landed. The tidings spread rapidly through the West Country, and men looked to their weapons, examined their consciences, and waited to see which way the wind blew. In Bath, the Mayor could not prevent celebratory bonfires from being lit in the streets, and some daring person briefly rang the Abbey bells.

Louise and Phoebe heard the news with heartfelt relief. For days after Charles's frightening invasion of their sanctuary, they had feared the worst, that the Prince's fleet had been destroyed and that Alex might be dead, although Louise, still certain that she would know if anything had happened to him, clung resolutely to her belief that he was alive. Then it was reported that the Dutch armada had been seen in the Straits of Dover: and, a few days later, that Alex had arrived in Exeter.

It was not so very far from Bath. Louise, within two weeks of her time, felt a wild and irrational desire to take horse and gallop in haste to her husband's side. It was, of course, quite impossible, for whatever happened she was confined to the house in Nowhere Lane, for the baby's sake, until it was born. But she began to fret impatiently, and for the first time during this pregnancy chafed at the ties and fetters that her condition had imposed upon her free and reckless spirit.

Phoebe reminded her, with her usual sound common sense, that Alex knew that they were in Bath. Somehow, he would surely send word to her, or even find the opportunity to come in person. The hope buoyed up Louise through the last tedious weeks of her pregnancy, taking her mind from the discomforts imposed by her burden, the cramps and weariness and the cumbersome bulk of her once slender and graceful body.

It was as well that she had no knowledge of the living conditions of an army, particularly an army compelled by policy to rely largely upon its own resources in a land that might soon become inhospitable. William's officers, including Alex, were kept ceaselessly busy during their prolonged sojourn in Exeter. The most pressing need was for horses, particularly draught animals, for there had not been enough time to find sufficient replacements for those lost in the storm. Moreover, the roads were deep in mud, their usual winter condition, and there were not enough carts or wagons to transport the baggage or the artillery train. William in desperation issued a proclamation promising the princely sum of four shillings a day for the use of a team of four oxen, proportionately more for six. Not surprisingly, the local people, already profiting handsomely by selling the army anything from broadcloth and shoes to eggs, apples and chickens, obliged with alacrity.

Alex had been given a commission as colonel of one of the loosely formed regiments of English exiles, and there was a small mountain of paperwork on the table in his quarters. William, ever meticulous, required everything to be written down, purchases, expenses, disbursements and recruits, and Alex, in common with all the other officers, found himself sitting up late into each night with paper, quill and ink. It was small wonder, he thought, that this was such a well-behaved army: the officers were working too hard to indulge in debauchery, and the men, in this appalling weather, were too ill, or too exhausted, to do anything other than rest and recuperate in their quarters as the rain poured down outside.

For the first three days, the roads leading to Exeter were ominously empty, and some of the fainter hearts began to panic. Where were the promised supporters? There were country people flocking in droves to enlist, but no sign of the gentlemen of quality whose prestigious support would ensure the Prince's success.

'They're all waiting for each other,' Alex told Tom Talmarsh, whose quarters were not far from his own. 'As soon as one musters the courage to come in, they all will. No one wants to be the first, but I'm damn sure that no one will want to be the last, either.'

It was, in fact, members of the Treason Club, friends to them both, who were among the first to ride into Exeter to offer their swords to the Prince. They included Tom Wharton, whose song 'Lilliburlero' had been sung by William's army as they marched, Charles Godfrey, Lord Colchester and several others, some of whom had also dined with Hugh Trevelyan and his niece a month previously. They were followed by Sir Edward Seymour, who wielded immense power and influence in the West Country, and who was prepared to assert his loyalty to William despite being personally on bad terms with him. The Earl of

Shrewsbury drew up a Document of Association, and the local gentry queued up to sign it, thereby irrevocably committing themselves to treason, and the cause of William of Orange. At last, the snowball was beginning to roll down the hill.

At the same time, news came in of risings in the north, as had been long planned, and soon York, Newcastle, Nottingham and Chester were in the hands of the Prince's supporters. The regiments of English exiles were swelled with a tide of volunteers, mostly gentlemen of the West Country. William, addressing a gathering of them, told them that that he wished that they had come in earlier, but their support was better offered late than never, and they were heartily welcome.

At last assured that James's troops would offer him little resistance, and the people less, William prepared to leave Exeter. An important defector, Lord Cornbury, the King's nephew, had brought word that the royal army was to muster on Salisbury Plain, to block the Prince's advance towards London. And on the twentieth of November, in rain and sleet and cold, William and his forces left Exeter, to meet their fate.

In London, the King's confidence was slowly but surely ebbing away. He had trusted in his navy, but so far, crippled both by contrary winds and by an apathetic indecision that stopped just short of mutiny, it had failed to fight. As yet unaware of the machinations of the Treason Club, he trusted now in his army. Whitehall was in a state of panic, and many begged him to make haste with his preparations for war, but the King told them that there was no need to hurry. The Prince could expect no support, and the royal forces now mustering at Salisbury in leisurely fashion easily outnumbered his son-in-law's puny army.

So James lingered for two weeks in London, deaf to the increasingly frantic voices besetting him on all sides, before deciding to lead his troops into battle in person. He arrived in Salisbury in the middle of a snowstorm, and found that the alarming rumours of confusion and desertion that had reached him in Whitehall, and which he had refused to believe, were in fact all too true.

Feversham, his commander-in-chief, had nearly been defeated by Monmouth's rabble army three years ago, and showed no sign now of any increase in his dismally low level of competence. No scouts had been posted, no-one knew whether the Prince's army had even left Exeter, and the desertion of Lord Cornbury and other important officers had had a drastic effect on morale. Cold, miserable and apprehensive, the soldiers huddled in their inadequate tents, and wished both King and Prince to the devil, while reports came in from all sides of further defections, and of the loss of the North.

The King collapsed into a mood of catastrophic despair. He could not sleep, and his will and energy were drained by the debilitating nosebleeds that had assailed him since arriving in Salisbury. Finally, he called a council of war. All his earlier confidence and belligerence had vanished: now he feared most of all for his wife and son, and valued their safety above that of his kingdom. In vain, his senior officers tried to persuade him to make a stand, to fight for his rights, to encourage his men. Many were still loyal: a few rousing speeches would do much to restore their spirits.

But James had completely lost heart. He gave orders for a retreat towards London, and woke the next morning to find that most of his senior officers – his nephew the Duke of Grafton, Lord Churchill, Lord Berkeley – had left the camp, presumably defecting to the Prince. Others, professional soldiers and courtiers alike, weighed up the odds, and abandoned their depressed and demoralised King, who seemed ready to surrender his realm to the invader without striking a single blow. But it was not until James returned to London that he discovered the most hurtful betrayal of all. The night before his arrival in Whitehall, his daughter Anne, accompanied by Sarah Churchill and by the Bishop of London, unclerically armed with sword and pistol, had left her lodgings at the Cockpit and fled northwards to join the rebels in Nottingham.

There were many courtiers he had left behind him,

apparently loyal beyond question, who now could not be found either, and who had undoubtedly gone to join the Prince of Orange. Among them was Sir Hugh Trevelyan, who had been many years in his service, and whom the King had thought to be a sincere convert to the true religion. If such men could desert him, if even his own daughters could turn against him, there was no hope left. James gathered his remaining advisers about him, and prepared to negotiate with his hostile son-in-law.

William, meanwhile, was advancing inexorably towards London. Apart from one or two minor skirmishes, he had met with no resistance: indeed, his march had taken on something of the aspect of a royal Progress. He was lodged and entertained each night by a succession of eager gentlemen, and took the time to indulge in his passion for hunting. The army paused at Axminster, where Lord Churchill and the Duke of Grafton joined them, and then moved on to Crewkerne. William himself stayed at Hinton St George, guest of the Poulett family, and spent a day hunting deer in the park. And Colonel Alex St Barbe, with a little time on his hands at last, rode the few miles from Crewkerne back to Chard, to visit his Aunt Silence.

He had not seen her for more than two years, since his first reconciliation with Louise, just after Nathaniel's death, and he had no idea how much she knew about the subsequent collapse of their marriage. He had set out with some apprehension, suspecting that Silence would have a few choice words to say to him regarding his treatment of his wife, and found his fears justified.

'I'm surprised you have the temerity to show your face here,' his aunt said, surveying him coldly over her spectacles. 'You have behaved disgracefully to poor Louise, so I hear. And yet she seems to have forgiven you. Is that really true?'

'It certainly is,' Alex told her. 'And before you read me a list of my undoubted faults, Aunt, I must inform you that I do not feel that I deserve it, either.'

'Do you not? Then perhaps there is some hope for you,' Silence said.

427

Her expression was still severely critical, but he thought that he saw a gleam in her eyes, and gave her the full benefit of his boyish grin.

'Nor can you charm me so easily,' she added sternly. 'You are just like my poor dear sister, who knew that she only had to smile to escape scot-free from all sorts of quite justified punishments. Unlike you, however, she was entirely free from malice, or cruelty, or callousness. I suspect those are qualities you inherited from my late husband's mother, who did her best to make everyone's life a misery.'

'You do me an injustice,' Alex said. Surprisingly, he felt no anger, only an urgent desire to set the record right. 'Oh, I admit to every sin in the calendar, Aunt – I betrayed Louise, I beat her, I raped her. The fact that I was drunk at the time is no excuse. I behaved despicably. But I *know* that I did, and I have learned my lesson. The miracle is that Louise still loves me, despite what I did to her – and I shall be grateful for ever more for her forgiveness.'

'I see.' Silence removed her spectacles and put them into a small leather bag on the table beside her. Her eyes, a warm hazel-brown, stared at him assessingly. 'Then do I have your word of honour, as the gentleman which you too readily admit that you are not, that you will never use her so abominably again?'

His gaze met hers. 'I do not have to swear it,' Alex said, after a long, significant pause. 'For you know it already, do you not? I love Louise more than anything else, and I will adore and cherish her for the rest of my days. Beside what I have found in her, my past life seems all sound and fury, signifying nothing.'

'I am glad to hear it,' Silence said, and smiled with sudden, overflowing warmth. 'Welcome home, Alex.'

They embraced, and he knew that, for perhaps the first time in his life, he enjoyed her wholehearted approval. He said, 'I did not only come to make my peace with you – important though that is to us both. I came to ask if you have any news of Louise. Did you know that she expects another child, very shortly?'

428

'I have had letters from Deb, and from Phoebe – they at least keep me a little up to date,' Silence said drily. 'Yes, I know about the new baby, although I have no news yet of its birth, which must have happened by now. With the Prince's invasion, the post is all at sea, and we have received no letters for over a week. I take it you are with the Dutch army?'

He told her as much as he could about the Prince, his motives and aims, and about the King, whose world seemed to be rapidly cascading down around his ears. Silence might be old now, but her intelligence was still acute. 'And what are the chances of this business passing off without bloodshed?'

'If the King is as downcast as Churchill and Grafton claim, fairly high, I should think. If he offers no further resistance, then the Prince will be able to march unmolested into Whitehall. After that . . . I do not know. It all depends on the King, on how far he is prepared to negotiate.'

'And William? Does he seek to snatch the throne from his beleaguered father-in-law? Or will he stay long enough to ensure a free Parliament, and then take himself and his army home again?'

Alex stared at her, and then grinned wryly. 'I would prefer not to answer that question, Aunt.'

'Then he means to be King, I take it. I must say, I cannot blame him, and if he will make a better ruler than King James – which will not be difficult – then I cannot oppose him either. And perhaps the thoughts of one old woman do not count, but Nick tells me that ninety-nine out of a hundred feel as I do. With such a mass of popular support, how can the Prince fail?'

'He will not fail,' Alex said. 'He has never entertained the possibility of it, not even when his fleet was scattered in that storm, and it was all to do again. A lesser man would have given up then in despair. The Prince worked day and night to regroup his ships, and hearten his men, and overcome adversity. Given the choice between him and that burst bladder in Whitehall, I'm not surprised most people prefer William.'

429

'Then let us pray that he gets what he wants, whatever that may be, as quickly as possible, and without fighting,' Silence said. 'I have lived through one civil war in my life, and I have no wish to see another. And what will you do, when it is all over?'

'Take Louise and the children back to Wintercombe, of course.'

'If all goes well with the birth.' Silence gave him a compassionate glance. 'Such things are never a foregone conclusion, as you have good cause to know. And what will you do about Charles?'

Alex's face hardened suddenly. 'You know what I will do. Like the Prince, I would wish it done without violence, but if I have to use force to eject him, then I will. He has offered no compassion or generosity either to me or to Louise, and I do not feel constrained to offer him anything in return, although I know you feel that for his father's sake he must be treated gently.'

'No longer,' Silence said. 'He has forfeited that right, through his malice and deception, and his obsessive desire for revenge. As I have said before, the blame was partly yours, in the beginning, but at least you have atoned for your behaviour. Charles has compounded his offences, and from all accounts cannot understand that he has done wrong. No, he can expect no more favours from me, and you may tell him that, though I doubt he will believe it. He has much in common, I think, with the King – they both refuse to acknowledge anything that does not fit in with their exceedingly restricted view of the world. Let us hope that Charles capitulates as readily as His Majesty seems to have done.'

'Amen to that,' Alex said, and smiled at her enquiring expression. 'No, Aunt, I have not transformed myself into a praying man, despite my repentance of most of my other sins. But if I were, I would be on my knees now, asking the Almighty to spur James into flight. Only if he leaves the country can all this tangle be speedily resolved – and then I can leave my military duties, and go in search of Louise.'

He stayed for dinner, spending most of the meal telling

Silence's husband and son the latest news of the Prince's march, and the situation further afield, and then rode back to Crewkerne with a greatly lightened heart. After the early death of his mother, his aunt had played a considerable part in his upbringing, and he had repaid her love and care by brutally rejecting her values and all she held dear. The sad irony was that only now, as she approached the end of her days, could he fully express his affection and respect for her. But at least they had made their peace, and he was assured of her approval.

Surprisingly, he found that it meant much more to him than he had thought it would.

The Prince's army left Crewkerne, and proceeded to Sherborne Castle in a snowstorm. They paused there for three days, and more deserters from the royal army joined them, including Princess Anne's husband, George of Denmark. All brought encouraging information about the confusion prevailing in the King's forces, and the complete demoralisation of the King himself.

William's wish for a bloodless revolution was becoming more and more likely to be fulfilled. But even as his opponents fell back in disarray, he could not afford to fling all sense of military caution to the winds. Plymouth was safe behind him, under Lord Bath, but the port of Bristol, the second in the kingdom, lay empty and unguarded. Troops from Ireland might land there, and so it was important to secure the city before advantage could be taken by his opponents of its governor's retreat.

He ordered two regiments, under the overall command of Lord Shrewsbury, to take Bristol. One was led by Sir John Guise, who was a native of Gloucestershire, and the other by Sir Alexander St Barbe.

Originally, another regiment had been assigned this duty by the Prince, but Alex had gone to William and asked him to let him take his men in its place. He did not mention the presence of Louise in Bath, a lure as potent as a magnet to iron: such personal considerations weighed little with William, who, much though he loved his wife, always gave first place in his mind to affairs of state. Instead, he pointed out that, as a native of Somerset, he knew the area well, and would be able not only to guide the troops to Bristol, but to organise the supporters of the Prince when the city had been secured.

To his concealed delight and relief, William agreed: and so, on the twenty-eighth of November, in cold, wet and windy weather, the two regiments, numbering some four or five hundred foot soldiers and dragoons, left Sherborne on the road to Wincanton, and thence to Bristol, some forty-five miles to the north.

Shrewsbury had been ordered to make all possible speed, so there would be no time for detours to Bath, or to Wintercombe. But Alex hoped that, once Bristol had been taken for the Prince, he would be able to slip away for a day or two, see Louise, and give Charles due warning that his time of ascendancy, like the King's, was over. The latest news from London had arrived at Sherborne just before he had left, and had spoken of the panic-stricken James collapsing like a wet rag. He had summoned a group of peers and bishops to advise him in his hour of need, and negotiations seemed to be imminent. Unless some miracle happened, the King was surely defeated, and William could assume control of the country at his leisure.

They passed through Wells, and over the bare Mendip hills, scarred and scattered with the lead mines from which much of the St Barbe prosperity came, and rode down into Bristol just before sunset, on the first day of December.

There were indeed no royal troops in the city: only that morning rioting had broken out, and the homes of three Papists had been attacked, looted and burned by a howling mob. The Mayor and aldermen, with the Bishop, knew the importance of preserving peace for the sake of trade and prosperity, and welcomed the arrival of the Prince's soldiers with grateful and heartfelt relief. Shrewsbury gave them a letter from the Prince, which calmed any remaining fears the good citizens might have had of playing host to a force of possibly hostile soldiers. William had, he said, come to England to defend religion, liberty and property,

432

and in order to earn the friendship of the people of Bristol, he had burdened them with only a small number of troops. Then, to the cheers of the crowds lining the streets, Shrewsbury was proclaimed governor of the city, on behalf of the Prince of Orange.

To Shrewsbury, a gentle and personable young man with considerable charm and tact, had gone all the glory: Alex and Sir John Guise were allotted the more mundane task of finding suitable quarters for their men within the city. Fortunately, there was no shortage of offers from the citizens, who were famous for their devotion to the causes of Whiggery and Dissent, and it did not take long to find billets, even for more than two hundred foot soldiers, and the same number of dragoons, with their fine Flanders horses.

At last, some time after dark, Alex's work was finished. He took his servant Gerrit, who had accompanied him from Holland, and a boy to light their steps, and made his way to Small Street, just behind the Key, where lived his uncle, Henry Orchard, and his wife.

Aunt Deb, cheerful, loud and a confirmed gossip, knew almost everything of note that happened in the St Barbe family. As Silence had pointed out, Louise must surely by now have given birth, and Deb, only twelve miles distant, would undoubtedly have news of her.

It might be bad: the child might have died, and Louise might also be dead, as so often happened despite the efforts of doctors and midwives. He did not particularly want to learn that he was a widower from the rather insensitive lips of his aunt: her inevitably overflowing sympathy was a prospect from which he shrank. But he had to know, one way or another: he had waited so long, and now that the means of discovery was here at hand, he could endure in ignorance no longer.

It was very late when he hammered on the door. The face of the maid, peering nervously round it, was eloquent testimony to the fear which the arrival of the soldiers, and the threat of Papist retaliation, had inspired.

'I wish to see Master Orchard, if he is at home,' Alex said, making his voice as level and reassuring as possible. 'I am his wife's nephew, Sir Alexander St Barbe.'

The girl eyed him up and down for a moment, seeing the sword, the plumed hat and the crimson coat worn by the dragoons who had entered the city earlier that day. Evidently still far from convinced, she opened the door a little wider. 'Do ee come in, sir, and wait, and I'll go tell Master Orchard.'

As Alex had expected, his uncle Henry was first and foremost a merchant, and would always owe his allegiance to the rising, rather than to the setting sun. He was a stout, shrewd, high-coloured man of fifty or so, with a very sharp nose jutting between his plump cheeks, and a general air of good humour, which was deceptive, and great prosperity and self-satisfaction, which was not. He greeted Alex with enthusiasm, asked tenderly after the Prince of Orange, and expressed his great pleasure and relief at this most recent turn of events. After all, it had probably saved England from Popery and civil war (neither of which were good for trade), and Bristol from riots and disorder instigated by a few unruly and despicable fanatics. He then invited his nephew to sup with his family in celebration, and without drawing breath took the younger man's arm and escorted him to the dining parlour.

Aunt Deb was there, of course, and her shy, plain, plump daughter, who had been Phoebe's companion for a while. Libby lowered her eyes and blushed rosily, and he smiled at her, remembering that he had been more than usually offensive in her presence when last they met.

The Orchards, as might be assumed from their generous size, kept an excellent table, and he was plied with good food. The wine was extremely palatable, which was hardly surprising: Henry imported, amongst other things, claret, sherry wine, port, sack, brandy and other spirits from all over Europe, and had supplied the buttery at Wintercombe for more than thirty years. His aunt and uncle kept up the flow of questions as he ate, mostly concerning the Prince's march, his adherents, and his plans. Alex endeavoured to answer them as best he could without compromising his commander: Deb was as notorious a gossip as her sister-in-law Bab, although entirely lacking her malice, and whatever he told them tonight would be all round Bristol by dinner time tomorrow.

All the while, however, one question was burning in his mind, and the answer to it would determine his whole future. They must already know: and although he had rehearsed it in his mind for days, he still could not bring himself to utter it. If Louise were dead, he would surely know it in his heart: and yet, as a rational man who did not believe any such foolish superstitions, he had also to acknowledge the very real possibility that he was now a widower, bereft of the love of his life, just as his father had been.

And the baby – was it dead too? Or did it live as Phoebe had lived, a misshapen scrap? Was it the boy whose arrival would end Charles's pretensions to Wintercombe, as Alex's heir? Or another girl, to be loved and cherished but never, however unfairly, to inherit his estates?

He had swallowed several glasses of the ruby-red claret before he found enough courage to cut through the flow of Deb's talk. 'I'm sorry to interrupt, Aunt, but I must know –have you had word of my wife?'

'Oh, I *knew* there was something I must tell you!' Deb cried, and her sudden smile lifted the sense of doom from his heart. 'And there was I, rattling on, never letting you put a word in – how can I forgive myself? Yes, we had the news of it last week from Phoebe – a fine healthy boy, and no trouble at all.'

After all his hopes, his anticipation of joy or disaster, her words came almost as an anticlimax. He stared at her, his heart leaping, his mind made slow and stupid with delight and astonishment, when he had almost convinced himself of tragedy. 'A boy?' he said at last. 'And Louise – is she well?'

'It was a very quick and easy birth, so Phoebe said in her letter, and she's already up and impatient to be out,' Libby told him, breaking her usual shy silence with a smile almost as broad as her mother's.

435

'A big, lusty, beautiful boy, that's how she described him,' Deb added. 'A vast quantity of black hair, and exactly like his father. Good news, eh, nephew, on top of all the rest? Once the Prince has settled the country, you'll be able to bring them all back to Wintercombe, and take up your rightful place again.'

'And what of that rogue Charles?' Henry asked. 'Setting himself up as the head of the family, driving you out, threatening your poor wife – oh, yes, Phoebe told me all about it when I took some claret to her last month. What will you do with him?'

'Clap him in gaol, I trust,' said Deb. 'The lies he's told, the things he's done – they don't bear thinking about! I'm not one of those who ascribe every ill to a Papist plot, but if he's an example of the breed then the sooner we're rid of them all, the better. You'd better be careful, nephew, that he doesn't offer you harm.'

'He won't,' Alex said. A wild, sweeping joy was beginning to overwhelm him, urging him to shout his triumphant happiness from the rooftops. If Charles had appeared at that moment, he would almost have been prepared to hug him. 'With the Prince victorious – not that he's had to strike a blow for it – and the King utterly cowed and defeated, he'll know by now that he has lost whatever power and influence he might have had. It's true, yes, that I made Wintercombe over to him of my own free will – but circumstances have changed since then, and no judge in the land will find in his favour now that there's a Protestant wind blowing. If he's wise, he'll be packing his bags at this very moment.'

'Amen to that, and good riddance,' said his uncle, and raised his glass. 'A toast would be appropriate now, I think. To your wife and your new son, may their lives be long and happy!'

Alex drank the health of Louise and the baby, who apparently had no name as yet: and of the Prince of Orange, the Earl of Shrewsbury, the Seven Bishops, and anyone else whose loyalty to William was public and unquestioned. Aunt Deb, correctly divining that her husband was intent on celebrating the good fortune of the country, the Protestant religion and the St Barbe and Orchard families with a lavish hand, ushered her daughter to bed quite early in the proceedings. Alex, who had had every intention of staying sober, found that the rich red wine slid down his throat with increasing and inebriating ease. He remembered little of the last part of the evening, save that Uncle Henry had revealed a previously unsuspected talent by singing 'Lilliburlero' several times over, in a surprisingly tuneful voice, and he had readily joined in.

He was escorted back to his quarters, still singing, by the long-suffering Gerrit, and woke the next morning with a headache that could not drown the echoes of joy in his mind. Only twelve miles to the east, half a day's ride away, were all the people he loved: Phoebe, Lukas, Kitty and above all Louise, and the baby son for whom they had both longed so much.

Bristol was quiet, no opposition was expected: indeed, the vast majority of the citizens were so fervently in favour of the Prince of Orange that their paltry new garrison seemed an unnecessary show of strength. After a reviving breakfast of bread, cheese and the very strong coffee that Gerrit, without comment, always brewed on mornings after his master had imbibed too freely, Alex dressed with some care, and went to see Shrewsbury.

The young Earl was popularly known as the King of Hearts, both for his good looks and for his powers of attraction. Women competed avidly for his attentions, and men flocked to be his friend. Alex had always found him rather insipid, despite his devoted adherence to the Prince's cause, and suspected that William had sent him to Bristol precisely because his manner and appearance, despite the accompanying soldiers, were so very far from being warlike and threatening. Shrewsbury's talents lay elsewhere, as courtier and diplomat: doubtless he would be called upon to play a leading part in any negotiations between the Prince and King James.

The Earl was in excellent spirits, and greeted Alex with a smile and the offer, accepted, to share a pot of chocolate with him. News had just arrived that Lord Delamere, who had taken a prominent and successful part in securing the north-west for the Prince, was on his way to Bristol with the Earl of Stamford and about three hundred and fifty horse, and could be expected later that day.

'A trifle superfluous, those horse,' Alex said drily. 'I doubt there's one man in Bristol who would dare say a word against the Prince, let alone rise against him.'

'It's as well to be safe,' Shrewsbury pointed out. 'And he probably wishes to wait on the Prince as soon as possible, and so ensure that his contribution to our success does not pass unnoticed. I've sent a message back to the Prince, of course, to tell him that Bristol is now safe in our hands. There were also several letters from the Bishop, the Mayor and various other worthy citizens, all doubtless assuring him of their undying loyalty and devotion.'

'Doubtless,' Alex said, noting the complete absence of cynicism in Shrewsbury's voice. He sipped his chocolate and added, 'My Lord, I have a favour to beg of you.'

The Earl was known to be unduly at the mercy of a sensitive and rather melancholy and reflective nature, but this morning his mood was buoyant. 'Anything in my power, my dear St Barbe – I will be happy to grant it, if I can.'

'I learned last night from my uncle here in the city that my wife gave birth only last week, to our son and heir. She lives in Bath, and I have not seen her for some considerable time – nine months, in fact,' he added, feeling an involuntary smile spread across his face. 'If you can spare me for the rest of today, I can return here tomorrow – '

'Of course!' Shrewsbury said at once, and gave Alex the benefit of his singularly sweet smile. 'My heartiest congratulations, sir – you must be delighted. And don't come hurrying back too soon – take two days over it, and when you return we'll see your son amply welcomed to the world. The merchants here have been falling over themselves to present me with fine wines and delicacies, so dine with me on Tuesday, eh? Then we can celebrate in style.'

At that precise moment, the thought of another carouse

in honour of his son's arrival did not exactly appeal to Alex, but he smiled, pronounced himself delighted to accept, and took his leave of Shrewsbury with more warmth than he had previously felt towards his commander. Then, with a light and eager heart, he sought out his lieutenant-colonel, made the necessary arrangements to cover his temporary absence, and by ten o'clock was riding out of the city on the Bath road, his servant Gerrit behind him, and a fitful but cheering winter sun lighting his way.

At last, there was no flaw or misfortune anywhere to spoil his happiness. Today, in two or three hours, he would see Louise, and their future lay whole and clear and glorious before them.

# Chapter Twenty-Two

## 'Time of triumph near'

'It's the end, I tell you!' Bab St Barbe stared in distress at her son, her fat white fingers obsessively stroking the chestnut hair on the back of her dog Floss. 'The King has given up – you said so yourself. The Prince of Orange will throw him in prison – seize the poor little Prince of Wales – and smother him and kill us all in our beds, as like as not!'

There were many times now when Charles actively loathed his mother, and this was one of them. He swallowed the urge to say something insulting and unforgivable, and turned to stare intently out of the window of her chamber. Below, Wintercombe's lovely garden lay dead and brown, the gravel raked and the knots bare, the earth concealing the bulbs which would leap up, in a month or so, to herald the spring.

If he was here to see it.

He thrust the unwelcome thought away from him, as he had done so often before, but always it would return. The Prince had landed, the Prince had swept all before him, and countless gentlemen, traitors all, had basely forsaken their rightful King and flocked to the invader's standard. And despite William's promise of peace to peaceful Catholics, Bab refused to believe him.

Reluctantly, Charles acknowledged to himself that her fear was not misplaced. For a very long time, English people had seen the spectre of Popery lurking at their doors. Now, hoping that it had been banished for ever by the Prince's triumph and the King's apparent capitulation, they might well turn violently against the Catholics living in their midst.

It was a prospect which had recently troubled Charles. The thought of having to defend his home and his mother against a mob of murderous fanatics was a horrible one, and he had determined to ensure that they were adequately protected. He had ordered his manservant, Robert Warren, to buy stocks of arms, powder and shot in secret, and these were now unobtrusively stored in a chest in his study, under lock and key. Anyone presuming to attack Wintercombe would learn a sharp lesson.

But he had no wish to reveal this to Bab: it would only confirm her fears, and he did not want his actions hindered by his terrified mother, begging him to save her. So he swallowed his anger and dislike, and spoke soothingly. 'Of course he will not, Mama. The Prince may be a misguided heretic, he may intend to usurp the throne, but he is a civilised man. Catholics live unmolested in Holland. We're in no danger from him, and neither is the baby Prince.'

'His Majesty should send him and his mother to France – they'll be safe there,' Bab said. She turned her protuberant grey-blue eyes appealingly to her son. 'So will we, Charles –we'll be made welcome there too.'

'For the last time, Mother,' Charles said, through savagely clenched teeth, 'we're in no danger here. No one would dare to attack Wintercombe. Oh, the mob might threaten some poor tradesmen who happen to be Catholics, but a great mansion such as this is quite safe, I assure you. And besides, this is *my* home, *my* house, and I have no intention of leaving it.'

Bab's mouth was trembling. She said urgently, 'But, Charles, dearest, what if that dreadful man comes here? What if Alex comes back?'

It was a prospect that had caused Charles many sleepless nights, not from fear, but from hate. He had lain awake savouring that confrontation, the words he would use, the abuse he would heap upon the man who had treated him with such contempt, and used his adored Louise like a common whore. He pictured his cousin's white, appalled face as the truth dawned on him, that unlike his royal master, Charles would not surrender his birthright without striking a blow. And the scene, vivid and compelling, always ended in the same way: the look of astonishment and

441

despair as Alex realised at last that Charles had triumphed after all; the flash of flame from one of the heavy flintlock pistols that Warren had bought; and his cousin falling backwards, to lie still and forever lifeless on the ground.

It would not, alas, be an unalloyed victory. The most unwelcome news had reached Wintercombe, earlier that week, of the birth of Louise's son. If it were indeed Alex's child, then it would inherit Wintercombe, and Charles must stand aside. But of course the baby might not live: the first one had died, after all. And in any case, he suspected that a strong case could be made that it was the result of an adulterous liaison, presumably with that slimy Frenchman who had been the subject of much scandalised gossip last year, so Bab had assured him. The thought of it made Charles feel physically sick. That she should prefer Alex to himself was bad enough: to spurn his own honest devotion in favour of some greasy mountebank was beyond belief. He could only presume that Alex had corrupted and defiled her to such an extent that she was no longer able to recognise or appreciate genuine love.

But even if the child proved to be the true heir to Wintercombe, the estate must be managed for him until he grew up, and Charles was the obvious candidate for such a task. He thought of that long minority, and the opportunities it afforded for diverting a proportion of the revenues to his own use. And there was still the chance that Louise, her husband dead and the Frenchman vanished, would turn at last to Charles for comfort.

If Alex arrived at Wintercombe, he would be perfectly within his rights to shoot the man out of hand, as a traitor. The blame could always be put on to one of the servants, especially if the circumstances were confusing. Savouring the prospect, he had followed the progress of the Prince of Orange with a mixture of dread and anticipation. Surely, Alex would not be able to resist the temptation to turn aside to Wintercombe, and gloat?

'If he comes here, I shall tell him to leave,' Charles told Bab. 'He's a traitor, after all, in armed rebellion against his rightful king. It would be my duty to arrest him, in fact.

And anyway, he signed Wintercombe over to me of his own free will. The house is mine, and I have legal possession of it. There's nothing he can do about that now – nothing at all.'

'But if he's with the Prince of Orange – if the King surrenders, or flees, then the Prince can give Wintercombe to Alex!'

'Remember, Mama dear, it's my property,' Charles said, smiling. 'Mine by right. And the Prince claims to be protecting property, does he not? All property, and the laws of the land. It would hardly be just if he took property away from Catholics just because they were Catholics, and handed it over to his own supporters. That would give many people cause for second thoughts. And after all, I haven't opposed the Prince. I'm not one of the King's advisers, that he professes to hate so much. All I've done is to live quietly and peaceably on my own estate, giving cause for offence to no one. No, Mama, the Prince of Orange cannot touch us here. Whatever happens, we're safe.'

He thought, eventually, that he had convinced her. Certainly, after no more than an hour's further persuasion and cajolery, she seemed to accept his arguments. And with her irrational fears calmed, for the moment at least, he could devote his energies once more to planning for the day when, inevitably, Alex would appear, and receive his just and long-awaited deserts at last.

It was snowing, lightly and coldly, when Alex arrived in Bath after a rather protracted journey fron Bristol. The wind had been blowing from the north-east, almost directly towards him, and his horse, a stout and well-kept Flanders mare, had proved most reluctant to face it. He had used all his considerable skills of horsemanship to persuade her, and at last, sullenly, her ears laid flat back, she had yielded to his firm and inexorable pressure. But he had been unable to urge her out of a trot, and the miles had passed very slowly, not helped by the rutted and frost-hardened road.

By the time he entered Bath, it was well past the hour for dinner, and he was extremely hungry: he had not wanted to waste precious minutes halting to eat. There were guards on the gate, stopping and questioning travellers, but they were evidently looking for suspicious Papists and foreigners, and he was waved through without much delay, glad that he had chosen to wear a plain suit rather than the red and gold of the Prince's dragoons.

He rode down Westgate Street, threading his way through the few who had business urgent enough to force them out on such a cold day, and turned right down Stall Street, to the White Hart. Here he dismounted, telling Gerrit to take the horses into the inn for stabling, and walked down the sidestreet to his sister's house in Nowhere Lane.

There was no one about, and the snow was falling more persistently now. He knocked, and heard, as he waited, the crying of a baby.

The door opened, and Mattie's familiar and suspicious face glared round it. 'What do ee want?' she demanded, and then her face cracked into a sudden smile of recognition. 'Oh, sir, I d'beg your pardon, I didn't know ee!'

'I'll turn into an icicle if you don't let me in, Mattie,' Alex said, grinning at her. 'Is that my son?'

The screams were certainly very loud. The maid flung the door wide, and bobbed a welcoming curtesy. 'Oh, yes, sir, and a fine lusty bobbish little lad he be – oh, do ee come in, sir, come in – oh, m'lady will be despeard joyful to see ee, and Mistress Phoebe and Master Lukas too – do ee let I take your coat and hat, sir.'

Once she had harboured the gravest doubts about him, he knew, but these were now plainly dispelled. Divested of his damp, snow-spangled outer garments, he ran a hand through his untidy hair, still growing raggedly back to its former length, and said, 'I've ridden from Bristol, Mattie, and I haven't eaten since breakfast – but I'll see my wife first. Is she upstairs?'

'Yes, sir, in her chamber, with Mistress Phoebe and the children – Master Lukas and little Mistress Kitty and the baby, of course. Shall I – '

'No, Mattie, you go find me some food, and get

444

something ready for Gerrit – he'll be here soon, he's seeing the horses settled at the White Hart. I'll announce myself,' Alex said, smiling, 'and surprise them. With that astonishing noise clogging their ears, I doubt they've heard me arrive.'

'Doctor Peirce d'say as how the babe have a fine pair of lungs to en, sir,' Mattie observed with a grin, and disappeared in the direction of the kitchen.

He climbed the stairs, following the yells of his son. As he came to the door of his wife's chamber, they quietened a little, and he could hear someone, presumably the nurse, crooning a lullaby. He stood for a moment, listening, and then lifted the latch.

They did not hear or see him. A fat young woman was holding a tiny, squalling, red-faced bundle in her arms, and beside her, Lukas was earnestly trying to hush his half-brother. Phoebe sat on a well-cushioned chair by the fire, a pained expression on her face, and the plump little girl standing next to her must be Kitty.

And Louise . . .

Louise reclined on a squab couch opposite her sister-in-law, surveying the scene with a look of wry resignation. She wore a loose gown of rose-coloured silk, and her hair, undressed, curled in profusion on her shoulders. He saw the print of tiredness in her face, but no sign of the dreaded childbed fever. Then, in mock despair, she put her hands over her ears, and Kitty, copying her, turned and saw Alex standing in the doorway.

She had seen him only once before, nine months previously, and she could not possibly remember him. But a glorious smile broke out on her chubby face, and she said something that was quite inaudible above the baby's crying. And then Louise followed the direction of the little girl's pointing finger, and noticed him.

Her shriek could be heard even through the noise filling the chamber. She leapt to her feet, cushions flying, and hurled herself into his arms.

For some time afterwards, there was considerable chaos. Everyone seemed to be talking, or shouting, at once, and he

445

found himself embraced not only by Louise, who was clinging to him as if she would never let him go again, but by Lukas and Phoebe too. Even little Kitty, determined not to be left out, had wrapped her arms round one of his legs. He discovered that it was impossible to speak: not only would no one have heard him, but there was an unaccustomed restriction in his throat. After so long, after so much unhappiness and despair, he had come home at last, to everything he had ever loved or wanted.

The noise suddenly diminished, and then was almost extinguished by the shutting of the door. 'I told Jane to take him back to the nursery,' Phoebe said. 'Now perhaps we can all hear ourselves think.'

Louise, her eyes wet with tears, drew away a little to look at her husband. As always, the power and reality of his physical presence overwhelmed her memories of him. In his eyes, that remarkable and compelling blue, she saw love, and delight, and the old and intoxicating desire that she shared with him. And then he smiled, like the sun rising, and bent his head to kiss her.

Much later, when all their questions had been more or less answered, and he had eaten, and the first joyous exuberance of welcome had dwindled into a breathless glow of happiness that was almost tangible, Louise took her husband by the hand and led him to the nursery. The fat girl was busy sewing, and rose with a smile and a bobbed curtsey. 'He've had a good feed, m'lady, and he be fast asleep now, thank the Lord.'

The wooden cradle stood before the fire, and inside it lay Alex's son, warmly wrapped and blessedly silent. His hair, black and very long and fine, stuck out beneath the lacy frill round his bonnet. Below it, the small face was surprisingly pale, with a dimpled chin, pursed mouth and ferociously peaked eyebrows.

'You could not accuse him of being a shy and retiring child,' Alex commented drily. He put his arm around Louise and hugged her close. 'But I suppose that with two such parents, it's hardly surprising. When was he born?'

'The seventeenth of November,' Louise told him, laying

446

her head against his shoulder. 'A good Protestant day – the anniversary of Queen Elizabeth's accession, is it not? They rang bells and lit bonfires here to celebrate it, and it seemed as if the whole city were giving him welcome.'

'So he is just past a fortnight old.' Alex bent to touch one small curled and dimpled fist. The baby stirred, and he started back in mock alarm.

Louise nudged him. 'Don't you *dare* wake him – I think he must be the noisiest baby in the whole world. But at least he sleeps a great deal, doesn't he, Jane? And has a hearty appetite, too.'

'Indeed he have, m'lady.'

Alex drew her close again, his eyes still on his son, as if unable to force himself away. 'So, is he named yet? Have you christened him?'

'Not yet,' Louise said, glancing up at him. 'In my mind there's only one possible name for him, but I wanted to ask your opinion first – I knew that we would hear from you soon. The rector at St James is becoming a little impatient, though. I think he fears that you won't have him baptised at all, or in some blasphemous satanic rite.'

'I'm surprised he's so eager,' Alex said. 'Has he *heard* the child? There's every chance that his screams will shatter the walls of the church like the trumpets at Jericho. Well? What is your choice of name for him? Joshua?'

'William,' Louise told him. 'In honour of the Prince.'

'And not in memory of my long-dead uncle, father of our beloved Charles?'

'Charles was not his fault, and Gran'mère loved him dearly. She would be so pleased that we had called him William, whoever was honoured.'

'I know she would. I called in at Chard, by the way, a few days ago. She and Nick are well, and I have made my peace with her – I thought that it was time. No, I have no objection to William – in fact, I would have suggested it myself.' Alex turned Louise to face him, his eyes alight with mischief. 'William St Barbe, the heir to Wintercombe, and the source of all our joy – and our deafness.'

As she giggled, he kissed her, ignoring the sentimentally

447

approving glances of the wet nurse Jane. Then he said softly, against her mouth, 'Treason's gift. If I had not come to England secretly, he would not exist, and I would not be here now. Conspiracy does have its benefits, you know.'

'I never doubted it,' Louise said, and her smile was as brilliant as his. 'But why claim the whole responsibility for yourself? I had journeyed to Suffolk to find you, after all, and I seem to remember, too, that you were rather less than pleased to see me, at first.'

'I may indeed have given that appearance – but believe me, sweet Louise, a dying man in the deserts of Arabia could not have looked upon an ocean of water with greater delight. Young William is watching us.'

Roused even by the soft voices above his cradle, the baby's eyes had opened, unfocused and vaguely blue. He gave a gurgle of wind, his face puckered, and his mouth opened to wail. Louise bent swiftly to rock the cradle, humming softly. As his son's face relaxed again into sleep, Alex, with some amusement, recognised the familiar notes of 'Lilliburlero'.

'He likes that tune,' Louise said, smiling, as they crept from the nursery. 'Small wonder, since all of Bath seems to be whistling it, or singing it.'

'The Prince's army marches to it. Tom Wharton claims he wrote it, or part of it, though for myself, I'd hesitate to claim the words – they make almost no sense at all. But at least everyone understands about the Protestant wind, and the melody sticks in your head as if glued there.' He paused, and then turned her gently to face him. They stood almost at the top of the stairs, and from below came cheerful sounds, and a savoury smell of cooking, as supper was prepared. 'Sweet Louise – am I truly forgiven?'

She stared at him in astonishment, and some perplexity. 'Of *course* you are – of *course*! How could you doubt it? I love you so much, God help me, and that is enough – I am willing now to take worse with better, to accept you as you are. That night – that dreadful night was an aberration, and perhaps some good has come of it, as well as evil. And I want to look to the *future* now, Alex – the future, rather than the past. We have Kitty, and William, and soon we will be able to go home.'

'Despite Charles?' Alex said softly. He looked around, and then drew her into her chamber, now empty, and shut the door. 'Charles will not readily give Wintercombe back without a fight. And, after all, he has a case – I made it over to him of my own free will. In law, it is his, until I die, and then William will inherit, as the next heir under the entail.'

'No,' Louise said. As he stared at her, she went on. 'Philip Cousins can tell you the full story – you should go see him tomorrow, but I will explain it now as best I can. When you wrote to him ordering him to make Wintercombe over to Charles, he had very serious doubts about the wisdom of it.'

She glanced at Alex to see how he was taking it: he merely grinned wryly. 'I'm not surprised. Go on.'

'It was Phoebe's idea, born out of sheer desperation, and it worked. At her suggestion, when Philip drew up the deed of transfer, he inserted a clause in the document allowing for the right of Charles to Wintercombe to be revoked, should you ever change your mind. And Charles was so delighted with his triumph over you that he never bothered to read it properly – he signed it without question.'

'So, do I have this aright? Charles is under the impression that he is Wintercombe's rightful and inalienable owner? He doesn't *know* that provision was made for the entail to return to me if I wanted it?'

'Apparently not.' Louise was watching him carefully. In the fading afernoon light, his face showed only a wry, ironic relief. He laughed suddenly. 'Well done, Philip, and my dear, devious little sister. They've probably saved me a great deal of trouble, not to mention the considerable expense of a lawsuit. But what in the devil's name will Charles say when he finds out?'

There was a brief, ominous silence. Louise shivered suddenly, although the chamber was comfortably warm. She said slowly, 'And, more to the point – what will he *do*?'

'Call me out, I expect,' Alex said. 'Or is that too honest and open for him? Charles prefers the knife under the

449

cloak, or the sword in a dark alleyway. But at least we have William now, and so two lives stand between him and Wintercombe.'

'But only one life between him and me,' Louise said. She turned to close the shutters. Outside in the darkening street, snow was still falling, and the cold struck at her through the panes of the window. She went on, trying to keep her voice calm and rational. 'He is still obsessed with me, God knows why, for I have done nothing to encourage him – the reverse, in fact. At intervals he has come here to pester me – it is as if he can keep himself under control for a while, and then like a boiling witch's cauldron, the lid spills off and all that poisonous evil comes bubbling up over the edge.' She essayed a rather bleak smile. 'The last time was about a month ago. He burst in, and Christian couldn't stop him.'

'Phoebe really must employ some stout fellow to keep her door. That scrawny little kitchen boy wouldn't deter a mouse. Well? What happened?'

His voice was light, but his eyes told a different story. Louise went on, trying to sound matter-of-fact. 'He saw me in all my glory. We'd only just returned from London, you see, and we'd stayed there with Hugh since June. He didn't know I was with child. It came as rather a shock to him,' she added, with a dry understatement worthy of Alex himself. 'He accused me of adultery, and then he left.'

'Just left? Tamely and meekly? That doesn't sound like Charles, he's as obstinate and thick-skinned as a rhinoceros. What are you not telling me, sweet Louise?'

'When we left London,' his wife said, not meeting his eyes, 'Hugh thought it best that we had some means of defending ourselves, on the journey home. He gave Phoebe a pair of pocket pistols, and I used one of them to threaten Charles.'

There was a startled pause. 'Good God,' Alex said. 'Was it loaded?'

'As it happens, no, but Charles wasn't to know that. He was completely convinced that I was going to shoot him – he left as meekly as a lamb. He did tell me that the Prince's fleet had been sunk in a storm and that you were probably dead, but fortunately we heard the true story soon afterwards. And since then, we have not seen him.'

'I'm not surprised,' Alex commented. 'Do you *know* how to load and fire a pistol?'

'Hugh showed us both, but I think Phoebe proved a more apt pupil. I could never have been one of those stalwart women in the war, loading their menfolk's muskets until the barrels grew hot.'

'Like Francis Heron's wife? She has some tales to tell – I should ask her for them, when next we meet.'

'That does not seem likely, alas,' Louise said. 'I think Hugh proposed marriage to Phoebe, did you know? I see you did. And of course, she turned him down. She hasn't told me in so many words, but it was obvious what happened. She was waspish, even for Phoebe, on the way back from London. Since William was born, though, she's been more like her usual self.'

'I can't think why. Having Stentor's natural heir living in the same house is not exactly conducive to peaceful study. And right on cue, there he is again.'

There was a sudden and angry wailing, only partly muffled by the two intervening doors. Louise smiled. 'Jane is very capable. Her own baby is weaned now, he's nearly a year old, but she was happy to suckle William – and nothing seems to ruffle her. Lukas thinks she must be deaf.'

'If she isn't, she soon will be.' Alex sat down on the bed, made as if to put his feet up, saw his wife's face, and desisted. 'Persevere, sweet Louise, and you may civilise me yet.'

'I doubt it,' she said, sitting beside him. 'Indeed, I don't want to tame you. A little wildness is very invigorating, after all, and I can't imagine anything worse than a boring marriage. Don't you agree?'

'Entirely. But with you, and William, I strongly suspect that life will be anything but tedious.' He leaned back against the bolster, studying the rather faded blue damask of the bed canopy above him. 'And, of course, we have

451

adroitly avoided the chief problem facing us. What in God's name are we to do about Charles?'

Louise looked at him in surprise. 'We tell him to go, of course.'

'And if he declines? Do we eject him violently, at point of sword or pistol? And what of dear Aunt Bab? If she refuses to budge, there's little we can do, short of rope and winch, to shift her. And I'll be damned if I share my house with her.'

'I doubt very much that she'll want to share it with *you*,' Louise pointed out. 'Alex, don't mistake me – I loathe, detest and abhor Charles, and more than that, he frightens me – he seems to have lost all sense of reality, where I am concerned at least. But he is a St Barbe, and it seems brutal and undignified, somehow, to send him packing by violent means of any kind. Can you not give him due warning first, so that he can leave gracefully?'

'I'd be wasting my time,' Alex said. 'Charles has been given any number of chances to back down, and so far has failed to heed them. I suspect that nothing less than pistol point *will* move him.'

'But even so . . .' Louise hesitated, seeing the look on his face. Alex had never been friendly with Charles, had never even given him the benefit of any doubt. Indeed, his early and insulting hostility had helped to transform their cousin from the pleasant, reserved young man of her first acquaintance, into the obsessed, deluded and desperate Charles who had screamed abuse at her and, however obliquely, had threatened her child.

And she herself, if she thought about it honestly, must share in some of the guilt. She went on firmly. 'I hold no brief for him, but I still feel he should be given one last chance to leave of his own free will. Gran'mère would agree, I am sure.'

'Alas, no – Charles has exhausted even her bountiful store of patience. She told me herself that in her view he had forfeited any right to gentle treatment. She knows full well what I intend to do, and I have her approval.'

'But . . .' She saw the expression in his cold blue eyes,

and lifted her chin, defiant and unafraid. 'Alex, please. He will lose everything, there will be nothing left for him – why not show some mercy and generosity to him in defeat? Who knows, one day your conscience may be glad of it.'

He stared at her, and then, suddenly and quite unexpectedly, he smiled. 'Do you never give over, sweet Louise? But I suppose you have a point. I shall make sure that he has due warning of his impending eviction. Would that please you?'

'It would indeed,' she said, and kissed him. 'It will give him the chance to make his plans, and go in his own time. And I am sure that Gran'mère will be grateful, too, despite what she said. Thank you, Alex, for yielding to persuasion.'

'If not to reason. Who knows, perhaps there are indeed some fragments of scruple, lurking unsuspected in the darker regions of my mind. And I have you to thank or to blame for it – and, dear Heaven, for that.'

William's screams erupted again. Alex grinned. 'One thing is certain – when Charles has gone, and as soon as the Prince can spare me, I shall come back and remove you and the children to Wintercombe, before murder is done. At least there it is possible to put a great many doors between my ears and that racket.'

'So that is the only reason you want to return to Wintercombe? To make it easier to ignore our son?' Louise enquired, in mock indignation.

Alex grinned again, and drew her close for another kiss. 'You know it is not. And even if my wishes did not enter into it, William and Kitty have the right to grow up there – it is the home of the St Barbes, and where they belong. And no one, certainly not Charles, will be able to deny them that.'

Philip Cousins, who had managed the stormy and complicated legal affairs of the St Barbe family for some years now, had thought himself immune to further surprise: but the arrival on his doorstep of Sir Alexander, last heard of in apparently lasting exile in Holland, took him somewhat aback. He concealed his amazement, however, ushered his client into his office, and saw him settled with a large pot of coffee and two cups between them before asking the obvious question. 'Are you intending to return to Wintercombe permanently?'

'Of course I am,' Alex said. He sipped the strong, dark streaming brew, very welcome on such a cold, raw morning, and grinned at his lawyer. 'Come, Philip, you know the situation even better than I do. I'd hardly be likely to take up residence tamely in Bath while Charles enjoys my inheritance, would I? Circumstances have changed, as you must be aware. Louise and I are reconciled, and we have a son and heir now.'

'So your sister told me. My heartiest congratulations – is he well?'

'In fine voice, certainly – it's a miracle you haven't heard him here in Westgate Street.'

'I doubt it, above the sound of my own brats.' Cousins smiled as the muffled shrieks of juvenile discord echoed appositely through the house. 'I have another son, by the way.'

'Then I must offer you congratulations in my turn – how many is that, now?'

'Four – three boys and the girl. I'll swear that Sarah makes enough noise for all of them. But you did not come here to discuss our respective families, pleasant though such talk may be. I take it that you are intent on ousting Charles?'

'Certainly,' Alex said. 'Louise and Phoebe have told me of that very neat stratagem which you executed on my behalf. I must thank you indeed for such a devious ploy – and for the wisdom and foresight which considered it necessary.'

'I must confess that it was your sister who thought of it first,' Cousins told him. 'She must take most of the credit for it. And it does not need very much wisdom, or foresight, to see that words spoken and things done in haste and anger may soon be repented at leisure. I knew that I would be in no danger of incurring your wrath. If you did not change your mind, you would never know what we had done on

454

your behalf – and if you did, then you would assuredly be glad of it.'

'As indeed I am. May I see this document? I am told that you have a copy.'

With a slow-growing smile on his face, he studied the parchment, solemnly signed and sealed by Charles St Barbe, and by Philip Cousins on behalf of Sir Alexander St Barbe, and then handed it back. 'You cunning devil. And he never noticed?'

'He was so delighted to have his hands on Wintercombe at last, he did no more than cast his eyes over it. I don't think he'd have noticed if it gave him title to the Tower of London. After all, he'd hardly have signed it if he'd realised what it said.'

'Which only serves to point the moral of this fable – you should always read any legal document with the greatest possible care, in case your lawyer plans to cheat you,' Alex said, grinning. 'Poor Charles. He'll be devastated when I tell him.'

'When *you* tell him? Do you think that's wise?'

'Probably not – but when was I ever wise? I leave such matters to you, and to my sister and my aunt. Anyway, I do not intend to lurk cowardly in Bath and allow you to perform any more skulduggery on my behalf. Louise has persuaded me that Charles deserves one last chance to redeem himself, God alone knows why, and so I have promised to give him fair warning of my return, so that he and his mother may leave with some dignity. I have to return to Bristol tomorrow – I'm with the Earl of Shrewsbury – but as soon as this matter of the King and the Prince of Orange is settled, one way or the other, I propose to take up residence once more at Wintercombe. And, not unnaturally, I'd like vacant possession.'

'You came with the Prince, then?' Cousins said, his eyes gleaming, and for the next ten minutes or so, they discussed the political situation with considerable interest and animation, on both sides.

'It depends on what the King does,' Alex said, after the other man had speculated at some length as to the outcome

455

of the Prince's invasion. 'From all accounts, he's collapsed like a burst bladder, which of course is just what the Prince wants. He may have come with an army, but he did not intend to use it in anger, except as a last resort.'

'And what else does he want? Merely a free Parliament, as he has claimed in his Declaration? Or is he aiming somewhat higher?'

'Somewhat higher, I think – although he hasn't said as much openly to his supporters at large. But he will take the throne only if it is offered to him – just as he would not invade unless invited. If James should prove obstinate at the last, then the Prince may yet be denied his desires. But even a free Parliament, to undo all the damage that the King has done, and confirm England's position as an enemy rather than an ally of King Louis, will be better than nothing. What William would *really* like, of course, is for the King to flee to France, and leave the field clear for him to become King. And certainly James seems spineless and demoralised enough to take such a craven course.' He smiled bleakly. 'I doubt even my cousin Charles will bow so tamely to the inevitable.'

'He may, though,' Cousins said. He fumbled amongst his papers and drew out a printed pamphlet. 'This has been circulating widely here for a day or so now, and stirred up considerable feeling.'

It was dated the twenty-eighth of November, from Sherborne Castle, and purported to be the third Declaration of the Prince of Orange. Alex skimmed through it quickly, and then handed it back to Cousins. 'I doubt this is the Prince's work – directly, at any rate. It's an open incitement to violence against Catholics, if they're thought to be armed – and such rumours are easily started.'

'Genuine or not, it's done its work already. That priest, Father Anselm or whatever his name is, has left Bath in some haste, and there have been disturbances outside Berkeley Carne's house. You are aware that his younger son is married to your cousin Amy, and that they have a son?'

'I seem to remember one of Phoebe's letters mentioning

456

it, yes. But the Carnes are rich and well respected – surely they have not suffered the attentions of the mob?'

'Troublemakers with nothing better to do can always be persuaded to throw a few stones and shout a few insults on the flimsiest excuse. In any case, the Watch soon dispersed them. But they may turn their attentions elsewhere – and your cousin Charles could prove to be one of their targets.'

Alex gazed at him. Then a slow, malicious smile spread across his face, and Cousins felt the hairs rise on his arms. 'Could he, indeed? Well, in that case I had best ride over to Wintercombe as soon as possible. A mob might be unlikely to take the trouble to tramp seven or eight miles over the hills in the depths of winter, merely for the fleeting pleasure of beating up a Papist, but you never know, do you?' Alex said softly. 'And it's only fair to give advance warning, after all.'

'Alex,' said his lawyer, urgently abandoning all pretence of formality, 'what are you planning? For God's sake, man, do you want to take possession of a smoking ruin? If word gets about that your cousin has arms at Wintercombe, true or not, then the mob will take that Declaration, even if it is spurious, as *carte blanche* to attack him. Do you want his murder on your conscience? Or his mother's? Whatever he has done to you, she at least deserves mercy.'

'Does she? In her own inimitable way, she has harmed us as much as Charles. No, Philip, don't worry – I have no intention of setting the mob on Wintercombe. But the fear of it may prove just the spur Charles needs to leave without too much humiliation. And when he has gone, you may take possession of it in my name, and install there my wife, and my children, until I come home again.'

'I'll do that, and gladly,' Philip said. He hesitated, and then added quietly, 'I would nevertheless advise you to be careful of your cousin. He has never seemed very dangerous in himself, but in desperation, as you have cause to know, he can be lethal.'

'I'm reminded of it every time the wind blows from the north, and I feel the ache where he put his sword through my leg.' Alex smiled, and laid his hand on the weapon slung from his shoulder. 'Have no fear, Philip – this time, I shall not be unarmed, or unprepared, and my servant will be with me, too. I can assure you, Charles will prove as full of fight at the sticking point as King James.'

# Chapter Twenty-Three

## 'The perjur'd murderer'

At Wintercombe, snow had been falling fitfully since dawn, and the racing grey clouds promised heavier by afternoon, and a cold night to come.

Bab prayed and read and ate in the stuffy warmth of her chamber, and thought of the Prince of Orange, whose coming surely must spell ruin for her and her son. Fear made her more than usually peevish, and even her maid, of necessity a very long-suffering young woman, was eventually driven to say, 'Don't worry, madam, I'm sure no one will harm you. The Prince said himself that he came in peace, and that only Catholics who were armed and offering resistance would be in danger.'

'But the mob – they have already attacked Catholics in Bristol, simply because they were Catholics – they weren't armed, and yet their houses were burned,' Bab said, her voice tremulous. 'The people in Philip's Norton have no love for us because of our religion. What if they should come here to drive us out?'

Her maid told her, soothingly and at some length, that no one would dare to do such a terrible thing. Inwardly, however, she was not so sure. Both in the servants' hall and in the village, opinion of Charles St Barbe had considerably deteriorated in the two years that he had been in charge of Wintercombe. As old Jem Coxe, the gardener, had pointed out, a piece of paper was all very well, but the place belonged to Sir Alexander by right, exile or no exile, and as soon as he returned from Holland, Master Charles should hand the house back to him and leave with a good grace. This covert and growing hostility had been increased by the slighting and scornful remarks which their master had made about the new heir, and his parents, in the hearing of many of the servants.

'The young Master be a truer St Barbe than that there Prince of Wales be a true son of the King,' Daniel Pardice had said with firm conviction, and his opinion was shared by almost everyone in the household. Pardice was universally respected for his honesty and fairness and his unswerving loyalty to the family he served, and he was well known to hold Sir Alexander and his lady in the highest regard, whilst having very little time for Master Charles. This, of course, might be because Master Charles was completely uninterested in horses, and had even tried to sell Sir Alexander's beloved and beautiful stallion Pagan, until Pardice dissuaded him: but on the whole, the Wintercombe servants followed the groom's judgement, and performed their duties, under their unwelcome usurper, with competence but no enthusiasm.

Bab's maid, eyeing her mistress, decided that, come the spring, she would find another position, with a woman whom she did not actively dislike.

There was a familiar double knock on the door, and Charles entered at his mother's bidding. Even Bab, looking at him with a fond maternal eye, noticed his haggard, sleepless appearance. He gave her a tired smile. 'Good afternoon, Mama. I trust I find you well?'

It was her favourite topic. With fretful verbosity, Bab described, in gruesome detail, exactly why he did not find her at all well. Once, Charles would have listened to her with every appearance of interested attention. Now, he fidgeted in his chair, yawned behind his hand, and at last interrupted her in the middle of an explanation of the probable cause of her back pains. 'I'm sure you must have been sitting in a draught, Mama – although how there can be any draughts in here, I cannot imagine.'

'There are draughts in plenty elsewhere – the wind fairly whistles through the parlour,' Bab said peevishly. 'Why will you not entertain the idea of rebuilding Wintercombe, Charles? It would be so much more comfortable and convenient if you did. We could have a salon on the first floor, *so* fashionable, and a grand staircase, and windows that fit properly – '

'For the last time, Mother, will you not understand that we cannot *afford* the expense of any such work? And in any case, I do not wish to alter Wintercombe. I like it perfectly well as it is.'

'If the mob come here and burn us out of our beds, you'll be forced to rebuild it,' Bab reminded him. 'What are you doing to protect us, Charles? You must do *something*. We cannot just sit here and wait for them to attack us – '

She was interrupted by an urgent hammering on the door of her chamber, alarmingly well timed. As she squawked in fear, her hands flying to her mouth, the dog Floss leapt off her lap and set up a frantic yapping. Charles cursed under his breath, and looked round. 'Yes – what is it?'

The imperturbable figure of Twinney the butler stood in the doorway, his hand on the shoulder of a small boy, wet, rosy-faced and panting, his hair spiked with twigs and his hands scratched. Charles recognised Joel Combe, whose family lived at the mill, about halfway between Winter-combe and Philip's Norton.

'Say your piece, Joel,' the butler prompted him.

The child seemed almost too overawed to speak, but he took a deep breath, and gasped out his message. 'Sir, Father sent I to ee quick as I could – I ran 'cross the fields – he said as to tell ee that Sir Alexander be a-coming here, sir!'

Charles's heart leapt, and then thudded in his chest, with terror and triumph mixed. At last, his hour had come, and his chance of revenge. He sent up a brief, urgent prayer, for a steady hand and an unswerving purpose, and then rose to his feet, ignoring his mother's clutching hands and cries of dismay. 'Sir Alexander? Are you quite sure? Is he alone, or are there soldiers with him?'

' 'Tis he for certain, sir, and there bain't no one with en but that foreign Dutchy,' said the boy.

'I wonder that he dares to show his face here,' Charles said, and smiled reassuringly at Bab. 'Have no fear, Mama – he is a traitor, come to fight against the lawful king, and he

461

will earn a traitor's deserts. Stay here, and I will tell you when it is safe again.'

He strode past the child and Twinney, calling for his servant. Warren appeared from the hall as he reached the foot of the stairs, and Charles gave him his orders in a low, hasty whisper. The man, smiling grimly, went to do his bidding: and now Charles was forced to wait, in a fever of impatience, for the arrival of his detested cousin.

The word had spread rapidly through the house. Servants crowded into the porch as Charles walked slowly down the steps, and he could see the stable lads in the shelter of the gatehouse, peering towards the track which led to Philip's Norton. It had been snowing steadily for some time, and the gravelled forecourt was covered to a depth of two or three inches. The wind was keen and bitterly cold, and Charles stayed in the lee of the house, narrowing his eyes against the unfamiliar whiteness of the landscape.

The stable boys began jumping up and down. One of them yelled jubilantly, his words blown away by the wind, but the sense of them quite plain. Behind Charles, someone cried, ' 'Tis he at last!', and there was a general clamour of delighted welcome.

He rounded on his disloyal household, his face so contorted with rage and disgust that one of the little kitchenmaids burst into tears. 'Stop that! Stop it, d'you hear me? The man's a traitor – a traitor to our King and our country, and he's not wanted here.'

They stared at him, and for the first time he felt the full force of their hostility. With a curse, he turned away again, and Warren sidled unobtrusively up to him. 'Here you are, sir. I've loaded and primed them both, as you said.'

He took one of the pistols. It felt heavy, and reassuringly deadly in his grasp. All the fog of misery and confusion had burned away from his mind. Oblivious to the horrified cries behind him, his intention and his duty clear and shining now before him, he walked into the centre of the courtyard, ignoring the wind and snow, his weapon in his hand and Warren by his side, to face the man he loathed above all others.

462

Alex was riding a tall black mare, her dark coat spangled with snowflakes. He wore a bulky greatcoat over a plain grey suit, and there was a sword at his hip and pistols thrust into holsters either side of the saddle. Under the broad-brimmed hat, white with plumes and snow, his face was that which had haunted Charles's worst nightmares: implacable, hostile, cruel.

He halted the horse a few feet away from his cousin, and surveyed him. 'How nice of you to come out to welcome me, Charles – and in such inclement weather, too. Shall we go indoors? I have some very urgent matters to discuss with you, in private.'

That mocking, spuriously civil tone had always enraged Charles. He said through clenched teeth, 'You are a rebel and a traitor, sir, and I will not allow you inside my house.'

'Your house? You mistake the matter, Cousin. It is my house, and I have come to give you due notice that it is my intention to claim it.'

'Claim it?' Charles laughed derisively. 'You have no claim to Wintercombe – you gave it to me of your own free will, two years ago, and I have the document which proves it.'

'So you may have – but did you actually read it before you signed?'

'What do you mean?' Charles's hand gripped the butt of the pistol by his side, but a voice, of reason or cowardice, whispered inside his head, 'Not yet.'

'If you had read it, you would have discovered a clause allowing for me to change my mind,' Alex told him. He looked down at Charles, standing stocky and enraged in the snow, and added, his voice insultingly friendly, 'This is assuredly not the place for such a discussion. Be reasonable, Cousin, and we'll adjourn indoors, and talk about it in private.'

'I don't care if the whole of Somerset hears it, nor if you freeze to death – I will not let you set foot in *my* house.' Charles brought the pistol up, and aimed it steadily at the other man's heart. 'I am not bluffing. You are a traitor, and

463

you deserve to die – in fact, it will give me the greatest pleasure to pull the trigger. Now go.'

Alex looked down the barrel, and smiled. 'Is it loaded? I doubt it. Louise's pistol wasn't, you know, but although you had the courage to force your way into her house and threaten her and the baby, you did not have sufficient left over to call her bluff. Just as well for you, really – I would not now be so forbearing if you had harmed her.'

Charles cried furiously, 'I wouldn't harm her – I love her – which is more than you do!'

Despite the cold, Alex's face was pale with anger, his blue eyes as hard and glittering and merciless as gemstones. 'Oh, you love her, do you? Is that why you accused her of adultery, without a shred of evidence outside your own warped imagination, and offered her insults for which I should by rights call you out? My wife is faithful, honourable and loving – I'm well aware that she's far more than I deserve, but at least I can learn from my past errors. You, it seems, can learn nothing. She finds you repugnant, and always will – and if I ever discover that you have abused her or insulted her or frightened her again, I'll show you no more mercy. Understand?'

Somehow, despite the threat of the pistol pointed at him, Alex had gained the advantage. In the porch, the servants muttered their anger and dismay. Charles said, his voice loud with fear and fury, 'You brute, you won't have the chance. Wintercombe is mine, d'you hear me? Mine, mine, *mine* – and no legal trickery can rob me of it! You have no right to be here – now get off my land, or I'll shoot you!'

'I do have the right – and if you will come inside and discuss it in privacy, as I requested, you will see that I speak the truth.' Alex's voice was even, reasonable, and spoke of temper held on a tight rein. 'And in any case, you are no longer my heir. That honour belongs to my newborn son, William St Barbe.'

Charles's face cracked. '*Your* son? You corrupted Lou and now she's cuckolded you with some slimy Frenchman, and you haven't the wit to see that you've made her a whore –'

With a sudden, savage movement, Alex went for his sword. And Charles, given the excuse he wanted, and borne on the vast wings of his own righteous anger, nursed and nourished by festering hatred for nearly four years, cocked the pistol and fired.

The shot was followed, almost instantly, by another from Warren, who had been ordered to shoot when his master did. The black mare, terrified, reared up, and Alex fell backwards. He hit the snow-covered ground hard, some twenty feet from Charles, and lay quite still.

The horse, snorting her fear, turned and galloped towards the gateway that led into the stables. Two of the lads ran to catch her. The maids were screaming, there was a thick smell of acrid powder-smoke, someone cried, 'He've killed en!'

In the middle of the commotion, Charles stood, the clear, calm centre of it, and felt a huge weight lift from his heart, as though he had cast aside some dreadful and crippling burden, and at last was free.

Twinney had run forward, and over by the gatehouse the Dutch servant, his broad face aghast with horror and disbelief, was dismounting in frantic haste. Charles turned to Warren, whose loyalty he now trusted alone of his household, and handed him the smoking pistol. Then he glared at the servants, crowded together, many weeping, all shocked and appalled. Few of them met his gaze, and several of the younger maids shrank away, as if he would slaughter them too.

His voice loud, Charles said, 'He would have killed me. You all saw it. He was a wicked and evil traitor, and he deserved to die.'

'Murderer!' one of the women cried, and there was a fresh outburst of sobbing.

Such accusations were beneath his dignity to answer. He ignored them, and walked over to the body of the man who had been his sworn enemy.

Alex lay sprawled untidily on his back, and there was blood soaking into the snow around his head. Twinney was bending over him, and the Dutch servant, who had always

465

seemed so stolid and phlegmatic, leapt up and screamed something at him in his foreign gibberish. As two of the stable boys restrained him, Charles, to his astonishment, saw that his cheeks were wet with tears.

Pardice had come running from the stables, his face set in such a mask of loathing and disgust that Charles momentarily recoiled. But he was only a groom, and his opinion did not count. Charles smiled at Twinney, and said, 'Is he dead?'

Twinney stared at his master for a very long moment, as he would at something repellent that had crawled from beneath a stone. Then he said venomously, 'Yes, you've murdered him, you treacherous Papist bastard – but you won't have Wintercombe, we'll see to that!'

Charles raised his eyebrows, and smiled again. 'You may consider yourself dismissed from my employ, Twinney – and after such insults, you're lucky to escape a whipping.' He felt a glorious lightness of heart. If it had not been alien to his dignity, and his natural reserve, he would have laughed and crowed and danced in triumphant delight. Instead, he could not stop smiling.

He gazed avidly down at the motionless, bloodstained body of the man whom he had yearned so much to kill, for so long. Alex's face in death was still, empty, the malicious eyes closed, and all that vivid, savage, insulting life fled, to threaten and abuse him no longer. The snow, falling harder, was already settling on his skin and on his clothes. Charles said, his voice ripe with victory, 'So perish all traitors to His Majesty! Take him away, Pardice, and get someone to clear up the mess.'

'Clear it yourself, murderer!' the groom said, his blue eyes full of loathing. 'I won't work no more for ee, not for all the gold in India.'

'Then you may get out of my sight,' Charles told him. 'I have no wish to see you again.'

'I'll see him buried afore I go,' Pardice cried fiercely. His voice cracked suddenly, and he turned away. Twinney caught hold of his arm, and muttered something. Painfully, the groom struggled to master himself, and bent over the body.

466

With vast satisfaction, Charles watched the three men, two English and one Dutch, gather up the mortal remains of Sir Alexander St Barbe. It was not an easy task, for he had been a big man, but they waved away all offers of help from the stable boys. Slowly, with a pathetic dignity, they carried the limp and lifeless corpse towards the stables, shuffling in the snow. In their track, there was a vivid scarlet trail of blood.

Charles stayed until they had gone, and then bent to pick up Alex's plumed hat, which lay a few feet away from where he had fallen. With gloating delight, he fingered the two holes in its bloodstained crown, marking the path of the bullet, and then turned to walk back to the warmth of the house. Warren had already taken charge of Alex's two pistols, and had carried them back inside, along with the ones that had already been fired.

Many of the servants still huddled in the porch, tear-streaked faces expressing every degree of fear, horror, shock. He stopped, and stared at them. 'What are you all gawping at? Get inside, now, and on with your work!'

'Murderer!' someone cried behind him, and a snowball smacked against his back. Such stupid and unruly behaviour was beneath contempt. He glowered at the women, and they shrank away from him in terror. Charles smiled, and walked past them, into his house.

Wintercombe was safe in his possession. The baby did not count: with luck, it would soon die. And then he would be the undisputed master of all the St Barbe estates.

Smiling even more broadly, Charles went up to his mother's chamber, to tell her the wonderful news.

# Chapter Twenty-Four

## 'Anguish, dangers and distress'

Like Philip Cousins, Louise had doubted the wisdom of Alex confronting his cousin at Wintercombe in person. It would have been better and safer, surely, if he had sent the lawyer to tell Charles that he and his mother must pack their bags and leave. But she herself had persuaded him to allow Charles some warning, and so she had swallowed her protests and her misgivings, and kissed him, and bade him only to take care.

'Oh, I will, sweet Louise,' Alex had said, sitting on the tall, restless black horse that would make an excellent brood mare when they returned to Wintercombe. 'But this is a duty I will lay on no one else. With luck, I should be back before dark.'

But dusk had come without him, and up in the hills where Philip's Norton and Wintercombe lay, the snow must surely be falling thick and heavy. Louise tried to ignore the sick and suffocating premonition of disaster that was creeping inexorably up on her. She played with Kitty, listened to Lukas's efforts to improve his French, and chatted blithely to Phoebe as if she had not a care in the world.

But later, when the children were in bed, and the clock on the mantelpiece in Phoebe's back parlour announced in gentle chimes that it was eight o'clock, and there was still no sign of him, she gave way at last to her fears. 'Something terrible has happened to him – I *know* it has!'

Phoebe's face was pinched and sharp with a similar concern, but she said calmly, 'It's still snowing hard. He may well have decided to stay in Philip's Norton overnight.'

'He *may*,' Louise said. She got up and paced restlessly around the room. 'But I can't help being so frightened for

468

him, Phoebe – I feared something might happen to him, and I still let him go!'

'Could you have prevented him?' her sister-in-law pointed out reasonably. 'You know Alex. And he is more than capable of looking after himself – and of besting Charles.'

'Yes, but Charles is treacherous.'

'And Alex isn't?'

Louise stared at her unhappily. 'Not to the same extent, no. He loathes Charles, but he also despises him. And he can afford to be magnanimous. Whereas Charles . . . Charles is desperate, and he has nothing whatsoever to lose now.'

Phoebe was looking thoughtful. She said at last, 'I do not feel, rationally, that you have any cause for fear . . . but I do understand. Shall I sit with you for a while? You must be in need of the company.'

'You don't have to, if you want to go to bed,' Louise told her. She knew that Phoebe was always weary in the evenings, and usually retired early.

'It won't be the first time I have lost sleep on his account –nor the last, either, if I know Alex. Besides, if William creates the same commotion this night as most others, peaceful slumber will be impossible. You should have called him Macbeth.'

Louise smiled reluctantly. 'Because he has murdered sleep? Perhaps we should.'

Precisely timed, her son's imperative demands for yet another feed erupted from above them. 'His father's child indeed,' said Phoebe drily. 'Let us hope that he grows up a little less turbulent – although his present habits suggest otherwise.'

'He is so different from Kitty – she's such a happy and sweet-natured little girl.' Louise smiled, thinking of her daughter, already a chatterbox, although no one save Kitty herself understood what she said. Phoebe, listening to her, had decided that it was indeed a language, though unknown to anyone else, and seemed to have its full complement of vocabulary, grammar and expression. And Alex, teasing his sister, had asked if she planned to compile a Dictionary of Kittyish.

Oh, Alex . . .

Sick with fear and longing, Louise foolishly allowed her thoughts to stray on the previous night, when they had lain in each other's arms, warm and loving and at peace, and she had known that whatever happened, whatever the future held of joy or anguish, at this moment her happiness was perfect, and complete, and united with his.

Only last night . . . Her eyes filled suddenly with tears, and she brushed them angrily away, upbraiding herself for a timorous fool. But she had experienced this feeling, this certainty of catastrophe, before: and acting in obedience to it, despite all her rational doubts, she had found Alex half-dead in a ditch, after the fighting at Philip's Norton between Monmouth's men and the royal army.

Then, she had rescued him from discovery, possibly even saved his life, and they had become lovers. But now she could not venture out into the snow, in defiance of sense and reason. The city lay quiet in the darkness, and the gates would be shut until morning. And out on the high, bleak downs that lay between Bath and Wintercombe, the drifts would lie deep and dangerous, an obstacle to all but the most hardy and desperate traveller.

So if he had not returned by now, then he would not come until tomorrow. There was nothing she could do, nothing at all. And yet she could not go to bed, and would not be able to sleep if she did.

'You remind me of those caged lions in the Tower.' Phoebe's astringent tones broke sharply in on her thoughts. 'And you have as much hope of escape as they do.'

'I'm sorry,' Louise said, and sat down in a flurry of amber velvet. 'I can't settle – I keep thinking too much.'

'Why not read? No better distraction exists.'

'For you, perhaps, but not for me. I'm not capable of losing myself in a book.' Louise gave a wry shrug. 'I may retire in a while. He will not come now until morning.'

'Unless he's gone to see Philip, or stopped at the White Hart – you know Alex, that's all too likely.'

470

'Once, maybe – but not now. He's changed.'

There was a thoughtful silence. Phoebe's eyes, reflecting, met the younger girl's. 'Yes,' she said consideringly. 'Yes, he has – and greatly for the better. I suspect that you are responsible for it. He loves you very dearly, and he is secure in the knowledge of your love, and the children's. It has been very good for him. And if the Prince proves triumphant, as he surely must, I suspect that Alex will be handsomely rewarded. A post at Court, perhaps?'

'He is devious and subtle enough for a life in politics, certainly.' Louise paused, wondering whether she dared broach the subject, and then cast circumspection to the winds. 'Like Hugh Trevelyan. What will happen to him, I wonder?'

'He'll survive, I'm sure. After all, he's clever enough to have been spying for William for months, if not years, while pretending to be a King-loving Papist – and it sickened me.' Phoebe slammed her book shut, glared at Louise over the top of it. 'As it sickened him, I think. But that's no concern of mine now.'

Louise decided to play the innocent. 'Whyever not? I thought you and he were good friends.'

'We were, but no longer,' Phoebe said curtly, and fumbled for her stick. 'Perhaps I will go to bed, after all.'

'No, you won't.' Louise leapt to her feet and snatched the cane away, just before Phoebe's hands could reach it. 'Not until you've told me *why*.'

Real anger flushed in her sister-in-law's thin cheeks. 'I certainly won't. It's none of your business.'

'Oh, yes, it is – you're my dear friend, and your happiness is certainly my business.' Louise sat down again, the disputed stick in her grasp, and impaled Phoebe with a stern gaze. 'Did Hugh propose marriage to you?'

'I told you to mind your own business,' Phoebe said fiercely. 'Now give me my stick back, and stop behaving so childishly.'

'He did – I'm sure he did, and about time too. And you turned him down, did you? Why?'

'Because I will be no one's wife, at the beck and call of a

471

man,' Alex's sister said, and in her voice, suddenly and revealingly, there was both bitterness and yearning. 'I was happy with his friendship, and now that is compromised. I will not be propositioned out of pity.'

'Pity has nothing to do with it – Phoebe, he *loves* you!'

There was a long, long silence. 'Yes,' Phoebe said at last. 'God alone knows why, but I suppose he does – and that is the problem.'

'Why? Surely – '

'Love conquers all? In plays and romances it might. In real life, matters are differently arranged.'

'I have not found it so,' Louise said softly, and in her face there was the glow of remembered joy. 'Oh, Phoebe, why did you refuse him? He is kind, amusing, intelligent – he admires you, he *knows* you, he will give you the space to be yourself, he would not cage you in. Think of what you might be in twenty years' time, in thirty – a dried-up, crabbed old spinster, a recluse who knows only books, living alone . . .'

'That is not such a dreadful fate,' Phoebe said, but she did not sound very convinced.

Louise pressed home her advantage. 'If Hugh has been working for the Prince, then surely the Prince will reward him. He'd still be at Court, in the centre of things, like Alex. And as his wife, you would have the entrée too – not to do as I would, to dance and enjoy yourself and fritter the time away, but to use your influence. Lady Churchill does it, through her husband. Short of being born royal, it is the only way a woman can make any mark in affairs of state. And politics fascinate you, you can't deny it.'

'You think I should marry Hugh so that I can meddle in *government*?' Phoebe demanded furiously.

'No – no, of course I don't!' Louise cried in exasperation. 'You should marry him because you love each other, and none of this ridiculous tarradiddle of excuses can convince me otherwise!'

There was an awful pause. Finally, Phoebe struggled painfully to her feet and stood lopsided, clinging to her chair. 'I would like my stick back, thank you,' she said, with cold anger. 'And then I shall go to bed. Good night, Cousin.'

And she limped with dignity from the room, leaving Louise alone with her thoughts, her regrets, and her overwhelming, desperate fears for Alex.

Something wet, stroking his face: pain, and nausea, and a shrieking agony inside his head, extinguishing all rational thought. He moved, and moaned, and a voice said, with satisfaction. 'Told ee he'd be round somewhen soon.'

He opened his eyes. There were dim shapes above him, and his mind, dazed and stupid, informed him eventually that they were faces. Familiar faces: a familiar smell, too, rich, aromatic and equine. Then one of the shapes moved, and a light shone brilliantly, stabbing straight into his brain. With a groan of pain, he screwed his eyes shut and turned his head away.

'Girt gawcum,' said the voice. 'Do ee hide that light directly, or I'll fetch ee such a whack.'

He knew who it was, but his mind refused to supply him with a name. Someone placed a cold, wet cloth over his forehead, and the relief was so overwhelming that he gasped.

Another voice began, strained and anxious, uttering words that made no sense at all.

'Speak good English, can't ee?' said the first voice. 'After a wallop like that, tworden surprise I nif he couldn't mind his own tongue, let alone yourn.'

At last, he remembered. 'Pardice?'

'Aye, sir, here I be.' The groom's voice softened, and became almost fatherly. 'You be in the stables, lad, and safe enough, for the moment. Master Charles d'think ee be dead.'

'*I* thought I was dead.' Alex lay quiet, his eyes still closed, grateful for the coolness across his brows. Some of the fog of bewilderment had dispersed, and he found that he could remember facing Charles, bandying insults until his cousin had called Louise a whore . . .

And after that, nothing. He opened his eyes again. This

473

time, the faces were clearer: Pardice, wrinkled and weather-hardened, his blue eyes concerned; Gerrit, his features blurred with distress; and young Henry Renolds, one of the stable boys, and presumably the one who had inadvertently revealed the lantern.

With an effort, he focused his gaze on the groom, and said, 'What happened?'

Pardice's face assumed an expression of extreme repugnance. 'He called your lady a whore, sir, and then you set a hand to your sword, as any man would do likewise, and he shot his pistol at ee – and so did that hang-gallise man of hisn.'

' 'Twere horrible, sir,' Renolds put in. 'He woulden stop a-smiling all the while, he were so glad he'd murdered ee!'

'He probably was.' Alex found that he could muster a smile himself, rather to his surprise. 'He'll be bitterly disappointed when he finds out the truth.'

'If he do, he'll make certain sure he do it right next time,' Pardice said grimly. 'But we bain't a-going to give en the chance, sir, depend on it!'

'I'm glad of that,' Alex said. He lifted his hand and made a tentative exploration of his head. 'Since I seem to have survived, I take it the damage isn't very serious?'

'A grig lower, and 'twould have been a mite worse,' Pardice told him drily. 'The ball took your hat off, raked the top of your head – you'll have a mark there, sir, to the end of your days, but no bones broke that I can tell.'

'So if I'm not dead – why did Charles think I was?'

'Allus bleed a lot, head wounds,' Pardice observed with satisfaction. 'And Master Charles be tarblish easy to gull, if he d'want suffen bad enough. He wished ee dead, and Twinney told en you were, and he believed en. *I* thought ee were gone, till Twinney told I different. Only he know the truth, aside from all on us here.'

It was becoming easier to think, now that the pain in his head had lessened a little. Alex marshalled his thoughts with urgency. 'How long have I been here?'

'Well, 'tis darkening outside – five o'clock, maybe,'

Pardice said. 'So you've been senseless four hour or more, I reckon. 'Tisn't snowing now – a clear night to come, and the moon near full. No, lad, do ee lie still, for God's sake, or you'll start up the bleeding again!'

'Help me sit up,' Alex ordered him. After a brief pause, the groom did as he asked. The agony in his head flared savagely, and he closed his eyes, his breathing deliberately calm, fighting the waves of pain and nausea. He felt dizzy and faint, but he had received blows on the head before, and knew what to expect, and how to alleviate the effects.

'All right, lad?' Pardice was supporting him, his voice full of anxiety, and for a wild, longing moment, Alex wished that it could be Louise by his side, so that he could lean all his weight against her, and sink into her love and concern . . .

Louise. She was in danger, and so was the baby, William. Charles would want to waste no time in telling her, with the utmost and gloating glee, that she was now a widow, her children orphaned, and a two-week-old baby the new and uncertain life standing between Charles and the legal and inalienable possession of Wintercombe.

'I'll do well enough,' he said. 'I must get back to Bath tonight.'

'To *Bath*? Be ee ramping mad?' Pardice said in horror. ' 'Twill kill ee surer than Master Charles and his pistol. No, lad, us'll take ee to the mill, or the George, Mistress Prescott will tend ee and Master Charles won't know – after what he've done, not one of we, save that Warren, will tell him aught.'

'I'm going to Bath,' Alex repeated stubbornly. The thought of a soft and comfortable bed in the George was wonderfully inviting, but he rejected it resolutely. 'Charles will soon discover I'm not dead after all. How long d'you think I'd live if he found me here, or in the village? The George is the first place he'll look. No, Dan, I must go. My wife will be worried – and she may be at risk from Charles, too. And in Bath, I can organise retribution.'

There was a brief, significant silence. Alex looked round

at his head groom, and gave him an exhausted, desperate smile. 'I know – I'm a fool three times over, and the journey will probably finish what Charles began. But I have to go, I can't stay here to be killed in cold blood. If I can reach Bath, he won't dare to touch me there.'

Pardice still looked very doubtful. At last he said, 'Very well, lad, on your own head be it. But you bain't fit to walk, never mind ride to Bath in two foot of snow with the cold like to freeze a furnace. For God's sake, let me go along of ee.'

'Charles will guess why you've gone.'

'That don't matter a grig,' the groom said. 'I told en as how I woulden do his filtry for all the gold in India. So I be free to go.'

'Please, do ee let I come too, sir!' Henry Renolds cried eagerly.

Pardice shook his head. 'Oh, no, ee won't. Do ee stay here and disremember all you've seen and heard this even. Understand? You haven't seen naught, nor heard aught.'

'Yes, sir,' said the boy, crestfallen but stalwart. 'I won't chackle to orryone, not if they tortured me I woulden!'

'Good.' Alex was beginning to feel that the journey to Bath might actually be possible. 'Is Pagan still here?'

'Aye, though no thanks to that Papist varmint,' Pardice told him. 'He wanted to sell en, but I soon put a stop to it. Do ee wish him saddled up, sir? Well, don't ee just stand by gawping, young Renolds, git a-going!'

The boy ran off obediently. Alex looked at the groom kneeling beside him, and smiled. 'I owe you my life, don't I? Thank you. It's an honour that I probably don't deserve.'

'No one deserve murdering in cold blood,' Pardice said, his voice suddenly gruff. 'Saving your cousin, maybe.'

'Don't worry,' Alex told him. 'I have no intention of sliding into the same error. In any case, his race is run. The Prince of Orange already has England in his grasp, and King James had proved helpless against him. And when he falls, men like Charles will fall too, and harder. All I have to do is to stay alive just a little longer.'

476

'And that might prove harder than ee think, lad,' Pardice said, his face as grim and bleak as his voice.

# Chapter Twenty-Five

## 'Vengeance to complete'

Eventually Louise had accepted the inevitable, and retreated to the lonely silence of her chamber. Eventually, too, she must have slept, for an urgent hammering on the front door jerked her rudely and abruptly awake.

From the limited light outside, it was just dawn. She leapt from the bed, almost bumping into Christian – who had stumbled sleepily in from her closet – flung on her loose heavy wrap, and ran down the stairs.

The knocking began again. Mattie, who always rose early, as did Phoebe, was drawing back the bolts. As Louise, her heart thudding in panic, reached the door, Lukas came tumbling down half-dressed for school, his hair tangled and unbrushed. 'Papa, is it Papa?'

'Please God it is,' Louise said, catching hold of him, as Mattie turned the key and with understandable caution peered round the door.

Two men stood there, supporting a third, much taller, between them. Louise, horror-struck, thought for a second that he was dead: and then Alex raised his head, and smiled, and said in a voice barely above a whisper, 'For Christ's sake, Mattie, let us in.'

The maid had already flung the door wide, with a rush of icy air. Outside, the cobbles of Nowhere Lane lay under a white and lumpy quilt of snow, rumpled with footprints. Three horses stood there wearily, and one of them, Louise noticed in a last frantic glance, was the beautiful dapple-grey stallion, Pagan.

'What's happened?' Lukas was crying in distress. He tried to embrace his father, but Louise restrained him.

'It's all right,' Alex said. 'I can manage now. See to the horses, Dan.'

With evident reluctance, Pardice relinquished his support and turned away to gather up the reins. Helped by Gerrit, Alex stumbled over the threshold and reeled against the wall, his hands clenched on the panelling to hold himself upright. His hair was dripping wet, and there was a scarlet gash parting it at the crown: his face was streaked with old blood, and haggard and grey with exhaustion. As Louise stared at him, appalled, a series of convulsive tremors shook his body.

Gerrit said something in Dutch, received a brief answer in the same language, and disappeared in the direction of the kitchen. Lukas, tears pouring down his face, wriggled out of Louise's grasp and ran to his father. 'Papa, what's happened? Are you badly hurt?'

'Don't worry, Luikje – it's not as bad as it looks, but if you embrace me too vigorously, I'll fall over.' Alex leaned back against the panelling, his eyes closed. 'Go help Gerrit, I've asked him to get a posset for me, and the cookmaid won't be able to understand him.'

'But, Papa – '

'I'll be all right – please, Luikje, go!'

After one last pleading look, the boy ran after Gerrit. Louise glanced at Phoebe, who was making her painful way down the stairs, and then went up to her husband. 'What happened? You're hurt – come and sit down, you can't stay there – '

'I can't move,' Alex said. 'Just a question of balance – I'll be right as a trivet in a moment.' He opened his eyes and squinted down at her, apparently having some trouble focusing. 'Charles tried to kill me. As you can see, he failed – by a hair's breadth, literally.' He laughed rather wildly. 'He thinks I'm dead. Hasn't he been here already, proposing marriage?'

'He tried to *kill* you? How? When?'

'He shot me. Good thing his aim was bad – it just scraped my head, and there are two holes in my hat, wherever it is. Twinney convinced him that I was dead, and Pardice kept me in the stables until I came round, and then he and Gerrit and I rode here.' He began to laugh again. 'What will he say

479

when he finds the dead man has walked? Twinney called him a treacherous Papist bastard, apparently – I wish I'd seen his face.'

Another shiver ran through him, and another. Suddenly alarmed, Louise touched her hand to his forehead. It was soaked with sweat, not water, and his skin was burning hot. She said sharply, 'You're ill! We must get you into bed – '

'It's the marsh fever,' Alex told her. His eyes, glittering bright, met hers at last, and he smiled. 'An old enemy – shouldn't have ridden all night, but I had to – had to get back to you before he came here. Gerrit – Gerrit knows what to do.' His legs buckled and he slid down the wall, still talking with febrile fluency. 'Find a 'pothecary – Jesuits' Powders will cure it – I knew I shouldn't have had so much of Uncle Henry's wine.'

'Alex!' Louise knelt beside him, her arms around him, ignoring his sodden coat. 'What shall we do, if Charles comes here? We shall have to hide you – '

'No need – you shoot him, of course,' said her husband. 'Only this time, make sure to load the damn thing first.'

It was the last vaguely coherent remark he uttered for some time. With the help of Gerrit, stalwart and muttering in Dutch (Lukas told Louise afterwards that most of it was unfit for a lady's ears), and Dan Pardice, whose small, wiry frame concealed considerable strength, Louise put him to bed in the front parlour, stripped off his soaking, blood-stained clothes, and tried to force a warming posset between his teeth. Never the most co-operative patient, Alex in the grip of a raging fever proved impossible for her to handle, and in the end, miserable and defeated, Louise let Gerrit take over, while Mattie, with a well-filled purse, went in search of an apothecary who might sell Jesuits' Powders.

She returned triumphantly half an hour later. By this time, Alex had fallen into an uneasy slumber, and Louise had taken the opportunity to speak to Lukas, who had refused point-blank to go to school, and who had sat for most of the time on the stairs, a wan, hunched and woebegone figure, excluded from the sickroom.

'Will he die?' the boy asked unhappily.

Louise shook her head with a conviction that, secretly, she did not really feel. 'Of course he won't. It's only a fever, and he's had it several times before, so Gerrit says, and recovered from it in a day or so.'

'Can I see him? Please?'

He looked so desperately miserable that she nodded, and, despite her better judgement, led him into the parlour.

Gerrit was there, with the air of capable, impassive stolidity that she had always liked about him, and Alex was talking, but not to his servant. She had brought Lukas right up to the bed before she realised what he was saying, and by then it was too late. She saw the boy's scarlet embarrassment, and knew that she too had flushed.

'Louise?' Alex said, and his voice rambled on, loving and passionate, commenting and describing, while she hastily escorted Lukas from the room.

Outside, he gave her a rather shamefaced grin. Her composure regained, she grinned back. 'At least he is thinking about me. Don't worry, Luikje – when Mattie brings the powders, we'll give them to him, and he'll soon be better.'

'Cousin Charles tried to kill him,' Lukas said. 'Will he come here and try again?'

'No, of course he won't – we have Gerrit and Dan to protect us now, and we're in the middle of Bath – please don't worry, Luikje, he's quite safe, and he'll soon be well again, you'll see.'

'He wasn't safe in the middle of London, when Cousin Charles tried to kill him before,' Lukas said, and a tear slid down his face. 'I *hate* Charles! I wish Father would kill *him* – we'll never be safe until he's dead!'

And Louise, burdened with a multitude of fears for her husband, knew, though she did not say so, that the child was right. What would Charles do when he discovered that he had not killed Alex after all?

Charles St Barbe spent a blissful night, entirely free of bad dreams and sleeplessness for the first time in many months, and woke refreshed and invigorated. He prayed for some

481

time, asking for God's blessing on his future life, and for forgiveness for his sins – a formality, this, since he knew that God would look with indulgence upon the necessary slaughter of a man so irredeemably wicked and corrupt. Then, aware that there were certain practical matters to arrange, he went out to the stables.

Pardice was not there, of course, but since he had left Charles's employ, that was not surprising. There were two horses missing, however, and one of them the very valuable grey which his cousin had set such store by. And the Dutchman, who would surely wish to attend his master's funeral, had also disappeared, with his mount.

Two men gone, but three horses. And the stable boys, when questioned, seemed frightened and ill at ease. They had no idea, they said, where the foreign servant had gone, and looked blank when asked why the grey had been taken.

'So Pardice has stolen him, has he?' Charles said. 'Well, that's a hanging matter. I'll send the word out – he won't get far. Now, where did they put the body?'

The boys did not know. In the end, cursing, Charles searched the stables himself, peering into each stall, until he was sure that Alex was not there. Nor was he laid in the hay-loft, or the coach-house, or the barn.

But why remove a dead man? An awful suspicion crept into Charles's mind, and he banished it immediately. He had certainly killed him: he had seen the blood, and the holes in Alex's hat, and the lifeless body. Twinney had assured him that his enemy was dead, and Pardice had called him a murderer.

The stable lads would know. There had been four, but when he called for them, only two appeared. He pushed them into his study and questioned them. He was a Justice, after all, and it was a felony to withhold information. Warren stood by with a switch, ready to assist if necessary, and in the end, after a beating, one of the boys cracked.

It was Lawrence Earle, the tall, thin, sensitive one, whom the younger maids teased unmercifully. Sobbing, he stammered out some fantastic tale that Sir Alexander was not dead, but had only been knocked senseless in the fall, and that Dan Pardice and the Dutchman had brought him round in the stables, and then ridden off, all three of them, in the middle of the night.

'You bain't no better'n a traitor!' Renolds, the other boy, shouted. 'I *told* ee to say naught!'

'Then it's true?' Charles demanded, feeling sick. 'Sir Alexander is not dead?'

'And no thanks to ee, murdering Papist!' the boy said defiantly. 'Find en if ee can – you won't get aught from I!'

Nor did they, for even Warren's heavy hand made no difference to his obstinacy, though he was sobbing with pain when Charles at last told his servant to desist. 'That's enough, Warren. We're wasting valuable time.'

'He'll come for ee,' Henry Renolds said, scrubbing the tears of pain from his face. 'You see if he don't – he'll hike ee out of Wintercombe so fast your feet won't touch the ground, and your silly old faggot of a mother too, and then 'twill be fit for decent folk to live in!'

Charles, icy calm despite the repressed fury boiling within, dismissed him from his service. With no references, turned off in disgrace, the boy would never find another position. He sent Earle, who was still blubbering like a baby, back to the stables, for until another groom and lads were engaged to replace Pardice, Renolds and those who had cravenly disappeared, there was no one else to look after the horses.

As Earle left, the housekeeper, Abigail Gaye, entered, her face unusually grave. Charles glanced at her impatiently. 'Yes, Abigail? What is it?'

'I've come to tell ee, sir, that I can't work in this house a moment longer. I be leaving today, sir.'

Stunned, Charles stared at her. The housekeeper's cheerful efficiency had kept Wintercombe running like clockwork for two years, and without her, the household would probably descend rapidly into chaos. 'In God's name, Abigail, why?'

'I think ee d'know why, sir.' The woman's manner had always been one of brisk willingness, but now even Charles could detect an undercurrent of contemptuous dislike in

483

her voice. 'You tried to kill Sir Alexander in cold blood, and I can't work for ee no more.'

She was a village girl, and had served the St Barbes loyally for twenty years. Charles said, angry and astonished, 'You cannot leave us now – not for such a ridiculous reason!'

'So ee think murder be ridiculous, do ee?' Abigail said, and in her tone was a disgust so overwhelming that Charles recoiled. ' 'Tis naught to do with ee being a Papist – I woulden serve ee if you was a Protestant or a Mohammedan neither! And I know for a fact that all on us servants d'feel the same. Goodbye to ee, and I hope ee rot in Hell!'

The door slammed behind her, leaving Charles standing, gaping foolishly, in the middle of the floor. That Abigail should use such language to her employer was beyond all belief. Pardice, Renolds, Twinney, and now the housekeeper, all deserting him . . .

With an effort, Charles pulled his thoughts together. Servants were easily hired. He would take care to find people who owed no loyalty to other St Barbes, or who, better still, were Papists themselves. Father Anselm in Bath might be able to recommend some, or his brother-in-law Edward Carne.

But all that could wait. For now, he must find Alex. Despite what Earle had said, he had surely been seriously hurt: indeed, there had been so much blood that Charles himself had not thought to question Twinney's assertion that he was dead. Furiously, he cursed the butler's lies, and his own folly in being so ready to believe them. But at least, even with Pardice and the Dutchman to help him, Alex could not have gone far in such a condition. He would surely still be in the village, and a search must be made immediately.

Easy to decide, not so easy to arrange. Save for Warren, and the elderly gardener Jem Coxe, there were no adult male members of the household left. But Charles, in his capacity as a magistrate, had the power of the law behind him. It would not prove difficult to discover where a hunted traitor was hiding.

Deliberately, he neglected to tell his mother the news that Alex had survived. Time was pressing, and he had no stomach for her inevitable lamentations and reproaches. He ordered Earle to saddle two horses, and then he and Warren, both armed with sword and pistol, rode into the village.

The most obvious hiding-place was the George, so they went there first. But Henry Prescott, even faced with a drawn pistol, proved infuriatingly obdurate. He had, like all the village, heard of Sir Alexander's return, but swore obstinately that he had not actually laid eyes on the man for over two years.

'Then you will not object if I search your premises,' Charles said, and pushed past him.

At this time of year, and in snowy weather, there were only a handful of travellers, and most of the chambers were unoccupied. He even climbed up to the great loft that ran the length of the inn, where the wool and cloth was stored at fair time, but it was echoing and empty, home only to the mice. Prescott, with a face like thunder, followed him everywhere, but said nothing until Charles had finished. 'Satisfied, sir?'

The sneering tone was lost on Charles. 'Yes, for the moment,' he said, and walked out of the door, Warren following.

Despite the snow on the ground, and the chilly air, people had gathered in some number around the market-place outside the George. As Charles appeared on the steps, a low, hostile murmuring rose from the crowded villagers. He stopped, seeing the opportunity to make his task lighter, and held up his hand for silence. 'I am seeking the traitor and rebel Sir Alexander St Barbe. He has escaped from my custody, and may well be hiding somewhere in this village. As a Justice, I am empowered to search for him, and I am also able to offer a substantial reward for his capture.'

He paused, seeing their attentive faces, and then continued with greater confidence. 'I will pay the sum of one hundred guineas to anyone who can tell me where he is, or who can lead me to him. He must be here in Philip's Norton – he is hurt, he cannot have gone far.'

'And if us d'know, us on't tell ee!' someone shouted, and there were cries of assent.

'You would hide a traitor?' Charles stared angrily at the recalcitrant villagers. 'May I remind you of His Majesty's proclamation when the Prince of Orange first threatened to set foot on our shores. To give aid or assistance to the Prince or his accomplices is to commit high treason, and will be punished accordingly.'

'Who by?' demanded a man in the front rank of the crowd. 'The King's beat, and all you Papists have had your day.'

There was laughter, and more cheers, and several people at the back shouted, 'Gold bless the Prince of Orange!'

The cry was taken up with hearty enthusiasm, and hats were flung into the air. Charles stared impotently at the people whom he had known for most of his life, and whom he had thought respected him. Then Prescott appeared at his side, and said, with contemptuous concern, 'They seem to be in an ugly mood, sir. Perhaps you'd best return to Wintercombe.'

'Not while that traitor might be lurking here,' Charles said in fury. He lifted his pistol threateningly, but the villagers failed to cower or flee: instead, they hissed and jeered, and one or two of the hardier spirits moved forwards, followed by the rest.

'I don't think he's here in Philip's Norton, sir,' Prescott said. 'Ned Pardice told me his cousin had gone with him to Bath, last night.'

'To Bath? Overnight? Then he'll have frozen to death, with luck.' Charles glared at Prescott. 'Is this true? Why didn't you say so before?'

'You didn't give me the chance, sir.' Prescott glanced at the crowd, who were now within a few feet of where they stood on the steps leading down into the street. 'For God's sake, go, or there'll be blood spilt.'

As he spoke, a stone rattled against the oaken door behind him. Consumed with rage and frustration, Charles

486

brandished the pistol at the faces below him. 'Get back – get back, will you, and let us through!'

It was a bitter disappointment, to mount his horse, and guide it through the menacing throng of people who had forgotten that he ranked amongst their betters, who spat, and threw things, and shouted abuse and insults. He was called a murderer, a traitor, a Papist and a rogue, and although every sinew ached to retaliate, to fire his pistol into the insolent faces and slash the sneers from their mouths with his sword, he withdrew into an icy carapace of dignity for sheer self-preservation: they had so far abandoned respect and decency that he would surely be set upon and killed if he offered them any violence.

But he made sure to commit their names to memory. Later, he would have his revenge.

The Jesuits' Powders, mixed with honey and water to disguise their bitter taste, were administered as the apothecary had directed, and then all they could do was wait. Alex spent all day in delirium, thrashing and tossing in the bed, speaking in English, in Dutch and Italian and French, reliving episodes in a career that had been more than usually eventful. Louise insisted on sitting with him, despite Gerrit's protests, and learned rather more than she would have wished about the previous women in his life.

But they belonged to his past, she reminded herself: no longer was she so unsure of his love that she must take refuge in pointless jealousy. She, and the children, were his future now. And she was assured of it when, in one of the rare, lucid intervals between bouts of delirium, he looked up at her, the shadow of a smile lurking at the corners of his mouth, and made a suggestion to her that was at once outrageous, temporarily impossible, and full of promise.

Fortunately, he had spoken in French, and she answered in the same language. '*Un peu plus tard, peut-être, mon amour.*'

'*Bien entendu, mignonne,*' Alex said, his voice sinking into a whisper. 'At Wintercombe . . .'

He drifted into a restless, difficult sleep, his hot hand

holding hers. She sat watching him, waiting for the powders to take effect, hardly daring to believe that they could cure him as easily as everyone seemed to think.

Phoebe brought her a cup of chocolate, and sat with her for a while. It made Louise feel a little uneasy, for she was well aware that she had overstepped the bounds the previous night. She had been anxious for Alex, and too keen to help Hugh and Phoebe come to an understanding, but although she knew that she might have been more tactful, she was also sure that she was right. Through fear of emotion, of involvement and hurt, Phoebe was afraid to leap into matrimony: and for her own good, neither her brother nor his wife was above giving her a strategic push.

She eyed her sister-in-law, wondering whether to mention it again, but something in the fierce set of Phoebe's brows warned her otherwise. In any case, it would do Alex no good to have them arguing over his sickbed.

He slept until after dark, and woke cool, clear-headed and ravenously hungry. Gerrit brought nourishing food, with the air of someone who had done this often before, and Lukas sat on the bottom of the bed, hugging his knees and smiling with delight and relief at his father's swift recovery.

'Those powders have worked a miracle,' Louise said, her own joy shining from her face, had she known it, like a lantern. 'It hardly seems possible that you are well again already.'

'There may be a relapse,' Alex told her. 'Marsh fever comes and goes, with precious little warning. This is my third bout of it – and my doctor in Holland said that I can expect more, at increasingly long intervals, until eventually they stop.' He grinned. 'Unless, of course, I resume my former excesses. From henceforth, therefore, I shall refuse any more invitations to celebrate William's birth in a lake of claret, and moderation will be my watchword.'

'And pigs have wings,' Phoebe commented darkly from the table, where she was writing a close-packed and detailed letter to Nick and Silence in Chard. She laid her quill down and looked severely at her nephew. 'Lukas, have you done the work that was set you? If you haven't attended school today, Master Carne will want to see it tomorrow.'

'No one has taken any notice of what he says, since the Prince landed,' Lukas complained. 'And Matthew told me that *his* father said that Master Carne would soon be shown the door, and Master Baker returned in his place.'

'That's as maybe – go do your work now.'

Phoebe's voice was one he never disobeyed, but Lukas nevertheless glanced appealingly towards his father. Alex jerked his head significantly at the door, and with a rueful expression of resignation, Lukas got down from the bed and went out.

As soon as the door had closed behind him, Alex pushed himself into a more upright position against the pillows and bolster piled behind him, and said briskly, 'And now to business.'

'Business?' Phoebe looked up, her expression sharp.

'Yes, little sister, business. To be precise, the business concerning Charles. Are we all agreed that this nonsense has gone on long enough?'

Louise glanced at the top of his head. The furrow left by their cousin's bullet showed dull red amidst the blackness of his hair. A fraction lower, and he would have died: and the thought of how nearly she had lost him made her shiver with renewed horror.

'I am,' she said. 'But what can we do? He is in possession of Wintercombe, however illegally, and we are not.'

'You can hardly eject him without an army at your back,' Phoebe pointed out.

Alex smiled, and it was not pleasant. 'Perhaps not. But that, sister dear, is precisely what I have in mind.'

And he proceeded to describe, in alarming detail, the means by which he proposed that Charles would be finally evicted from Wintercombe.

The day that Charles discovered that he had not, after all, slain his cousin and *bête noire* was black indeed. He had been forced to suffer gross abuse and indignities at the hands of his inferiors, and he had returned to Wintercombe humiliated and empty-handed. He had then spent some considerable time screwing his courage up to the point where he felt able to face his mother, and tell her the appalling truth.

As he had expected, Bab took the news badly. She cried, she wailed, she called for hartshorn and for her maid, who seemed to have disappeared, and her huge bulk shuddered with terror and distress. Charles did his best to reassure her, but without success: and in the end, as he had known that she would, she turned the blame on him. He should have made sure of his aim, he should have blasted away his cousin's black heart, and made an end of him for ever.

'I thought he was dead,' Charles protested defensively. 'He *looked* dead, and there seemed to be enough blood for it – how was I to know? And what could I have done if I had found out then that he was not? Would you have had me put another bullet through him in cold blood as he lay there?'

Bab, sobbing, gave him to understand that this was precisely what she would have wanted: and, furthermore, that by not thus obliging her, he stood condemned, in her eyes, as an unfilial coward, and a poltroon.

It was then that Charles left her, terrified not of what she said, but of what he feared he might do to her if he stayed. He knew that if he had the means to do her harm in his hands then, sword or club or pistol, he would have used it.

For the rest of the day, he prayed alone in his chamber, for guidance through the maze of terrible and conflicting emotions, hatred and fear and despair, that now threatened to overwhelm him.

And while he remained in agonised seclusion, tormented and utterly alone, one by one the remaining servants gathered their few possessions, and crept quietly away to family or friends. Like Abigail, Pardice and Twinney, they balked at serving a man who had tried, in public, to provoke his own cousin to violence by falsely slandering his wife, and had then quite deliberately shot him.

He emerged at dusk, to a chilly, dark and silent house. Never had he known Wintercombe so quiet: even at night, it had always contained the muted sounds and signs of a

490

large and busy household. Now, the fires had died from lack of attention, the air was cold, no candles had been lit, no tempting smells issued from the kitchen, and there was no distant, cheerful chatter as supper was prepared.

At first bewildered, Charles ran through the house with increasing urgency and rage as the awful truth dawned on him. There was no one left – no one – they had all deserted him. He called frantically for Warren, whose loyalty had seemed to be beyond question, and his manservant's name echoed unanswered among the high, dim rafters of the hall, announcing the final betrayal.

Then he heard his mother's voice. 'Charles! Charles, where are you? Charles, *help me!*'

For years, Bab had relied on the services of a succession of more or less docile maids to perform the smallest task for her. Left alone, she was completely incapable of doing anything for herself, a situation exacerbated by her enormous bulk.

For a moment, Charles stood still in the empty fastness of the hall, his hands over his face. But he could not ignore her: the voice that had at once commanded and repelled him, all the days of his life, rang out again, imperious, insistent, urgent.

With a groan, he turned and went obediently upstairs.

The Prince's third Declaration, from Sherborne, had proclaimed that Catholics were to be left in peace, save for those who were armed and were therefore a danger to the righteous forces of Protestantism. Though the Prince repudiated authorship, few believed him. To most ordinary people, the implication of a Papist conspiracy chimed exactly with their own suspicions, while many of their betters could see that the terror of reprisal which the Declaration inspired in most Catholics had led to the collapse of all remaining resistance to the Prince.

Even the King's most devoted adherents, Father Petre, Lord Chancellor Jeffreys and the rest, thought now only of saving their own skins. The London apprentices rose, joyfully, to pull down the mass houses that had proliferated

491

under the King's indulgent eye, and the whole country was set in a panic at the thought of bands of Catholic soldiers, at liberty after the disintegration of the King's army, wandering the land to loot and murder at will.

In such a climate of terror, rumour, suspicion and hatred, no Catholic was safe. Even Berkeley Carne, wealthy and respected, had been threatened, his windows broken and abuse hurled at his family. The city fathers, fearful of riots breaking out in the narrow streets of Bath, threw a couple of ringleaders into gaol, and put a guard on the Carnes' house and on those of the few other prominent Catholics who dared to remain in the city. As in Bristol, further trouble seemed to have been averted, and they saw no need to ask the Earl of Shrewsbury, who passed by on his way to rejoin the Prince at Hungerford, for the loan of a few soldiers to help keep order.

Shrewsbury had already been informed that his Colonel of Dragoons was lying sick in Bath, for Alex had sent Pardice with the message, presenting his apologies both to the Earl and to the Prince, and hoping that he would be fit to return to William's service within a week.

It should take no longer to carry out his plans, and the Prince's victory seemed so overwhelming that he would not be needed for a while. The fever had been intense, but the course of powders had soon put an end to it, and Doctor Peirce, brought in at Louise's insistence, had stayed only ten minutes and charged a considerable fee to tell him what he already knew. Since Alex also refused, in the strongest terms, to be bled, the good physician had left in high dudgeon, proclaiming that whatever happened to his patient hereafter, he could not be held responsible.

Alex was well aware that while bleeding might not be necessary for a quick and complete recovery, rest and good nourishment certainly were. And with his younger son's wails disturbing the household at regular intervals, he was unlikely to enjoy much peace and quiet. But he was determined to carry out the bold and drastic course of action which he had already disclosed to his wife and his sister.

In their opinion, it was dangerous and foolhardy in the extreme, and Philip Cousins, summoned to the house the morning after Alex's arrival, agreed with them in no uncertain terms. 'You're mad even to think of it, Alex! Let the mob run loose, and there'll be no end to it!'

'I am not without experience in dealing with such people,' Alex pointed out. He was up, and dressed, and apart from a certain gauntness about his face, revealed few signs of his recent illness. The wound in his scalp had been cleaned and carefully stitched by Gerrit, whose huge, blunt fingers possessed an unlikely delicacy of touch, and the mark now hardly showed. 'I have taken lessons from Shaftesbury, remember, and he had a genius for manipulating the mob. My attempts at reasonable persuasion have been met with unreasonable force, and I am sick of forbearance. Charles deserves everything I plan to do to him, and more, and if he proves as brave a man as His Majesty, he'll slink away from Wintercombe with his tail between his legs at the first sign of trouble. And it's not as if I am doing wrong – I have the Prince's own sanction, after all, to deal thus with armed Catholics.'

He looked at the lawyer with spurious innocence, and Cousins shook his head. 'You yourself doubted that the Prince had anything to do with that Declaration.'

'Not directly, no, but it has served his purpose very well – and mine, come to that. The times are against Charles, and he ignores that unpalatable fact at his peril. I'm well aware I'm playing with fire, Philip, and this time I do not intend to burn my fingers. But I intend to finish this matter once and for all, so that my wife and children no longer need live in fear for their safety, and mine.'

Louise, listening to him, thought of Charles, cornered at Wintercombe like some desperate animal driven back into its lair, and shivered. It seemed that this terrible, destructive enmity would only end when one of them was dead: and she prayed that Alex, plotting Charles's downfall with a boldness that frightened and disturbed her deeply, would not be the one to lose his life.

*

Charles had spent a miserable night, and most of the following day, tending the multitudinous needs of his mother. He had helped her to the close-stool, he had supplied her with meagre meals from kitchen scraps – the servants, departing, had not scrupled to lay their hands on anything they fancied – he had undressed her, and he had even fed her dog, and was growled at and nipped for his pains. Nor had Bab failed to make it quite clear that she held him alone responsible for their present misfortunes. Due to his astounding incompetence, he had failed to kill Alex, he had failed to stop the servants leaving, or pilfering, and now he had failed to engage more servants to replace those who had deserted them.

Charles stared at her in helpless rage and loathing. 'Mother, I will do my best, but I could hardly rush out in the middle of the night and scour the village for maids, now could I? For God's sake be reasonable!'

But at her insistence, he rode into Philip's Norton to seek out people who would be prepared to work for him. Any idea of searching for his cousin had long since disappeared: he could spend days on a wild-goose chase all over north Somerset, and return to find Wintercombe's door barred against him and Alex laughing at him from inside the house. Even to go such a short distance filled him with unease, but there was no help for it: he did not need Bab's continual nagging to convince him of the urgency of hiring more staff to run the house.

But the villagers were not interested, and said so, with a ripe derision that made him hot with humiliated rage. They would happily serve all other St Barbes, it seemed, save him and his mother, and everyone spoke warmly of Alex, and of the Prince of Orange, and expressed profound delight at the apparent downfall of His Majesty.

At last, he could stand no more, and rode home, his passage along the Wellow Lane attended by a crowd of hooting urchins shouting abuse and pelting him with rubbish. In the end, as they were only children, he fired his pistol over their heads, and watched them scream and scatter with sour satisfaction.

The feeling did not last long. He spent a considerable time tending to the horses, who had been tied up since the previous evening without food or water, and then, weary, hungry and full of resentful rage, forced himself inside to face his mother.

As he had feared, her catalogue of complaint was endless, and became more and more preposterous as the evening wore on. It seemed that everything was his fault, from the severity of the weather to the Prince's invasion and the apparent collapse of the King's forces. Indeed, he was so feeble and incompetent he could not even engage a servant to look after her, and so she was forced to submit to his clumsy and unenthusiastic ministrations, a situation neither proper nor seemly.

It went on and on and on, and at last, his protests unheeded, he found himself unable to stand there any longer under such a hail of accusation and abuse. In desperation, he turned on his heel and fled to the sanctuary of his chamber, locking the door behind him.

Often before, he had felt this dreadful murderous rage, this longing to kill and maim. But never, until the disastrous events of the past few days, had he been tempted to injure his mother. And he knew that if she spoke to him like that again, he would find it impossible to keep his hands from her.

He went into the stables the next morning, and found the horses once more restive and hungry. He ignored their hopeful stamps and whickers, saddled the workmanlike bay gelding he usually rode, and set off for Frome, with a bag of coin clinking at his saddlebow. There, they would neither know nor care what he had or had not done to his cousin Alex: and he would surely be able to hire enough servants to ensure that the household ran smoothly, until more satisfactory and permanent arrangements could be made.

It took all day, and left him exhausted, raging and frustrated. Despite the cold, and the depressed state of the cloth trade, few were willing even to consider serving in the employ of such a notorious Papist. Frome was, after all, only five or six miles away from Wintercombe, and he found that alarming rumours had been circulating about him there, for some considerable time.

There were, however, as he had hoped, several who were desperate or greedy enough to accept his generous offer of a crown in the hand now, and three pounds a year in addition, to work at Wintercombe. He hired two slatternly maids, a doubtfully respectable widow who claimed to be able to cook, and a sullen-faced, pockmarked man who said he was a skilled groom, but looked as if he might have most recently earned his living as a highwayman. He arranged for a man and a cart, at exorbitant expense, to carry them back to Wintercombe, and set off ahead of them under a lowering sky, anxious to be home before any further falls of snow.

It was growing late when he finally arrived at Philip's Norton. He had taken care to avoid the village that morning, taking a long detour across the fields to the west, and wasting much time in doing so. Now he was weary, and impatient to get back. Surely, at this hour on a chilly winter afternoon, there would be few people abroad to see him.

South Street stretched before him, meandering up to the George and the Market Cross. The smoke from many fires lay in a low, flat, acrid cloud above the muddy road, and the first few flakes began to fall as his tired horse passed the Slopers' house. He caught sight of movement at many windows as he rode past, but to his relief no one came running out into the street to shout abuse, or throw things at him. Perhaps, after all the high words and insults of the previous day, they had come at last to their senses.

There were lamps lit at the George, and a welcoming glow from the windows. The taproom would be warm, and the beer – mulled perhaps, with a poker red-hot from the fire thrust sizzling into the tankard – was a powerful temptation. But Charles could not face the looks, the muttered sneers and open insolence that might greet his appearance. When even the polite and urbane Twinney, the cheerful and good-natured Abigail, had addressed him in the most insulting terms, he could expect no less from the Combes, Pardices, Slopers, Fripps and other respectable villagers who frequented the George in preference to its disreputable neighbour, the Fleur-de-Lys, over the way.

In any case, although unpleasantness awaited him at Wintercombe, he must face up to it. He turned his yearning gaze from the George and pressed on: along North Street, turning left down the lane where much of the fighting had taken place three years ago, when Monmouth's rebels had held off the might of the royal army; then right at Lyde Green and so down past the mill, dank and cheerless and waterlogged, to Wintercombe.

He was so engrossed in his thoughts and his misery that he did not at first hear the sounds growing louder ahead of him. It was only when his exhausted mount breasted the rise in the track leading to Wintercombe, and his home became visible before him, that he realised that the confused shouting was close, and loud, and growing louder, and that there were flickering lights massed in the courtyard in front of the house.

Bewildered, Charles let the horse carry him on, almost level with the gatehouse, before he could collect his dazed thoughts enough to bring the animal to a halt. People were packed into the square of gravel on the other side of the low wall which separated the track from the courtyard, and although there were still some light in the sky, the brilliance from a score or more of leaping torches dazzled him. He stared, stupefied with horror, at the unruly, yelling mob who, without doubt, had come to exact their spiteful vengeance upon him.

Someone had seen him. There was a howl of fury, and several young men leapt over the wall and surrounded him. More, less agile, were streaming through the gatehouse and running towards him.

He had no time to use the pistols he carried: he drew his sword and slashed wildly at the hands grabbing at his horse's bridle, while the animal, frightened out of its weariness, snorted and sidestepped in alarm.

The men crowding round him dodged his blade with ease, and one of them knocked it contemptuously out of his hand with a blow from a cudgel. Helpless, clutching his jarred wrist in agony, he could only watch as they seized his gelding's reins, and then the clutching fingers began to reach for him.

'Let go!' Charles screamed, in terrified rage. 'Get your hands off me, you bastards!'

'Stop!'

The voice was one he knew, one that he had thought silenced for ever, only three days ago. Beyond the faces of the mob, distorted with hate, he saw his cousin Alex appear, tall, cool and casually elegant on the magnificent dapple-grey stallion Pagan. He looked as if he had just returned from a gentle hack across the fields: if any ill effects remained from his injuries, they were not discernible. His mind overwhelmed with all-consuming hatred, Charles stared impotently at his cousin, his emotions stark and ugly on his face.

'Don't touch him,' Alex said. The stallion, under perfect control, stood calmly beneath him, its ears flicking at the sound of his voice. 'If vengeance is anyone's, it is mine – but keep a good hold of his horse. Good afternoon, Charles. Was your jaunt successful?'

For a dreadful moment, bursting with fury, Charles could only stutter. At last, conscious of sniggers around him, he forced the words through shut teeth. 'Go away – get out – you are a traitor, and you have no right to be here.'

'We have had this conversation before, and repetition is tedious. I'll say merely that you mistake the matter. Wintercombe is mine, legally and inalienably, and since you would not listen to reason, I have come with my friends to ensure that you take heed this time.'

'You call this rabble, this scum, your friends? Just what I would have expected!'

'Look around you. Notice any familiar faces? Yes, I see you do. I would call them scum at your peril, Charles. Twinney? See if he is armed.'

Charles's erstwhile butler, his face its usual polite mask, pushed his way through the crowd. As he pulled the pistols out of their holsters, there was a growl of anger, which subsided reluctantly as Alex continued.

'The Prince of Orange, in his wisdom, has decreed that no violence be directed at Catholics who are peaceable. Those who carry arms and threaten violence and resistance, however, may, and I quote, be delivered up to the discretion of the soldiers. I hold a commission from the Prince of Orange, Charles, and I would be entirely within my rights to shoot you out of hand – as, three days ago, you shot me. Give me the pistols, Twinney.'

The butler made his way back to the grey stallion, the heavy weapons cradled in his hands. Alex took them and pointed one at Charles, a malicious smile on his face. 'Shall I pull the trigger? I don't think so – my aim might not be as bad as yours, and despite everything I find I cannot kill you in cold blood, however richly you may deserve it. Which reminds me that I must warn you to prepare yourself – I have some bad news for you.'

Charles stared at his cousin. 'What do you mean? What news? Is it – is it my mother?'

Alex studied him, and nodded, as if his expectations had been confirmed. He said, 'It doesn't seem to be much of a surprise to you, does it? Were you provoked beyond endurance? I can't say I blame you.'

'What do you mean?' Charles cried in terror. 'What's happened to her? What have you done to her, you bastard?' He drove his spurs into his horse's flanks, but the gelding, caught fast, could not obey: it squealed in pain, and tried to pull away from the man holding the reins. Charles aimed wild blows with his fist at the nearest faces, sobbing with despair, while the men dodged and laughed and taunted him.

'Enough,' Alex said sharply. 'Dismount him, and bring him to me.'

Rough hands pulled him from the saddle: he struggled, and was cuffed into submission like a recalcitrant child. Then, his head ringing from the blows, he was dragged through a forest of buffeting, contemptuous fists to face his cousin on the edge of the crowd.

His face streaked with blood and tears and mucus, even in this extremity Charles had managed, somehow, to

499

control his emotions and assume a kind of desperate dignity. He stared at Alex through swollen lids, and said, 'Tell me – what has happened to my mother?'

Alex's expression now was sombre, with no hint of the infuriating mockery he had so often used to inflame his cousin's rage. He said quietly, 'She is dead, Charles.'

'Dead? Dead?' The other man's voice rose to a howl of anguish. 'She was alive and well when I left her this morning – she can't be – you're lying to me, you bastard, you killed her!'

'I have done nothing to her. I found her, an hour ago, at the foot of the stairs, and I think she had been dead for some while, for the body was quite cold. It appears to have been an accident – she may have had an apoplectic fit, or perhaps tripped over something, possibly her dog. Either way, her neck is broken, and she is dead, but not, I swear to you, by my agency. If she was indeed alive when you left her, then she must have died soon afterwards. She should not have been left on her own, Charles.'

'I had to!' he shouted. 'It was impossible – I had to get servants – of course I had to leave her, how else was I to hire them? You hated her, you killed her, you murderer!' He struggled, and the grip on his arms tightened painfully, until he subsided with a sob.

'*I* am no murderer,' Alex said softly. In the face of his cousin's frenzied accusations, he had remained as controlled and still as the stallion he rode. 'That is one charge which I can quite truthfully deny. Only you know whether it was really an accident, Charles, and I am not going to judge you for it, now or hereafter. All I want is for you to leave Wintercombe for ever, and never to see or hear of you again. Now, do you wish to see your mother?'

All around, the rabble stood silent, avid, menacing, watching the confrontation with greedy and curious eyes. Charles glanced round at them, seeing many villagers, and several Wintercombe servants, their faces appallingly familiar amidst the brutal anonymity of the mob. He thought of his mother, foolish, malicious, wronged, and his heart clenched savagely with grief and guilt. Tears stood in his eyes: he said, on a harsh sob, 'Please – take me to her.'

With a little more gentleness, he was propelled through the gatehouse, and across the courtyard to the porch. It was almost dark now, and the snow was falling more steadily, with white, whispering grace. The torches cast huge, dancing, slanting shadows away from him as, frozen with cold and despair, he stumbled up the steps, along the screens passage, and into the Hall.

They had laid Bab St Barbe on a trestle table by the wall, beneath the high windows that overlooked the garden. Above her, the stern faces of her long-dead husband's grandparents glared down at her, for she was none of their own. Someone had closed her eyes, but death had locked her sagging jaw open, and set her face into a bruised and battered mask of final horror. It was the expression of a woman who had died violently, whether by accident or by design.

Charles stared for a long time at the woman who had borne him, and to whom he had been tied all his life in bonds of adoration and guilt and secret, tormented dislike. Then, he turned his head away.

Alex drew the cloth back over his aunt's dead face, and gave Charles a look of contemptuous pity. He said softly, 'She did not deserve to die thus, in such fear. You have much to answer for, Charles, but I am sick beyond belief of this feud between us. Wintercombe is mine, understand that – Louise is mine too, unto the ends of our lives and beyond. I will keep you here tonight, and you may attend the burial tomorrow, but after that, you must leave. There should be a ship at Bristol which is bound for France, and I shall put fifty guineas into your pocket. And before God, if I ever see you again in this country, or hear that you have returned, I shall not scruple to use any means I choose to protect my life, my family and my property from you. Do you understand me?'

Charles lifted his head, his expression venomous with loathing. Alex met his gaze with the same controlled calm that he had displayed throughout. 'Do you understand

501

me?' he repeated. 'The game is over, Charles. Your mother has lost her life because of it, and you have now tried to kill me twice, besides causing terrible distress to Louise and Phoebe and the children. I will have no more blood spilt by your agency, Cousin – the end is here, now, and for ever. How many more innocents do you wish to suffer in your insane pursuit of vengeance?'

Charles cried, his voice strained and frantic, 'I should have killed you three days ago – I should have made sure – and then the game *would* be over, and she – she would still be alive!'

'No, she would not,' Alex said. He walked up to Charles, so close that his cousin could have struck his face, if his arms had not been pinioned. 'Listen to me, Charles. Whatever the truth of it, *you* are responsible for her death – *you* and no other. If she died after you went out this morning, she died because you left her alone. Let your slippery, self-justifying conscience deal with that, if it can, for I will not shoulder your guilt. You may lay many things with justice at my charge, but Bab's death is not one of them.' He glanced at Pardice and Gerrit, who were holding his cousin secure in their grasp, and nodded. 'Take him away, and lock him up in the gatehouse.'

Alex stood by his aunt's monstrous shrouded bulk as Charles, screaming incoherent threats and protests, was hauled unceremoniously away. For a brief moment, he was alone. Exhausted by the events of this long day, spent collecting, organising and leading the mob of Bath apprentices and men from Philip's Norton and the surrounding villages, he leaned his back against the cool stone wall and closed his eyes. The confrontation with Charles had sickened him: as, too, did the strong suspicion that his cousin had somehow, directly or indirectly, caused Bab's death.

He breathed deeply, trying to restore some sense of calm after such turbulence, and felt the tension slipping away from him at last. Then the stillness began to creep into his heart, the subtle, lovely, unmistakable familiarity of the house where he had been born, the home of his forbears and the inheritance of his children.

And all around him, he felt Wintercombe reach out to him, and recognise him, and welcome him back.

# Chapter Twenty-Six

## 'A wise alliance'

On the eleventh of December, King James, forsaken by all those whom he had most trusted, gave way to overwhelming fear and despair, and fled London. He had already sent the Queen and the six-month-old Prince of Wales to safety in France: now, no longer protected by his disintegrating army and navy, and with the Prince of Orange advancing unopposed towards London and demanding humiliating terms, his nerve had utterly failed him.

Characteristically, however, he could not even manage a successful escape: he was seized, subjected to brutal indignities at the hands of a group of sailors, and imprisoned at an inn in Faversham, in Kent. After three days, he was escorted back to London under armed guard, and received a surprisingly enthusiastic reception as he rode through the City, although most people, at heart, supported the Prince of Orange.

William, encamped by now at Henley, was not best pleased to learn that his father-in-law had botched his escape. It would have been remarkably convenient to have the King fled safely to France, leaving the way clear for the Prince to assume the throne by default – if it were to be offered to him, of course, a prospect that had seemed more and more likely.

Moving to Windsor, he discussed the problem with a number of lords. Exile, house arrest, close imprisonment, all were suggested, in tones shockingly hostile to the King. Finally, it was decided that he should be kept under guard at the house at Ham belonging to the Duchess of Lauderdale, mother of Tom Talmarsh. Three lords, Halifax, Delamere and Shrewsbury, were charged with the unpleasant duty of informing James about their plans for his future.

They arrived at Whitehall in the early hours of Tuesday, the eighteenth of December, and the King's Guard was replaced by a detachment of Dutch soldiers under Count Solms. James, still hoping for escape, pointed out that Ham House was damp and untenanted, the Duchess being at present in Scotland. He asked instead to be allowed to go to Rochester, and the three lords agreed with alacrity. The next morning, the King left Whitehall and set off by barge down the Thames, escorted by more Dutch troops.

Towards evening of the same day, in pouring rain, the Prince of Orange entered the capital, accompanied by several regiments of foot and dragoons, and coachloads of his supporters following behind. All along the road, through Knightsbridge and up to Hyde Park, the way was lined with cheering people, many with orange ribbons in their hats, or waving oranges on sticks. But William himself had little taste for pomp and ceremony when it did not serve his immediate purpose. He avoided most of the crowds by taking the quieter route through the Park to St James's Palace, where he planned to stay with his entourage until the matter of the English throne was finally settled.

Amongst his train was Sir Alexander St Barbe. It was twelve days now since he had risen from his sickbed and roused the mob to drive Charles from Wintercombe. Despite the misgivings of his family, and of Philip Cousins, his stratagem had worked as smoothly as he had hoped: indeed, given the quantity of coin he had distributed, he would have been astonished if his plan had miscarried.

The only unforeseen misfortune had been the demise of his aunt Bab. He was still not certain whether her fall had been a genuine accident, or whether Charles, goaded at last into violence, had pushed her down the steep, winding stone stairs to her death. But whatever the truth of it, he had found her lying at their foot, her body grotesquely twisted by the fall, and guarded by her little dog. It snarled and snapped when they tried to move its mistress's corpse, and had proved such a nuisance that when the carpenter, Thomas Tilley, came to put Bab in her coffin, he lost his temper and clubbed it over the head with his hammer.

So Bab had gone to her last resting place, in the St Barbe vault under the church in Philip's Norton, with the corpse of her beloved dog Floss laid beside her in the coffin. And Charles, white-faced, silent, bowed beneath the finality of his defeat, had presided apparently without emotion at the funeral of his mother, whom he might have murdered, before returning to Wintercombe under the discreet guard of Gerrit and Dan Pardice.

Alex had given him leave to take whatever personal possessions he wished, but it seemed that all Charles wanted was contained in the small, shabby canvas bag strapped behind his saddle. As promised, he was given fifty guineas, enough to preserve him from penury for some considerable time, and his passage would be paid for him.

There were no farewells, no final scene blistering with the disgust and loathing both men felt for each other. As so often in his childhood, when submitting to unendurable humiliation, Charles had locked himself away inside an armour of cold and dignified reserve. The screams, the pleas, the threats and insults, might never have been uttered: he rode away from Wintercombe, closely attended by Gerrit and Dan and four more men, all armed, and gave the home of his heart not a backward glance.

Once he had gone, the servants presented themselves in a body at Wintercombe's door, and begged to be allowed to return. Alex, more touched by their loyalty to him than he would ever admit, save to Louise, accepted their entreaties and issued his instructions. He would now return to Bath, and in a day or so would bring his wife, his children and his sister. In the mean time, the house was to be cleaned and restored to its former glory, and all trace of Bab's extravagant hand removed.

The St Barbe coach duly rolled up in the courtyard on a wintry afternoon blessed by rare sunshine, and when Louise stepped down carrying her son William, quietly asleep for once, there was a line of beaming servants on either side of the front door, their livery fresh and neat, waiting to welcome their lady and her children home. They cheered loudly, and then their eagerness and enthusiasm

506

overcame the formality of the occasion. William, waking, found himself the centre of much cooing attention, and reacted predictably. The furious yells of the heir to Wintercombe, bouncing round the rafters of the Hall like a shuttlecock, made a singularly appropriate fanfare for a triumphant return.

Alex stayed for two days, to see them all settled, and to await Gerrit's return from Bristol with the news that Charles had been put aboard a ship bound for Le Havre. Then, with reluctance, but mindful of his duty, he rode away to rejoin the Prince. He still tired easily, and it had not been very wise to rise so quickly from his sickbed, but if he lingered any longer at Wintercombe, the Prince would doubt his loyalty, and there would be no reward for his service.

He knew now what he wanted, the two lives he wished to lead hereafter. One, with Louise and their children at Wintercombe, managing his inheritance, breeding and racing horses, was already secure. But the other, taking part in great affairs, moving in court circles, employing his mind and his gifts for the benefit of a man whom, alone amongst those he had met over the years, he felt he could serve, depended on the good will and favour of the Prince of Orange.

Louise understood: Louise had let him go, with love, and a smile, and the promise that, when he returned to her, she would be waiting for him.

'And perhaps,' she added, with the dazzling, mischievous smile he had grown to love so much, 'your younger son will have learned a little moderation when next you see him.'

'I doubt it,' he had told her, and bestowed a swift kiss on her lips: another promise. 'For since both his parents tend to the extreme, what chance has he of temperance?'

He had driven away, with Gerrit as ever loyally by his side, and for the first time she felt no impulse to grieve at their parting, for their future together was assured at last.

He had found William at Windsor, and presented his apologies, putting the blame for his absence on ill health.

507

His commander regarded him closely, but made no comment beyond expressing, in his usual taciturn style, the hope that Sir Alexander was now fully recovered.

Certainly, the Prince had no time to waste on further investigation into Alex's activities in Somerset, for he was fully occupied with the dense, subtle, tactical manoeuvres that would ensure that King James was soon replaced by King William. James's attempt to desert his country and his responsibilities had turned all but his most blindly devoted supporters against him. It was quite obvious to everyone, after the recent riots, that the only hope of secure and lawful government lay with the Prince of Orange: and William, for his part, was completely in command of the situation.

So, he had already permitted James to go to Rochester: and there, as the Prince had wanted all along, the King was allowed to slip away a few days later, and take ship for France. On Christmas Day, in cold and snowy weather, he arrived at Calais. By fleeing, he had effectively abdicated in William's favour.

It was over: all that remained now was to put the unofficial fact of the Prince's accession on to a legal footing. A Parliament was called, and the writs were sent out, though with some difficulty: not only was the weather bad, with snow and frost, but the King, on his first flight from London, had dropped the Great Seal into the Thames. Even so, the elections took place remarkably smoothly, with no recurrence of the riots, panics and disturbances that had alarmed the kingdom as James's authority collapsed.

Many of the men now elected had never sat before: some, like John Wildman, had come over with William, or had joined him in the early days, and gained much support because of it. The County of Somerset had returned two comparatively young men, George Horner of Mells, and Sir Alexander St Barbe of Wintercombe, who despite his dubious past was after all a Whig, and unequivocally the Prince's man.

Parliament met, and discussed the issues with some heat, and a great deal of activity behind the scenes. The task before the new Members was a daunting and onerous one:

they must find solutions to enormous and fundamental problems concerning the government of the country, which previous Parliaments had failed lamentably to resolve. Many wild ideas had been bandied about: a regency for the Prince of Wales; a regency for the Princess of Orange; a Council, chaired by William, of a select group of Lords and Commons. But, on the thirteenth of February, Parliament formally offered the throne of England to the Prince and Princess of Orange as joint sovereigns, although in practice, as he wished, all the business of government would fall upon William's shoulders.

Once the important issue of the kingdom's future had been settled, Parliament fell to bickering. The Prince, forced to distribute offices between the Tories and Whigs, found that he had pleased nobody. And the backstabbing, vituperation and viciousness fomenting in Whitehall and Westminster as men struggled for positions and influence would, as Alex pointed out acerbically in a letter to his wife, have made the intrigues of ancient Rome seem innocent and harmless by comparison.

But this world, however selfish and corrupt, was Alex's natural element. William had originally been suspicious of him as an extreme Whig and a republican, but seemed now to place considerable trust in him. He was given, as he wished, a comparatively minor but still important post in the Government. The new king disliked the backstairs, bedchamber intrigue that had characterised the reigns of both his immediate predecessors, and Alex, well aware of this, was not interested in the type of position that Sir Hugh Trevelyan had once occupied.

During the momentous events of December, his friend had kept his head low. After all, he was an intimate of King James, and apparently a convert to the Roman religion. But Alex had been careful to point out to William the true and invaluable nature of Trevelyan's service to him. Hugh disarmed suspicion by publicly attending Protestant church services, and used his still considerable contacts and influence to good effect. By the end of February, he had secured a place in the household of the new Queen Mary, largely on the enthusiastic recommendation of her sister Anne, one of whose ladies happened to be Sir Hugh's niece Sophie.

There was a flurry of letters between Alex and his wife, ensconced happily at Wintercombe: and when Parliament adjourned temporarily for Easter, at the end of March, the new member for Somerset took the opportunity to return briefly to his family. The double coronation had been set for the eleventh of April, and his presence would naturally be required: moreover, the Queen had expressed an interest in his wife, and had asked to meet her. He had taken a house close to Whitehall, and planned to bring Louise back with him.

In his coach, a welcome companion, was Sir Hugh Trevelyan. He had been to Wintercombe only once, when King James had been feasted there by Charles St Barbe, nearly two years ago. His return now was not purely for reasons of friendship and courtesy, for, encouraged by Alex, he had resolved once more to propose marriage to Phoebe.

They were welcomed with much joy, especially by Louise. She had missed Alex sorely over the past months, although his letters to her, full of news and intrigue that she passed on to Phoebe, and loving phrases that she kept to herself, now formed a thick pile in the rosewood box in her bedchamber. The children, too, were delighted to see them. Lukas, released from school for the holiday, had grown two inches since Christmas, and now possessed a competent grasp of French and Greek; Kitty could say a fair number of words, in English rather than her own language, and had been taught, with some effort, to make a rather wobbly curtsey to her father; and William, four months after his birth, was already breeding a tooth, and characteristically announcing his dislike of this process with all the considerable power of his lungs.

Late that night, after a cheerful and noisy supper, followed by a lively and interesting discussion of the political situation and the coming coronation, Louise retired at last to bed with her husband. They had not made

510

love since William's conception, more than a year ago, for in Bath in December it had been too soon after the baby's birth, and then Alex had been ill. But they had spent several nights in each other's arms, and if he had desired her then, he had controlled it for her sake.

Now, knowing what was to come, she had taken particular pains to prepare herself, her abundant hair loose on her shoulders, her body washed and subtly scented, and clothed only in a new loose silk robe, that fell softly over the roundness of her breasts, and revealed more than it hid.

She was brushing her hair when he entered from his own chamber, clad likewise in a light Turkish robe tied with a sash around the waist. She met his eyes in the mirror, and smiled. 'I have not seen that before. Did you buy it in London?'

'I did – do you like it? Because if you do not, I will remove it forthwith.' He came to stand very close to her, so that the two silks, his blue, hers rose, were almost touching, and she could feel the warmth of his body at her back. His hands slid on to her shoulders, and downwards to cup her breasts: and as she drew her breath in sharply, he bent and laid his lips against her hair. 'Are you going to put that brush down, sweet Louise, and come to bed with me?'

It was the reunion she had longed for, wildly pleasurable, a joyous celebration of their love and their happiness. Afterwards, lying sated, for the moment, in his embrace, she said softly, 'Has Hugh come back to ask Phoebe again?'

'Certainly he has – and I think that this time he will tread more carefully.' Alex smiled, his blue eyes reflective. 'My sister has still as many spines as a hedgehog, and no compunction about whom she wounds with them, but perhaps she will realise that the one whom she is hurting the most is herself. And if Hugh, with all his advantages and qualities, cannot turn her aside from a spinster's life, then no one will.'

'But have you not considered that she might be right?' Louise saw his raised eyebrows, and went on in explanation. 'Maybe she is not meant for matrimony after all. Think how fiercely she values her independence, and how unhappy she would be if anyone sought to remove it from her – even if it were done out of love, or friendship.'

'Hugh understands that – God knows he should, I've harped on it often enough. And you, I suspect, have been working on Phoebe.'

'To little effect, I fear – or if my attempts at persuasion have had some impact, then she has disclosed none of it to me.' Louise stared with unusual seriousness at her husband's face, so close to her own that it was almost out of focus. 'Alex, what if we are doing her no favours by this meddling? What if she really would be better off single, unhampered by marriage? It's a bond, in both senses of the word – even if Hugh does not want to imprison her, she may well come to feel that he has.'

'On the other hand,' Alex pointed out, 'spinsterhood itself is a cage. If she can envisage no life for herself outside scholarship, immersing herself in the pursuit of knowledge for its own sake, then, yes, her present situation is entirely appropriate. But if she wishes to move in Court circles, to take part in the world of affairs, she must marry, for the sake of propriety if for no other reason. Hugh has a position in the Queen's household, and I don't doubt that before long he will have regained most of his former influence and standing. Even though some regard him as a cynical turncoat – himself not least – William knows that he played a secret and important part in the overthrow of King James. And as his wife, Phoebe would find many doors opened to her. The King and Queen are serious, cultured people, interested in learning and in the arts. There are plans well afoot to refurbish the palace at Hampton Court – William loathes Whitehall and all its associations, and the London air is not good for his health. You'd be surprised at how many kindred and congenial spirits Phoebe might discover at Court, if she married Hugh.'

'I said as much to her months ago,' Louise told him, with a wry smile. 'She did not take at all kindly to the idea that she should marry Hugh to "meddle in government", as she put it. And since then, I have not dared mention it again.'

'And her welcome today was wary, at best,' Alex said. He

512

grinned. 'Hugh is undoubtedly the most courageous, or the most foolhardy, man of my acquaintance. There are few indeed who would brave Phoebe's wrath once, let alone risk it a second time. And in view of that fact, I can only assume that despite everything, he must truly love her.' He took her face in his hand and kissed her nose, then her mouth. 'As I love you – beyond any measure or counting. Well, we have all our hearts' joy, and so have King William and his Queen – so why should not Hugh and Phoebe be given theirs, and end all our stories happily?'

As her brother had accurately observed, Phoebe had not been best pleased by the arrival of Hugh Trevelyan. She had not expected it, and the sight of his long, fine-featured face under a periwig that looked preposterous beside Alex's natural hair, cast a considerable blight over her brother's homecoming. She greeted her would-be suitor with cool friendliness, however, and exerted herself to behave almost as normal. She found herself, doubtless by Louise's contrivance, seated next to him at supper, and managed to keep their conversation on the safe subject of his son James's progress at school.

But when she lay at last alone in her bed, in the chamber beyond the Hall that she had occupied at Wintercombe since her childhood, she brought herself sternly to consider the facts once more. For he would undoubtedly ask her again: she had seen in his eyes, before she looked away, that his feelings had not changed. And despite all her fierce denials of love, her curiosity had reluctantly roused itself.

What would it be like to share her life, her home, her bed, with a man? She could not imagine herself submitting to his demands, and yet submit she must, or it would be no marriage, and grossly unfair to a man whom, in spite of everything, she still liked very much indeed. Passion, as experienced to such devastating effect by Alex and Louise, was totally alien to her nature: but she wondered if, in the fullness of time, even a union based on friendship might not eventually come to admit some mutually pleasurable physical expression of affection . . .

513

Her mind recoiled at the thought. She was crippled, thin, ugly, a virgin, and most likely barren. The idea of lovemaking was revolting – she could not imagine why Hugh would wish to do it with her. And such a gross intrusion seemed to be the greatest possible violation of the privacy of self which she had guarded so jealously, all her life, from everyone save her father, her brother, and now Lukas and Louise.

Once, she had admitted Hugh Trevelyan to that tiny group of intimates. And that impulse of liking and friendship now threatened all the narrow, fierce, selfish independence upon which she had based her adult life.

There was no way out of her predicament. Even her sharp, logical intellect could see no compromise between losing a dear friend, and setting aside all the asumptions and principles which she valued so much. She must either betray Hugh, or herself.

Caught on the horns of an impossible dilemma, she slept little, and excused herself from all activity the next morning, pleading illness. She was not thinking as clearly as usual, or she would have foreseen the inevitable consequence of such an announcement: there was a procession of concerned visitors to her bedside, disturbing her still more with well-meaning and misplaced sympathy.

It was Alex, of course, who proved characteristically to be the most perceptive, and the most disruptive. He sent Mattie briskly out of the room, despite Phoebe's protests, and then sat on the bed and fixed his sister with a gaze that permitted no evasion. 'This is very unlike you, to skulk in your chamber refusing battle.'

She had long ago acknowledged the futility of arguing with him, but nevertheless glared back. 'I find the situation intolerable. Why did you bring him with you?'

Alex opened his sapphire eyes to their widest and most innocent extent. 'I, little sister? He asked most eagerly to come, and I was in no mind to refuse him.'

'Liar,' Phoebe said. 'I know exactly what you're thinking, and what you want, and I will not dance to your music, brother – nor to anyone else's, for that matter. Is that quite clear?'

Alex gave her a mockingly rueful grin, and sketched a gesture of surrender. 'I yield to your superior strength, and retire bloody, but unbowed.'

'Good,' Phoebe said tartly. 'Now will you kindly get off the bed and leave me in peace? I didn't sleep a wink last night.'

It was a mistake to admit it, she knew as soon as the words had left her mouth. Alex smiled wider. 'Which would hardly be the case if your conscience were easy. Let me spell it out for you plain. You regard Hugh with great liking and affection: you wish to have him as your friend: but the thought of marrying him greatly alarms you, and moreover threatens your happy little life in Bath. Am I right?'

'Perhaps,' Phoebe said guardedly. Sitting up in bed, wrapped in an old furred gown and propped against bolsters that were no whiter than her thin, shadowed face, she did not in the least look like the object of anyone's desire. 'But it is *my* life, brother, however little, and I am sick of your interference in it. Who are you to order my happiness according to what *you* think is best for me? Father never made that mistake.'

'But Hugh had not then appeared on the scene,' Alex reminded her. 'And be sure of this, little sister – whatever your feelings on the matter, there won't ever be another man who can offer you what he does. It is Hugh, or no one. And I've seen how you love Lukas, and Kitty – you can't keep that hidden. Do you really want no children of your own?'

'I'm probably barren – two or three doctors have said as much.'

'How do they know? Virgins generally are,' Alex pointed out, with unanswerable logic. 'Listen, Phoebe – I will say no more for now – '

'Just as well – you have said quite enough already.'

'But think on it – don't dismiss him out of hand.' Alex rose to his full and considerable height, and stood looking thoughtfully down at his sister. 'I do not wish to interfere, or to coerce you, or even persuade you against your better judgement. I know how you value your independence, in

515

your life as in your mind. I want only your happiness, and I feel, honestly, that if any man is capable of giving it to you, then Hugh Trevelyan is. Please, *think* on what I have said. And whatever else you decide to do, remember that skulking in here like a felon won't serve your cause.'

And with one last, infuriating grin, he left her alone.

Damning her brother to the nethermost confines of Hell, Phoebe burrowed down under the bedclothes, and tried to shut away the voices that screamed at her from all sides. She wrestled with her thoughts until dinner time, and then called Mattie, and told her that she wished to be dressed.

With some surprise, and not a little curiosity, the maid brought the garments that Phoebe requested. The blue mantua was her only gown that was remotely fashionable, and a considerable improvement on her usual shabby garb. With a lace tippet to disguise the starkness of her thin shoulders, and her black, glossy hair dressed with some art to conceal its essential want of curl, she felt much more confident. Appearance, after all, was everything, and even Louise, if dowdily dressed and lacking the essential sparkle of her personality, would never attract anyone's attention. But she knew how to impress, how to draw all eyes upon her despite her unmodishly olive skin and undeniably aquiline nose, and Phoebe, who was extremely observant, had long ago fathomed her entrancing sister-in-law's secrets.

Never, though, had she thought to employ them herself: but never before, either, had she felt compelled to appear at her best. She would skulk no longer, but go boldly out to meet her fate, whatever it might be.

As usual before dinner, the family had congregated in the Great Chamber, which occupied the whole of the first floor on the east side of the house. Long ago, this large and lovely room had been haven to Silence, in the days when she had kept Wintercombe safe from the perils of civil war. Later, Alex had occupied it on his return from Holland, until his marriage to Louise had prompted alternative arrangements. Now, it was used for formal and informal gatherings such as this, when guests were present and the much smaller winter parlour would seem cramped.

Alex and Louise were there, of course, with Lukas, and Hugh. She stood in the doorway, head high, leaning on her stick, daring them to comment on her appearance. And it was her nephew, apparently unaware of all the undercurrents of emotion, who came forward, smiling, to take her arm and lead her to a chair by the fire.

Phoebe thought afterwards, ruefully, that she might as well have put on her old rusty black after all, for all the comment made on her unaccustomed finery. But she found, rather to her surprise, that she could talk to Hugh quite easily, so long as it was in the course of general conversation. And he, too, seemed disinclined to engage her individual attention. Her spirits began to lift a little. Perhaps mere friendship might be possible after all.

After the meal, since the weather was fine and springlike, Alex and Louise decided to ride out towards Wellow, and Lukas begged to accompany them on his new pony. At that point, Phoebe slipped quietly out of the room. She knew that it was discourteous, but Alex's intention was plain, and she had no wish to be thrust quite so blatantly into Hugh's exclusive company.

She made her way, as speedily as her crippled limbs would carry her, down the flights of steps leading through the terraced garden to the orchard below. There were niches set in the last wall close by the apple trees, already in bud. Most of them held straw bee-skeps, but she found an empty one, warmed by the new April sunshine, and sank gratefully into it. Only those familiar with Wintercombe knew of these secluded recesses, and Hugh would never find her here. She hoped that Alex and Louise had persuaded him to go riding with them, and leaned back against the smooth dressed stonework, her eyes closed, enjoying the peace and the sweet music of spring birdsong.

She must have dozed off, for the next she knew was the arrival of a shadow, blocking out the sun, and a voice saying softly, 'I'm sorry – have I disturbed you?'

Her eyes flew open. Hugh Trevelyan stood apologetically in front of her. He had changed the extravagant suit of red velvet, which he had worn at dinner, for a much plainer one of blue cloth, and wore what Phoebe guessed must be his fifth-best periwig.

Despite her annoyance, she managed a smile. 'Not really.'

'Which means that I have,' said Hugh. 'I am sorry – I will go.'

'No!' The word came out more sharply than she had intended, and she repeated it, in gentler tones. 'No, please don't. Has my incorrigible brother left you to fend for yourself?'

'Only at my insistence. And besides, although I am content to sit upon a horse for the purposes of travel, as a pastime for its own sake it holds little appeal for me. I must allow, though, that bay he rides is a fine horse, and very spirited.'

'Blaze? Too spirited, in my opinion – Alex says he's the devil to control. His other stallion, Pagan, is a perfect gentleman, and even I can appreciate his magnificence. He's running with the mares at present, though, down in the valley, so Alex rides the bay. Both stallions are intended to be the foundation sires for a breed of fine racing horses – Alex and Louise have great plans.' She smiled. 'It's an interest I don't share with them, I'm afraid.'

'Nor I, as you may have already discerned.' He glanced around him. 'Do you mind if I sit? There is a convenient log over there, which might protect me from the perils of damp ground.'

'Of course,' Phoebe said courteously, and watched as he dragged the branch closer. He was not as tall as her brother – very few men were – but he was still of a good height, and carried himself well for a man who must be past forty. She realised that she did not know his exact age, and then, further, that it did not matter.

Hugh dusted the moss and bark from his hands and sat down almost at her feet, with an exaggerated care that made her smile. He said, 'Did Alex tell you? There is news of your cousin.'

'Cousin? Do you mean Charles? Or Bram?'

'Bram is the one who was transported to the Barbadoes, is

he not? Yes, that cousin. It seems that King William will be happy to grant him a pardon, along with all the other rebels. If he is able to buy his passage home, he will be free to do so. Or, of course, the money for it can be sent out to him.'

'If he chooses to take it,' Phoebe said.

'Alex said he might not,' Hugh commented. 'He has apparently done very well for himself. One of my brother's neighbours, Sir Robert Davers of Rougham, was born in the Barbadoes, and recently returned from a visit there. He knew of your cousin Bram, and was able to give Alex a glowing report of him. Davers is one of the Members for St Edmunds Bury, and met your brother at the sessions of Parliament.'

'I am glad that Bram has done so well. But he has the greatness of spirit to rise above the worst adversity, and turn it to his advantage. Unlike Charles.'

Hugh glanced up at the bitterness in her voice. 'There is no news of him, I take it?'

'As Alex has presumably told you, he was put on a ship bound for France, just before Christmas. Since then there's been no word, but I would not have expected any. You know what he tried to do?'

'Yes, and I think Alex was extremely merciful, under the circumstances. After all, this is the second time that Charles has tried to kill him, and the second time, too, that he has been sent overseas. Are you not afraid that he will come back again? Wintercombe seems in some peculiar way to be his lodestone – he cannot keep away from it.'

'He considers it to be his own rightful property – and he has the same view of Louise. He has never, ever accepted that she loves Alex, and not him. And although my father meant well when he placed the estate under an entail, it has done much to foster and encourage the rivalry between them. Until his son was born, Charles was Alex's heir. And babies die so readily, even children as vigorous as William seems to be. It is horrible to say so, but I do believe that if Alex had been killed that day, Charles would have persuaded himself by now that William was better off dead, too.'

Hugh was silent, his long face thoughtful. Phoebe, studying him, saw his slender, fine, well-kept hands, the sunlight illuminating the contours of his face, the unusual grey-green of his eyes. Something unwelcome and unfamiliar woke inside her, and abruptly, denying it, she looked away.

He did not seem to have noticed anything untoward. He said seriously, 'If that is true, then I hope he stays in France. But if his desire for Wintercombe has reached the point of obsession – which it must have done – I cannot imagine that he will stay in France for ever. There must be a good chance that he will return one day, vowing vengeance.'

'I know there is,' Phoebe said. 'But Alex seems to think that he has gone for good, and it was he who ordered him into exile. Perhaps Charles has indeed finally accepted reality, although personally I doubt it very much. I think he has long since strayed beyond the bounds of reason. Alex suspects that he may even have killed his mother, although there was no proof of it and it's perfectly possible that her death was an accident.'

'It should not be too difficult to discover his whereabouts in France,' Hugh pointed out. 'He has probably found his way to James's court at St Germain, like all the other Catholic exiles. William has his spies there, of course – I will make enquiries, if you like.'

'It might be wise. Even if Alex no longer sees him as a danger, I most certainly do. And when James decides, as he surely must, to try and regain his throne, then we are faced once again with the evils of a civil war. And Charles will undoubtedly come with him, and revive that corrosive, horrible feud, to all our perils.'

She shivered, and Hugh, his face displaying concern, rose to his feet. 'Are you cold?'

'No – a shadow crossed my grave, or my brother's.' Phoebe smiled at him. 'But I think I will go back indoors, nevertheless. It is barely April, after all, and this lovely sunshine disguises a distinct chill in the air.'

He helped her to her feet without fuss, and she took his

arm. They walked slowly up the steps leading back to the terraced gardens, and thence to the house. She paused for breath by the sundial, with its Latin inscription, as dear and familiar to her as a line in her favourite book.

' "I do not count the hours unless they are sunny ones",' Hugh translated softly beside her. 'The same phrase is written on the sundial above the porch at Goldhayes.'

'Perhaps it is a common motto for them. But a delightfully appropriate one, for all that.'

The thin shadow, cutting across the dull brass of the dial, showed that it was nearly three o'clock. Phoebe stared at it, suddenly and intensely aware of the strength and warmth and support of the man beside her, on whom she leaned. She took a sharp breath, and said, 'Hugh . . .'

'Yes?'

She turned, clumsily, to face him. He was very much taller than she was and she felt suddenly dowdy and insignificent beside this urbane, accomplished and powerful man. Regretting her impulse already, she shook her head impatiently. 'Oh, it's nothing. I do feel cold, after all.'

'Phoebe . . . may I say something to you?'

His voice was uncharacteristically urgent, and she looked at him reluctantly. 'I suppose so.'

'Phoebe, I do not wish – I never intended to presume on your friendship, or to compromise the affection that lay between us. If I did, then I am heartily sorry for it.' He held out his hand, and after a moment's hesitation, she took it. Her ink-stained paw was lost inside his. He withdrew his own fingers, and smiled. 'May we continue to be friends?'

'Of course,' Phoebe said, and returned his smile. 'And I am sorry, too, that I was so discourteous. Your proposal did me much honour, and I did not give it the attention it deserved.'

He had become very still. She went on, acutely aware of the intensity of his gaze. 'I rejected you out of hand, largely from my own perversity, and also because . . . perhaps because I had not expected it. I am nearly twenty-eight, Hugh, and a confirmed old maid. No man has ever before shown the slightest bit of interest in me, unless for my learning, and I am sure that the ancient scholars who were friends of my father, and with whom I correspond regularly, think that I am a dried-up old spinster with no idea of the real world at all. And indeed, *I* thought that was what I was.'

'And now?'

'And now, I see that I was mistaken.' She fixed his eyes with her own, showing herself no mercy. 'Not entirely so – the delights of scholarship still attract me. I love to read, and discover, and dream, and I always will. That is a part of me which no one can threaten. But over the past few years, I have been shown that there is more to life than books. There are other things that are just as important to me now – friendship, loyalty, even love. And for that, though it goes much against the grain to admit it, I have largely to thank my brother Alex. And you.'

His expression was unreadable, and she paused, suddenly lost, wondering what he was thinking. Had she given him false hope? Or had she unknowingly angered him? They had been friends for more than three years, but still she knew so little about the real man beneath all that smooth veneer of diplomacy, courtesy and kindness.

'Go on,' he said.

He had withdrawn from her slightly, and the sundial, warm yellow stone and old, battered brass, now supported all her weight. Sunny hours: would these count amongst them, when she came to look back on her life?

With no help from him, it was extraordinarily difficult to bare her soul. She had never needed to, with Alex, for her brother knew her so well that words were often superfluous. She said at last, stubbornly blunt, 'I did not intend to be unkind. But I will lay my cards on the table now, and you can take or leave them as you choose. After all, it is only fair – marriage is a bargain, a transaction like any other matter of business, and it is surely politic to let you know what it really is that you think you want so much.' She stared at him, her eyes sombre. 'I have said this before, but I will say it again, more plainly perhaps. I am crippled. I have been told, by several excellent doctors, that I am unlikely to bear children. My own mother suffered much pain and difficulty, and died giving birth to me.'

He gestured impatiently, and she added, 'It is *not* of no account, Hugh! It was *marriage* that you proposed, not ordinary friendship, and such things matter – I cannot believe that they do not to you.'

'I have my son,' Hugh said. 'I lost my first wife in childbirth, and his brother. I am content with what I still have.'

'But *think*!' said Phoebe angrily. 'You love me, or so I am told. And love requires its own expression. You have only to watch Alex and Louise to see that – to see the passion that joins them still. Sooner or later, you will want to make demands on me, and denying them will only give you unhappiness. And I – Hugh, forgive me, but I do not think that I am capable of returning such feelings, in that way.'

'You say that.' His voice was very low, almost a whisper. 'How do you know?'

'Because I know myself. And besides, it would be ridiculous.' She spread her hands wide, in painful self-mockery. 'Look at me, Hugh – *look* at me! Do you really want this scrawny bag of bones in your bed? Do you want to be the laughing stock of Whitehall because of it? Your first wife was beautiful, apparently.'

'She was, yes. But there are other kinds of beauty, too.'

Phoebe laughed. It was a hollow, bitter sound. 'No part of me is beautiful, neither within or without. My brother has the monopoly on looks, and I am left as you see. And until now, I have not cared a jot.'

'Until now?'

'*Now* I care!' She was shouting, and brought her voice down to a more seemly level. 'The unadorned truth is that, yes, part of me *does* want to marry you – to be loved and cherished, to have your children and diminish into a wife, as Louise will surely do, no matter how she may struggle against it. But another part of me knows full well that it is utterly impossible – *impossible*, however much you may smile and deny it! What kind of wife would I make for you? You need some great and courtly lady, a wealthy widow perhaps, who will do all the right things, and grace your bed and your board, who will wear fine clothes and jewels without looking ridiculous, and never say what she really thinks.'

'No,' Hugh said. 'I need you.'

Phoebe shook her head, slowly and emphatically. 'No, you don't. You may *think* you do, but you don't.'

'At least allow me to know my own mind!' Hugh set his hands on her shoulders, and it took a supreme effort of will to stop herself flinching. 'Oh, Phoebe, dear girl, how can you convince me? Or I convince you? Except . . .'

She saw it coming, and from pride would not turn away: and so received her first kiss.

It was not so unpleasant as she had feared: and when it was over, she looked at his face and saw love, and understanding, and not a little delight, all mingling together. 'There,' he said, smiling. 'Not so very bad, was it?'

She could not summon the uninhibited joy that was one of her brother's most endearing qualities, but she gave him a reluctant smile in return. 'No, I suppose not.'

'It's nothing to fear, you know. Dear girl, I have loved you for a long time now – and despite all the disadvantages which you have twice been at such pains to set before me, I love you still – and I suspect that I will continue in my sad delusion until the day I die. That is as maybe. And feeling thus, I want only for you to be happy – and if you think that you would be better off as you are, then I will gladly consent, and accept your friendship, and never trouble you further with inconvenient proposals. And if you should ever change your mind, you have only to say, and we can be wed. I will make no demands on you, before or after any marriage, until you wish it. You may have all the freedom you want, to read and talk with whosoever you wish. You can, if you so choose, be as independent as you are at present. Such arrangements are not uncommon, after all – no eyebrows will be raised.'

'But what advantage would you gain? It would be worse for you than a conventional marriage, and worse by far than staying single.'

'I doubt it – because I hope, perhaps with very little cause, but still I hope that, sooner or later, you will begin to change your mind.'

Phoebe looked up at him, in some exasperation. 'Allow *me* to know my own mind!'

He grinned wryly. '*Touché*, dear girl. "I am two fools, I know, For loving, and for saying so".'

'But not, thank God, in "whining poetry",' Phoebe said. 'I did not know that you were familiar with the poems of John Donne.'

'My brother Francis has a great liking for them, and, I confess, so do I, however rough and ready and old-fashioned they seem today.' He gazed down at her, his expression still rather twisted. 'There is so much that we do not know about each other – that we have kept hidden, without intending to, perhaps out of habit. I have been alone, save for James, for a very long time – and you perhaps for all your life.'

'No,' Phoebe said. 'I was very close to my father. And now . . .' She took a deep breath. 'Hugh – what I fear most is that if you were to marry me, you would come to regret it. Not that *I* would – I have never asked for very much from life, anyway. But I doubt that I would be able to live up to your expectations.'

'But you don't know for certain, do you? And if you never try, you'll never know.' He grinned. 'Sometimes, it is perhaps the right thing to do, to plunge in regardless of the consequences.'

'My brother told you that, did he?' Phoebe enquired tartly. She was growing increasingly weary, and her hip had begun the dull, nagging ache that would soon become unbearable if she did not sit down. She must go in, now, and leave this inconvenient and unwanted conversation, or argument, that had laid altogether too many truths naked to each other's gaze. She did not want to marry – she did *not* – but, oh, she was so very tired of loneliness.

The loneliness, stretching before her; the books, which fed her soul but neglected her heart; the affection and friendship of Alex and Louise, who yet really only had eyes for each other; watching their children grow, becoming their maiden aunt, a harmless but eccentric appendage; the companionship of her cousin Libby, until she inevitably married, and then a succession of other girls, young and lively, and an ever-increasingly gulf between them, of age and attitude . . .

She could see it all so clearly. And she knew how she would end: as a crippled, irascible old lady in her dotage, whom her family would regard with tolerant pity, and forget as soon as her life was done, all her learning dust and her sterile intellect come to nothing.

Of all men and women, she was most like her father. And he had owned such pleasure and pride in her, as he would have in Alex if they had not quarrelled so bitterly. He had loved both his children, as Alex loved his.

And she was jealous of her brother, as she always had been, ever since their childhood. Jealous of his health, his looks and vitality, the freedom which was denied to her, save at the peril of her reputation, and above all jealous of his love for Louise, and his children.

No, jealous was the wrong word. She *envied* him: and so, being envious, she must logically conclude that she too wanted these things.

Well, looks and vigour were denied her, and always would be. But a man who professed to love her, God alone knew why, was standing at her side, offering her marriage. And she, poor timorous fool, feared to take that gift, even when offered to her on a golden platter. In her darkest, most secret heart she wished desperately for love, and children, even if they were purchased at the cost of her cherished and selfish independence. And such a high price was not being asked of her.

With Hugh, she might indeed have her cake, and eat it too, if she could only muster the courage to surrender.

'Phoebe? Phoebe, are you all right?'

He was looking at her with some concern. She smiled, and nodded. 'Yes, Hugh, quite all right, thank you. But I would very much like to go in, and sit down.'

It was exceedingly pleasant to lean on his arm like this.

Dependence might have some advantages, after all. And as they climbed the last steps, and came to the door that led into the screens passage, she arrived at a decision. He had been so very patient: he had not insisted on an immediate answer. And so, he deserved one now.

'Wait, before we go in,' she said, and turned to look up at him. Her face was very pale, with a thin, thoughtful line between her brows, but her sapphire-blue eyes, so like her brother's, were clear and unshadowed. 'Hugh – I am sorry. Sorry that we were ever at cross-purposes, or that our friendship was disrupted by my agency.'

'That does not matter – we are friends again now.'

'I am glad of it. But . . . I have been thinking. You already know how I feel. I have explained it all to you twice, and I won't bother you with it again.' She took a long, steadying breath. 'And you have said what your feelings are, and made me an offer which is more than anyone else will ever make, for you are more generous by far than any man I know. And I am well aware of that generosity, and I –I find that it is very hard to refuse, despite all my fine words and speeches. If – if you still wish to marry me, on the terms that you have just set forth – then, my dear, I will be happy to accept.'

The slow-dawning smile on his face lit an answering one from her. He said, as if he did not quite believe it, 'You *accept*? Why?'

'Please don't make me spell it out too plain, or I might change my mind. But I have realised that such an offer will come to me only once in my life – indeed, I am more than fortunate to have received it at all. And where else will I find a man willing to allow me my freedom, if I want it?'

'And will you want it?'

'I don't know,' Phoebe answered him honestly. 'In time I may perhaps find it less attractive than I had thought. But the real reason is that, devious and accomplished courtier that you are, I feel that I can trust you. And *that* is something I will never, ever say to my brother, dearly though I love him. The sky will fall first.'

'So.' Hugh took her hands in his. 'Am I then to understand that we are now betrothed?'

527

'In a word – yes.'

And her second kiss was even more pleasant than the first.

# Chapter Twenty-Seven

## 'Sinister destinies'

They told Alex and Louise on their return from riding, and there were many congratulations and expressions of happiness. But, as Louise mischievously pointed out, it was not entirely unexpected, since she and her husband had purposely left Hugh and Phoebe alone together, so that he might have another chance to propose to her.

'But you could not possibly have been certain that I would consent,' Phoebe said.

Alex laughed. 'Given your usual pig-headed and contrary nature, little sister, I was sure you would accept, if only out of the desire to astound me.'

It was a merry supper indeed. A great many healths were drunk, particularly to the prospective bride and groom, and at last Phoebe and Louise left the men lingering over their brandy, and retired to the winter parlour.

'I am so very glad for you,' Louise said to her sister-in-law. 'But to be honest, I never thought you would succumb. You spoke so hotly against the very idea.'

'A woman's prerogative, is it not, to change her mind?' Phoebe said drily. 'No. If the truth be known, I looked into my future, and did not like what I saw. Hugh gave me the chance to amend it, and at last I realised the true extent and generosity of his offer. No other man would have been so patient – but then, I do not want any other man.'

'Do you love him?'

Phoebe's face was made fresh and soft by the flatteringly gentle light of the candles. 'To be honest, I do not know. I *like* him, very much, and I do feel great affection for him. And I trust and respect him, too. As for passion, however, that is still alien to me, and perhaps it always will be. But he knows it. Whatever else, this will not be a marriage based on deception.'

'And you will live in London?'

'Yes, and at his house in Suffolk, so I will meet all the Heron family at long last. But he also spoken of keeping the lease on the house in Nowhere Lane, so have no fear, you will not be rid of me so easily.'

'Well, with Alex in Parliament, and at Whitehall, we will spend much time in London too,' Louise said. She sighed, and bent to push a few more lumps of coal on the fire. 'Is it right, to feel so happy? After all we have endured, all the pain and misery and separation, I still cannot quite believe that we are safe. And to have you and Hugh come to an understanding at last . . . it seems almost too good to be true. I look at Kitty, and at William, and above all at Alex, and I love them so much, I could not bear it if anything happened to them now.'

'You may be forced to bear it,' Phoebe pointed out. 'There is no certainty in life, after all. But Nathaniel's death did not defeat you, disastrous though the consequences turned out to be. And now that your cup is truly full to overflowing, I suggest that you banish all your melancholy thoughts, and drink it down with relish.'

'As Alex is probably even now drinking down his brandy,' Louise said, with a rueful grin.

He was, indeed, rather less than sober when he and Hugh rejoined them a while later. After several chaotic and hilarious games of whist and piquet, notable chiefly for the brazen way in which he attempted to cheat, Louise decided that it was time to retire to bed. Phoebe, who had been remarkably tolerant of her brother's antics, was worn out after the emotional turmoil of this momentous day, and disappeared with alacrity, after bestowing a chaste kiss on her betrothed's rather flushed cheek. Hugh then vanished in the direction of his guest chamber, where his valet was patiently waiting his arrival, and Louise and Alex were left alone in the parlour.

'Time we were in bed,' she said, and the longcase clock in the Hall, its chimes rather muted by distance, pointedly struck tenfold.

'Exactly,' Alex said. He caught her in his arms and kissed

530

her, his hands busy meanwhile, rather clumsily, with the fastenings of her gown. 'But first . . . there is no law that dictates that lovemaking must only take place in bed, is there?'

'You're drunk,' Louise said, playfully trying to fend him off. 'Someone will come in – oh, Alex, don't!'

'Why not? You like it – you know you do.' He nuzzled her hair, then her ear. 'And besides, I've locked the door. No one can get in – or out.'

Louise giggled as his hands strayed lower, arousing her desire with arrogant and practised ease. 'You're incorrigible. Why did I ever marry you?'

'You know why.' Grinning, he pulled her down with him on to the Turkey rug in front of the fire. Laid on her back, laughing at his effrontery, she saw his face above her, full of hunger, and joy, and the wild mischief that had first drawn her to him, years ago in France when she was a child. 'This is why,' he said, and she ceased her token resistance with a gasp, and gave herself up entirely to pleasure.

Afterwards, he lay drowsily in her arms, smelling of brandy and sweat and himself, and said, 'I think after all, bed is more comfortable.'

'Certainly it is if you're the one underneath,' Louise pointed out. 'No matter. I mean to exact my revenge, at a time and a place to suit my convenience. You don't look very apprehensive.'

'Oh, I am, I am,' he assured her. 'Behold me, quaking in my boots.'

'You're not wearing any. I'll repeat my earlier suggestion. Shall we go to bed?'

And this time, he assented.

In the dying firelight, they helped each other arrange creased and tangled clothing, Louise fastening buttons and laces with rather more dexterity than her errant husband. Then they stood together, so close that they might have been one, and he said, kissing her, 'Why are you smiling?'

'I was remembering another time when we did this . . . in a cowshed.'

That had been the first occasion when they had

succumbed to the mutual and passionate hunger, lust, desire, love, that had been the mainspring of both their lives, ever since. And she saw, from the sudden fierce delight kindling on his face, that his memories were still as vivid as hers.

'One day,' he said softly, his hands already straying again, 'one day, I shall take you down there, sweet Louise, and spend the rest of the year picking hayseeds out of your hair. And if we have an audience of twenty bullocks or twenty yokels, I shall not care. *Now* shall we go upstairs?'

In her chamber, they made love again, more conventionally this time, but with no less delight, and fell asleep still entwined together in the confused embrace of her feather bed. The candle, unextinguished, guttered to its end in a puddle of melted wax, and went out, while all around them Wintercombe lay in quiet and darkness, and waited for the dawn, seven hours hence.

And outside, on the edge of the field overlooking the north side of the house, a watcher noted the lights disappear one by one, until at last the house was reduced to a dim bulky shadow against the cloud-shrouded sky. Only when he was sure that no one could be awake inside, did he move, slowly and stiffly, from his hiding-place behind the hedge. He crept past the gatehouse, its doors propped shut, and climbed over the gate that led into the stable yard. The house would be locked and bolted and barred, but he knew that the stables were never so closely defended. And soon the inhabitants of Wintercombe would be lured from their dry, warm, comfortable beds, to take their allotted parts in his careful, final strategy of vengeance.

The noise woke Louise from a blissful, sated slumber. The air felt chilly on her bare skin: bewildered, she fumbled for some covering, and encountered the hand of her husband, doing likewise. He muttered something sleepily, and she pulled a blanket over them both.

And then, the distant cries began, abruptly and shockingly, to make sense.

'Fire! *Fire!*'

Alex flung the cover off and leapt out of bed. She heard him blundering about in the dark, swearing under his breath, until he found his breeches. She remembered where the tinderbox was, but by the time she had managed to locate it, and had lit a spill with urgent, fumbling fingers, he was at the door, still pushing his arms into the sleeves of his shirt. 'Get the children and get everybody out,' he said, and was gone.

She jammed the spill into the candlestick, and by its limited light found and put on her shift and the silk nightrobe. Then, she ran like a hare for the nursery.

The maids were already rousing the children. William was thankfully still asleep in his nurse's arms; Kitty, her hair tousled under her lace-edged cap, had the blank, dazed look of one not properly awake. Lukas ran up, saying breathlessly, 'It's all right – the fire's in the stables, not in the house. Papa will put it out before it spreads.'

The chamber where the children slept overlooked the garden, but the room next door gave on to the stable yard. With Lukas at her heels, she ran to its window, pulled the shutters back and looked out.

The fire was young, as yet, but she knew how terrifyingly quickly it might spread, in a stable packed with inflammable hay and straw. At present, the bright, leaping flames were confined to the nearer end, where the stalls joined the tackroom. The roof was tiled in stone, and the building stood apart from both the barn and the house itself, separated from each by a gap of some ten feet. Lukas was right: the flames would surely be extinguished long before Wintercombe was threatened.

But it was sensible to take precautions. She paused only to see Alex, pulling on some kind of coat over his conspicuous white shirt, arrive below her in the yard, and to note with some detached part of her mind, the transformation of the haphazard gaggle of servants into brisk efficiency under his direction. Then, she ran back to the nursery.

It did not take long for the rest of the household to gather, in varying states of panic and undress, in the Hall. Lukas was there, and the nursemaids carrying William and Kitty, and Phoebe with Mattie and Christian. She ran her eye along the rest, noting that all the men and boys were absent, presumably helping to fight the blaze.

'It's only a small fire in the stables, at present,' she told them calmly. 'There's no need to worry, but Sir Alexander has told me to ensure your safety. The summerhouse in the garden is well away from any possible danger, so I suggest you all go there immediately. And on no account come back into the house until word is given – if the fire does spread, you would risk your lives, and besides, we need to make sure that everyone is accounted for.'

'Can't us help to put en out, m'lady?' Abigail asked. 'Us be as good as the men, any day – us'll fill and throw a bucket so well as they!'

A chorus of voices agreed. In the end, Louise sent only the nurses, with the children and two or three of the younger maids, to the summerhouse. Then, at the head of a procession of servants, she hurried to the kitchen, where a door led to the vegetable garden, and Wintercombe's well.

Phoebe, hag-lit in the firelight, kept well out of everyone's way, but she was quite plainly seething with frustration at her inability to help. The others clustered round Gerrit, who was winding the well, dropping empty buckets down, drawing full ones up, like a man possessed. As each brimming pail spashed to the top, he unhooked it and handed it to the next eager firefighter, who carried it to the flames as quickly as possible, without spilling too much.

Twinney was there, and she touched his arm. 'Where's Sir Alexander?'

'He's with Sir Hugh, my lady, getting the horses out.'

A wild, high scream, from a beast in an extremity of pain or terror, tore through his words as he spoke. Louise gave him a brief smile, and ran through the gateway into the stable yard.

In the few minutes since she had looked down from the nursery, the fire had grown considerably. The scene was lit with an evil, flickering glare, like a depiction of Hell, illuminating the scurrying figures of men with buckets, men with pitchforks, and the wild, plunging shapes of the rescued horses. There were three of them, two brood mares and a new foal, loose in the confusion: there had evidently been no opportunity to lead them out of the way, into the paddock behind the yard.

Hugh emerged with Pardice from one of the stable doors, each leading a coach horse. Matched chestnuts, purchased for their strength and stamina, they were mad with terror, squealing and rearing, so that even the strongly built courtier risked having the head collar torn from his hand. She ran across to them. 'Take them to the paddock gate – I'll open it for you.'

Somehow, Hugh and the groom managed to guide the frantic beasts to the opening. She pulled the gate wide, and they let them go. Neighing and snorting, the two chestnuts vanished into the darkness. Henry Renolds, the most sensible of the stable boys, ran up leading the foal, its dam following anxiously behind. A slap and a shout, and they too disappeared into the safety of the paddock.

'Better loose in there for the night than burned to a crisp or trampling us to death in the yard,' Hugh said breathlessly. Over his shirt and breeches, he wore an old buff coat that had once belonged to Alex's grandfather in the days of civil war: it was presumably as protection against the flames. Without his periwig, his close-cropped fair hair made him look completely unfamiliar. He turned to follow Pardice back to the stable, and she grabbed his arm. 'How bad is it, Hugh? Where's Alex?'

'Persuading the other pair of coach horses, the last I saw of him. It's spreading very quickly, and there are nearly a dozen more to save – including that bay stallion. Listen to him!'

Above the shouting and the fierce, greedy crackle of the flames, she could hear Blaze squealing, and the drumming of his hooves on the wooden partition of his loosebox. At least there, she thought, he is furthest from danger.

'I must go,' Hugh said, and he and Renolds ran back towards the fire. To her inexpressible relief, she saw her husband emerge from the blazing building, pulled by one of the remaining coach horses. She started towards him, but he thrust the head collar rope at Renolds, and with a grin and a wave of his arm in her direction, dived back in.

Henry led the horse up, and Twinney followed, with the remaining loose mare. Once more she heaved the gate open, and the two horses, liberated, dashed through. Frantically, she listed the inhabitants of the stables in her mind. Three brood mares, two with very young foals at foot, the third yet to give birth; the stallion, Blaze; four coach horses; her own riding mare Saffron; the aged, comfortable nag that was Phoebe's mount on the rare occasions when she rode anywhere; Lukas's new grey pony; and five assorted riding horses for the use of guests and servants. Eighteen in all, and so far only five of them, and a foal, were safe. Fortunately, Pagan was out at grass with a selection of young mares, and far away from any danger.

The lanky figure of Earle, one of the stable boys, erupted from the door amidst a burst of grey smoke, dragging the other foal. Behind him came its dam, so close she almost knocked him over. Louise opened the gate for them, glad to be doing something useful. She shouted at the boy, 'Saffron! Is she safe?'

'Sir Alexander told we to get out they as were anear the fire first,' Earle said, panting. His straggly fair hair was singed and his face, black with smoke, had shiny trickles of sweat or tears running down it in pink rivers. ''Tis the last of they chestnuts next, then Master Lukas's pony. Must go, m'lady, the roof be afire!'

Tied by her self-imposed duty at the gate, she watched in an agony of fear and frustration. For anyone, man or horse, to be burned to death was a dreadful, horrible fate, and it threatened to befall her sweet golden mare Saffron. And, far worse, Alex was in mortal danger too. Only a few hours ago, she had disclosed to Phoebe her fears that she might be too happy, as if she had sensed somehow that disaster was about to strike them, as if capricious fortune had decided that no one could be allowed such perfect joy in life. And she prayed desperately that he would not put himself at risk.

The roof had indeed caught, there were plumes of smoke

wreathing from between the stone tiles at the further end of the stables, and the scrambling, desperate figures, with their paltry buckets of water, seemed to be having as much effect on the inexorable spread of the fire as if they were trying to extinguish the flames of Hell.

But at least they were still bringing the horses out. The remaining coach horse, blindfolded with someone's shirt; her lovely Saffron, snorting with terror, but safe; Lukas's pretty iron-grey pony, only purchased two weeks ago; two of the riding horses, in Alex's capable grasp. Like Hugh, he wore an old buff leather coat, soaked with water, and his face was smudged and filthy, his eyes streaming with the effects of the smoke. As the two nags bolted for freedom, he paused to kiss her, and said briefly, 'It's not so bad. With luck, we'll even save Blaze. Devil though he is, I wouldn't want to lose him. But the stables will go, we just haven't enough water. Putting it on by the bucketful is useless. And of course the hay in the loft is alight.' He grinned, and kissed her again. 'Don't worry, sweet Louise, I'll be careful. Are the children well out of the way?'

'They're in the summerhouse. How did it start?'

'Can't say. Pardice doesn't know. If it turns out that one of the lads had an illicit smoke, I swear I'll murder him. I've got to go.' He blew her a kiss, and ran.

Inside the stables, he met pandemonium. The roar of the fire, the screams of the remaining horses, drowned all other noise. Already, the flames had consumed the first five or six stalls, with a gap of only three empty ones before those still occupied. Dan Pardice, grimly patient, was attempting to persuade Phoebe's elderly mount to move, but in an extremity of terror, it was refusing to budge. The smoke billowing past in acrid, throat-catching clouds, made it difficult to see, to breathe, to think. And above them, the hayloft, still stacked with enough to last until July, was well ablaze.

But at least almost all the horses were safe now. Alex shouted, 'Leave it!' at Pardice as he passed him. Hugh was dragging one of the riding horses, blindfolded and shaking, through the further door. Only three left: and Blaze, of course.

Rather than trying to handle the maddened stallion, it might be prudent just to open the loosebox door, and let him go. Alex knew that the risk of being trampled in the rush was probably somewhat less than the danger that he would be smashed to a pulp by the flailing hooves, as soon as he entered the loosebox. And much though he loved his horses, he had no intention of dying for them.

At the further end, a roar and a sudden sheet of flame announced the partial collapse of the roof. Phoebe's nag, at last brought abruptly to its senses, neighed wildly and blundered out of the stall. It barged past Henry Renolds, running in, and plunged out into the open air. Two more, and Blaze.

Hugh and one of the other stable boys were dragging the occupants of the last two stalls to safety. As they left, the bay stallion reared up again and assaulted the door of his loosebox, with the force of a battering ram. It was fastened with a bolt, and under the repeated and powerful blows of the stallion's hooves, it had almost given way. For a brief, blessed moment the great horse subsided again, gathering his strength, his eyes rolling, his flanks heaving, drenched and dripping with foam and sweat.

Pardice, his eyes streaming, looked at Alex. 'Begging your pardon, sir, but I woulden touch en, not for all the gold in the Indies. Shall I just open the door?' He coughed as the smoke caught at his lungs, and Alex thumped him briskly on the back. 'Thank ee, sir. What do ee reckon?'

'Let him go,' Alex said. 'He can take his chance – the rest of the roof will fall in at any moment, and I don't intend to be still in here when it does.'

And a voice, hoarse, desperate, unrecognisable, said, 'So you think, Cousin.'

Alex whipped round. Charles stood at the door of the other, empty loosebox. Unkempt, straw-scattered, smoke-blackened, he was nevertheless not a comic figure. And in each hand he held a pistol, pointing with deadly menace straight at the two men standing a few feet away from him.

Pardice's face twisted with rage and loathing. 'You

started all this, diden ee!' he shouted. 'You be mad – ramping mad!'

'Stand still – don't move, or I'll shoot you,' Charles said. He coughed, and gestured savagely with his right hand. 'Get in there – with the horse. Both of you. They'll all just think it was an accident.'

'This is our quarrel,' Alex said urgently. 'It has nothing to do with Pardice – let him go!'

'To bring everyone in here in time to save you?' Charles said. 'I think not.' He smiled, and the rictus, stretching his mouth below his staring, red-rimmed eyes, gave chilling point to the groom's accusation. 'If the horse doesn't kill you, the fire will – and no one will suspect a thing. *Get in!*'

Just to Pardice's left, the door was ajar. He made as if to move to the loosebox, and then suddenly dived for the opening. Charles whirled, and fired, but already the groom had vanished. The deafening crash of the pistol set Blaze screaming again in terror, and Charles, cursing, his eyes wild, flung the empty weapon down and turned the other upon Alex.

Louise, still by the gate, heard the explosion, and at the same moment saw Pardice fling himself out of the stable door. He tripped and fell flat on the cobbles, and as she ran to him, waved her away with a frantic gesture. 'No, m'lady – get away – he've a gun, he'll shoot ee, he be mad!'

'A *gun*?' Louise, her hand outstretched to help him up, stared at him in horrified bewilderment. 'Who's got a gun?'

'Master Charles,' said the groom, panting. 'He set the fire for sure, m'lady – '

'Alex!' She turned frantically towards the stables. '*Alex* is in there! Charles will kill him!'

'No, m'lady, don't – ' Pardice had scrambled to his feet, and grabbed her arm. 'Let I fetch Sir Hugh – don't ee go in there, for God's sake!'

Reason, sense, everything but her terror for Alex had vanished. 'Let me *go*!' Louise screamed, struggling in his grasp: and when he did not oblige, she bent her head and bit his arm. With a cry of pain, Pardice released her, and she ran for the smoke-filled door.

'Open the loosebox,' Charles said, gesturing. 'Now. Or I'll shoot you.'

Alex stared at him, his expression full of mockery. 'I hope your aim hasn't improved since the last time you tried it.' Behind him, he could feel the heat of the fire on his back. Without the protection of the wet leather buff coat, the sparks falling about him would have done serious damage.

Charles, clad only in shabby broadcloth, seemed heedless to the danger. He grimaced with hatred. 'I won't miss. You're so close, I'll blast a hole right through you. *Now open that door!*'

The pistol was cocked, ready to fire. Blaze, maddened with fear, hurled himself again at the loosebox door. Alex stepped sideways, his eyes on his cousin, until his hand was on the bolt. He was only a yard or so from the outside door, and it would be easy enough to dash for freedom, as Pardice had done, but, as Charles had said, in this restricted space he would be almost impossible to miss.

Someone screamed his name, and Louise, barefoot in her shift, her beautiful silk robes torn and dirty, burst into the stable. Charles, taken completely by surprise, turned violently towards her, and the pistol went off with a crash that shattered hearing.

And Alex wrenched back the bolt.

Blaze flung himself for the last time at the door of his loosebox. It gave way and he plunged out, knocking Charles flying backwards into the gutter running down the passageway beside the stalls. Crazed with fear and rage, the stallion reared up, screaming, and Alex grabbed his wife's arm and hurled her bodily back out into the night.

Charles, his face contorted with terror, was trying to struggle out of reach of the stallion's flailing hooves. Above him, the horse reared again, striking him a vicious blow on his arm as he tried to shield his head. He screamed, and screamed again. 'No – get him away – get him away from me!'

But Blaze was beyond the power of anyone to control. Charles cowered away from the thrashing, lethal hooves, and tried desperately to crawl out of their reach.

And then, with catastrophic lack of warning, the roof collapsed on top of them all in an explosion of flame and smoke.

Louise, sprawling winded and bruised on the stones of the yard, where her husband had flung her for her own safety, was instantly surrounded by a crowd of anxious, helpful people. Crowing for breath, she tried to shout, to tell them that a madman was threatening Alex, but as in some ghastly nightmare, could not utter a word. She saw Hugh's anxious face, and Lukas, who was meant to be safe in the summerhouse. She struck their hands away, and struggled desperately to her feet.

And then, with a roar and a wild flowering of flame, the rest of the roof caved in on the stables below.

Somewhere, high above the sound, was a shrill, dreadful scream: but whether from a human or an animal throat, it was impossible to tell. Smoke burst from all the open doors, and in the middle of it, a man running, his hands over his head, a black shape outlined stark against the fierce brilliance of the leaping fire behind him. The horse trough, still part full, stood in the centre of the yard: pouring smoke and flames like a brand plucked from a furnace, he flung himself full length into the water.

Louise was there first, screaming his name, her hands reaching for him. For a terrible instant, as he lay quite still, face down, she thought that he was dead: and then the surface shook, and parted, and Alex, singed and raw and streaming water, struggled on to his hands and knees, shaking his head like a dog.

He was alive. There were marks on his face, his hair had caught, his hands were burned, but he was alive. The thick buff coat had probably saved him. He sat back on his heels, his expression almost dazed, as if he could not quite believe in his survival. She said, her voice shaking, 'Alex? Alex, are you all right?'

'A trifle scorched,' he said, his voice low and hoarse from smoke. 'Nothing that won't mend. I'm sorry if I hurt you – I had to see you safe – he was mad, he would have killed anyone in his path, even you.'

She knew the truth already, but for the benefit of everyone gathering round them, she asked him anyway. 'Charles? What happened to him?'

'He's dead,' Alex said, and in his eyes, bleak and shadowy despite the brilliant glare of the fire, she saw grief, and anger, and bitter, futile regret. 'The stallion knocked him down and trampled him, and then the roof fell on them both. They're dead. And before God, I wish it had not ended like this.'

Then, he buried his face in his hands, and she leaned over into the trough and held him close, cold and wet as he was. For he knew, none better, that the ultimate responsibility for that dreadful, fatal feud lay on his shoulders. And since he was not, at heart, the careless, cruel and callous libertine that Charles had always imagined him to be, he would probably find it difficult to come to terms with the terrible consequences of what he had done.

But she could help him: she, who knew his many strengths, as well as his weaknesses, as thoroughly as he knew them himself. Charles was dead, and however horrible the manner of his end, he could harm them no longer. And, suddenly, she had no more fear for her future with Alex, whatever it might bring of joy, or sorrow.

'You can't sit in there all night.' It was Phoebe's voice, briskly practical. 'For God's sake, Alex, get out, and we can put some salve on those burns.'

He removed his hands from his face, and Louise, with loving and infinite gentleness, took them in hers. She looked at him, and surprised, somewhere in his exhausted, pain-stricken face, a spark of the old irreverent humour. 'I'm starting to feel a little ridiculous,' he said, and began to laugh rather helplessly. 'But I don't think I can get out unaided – and certainly not with you in my way, dear lady.'

She hastily moved aside, and a dozen willing hands helped her husband from the trough and on to dry land.

Louise, shaking with relief and reaction, took him into her arms, and he winced. 'Be careful! You'll have to treat me very gently, for a week or so at least.'

'For God's sake,' Phoebe said again, sternly. 'Go inside, the pair of you, before you both catch a chill on the lungs. Mattie and Christian and I can see to your hurts – and the fire can't spread any further now. It's dying down already.'

Slowly, supported by Louise and Lukas and surrounded by a bevy of eager helpers, Alex made his way back to the house, leaving a trail of wet footprints. Behind them, the flames were indeed diminishing, the hideous bright glare growing slowly duller, as the rest of the servants ran to and fro with the meagre buckets of water that were now beginning to make some difference.

Alex turned at the door, to look back at the pyre which had, at last, obliterated the terrible tangle of greed, jealousy, failure and hatred that had tormented his cousin Charles. And then, shaking off the final burdens of the past, he took his wife's hand, and his son's, and walked a free man into Wintercombe.

# Historical Note

It is difficult for most people today to understand the depth and extent of the fear and hatred which Roman Catholicism inspired in English Protestants three hundred years ago. Perhaps the nearest modern analogy is the 'Reds under the bed' terror of Communism in America during the McCarthyite witch-hunts and the Cold War. In the seventeenth century, quite sane, educated and sensible people believed that the 'Papists' were behind an astonishing and ludicrous variety of misfortunes, including the Great Fire of London and the comparatively early death of Charles II. So although I have put a number of anti-Catholic statements into the mouths of many of my characters, I should perhaps point out, for the benefit of those of my friends, relatives and readers who are Catholics, that they in no way reflect my own views!

The St Barbe and Heron families are fictional, but many others portrayed in the book are not, including the Carne family (except Edward), Henry Sidney, John Wildman, Thomas Talmarsh (or Tollemache) and Edmond Everard, who does indeed seem to have been a spy for James II. The full complexity of William of Orange's intelligence network has yet to be unravelled, but operated broadly as I have described it. The King did indeed visit the site of the skirmish at Norton St Philip, as mentioned in the Churchwardens' Accounts, and most of the Wintercombe servants are recorded in various contemporary parish documents.

As this is probably the last of my chronicles of the St Barbe family, I would like to thank all those who have made the writing and the research for the four books so enjoyable. Firstly, the Floyd family, whose home at Great Chalfield in Wiltshire is the original of 'Wintercombe'; Mrs Pat

Lawless, whose wide knowledge of the history and families of Norton St Philip was such a great help; Dave Ryan, of Caliver Books and the English Civil War Society; the staff of the Somerset County Records Office, Bath City Archives, Melksham Library and the London Library, without whose supply of books and specialist knowledge my task would have been made much more difficult; and the various members of my family, and friends, who have offered help, support and encouragement over the last five or six years.

And finally, of course, I am as always deeply indebted to my mother, whose constructive criticism and gimlet eye for errors and unlikely flights of fancy have always brought me gently but inexorably back to earth; and to my husband, Steve, whose cheerful, enthusiastic support and technological backup have been so invaluable, so many times.

P.D.A.B.
January 1992